Praise for Anna Todd and the After series

"Todd [is] the biggest literary phenom of her generation."
—*Cosmopolitan*

"I was almost at the point like with *Twilight* that I just stop everything and my sole focus was reading the book . . . Todd, girl, you are a genius!!!"
—*Once Upon a Twilight*

"The Mr. Darcy and Lizzy Bennett of our time . . . If you looked up 'Bad Boy' in the fiction dictionary, next to it would be a picture of Hardin alongside *Beautiful Bastard* and Mr. Darcy."
—*That's Normal*

"The one thing you can count on is to *expect the unexpected.*"
—*Vilma's Book Blog*

"Anna Todd manages to make you scream, cry, laugh, fall in love, and sit in the fetal position . . . Whether you have read the Wattpad version or not, *After* is a can't-miss book—but get ready to feel emotions that you weren't sure a book could bring out of you. And if you have read the Wattpad version, the book is 10x better."
—*Fangirlish*

"A very entertaining read chock-full of drama drama drama . . . This book will have you from the first page."
—*A Bookish Escape*

"I couldn't put this book down! It went with me everywhere so I could get my Hessa fix every spare moment I had. Talk about getting hooked from page one!"
—*Grown Up Fangirl*

I want more. ☹
—Readers everywhere

ALSO BY ANNA TODD

After

After We Collided

After Ever Happy

AFTER WE FELL

ANNA TODD

G

GALLERY BOOKS

New York London Toronto Sydney New Delhi

G
Gallery Books
A Division of Simon & Schuster, Inc.
1230 Avenue of the Americas
New York, NY 10020

This book is a work of fiction. Any references to historical events, real people, or real places are used fictitiously. Other names, characters, places, and events are products of the author's imagination, and any resemblance to actual events or places or persons, living or dead, is entirely coincidental.

The author is represented by Wattpad.

First Gallery Books trade paperback edition December 2014

GALLERY BOOKS and colophon are registered trademarks of Simon & Schuster, Inc.

Interior design by Davina Mock-Maniscalco
Cover design by Damonza
Cover image © Ase/Shutterstock

Manufactured in the United States of America

20 19 18 17 16 15 14 13

Library of Congress Cataloging-in-Publication Data is available.

ISBN 978-1-4767-9250-7
ISBN 978-1-4767-9256-9 (ebook)

To J,
for loving me in a way
most people only dream of.

And to the Hardins of the world,
who deserve to have their stories told, too.

prologue

TESSA

As I stare into the familiar face of this stranger, memories flood me.

I used to sit there, brushing the hair on my blond Barbie doll. Often, I'd wish that I *was* the doll: she had it made. She was beautiful, she was always groomed, always exactly who she was supposed to be. Her parents must be proud, I used to think. Her father, wherever he was, was probably a big CEO, traveling the world to make a life for his family while her mother stayed back and took care of the house.

Barbie's father would never come home stumbling and yelling. He wouldn't scream at her mother so loudly that Barbie would hide in the greenhouse to get away from all the noise and the breaking dishes. And if, by chance, some small, easily explainable misunderstanding had caused an argument between her parents, Barbie always had Ken, her perfect blond boyfriend, to keep her company . . . even in the greenhouse.

Barbie was perfect, so she would have the perfect life, with perfect parents.

My father, who left me nine years ago, is standing in front of me, dirty and haggard. Nothing like he should be, nothing like I remember. A smile covers his face as he stares at me, and another memory surfaces.

My father, the night he left . . . my mother's face set in stone. She didn't cry. She just stood there, waiting for him to walk out the door. That night she changed; she wasn't the same loving mother anymore after that. She became something unkind, and distant, and unhappy.

But she was there after he decided not to be.

chapter one

TESSA

Dad?" This man in front of me couldn't possibly be my father, despite the familiar brown eyes staring back at me.

"Tessie?" His voice is thicker sounding than I recall from my distant memories.

Hardin turns to me, eyes blazing, and then back to my father.

My father. Here, in this bad neighborhood, with filthy clothes on his back.

"Tessie? Is that really you?" he asks.

I'm frozen. I have no words to say to this drunken man wearing my father's face.

Hardin puts a hand on my shoulder in an attempt to elicit a reaction from me. "Tessa . . ."

I take a step toward the strange man, and he smiles. His brown beard is peppered with gray; his smile isn't white and clean like I remember . . . how did he end up this way? All the hope I once held that my father would've changed his life around the way Ken did has vanished, and the realization that this man is actually my father hurts worse than it should.

"It's me," someone says, and after a moment I realize the words came from me.

He closes the space between us and wraps his arms around me. "I can't believe it! Here you are! I've been trying to—"

He's cut short by Hardin pulling him away from me. I step back, unsure how to behave.

The stranger—my father—looks between Hardin and me,

alert and in disbelief. But shortly he eases back into a nonchalant posture and keeps his distance, for which I'm glad.

"I've been trying to find you for months," he says, wiping his hand across his forehead, leaving a smudge of dirt on his skin.

Hardin stands in front of me, ready to pounce. "I've been here," I say quietly, peering around his shoulder. I'm thankful for his protection, and it dawns on me that he must be completely confused.

My father turns to him, looks him up and down for a while. "Wow. Noah sure has changed a lot."

"No, that's Hardin," I tell him.

My father shuffles around him a little and inches closer to me, and I can see that Hardin tenses when he moves. This close, I can smell him.

It's either the liquor on his breath, or the by-product of abusing liquor, that has him confusing the two; Hardin and Noah are polar opposites, and could never be compared to each other. My father swings an arm around me, and Hardin gives me a look, but I shake my head slightly to keep him at bay.

"Who's he?" My father keeps his arm around me for an uncomfortably long time while Hardin just stands there, looking like he's going to explode—not necessarily out of anger, I realize; he just seems to have no clue what to say or do.

That makes two of us. "He's my . . . Hardin's my . . ."

"Boyfriend. I'm her boyfriend," he finishes for me.

The man's brown irises go wide as he finally takes in Hardin's appearance.

"Nice to meet you, Hardin. I'm Richard." He reaches his dirty hand out to shake Hardin's.

"Ehm . . . yeah, nice to meet you." Hardin is clearly very . . . unsettled.

"What are the two of you doing out around here?"

I take this opportunity to move away from my father and stand next to Hardin, who snaps back to himself and pulls me to his side.

"Hardin was getting a tattoo," I answer robotically. My mind is unable to comprehend all that's happening right now.

"Ah . . . Nice. I've used this place before myself."

Images of my father having coffee before leaving the house every morning to go to work fill my mind. He looked nothing like this, he spoke nothing like this, and he sure as hell didn't tattoo himself back when I knew him. When I was his little girl.

"Yeah, my friend Tom does them." He pushes up the sleeve of his sweatshirt to reveal what resembles a skull on his forearm.

It doesn't look like it belongs on him, but as I continue to examine him I begin to see that maybe it does. "Oh . . ." is all I can manage.

This is so awkward. This man is my father, the man who left my mother and me alone. And he's here in front of me . . . drunk. And I don't know what to think.

Part of me is excited—a small part that I don't want to acknowledge at the moment. I had secretly been hoping to see him again since the day my mother mentioned he was back in the area. I know it's silly—stupid, really—but in a way he seems better than before. He's drunk and possibly homeless, but I have missed him more than I realized, and maybe he's just had a rough time lately. Who am I to judge this man when I don't know anything about him?

When I look at him, and at the street surrounding us, it's bizarre to see that everything is moving along as it normally should. I could have sworn time stopped when my father stumbled in front of us.

"Where are you living?" I ask.

Hardin's defensive gaze is set on my father, watching him like he's a dangerous predator.

"I'm in between places right now." He wipes his forehead with his sleeve.

"Oh."

"I was working down at Raymark, but I got laid off," he tells me.

I vaguely recall hearing the name Raymark before. I think it's some manufacturer. He's been doing factory work?

"What have you been up to? It's been, what . . . five years?"

I can feel Hardin stiffen next to me as I say, "No, it's been nine."

"Nine years? I'm sorry, Tessie." His words are slightly slurred.

His nickname for me makes my heart sink; that name was used in the best of times. In the time when he would lift me up onto his shoulders and run through our small yard, the time before he left. I don't know what to make of this. I want to cry because I haven't seen him in so long, I want to laugh at the irony of seeing him here, and I want to yell at him for leaving me. It's confusing to see him this way. I remember him as a drunk, but he was an angry drunk then, not a smiling, showing-off-tattoos-and-shaking-hands-with-my-boyfriend drunk. Maybe he's changed into a nicer man . . .

"I think it's time to go," Hardin states, looking at my father.

"I really am sorry; it wasn't all my fault. Your mother . . . you know how she is." He defends himself, his hands waving in front of him. "Please, Theresa, give me a chance," the man begs.

"Tessa . . ." Hardin warns beside me.

"Give us a second," I say to my father. I grab Hardin by the arm and lead him a few feet away.

"What the hell are you doing? You aren't actually going to—" he begins.

"He's my *dad*, Hardin."

"He's a fucking homeless drunk," he spits with annoyance.

Tears prick my eyes from Hardin's truthful but harsh words. "I haven't seen him in nine years."

"Exactly—because he left you. It's a waste of time, Tessa." He glances behind me at my father.

"I don't care. I want to hear him out."

"I mean, I guess so. It's not like you're inviting him to the apartment or anything." He shakes his head.

"If I want to, I will. And if he wants to come, he's coming over. It's my place, too," I snap. I look over at my father. He's standing there, wearing dirty clothes, staring down at the concrete in front of him. When was the last time he slept in a bed? Had a meal? The thought makes my heart ache.

"You aren't seriously considering having him come home with us?" Hardin's fingers slide through his hair in a familiar gesture of frustration.

"Not to live or anything—just for tonight. We could make dinner," I offer. My father looks up and makes eye contact with me. I look away as he starts to smile.

"*Dinner?* Tessa, he's a goddamn drunk who hasn't seen you in almost ten years . . . and you're talking about making dinner for him?"

Embarrassed at his outburst, I pull him by the collar closer to me and speak low. "He's my *father*, Hardin, and I don't have a relationship with my mother anymore."

"That doesn't mean you need to have one with *this* guy. This isn't going to end well, Tess. You're too damn nice to everyone when they don't deserve it."

"This is important to me," I tell him, and his eyes soften before I can point out the irony of his objections.

He sighs and tugs at his messy hair in frustration."Dammit, Tessa, this isn't going to end well."

"You don't know how it will end, Hardin," I whisper and look over at my father, who's running his fingers over his beard. I know Hardin may be right, but I owe it to myself to attempt to get to know this man, or at least to hear what he has to say.

I go back over to my father, instinctive apprehension making my voice waver a little. "Do you want to come to our place for dinner?"

"Really?" he exclaims, hope threading through his face.

"Yeah."

"Okay! Yeah, okay!" He smiles, and for a brief moment the man I remember flashes through—the man before the liquor, that is.

Hardin doesn't say a word as we all walk to the car. I know he's angry, and I understand why. But I also know that his father has changed for the better—he runs our college, for goodness' sakes. Am I so foolish for hoping to witness a similar change in my father?

When we approach the car, my father asks, "Whoa—this is yours? It's a Capri, right? Late-seventies model?"

"Yep." Hardin climbs into the driver's seat.

My father doesn't question Hardin's terse response, and I'm glad for it. The radio is set low, and as soon as Hardin revs the engine, we both reach for the knob at the same time, in hopes that music will drown out the uncomfortable silence.

The whole drive to the apartment, I wonder how my mother would take this. The thought gives me chills, and I try thinking about my upcoming move to Seattle.

Nope, that's almost worse; I don't know how to talk about it with Hardin. I close my eyes and lean my head against the window. Hardin's warm hand covers mine, and my nerves begin to calm.

"Whoa, this is where you live?" My father gapes from the backseat when we pull up to our apartment complex.

Hardin gives me a subtle here-it-comes look, and I respond, "Yeah, we moved in a few months ago."

In the elevator, Hardin's protective gaze heats my cheeks, and I give him a small smile, hoping to soften him. It seems to work, but being in our home area with this virtual stranger is just so awkward that I begin to regret inviting him over. It's too late now, though.

Hardin unlocks our door and walks inside without turning around, immediately heading to the bedroom without a word.

"I'll be right back," I tell my father and turn to leave him standing alone in the foyer area.

"Do you mind if I use your bathroom?" he calls after me.

"Of course not. It's just down the hall," I say, pointing to the bathroom door without looking.

In the other room, Hardin's on the bed, removing his boots. Looking over to the door, he gestures for me to close it.

"I know you're upset with me," I quietly remark as I walk over to him.

"I am."

I take his face between my hands, my thumbs running over both his cheeks. "Don't be."

His eyes close in appreciation of my gentle touch, and I feel his arms wrap around my waist. "He's going to hurt you. I'm only trying to prevent that from happening."

"He can't hurt me—what could he possibly do? I haven't seen him in how long?"

"He's probably out there shoving our shit in his bloody pockets now," Hardin huffs, and I can't help but giggle. "It's not funny, Tessa."

I sigh and tilt his chin up to make him look at me. "Can you please try to lighten up and be positive about this? It's confusing enough without you sulking around and adding to the pressure."

"I'm not sulking. I'm trying to protect you."

"I don't need you to—he's my dad."

"He's not your dad . . ."

"Please?" I run my thumb along his lip, and his expression softens.

Sighing again, he finally answers, "Fine, let's go have dinner with this guy, then. God knows he hasn't eaten anything that didn't come from a fucking Dumpster in a while."

My smile fades and my lip quivers against my will. He notices.

"I'm sorry; don't cry." He sighs. He hasn't stopped sighing since we ran into my father outside the tattoo shop. Seeing Hardin's *worry*—even if, like everything else he does, it's tinged with anger—only adds to the surrealness of the situation.

"I meant everything I said, but I'll try not to be a dick about it." He rises to his feet and presses his lips to the corner of my mouth. As we exit our bedroom, he mumbles, "Let's go feed the beggar," which doesn't help my mood much.

The man in the living room looks so out of place, gazing around the space, noticing the books on our shelves.

"I'm going to make dinner. You can watch television?" I suggest.

"I can help?" he offers.

"Um, okay." I half smile, and he follows me into the kitchen. Hardin stays in the living room, keeping his distance, as I suspected he would.

"I can't believe you're all grown up and living on your own," my father says.

I reach into the refrigerator to grab a tomato while I try to collect my scattered thoughts. "I'm in college, at WCU. So is Hardin," I reply, leaving out his looming expulsion for obvious reasons.

"Really? WCU? Wow." He sits down at the table, and I notice that the dirt has been scrubbed from his hands. The spot on his forehead is gone, too, and a wet spot on the shoulder of his shirt makes me think he was trying to clean a stain from it. He's nervous, too. Knowing that makes me feel a little better.

I almost tell him about Seattle and the exciting new direction my life is going in, but I have yet to tell Hardin. My father's resurfacing has added another detour to my road map. I don't know how many problems I can deal with before everything ends up collapsing at my feet.

"I wish I'd been around to see all this happen. I always knew you'd make something of yourself."

"You *weren't* around, though," I say tersely. Guilt plagues me as soon as I say the words, but I don't wish to take them back.

"I know, but I'm here now, and I'm hoping I can make up for that."

Those simple words are actually a bit cruel, giving me hope that he might not be so bad after all, that maybe he just needs help to stop drinking.

"Are you . . . Are you still drinking?"

"I am." He looks at his feet. "Not as much. I know it looks otherwise right now, but it's been a hard few months . . . that's all."

Hardin appears in the doorway of the kitchen, and I know he's battling with himself to stay quiet. I hope he can.

"I've seen your mom a few times."

"You have?"

"Yeah. She wouldn't tell me where you were. She looks really good," he says.

This is so awkward, him commenting on my mother. Her voice plays in my head, reminding me that this man abandoned us. That this man was the reason she is the way she is today.

"What happened . . . with the two of you?" I place chicken breasts in a pan, the oil crackling and popping as I wait for an answer. I don't want to turn and face him after asking such a direct and abrupt question, but I just couldn't stop myself from inquiring.

"We just weren't compatible; she always wanted more than I could give her, and you know how she can be."

That I do know, but the way he's casually talking about her in such a dismissive tone doesn't sit well with me.

Shifting the blame from my mother back to him, I turn quickly and ask, "Why didn't you call?"

"I *did*—I always called. I sent you gifts every birthday. She didn't tell you that, did she?"

"No."

"Well, it's true—I did. I missed you so much all this time. I can't believe you're here, in front of me now." His eyes are luminous and his voice shaky as he stands and walks toward me. I don't know how to react; I don't even know the man anymore, if I ever did.

Hardin steps into the kitchen to create a barrier between us, and once again I'm glad for his intrusion. I don't know what to think of all of this; I need to keep physical space between this man and me.

"I know you can't forgive me." He nearly sobs, and my stomach drops.

"It's not that. I just need time before I jump into having you in my life again. I don't even know you," I tell him, and he nods.

"I know, I know." He sits back down at the table, leaving me to finish preparing dinner.

chapter two

HARDIN

Tessa's piece-of-shit sperm donor scarfs down two plates of food before even stopping to take a breath. I'm sure he was starving, living on the streets and all. It's not that I don't feel bad for people who are down on their luck and have hit hard times—it's that this specific man is a drunk and he abandoned his kid, so I don't feel bad for him for a goddamn second.

After gulping down some water, he beams at my girl. "You're quite the cook, Tessie."

I think I'll scream if he calls her that one more time.

"Thank you." She smiles, like the nice person *she* is. I can tell his bullshit is seeping in, filling the emotional cracks he created by leaving her when she was a child.

"I mean it; maybe you could teach me this recipe sometime."

For you to use *where*? In your nonexistent kitchen?

"Sure," she says and stands to clear her plate, grabbing mine on the way.

"I can go now. I appreciate dinner," Richard—*Dick*—says and stands.

"No, you can . . . you can stay tonight, if you want, and we can take you back . . . *home* in the morning," she says slowly, unsure what words to use to describe his situation.

What I'm sure of is that I don't like this shit at all.

"That would be great," Dick says, rubbing his arms.

He's probably itching for a drink right now, the fucking prick.

Tessa smiles. "Great. I'll go get a pillow and some sheets from the bedroom." Looking at her dad and me for a moment, she must notice how I'm feeling, because she asks, "You two'll be okay for a minute, right?"

Her dad laughs. "Yeah, I want to get to know him anyway."

Oh no, you don't.

She frowns at my expression and saunters out of the room, leaving us alone in the kitchen.

"So, Hardin, where did you meet my Tessa?" he asks. I hear her close the door and wait a couple of beats to make sure she's not in earshot. "Hardin?" he repeats.

"Let's get something straight," I snarl and lean across the table, startling him. "She isn't *your* Tessa—she's *mine*. And I know what the fuck you're up to, so don't think for a goddamn second you're fooling me."

He raises his hands meekly. "I'm not up to anything, I—"

"What do you want, money?"

"What? No, of course I don't want money. I want a relationship with my daughter."

"You've had nine years to build one, and yet you're only here because you ran into her in a damn parking lot. It's not like you came looking for her," I bark, having visions of my hands around his neck.

"I know." He shakes his head, looking down. "I know that I made a lot of mistakes, and I'm going to make up for them."

"You're drunk—right now, sitting in my kitchen, you're fucking drunk. I know a drunk when I see one. I have no sympathy for a man who leaves his family and doesn't even have his shit together nine years later."

"I know your intentions are good, and it makes me happy to see you try to defend my daughter, but I'm not going to mess this up. I only want to get to know her . . . and you."

I stay silent, trying to calm my irate thoughts.

"You're much nicer when she's around," he observes quietly.

"You're worse of an actor when she's not around," I retaliate.

"You have every right not to trust me, but for her sake, give me a chance."

"If you hurt her in any way, you are dead." Maybe I should feel a little remorse about threatening Tessa's father like this, but I only feel anger and distrust toward the pathetic drunk. My instincts tell me to protect her, not to sympathize with a drunk stranger.

"I won't hurt her," he promises.

I roll my eyes and take a drink from my glass of water.

Thinking his statement somehow settles it, he tries to joke, "This talk—our roles should be reversed, you know?"

But I ignore him and walk into the bedroom. I have to, before Tessa comes out to find me strangling her father.

chapter three

TESSA

I have a pillow, a blanket, and a towel in my hands when Hardin storms into the bedroom

"Okay, what happened?" I ask, waiting for him to explode, waiting for him to complain that I invited my father to stay without really consulting him first.

Hardin goes to the bed and lies down on it, then looks over at me. "Nothing. We bonded. Then I felt like I'd had enough quality time with our guest, and decided to come in here."

"Please tell me you weren't horrible to him." I barely know my father. The last thing I want is more tension.

"I kept my hands to myself," he says and closes his eyes.

"Guess I'll take him a blanket and apologize for your behavior, as always," I say with annoyance.

In the living room, I find my father sitting on the floor, picking at the holes in his jeans. He looks up when he hears me. "You can sit on the couch," I tell him and place my bundle on the arm of the couch.

"I . . . well, I didn't want to get anything on your couch." Embarrassment colors his expression, and my heart aches.

"Don't worry about that . . . you can take a shower here, and I'm sure Hardin has some clothes you can wear for the night."

He doesn't look at me, but lightly protests, "I don't want to take advantage."

"It's okay, really. I'll bring out some clothes; go ahead and take a shower. Here's a towel for you to use."

He gives me a wan smile. "Thank you. I'm so glad to see you again. I've missed you so much . . . and here you are."

"I'm sorry if Hardin was rude to you. He's . . ."

"Protective?" he finishes for me.

"Yeah, I guess he is. He comes off very rude sometimes."

"It's okay. I'm a man; I can take it. He's just looking out for you, and I don't blame him. He doesn't know me. Hell, neither do you. He reminds me of someone I used to know . . ." My father stops and smiles.

"Who?"

"Me . . . I was just like him. I didn't have respect for anyone who didn't earn it, and I ran over anyone who got in my way. I had the same chip on my shoulder that he has; the only difference is he has a lot more tattoos than me." He chuckles, and the sound breathes life into memories I had long forgotten.

I enjoy the feeling and smile along with him until he stands up and grabs the towel. "I'm going to take you up on that shower now."

I tell him that I'll bring him a change of clothes and place them outside the bathroom door.

Back in our room, Hardin is still on the bed, eyes closed and knees bent in front of him.

"He's taking a shower. I told him he could wear some of your clothes."

He sits up. "Why would you do that?"

"Because he doesn't have any clothes." I walk toward the bed, arms extended to calm him.

"Sure, Tessa, go ahead and give him my clothes," he says harshly. "Should I offer him my side of the bed, too?"

"You need to stop, *now*. He's my father, and I'd like to see where this is going to go. Just because you can't forgive your father doesn't mean you have to sabotage my attempts to have some kind of relationship with mine," I reply, equally harshly.

Hardin stares at me. His green eyes narrow, no doubt from the effort not to say out loud the hateful words he's spewing at me in his head.

"That's not what this is; you're too naive. How many times do I have to tell you this? Not everyone deserves your kindness, Tessa."

I snap, "Only you, right? You're the only one I should forgive and give the benefit of the doubt to? That's bullshit, and really pretty selfish of you." I dig through his bottom drawer to grab a pair of sweats. "And you know what? I'd rather be naive and capable of seeing the good in people than be a jerk to everyone and assume that everyone is out to get me."

I gather up a shirt and some socks and storm out. As I'm placing the pile of clothes by the bathroom door, I hear my father's voice singing softly over the sound of the water. I press my ear to the door and can't help but smile at the wonderful noise. I remember my mother talking about my father's singing and how obnoxious it always was, but I find it lovely.

I turn the television back on in the living room and set the remote on the table to encourage him to watch what he wants. Does he watch television?

I straighten up the kitchen, leaving some leftovers out on the counter in case he's still hungry. *When was the last time he had a real meal?* I wonder again.

The water is still running in the bathroom; he must be enjoying his hot shower, which tells me that he probably hasn't had a bath in a while.

Hardin has his new leather binder that I got him on his lap when I finally go back to the bedroom. I walk by him without making eye contact, but then feel his fingers wrap around my arm to stop me.

"Can we talk?" he asks, pulling me to stand between his legs. His hands quickly move his binder out of the way.

"Go ahead, talk."

"I'm sorry for being a dick, okay? I just don't know what to think of all this."

"All of what? Nothing has changed."

"Yes, it has. This man who neither of us really knows is in my house, and he wants to become close with you after all these years. It doesn't add up, and my first instinct is to be defensive. You know that."

"I hear what you're saying, but you can't be hateful and say those things to me—like calling him a beggar. That really hurt my feelings."

He spreads my hands open with his, lacing his fingers through mine while pulling me even closer to him. "I'm sorry, baby, I really am." He brings our hands to his mouth, slowly kissing each of my knuckles, and my anger dissolves at the touch of his soft lips.

I quirk one eyebrow. "Are you going to stop with the cruel comments?"

"Yes." He turns my hand over in his, tracing the lines etched into my palm.

"Thank you." I watch as his long finger travels up my wrist and back down to my fingertips.

"Just be careful, okay? Because I won't hesitate to—"

"He seems okay, though, doesn't he? I mean he's nice," I say quietly, interrupting his sure-to-be-violent promise.

Hardin's fingers stop their movements. "I don't know; he's nice enough, I guess."

"He wasn't nice when I was younger."

Hardin looks at me with serious fire in his eyes, though his words have a gentle tone to them. "Don't talk about that while he's this close to me, please. I'm trying my best here, so let's not push it."

I climb onto his lap, and he lies down with my body against his.

"Tomorrow's the big day." He sighs.

"Yeah," I whisper against his arm, nuzzling in his warmth. Hardin's expulsion hearing for beating up Zed is scheduled for tomorrow; not our finest hour.

Suddenly a small feeling of panic shoots through me at the memory of the text Zed sent me. I'd almost forgotten about it altogether after seeing my father outside the shop. My phone had vibrated in my pocket as we waited for Steph and Tristan's return, and Hardin had stared at me silently while I read it. Fortunately he didn't ask me what was up.

I need to talk to you tomorrow morning, alone please? Zed had written.

I don't know what to make of the message; I don't know if I should talk to him about anything, considering he told Tristan he was going to press charges against Hardin. I hope he just said that to impress him, to keep his reputation. I don't know what I'll do if Hardin gets in trouble—*real* trouble. I should respond to the message, but I don't think it's the best idea to meet Zed or to talk to him alone. Hardin's already in enough of a mess without me adding to it.

"Are you listening to me?" Hardin nudges me, and I look up from the comfort of his embrace.

"No, sorry."

"What's on your mind?"

"Everything: tomorrow, the charges, expulsion, England, Seattle, my father . . ." I sigh. "Everything."

"You'll come with me, though? To find out about the expulsion?" His voice is smooth, yet nervous.

"If you want me to," I say.

"I need you to."

"Then I'll be there." I have to change the subject, so I say, "I still can't believe you got that tattoo. Let me see it again."

He gently rolls me off of him so he can turn over. "Lift my shirt."

I lift the bottom of his black T-shirt until his entire back is laid bare, and then I pull back the white bandage covering the newly engraved words.

"There's a little blood on the bandage," I tell him.

"That's normal," he says, humor at my ignorance coming through his words.

I outline the reddened area with my finger, taking in the perfect words. The tattoo he got for me is my new favorite. The perfect words—words that have so much meaning for me, and for him as well, apparently. But they're tainted by the news I've chosen to withhold about moving to Seattle. I'll tell him tomorrow, as soon as we find out about the expulsion. I promise myself one hundred times that I will; the longer I wait, the more angry he'll be.

"Is that enough of a commitment for you, Tessie?"

I scowl at him. "Don't call me that."

"I hate that nickname," he says, turning his head up to look at me while still lying on his stomach.

"Me, too, but I don't want to tell him that. Anyway, the tattoo is enough for me."

"You're sure? Because I can go back and get your portrait underneath." He laughs.

"No, please don't!" I shake my head, and his laughter rises.

"You're sure this'll be enough?" He sits up and tugs his shirt back down to cover his body. "No marriage," he adds.

"That's what this was? You got a tattoo as an alternative to marriage?" I don't know how I feel about this.

"No, not exactly. I got the tattoo because I wanted to, and because I haven't gotten one in a while."

"Thoughtful."

"It's for you, too, to show you that I want this." He gestures between us, taking my hand in his. "Whatever this is that we have, I don't ever want to lose it. I've lost it before, and even now I don't completely have it back, but I can tell it's getting there."

His hand feels warm, and so right holding on to mine.

"So once again, I used the words of a far more romantic man than myself to get the point across." He smiles a bright smile, but I see the terror beneath it.

"I think Darcy would be appalled by your use of his famous words," I tease.

"I think he would high-five me," he boasts.

My laughter comes out like a bark. "High-five? Fitzwilliam Darcy would never do such a thing."

"You think he's above high fives? He's not; he would sit here and have a beer with me. We would bond over how annoyingly stubborn the women in our lives are."

"The two of you are lucky to have us, because the Lord knows no one else would put up with either of you."

"Is that so?" he challenges with a dimpled smile.

"Obviously,"

"You're right, I suppose. But I'd trade you for Elizabeth in a heartbeat."

My mouth presses into a straight line, and I raise a brow, expecting an explanation.

"Only because she shares my views on marriage."

"But she still got married," I remind him.

In a very un-Hardin-like move, he takes my hips in his hands and pushes me back on the bed, so my head lands on the mountain of decorative pillows that he despises—a fact he never fails to remind me of. "That's it! Darcy can have both of you!" His laughter fills the room, and mine is equally powerful.

These little dramas during which we bicker over fictional characters and he laughs like a child are the moments that make all the hell we've put each other through worth every second. Moments like these shield me from the harsh realities we've experienced throughout our relationship, and all the obstacles that still lie in front of us.

"I can hear he's out of the bathroom," Hardin says, his tone guarded.

"I'm going to say good night." I wrestle out of Hardin's grip, placing a swift kiss on his forehead.

In the living room, I find that Hardin's clothes look odd on my father, but at least they fit better than I'd expected.

"Thanks again for the clothes. I'll leave them here when I go in the morning," he tells me.

"It's okay, you can take them . . . if you need them."

He sits on the couch and rests his hands on his lap. "You've already done enough for me, more than I deserve."

"It's okay, really."

"You're much more understanding than your mom." He smiles.

"I'm not sure I understand anything right now, but I want to try to get to that point."

"That's all I'm asking for, just a little time to get to know my little . . . well, my *adult* daughter."

I give him a tight smile. "I'd like that."

I know he has a long way to go, and I'm not forgiving him overnight. But he's my father, and I don't have the energy to hate him. I want to believe that he can change; I've seen it happen before. Hardin's father, for example, has completely turned his life around, even if Hardin can't let go of their painful past. I've seen Hardin change, too. And since there aren't many people more stubborn than him, I figure there's hope for my father, no matter how bad he may have gotten.

"Hardin hates me. I've got my work cut out for me here."

His sense of humor is contagious, and I chuckle. "Yes; yes, you do." I look down the hall at my scowling boyfriend in his solid black clothes, watching us with suspicious eyes.

chapter four

TESSA

"Turn it off," Hardin groans as the alarm rings throughout the dark bedroom.

My fingers fumble for my phone, and finally, with a swipe of my thumb across the screen, the unwelcome sound stops. My shoulders feel heavy as I sit up in bed, the weight of today's tensions threatening to pull me back down: the university's decision whether to expel Hardin, the possibility of Zed pressing charges against him, and lastly, Hardin's potential reactions to my telling him I'm planning to follow Vance Publishing to Seattle, and that I want him to come even though he's professed to hate the city.

I can't decide which of these terrifies me the most. By the time I turn the bathroom light on and splash cool water against my face, I realize that the assault charges are the worst. If Hardin is sent to jail, I honestly have no idea what I would do, or what he would do. The thought alone makes me nauseous. Zed's request to meet with me this morning resurfaces, and my mind reels with all the possibilities of what he could want to talk about, especially since he said something about having fallen "in love" with me the last time I saw him.

I inhale and exhale into the soft towel hanging on the wall. Should I reply to Zed and at least see what he has to say? Maybe he can offer an explanation for why he told Tristan one thing and me another about pressing charges. I feel guilty for asking him not to, especially considering how badly Hardin hurt him, but I love Hardin, and Zed had the same intentions as Hardin did, to win a bet, in the beginning. Neither of them is purely innocent here.

Before I can overthink the possible repercussions, I text Zed. I'm only trying to help Hardin. I remind myself of that over and over after I hit send and obsess over my hair and makeup.

WHEN I SEE that the blanket is folded neatly on the arm of the couch, my heart sinks. He left? *How will I get hold of him—*

The soft sound of a cabinet opening in the kitchen picks my heart up from the floor. Going into the dark room, I switch the light on and see my father startle and drop a spoon onto the concrete floor with a clatter.

"Sorry, I was trying to be as quiet as possible," my father says as he quickly bends to retrieve the utensil.

"It's okay. I was up. You could have turned the light on." I laugh quietly.

"I didn't want to wake anyone. I was just trying to make some cereal; I hope that's okay."

"Of course it is." I start the coffee pot and check the clock. I need to wake Hardin in fifteen minutes.

"What are your plans for today?" he asks with a mouth full of Frosted Flakes, Hardin's favorite.

"Well, I have class, and Hardin has a meeting with the university board."

"The university board? That sounds serious . . ."

I look at my father and wonder, *Should I tell him?* But then, figuring I have to start somewhere, I say, "He got in a fight on campus."

"And they're making him talk in front of the board? In my day, you got a slap on the wrist, and that was that."

"He destroyed a lot of property, expensive property, and he broke the guy's nose." I sigh and stir a spoonful of sugar into my coffee. I need the extra energy today.

"Nice. So what was the fight about?"

"Me, sort of. It was something that was building over time, and it finally just . . . exploded."

"Well, I like Hardin even more now than I did last night." He beams. Though I'm glad that he's warming to my boyfriend, it's not for a good reason. I don't want the two of them bonding over violence.

I shake my head and gulp down half my coffee, letting the hot liquid soothe my frantic nerves.

"Where's he from?" He sounds genuinely interested in learning more about Hardin.

"England."

"Thought that was the accent. Though sometimes I can't tell it from Australian. So his family's still there?"

"His mother is. His father's here. He's the chancellor at WCU."

Curiosity fills his brown eyes. "Ironic, then, about the expulsion."

"Very." I sigh.

"Your mother's met him?" he asks, then takes a big spoonful of cereal.

"Yes, she hates him." I frown.

" 'Hate' is a strong word."

"Trust me, in this case it's not strong enough." The ache from the loss of my relationship with my mother is much less potent than it used to be. I don't know whether that's a good thing or not.

My father puts down his spoon and nods several times. "She can be a little hardheaded; she just worries about you."

"She doesn't need to. I'm fine."

"Well, let her be the one to come around, then; you shouldn't have to choose one or the other." He smiles. "Your grandma didn't approve of me either—she's probably scowling at me from her grave as we speak."

This is all so strange, sitting in my kitchen with my father, bonding over cereal and coffee after all these years. "It's just hard because we've always been close . . . as close as she's capable of, at least."

"She always wanted you to be just like her; she made sure of that from a young age. She's not a bad person, Tessie. She's just afraid."

I look at him quizzically. "Of what?"

"Everything. She's afraid of losing control. I'm sure seeing you with Hardin terrified her and made her realize she doesn't have control over you anymore."

I stare at the empty cup in front of me. "Is that why you left? Because she wanted to control everything?"

My father sighs softly, an ambiguous sound. "No, I left because I have my own issues and we weren't good for one another. Don't worry about us." He chuckles. "Worry about yourself and your troublemaker of a boyfriend."

I can't picture the man in front of me and my mother being able to hold a conversation; they are just so different. When I glance at the clock, I realize it's past eight.

I get up and put my cup in the dishwasher. "I need to wake up Hardin. I threw your clothes in the wash last night. I'll get dressed and bring them out."

I go into the bedroom and see that Hardin is awake. As I watch him pulling a black T-shirt over his head, I suggest, "Maybe you should wear something a little more formal to the meeting?"

"Why?"

"Because they're deciding your educational future, and a

black T-shirt doesn't show much effort on your end. You can change right after, but I really think you should dress up."

"Fuuuuuck." He exaggerates the word and throws his head back.

I walk past him and into the closet to retrieve his black button-up shirt and pants.

"No dress slacks—for the love of God, no."

I hand the pants to him. "It's only for a little while."

He holds the garment like it's nuclear waste or an alien artifact. "If I wear this shit and they still kick me out, I'll burn that whole campus to the ground."

"You're so dramatic." I roll my eyes at him, but he doesn't look amused as he steps into the dress pants.

"Is our apartment still operating as a homeless shelter?"

I drop the shirt, still on the hanger, onto the bed and march to the door.

Frantic fingers lace through his hair. "Dammit, Tess, I'm sorry. I'm getting anxious, and I can't even fuck you to settle me down because your dad is on our couch."

His vulgar words stir my hormones, but he's right: my father in the other room is a big impediment. I walk over to Hardin, whose long fingers are struggling with the top button on his shirt, and gently move his hands out of the way. "Let me," I offer.

His eyes soften, but I can tell he's beginning to panic. I hate seeing him this way; it's so foreign. He's so controlled all the time, never caring much for anything—except me, and even then he's still pretty good at hiding his feelings.

"Everything will be fine, babe. It'll work out."

"Babe?" His smile is instant, and so is the flush in my cheeks.

"Yes . . . babe." I adjust the collar of his shirt, and he leans over to kiss the tip of my nose.

"You're right; worst-case scenario, we go to England."

I ignore his comment and return to the closet to pick out my own clothes for the day. "Do you think they'll let me accompany you inside?" I ask him, unsure what to wear.

"You want to?"

"If they allow it." I grab the new purple dress that I planned to wear to Vance tomorrow. I undress and put it on as quickly as possible. I slip on some black heels and exit the closet with my hands holding up the front of the dress. "Can you help me?" I ask Hardin, turning my back to him.

"You're purposely torturing me." His fingertips travel across my exposed shoulders and down my back, leaving goose bumps in their wake.

"Sorry." My mouth is dry.

He slowly raises the zipper, and I shiver as his lips press against the sensitive skin on the back of my neck. "We need to get going," I tell him, and he groans, fingers digging into my hips.

"I'm going to call my dad on the way. Are we dropping the . . . your dad off somewhere?"

"I'll ask him now; can you grab my bag?" I say, and he nods.

"Tess?" he calls as my hand hits the doorknob. "I like that dress. And you. Well, I love you, of course . . . and your new dress," he rambles. "I love you, and your fancy clothes."

I curtsy and do a little three-sixty so he can see me. As much as I hate Hardin being nervous, it's also very appealing to me, because it reminds me that he's not so tough after all.

In the living room, my father is sitting on the couch, having fallen back asleep. I don't know if I should wake him up or just leave him here to rest until we get back from campus.

"Let him sleep," Hardin answers, sensing my thoughts as he walks up behind me.

I quickly scribble a note for him explaining when we'll return, along with our phone numbers. I doubt he has a cell phone, but I leave them just in case.

The drive to campus is short, too short, and Hardin looks like he's going to either scream or punch something at any moment. When we arrive, he scans the parking lot for Ken's car.

"He said to meet him here," Hardin says, checking the screen on his phone for the fifth time in five minutes.

"There he is." I point to the silver car pulling into the lot.

"Finally. What the fuck took him so long?"

"Be nice to him; he's doing this for you. Please, just be nice to him," I beg, and he sighs in frustration but agrees.

Ken has brought his wife, Karen, and Hardin's stepbrother, Landon, which surprises Hardin and makes me smile. I love them so much for supporting him, even when he acts like he doesn't want their help.

"Don't you have anything better to do?" Hardin says to Landon as they approach us.

"Don't you?" Landon retaliates, which makes Hardin laugh.

Listening to their exchange, Karen smiles with a brightness completely at odds with how she first appeared when she emerged from Ken's car.

As we walk toward the administrative building, Ken says, "I'm hoping this won't last long. I've been calling everyone I can to pull as many strings as possible, so I'm praying for the best." He stops for a minute and turns to Hardin. "Let me do the talking in there—I mean it." Watching for his son's response, he waits for him to agree.

"Okay, yeah," Hardin says without argument.

Ken nods and swings the big wooden doors open, leading us all inside. Over his shoulder, Ken says authoritatively, "Tessa, I'm sorry, but you can't come inside the room with us. I didn't want to push it, but you can wait right outside." He turns and gives me a sympathetic smile.

But Hardin immediately goes into full panic mode. "What do you mean she can't come inside? I need her in there!"

"I know you do. I'm sorry, but it's family only," his father explains as he leads us down the hall. "Unless she was a witness, but even then, that's a huge conflict of interest."

Ken stops us in front of a conference room and muses, "It's not like *I'm* not engaged in a conflict of interest, being the chancellor. But you're my son, and let's at least have only one conflict, okay?"

I turn to Hardin. "He's right, and it'll be better this way. It's okay," I assure him.

He lets go of my hand and nods, looking past me to shoot daggers at his father, who sighs and says, "Hardin, please try your best to—"

Hardin holds up one hand. "I will, I will," he says and kisses my forehead.

As the four of them walk into the room, I want to ask Landon to wait with me, but I know Hardin needs him in there, whether he'll admit it or not. I feel so useless just sitting here outside this room while a group of stuffy men in suits decides Hardin's educational future. Well, maybe there's one way I can help . . .

I pull my phone out and text Zed. I'm at the administrative building, can you come here?

I stare at the screen, waiting for a reply, and my phone lights up less than a minute later: Yes, I'm on my way.

I'll be outside, I send.

With one last glance at the door, I head outside. It's cold, too cold to be waiting out here in a knee-length dress, but I don't have much of a choice.

AFTER WAITING AWHILE, I've just decided to go back inside when Zed's old truck pulls into the parking lot. He steps out, wearing a black sweatshirt and dark-wash jeans. The deep bruising on his face shocks me, despite the fact that I just saw him yesterday.

He tucks his hands into the pocket on the front of his sweatshirt. "Hey."

"Hey. Thanks for meeting me."

"It was my idea, remember?" He smiles, and I feel slightly less unsettled.

I smile in return. "I guess you're right."

"I want to talk to you about what you said at the hospital," he says, which was exactly what I was planning to talk about.

"So do I."

"You go first."

"Steph said you told Tristan you're pressing charges against Hardin." I try not to look at his bruised and bloodshot eyes.

"I did."

"But you told me you *wouldn't* press charges. Why lie to me?" I'm sure the hurt is clear in my shaky voice.

"I didn't lie to you; I meant it when I said it."

I step closer to him. "So what changed your mind?"

He shrugs. "A lot of things. I thought about all the shit he's done to me, and to you. He doesn't deserve to just walk away from this." He gestures to his face. "Look at me, for God's sake."

I'm not sure what to say to Zed in this moment. He has every right to be upset with Hardin, but I wish he wouldn't take legal action against him.

"He's already in trouble with the university board," I say, hoping to change his mind.

"He's not going to get in trouble; Steph told me his dad's the chancellor," he scoffs.

Dammit, Steph—why would you tell him that? I nod to acknowledge what he said. "That doesn't mean he won't get in trouble."

But my saying this only makes him exasperated. "Tessa, why are you always so quick to defend him? No matter what he does, you're right there to fight his battles for him!"

"That's not true," I lie.

"Yes, it is!" He throws his hands up in disbelief. "You *know* it is! You told me you'd think about what I said about leaving him, but then I see you with him at a tattoo shop days later. It doesn't make sense."

"I know you don't understand, but I love him."

"If you love him so much, then why are you running away to Seattle?"

His words rattle me. I pause for a second, but say, "I'm not running to Seattle. I'm going there for a better opportunity."

"He's not coming with you. Our group of friends talk, you know?"

What? "He was planning to," I lie. But I can tell Zed sees right through it.

With challenge in his eyes, he looks off to the side, then levels his stare at me. "If you can tell me that you have no feelings toward me, none at all, I'll drop the charges."

Right then, the air seems to grow colder, the wind stronger. "What?"

"You heard me. Tell me to leave you alone and never speak to you again, and I'll do it." His request reminds me of something Hardin said to me long ago.

"But I don't want that; I don't want to never talk again," I admit.

"So what do you want, then?" he asks, his voice tinged with sadness and anger. "Because you seem to be just as confused as I am! You keep texting me and meeting up with me; you kiss me, sleep in the same bed as me; you always come to me when he hurts you! What do you want from me?"

I thought I'd made my intentions clear at the hospital. "I don't know what I want from you, but I love *him* and that's never going to change. I'm sorry that I gave you mixed signals, but I—"

"Tell me why you're going to Seattle in a week and haven't told him!" he shouts back at me, his arms waving in front of his body.

"I don't know . . . I'm going to tell him when I get the chance."

"You won't tell him because you know he'll leave you," Zed snaps, his eyes looking past me.

"He . . . well . . ." I don't know what to say—because I really fear Zed's right.

"Well, guess what, Tessa? You can thank me later."

"For what?" I watch as his lips turn up into a wicked smile.

Zed lifts his arm up, gesturing behind me, and a shiver rakes through me. "For telling him for you."

I know that when I turn around, Hardin will be standing there. I swear I can hear his ragged breathing over the harsh winter wind.

chapter five

HARDIN

When I'd stepped outside, the wind whipped around me, carrying the one voice I didn't expect to hear right now. I'd just had to endure hearing a lot of people say a lot of bad things about me, and I just had to remain quiet. And afterward, all I wanted to hear was the voice of my girl, my angel.

And there was her voice. But there was also *his*. I turn the corner, and indeed, there he is. There *they* are. Tessa and Zed.

My first thoughts were: *Why the fuck is he here? Why the fuck is Tessa outside talking to him? What part of "stay the fuck away from him" does she not fucking get?*

When that motherfucker raised his voice at her, I started walking toward them: nobody yells at her like that. But when he mentioned Seattle . . . I was stopped in my tracks. *Tessa is planning to go to Seattle?*

And Zed knew, but I didn't?

This isn't happening, this can't actually be happening. She would never plan to leave without telling me . . .

Zed's wild eyes and shit-eating grin mock me as I try to collect my fucked-up thoughts. When Tessa turns to me, her movements are painstakingly slow. Her blue-gray eyes are wide, pupils blown out in surprise when they meet mine.

"Hardin . . ." I can see she's saying the words, but her voice is small, lost in the wind.

Unsure what to say, I stand still while my mouth drops open, closes, opens—back and forth in an endless pattern until the words finally fall from my lips. "So this was your plan, then?" I manage.

She pushes her hair back from her face, her mouth turns to a frown immediately, and she rubs her hands up and down her arms, which are crossed in front of her chest.

"No! It's not like that, Hardin, I—"

"You two are quite the fucking schemers, aren't you? You . . ." I point to the bastard. "You fucking scheme and plot behind my back and try to make a move on my girl, over and fucking over. No matter what I do, no matter how many times I pound your goddamned face in, you still keep crawling back like a fucking cockroach."

Amazingly, he dares to speak. "She's—"

"And *you* . . ." I point to the blond girl who has my world under the sharp heel of her black shoe. "You—you keep playing mind games with me, acting like you give a fuck, when really you've been planning to leave me this entire time! You know I won't go to Seattle, yet you're planning to run off—without telling me!"

Her eyes glassy, she pleads with me. "That's why I hadn't told you yet, Hardin, because—"

"Stop fucking talking," I say, and her hand moves to her chest, like my words are causing her pain.

Maybe they are. Maybe I want them to, so she can feel what I feel.

How could she humiliate me this way—in front of Zed, of all people?

"Why is he here?" I ask her.

There is no evidence of his smug grin when she turns to look at him before looking back at me. "I asked him to meet me here."

I stagger back in mock surprise. Or maybe it's real surprise—I can't tell what these feelings really are, rushing through me so quickly. "Well, there we go! The two of you obviously have something special here."

"I only wanted to talk to him about the charges. I'm trying to *help* you, Hardin. Please, just *listen* to me." She steps toward me, moving her hair from her face again.

I shake my head. "Bullshit! I heard your entire conversation. If you don't want him, tell him right now, in front of me."

Her watery eyes plead silently for me to give in and not make her humiliate him in front of me, but it doesn't sway me.

"Now, or I'm done with you." My own words burn like acid on my tongue.

"I don't want you, Zed," she says, facing me. Her words are rushed, panicked, and I know it's hurting her to say them.

"At all?" I ask, mimicking Zed's grin from earlier.

"At all." She frowns, and he runs his hands through his hair.

"You never want to see him again," I instruct. "Turn and tell him that."

But it's Zed who speaks up. "Hardin, just stop. Leave it alone. I got the message. You don't have to play into his sick game, Tessa. I get it," he says. He looks pathetic, like a sad child.

"Tessa . . ." I start, but when she looks up at me, what I see behind her eyes nearly brings me to my knees. Disgust—she is full of disgust for me.

She takes a step toward me. "No, Hardin, I won't do it. Not because I want to be with him—because I don't. I love you—only you—but you're only doing this to prove a point, and it's ugly, and it's cruel, and I won't help you." She bites the inside of her cheek, trying not to cry.

What the hell am I doing?

With fiery intensity, she tells me, "I'm going home; when you want to talk about Seattle, that's where I'll be." With that, she turns to walk away.

"You don't have a way to get home!" I call to her.

Zed reaches out an arm in her direction. "I'll take her," he says.

Which breaks something in me. "If I wasn't already in a bunch of shit because of you, I would *kill* you right now. I don't just mean break a bone, I mean I would literally crack your skull open against the concrete and watch you bleed out all over this—"

"Stop it!" Tessa yells as she turns, covering her ears.

"Tessa, if you—" Zed says softly.

"Zed, I appreciate everything you've done, but you really need to stop." She tries to sound stern but fails miserably.

With a final sigh, he turns on his heel and walks away.

I head to the car, and as soon as I'm near it, my father and Landon appear—of fucking course. I hear the click of Tessa's heels behind me.

"We're going," I tell them before they can get a word in.

"I'll call you in a little while," she says to Landon.

"You're still going Wednesday, right?" he asks her.

She smiles at him, a fake smile to mask the panic behind her eyes. "Yeah, of course."

Landon glares at me, obviously noticing the tension between us. *Does he know about her plan? Probably—he probably helped her develop it.*

I climb into the car, not even trying to hide my lack of patience.

"I'll call you," she says again to Landon and waves goodbye to my father before getting in. I immediately turn the music off as she buckles her seat belt.

"Go ahead," she says, no emotion in her voice.

"What?"

"Go ahead and scream at me. I know you're going to."

I'm stunned into silence by her assumption. Granted, I had planned on yelling at her, but the way she just expects it throws me off guard.

But of course she expects it—that's what always happens. That's what I do . . .

"Well?" Her lips are pressed in a hard line.

"I'm not going to yell at you."

She glances over at me momentarily before focusing at some point out beyond the window.

"I don't know what to do except scream at you . . . that's the problem." I sigh in defeat, my forehead resting against the steering wheel.

"I wasn't planning this behind your back, Hardin, not purposely."

"It sure as hell seems that way."

"I would never do that to you. I love you. You'll understand when we go over it."

Her words bounce right off of me as anger takes over. "I *understand* you're moving—soon. I don't even know when—and *we live together*, Tessa. We share a fucking bed, and you're going to just leave me? I always knew you would."

I hear the click of her seat belt and then feel her hand pushing me back by the shoulders. Within seconds she's on my lap, bare thighs straddling me, cold arms wrapped around my neck, her tear-soaked face buried in my chest.

"Get off of me," I say, attempting to unwrap her arms from me.

"Why do you always assume I'm going to leave you?" She tightens her grip.

"Because you will."

"I'm not going to Seattle to leave you, I'm going for myself and my career. It's always been my plan to go there, and this is an incredible opportunity. I asked Mr. Vance while we were figuring out what we were going to do, and I planned on telling you so many times, but you either cut me off or didn't want to talk about anything serious."

All I can think of is her packing her bags and leaving me with nothing but some bullshit note on the counter. "Don't you dare try to blame me." My voice doesn't hold as much conviction as I intended.

"I'm not blaming you, but I knew you wouldn't be supportive; you know how important this is to me."

"What are you going to do, then? If you go, I can't be with you. I love you, Tessa, but I'm not going to Seattle."

"Why? You don't even know if you'd like it or not. We could at least try it, and if you hate it, we could go to England . . . maybe," she says with a sniffle.

"You don't know if you'll like Seattle either." I look at her with blank eyes. "I'm sorry, but you have to choose: me or Seattle."

She looks up at me for a moment, then moves back to the passenger seat without a word.

"You don't have to decide right now, but time is running out." I put the car in drive and pull out of the small space.

"I can't believe you're making me choose." She doesn't look at me.

"You knew how I felt about Seattle. You're lucky I kept my cool back there when you were with him."

"I'm 'lucky'?" she scoffs.

"This day is shit already; let's not fight about it. I'm going to need an answer by Friday. Unless, of course, you'll be gone by then." The idea sends a chill through my body.

I know she'll choose me—she has to. We can go to England and get away from all this bullshit. She hasn't said a word about missing classes today, which I'm glad for, since that's another fight I don't want to have.

"You're being so selfish," she accuses.

I don't argue, because I know she's right. But I do say, "Well, some might say selfish is also not telling someone when they plan on leaving them. Where are you going to live? Do you already have a place?"

"No, I was going to look for one tomorrow. We leave Wednesday for the trip with your family." It takes me a moment to realize who she's referring to.

"We?"

"You said you'd go . . ."

"I'm still trying to recover from this Seattle shit, Tessa." I know I'm being an asshole, but this is so fucked up. "And let's not forget you calling Zed," I add, doubling down.

Tessa stays silent as I drive. I have to look over at her multiple times to make sure she's still awake.

"Are you not speaking to me now?" I finally ask her as we approach the parking lot of our . . . *my* apartment.

"I don't know what to say." Her voice is quiet, defeated.

I park, and it hits me. *Shit.* "You're dad's still here, isn't he?"

"I don't know where else he would go . . ." she says without looking at me.

We get out of the car, and I say, "Well, when we get upstairs, I'll ask him where he needs to be dropped off at."

"No, I'll take him," she mumbles.

Even though my girl's walking next to me, she seems miles away.

chapter six

TESSA

I'm too disappointed in Hardin to argue, and he's too pissed at me to speak without screaming. He actually handled the news better than I thought he would, but how could he make me choose? He knows how important Seattle is to me, and it's not like he has a problem with me giving something up for him—that's what hurts me the most. He always says he can't be away from me, that he can't live without me, yet he's giving me an ultimatum, and it's not fair.

"If he took off with any of our shit . . ." Hardin begins as we get to the door.

"Enough." Hopefully my exhaustion is heard through my soft dismissal, so he won't press it.

"Just saying."

I push my key into the lock and twist, momentarily considering the possibility of what Hardin has mentioned. I don't know the man, really.

Any paranoia I have disappears when we walk inside. My father's body is slumped over the arm of the couch. His mouth is wide open, and deep snores escape from his parted lips.

Without another word, Hardin walks into the bedroom and I go to the kitchen for a glass of water and a minute to think about my next step. The last thing that I want to do is fight with Hardin, but I'm beyond sick of him only thinking of himself. I know he has changed so much, tried so hard, but I've given him chance after chance, resulting in an endless breakup-makeup cycle that would make even Catherine Earnshaw cringe. I don't know how long I can keep my head above water when I'm fighting off the tidal wave that we call a relationship. Every time I feel like I've learned to tread its waters, I'm sucked back under by yet another conflict with Hardin.

After a few moments, I get up and look over at my father: still snoring in a way I would find amusing if I wasn't so preoccupied. Deciding on a course of action, I head into the bedroom.

Hardin is lying on his back, his arms tucked under his head as he stares at the ceiling. I'm about to speak when he breaks the silence.

"I got expelled. Just in case you were wondering."

I turn to him quickly, my heart racing. "What?"

"Yep. Sure did." He shrugs his shoulders.

"I'm so sorry. I should have asked earlier." I thought for sure Ken could get his son out of this mess. I'm devastated for him.

"It's okay. You were otherwise occupied with Zed and plans for Seattle, remember?"

I sit on the edge of the bed, as far from him as possible, and try my best to bite my tongue. It's a wasted effort. "I was trying to find out about the charges against you. He says he's still—"

He interrupts me with his eyebrows raised in mockery. "I heard him. I was there, remember?"

"Hardin, I've had enough of your attitude. I know you're upset, but you need to stop being so disrespectful." I speak slowly, hoping the words sink in.

He's dumbfounded for a moment, but he quickly recovers. "Excuse me?"

I try to keep the most neutral, if stern, expression I can manage. "You heard me: stop talking to me like that."

"I'm sorry—I get kicked out of school, then find you with *him*, then learn you're going to Seattle. I'd say I'm entitled to be a little angry."

"Yes, you are, but you aren't entitled to be a jerk. I was hoping we could actually talk about this and work it out like adults . . . for once."

"What's that supposed to mean?" He sits up, but I keep my distance.

"It means that after six months of this back-and-forth, I thought we could possibly solve a problem without one of us leaving or breaking things."

"Six months?" His jaw drops.

"Yes, six months." Awkwardly, I avoid his eyes. "Well, since we met."

"I hadn't realized it's been that long."

"Well, it has." *It feels like a lifetime to me.*

"It doesn't feel like that long . . ."

"Is that a problem for you? We've been seeing each other too long?" I finally meet his green eyes.

"No, Tessa, it's just odd to think about, I guess. I've never been in an actual relationship, so six months is a long time."

"Well, we haven't been dating the entire time. Most of it was spent fighting or avoiding one another," I remind him.

"How long, exactly, were you with Noah?"

His question surprises me. We've had a few talks regarding my relationship with Noah, but they usually last less than five minutes, ending abruptly because of Hardin's jealousy.

"We were best friends since I can remember, but only started dating halfway through high school. I think we'd basically been dating before then but we just didn't realize it." I watch Hardin with careful eyes, waiting for a reaction.

Talking about Noah makes me miss him—not in a romantic way, but in that way you miss your family after not seeing them for an extended period.

"Oh." He rests his hands in his lap, making me want to reach across and hold them. "Did you fight?"

"Sometimes. Our fights were over things like what movie to watch, or him being late to pick me up."

He doesn't look up from his hands. "Not like we fight, then?"

"I don't think anyone fights like we do." I smile in an attempt to reassure him.

"What else did you do? With him, I mean," he says, and I swear that sitting in Hardin's place on the bed there is now a small child, green eyes bright, hands nearly shaking.

I give a gentle shrug. "We didn't do much, really, outside of studying and watching hundreds of movies. We were more like best friends, I guess."

"You loved him," the child reminds me.

"Not the way that I love you," I tell him, just like I have countless times before.

"Would you have given up Seattle for him?" He picks at the rough skin around his fingernails. When he looks at me, his insecurity shines through his eyes.

So this is why we're talking about Noah: Hardin's low self-esteem has once again taken his thoughts there, to that place where he compares himself to whatever or whomever he thinks that I need.

"No."

"Why not?" I reach for his hand to comfort the childlike worry inside of him.

"Because I shouldn't have to choose at all, and he always knew about my plans and dreams, so I wouldn't have had to choose."

"I don't have anything in Seattle." He sighs.

"Me . . . you'd have me."

"That's not enough."

Oh . . . I turn away from him.

"I know that's fucked up, but it's true. I have nothing there, and you'll have this new job, and you'll make new friends—"

"You'd have a new job, too. Christian said he'd give you a job—and we would make new friends together."

"I don't want to work for him—and the people you'd choose as friends are more than likely not going to be the same people I would choose. It would just be so different out there."

"You don't know that. I'm friends with Steph."

"Only because you were roommates. I don't want to move there, Tessa, especially now that I've been expelled. It makes more sense for me to just go back to England and finish university there."

"This shouldn't only be about what makes sense for you."

"Considering that you went behind my back and saw Zed yet again, you aren't exactly in any position to be calling the shots."

"Really? Because you and I haven't even established that we're together again. I agreed to move back in, and you agreed to treat me better." I stand up from the bed and begin to pace across the concrete floor. "But you went behind my back and beat him up, resulting in your expulsion—so if anyone isn't in a position to call the shots, it's you."

"You were hiding this from me!" He raises voice. "You've been planning to leave me and didn't tell me!"

"I know! I'm sorry for that, but instead of arguing over who's the *most* wrong here, why don't we try to fix it or come to some sort of compromise?"

"You . . ." He stops and stands up from the bed. "You don't . . ."

"What?" I press.

"I don't know, I can't even think straight because of how mad I am at you."

"I'm sorry for you finding out that way, but I don't know what else to say."

"Say that you won't go."

"I'm not making that choice right now. I shouldn't have to."

"When then? I won't wait around—"

"What are you going to do, then—leave? What happened to 'I never wish to be parted from you from this day on'?"

"Really? You're going to bring that up? You don't think an ideal time to bring up Seattle would be before I got a fucking tattoo for you? The irony isn't lost on me." He steps closer to me, challenging me.

"I was going to!"

"But you didn't."

"How many times are you going to mention that? We can go back and forth all day, but I really don't have the energy. I'm over it," I say.

"Over it? You're *over* it?" He half laughs.

"Yes, over it." It's true, I'm over fighting with him about Seattle. It's suffocating and frustrating, and I've had just about enough.

He grabs a black sweatshirt from the closet and pulls it over his head before slipping his boots onto his feet.

"Where are you going?" I demand.

"Away from here," he huffs.

"Hardin, you don't have to leave," I call as he opens the door, but he ignores me.

If my father wasn't in the living room, I'd chase after him and force him to stay.

But honestly, I'm tired of chasing him.

chapter seven

HARDIN

Tessa's father is awake now, sitting on the couch with his arms crossed in front of his chest and staring blankly out the window.

"Do you need a ride somewhere?" I ask him. I'm not thrilled with the idea of taking him anywhere, but I sure as hell despise the idea of leaving him alone with her.

He snaps his head my direction as if startled. "Um, yeah, is that okay?" he asks.

"Yeah," I quickly answer.

"Okay, I just want to say goodbye to Tessie." He looks toward our bedroom.

"Fine. I'll be in the car."

I head out the door, unsure of exactly where I'm going after I drop the old fool off, but I know it's not good for either of us if I stay here. I'm so angry with myself. I know she's not the only one to blame here, but I'm used to lashing out at people, and she's always with me, making her an easy target. Which makes me a pathetic motherfucker, I know. I keep my eyes trained on the entrance to our apartment building, waiting for Richard. If he doesn't come soon, I'll leave his ass here. But then I sigh at the thought, since I really don't want to leave him here with her.

At last, the Father of the Year steps through the door and pulls down the sleeves of his shirt. I had expected him to wear the clothes of mine that Tessa gave him, but he's dressed in his clothes from yesterday, only now they're clean. Damn Tessa, she's too fucking nice.

I turn the volume up on the radio as he opens the passenger door, hoping that the music will halt any conversation he might try to make.

No luck. "She said to tell you to be careful," he says as soon as he gets in, then buckles his seat belt like he's trying to show me how to do it. Like he's some airline hostess. I give him a small nod and pull onto the street.

"How did your meeting go today?" he asks.

"Really?" I raise my brow at him.

"Just wondering." He taps his fingers on his leg. "I'm glad she went with you."

"Okay."

"She seems to be a lot like her mother."

I shoot a look at him. "The hell she is. She's nothing like that woman." *Is he trying to get himself thrown out onto the highway?*

He laughs. "The good qualities only, of course. She's very headstrong, just like Carol. She wants what she wants, but Tessie is much sweeter, gentler."

Here we go with the Tessie bullshit again.

"I heard the two of you fighting. It woke me up."

I roll my eyes. "Excuse us for waking you up at noon while you were sleeping on our couch."

Again, I'm met with a chuckle. "I get it, man—you're angry at the world. I was, too. Hell, I still am. But when you find someone who's willing to put up with your shit, you don't have to be so angry anymore."

Well, old-timer, what do you suggest I do when your daughter is the one making me so goddamn angry? "Look, I'll admit you aren't as bad as I thought you were, but I didn't ask for your advice, so don't waste your time giving it to me."

"I'm not giving you advice, I'm speaking from experience here. I'd hate to see the two of you end things."

We aren't ending things, Dick. I'm just trying to get my point across. I want to be with her, and I will be; she just needs to give in and come with me. I'm beyond fucking angry that she'd bring Zed into this shit again, regardless of her reasoning.

I turn the damn radio off. "You don't even know me—or her, for that matter. Why would you care?"

"Because I know you're good for her."

"Do you?" I reply, sarcasm in full bloom. Thankfully we're getting closer to his side of town, so this horrid conversation will be ending soon.

"Yes, I do."

Then it strikes me, and I'll never admit it to anyone, but it's actually sort of nice to have someone say I'm good for her, even if it's her drunk asshole of a father. I'll take it.

"Are you going to be seeing her again?" I ask, and then quickly add, "And where exactly am I taking you?"

"Just drop me near the shop where we met yesterday; I'll figure it out from there. And yes, I hope to be seeing her again. I have a lot of shit to make up for."

"Yeah, you do," I agree.

The parking lot next to the tattoo parlor is empty, which makes some sense, since it's not even one in the afternoon yet.

"Can you drive me to the end of this street?" he asks.

I nod and pass the shop. The only thing at the end of this street is a bar and a run-down Laundromat.

"Thanks for the ride."

"Yep."

"Do you want to come inside?" Richard asks, nodding toward the small bar.

Getting a drink with Tessa's homeless drunk father doesn't sound like the most intelligent thing to do at the moment.

However, I'm not known for making good decisions. "Fuck it," I mumble and turn the car off and follow him inside. It's not like I had anywhere in mind to go anyway.

The bar is dark and smells like mold and whiskey. Following him to the small counter, I grab a stool, leaving an empty seat between us. A middle-aged woman wearing what I *pray* are her teenage daughter's clothes walks toward us. Without a word she slides Richard a small glass filled with whiskey and ice.

"And for you?" she asks me, her voice raspy and deeper than mine.

"Same as him."

Tessa's voice warning me not to do this is clear as a bell between my ears. I push it away, push her away.

I raise the glass, and we toast and each take a sip. "How can you afford to be a drunk if you don't work?" I ask.

"I clean the place every other day, so I drink for free." Shame is clear in his voice.

"Why not be sober and get paid, then?"

"I don't know; I tried and tried." He stares at his glass with hooded eyes, and for a second they resemble mine. I can see a shadow of myself in them. "I'm hoping now it'll get easier if I can see my daughter more often."

I nod, not even bothering to hit him with a snide remark, and instead wrap my fingers around the cool glass. I welcome the familiar burn of scotch as I tip my head back and finish the rest. When I push it across the semipolished bar top, the woman makes eye contact and then starts pouring me another.

chapter eight

TESSA

Your *dad*?" Landon says incredulously through the phone.

I forgot that I hadn't had a chance to tell him about my father's return.

"Yeah, we ran into him yesterday . . ."

"How is he? What did he say? What was it like?"

"He's . . ." I don't know why, but I feel embarrassed to tell Landon that my father is still drinking. I know he'd never judge me, but I'm still apprehensive.

"Is he still . . ."

"Yeah, he is. He was drunk when we saw him, but we brought him back here and he stayed the night." I twirl a lock of hair around my index finger.

"Hardin let him?"

"He didn't have a say in it; it's my place, too," I snap. But then I immediately feel bad and apologize. "I'm sorry, I've just had it with Hardin thinking he controls everything."

"Tessa, do you want me to leave campus and come over?" Landon's so kind; you can hear it in how he talks.

"No, I'm just being dramatic." I sigh and look around the bedroom. "I think I'll come there, actually. I can still make my last class." I could really use some yoga right about now, and some coffee.

I listen to Landon as I dress myself for yoga. It seems like a waste to drive all the way to campus for one class, but I don't want to sit around this apartment and wait for Hardin to come home from wherever he ran off to.

"Professor Soto asked about your absence today, and Ken said he wrote a character witness statement for Hardin. What's up with that?" he asks.

"Soto did? I don't know . . . He offered to help him before, but I didn't think he meant it. I guess he just likes him or something?"

"Likes him? Likes *Hardin*?" Landon laughs, and I can't help but join him.

My phone drops into the sink as I pull my hair into a ponytail. I curse at myself and get it back to my ear just in time to hear Landon say he's headed to the library before his next class. After our goodbyes, I hang up and start to text Hardin, to let him know where I'll be. But then I close the app instead.

He'll come around about this whole Seattle thing; he has to.

By the time I get to school, the wind has picked up yet again and the sky has turned an ugly shade of gray. After grabbing a coffee, I still have thirty minutes before yoga. The library is on the other side of campus, so I don't have time to go there and see Landon. Instead I end up waiting outside Professor Soto's classroom. His class should be ending any—

My thoughts are cut off by the crowd of students practically rushing out the doors and into the hall. I lift my bag farther up my shoulder and push my way through them to get inside. The professor is standing with his back turned toward me as he pulls his leather jacket over his arms.

When he turns, he greets me with a smile. "Ms. Young."

"Hi, Professor Soto."

"What brings you by? Did you need the topic for today's journal that you missed?"

"No, Landon gave it to me already. I came by to thank you." I shift uncomfortably on the heels of my gym shoes.

"For what?"

"Writing that character witness statement for Hardin. I know he hasn't been that pleasant to you, so it's very appreciated."

"It's nothing, really. Everyone deserves a quality education, even hotheads." He laughs.

"I guess so." I smile at him and look around the classroom, unsure what to say next.

"Besides, Zed deserved what he got, anyway," he says suddenly.

What?

I look back at him. "What do you mean?"

Professor Soto blinks a few times before collecting himself. "Nothing, I'm just . . . I'm sure Hardin had a good reason for going after him, that's all. I better get going, I have a meeting to get to, but thanks for coming by. I'll see you in class Wednesday."

"I won't be here Wednesday; I'm going on a trip."

With a light hand he waves this off. "Well, have fun, then. I'll see you when you return." He quickly walks off, leaving me bewildered by what he could have meant.

chapter nine

HARDIN

My unlikely drinking partner, Richard, has escaped to the restroom for the fourth time since we've arrived. I get the feeling that Betsy the Bartender may taken have a slight liking toward the man, which makes me really fucking uncomfortable.

"Another?" she asks.

With a nod, I dismiss the burly woman. It's now after two in the afternoon, and I've had four drinks, which wouldn't be so bad if they weren't straight scotch with a smidgen of ice.

My thoughts are cloudy and my anger has yet to subside. I don't know who or what to be more mad about, so I've given up on reasoning things out and have decided to just run with a general state of pissed-the-fuck-off.

"Here ya go." The bartender slides my drink in front of me as Richard takes the stool directly next to me. I was under the impression he understood the importance of the empty stool between us. Guess not.

He turns to me, raking his hand over the rough whiskers of his beard. The sound is disgusting. "Did you order me another?"

"You should shave that." I offer my somewhat intoxicated opinion.

"This?" He does that thing with his hand again.

"Yes, that. It's not a good look," I say.

"It's okay—keeps me warm." He laughs, and I take a drink to stop myself from joining him.

"Betsy!" he calls. She nods and pulls his empty glass from the counter. Then he looks at me. "Are you going to tell me what it is you're drinking over?"

"Nope." I move my scotch in a circle, causing the solitary ice cube to clink against the glass.

"Fine; no questions, then. Only booze," he says with some glee.

My hatred toward him has dissolved for the most part. That is, until I picture the blond ten-year-old girl hiding in her mum's greenhouse. Her blue-gray eyes are wide, fearful almost . . . and then the blond boy in the fucking cardigan shows up to save the day.

"One question," he presses, jarring me from my thoughts.

I take a deep breath and an even deeper drink to keep myself from doing something idiotic. I mean, more idiotic than drinking with my girlfriend's alcoholic father. This family and their fucking questions. "One," I say.

"Did you really get kicked out of college today?"

I look over at the neon Pabst sign, thinking over the question, wishing I hadn't had four . . . no, *five* drinks. "No. But she thinks I did," I admit.

"And why does she think that?" *Nosy fucker.*

"Because I told her that I did." I swing my gaze to him and say with dead eyes, "That's enough confessions for one night."

"Have it your way." He smiles and raises his glass to hit mine but I pull away, shaking my head. I can tell by his laughter that he hadn't expected me to toast with him anyway and he finds me very amusing, the same way that I find him very annoying.

A woman around his age appears at his side and takes the stool next to him. She wraps her thin arm around his shoulder and he greets her warmly. She doesn't strike me as the homeless type, but she obviously knows him. He probably spends the majority of his time in this shithole of a bar. I use this distraction to check my phone for messages or calls from Tessa: nothing.

I'm relieved but annoyed that she hasn't attempted to talk to me. Relieved because I'm drunk, but annoyed because I miss her already. Each glass of scotch that slides down my throat makes me want her more, makes the hollowness of her absence grow.

Fuck, what has she done to me?

She's so damn infuriating, always trying to push my buttons. It's like she literally sits around and devises new ways to enrage me. Matter of fact, she probably does. She's probably sitting cross-legged on the bed with that stupid fucking planner on her lap, a pen between her teeth and another behind her ear, coming up with things to do or say that will drive me insane.

Six months we've been together now—six months. That's a long-ass time, longer than I ever thought I could stand to spend with one person. Granted, we haven't been dating the entire time, and a lot of those months were spent—no, *wasted*—with my trying to stay away from her.

Richard's voice breaks my thoughts. "This is Nancy."

I nod at the woman and stare back down at the dark wood of the bar top.

"Nancy, this well-mannered young man is Hardin. He's Tessie's boyfriend," he proudly says.

Why would he be proud of me dating his daughter?

"Tessie has a boyfriend! Is she here? I'd love to finally meet her. Richard here has told me so much about her!"

"She isn't here," I grumble.

"That's too bad; how did her birthday party go? It was last weekend, right?" she asks.

What?

Richard looks to me, clearly imploring me to go along with some lie he's obviously told. "Yeah, it was nice," he answers for me before gulping down the rest of his drink.

"That's nice," Nancy says, then points toward the entrance. "Oh, there she is!"

My eyes dart to the door, and for a moment I think she's talking about Tessa, but that wouldn't make sense. She's never met her. Instead a too-thin blonde walks across the small room and over to us. This dive bar is getting too damn crowded.

I hold my empty glass in the air. "Another."

After an eye roll and a whispered "Asshole," I'm given another drink.

"This is my daughter, Shannon," Nancy informs me.

Shannon looks me up and down with eyes that appear to have spiders stuck to them. This chick is wearing way too much makeup.

"Shannon, this is Hardin." Richard speaks, but I don't make any motion toward greeting her.

Many months ago I probably would have paid at least a little attention to the desperate girl. I maybe would have even let her blow me in the disgusting bathroom here, but now I just want her to stop fucking staring at me.

"I don't think it'll go any lower without taking it off," I say regarding the obnoxious way she keeps tugging at the hem of her shirt to show off the small bit of cleavage she can manage.

"*Excuse* me?" she huffs, placing her hands on her narrow hips.

"You heard me."

"Okay, okay. Let's all just settle down here," Richard says, putting his hands in the air.

With that, Nancy and her slutty daughter walk away to find a table.

"You're welcome," I say to him, but he shakes his head.

"You're an unpleasant son of a bitch." Before I can react, he adds, "Just how I like 'em."

* * *

THREE DRINKS LATER, I can barely sit on the bar stool. Richard, who obviously drinks for a living, literally, appears to have the same problem, as he's leaning way too close to me.

"So then when I get out the next day, I had to walk two miles! Of course it started raining . . ."

He continues on, telling me about the last time he was arrested. I continue to drink and pretend that he isn't talking to me.

"If I'm supposed to keep your secret, you should at least tell me why you told Tessie you were expelled," he says at last.

I somehow knew he would wait until I was full-on drunk to bring this up again. "It's easier if she thinks that," I admit.

"How's that?"

"Because I want her to go to England with me, and she isn't exactly thrilled with the idea."

"I don't get it." He pinches the bridge of his nose.

"Your daughter wants to leave me, and I can't let that happen."

"So you tell her you got kicked out of school so she'll go to England?"

"Basically."

He looks down at his drink, then over at me. "That's really stupid."

"I know." And it *does* sounds really fucking stupid when spoken out loud, but it somehow makes sense inside my fucked-up head.

"Who are you to give advice to me, anyway?" I say to him at last.

"No one. All I'm saying is you'll end up just like me if you keep it up."

I want to tell him to fuck off and mind his own damn business, but when I look up at him I see the resemblance I noted when we first sat down at the bar. Fuck.

"Don't tell her," I remind him.

"I won't." Then he turns to Betsy. "Another round."

She smiles at him and begins to make our drinks. I don't think I can handle another.

"I'm good. Right now you have three eyes," I tell him.

He shrugs. "More for me."

I'm a shit boyfriend, I think to myself, wondering what Tessie—*fuck*, Tessa—is doing right now.

"I'm a shit father," Richard says.

I'm too drunk to comprehend the difference between thinking and speaking, so I don't know if him saying this is coincidence or I was speaking out loud—

"Move down," a gruff male voice says to the left of Richard.

I glance over to see a short man with an even fuller beard than my drinking companion's.

"There aren't any more stools, partner," Richard replies slowly.

"Well, then you better move," the man threatens.

Fuck, not this. Not now.

"We aren't moving." I dismiss the man.

The man who then makes the mistake of grabbing Richard by the collar and roughly yanking him upright.

chapter ten

TESSA

The walk back to my car after yoga feels much longer than usual. The heaviness of Hardin's expulsion and the move to Seattle were lifted from me during meditation, but now, outside the walls of the classroom, the weight is back and multiplied by ten.

As soon as I begin to pull out of the parking spot, my phone vibrates on the passenger seat. Hardin.

"Hello?" I stop and shift the gear into park.

But it's a woman's voice that barks through the speaker, and my heart stops. "Is this Tessa?"

"Yes?"

"Good, I've got your father and . . ."

"Her . . . boyfriend . . ." I hear Hardin groan in the background.

"Yeah, your *boyfriend*," she says snidely. "I'm gonna need you to pick these two up before someone calls the cops."

"Calls the cops? Where are they?" I shift back into drive.

"Dizzy's on Lamar Avenue; you know the place?"

"No, but I'll Google it."

"Huh. Of course you will."

Ignoring her attitude, I hang up the phone and hastily get directions to the bar. *Why the hell are Hardin and my father at a bar at three in the afternoon? Why the hell are Hardin and my father even together?*

This makes no sense to me—and what about the cops? What did they do? I should have asked the woman on the phone. I can only hope they didn't get into a fight with *each other*. That's the last thing any of us needs.

My imagination has run wild by the time I make it to the bar, and has concluded that Hardin's either murdered my father or vice versa. There are no cop cars outside the small bar, which is a good sign, I suppose. I park directly in front of the building and hurry inside, wishing I had worn a sweatshirt instead of a T-shirt.

"There she is!" my father calls out jubilantly.

I can tell he's loaded as he stumbles over to me.

"You should have seen it, Tessie!" He claps his hands. "Hardin just whooped some serious ass!"

"Where is he—" I start, but right then a bathroom door opens and Hardin walks out, wiping his bloody hands on a red-stained paper towel.

"What happened?" I yell to him from the opposite side of the room.

"Nothing . . . calm down."

I gape as I walk over to him. "Are you *drunk*?" I ask, then twist slightly to look at his eyes: bloodshot.

He looks off to the side. "Maybe."

"This is unbelievable." I cross my arms as he tries to take my hand.

"Hey, you should be thanking me for having your dad's back. He'd be on the floor right now if it wasn't for me." He points to a man sitting on the floor holding a bag of ice against his cheek.

"I won't be thanking you for anything—you're drunk in the middle of the afternoon! And with my father, of all people. What the hell is wrong with you?" I storm away from him, back toward the bar, where my father is now sitting.

"Don't be mad at him, Tessie; he loves you." My father is defending him.

What the hell is going on here?

As Hardin walks over, I ball my fists at my sides and shout,

"So what, you two get drunk together and now you're best friends? Neither of you should even be drinking!"

"Baby," Hardin says into my ear and attempts to wrap his arm around me.

"Hey," the woman behind the bar says, knocking on the counter to get my attention. "You gotta get them out of here."

I nod at her and glare at the drunken idiots who are my lot. My father's cheek is pink, giving the impression he was hit, and Hardin's hands are already swelling.

"You can come to our house for tonight so you can sober up, but this isn't acceptable behavior." I want to scold them both, like the children they are. "For either of you."

I exit the smelly little space and am at the car before they make it to the door. Hardin scowls at my father as the older man tries to rest an arm on his shoulder. I get into my car, disgusted.

Hardin's intoxication puts me on edge. I know how he is when he's drunk, and I'm not sure I've ever seen him this drunk before, not even that night he destroyed all the china. I miss the days when Hardin didn't drink anything but water at parties. We have a list of problems right now, and him drinking only adds fuel to the flames.

APPARENTLY, MY FATHER has graduated from being an angry drunk to one who tells endless jokes, most of which are tasteless and obnoxious. The whole ride home he laughs too hard at his own words, with Hardin joining him every now and then. This isn't how I envisioned this day at all. I don't know what it was that made Hardin warm up to my father, but now that they're both drunk in the middle of the day, I don't like their "friendship" at all.

When we get home, I leave my father in the kitchen eating more of Hardin's Frosted Flakes and head for the bedroom—where most of our arguments seem to begin and end.

"Tessa," Hardin begins as soon as I close the door.

"Don't," I say coldly.

"Don't be mad at me—we were just having a drink." His tone is playful, but I'm not in the mood for it.

" 'Just having a drink'? With my father—an alcoholic who I'm trying to build a relationship with, who I wanted to maybe think about getting sober. That's who you were 'just drinking' with?"

"Baby . . ."

I shake my head. "Don't you 'baby' me. I'm not okay with this."

"Nothing happened." He wraps his fingers around my arm to pull me to him, but when I pull away it causes him to stumble to the bed.

"Hardin, you got in a fight again!"

"Not a big one. Who cares?"

"I do. I care."

He looks up at me from his place on the edge of our bed, his green eyes laced with red, and says, "Then why are you leaving me? If you care so much?"

My heart sinks a little farther into my chest.

"I'm not leaving you; I'm asking you to come with me." I sigh.

"But I don't want to," he whines.

"I know, but this is the one thing I have left—apart from you, of course."

"I'll marry you." He reaches for my hand, but I step back.

My breath hitches. I'm sure I couldn't have heard that correctly. "*What?*" I raise my hands, blocking him from coming closer.

"I said I'll marry you if you choose me." He stands up, stepping toward me.

The words, even though they're meaningless because of the amount of alcohol coursing through him, still excite me. "You're drunk," I say.

He's only offering marriage because he's drunk, which is worse than not offering at all.

"So? I still mean it."

"No, you don't." I shake my head and dodge his touch again.

"Yes, I do—not now, of course, but in like . . . six years or so?" He scratches his thumb across his forehead, thinking.

I roll my eyes. Despite my fluttering heart, this last bit of hedging, offering to marry me in a vague "six years or so," shows that reality is creeping back into his thoughts, even as he drunkenly tries to convince me otherwise. "We'll see how you feel about this tomorrow," I say, knowing he surely won't remember it tomorrow.

"Will you be wearing those pants?" His lips form a wicked smile.

"No; don't even start talking about these damn pants."

"You're the one who wore them. You know how I feel about them." He looks down at his lap, then points at it and looks up waggling his eyebrows.

Playful, teasing, drunk Hardin is sort of adorable . . . but not adorable enough to make me lose my ground.

"Come here," he begs, mock-frowning.

"No. I'm still upset with you."

"Come on, Tessie, don't be mad." He laughs and rubs his eyes with the back of his hands.

"If either of you calls me that one more time, I swear—"

"Tessie, what's wrong, Tessie? You don't like the name Tessie, Tessie?"

Hardin grins wide, and I feel my resolve fading the longer I stare at him.

"Are you going to let me take those pants off of you?"

"No. I've a lot to do today, and none of those things involve you taking my clothes off. I would ask you to come along, but you decided to get wasted with my father, so I have to go alone."

"You're going somewhere?" His voice is smooth yet raspy, thick from the liquor.

"Yes."

"You're not wearing that, though, right?"

"Yes, I am. I can wear whatever the hell I want to wear." I grab a sweatshirt and head for the door. "I'll be back later; don't do anything stupid, because I won't bail you or my father out of jail."

"Sassy. I like it, but I can think of something else to do with that smart mouth of yours." When I ignore his crude remark, he coos, "Stay with me."

I quickly leave the room and the apartment before he can persuade me to stay. I hear him call "Tessie" as I reach the door and have to cover my mouth to hide the giggle that escapes. This is my problem: when it comes to Hardin, my brain doesn't see the difference between right and wrong.

chapter eleven

TESSA

By the time I make it to my car, I already wish I'd have stayed in the bedroom with Hardin and his playful mood.

But I have too much to do. I have to call the woman back about the apartment in Seattle, get a few things for the trip with Hardin's family, and, most importantly, clear my head about Seattle. Hardin offering me marriage nearly swayed me, but I know he won't mean it tomorrow. I'm trying desperately not to overthink his words and let them change my mind, but it's much harder than I expected.

I'll marry you if you choose me.

I was surprised—shocked, really—when the words were spoken. He seemed so calm, his voice so neutral, as if he were announcing what we were having for dinner. I know better, though; I know he's getting desperate. The liquor and his desperation to keep me from moving to Seattle are the only reasons behind his offer. Even so, I can't stop replaying the words in my mind. Pathetic, I know, but if I'm being honest, that mix of hopefulness and knowing better than to feel that way is how I feel.

By the time I get to Target, I still haven't called Sandra (I believe that's her name) to discuss the apartment. It looks like a nice place from the pictures on the website. Not nearly as big as our current space, but it's good enough, and I can afford to live there on my own. It doesn't have bookshelves for walls or the exposed-brick wall that I have grown to love so much, but it'll do.

I'm ready for this, for Seattle. I'm ready to take this step for my future; I've been waiting for this since I can remember.

I stroll through the store, daydreaming about Seattle and my situation, and soon I find my basket full of random things, none of which I actually need for the trip. Tablets for the dishwasher, toothpaste, a new dustpan. Why am I buying this if I'm moving anyway? I put the dustpan back, along with some colorful socks I tossed in there for no apparent reason. If Hardin doesn't come along, I'll need to start over and buy all new dishes, all new everything. It's a huge relief that the apartment comes furnished, since that crosses out at least a dozen things from my to-do list.

After Target, I'm not really sure what to do with myself. I don't want to return to the apartment with Hardin and my father, but I don't have anywhere else to go. I'm going to be spending three days with Landon, Ken, and Karen, so I don't want to drive to their house and bother them. I really need friends. Or one friend, at least. I could call Kimberly, but she's probably busy planning her own move. Lucky girl. It's Christian's company that's taking her to Seattle, granted, but I can tell by the way he looks at her that he'd follow her anywhere.

While scrolling through my phone to call Sandra, I almost tap Steph's name.

I wonder what she's doing. Hardin would probably lose his mind if I called her to hang out. Then again, he's in no position to tell me what to do, being completely belligerent and wasted in the middle of the day.

I'm calling her, I decide. And she answers quickly.

"Tessa! What're you up to?" she says loudly, trying to talk over the voices in the background.

"Nothing. I'm sitting in the parking lot at Target."

"Oh, fun shit, then?" She laughs.

"Not really. What are you doing?"

"Nothing; going to lunch with my friend."

"Oh, okay. Well, call me later or something," I say.

"You can meet us there if you want; it's just the Applebee's right off campus."

Applebee's reminds me of Zed, but the food was incredible and I haven't eaten yet today.

"Okay, I'll come if you're sure that's okay?" I ask.

I hear a car door shut in the background. "Yes! Get your ass over here. We'll be there in about fifteen minutes or so."

I call Sandra on my way back toward campus and leave her a voicemail. I can't ignore the relief that I feel when her voicemail picks up instead of her actual voice, but I'm not really sure what that's about.

Applebee's is really crowded by the time I arrive, and I don't see Steph as I scan the room for bright crimson hair, so I put my name in with the hostess.

"How many?" The hostess asks me with a friendly smile.

"Three, I think?" Steph said she was with her friend, so I assume she meant only one person.

"Well, I've got a booth available now, so let me give it to you just in case." The girl smiles and grabs four menus from the stand behind her.

I follow her to the booth toward the back of the restaurant and wait for Steph to arrive. I check my phone for any correspondence from Hardin, but there's none; he's probably passed out by now. When I look back up, my adrenaline immediately spikes at the sight of flaming-pink hair.

chapter twelve

HARDIN

I open the cabinet in search of something to eat. I need to soak up the liquor coursing through me.

"She's so mad at us," Richard says, watching me.

"Yeah, she is." I can't help but smile at the way her face was flushed with anger, her small fists bunched at her sides. She was furious.

It's not funny . . . well, it *is*, but it shouldn't be.

"Is my daughter one to hold grudges?"

I look at him for a minute. It's weird for a father to have to ask a boyfriend about his own daughter's habits. "Obviously not. You're in our kitchen eating all my damn cereal." I shake the empty box.

He smiles. "Guess you're right," he says.

"Yeah, usually am." Actually, that couldn't be further from the fucking truth. "Guess it sucks for you that you showed up now, when she's moving in less than a week," I say as I place a Tupperware container in the microwave. I'm not exactly sure what's in it, but I'm starving and too drunk to cook for myself, and Tessa isn't here to cook for me. *What the fuck am I going to do when she leaves me?*

"It does," he says with a grimace. "I'm just glad Seattle isn't too far."

"England is."

After a long pause, he says, "She won't go to England."

I give him a fuck-off look. "What the fuck do you know?

You've known her for, what, two days?" I'm about to really go off when the obnoxious beep of the microwave interrupts us.

"I know Carol, though, and she wouldn't go to England."

So he's back to being the annoying drunk he was yesterday.

"Tessa isn't her mother, and I'm not you."

"Okay," he says and shrugs.

chapter thirteen

TESSA

Molly.

I pray that her presence here is a complete coincidence, but when Steph appears behind her, I sink back into the booth.

"Hey, Tessa!" Steph says and sits across from me, scooting in close to the wall so her "friend" can sit next to her. *Why would she invite me to have lunch with her and Molly?*

"Long time no see," Molly the skank says to me.

I don't know what to say to either of them. I want to get up and walk out, but instead I half smile and just say, "Yeah."

"Have you ordered?" Steph asks, completely ignoring the fact that she brought with her my biggest—my *only*—enemy.

"No." I reach into my bag to pull out my phone.

"No need to call Daddy, I'm not going to bite." Molly smirks.

"I wasn't calling Hardin," I tell her. I was actually going to text him; there's a clear difference.

"Sure you weren't," she replies, and laughs.

"Stop," Steph snaps. "You said you'd be nice, Molly."

"Why did you even come?" I ask the girl that I loathe more than anyone in the entire world.

She shrugs. "I'm hungry," she says matter-of-factly, clearly mocking my emotions.

I grab my sweatshirt and move to get up. "I should just go."

"No, stay! Please, you're moving, and I won't see you again," Steph says, pouting.

"What?"

"You're leaving in a few days, aren't you?"

"Who told you that?"

Molly and Steph look at each other before Steph answers. "Zed, I think; it doesn't matter, though. I thought you'd tell me."

"I was going to; there was just a lot going on. I was going to tell you here . . ." I say, then look at Molly as if to explain my reluctance to continue.

"I still wish you'd've told me. I was your first friend here." Steph sticks out her bottom lip in a way that makes me feel bad but still seems a little comical, so I'm thankful when a server arrives to take our drink order.

While Steph and Molly are ordering their sodas, I text Hardin. You're probably passed out, but I'm at lunch with Steph, and she brought Molly :/ I hit send and look back up at the two girls.

"So, are you excited to be leaving? What are you and Hardin going to do?" Steph asks.

I shrug and look around the room. I'm not discussing my relationship in front of Satan's daughter.

"You can talk in front of me. Trust me, I'm not interested in your boring-ass life," Molly scoffs, taking a sip of her water.

"Trust you?" I laugh, and my phone vibrates.

Come home. Hardin texts back.

I don't know what I expected him to say, but I'm disappointed in his advice, or lack of it.

No, I'm hungry. I reply.

"Look, you and Hardin are cute and all, but I don't really give a shit about your relationship anymore," Molly informs me. "I have my own relationship to worry about now."

"Great. Good for you." I feel bad for whoever the idiot is.

"Speaking of which, Molly, when are we going to meet this mystery man?" Steph asks her friend.

Molly dismisses her with a flip of the hand. "I don't know; not right now."

The waitress returns with our drinks and takes our orders. As soon as she leaves, Molly turns to me, her real prey. "Anyway, so how pissed at Zed are you that he's planning to put Hardin in jail?" she asks, and I nearly spit out my water.

The idea of Hardin going to jail sends ice through my veins. "I'm trying to stop that from happening."

"Good luck with that. Unless you plan on fucking Zed, there's nothing you can do." Again she smirks, tapping her neon-green fingernail on the table.

"That's not an option," I growl.

I've got something you can eat here. Really, though, come home before something happens and I can't save you.

Save *me*? From what? Molly and Steph? Steph is my friend, and I've already proved once before that I can take Molly, and I'd do it again in a heartbeat. She's annoying and I can't stand her, but I'm not afraid of her like I once was.

I can tell by Hardin's perverted message that he's still intoxicated.

I mean it, leave there, his next message says when I don't reply.

I shove my phone into my bag and direct my attention to the girls.

"You've already done it before, so what's the difference?" Molly says.

"Excuse me?" I say.

"I'm not judging you. I've fucked Hardin. Zed, too," she reminds me.

I'm so frustrated that I want to scream. "I didn't sleep with Zed," I say through my teeth.

"Mm-hmm . . ." Molly says, and Steph glares at her.

"Did someone say that—that I slept with Zed?" I ask them.

"No," Steph answers before Molly can speak. "And anyway, enough talk about Zed. I want to know about Seattle. Is Hardin coming, too?"

"Yeah," I lie. I don't want to admit, especially in front of Molly, that Hardin refuses to join me in Seattle.

"So neither of you will be here anymore? That will be so strange," Steph says with a little frown.

It'll be strange to start over at a new campus after everything I've been through at WCU. That's exactly what I need, though—a new start. This entire town is tainted with memories of betrayal and false friendships.

"We should have a get-together this weekend—one last hurrah," Steph says.

I groan. "No, no parties."

"No, no, not a party, just our group." She looks at me with something like pleading in her eyes. "Let's be honest: we'll probably never see each other again, and Hardin should hang out with his old friends at least one more time."

I hestitate and have to look away from her, glancing over at the bar area.

Molly's voice interrupts the silence. "I won't be there, don't worry."

I look back at them, and right then our food arrives.

But I've lost my appetite. *Are people really saying that I slept with Zed? Has Hardin heard this supposed rumor? Will Zed really put Hardin in jail?* My head hurts.

Steph eats a few fries, and before she finishes chewing she says, "Talk to Hardin and let me know. We could have it at someone's apartment—Tristan and Nate's, even. That way no random douche bags will show up."

"I can ask . . . I don't know if he will or not." My eyes move down to my screen. Three missed calls. One text: Answer your phone.

I'm leaving after I eat, calm down. Drink some water, I respond and pick at my own fries a little.

But the tension obviously gets to Molly, and she starts talking like a pot boiling over. "Well, he *should* like that idea—we were his friends long before you came along and ruined him."

"I didn't ruin him."

"Yes, you did. He's so different now—he doesn't even call anybody anymore."

"His friends," I scoff. "Nobody calls him either. The only one who even contacts him anymore is Nate."

"That's because we know—" Molly begins.

But Steph puts her hand in the air. "Enough; oh my God," she groans, rubbing her temples.

"I'm going to ask for a takeout box and go home. This was a bad idea," I tell her. I don't know what she was thinking bringing Molly here anyway; she could have at least warned me.

Steph looks at me sympathetically. "I'm sorry, Tessa. I thought you guys could get along since she's not trying to fuck with Hardin anymore." Then she glares at Molly, who shrugs.

"We *are* getting along—better than before," Molly says.

I want to smack that smug look off her face. But Steph's ring tone interrupts my violent thoughts.

A puzzled look crosses her face. Then she says, "It's Hardin, he's calling me," and holds her phone up for me to see.

"I haven't been texting him back; I'll call him in a minute," I tell her, and she nods okay and ignores the call.

"Jeez, stalker much?" Molly bites down on the end of a french fry.

I bite my tongue and ask the server for a to-go box. I've barely touched my food, but I don't want to cause a scene in the middle of a restaurant.

"Please think about Saturday. We can even make it like a dinner thing instead of a party," Steph offers. Then she gives me her best smile. "Please?"

"I'll see what I can do, but we're going on a trip until Saturday morning."

She nods again agreeably. "You can choose the time."

"Thanks. I'll let you know," I tell her and pay my bill.

I don't like the idea, but in a way she's right—we won't ever see any of them again. Hardin's going somewhere; maybe not Seattle, but he isn't staying here now since his expulsion, and he probably should see his old friends one last time.

"He's calling again," Steph tells me; she doesn't bother trying to hide her amusement.

"Tell him I'm on my way." I stand up and head for the door.

When I turn back around, Steph and Molly are talking, and Steph's phone is resting on the table in front of them.

chapter fourteen

HARDIN

"Tessa, if you don't call me back, I'll come looking for you, hammered or not," I threaten, then throw my phone against the couch too hard, so it bounces up off the back and hits the concrete.

"She'll come back," *Dick* assures me ever so helpfully.

"I know that!" I shout at him and grab my phone. Fortunately, the screen's not cracked. I glare at the old drunk and then stalk into the bedroom.

Why the fuck is he here, again? And why the fuck isn't Tessa? Nothing good can come out of her being in the same room with Molly.

Just as I start plotting how to go out and find her when I have no keys, no car, and a blood alcohol level that is far beyond the legal limit, I hear the front door open.

"He's, uh, lying down," Richard says loudly, with incongruous cheerfulness. I suspect he's trying to give me some sort of warning of Tessa's arrival.

I pull the door open before she can and sweep a long arm to invite her in. She doesn't look the least bit intimidated or concerned by the deep scowl on my face.

"Why didn't you answer when I called you?" I demand.

"Because I told you I was leaving soon. And I did."

"You should have answered. I've been worried."

"Worried?" She's clearly surprised by my choice of words.

"Yes, worried. Why the hell were you with Molly?"

She puts her purse on the back of the chair. "Beats me. Steph invited me to lunch and brought her along,"

Fucking Steph. "Why the fuck would she do that? Was she mean?"

"No meaner than usual." She raises her brow, watching me.

"Steph's a bitch for bringing her. What were they saying?"

"I don't know, but I think people are spreading rumors about me." She frowns and sits on the chair to remove her shoes.

"What? What sort of rumors?"

What I really mean to ask is: Who do I have to kill?

Fuck, I'm still drunk. How is this possible? It's been at least three hours. I vaguely remember being told some time ago that each drink takes an hour to sober up from; I'm fucked for at least the next ten or so hours, then. That is, if I'm remembering correctly.

"Did you hear me?" Tessa's voice is calm, worried even.

"No, sorry," I mumble.

Her cheeks flush. "I think people are saying that Zed and I . . . *you* know."

"You what?"

"That we . . . slept together." Her eyes are weary and her voice is soft.

"Who's saying that?" I try to keep my voice at the same level as Tessa's despite the slow burn of anger building inside me.

"Supposedly there's a rumor about it; Steph and Molly were talking about it."

I don't know whether to try to comfort her or let my anger take over. I'm too drunk for this shit.

She holds her hands in her lap and looks down. "I don't want people to think of me in that way."

"Don't listen to them, they're fucking idiots. If there is a rumor, I'll be sure it's cleared up." I drag her over to sit with me on the bed. "Don't you worry."

"You're not mad at me?" she asks, blue-gray eyes meeting mine.

"Yes," I say. "I'm upset because you weren't answering, and then Steph didn't fucking answer. But I'm not mad about this rumor shit—not at you, at least; they probably just made it up because they wanted to be assholes." The thought of Steph and Molly saying shit to Tessa to purposely hurt her feelings really fucking irks me.

"I don't understand why she brought Molly, who then, of course, had to remind me that she slept with you." She cringes. So do I.

"She's a fucking whore who doesn't have shit else to do but reminisce over the days I used to fuck her brains out."

"Hardin," Tess whines at the too-descriptive reminder.

"Sorry; you know what I mean."

She unhooks the clasp on her bracelet and gets up to place it on the desk. "Are you still drunk?"

"A little."

"A little?"

I smile. "A little more than a little."

"You're being so weird." She rolls her eyes and pulls that damn planner out of the desk drawer.

"How so?" I walk over to stand behind her.

"You're drunk and being all nice about everything. Like you were mad that I wasn't answering you, but now you're being . . ." She looks up at my face. " '*Understanding*,' I guess is the word, over this Molly thing."

"What did you expect me to do?"

"I don't know . . . yell at me? You don't have the best temper when you're drunk," she says softly.

I can tell she's trying not to upset me, but wants to let me know she's not going to dance around the issue. "I'm not going to yell at you; I just didn't want you around them. You know how they are, especially Molly, and I don't want anyone hurting you." Then I add, emphasizing each word, "In any way."

"Well, they didn't, but . . . I know it's stupid, but for once I just wanted a normal lunch with a friend."

I want to tell her Steph isn't an ideal choice for a friend, but I know she doesn't have any, aside from Landon and me . . . and Noah.

And Zed.

Well, not Zed anymore. That shit is over, and I'm fairly certain that kid won't be showing his face around here for a while.

chapter fifteen

TESSA

The fact that Hardin is being reasonable surprises me, and I'm able to relax a little bit. He crosses his legs and leans back on his palms. I'm not sure if I should bring up Seattle now, since he seems to be in an easy mood, or if I should wait.

But if I wait, who knows when he'll be ready to talk about it.

I glance at him, notice his green eyes watching me, and decide to ease into it. "Steph wants to have a going-away party," I tell him and wait for his reaction.

"Where's she going? LSU?"

"No. It's for me," I explain, leaving out the small detail of telling them he's coming along to Seattle.

He gives me a look. "You told them you're moving?"

"Yes. Why wouldn't I?"

"Because you haven't decided yet, right?"

"Hardin, I'm going to Seattle."

He shrugs nonchalantly. "You still have some time to think about it."

"Anyway . . . what do you think about this party? She said it could be a dinner-party-type get-together at Nate and Tristan's place instead of the frat house," I explain, but Hardin's still intoxicated and he doesn't seem to be listening to me. I look over my moving schedule for next week. I really hope Sandra calls me back soon about that apartment; otherwise I won't have a place to live when I get there, and I'll be stuck living out of a suitcase in some motel room. Ugh, motel rooms.

"No, we aren't going," he surprises me by saying.

I turn to him. "What? Why not? If it's a dinner it won't be so bad—no Truth or Dare or Suck and Go, you know?"

He chuckles and looks up at me with amusement clear on his face. "Suck and *Blow*, Tess."

"You know what I mean! It'll be the last time we—well, *I* see them, and they have sort of been my friends, in a really strange way." I don't want to think about the beginning of my "friendship" with the group.

"Let's just talk about it later. This shit is giving me a headache," he groans.

I sigh in defeat. I can tell by his tone that he's not going to continue the discussion.

"Come here." He sits back down on the mattress and opens his arms to me.

I close the planner and go to join him on the bed; as I stand between his legs, his hands move to my hips. He looks up at me with a crooked smile.

"Aren't you supposed to be mad at me or something?"

"I'm getting overwhelmed, Hardin," I admit.

"Overwhelmed by what?"

I throw up my arms. "Everything. Seattle, transferring to another campus, Landon leaving, your expulsion—"

"I lied," he says plainly and nuzzles his face into my stomach.

What now? "What?" I thread my fingers through his hair and lift his head to look up at me.

He shrugs. "I lied about the expulsion."

I take a step away from him; he tries to pull me back, but I don't allow it. "Why?"

"I don't know, Tessa," he says, and stands. "I was upset about you being outside with Zed and all this Seattle shit."

My mouth drops. "So you told me you were expelled because you were pissed at me?"

"Yeah. Well, that and another reason."

"*What* other reason?"

He sighs. "You're going to be angry." His eyes are still red, but he seems to be sobering up quickly.

I cross my arms over my chest. "Yeah, probably. But tell me."

"I thought you'd feel bad for me and come to England."

I don't know what to think about his confession. I should be upset. I *am* upset. I'm pissed the hell off. The nerve of him, to try and guilt me into moving to England with him. He should have just been honest from the start . . . but still I can't help but feel a *little* better about finding it out straight from his mouth instead of the usual way his lies are revealed.

He looks at me with questioning eyes. "Tessa . . . ?"

I look at him and *almost* smile. "Honestly, I'm just surprised you came clean before someone else told me."

"Me, too." He closes the distance between us, bringing his hand to my neck, the span of his fingers covering my jaw. "Please don't be mad at me. I'm an asshole."

I blow out a harsh breath, but love his touch. "That's a terrible defense."

"I'm not defending myself. I'm a dick. I know this, but I love you and I'm sick of all the shit. I knew you'd find out sooner or later anyway, especially with this dreadful trip with my father's family."

"So you told me because you knew I'd find out?"

"Yeah."

I pull my head back a little and look at him. "You would have kept it from me and still tried to force me to go to England with you out of pity?"

"Basically . . ."

What the hell am I supposed to say to that? I want to tell him he's insane, that he's not my father and needs to stop trying to manipulate me, but instead I just stand there with my mouth open like a fool. "You can't try to force me into things by lying and manipulating me."

"I know it's fucked up," he says, with a look of worry in his green eyes. "I don't know why I am the way I am. I just don't want to lose you, and I'm desperate here."

I can tell by his expression that he really doesn't understand how he's been acting. "No, you don't know. Otherwise you wouldn't have lied."

Hardin puts his hands on my hips. "Tessa, I'm sorry, I really am. You have to admit that we're both getting much better at this relationship shit."

He's right; in a messed-up way we really are much better at communicating than we used to be. Far from a normal-functioning relationship, but normal has never been our thing.

"So, the marriage thing—that isn't going to make you come with me?"

My heart beats uncontrollably in my chest, and I'm sure he can hear it. But I say simply, "We'll talk about it when you're not drunk."

"I'm not that drunk."

I smile and pat his cheek. "Too drunk for that type of conversation."

He smiles and pulls me closer. "When will you be back from Sandpoint?"

"You're not coming?"

"I don't know."

"You said you would. We've never traveled together before."

"Seattle," he says, and I laugh.

"Actually, you showed up there uninvited, and left the next morning."

He runs a hand through my hair. "Technicalities."

"I really want you to come. Landon is moving soon." The thought of that alone pains me.

"So?" he asks, shaking his head.

"And your father would love it if you came, I'm sure."

"Oh, him. He's just upset with himself because they gave me a bullshit fine and put me on academic probation; the slightest fuckup and I'm done."

"Then why not transfer to the Seattle campus with me?"

"I can't hear the word 'Seattle' again tonight; I've had a long day and have a headache from hell now . . ." He kisses my forehead.

I snap my head back slightly, away from him. "You got drunk with my father and lied about being expelled—we're talking about Seattle if I want to," I say sharply.

He smiles. "And you wore those pants out after teasing me with them, and didn't answer my calls." He runs his thumb along my bottom lip.

"You don't need to call me that many times. It's suffocating. Molly even called you a stalker," I say, but smile beneath his gentle touch.

"Did she, now?" He continues tracing the outline of my lips, and they part involuntarily.

"Yeah," I breathe.

"Hmm . . ."

"I know what you're doing." I reach down and remove his other hand from my hip, where his fingers have begun to slip below the waistband of my pants.

He smiles. "What's that?"

"You're trying to distract me so I won't be mad at you."

"How's that working for me?"

"Not well enough. Besides, my father is here, and there's no way I'm having sex with you when he's in the other room." I reach around and smack him playfully on the butt.

Which only makes him thrust himself against me a little. "Oh, you mean like when I fucked you right there"—he points to the bed—"while my mum was sleeping on the couch?" He thrusts gently against me again. "Or the time I fucked you in the bathroom at my father's, or the multiple times I fucked you while Karen, Landon, and my father were just down the hall?" He reaches down and touches my thigh softly. "Oh, wait, you must mean like when I bent you over your desk at work—"

"Okay! Okay! I get it, I get it." I flush, and he laughs.

"Come on, Tessie, lie down."

"You're sick." I laugh and step away from him.

"Where are you going?" he says with a pout.

"To see what my father's doing out there."

"Why? So you can come back in here and—"

"No! Gosh—go to sleep or something!" I exclaim. I'm glad he's still being playful, but despite his confession, it's still annoying that he lied to me and is being so stubborn about even really *discussing* Seattle.

I thought for sure that when I got home from my late lunch at Applebee's, he'd be furious at me for not answering his texts. I never suspected that we'd talk things out and he'd admit to lying about being expelled. Maybe Steph had reassured him that I was on my way, so he had time to calm down. Then again, Steph's phone was on the table when I turned back around . . .

"Did you say Steph didn't answer when you called?" I ask.

"Yes; why?" He looks at me, confused.

I shrug, unsure what to say. "I'm just wondering."

"Why, though?" His tone is off.

"I told her to tell you I was on my way, and I'm just wondering why she didn't."

"Oh." He looks away, reaching for a cup on the dresser. This whole conversation is so awkward—Steph not telling him that I was on my way, him avoiding my eyes.

"I'm going out there. You can join us if you want."

"I will. I'm just going to change."

I nod and turn the door handle.

"What about your dad, though? He just came back into your life, and you're going to leave?" His words stop me in my tracks. It's not like I hadn't thought about it before, but Hardin lobbing that question at me like a missile when my back is turned doesn't sit right with me.

I take a moment to recover before leaving the room. When I get to the living room, my father is asleep again. Binge drinking at noon must be exhausting. I turn off the television and head to the kitchen for some water. Hardin's words about leaving so soon after seeing my father again keep replaying in my mind. But the thing is, I can't put my future on hold for a father whom I haven't seen for nine years. If the circumstances were different I would consider rethinking this, but he's the one who left me.

When I get back to the bedroom door, I hear Hardin's voice speaking from inside.

"What the fuck was that shit today?" he says, his voice muffled.

I press my ear to the door. I should just walk in, but I get the feeling I'm not supposed to hear the conversation. Which means I really should hear the conversation.

"I don't give a fuck, it shouldn't have happened. Now she's all upset and shit, and you're supposed to . . ." I can't make out the rest of the sentence.

"Don't fuck this up," he snaps.

Who is he talking to? And what are they supposed to be doing? Is it Steph? Or, worse, Molly?

I hear his footsteps approaching the door, and I quickly scoot into the bathroom and close the door.

Moments later, knuckles tap against the wood. "Tessa?"

I open the door. I know I must appear flustered. My heart is pounding against my rib cage, and my stomach is in a knot. "Oh, hey. Was just finishing up in here," I say, but my voice too small.

Hardin cocks an eyebrow at me. "Okay . . ." He looks down the hall. "Where's your dad? Is he asleep?"

"Uh, yup," I say, which makes him grin wide.

"Well, c'mon back to the bedroom, then," he says and takes my hand in his, turning and pulling me gently.

As I follow Hardin back into the bedroom, paranoia begins to seep into my thoughts like a familiar friend.

chapter sixteen

TESSA

The microscopic section of my mind that holds a place for common sense is attempting to send warning signals to the rest of my brain, the space held by Hardin and all things Hardin. The sensible side—what's left of it, anyway—is telling me that I need to ask questions, that I can't just brush this off. I do that too much as it is.

That's the microscopic section. The larger section wins. Because, do I really want to cause a fight with him or accuse him of something that I might just be misunderstanding? He could have just been angry at Steph for inviting Molly along to lunch earlier. I couldn't hear all that well, and he might have been sticking up for me. He was just so forthcoming about having lied about being expelled—why would he be lying to me now?

Hardin sits back on the bed, grabbing my hands in his, pulling me over to sit on his leg. "Well, we've exhausted all the serious topics, and your dad's asleep. I guess we'll have to find another way to occupy ourselves . . ." His grin is ridiculous yet infectious.

"Is sex all you think about?" I reply and push his chest playfully.

He lies back on the bed, one hand across the small of my back and one behind my thigh, pulling me on top of him. I straddle him, my thighs on either side of his, and he pulls me down so that our faces are nearly touching.

"No, I think of other things, too. For example, I think of those lips open around me . . ." He brushes his lips against mine. I can taste the hint of mint on his breath when he kisses me; the pressure is hard enough to send a wave of electricity through me, but gentle enough to leave me wanting more.

"I think of my face buried between your legs while you—" he starts to say, but I reach up and cover his mouth with my hand. The way his tongue playfully darts out to lick my palm causes me to pull away quickly.

"Eww." I crinkle my nose and wipe my wet palm on his black shirt.

"I'll be quiet," he softly says, lifting his hips from the mattress to press himself against me. "That's more than you can say, of course."

"My father . . ." I remind him, with much less conviction this time.

"Who gives a fuck? This is our place, and if he doesn't like it, he can leave."

I give him a semiserious look. "Don't be rude."

"I'm not, but I want you, and I should be able to have you whenever I want to," he says, and I roll my eyes.

"I have a say in this, too; it's my body you're talking about." I pretend like my heart isn't pounding and I don't have that familiar ache for him.

"Obviously, yes. But I know that if I do this . . ." He reaches his hand down between our bodies and under the waistband of my pants and panties. "See, I knew you'd be ready when I started talking about eating . . ."

I press my lips against his to silence his dirty mouth, and he swallows the gasps he's causing me to make as his fingers graze over my clit. He's barely touching me, deliberately trying to torture me.

"Pleasssse," I hiss, and he applies more pressure, pushing a slick finger inside of me.

"Thought so," he taunts and pumps his finger slowly.

All too soon he stops his motion and moves me to lie beside him. Before I can complain, he sits up and grips the top of my pants, the pair he seems to be so infatuated with, and pulls them roughly down my thighs. I lift my hips to assist him, and then he works off my panties, too.

Without speaking, he gestures for me to move up toward the top of the bed. I push myself back using my elbows and rest my back against the headboard. He lies on his stomach in front of me, hooking both arms around my thighs, opening them.

He smirks. "At least try to be quiet."

I begin to roll my eyes, but then his warm breath hits me—soft at first, then increasing in pressure when he gets closer. Without warning, his tongue slides across me, and I reach over and grab a decorative pillow, the yellow one that Hardin calls hideous on a regular basis. I cover my face with it, using it to muffle the involuntary sounds falling from my lips as his tongue moves faster and faster.

Abruptly, the pillow is ripped away from my face. "No, baby, watch me," Hardin instructs, and I nod slowly. He brings one thumb to his lips, and his tongue glides over me. Moving his hand back between my thighs, he hits my most sensitive spot. My legs tighten—his touch feels heavenly against my clit, his finger moving in slow circles with just the lightest touch of the tip of his finger torturing me.

Obeying his command, I gaze down at him between my thighs, his hair messy and pushed back, standing in a wave above his forehead, a lone lock falling down only to be pushed back again when he dips his head down. Half seeing, half imagining his mouth moving against me increases the sensation drastically, and I know, I just *know*, I won't be able to stay quiet as the slow buildup of my release begins. With one hand covering my mouth and one buried in his curls, I begin shifting my hips to meet his tongue. It just feels too good.

I tug at his hair and feel him moan against me, sending me closer and closer . . .

"Harder," he gasps.

What?

He reaches up to the hand that I've threaded through his hair, and places his hand on top of mine to tug at the roots of his hair . . . He wants me to pull his hair?

"Do it," he says with a wanting look, and then begins to move his fingers in fast circles and lowers his head to add his tongue to the sensation. I tug at his hair, hard, and he looks up at me, his eyes fluttering closed. When they open they're a bright, burning jade. He holds my gaze as my vision blurs and disappears momentarily.

"Come on, baby," he whispers.

I notice his hand reach down between his legs, and I can't hold it any longer. I watch his hand stroking his hard cock, bringing himself to orgasm with me. I will never get used to the way his actions make me feel. Watching him touching himself, feeling the hot puffs of air against me as his breathing grows heavier . . .

"You taste so fucking good, baby," he moans against me, his hand moving quicker between his legs. I barely feel my teeth sinking into my palm as I ride out my high, still pulling at his hair.

I blink. And blink some more, lazily.

As I come back to consciousness, I feel him adjust his weight and lay his head on my stomach. I open my eyes to find him with his closed, his chest moving up and down, his breath shallow.

I lift him by his shoulder and attempt to move between his legs.

He stops and looks at me. "I . . . um, I'm already done," he says.

I stare at him.

"I already came . . ." His voice is thick with exhaustion.

"Oh."

He smiles a lazy, half-drunk smile and stands up from the bed. He strides over to the dresser and opens his bottom drawer, grabbing a pair of white gym shorts.

"I need to shower and change, obviously." He points to the crotch of his jeans, where, despite their dark color, the wet spot is evident.

"Just like old times?" I smile, and he looks at me, smiling back.

Hardin comes over and places a kiss on my forehead, then one on my lips. "Good to know you haven't lost your touch," he says, walking to the door.

"It wasn't *my* touch," I remind him, and he shakes his head, leaving the room.

I reach for my clothes at the end of the bed, praying that my father is still asleep on the couch, and that if by chance he *is* awake, he doesn't stop Hardin on his way to the bathroom. Seconds later the bathroom door closes, and I stand to get dressed.

When I'm done I check my phone for a voicemail from Sandra, but there's nothing. What I do see is the small envelope in the corner of my screen indicating a new text message; maybe she's busy and decided to text me.

I click it open and read: I need to talk to you.

I sigh when I next read the sender's name: Zed.

I delete the message and set my phone back on the desk. Then curiosity gets the best of me, and I look around for Hardin's phone. My heart pounds as I remember the last time I went snooping through it. That didn't end well.

But this time I know he's not hiding anything. He wouldn't be. We're in a completely different place now than we were before. He got a tattoo for me . . . he just won't move for me. I have nothing to worry about. *Right?*

I check the dresser after not seeing it on the desk, then figure he must have taken it with him to the bathroom. Because that's normal, right?

I have nothing to worry about; I'm just stressed and paranoid, I remind myself.

Before I continue down the rabbit hole of worry, I remind myself that I shouldn't be going through his cell phone anyway, that I would be furious if he did that to me.

He probably does, though. I just haven't caught him.

The bedroom door clicks open, and I jump as if I've been caught doing something I shouldn't be. Hardin strides in, shirtless, barefoot, wearing the gym shorts, the black line of his boxers showing.

"You okay?" he asks, rubbing a white towel over his soaked hair. I love the way his hair appears black when it's wet; the contrast with his green eyes is something one can only dream about.

"Yeah. That wasn't a long shower." I sit down on the chair. "I should have gotten you dirtier," I say, trying to distract him from the slight quaver in my voice.

"I was in a hurry to see you," he says unconvincingly.

I smile. "You're hungry, aren't you?"

"Yeah," he admits with an amused grin. "I got hungry."

"Thought so."

"Your dad's still asleep—is he going to stay here while we're gone?"

Excitement overtakes any worry I had. "You're coming?"

"Yeah, I guess. If it's as lame as I know it will be, I'm only staying one night."

"Okay," I say with understanding. But inside I'm beaming, knowing that he won't leave early. He just has to keep up appearances by complaining about this sort of thing.

He licks his lips, and I think back to him between my thighs. "Can I ask you something?" I say.

His eyes meet mine, and he nods. "Yeah?" He sits on the bed.

"When you . . . you know, was it because I was pulling your hair?"

"What?" He laughs lightly.

"When I pulled at your hair, you liked it?" I flush.

"Yeah, I did."

"Oh." I can't imagine the shade of red I'm turning right now.

"Is that weird to you? That I liked it?"

"No, I'm just curious," I tell him truthfully.

"Everyone has certain things they like during sex; that's one of mine. I didn't know it until just now, though." He smiles, completely unfazed that we're talking about this.

"Oh yeah?" I get excited at the thought that he learned something new while with me.

"Yeah," he says. "I mean, my hair's been pulled on by other girls, but it's different with you."

"Oh," I say for the tenth time, but this one leaves me feeling flat.

Likely unaware of my reaction, Hardin looks at me with curiosity gleaming in his green eyes. "Is there something *you* like that I haven't done?"

"No, I like everything you do," I say softly.

"Yeah, I know, but is there something you've thought about doing before that we haven't done?"

I shake my head.

"Don't be embarrassed, baby—everyone has fantasies."

"I don't." At least, I don't think I do. I haven't had any experience outside of Hardin, and I don't know of anything else besides what we've done.

"You do," he says with a smile. "We just have to find them."

My stomach flutters, and I don't know what to say.

But then my father's voice breaks our conversation. "Tessie?"

My first thought is that I'm relieved that his voice sounds like it's coming from the living room and not the hallway.

Hardin and I both stand.

"I'm going to use the restroom," I say.

He nods with a wicked grin and heads into the living room to join my father.

When I get into the bathroom, Hardin's phone is sitting on the edge of the sink.

I know I shouldn't, but I can't stop myself. I immediately go to the call log, but it doesn't show. All the calls have been cleared. Not a single one is shown on the screen. I try again, and then look at the text-message screen.

Nothing. He's deleted everything.

chapter seventeen

TESSA

Hardin and my father are both seated at the kitchen table when I emerge from the bathroom, Hardin's phone in hand.

"I'm wilting away here, babe," Hardin says when I reach them.

My father looks over sheepishly. "I could eat . . ." he begins, like he's unsure.

I place my hands on the top of Hardin's chair and he leans his head back, his damp hair touching my fingers. "Then I suggest you make yourself something to eat," I say and place his phone in front of him.

He looks up at me with a completely neutral expression. "Okay . . ." he says and gets up and goes to the refrigerator. "Are you hungry?" he asks.

"I have my leftovers from Applebee's."

"Are you upset with me about taking him drinking today?" my father asks.

I look over at him and soften my tone. I could tell what my dad was like when I invited him in. "I'm not upset, but I don't want it to become a regular thing."

"It won't. Besides, you're moving," he reminds me, and I look across the table at the man I've only known for two days now.

I don't reply. Instead I join Hardin at the fridge and pull the freezer door open.

"What do you want to eat?" I ask him.

He looks at me with wary eyes, clearly trying to assess my

mood. "Just some chicken or something . . . or we can order some takeout?"

I sigh. "Let's just order something." I don't mean to be short with him, but my mind is whirling with possibilities of what was on his phone that he felt needed to be deleted.

Once ordering food becomes the plan, Hardin and my father begin bickering over Chinese or pizza. Hardin wants pizza, and he wins the argument by reminding my father who will be paying for it. For his part, my father doesn't seem offended by Hardin's digs. He just laughs or flips him off.

It's a strange sight, really, to watch the two of them. After my father left, I would often daydream about him when I saw my friends with their fathers. I had created a vision of a man who resembled the man I grew up with, only older, and definitely not a homeless drunk. I had always thought of him carrying an attaché case stuffed with important documents, walking to his car in the morning, coffee mug in hand. I didn't imagine he'd still be drinking, that he'd be ravaged by it like he's been, and that he'd be without a place to live. I can't picture my mother and this man being able to hold a conversation, let alone spending years married to each other.

"How did you and my mother meet?" I say, suddenly voicing my thoughts.

"In high school," he answers.

Hardin grabs his phone and leaves the room to order the pizza. Either that or to call someone and then quickly delete the call log.

I sit at the kitchen table across from my father. "How long were you dating before you got married?" I ask.

"Only about two years. We got married young."

I feel uncomfortable asking these questions, but I know I wouldn't have any luck getting the answers from my mother. "Why?"

"You and your mom never talked about this?" he asks.

"No; we never talked about you. If I even tried to bring the subject up, she shut down," I tell him, and watch his features transform from interest to shame.

"Oh."

"Sorry," I say, though I'm not sure what I'm apologizing for.

"No, I get it. I don't blame her." He closes his eyes for a moment before opening them again. Hardin strolls back into the kitchen and sits down next to me. "To answer your question, we got married young because she got pregnant with you, and your grandparents hated me and tried to keep her away from me. So we got hitched." He smiles, enjoying the memory.

"You got married to spite my grandparents?" I ask with a smile.

My grandparents, may they rest in peace, were a little . . . intense. *Very* intense. My childhood memories of them include being shushed at the dinner table for laughing and being told to take my shoes off before walking on their carpet. For birthdays, they would send an impersonal card with a ten-year savings bond inside—not an ideal gift for an eight-year-old.

My mother was essentially a clone of my grandmother, only slightly less poised. She tried, though; my mother spends her days and nights trying to be as perfect as she remembers her own mother being.

Or, I suddenly think, *as perfect as she imagines her being.*

My father laughs. "In a way, yes, to piss them off. But your mother always wanted to be married. She practically dragged me to the altar." He laughs again, and Hardin looks at me before laughing as well.

I scowl at him, knowing he's concocting some snarky comment about me forcing him into marriage.

I turn back to my dad. "Were you against marriage?" I ask.

"No. I don't remember, really; all I know is I was scared as hell to have a baby at nineteen."

"And rightfully so. We can see how that worked out for you," Hardin remarks.

I shoot him a glare, but my father only rolls his eyes at him.

"It's not something I recommend, but there are a lot of young parents that can handle it." He lifts his hands up in resignation. "I just wasn't one of them."

"Oh," I say. I can't imagine being a parent at my age.

He smiles, clearly open to giving me what answers he can. "Any more questions, Tessie?"

"No . . . I think that's all," I say. I don't exactly feel comfortable around him, though in a strange way I feel more comfortable than I would if my mother were sitting here instead of him.

"If you think of any more, you can ask me. Until then, do you mind if I take another shower before dinner comes?"

"Of course not. Go ahead," I say.

It seems like he's been here longer than two days. So much has happened since he appeared—Hardin's expulsion/nonexpulsion, Zed's appearance in the parking lot, my lunch with Steph and Molly, the ever-disappearing call log—just too much. This overstressful, constantly growing pile of issues in my life doesn't appear to be letting up anytime soon.

"What's wrong?" Hardin asks when my father disappears down the hall.

"Nothing." I stand up and take a few steps before he stops me by touching my waist and turning me around to face him.

"I know you better than that. Tell me what's wrong," he softly demands, placing both hands on my hips.

I look him dead in the eyes. "You."

"I . . . *what*? Talk," he demands.

"You're acting weird, and you deleted your text messages and calls."

His features twist in annoyance, and he pinches the bridge of his nose. "Why would you be looking through my phone, anyway?"

"Because you're acting suspicious, and—"

"So you go through my shit? Didn't I tell you before not to do that?"

The look of indignation on his face is so brazen, looks so practiced, that my blood gets boiling. "I know I shouldn't be going through your things—but you shouldn't give me a reason to. And if you don't have anything to hide, why would you care? I wouldn't mind if you looked through my phone. I have nothing to hide." I dig mine out of my pocket and hold it out. Then I start to worry that maybe I *didn't* delete the text from Zed on there and I panic, until Hardin waves it away like my trust is a gnat.

"You're just making up excuses for how psychotic you are," he says, his words burning me.

I don't have anything to say. Well, actually, I have a lot to say to him, but no words come from my mouth. I push his hands from my hips and storm off. He said he knows me well enough to sense when something's wrong with me. Well, I know him well enough to sense when he's close to being caught at something. Whether it be a small lie or a bet for my virginity, the same thing happens each time: first he acts suspicious, then when I bring it up to him he gets angry and defensive, and finally he spits harsh words at me.

"Don't walk away from me," he bellows from behind me.

"Don't follow me," I say and disappear into the bedroom.

But he appears in the doorway a second later. "I don't like you going through my shit."

"I don't like feeling like I *have* to."

He closes the door and leans his back against it. "You don't have to; I deleted that stuff because . . . it was an accident. It's nothing for you to be all worked up over."

"Worked up? You mean 'psychotic'?"

He sighs. "I didn't really mean that."

"Then stop saying things you don't mean. Because then I can't tell what's true and what's not."

"Then stop going through my shit. Because then I can't tell if I should trust you or not."

"Fine." I sit down at the desk.

"Fine," he repeats and sits down on the bed.

I can't decide if I believe him or not. Nothing adds up, but in a way it does. Maybe he did delete the texts and calls by accident, and maybe he *was* talking to Steph on the phone. The bits and pieces of the conversation that I caught fuel my imagination, but I don't want to ask Hardin about it because I don't want him to know I overheard them. It's not like he'd tell me what they talked about anyway.

"I don't want there to be secrets between us. We should be past that," I remind him.

"I know, *fuck*. There aren't any secrets; you're being crazy."

"Stop calling me crazy. You of all people shouldn't be calling anyone that." I regret the words as soon as they're out, but he doesn't seem fazed.

"I'm sorry, okay? You're not crazy," he says, then smiles. "You just go through my phone."

I force a smile in return and try to convince myself that he's right, that I'm being paranoid. Worst-case scenario, he's hiding something from me. I'll find out eventually, so there isn't any point in obsessing over it now. I've found out everything else.

I mentally repeat the logic over and over until I'm convinced.

My father yells something from the other room, and Hardin says, "I think the pizza's here. You're not going to be mad at me all night, are you?"

But he leaves the room without giving me a chance to answer.

I swivel on my seat and look at where I laid my phone on the desk. Curious, I check it, and sure enough, I have another new text from Zed. I don't bother to read it this time.

THE NEXT DAY is my last at the old office, and I drive slower than usual to work. I want to take in every street, every building on the way. This paid internship has been a dream come true. I know I'll be working for Vance in Seattle, but this area is where it started, where my career started.

Kimberly is sitting at her desk when I step off the elevator. Multiple brown boxes are stacked near the side of her desk.

"Good morning!" she chirps.

"Good morning." My voice isn't capable of sounding as cheery as hers. I'd come off nervous and awkward.

"Ready for your last week here?" she asks as I fill a small Styrofoam cup with coffee.

"Yes—my last *day*, actually. I'm going on a trip for the rest of the week," I remind her.

"Oh yeah, I almost forgot. Wow! Your last day! I should have gotten you a card or something." She smiles. "But then, I could just give it to you next week at your new office."

I laugh. "Are *you* ready to go? When will you be leaving?"

"Friday! Our new house is already unpacked and ready for us to arrive."

I'm quite certain that Kimberly and Christian's new home is lovely, large and modern, much like the house they're moving from. Kimberly's engagement ring sparkles under the light, and I can't help but stare at the beautiful band every time I see it.

"I'm still waiting for the woman to call me back about my apartment," I tell her, and she turns to look at me.

"What? You don't have an apartment yet?"

"I do—I sent her the paperwork already. We just have to go over the details of the lease."

"You only have six days," Kimberly says, looking panicked for me.

"I know, I have it under control," I assure her, hoping it's true.

If this had been happening a few months ago, I'd have had every detail of this move planned, but lately I've been too stressed to focus on anything, even the move to Seattle.

"Okay; if you need help, just let me know," she offers as she turns her attention to the phone ringing on her desk.

When I get back to my office, there are a few empty boxes on the floor. I don't have many personal items, so it shouldn't take long to pack.

Twenty minutes later, as I tape the last box closed, there's a gentle knock at the door. "Come in," I say loudly.

For a moment I wonder if it's Hardin, but when I turn around Trevor is standing in the doorway wearing light jeans and a plain white T-shirt. I'm always caught off guard when he's dressed casually; I'm so used to seeing him in a suit.

"Are you ready for the big move?" he asks as I attempt to lift a box that I packed too full.

"Yeah, almost. Are you?" He walks over and picks up the box for me, placing it on the desk.

"Thanks." I smile and wipe my hands on the sides of my green dress.

"I am. I'm heading out today as soon as I finish up here."

"That's amazing. I know you've been ready to move to Seattle since last time we were there."

I can feel embarrassment spread over my cheeks as I watch it spread across his. "Last time we were there," Trevor took me to a nice dinner, only to have me reject his kiss and then later be threatened and shoved by Hardin. I have no idea why I just brought that up.

He looks at me blankly. "That was an interesting weekend. Anyway, I know you have to be pumped, too. You've always wanted to live in Seattle."

"Yeah, I can't wait."

Trevor looks around my office. "I know it's none of my business, but is Hardin moving to Seattle with you?"

"No." My mouth answers before my mind can catch up. "Well, I'm not sure yet. He says he doesn't want to, but I'm hoping that he'll change his mind . . ." I continue to ramble, the words coming out quickly, too quickly, and Trevor looks somewhat uncomfortable as he shoves his hands into his jean pockets before finally interrupting me.

"Why wouldn't he want to go with you?"

"I'm not sure, really, but I hope he does." I sigh and sit down in my leather desk chair.

Trevor's blue eyes meet mine. "He's crazy if he doesn't."

"He's crazy either way." I laugh, trying to diminish the growing tension in the room.

He laughs, too, and shakes his head. "Well, I better finish up so I can get on the road. But I'll see *you* in Seattle."

With a smile he leaves my office, and for some reason I feel slightly guilty. I reach for my phone and text Hardin, casually letting him know that Trevor stopped by my office. For once, Hardin's jealousy appeals to me—maybe he'll find himself too jealous of Trevor and decide to move to Seattle after all? It doesn't seem likely, but I can't help but hold on to the last thread of hope that he'll change his mind. The clock is running out; six days is not very long for him to plan. He'd have to put in a transfer request, which shouldn't be a problem, considering Ken's position.

Six days doesn't seem long enough for me either, though I'm ready for Seattle. I have to be. This is my future, and I can't center it around Hardin when he isn't willing to compromise. I offered a fair plan: we move to Seattle first, and if it doesn't work out, we can go to England. But he didn't give it a second thought before declining. I'm hoping this whale-watching trip we have planned with his family will make him see that he can join me, Landon, Ken, and Karen in trying new things, that doing something fun and positive isn't too difficult.

Then again, this is Hardin I'm talking about, and nothing is easy when it comes to him.

The phone on my desk rings, distracting me from my stressful thoughts about Seattle. "You have a visitor," Kimberly says into my ear, and my heart leaps at the thought of seeing Hardin.

It's only been a few hours, but I always miss him when we're apart. "Tell Hardin to come on back. I'm surprised he even waited for you to call me," I say.

Kimberly clicks her tongue. "Um, it's not Hardin."

Maybe Hardin brought my father here? "Is it an older man with a beard?"

"No . . . young guy . . . like Hardin," she practically whispers.

"Does he have bruises on his face?" I ask, despite the fact that I already know the answer.

"Yeah; should I make him leave?"

I don't want to make her force Zed to leave, and he hasn't done anything wrong, except to not listen to Hardin's instructions to stay away from me. "No, it's fine. He's my friend. You can let him back."

Why would he come here? I'm sure it has something to do with me ignoring him, but I don't understand what could be so urgent that he'd drive forty minutes to tell me.

I hang up the phone and debate whether or not to text Hardin and tell him about Zed's arrival. I toss my phone into my desk drawer and close it. Nearly the last thing I need is for Hardin to come here, since he won't be able to control his anger and will surely cause a scene on my last day at work.

The *last* thing I need is for him to get arrested, again.

chapter eighteen

TESSA

When I pull open the door to my office, Zed is standing in the hall like the angel of death. He's dressed in a black-and-red-plaid sweatshirt, dark jeans, and sneakers. The swelling on his face hasn't gone down much, but the bruising around the edges of his eyes and nose have lightened from dark purple to a greenish blue.

"Hey . . . I'm sorry for coming here like this," he says.

"Is something wrong?" I ask and walk back over to my desk.

He stands awkwardly in the doorway for a moment before stepping into the room. "No. Well, yes, I've been trying to talk to you since yesterday, but you haven't been answering my texts."

"I know; it's just that Hardin and I already have enough issues without me creating even more, and he doesn't want me to talk to you anymore."

"You're letting him tell you who you can talk to now?" Zed sits down in the chair directly in front of my desk, and I take a seat behind it. The way we're seated gives an official, more serious tone to our conversation. It's not uncomfortable, just too formal.

I look out the window before answering.

"No, it's not like that. I know he's a little overbearing and may go about things the wrong way, but I can't say I blame him for not wanting me to be friends with you anymore. I wouldn't want him to spend time with someone he has feelings for either," I say, and Zed's eyes widen.

"What did you say?"

Dammit. "Nothing, I just meant . . ." The air grows thick, and I could swear that the walls are closing in on me. Why did I just say that? Not that it isn't true, but it won't help the situation here.

"You have feelings for me?" he asks, his eyes lighting up with each syllable.

"No . . . well, I did. I don't know," I ramble, wishing I could slap myself for being so quick to speak without thinking.

"It's okay if you don't, but you shouldn't have to lie about it."

"I'm not lying; I did have feelings for you. I may still have some, honestly, but I don't know. It's all confusing to me. You always say the right things, and you've always been there for me. It would make sense if I did develop those feelings. I've told you before that I care about you, but we both know it's a lost cause."

"Why's that?" he asks. I'm not sure how many more times I can reject him before he understands where I'm coming from.

"Because it's pointless. I'll never be able to be with you. Or anyone, for that matter. No one but him."

"You're only saying that because he has you trapped."

I try to push down the anger that is slowly building as I listen to Zed's words about Hardin. He's certainly entitled to have ill feelings toward him, but I don't like the way he's insinuating that I have no power or control when it comes to my relationship.

"No; I'm saying that because I love him. And as much as I don't want to say it that boldly to you right now, I know that I have to. I don't want to lead you on more than I already have. I know you don't understand why I stay with him through all of this mess, but I love him so much, more than anything, and he doesn't have me trapped. I want to be with him."

It's true. Everything I just said to Zed is true. Whether Hardin comes to Seattle with me or not, we can try to make it work. We can use Skype, see each other on the weekends until he goes to England. Hopefully by then he won't want to be away from me after all.

Maybe the distance will make Hardin's heart grow fonder, his tone softer. It may be the key to getting him to agree to move with me. Our history has proven that we aren't very good at staying away from one another; whether deliberately or not, we always end up together in some way. It's hard to remember a time when my days and nights didn't revolve around this man. I've tried again and again to picture a life without him, but it's nearly impossible.

"I don't think he gives you the chance to really think about what you want or what's good for you," Zed says with conviction, though his voice does crack. "He only cares about himself."

"And that's where you're wrong. I know you guys have some issues between the two of you, but—"

"No, you don't know about our issues at all," he says quickly. "If you did—"

"He loves me, and I him," I interrupt. "I'm sorry that you were brought into the middle of this. I'm so sorry; I never wanted to hurt you."

He frowns. "You keep saying that to me, and yet it keeps happening."

I hate confrontation more than anything, especially when it involves hurting someone that I care for, but these things have to be said so that Zed and I can close the book on this . . . I'm not even sure how to categorize it. *Situation? Misunderstanding? Bad timing?*

I look at Zed, hoping he can read the sincerity in my eyes. "It wasn't my intention. I'm sorry."

"You don't have to keep apologizing. I already knew this when I made the decision to come here. You made it pretty clear how you felt outside of the administration building."

"Then why did you come?" I ask softly.

"To talk to you." He looks around the room, then back at me. "Never mind. I don't know why I came here, really." He sighs.

"Are you sure? You seemed pretty determined a few minutes ago."

"No. It's pointless, like you said. I'm sorry for coming."

"It's okay, you don't have to apologize," I tell him.

We both keep saying that, I think.

He points down at the boxes on the floor. "You're still going, then?"

"Yeah, I'm almost ready to leave."

The air between us has become incredibly thick, and neither of us seems to know what to say to the other. Zed stares out the window at the gray sky, and I stare at the carpet beyond him.

At last he stands up and speaks, though I can barely hear his words through the sadness in his voice. "I better go, then. Sorry again for coming here. Good luck in Seattle, Tessa."

I stand up as well. "I'm sorry for everything. I wish things could've been different."

"So do I. More than you know," he says and stands up from the chair.

My heart aches for him. He's always been so sweet to me, and I've done nothing but lead him on and reject him.

"Have you made up your mind whether you're going to press charges or not?" This isn't the right time to be asking this, but I don't think I'll ever see or hear from him again.

"Yeah, I'm not going to. I'm over this whole thing. There's no point in dragging it out. And I did tell you that if you told me you didn't want to see me again I would drop them, didn't I?"

Suddenly I feel like if Zed just looks at me in a certain way, I'll probably start crying. "Yeah," I quietly respond. I feel like Estella in *Great Expectations*, toying with Pip's emotions. My own Pip stands in front of me, caramel eyes fixed on mine. And this is a role I don't really want to play.

"I truly am sorry for everything. I wish we could be friends," I say.

"Me, too, but you're not allowed to have friends." He sighs, running his fingers over his bottom lip, pinching it in the middle.

I decide not to comment on his statement: this isn't about what I'm "allowed" to do. I do, however, make a mental note to discuss this perception that other people have with Hardin and make sure he understands that it bothers me that his attitude makes them think this about me.

As if on cue, my office phone rings, breaking the silence between Zed and me. I hold my finger so he doesn't leave and pick it up.

"Tessa." Hardin's rough voice carries through. *Shit.*

"Hey," I say, my voice shaky.

"Are you all right?"

"Yeah, I'm fine."

"You don't sound fine," he says. *Why does he have to know me so well?*

"I'm fine," I assure him again. "Just distracted."

"Sure. Anyway, I need to know what you want me to do with your dad. I tried to text, but you weren't answering me. I've got shit to do, and I don't know if I should leave him here or what."

I look over at Zed. He's standing by the window now, not looking at me. "I don't know, can't you take him with you?" My heart is racing.

"No; hell, no."

"So leave him there," I say, just wanting this conversation to end. I'm going to tell Hardin about Zed's visit, but I can't imagine how pissed he would be if he knew he was here now, and I sure as hell don't want him to find out.

"Fine, you can deal with him when you get here."

"Okay, well, I'll see you when I get home—"

Music begins to play through my office, and it takes me a minute to realize it's coming from Zed. He reaches into his pocket and silences it, but not before Hardin notices.

"What was that? Whose phone was that?" he demands.

My blood suddenly runs cold, until I take a moment to think about this. I shouldn't be so afraid or nervous for Hardin to know Zed's here. I didn't do anything wrong; he came, and he's leaving. He already gets irritated when Trevor comes by my office, and Trevor's a coworker and entitled to stop in anytime he wants.

"Is fucking Trevor there?"

"No, it's not Trevor. Zed's here," I say and hold my breath.

The line is silent. I look at the screen to make sure the call is still connected. "Hardin?"

"Yeah," he says and lets out a ragged breath.

"Did you hear me?"

"Yes, Tessa, I heard you."

Okay? Why isn't he screaming through the phone or threatening to kill him yet?

"We'll talk about it later. Make him leave. Please," he calmly requests.

"Okay . . ."

"Thank you, I'll see you when you get home," Hardin says and hangs up the phone.

When I put my phone down, slightly bewildered, Zed turns to me and says, "Sorry, I know he's going to freak out on you."

"No, he won't. He'll be fine," I say back, knowing it's not true, but it sounds good, anyway. Hardin's reaction to Zed being in my office caught me off guard. I'd never have expected him to be so calm. I expected him to say he was on his way here. I sure hope he's not.

Zed walks toward the door again. "Okay. Well, I guess I should go."

"Zed, thank you for coming by. I probably won't see you again before I leave."

He turns, and emotion flashes in his eyes, but it disappears before I can decide which emotion it was. "I won't say meeting you hasn't complicated my life, but I wouldn't take it back. I'd go through all of this shit again—the fights with Hardin, the friendships I've lost, all of it. I would go through it again, for you," he says. "I guess it's just my luck; of course I can't meet a girl who doesn't already love someone else."

His words always get to me, always. He's so sincere all the time, and I admire that about him.

"Bye, Tessa," he says.

His words hold much more than a simple friendly goodbye, but I can't project too much into them. If I say the wrong thing, or anything at all, I'll only be leading him on, again.

"Bye, Zed." I half smile, and he takes a step toward me.

For a moment I panic, thinking he's going to kiss me, but he doesn't. He wraps his arms around me in a strong but brief hug before placing a light kiss on my forehead. He steps away immediately after and grabs hold of the door handle, almost like it's a cane.

"Be careful, okay?" he says, opening the door.

"I will. Seattle isn't too bad." I smile. I feel very resolved now, like I have finally given him the closure he needed.

He frowns and turns to leave the room. As he closes the door behind him, I hear him say gently, "I'm not talking about Seattle."

chapter nineteen

TESSA

As soon as the door shuts and Zed is gone—gone for good—I close my eyes and lay my head back against the chair. I don't know what I'm feeling. All of my emotions are jumbled, swirling around me in a cloud of confusion. Part of me feels relieved to end this back-and-forth between Zed and me. But another, smaller part feels a significant loss. Zed is the only one of Hardin's so-called friends who's been there for me constantly, and it's strange to realize that I'll never see him again. The tears burn, unwelcomed, down my cheeks as I try to collect myself. I shouldn't be crying over this. I should be happy that I can finally close the book on Zed, tuck it away, leaving it only to collect dust, never to be opened again.

It's not that I want to be with him, it's not that I love him, it's not that I would ever choose him over Hardin; it's just that I do care for him, and I wish things had played out differently. I wish I would have kept our relationship strictly platonic—maybe then I wouldn't have to completely cut him out of my life.

I don't know why he came back in here, but I'm glad he left before he could say anything to confuse me or hurt Hardin further.

My office phone rings, and I clear my throat before answering. When I say "Hello," I sound pathetic.

Hardin's voice carries through strong and clear. "Did he leave?"

"Yeah."

"Are you crying?"

"I'm just . . ." I start.

"What?" he implores.

"I don't know, I'm just glad it's over." I wipe at my eyes again.

He sighs through the line and surprises me by simply saying, "Me, too."

The tears are no longer falling, but my voice is hideous. "Thank you"—I pause—"for being understanding about this."

That went much better than I'd expected, and I don't know if I should be relieved or slightly worried. I decide to go with relieved and finish the last of my time at Vance as peacefully as possible.

Around three, Kimberly stops by my office; behind her is a girl who I'm sure I've never seen at the office before.

"Tessa, this is Amy, my replacement," Kimberly says, introducing the quiet yet stunning girl.

I get up from where I'm reading, trying to reassure Amy with a friendly smile. "Hi, Amy. I'm Tessa. You'll love it here."

"Thank you! I *already* love it," she says excitedly.

Kim laughs. "Well, I just wanted to stop by your office while we were pretending to be taking a tour of the building."

"Oh yes. You're teaching her to replace you, all right," I tease.

"Hey! Being engaged to the boss has its perks," Kim jokes back.

Beside her, Amy laughs, and then Kimberly leads her down another hallway. My last day here finally ends, and I find myself wishing it could have gone slower. I'm going to miss this place, and I'm slightly nervous to go home to Hardin.

I take one last look around my first office. My eyes focus on the desk first. My stomach tightens as memories of Hardin and me on the desk flood my senses. It seems so extreme: having sex in an office when anyone could walk in at any moment. I was too distracted by Hardin to think of anything else . . . which seems to be a pattern in my everyday life.

* * *

ON THE WAY HOME I stop by Conner's to get a few groceries—just enough to make dinner tonight, since we're leaving in the morning. I'm excited but nervous about the trip. I hope Hardin can keep his temper in check for the two-day vacation with his family.

Since that doesn't seem likely, my next hope is that the boat is big enough for the five of us to have a little breathing room.

Back at the apartment, I unlock the front door and push it open with my foot, picking up the grocery bags from the floor as I step inside. The living room is a mess; empty water bottles and food wrappers litter the coffee table. My father and Hardin sit on opposite ends of the couch.

"How was your day, Tessie?" my father asks, craning his neck to look over at me.

"Good. It was my last day there," I tell him even though he already knows. I begin to clear their trash from the table and floor.

"I'm happy you had a good day," my father says.

I look at Hardin, who doesn't look at me. His gaze is fixed on the television screen.

"I'm going to make dinner, then get in the shower," I tell them, and my father follows me into the kitchen.

As I unload the grocery bags and put the ground beef and box of taco shells on the counter, my father watches me with interest. At last, he says, "One of my friends said he can pick me up here later, if that's okay. I know you're leaving tomorrow for a few days."

"Yeah, that's fine. We can drop you off in the morning if that would be better for you," I offer.

"No, you've already been so generous. Just promise me you'll let me know when you get back from your trip."

"Okay . . . how will I get in touch with you?"

He rubs the back of his neck. "Maybe just drive down Lamar? I'm usually out there."

"Okay, I will."

"I'll go call him back now and let him know I'm ready." He disappears from the kitchen.

I hear Hardin teasing my father about the fact that he has to memorize phone numbers because he doesn't own a phone, and I roll my eyes when my father begins the when-I-was-a-kid-no-one-had-cell-phones speech.

Tacos with ground beef are easy to make and don't require too much thought. I wish Hardin would come into the kitchen and talk to me, but I suppose it's better if he waits until my father leaves. I set up the table for dinner and call for the two of them. Hardin enters first, barely making eye contact with me, followed by my father.

As he sits, my father says, "Chad will be here soon to get me. I appreciate you guys letting me stay. It was mighty generous of you two." He looks back and forth between Hardin and me. "Thank you so much, Tessie, H-bomb," he adds. The way Hardin rolls his eyes at my father, I can tell this is some inside joke between them.

"It's no problem, really," I tell him.

"I'm just so glad we found each other again," he says and starts eating his meal with an animated ferocity.

"Me, too . . ." I smile, still not able to process that this man is my father. The man that I haven't seen in nine years, the man who I had so many ill feelings toward, is just sitting in my kitchen eating with my boyfriend and me.

I look over to Hardin, expecting a rude comment from him, but he says nothing and quietly eats his meal. His silence is driving me mad. I wish he'd just say something . . . anything, really.

Sometimes his silence is far worse than his yelling.

chapter twenty

HARDIN

After we finish eating, Tessa gives her father her final, somewhat stiff goodbye and heads into the bathroom for a shower. I was planning on getting in the shower with her, but Richard's friend is taking all damn night to pick his ass up.

"Is he coming *today* or . . ." I begin.

Richard nods about twenty times, but then looks at the window with a slightly worried expression. "Yeah, yeah, he said he'd be here soon. He probably just got lost or something."

"Sure," I say.

He smiles. "Won't you miss having me around?"

"I wouldn't go that far."

"Well, maybe I'll find myself a job and see you both in Seattle."

"Neither of us will *be* in Seattle."

He looks at me sagely. "Sure," he repeats, using my word from moments ago.

A knock at the door ends our obnoxious conversation, and as he goes to answer it, I stand up. Just in case he needs an extra little push out the door.

"Thanks for picking me up, man," Tessa's dad says to his friend, who remains in the doorway but peeks his head in farther. He's tall, with long black hair swept back in a disgusting, greasy ponytail. His cheeks are sunken in, his clothes are ratty, and his fingernails are black lines on filthy, bony hands.

What the fuck.

The man's gravelly voice matches his appearance when he asks with some awe, "This is your daughter's place?"

This man is no drunk.

"Yeah. Nice, huh? I'm proud of her." Richard smiles, and the guy pats his shoulder, nodding in agreement.

"Who's this?" the man asks.

They both look over at me. Richard smiles. "Oh, him? That's Hardin, Tessie's boyfriend."

"Cool, I'm *Chad*," he states, saying it almost like he's a local personality I should somehow know.

Not a drunk. So much worse.

"Okay," I say, watching his eyes as they move around our living room. I'm relieved that Tessa's in the shower and doesn't have to meet this creep.

When I hear the bathroom door open, I curse at myself. I spoke too fucking soon. Chad lifts his long-sleeved shirt to scratch at his arms, making me feel like Tessa for a moment as I get a sudden urge to mop the fucking floor.

"Hardin?" Her voice travels down the hall.

"You should go now," I tell the scraggly pair before me in the most threatening tone possible.

"I want to meet her," Chad says with a dark twinkle in his eye, and I have to concentrate to keep myself in my place and not throw both these bags of bones into the hallway and out the window.

"No. You don't," I say.

Richard looks at me. "Okay . . . okay . . . we're going," he says and starts ushering his friend out. "I'll see you later, Hardin. Thanks again. Stay out of jail." And with a smirk and that parting shot, he leaves the apartment.

"Hardin?" Tessa calls again as she enters the living room.

"They just left."

"What's wrong?" she asks.

"*What's wrong?* Hmm . . . let's see. Zed came to your office, and your drunk of a dad just brought some creepy fucking dude into our apartment." A brief pause, and I add, "Are you sure your dad only drinks?"

"What?" The shoulder of her T-shirt—well, *my* T-shirt—slips down to bare her shoulder. She pushes it back up and sits down on the couch. "What do you mean, 'only drinks'?"

Looking at her, I don't want to plant the seed that her dad's not only a homeless drunk but a drug addict, too. He doesn't look as bad as the asshole who just came to pick him up, but I still have a weird feeling about this shit. Even so, I just say, "I don't know. Never mind, I was just thinking out loud."

"Okay . . ." she quietly answers.

I know her well enough to be certain that the thought of her father being on drugs hasn't crossed her mind and that she'd never guess I'm thinking it from what I said.

"Are you mad at me?" Her voice is soft, too timid.

I know she's waiting for me to explode any moment. I have been purposely avoiding conversation with her for a reason. "No."

"Are you sure?" She looks at me with those big, beautiful eyes, begging for me to say something.

They do the trick.

"No, I'm not sure. I don't know. I'm really mad, yeah, but I don't want to fight with you over it. I'm trying to change, you know? Keep my shit together and not flip out on you over every little thing." I sigh, rubbing the back of my neck. "Even though this *isn't* a little thing. I've told you time and time again not to see Zed, but you still do." I look at her coldly—not to be mean, but because I have to see how her eyes react when I add, "How would you feel if I did that to you?"

She practically crumples before my eyes. "I would feel terrible. I know I've been wrong for seeing him," she says without defense.

Well, I wasn't expecting that. I was expecting her to yell at me and stick up for that shithead Zed, like always. "Yes, you have," I say, then sigh. "But if you say you told him it's done, then it's done. I've done everything I can do to keep him away from you, but he doesn't stop. So you have to be the one to keep him away."

"It's done, I swear. I won't see him again."

She looks up at me, and I shudder at the thought of her on the phone earlier, her crying over their goodbye.

"We aren't going to that party on Saturday," I say, and her face falls.

"Why not?"

"Because I don't think it's a good idea." Actually, I *know* it isn't.

"I want to go." She presses her full lips into a line.

"We aren't going," I tell her again.

Her spine shoots up a little, and she pushes back. "If I want to go, I'll go."

Fuck, she's so fucking stubborn. "Can we please just discuss it later? We have shit to do if you want me to go on this fucking stupid-ass boat shit."

She smiles playfully. "Could you fit any more curse words in that sentence?"

And I smile as I have a vision of her bent over my knee for being so smarmy. She'd probably like that, actually: lying across my lap, my hand hitting her skin, not too hard, just hard enough to turn the skin pink . . .

"Hardin?"

My perverted thoughts interrupted, I push them away . . . for now. She would hide behind her hands if I told her what I was daydreaming about.

chapter twenty-one

TESSA

I shake his arm again, roughly this time. "Hardin! You have to get up—*now*. We're going to be late."

I'm already dressed and ready, our bags have already been placed in the car, and I've given him as much time to sleep as possible. Heck, last night I even did all the packing, not that he would've done a very good job of it anyway.

"Not . . . going," he groans.

"Please get up!" I whine and tug at his arm. God, I wish he was a morning person like me.

He covers his face with the pillow, and I grab it and toss it onto the floor. "No, go away."

I decide to take a different approach and bring my hand to the front of his boxers. He fell asleep in his jeans last night, and I had a hell of a time tugging them down his legs without waking him. But now he's been left vulnerable, and manipulable.

My fingernails gently graze the inked skin just above the waistband . . . He doesn't budge.

I dip my hand fully into his boxers, and he opens his eyes. "Good morning," he says with a lusty smile.

I remove my hand and stand up. "Get up."

He yawns dramatically and looks down at his boxers and says, "Looks like I . . . already . . . am." When he doesn't look back up, I see he's pretending to be asleep again, and soon he starts making loud cartoon snoring noises. It's inconvenient, but adorable and playful; I hope he remains this way for the rest of the week—really, I'll settle for the rest of the day.

I reach into his boxers again, and when his eyes pop open to look at me like an eager puppy, I say, "Uh-uh," and pull my hand back out.

"Not fair," he whines.

But he does get up, pulling yesterday's jeans back on. He walks over to the dresser and grabs a black shirt, looks at me, then puts it back and pulls out a white one. He runs his fingers through his hair, making it stand straight up before pushing it back down.

"Do I have time to brush my teeth?" His tone is sarcastic, and his voice is raspy from sleep.

"Yes, hurry up. Brush your teeth so we can go," I instruct and do a quick walk-through of the apartment to make sure everything is in order.

Minutes later, Hardin joins me in the living room, and we finally leave.

KEN, KAREN, AND LANDON are waiting for us in the driveway when we arrive.

I roll down the window. "Sorry we're a few minutes late," I apologize as we pull up next to where they stand.

"It's okay! We figured we'd all ride together since it's quite a drive," Karen says with a smile.

"Fuck, no," Hardin whispers next to me.

"Come on." She gestures to the black SUV filling the other half of the driveway. "Ken bought me this for my birthday, and we never use it."

"No; hell, no," Hardin says a little louder.

"It'll be fine," I say quietly, to him.

"Tessa . . ." he begins.

"Hardin, please don't make this difficult, please," I beg. Maybe, just maybe, I blink my eyes seductively, hoping that will work.

After looking at me for a moment, his eyes finally soften. "Fine. Fuck, you're lucky I love you."

I squeeze his hand. "Thank you." Then I turn back to Karen. "Okay," I say with a smile and turn off my car.

Hardin puts our bags into the back of Karen's SUV, scowling the whole time.

"This is going to be fun!" Landon laughs as I climb into the car.

Hardin sits next to me in the back row after making a comment about not having to sit next to Landon. As Ken pulls onto the street, Karen turns on the radio and begins to sing along softly.

"This is some shit straight from a corny comedy," Hardin says and puts his hand over mine before pulling them both to his lap.

chapter twenty-two

TESSA

"Wisconsin!" Karen says loudly, clapping her hands together, then pointing at a passing truck.

I can't help but laugh at Hardin's horrified expression. "Oh my fucking God," he huffs, laying his head back on the seat.

"Would you stop? She's having fun," I scold him.

"Texas!" Landon calls out.

"Just open the door, and I'll jump out here," Hardin adds.

"So dramatic," I tease and look over at him. "So she plays the license-plate game? I'd think you could relate—you and your friends seem awful fond of silly games, too, like Truth or Dare."

Before Hardin can say something smart back, Karen exclaims, "We're so excited for you two to see the boat and the cabin!"

I look over at her. "Cabin?" I ask.

"Yeah, we have a small cabin on the water there. I think you'll like it, Tessa," she says.

I'm so relieved to find that I won't have to sleep on the boat, like I'd assumed.

"I'm hoping the sun stays out—this weather is nice for February. It's even better in the summer. Maybe we can all come back?" Ken asks, looking in the rearview mirror.

"Yeah," Landon and I answer in unison.

Hardin rolls his eyes. Apparently he's going to stick to his pouty, childlike persona for the remainder of the drive.

"Do you have everything ready for Seattle, Tessa?" Ken asks.

"I spoke with Christian yesterday, and he's really looking forward to you coming."

I feel Hardin's eyes on me, but I'm not going to let that stop me. "I plan to start packing when we get back, but I've already enrolled in my classes at the new campus," I tell him.

"That campus is nothing compared to mine," Ken teases, and Karen laughs. "No, it really *is* a nice campus. If you have any trouble, let me know."

I smile, happy to have him on my side. "Thank you, I will."

"Come to think of it," he goes on, "we're getting a new professor from the Seattle campus next week. He's replacing one of our religion professors."

"Oh, which one?" Landon asks, looking at me with a raised brow.

"Soto, the young one." Ken looks in the rearview mirror again. "He's your professor right now, isn't he?"

"Yeah, he is," Landon answers.

"I don't remember where he's going, but I think he's transferring out," Ken says.

"Good thing," Landon remarks under his breath, but I catch it and smile at him. Neither one of us really likes Professor Soto's style and lack of academic rigor. Though I did enjoy the journaling he had us do.

Karen's voice is soft, and it slides between my thoughts. "Do the two of you have a place already?"

"No. I had an apartment, or so I thought, but the woman seems to have dropped off the face of the earth. It was perfect, too, right in my budget and close to the office," I tell her.

Hardin shifts a little beside me, and I want to add that he isn't joining me in Seattle, but I'm hoping to use this trip to convince him otherwise, so I stay quiet.

"You know, Tessa, I have a few friends in Seattle. I can see about getting you a place before Monday, if you'd like," Ken offers.

"No," Hardin says quickly.

I look over at him. "*Actually*, I *would* like that," I say and meet Ken's reflected gaze. "Otherwise I'll be spending a fortune staying at a hotel until I can find a place."

Hardin waves his dad off. "It's fine. I'm sure Sandra will call her back."

That's strange, I think and look at him. "How'd you know her name?" I ask.

"What?" He blinks a couple of times. "You've only said it one hundred times."

"Oh," I say, and he spreads his hand across my thigh, squeezing gently.

"Well, just let me know if you want me to call anyone," Ken offers again.

AFTER ANOTHER TWENTY MINUTES or so, Karen looks back at us, excitement bursting through her expression. "So how about I Spy?"

Landon's lips turn up into a vibrant smile. "Yeah, Hardin, how about I Spy?"

Hardin leans against me, his head on my shoulder, and his arm wraps around me. "I'm good. I mean, it sounds wonderful, but it's nap time for me. I'm sure Tessa and Landon would love to play."

Despite his mocking the game, the public intimacy warms me and makes me smile. I remember a time when Hardin would only hold my hand under the dinner table at his father's house, and now he doesn't seem fazed to be holding me in front of his family.

"Okay! I'll go first," Karen says. "I spy with my little eye . . . something . . . blue!" she squeals.

Hardin chuckles lightly, against me. "Ken's shirt," he whispers and nuzzles further into me.

"The navigation screen?" Landon guesses.

"No,"

"Ken's shirt?" I ask.

"Yes! Tessa, it's your turn now."

Hardin pinches me a little in acknowledgment, but I'm focused on Karen's massive smile. She's having way too much fun with these cheesy games, but she's too sweet for me to not to play along.

"Okay, I spy something"—I look down at Hardin—"black."

"Hardin's soul!" Landon shouts, and I laugh.

Hardin opens one eye and sticks up a middle finger at his stepbrother.

"You're right!" I exclaim, giggling.

"Well then, the lot of you can shut up so me and my black soul can get some sleep," he says, eyes closed.

We ignore him and continue, and only a few minutes later Hardin's breathing turns heavy and he begins to snore lightly into my neck. He mumbles for a moment before sliding down, putting his head on my lap and bringing his other arm around my waist. Landon seems to take that as a cue and lies across the middle seat, joining Hardin in sleep. Even Karen times out and ends up falling asleep.

I enjoy the silence as I stare out the window, watching the lush scenery shoot past us.

"We're getting close, only a few more miles," Ken says to the car, to nobody in particular.

I nod in acknowledgment and run my fingers through Hardin's soft hair. His eyelids flutter lightly under my touch, but he doesn't wake up. I trail my fingers down his back, slowly, taking in the view of him sleeping so peacefully, his arms wrapped tightly around my body.

Soon we turn onto a small street, the entirety of it lined with large pine trees. Silently, I watch out the window as we turn onto another street and round a corner, bringing the coast into view with sudden immediacy. It's beautiful.

Glittering blue water meets the shoreline, creating a gorgeous contrast. The grass is brown, though, dead from a harsher-than-normal Washington winter. I can't imagine how beautiful this place must be in the summer.

"Here we are," Ken says, pulling into a long driveway.

I look toward the front of the car and see a large wooden cabin. Clearly, the Scotts' definition of "small cabin" is very different from mine. The one I'm looking at is two stories tall, made entirely of dark cherrywood, and has a white-trimmed porch wrapping around the ground floor.

"Hardin, wake up." I run my index finger over his jawline.

His eyes open, and he blinks rapidly, confused for a moment, then he sits up and wipes his eyes with his knuckles.

"Honey, we're here," Ken says to his wife, and she lifts up her head, followed by her son.

Still a little dazed, Hardin carries our bags inside, where Ken shows him to the room we're staying in. I follow Karen into the kitchen while Landon takes his bags to his room as well.

The cathedral-style ceiling in the living room is repeated in the kitchen on a smaller scale. It takes me a moment to figure out what's so peculiar about this room, but then I see that the kitchen here is a smaller, yet equally elegant version of the Scotts' kitchen at home.

"This place is beautiful," I say to Karen. "Thank you for inviting us."

"Thank you, dear. It's nice to finally have company in it." She smiles and opens the refrigerator. "We love having the two of you here. I'd never have thought that Hardin would come along on a family trip. I know it's a short one, but this means the world to Ken," she says, speaking softly to ensure I'm the only one to hear.

"I'm glad he came along, too, I think he'll enjoy himself." I say the words hoping that once they're out there in the air, they'll come true.

Karen turns and grabs my hand warmly. "I sure will miss you when you go to Seattle. I haven't had much time with Hardin, but I'll miss him, too."

"I'll still be around. It's only a couple hours away," I assure her. And myself, really.

I'm going to miss her and Ken. And I can't even allow my mind to wander into thoughts of Landon's looming departure. Even though I'm leaving for Seattle before he leaves for New York, I'm not ready for him to be so far away. Being in Seattle, I'll still be in the same state at least. But New York is far, so far.

"I hope so. With Landon gone, too, I'm afraid I'll be lost. I've been a mother for nearly twenty years . . ." She begins to tear up. "I'm sorry, I'm just so proud of him." She dabs at her eyes with her fingers, stopping the tears, and looks around the kitchen, like she'll find a task that will stop this feeling she's having. "Maybe the three of you can run to the store down the road while Ken gets the boat ready."

"Yeah, of course we can," I say as the three men enter the room.

Hardin comes up behind me. "I left the bags on the bed for you to unpack. I know I'd do it wrong."

"Thank you," I say, grateful that he didn't even try. He likes to shove things haphazardly into dresser drawers, and it drives me mad. "I told Karen we'd go to the store for her while your father gets the boat ready."

"Okay." He shrugs.

"You, too." I turn to Landon, who nods.

"Landon knows where it is; it's just down the road. You can walk or take the car. The keys are hanging by the door," Ken says as we head out.

The weather is forgiving today, and the sun makes it feel much warmer than it should be this early in the year. The sky is a clear blue. I can hear the waves crashing and smell the salt in the air each time the wind blows. We decide to walk down to the small store at the end of the street, and I'm comfortable in jeans and a short-sleeved shirt.

"This place is so nice, it feels like we're in our own world," I say to Hardin and Landon.

"We *are* in our own world. No one bothers to come to the beach in fucking February," Hardin comments.

"Well, I think it's nice," I say, ignoring his attitude.

"Anyway"—Landon looks at Hardin, who is kicking at the rocks as we walk down the gravel road—"Dakota has an audition for a small production this week."

"Really?" I say. "That's so great!"

"Yeah, she's really excited. I hope she gets the part."

"Didn't she just start school, though? Why would they give the part to an amateur?" Hardin's voice is calm, wondering.

"Hardin . . ."

"They would give her the part because regardless of her being an amateur or not, she's an excellent dancer and has been studying ballet her entire life," Landon fires back.

Hardin holds up his hands comically. "Don't get testy, I'm just saying."

But Landon defends his love. "Well, don't, she's talented, and she's going to get the part."

Hardin rolls his eyes. "Okay . . . damn."

"It's nice that you support her." I smile at Landon in an attempt to break up the tension brewing between him and Hardin.

"I'll always support her, no matter what she does. That's why I'm moving all the way to New York." Landon looks at Hardin, and Hardin's jaw tenses.

"So this is how this trip is going to be, then? The two of you fucking ganging up on me? Count me fucking out, then. I didn't even want to come on this shit anyway." Hardin spits.

The three of us stop walking, and Landon and I both turn to Hardin. I'm thinking about how to calm him down, when Landon suddenly says, "Well, then you shouldn't have come. We'd all have a better time without you and your sour attitude anyway."

My eyes widen at Landon's harsh remark, and I feel the urge to defend Hardin, but I stay quiet. Besides, Landon's right, mostly. Hardin shouldn't make it his goal to ruin our trip by having an attitude for no good reason.

"Excuse me? You're the one with a fucking 'attitude,' because I said your girlfriend was an amateur."

"No, you started being a jerk in the car," Landon says.

"Yeah—because your mum wouldn't stop singing along to every fucking song on the radio and yelling state names"—Hardin's voice rises precipitously—"while I was trying to *enjoy* the *scenery*."

I step between them as Hardin tries to move toward Landon. Landon takes a deep breath and stares at Hardin, challenging him. "My mom is trying to make sure we all have a nice time!"

"Well, then maybe she should—"

"Stop it, you guys. You can't fight like this the entire time we're here. No one will be able to stand it, so please just stop," I beg, not wanting to take sides between my best friend and my boyfriend.

They look at each other for a few more tense moments. I nearly laugh at the way they behave like brothers despite the fact that they try so hard not to.

"Okay." Landon says finally, and sighs.

"Fine," Hardin huffs.

The rest of our walk is silent, aside from Hardin's boots kicking at the rocks and Landon's soft humming. The calm after the storm . . . or before it.

Or just between them, I suppose.

"WHAT ARE YOU GOING TO WEAR on the boat?" I ask Landon as we walk up the driveway to the cabin.

"Shorts, I think. It's warm right now, but I'll probably bring a sweatsuit."

"Oh." I wish it was warmer so I could wear a swimsuit. I don't even own one, but the idea of shopping for one with Hardin makes me smile.

I can picture him, saying crude and perverted things; he'd probably end up in the dressing room with me.

I don't think I'd stop him.

I need to stop thinking these types of things, especially while Landon is talking about the weather, and I should at least appear to be listening.

"The boat is insane, it's so big," Landon says.

"Oh . . ." I cringe. Now that we're closer to the boat ride, my nerves are beginning to take over.

Landon and I go into the kitchen to unpack the groceries, and Hardin heads into the bedroom without a word.

Landon looks over his shoulder to where his stepbrother disappeared to. "He's pretty sensitive when it comes to talking about Seattle. He still hasn't agreed to go, has he?"

I look around the room to be sure no one can hear us. "No, not exactly," I say and chew on my bottom lip in embarrassment.

"I don't get it," Landon says, looking through the bags. "What's so bad about Seattle that he won't go with you? Does he have some sort of history there?"

"No . . . well, not that I know of . . ." I start to say, but then Hardin's letter comes to mind. I don't remember him mentioning any hardships he'd gone through in Seattle. Could he have left them out?

I don't think so. And I hope not. I'm not ready for any more surprises.

"Well, there has to be a reason, because he can't even go to the bathroom without you, so I can't imagine him being okay with you moving away without him. I thought he'd do anything to keep you close to him . . . *literally* anything," Landon says with emphasis.

"Me, too." I sigh, not knowing why Hardin has to be so stubborn. "And he does go to the bathroom without me. Sometimes," I joke.

Landon laughs along. "Barely; he probably installed a hidden camera on your shirt to keep track of you."

"Cameras aren't my thing. I'm more of a tracking-device type of guy." Hardin's voice makes me jump, and I look over to find him leaning in the doorway of the kitchen.

"Thanks for helping prove my point," Landon says, but Hardin chuckles, shaking his head. He seems to be in a better mood, thank goodness.

"Where is this boat? I'm bored listening to you two talk shit about me."

"We weren't, we were joking," I tell him and walk over to hug him where he's standing.

"It's fine, I do the same when you're not around," he says in a mocking tone, although I can't help but detect a hint of seriousness behind the words.

chapter twenty-three

TESSA

"Dock's a little shaky, but sturdy enough. I need to get someone out here to remodel it . . ." Ken muses as we follow him out to the where the boat's moored.

With their backyard leading directly to the water, the view is incredible. The waves crash along the rocks lining the shore, and instinctively I step behind Hardin.

"What's wrong?" he asks quietly.

"Nothing. I'm just a little nervous."

He turns around to face me, sliding both of his hands into the back pockets of my jeans. "It's only water, baby, it'll be okay."

He smiles, but I can't tell if he's mocking me or being sincere. It's only when his lips brush my cheek that my doubt disappears.

"I forgot you don't like water." He pulls me closer.

"I like water . . . in swimming pools."

"And streams?" His eyes glitter with humor.

I smile at the memory. "Only one stream in particular."

I was nervous that day, too. Hardin only convinced me to get into the water by bribing me. He had promised to answer one of my endless questions about him in exchange for me getting into the water with him. Those days seem so distant—so ancient, really—but the ongoing theme of secrecy still litters our present.

Hardin takes my hand in his as we follow his family down the dock to the incredibly intimidating vessel waiting at the end. I don't know much about boats, but I think this one may be a giant-sized pontoon boat. I know it's not a yacht, but it's bigger than any fishing boat I've ever seen.

"It's so big," I whisper to Hardin.

"Shh, don't talk about my dick in front of my family," he teases.

I love this playful yet grumpy mood he's in; his smile is contagious. Then the dock creaks beneath my feet, and I squeeze tight against Hardin in panic.

"Watch the step," Ken calls back to us as he climbs onto the ladder connecting the boat and the dock.

Hardin's hand moves to my back as he helps me up the ladder. I try to force myself to imagine that it's just a small ladder at a playground, not something attached to an enormous boat. The reassurance that comes with Hardin's touch is the only thing keeping me from running back up the shaky dock, into the cabin, and hiding under the bed.

Ken helps us each onto the deck, and once there, I can see how nice the boat is, decorated in white wood and caramel leather. The seating area is large, big enough for all of us and then some to sit comfortably.

When he tries to help Hardin aboard, his son waves him off. When he's fully on the deck, he looks around and says plainly, "It's nice to see that your boat is nicer than Mum's house."

Ken's proud smile fades.

"Hardin," I whisper, tugging at his hand.

"Sorry," he huffs.

Ken sighs but seems to accept his son's apology before walking over to the other side of the boat.

"You okay?" Hardin leans into me.

"Yeah, just be nice, please. I'm already nauseous."

"I'll be nice. I already apologized." He takes a seat on one of the lounges, and I join him.

Landon takes the grocery bag and leans down to unpack

cans of soda and bags of snacks. I gaze across the expanse of the boat and out onto the water. It's beautiful, and the sun is dancing across the surface.

"I love you," Hardin says softly into my ear.

The boat's engine comes to life with a light hum, and I scoot closer to Hardin. "I love you," I say back, still looking out onto the water.

"If we get out far enough we may see a few dolphins, or if we're lucky, a whale!" Ken says loudly.

"A whale would surely knock this boat over in no time flat," Hardin remarks, and I gulp at the thought. "Shit, sorry," he apologizes.

The farther and farther we get from the shore, the calmer I become. It's odd: I thought it would be the opposite, but there's a certain serenity that comes with being so disconnected from the land.

"Do you see dolphins a lot out here?" I ask Karen as she sips on her soda.

She smiles. "No, only once. But we still try!"

"I can't believe the weather today, it feels like June," Landon remarks, pulling his T-shirt over his head.

"Are you working on your tan?" I ask him, taking in his pale torso.

"Or your ghost impression?" Hardin adds.

Landon rolls his eyes but otherwise ignores the remark. "Yep, even though I won't need a tan in the city."

"If the water wasn't ice cold, we could all go for a swim closer to shore," Karen says.

"Maybe in the summer," I remind her, and she nods happily.

"At least we still have the Jacuzzi back at the cabin," Ken says.

Enjoying the moment, I look up at Hardin, but he stays quiet, staring off into the distance.

"Look! There!" Ken points behind us.

Hardin and I both turn quickly, and it takes me a moment to see what he's spotted. It's a pod of dolphins leaping through the water. They aren't close to the boat, but they're close enough that we can see the way they move in sync through the waves.

"It's our lucky day!" Karen laughs.

The wind blows my hair across my face, blocking my view for a moment, and Hardin's hand reaches up to tuck it back behind my ear. It's always the simple things he does, the small ways he finds to touch me without thought, that make my stomach flutter.

"That was so neat," I say to him once the dolphins have fully passed by.

"Yeah, it was, actually," he says, sounding surprised.

AFTER TWO HOURS of conversation about boating, the beautiful summers along this spot of coastline, sports, and an awkward mention of Seattle that Hardin halted almost as soon as it began, Ken leads us back to the shore.

"That wasn't so bad, was it?" Hardin and I ask each other at the same time.

"Guess not." He laughs, helping me down the ladder to the dock.

The sun has marked his cheeks and the bridge of his nose, and his hair is unruly and blown out from the wind. He's so lovely, it hurts.

We all walk across the backyard, and all I can think about is how much I want to hold on to that peaceful sensation of being out on the water.

As we enter the cabin, Karen announces, "I'll make us all lunch—I'm sure everyone is hungry," and disappears into the kitchen.

The rest of us stand there silent and content as she walks off.

Finally, Hardin asks his father, "What else is there to do here?"

"Well, there's a nice restaurant further in town—we were planning for all of us to have dinner there tomorrow. There's an old-fashioned movie theater, a library—"

"So, a bunch of lame shit, then?" Hardin says, his words harsh but his tone playful.

"It's a nice place, you should give it a chance," Ken says, not in the least bit offended.

The four of us head into the kitchen and stand around while Karen puts together a platter of sandwiches and fruit. Hardin, who is being overly affectionate today, rests his hand on my hip.

Maybe this place is good for him.

AFTER LUNCH, I help Karen clean the kitchen and make lemonade while Landon and Hardin discuss how terrible modern literature is. I can't help but laugh when Landon mentions Harry Potter. This sends Hardin into a five-minute-long speech on why he never has read and never will read the books, and Landon tries desperately to get him to change his mind.

After the lemonade is finished and greedily drunk down, Ken says to us all, "Karen and I are going to head down to our friend's cabin a few doors down for an hour or two, if you all want to come."

Hardin looks over at me from across the room, and I wait for him to answer. "I'll pass," he finally says, still looking at me.

Landon looks back and forth between Hardin and me. "I'll come," he says plainly, but I swear I catch him smirk at Hardin before he stands up to join Ken and his mom.

chapter twenty-four

HARDIN

I am thinking they will never leave, but as soon as they do, I pull her over to the couch with me.

"You didn't want to go?" she asks.

"Fuck, no—why the hell would I want to go? I'd much rather stay here with you. Alone," I say and brush the hair back from her neck. She squirms a little from the light shiver my touch spreads across her skin. "Did you want to go sit and listen to a roomful of boring-ass people talk about boring-ass shit?" I ask her, my lips barely grazing her jaw.

"No." Her breathing has already changed.

"You're sure?" I tease and run my nose along her neck, nudging her to tilt her head.

"I don't know, it may have been more fun than this," she says.

I chuckle into her neck, kissing her where the goose bumps on her skin appear from my breath. "Not fucking likely. We do have a hot tub in our room, remember?"

"Yeah, but it's no good, because I don't have a swimsuit . . ." she starts.

I suck lightly at her neck and imagine what she'd look like in a bathing suit.

Fuck.

"You don't need one," I whisper.

She moves her head back and looks at me like I'm crazy. "Yes, I do! I'm not getting in a hot tub with no clothes on."

"Why not?" It sounds like a pretty fun time to me.

"Because your family is here."

"I don't know why you always use that as an excuse . . ." My hand travels down to her lap, and I press against the seam of her jeans. "Sometimes I think you may like that."

"Like what?" she asks, practically fucking panting.

"The possibility of being caught."

"Why would anyone like that?"

"A lot of people do—the thrill of being caught, you know?" I apply more pressure between her legs, and she tries to clamp them shut, struggling against what she wants and what she thinks she *shouldn't* want.

"No, that's . . . I don't know, but I don't like it," she lies. I'm pretty damn sure she does.

"Mm-hmm . . ."

"I don't!" she cries, defending herself, her cheeks flushed and eyes wide in embarrassment.

"Tess, it's okay that you do. It's pretty fucking hot, really," I assure her.

"I don't."

Sure, Tessa. "Okay, you don't." I raise my hands in defeat, and she whimpers a little from the loss of contact. I knew there was no way in hell she'd admit it, but hey, it was worth a try.

"Are you going to come into the Jacuzzi with me?" I ask and remove my hand from her.

"I'll come up there . . . but I'm not getting in."

"Suit yourself." I smile and stand up. I know she'll end up in there; she'll just need more persuading than most girls. Come to think of it, I've never actually been in a Jacuzzi with a female before, naked or not.

Wrapping her small hand around my wrist, she follows me upstairs to the room that is considered ours for the next few days.

The balcony connected to it is what made me claim it in the first place. The moment I saw that Jacuzzi sitting there, I had to get her into it.

The bed isn't bad either; it's small, but we don't need a big bed with the way we sleep any damn way.

"I really do love it here; it's so peaceful," she says and sits on the bed to take her shoes off.

I open the double doors to the balcony. "It's okay." If my father, his wife, and Landon weren't here, it would sure as hell be better.

"I don't have anything to wear tomorrow to that restaurant your father was talking about."

I shrug and lean down to turn the faucet on the Jacuzzi. "We won't go, then."

"I want to go. I just didn't know we were going out somewhere before I packed."

"It's poor planning on their fault, then," I say and study the gauges to make sure they look like they're working. "We'll just wear jeans. Seems like a casual area."

"I don't know."

"Well, if you don't want to wear jeans, we can find a store in this dump to get you something else," I offer, and she smiles.

"Why are you in such a good mood?" Tessa raises an eyebrow at me.

I dip a finger into the water. Almost there; this thing heats up *quickly*. "I don't know . . . I just am."

"Okay . . . should I be worried?" she asks, stepping out to join me on the balcony.

"No." *Yes.* I gesture to the wicker chair next to the hot tub. "Will you at least sit out here with me while I enjoy the relaxation that is sitting in scalding-hot water?"

She laughs and nods, taking a seat. I watch her innocent eyes as she stares at me while I pull my shirt over my head and take my pants off. I leave my boxers on; I want her to take them off.

"You sure you don't want to come in?" I ask her, and lift my leg over the edge and climb in. *Fuck, it's hot as hell.* A few seconds later the burn disappears, and I lean back against the hard plastic.

"I'm sure," she says and looks out at the woods surrounding us.

"No one can see us. You really think I'd ask you to come in here naked if someone could?" I ask. "I mean, me with my 'jealousy' issues and whatnot."

"What if they come back?" she asks quietly, as if someone can hear her.

"They said an hour or two."

"Yeah, but . . ."

"I thought you were learning to live a little?" I tease my beautiful girl.

"I am."

"You're sitting there pouting in a chair while I'm enjoying the view," I point out.

"I'm not pouting," she says, and pouts more.

I smirk at her, knowing it will irritate her further. "Okay," I say, closing my eyes as she purses her lips. "I sure am lonely in here. I may have to take care of myself."

"I don't have anything to wear."

"Déjà vu," I remark, thinking about our experience at the stream for the second time today.

"I—"

"Just get in the damn water," I say, without opening my eyes or changing my tone. I speak to her like it's inevitable, because we both know it is.

"Fine, I am!" she says, trying to convince herself she's exasperated and doesn't really want this as much as she does.

That wasn't as hard as I thought it would be. When I open my eyes, I nearly choke. She's lifting her shirt over her head, and of course she's wearing that damn red bra.

"Take the bra off," I say.

She looks around again, and I shake my head. The only thing she can see from this balcony is the water and trees.

"Take it off, baby," I coax, and she nods, sliding the straps down her arms.

I'll never get enough of her. No matter how many times I touch her, fuck her, kiss her, hold her . . . it will never be enough, I'll always want more. It's not even about the sex, which we have often; it's that I'm the only one who's ever been with her, and she trusts me enough to get naked on a fucking balcony.

So why then am I such a fuckup? I don't want to fuck this up with this girl.

Her jeans join her T-shirt and bra on the chair—folded perfectly, of course.

"Panties, too," I remind her.

"No, yours are on," she fires back and steps into the water. "Ouch!" she squeaks, pulling her foot back before easing in. Once she's all the way in, she sighs, her body having gotten used to the water.

"Come here." I reach for her and pull her onto my lap.

I suppose the uncomfortable plastic seats can be useful after all. The way her body feels against me, in combination with the pulsing jets, makes me want to rip those panties right off.

"It could be like this in Seattle, all the time," she says, and her arms wrap around my neck.

"Like what?" The last thing I want to do is talk about fucking Seattle. If I could find a way to wipe that damn city off the map, I would.

"Like this." She gestures between us. "Just us, no problems with your friends, like Molly, no bad history. Just you and me in a new city. We could start all over, Hardin, together."

"It's not that simple," I tell her.

"Yes, it is; no more Zed."

"I thought you were going to come in here and fuck me, not talk about Zed," I tease, and she tenses.

"Sorry, I . . ."

"Calm down, I'm joking. Well, about the Zed thing." I shift her body on mine so she's straddling my lap, her bare chest flush against mine. "You're everything to me; you know that, don't you?" I repeat the question I've had to ask her so many times.

She doesn't answer this time. Instead she rests her elbows on my shoulders, threads her fingers through my hair, and kisses me.

She's hungry. Just like I knew she'd be.

chapter twenty-five

HARDIN

I attempt to pull her nearly naked body even closer to me as she deepens the kiss. Her hands grip my arms, and I guide my hand down between her thighs.

No point in wasting any time here.

"Should have taken these off," I tell her, tugging at the side of her thin, soaked panties.

She lets out a breathless laugh before sucking in a sharp breath when my fingers enter her. Her moans are cut off by my mouth against hers. She pulls my bottom lip between hers, and I nearly lose it. She's so fucking sexy and seductive, and she doesn't even fucking *try*.

When she begins to rock her hips, pushing herself onto my hand, I grip her waist, move her from my lap, and place her next to me, her legs spread wide, my fingers still pleasing her.

These fucking panties are getting on my nerves.

She startles, then pouts when I remove my fingers from her and hook them around her panties, tugging them down as quickly as possible and leaving her to kick them off the end of one foot into the water beside her. I watch for a second as the jets carry them to the other side of the tub; there's something mesmerizing about seeing that final barrier float away so smoothly.

But quickly, Tessa grabs my wrist to force me to touch her again.

"What do you want?" I urge, wanting to hear the words from her.

"You." She smiles sweetly, then spreads her legs further, showing how dirty she really is.

"Turn around, then," I tell her.

Without giving her a chance to respond, I turn her body around, and she lets out a yelp. I panic for a moment, but then realize that her little pussy is directly lined up with the jets. Of course, she's moaning. She'll be fucking screaming in a minute.

I kneel behind her—I love taking her this way. I can feel so much more of her, I can touch the creamy skin on her back and pay attention to every muscle moving under her skin—and I watch every breath she fights for as I rock into her.

I move her long hair to the side and move closer, slowly pushing farther into her. Her back arches into me, and I take her breasts in my hands as I begin to move in and out of her slowly.

Fuck, it feels so damn good, better than ever. It has to be the hot water pushing around us as I inch in and out of her. She moans, and I reach down to make sure she's still being hit with the rushing water. Her eyes are screwed shut, and her mouth is wide open. Her knuckles are nearly white from gripping the edge of the tub.

I want to move faster, to pound into her, but I force myself to stay at this slow, torturing pace.

"Har-dinnn," she moans.

"Fuck, it's like I can finally feel every inch of you." The moment I say the words, I panic and pull away from her.

A condom.

I didn't even think to use a fucking condom. What has she done to me?

"What's wrong?" she pants, a thin layer of moisture covering her face.

"I don't have a condom on!" I run my hands over my wet hair.

"Oh," she says calmly.

"Oh? What do you mean, Oh?"

"So put a condom on?" she suggests with a doe-eyed look.

"That's not the point!" I stand up in the tub. She doesn't say anything. "If I hadn't thought about it, you could have gotten pregnant."

She nods understandingly. "Okay, yeah, but you did remember."

Why is she so calm about this? She has this grand plan to move to Seattle—a baby would definitely fuck that up. *Wait . . .*

"Is that your plan or something? If I get you pregnant, you think I'll go with you?" I sound like a fucking conspiracy theorist, but it does make sense.

She turns around, laughing. "You aren't serious!" And when she tries to wrap her arms around me, I move out of the way.

"I am."

"Come on, that's insane. Come here, babe." She tries to grab me again, but I dodge her, moving to the opposite side of the Jacuzzi.

Hurt flashes as clear as a goddamn neon sign across her face, and she covers her boobs with her hands. "*You're* the one who forgot about a condom, and now you're saying that I'm trying to trap you by getting pregnant?" She shakes her head in disbelief. "Just *listen* to yourself."

Well, it wouldn't be the first time some crazy chick did that. I slide over to get a little closer now, but she quickly rises onto her knees on the bench. I give her an impassive look, saying nothing.

Watching me, her eyes brim with tears as she stands up in the water and climbs out of the tub. "I'm going to take a shower." She disappears into the bedroom, slamming first the door to the deck and then the bathroom as she goes.

"Fuck!" I yell, smacking a palm at the bubbling water, wishing it could hit me back. I *do* need to listen to what I'm saying—this isn't some random crazy bitch. This is Tessa. What the hell is wrong with me? I'm so fucking paranoid. My guilt over this

Seattle shit is causing me to lose my fucking mind. What's left of it, anyway.

I have to fix this, or at least try to. I owe it to her, especially after I just accused her of the dumbest shit possible.

Ironically, in a twisted way, I almost wish I hadn't remembered the condom myself . . .

No. No, I don't. I just don't want her to leave me, and I don't know what else to do to get her to stay. A baby isn't the answer, that's for damn sure. I've done everything I possibly can except lock her in the apartment. Sure, it's an idea that's actually crossed my mind a few times, but I don't think she would like it too much. Plus she'd probably get a vitamin-D deficiency. And stop going to yoga . . . and so stop wearing those pants.

I need to go inside and apologize for embarrassing her and being a dick to her before the entire gang returns. Maybe I'll get lucky, and they'll get lost in the woods for a few hours.

But first, I have something else I need to do. I climb out of the hot tub and walk into the room; it's cold as hell now that I'm only wearing soaked boxers. I glance back and forth between my phone and the bathroom door connected to our room. The shower's still running, so I grab my phone and a blanket from the back of the chair before stepping back out onto the balcony.

I scroll through my contacts and find the name Samuel; real fucking clever decoy, there. I don't know why I saved this woman's number anyway; I guess I knew somehow I'd get tangled in a fucking web and have to call the bitch back. I changed the name in case Tessa went snooping through my shit, which I knew she would do. I thought she'd caught me when she asked about my deleted history and heard me yelling at Molly on the phone.

In some ways, I'm sure she'd rather see Molly on my call log than this person.

chapter twenty-six

TESSA

I can't believe Hardin had the nerve to accuse me of trying to get myself pregnant, or even *thinking* that there's even a small chance that I would do something like that to him . . . or to myself. The whole thing's just absurd and stupid all around.

Everything was going so great—incredible, really—until he mentioned the condom. He should have just gotten out of the water and grabbed one; I know he has a pile of them in the top of his suitcase. I watched him shove them in there after I neatly packed our bags.

He's probably just frustrated over this whole Seattle mess, so he overreacted, and maybe I did, too. As a result of my annoyance with Hardin's rude comments and his ruining our . . . moment in the hot tub, I need a hot shower. Seconds later the water begins to work against my strained muscles, relaxing my nerves and clearing my head. We both overreacted, him more than me, and the argument was so unnecessary. I reach for the shampoo. And then realize I was so rattled while getting away from him that I forgot to grab my toiletry bag. Great.

"Hardin?" I call. I doubt he can hear me over the shower and hot tub, but I pull the floral shower curtain back and watch for him just in case. When he doesn't appear in the doorway after a few seconds, I grab my towel and wrap it around my body. Trailing water into the bedroom, I reach the suitcases lying on the bed, when I hear Hardin's voice.

I can't quite hear what he's saying, but I catch his tone of false niceness, which tells me he's trying to be polite and not show his frustration. Which tells me that this conversation is something he deems important enough to not act like himself.

I pad quietly across the wooden floor, and since he's on speaker, I hear someone say, "Because I'm a Realtor, and my job is to fill empty apartments."

Hardin sighs. "Well, do you have any more empty apartments to fill?" he asks.

Wait, Hardin's trying to get me an apartment? I'm as shocked as I am excited at the thought. He's finally coming around to the idea of Seattle, and he's actually trying to help me instead of push against me. For once.

The woman on the other end, who, I realize, has a very familiar voice, replies, "You gave me the impression that your friend Tessa was not someone I should be wasting my time giving an apartment to."

What? Wait . . . is that . . . ?

He wouldn't.

"Here's the thing . . . she isn't as bad as I made her out to be. She hasn't actually trashed any apartments or left without paying," he says, and my stomach turns.

He *did*.

I burst through the doors to the deck. "You sick, selfish bastard!" I scream, the first words that come to mind.

Hardin spins to me, face paling, mouth opening wide. His phone tumbles to the floor, and he just stares at me like I'm some terrible creature who's come to destroy him.

"Hello?" Sandra's voice says through the speaker, and he reaches down to grab his phone to silence her.

Anger courses through me. "How could you? How could you do that?"

"I—" he begins.

"No! Don't even waste my time with an excuse! What the hell

were you thinking?" I yell with one arm sweeping in his direction violently.

I storm back into the bedroom, and he follows me, pleading, "Tessa, listen to me."

I turn around, feeling wounded, and strong, and hurt, and enraged. "No! You listen to me, Hardin," I say through my teeth, trying to lower my voice. But I can't. "I'm so sick of this, I'm sick of you trying to sabotage everything in my life that doesn't revolve around you!" I scream, balling my fists tightly at my sides.

"That's not what I—"

"Shut up! Shut the hell up! You are the most *selfish*, *arrogant*—you're just . . . ugh!" I can't think straight; angry words fly from my mouth, my hands moving through the air in front of me.

"I don't know what I was thinking. I was trying to clear it up just now."

I shouldn't be so surprised, really. I should have known that Hardin was behind Sandra's sudden disappearance. He doesn't know when to stop meddling in my life, my career, and I'm sick of it.

"Exactly; this is exactly what I'm talking about. You're always doing something. You're always hiding something. You're always finding new ways to try to control every single thing I do, and I can't take it anymore! This is too much." I can't help but pace back and forth across the room, and Hardin watches me with cautious eyes. "I can handle you being a little overprotective, and I can handle you getting in a fight now and then. Hell, I can even handle you being a complete asshole half the time, because deep down I always knew you were doing what you thought was best for me. But not this. You're trying to ruin my future—and I *won't fucking have it*."

"I'm sorry," he says. And I know that he means it, but—

"You're always fucking sorry! It's always the same shit: you do something, hide something, say something, I cry, you say you're sorry, and *bam!* All is forgiven." I point a harsh finger at him. "But not this time."

I have the urge to slap Hardin right across his face, but I look around for something to take my anger out on instead. I grab a frilly pillow from the bed and throw it onto the floor. Then I throw a second one. It doesn't do much for the anger flaming inside me, but I'd feel even worse if I destroyed anything of Karen's.

This is so exhausting. I don't know how much more I can take before I break.

Fuck that, I won't break. I'm sick of breaking—that's all I ever do. I need to pick up my own pieces, put them back together neatly, and hide them away from Hardin to keep them from ending up in a pile at his feet again.

"I'm sick of the endless cycle. I've told you before, and you don't listen. You find new ways to continue the cycle, and I'm done, I'm so fucking done!"

I don't know if I've ever been this angry at him. Yes, he's done worse things, but I've always moved on from that. We were never in a place like this before, a place where I thought he was done hiding things from me, and I thought he understood that he can't mess with my career. This chance means everything to me. I've spent my life watching what happens to a woman who has nothing of her own. My mother never had anything that she herself earned, anything that was hers, and I need that. I need to do this. I need this chance to prove that even though I'm young, I can make a life for myself that my mother never could make for herself. I can't let anyone take this from me, the way my mother let it slip from her.

"Done . . . with me?" His voice is shaky, and it cracks. "You said you're done . . ."

I don't know what I'm done with. It should be him, but I know myself better than to answer that right now. Normally I would be crying by this point and forgiving him with a kiss . . . but not tonight.

"I'm so fucking exhausted, and I can't stand it. I can't keep doing this like this! You were going to let me move to Seattle without anywhere to live just to try to force me not to go!"

Hardin stands before me in silence, and I take a deep breath, expecting my anger to diminish, but it doesn't. It grows and grows until I am literally seeing red. I grab the rest of the pillows, imagining that they're actually glass vases that shatter to the floor, leaving a mess for someone else to clean up. The problem is that I would be the one doing the cleaning—he wouldn't take the chance of cutting himself in order to spare me.

"Get out!" I scream at him.

"No, I'm sorry, okay, I—"

"Get the fuck out. *Now*," I spit, and he looks at me like he has no idea who I am.

Maybe he hasn't.

He hunches over and leaves the room—and I slam the door behind him before going back out to the balcony. I sit down on the wicker chair and stare out at the sea, trying to calm myself down.

No tears come, only memories. Memories and regrets.

chapter twenty-seven

HARDIN

I know she's exhausted—I can see it on her face each time I fuck up. The fight with Zed, the lie about the expulsion . . . every infraction takes a toll on her; she thinks I don't notice, but I do.

Why did I have to put Sandra on speakerphone? If I hadn't done that, I could have cleaned this shit up and told her about my fuckup after I fixed it. That way she couldn't be as upset.

I wasn't thinking about what Tessa would do when she found out, and I sure as hell wasn't thinking about where she'd live if she didn't change her mind about moving. I suppose I thought that being the control freak that she is, she'd postpone her trip if she didn't have anywhere to stay.

Way to fucking go, Hardin.

I meant well—well, I didn't at the time, but now I do. I know it's fucked up for me to mess with her apartment in Seattle, but I'm grasping at straws here, trying to get her not to leave me. I know what will happen in Seattle, and it's not going to end well.

True to my nature, I take a swing at the wall next to the staircase.

"Fuck!"

True to my luck, I find out it's not drywall. It's real fucking wood, and hurts so much worse. I cradle my fist with my other hand and have to stop myself from repeating my idiotic reaction. I'm lucky it didn't break anything. Sure, it will bruise, but what else is new.

I'm sick of the endless cycle. I've told you before and you don't listen. I stomp down the stairs and throw myself on the couch like a temperamental child. That's what I am really, a fucking child. She knows it, I know it—hell, everyone fucking knows it. I should just print the shit on a goddamn T-shirt.

I should just go up there and try to explain myself again, but honestly, I'm a little scared. I've never seen her so mad before.

I need to get the hell out of here. If Tessa hadn't forced me to ride with the entire fucking Partridge family, I could leave now and end this stupid-ass trip early. I didn't even want to come in the first place.

I guess the boat was sort of okay . . . but the trip in general is bullshit, and now that she's mad at me, there's literally no point in me being here. I stare up at the ceiling, unsure what I'm supposed to do now. I can't just sit here, and I know if I do, I'll end up back upstairs pushing Tessa further.

I'll take a walk. That's what normal people do when they're angry, not punch walls and break shit.

I need to get some damn clothes on before I do anything, but I can't go back up there or she'll murder me, literally.

I sigh as I get up. If I wasn't so confused by Tessa's behavior, I'd care more about what I'm about to do.

The door to Landon's room opens, and my eyes roll immediately. His clothes are stacked neatly on the bed; he must have been planning to dutifully put them away before his mum and my dad dragged him along with them.

I sift through the hideous crap and desperately search for something that doesn't have a fucking collar. Finally, I find a plain blue T-shirt and a pair of black sweatpants.

Fucking lovely. I've now resorted to sharing clothes with Landon. I hope Tessa's rage doesn't last long, but for once I don't know what will happen next. I hadn't expected her to react half as bad as she did; it wasn't really the words she used toward me, it was the way she looked at me the whole time. That look said more than she ever could and, in turn, scared me more than her words alone ever could.

I glance at the door to what was our room up until twenty minutes ago, then head back down the stairs and out the door.

I barely make it down the damn driveway before my favorite stepbrother appears. At least he's alone.

"Where's my dad?" I ask him.

"Are you wearing my clothes?" he responds, clearly confused.

"Um, yeah. I didn't have a choice, don't make a big deal of it." I shrug, knowing by the smile on his face he was planning on doing just that.

"Okay . . . What did you do now?"

What the hell? "What makes you think I did something?"

His brow arches.

"Okay . . . so I did something, something really fucking stupid," I huff. "But I don't want to hear your shit, so don't worry about it."

"Fine." He shrugs and begins to walk away from me.

I was hoping for a few words from him, he's okay with advice sometimes. "Wait!" I call and he turns around. "You're not going to ask me what it was?"

"You just said you don't want to talk about it," he replies.

"Yeah, but I . . . well." I don't know what to say, and he's looking at me like I've grown two heads.

"Do you *want* me to ask you?" He looks pleased, but thankfully he's not being too much of an asshole about it.

"I'm the reason . . ." I begin, but just then I see Karen and my dad starting to walk up the driveway.

"The reason what?" Landon asks, looking back at them.

"Nothing, never mind." I sigh, running my fingers through my damp hair in frustration.

"Hey, Hardin! Where's Tessa?" Karen asks.

Why does everyone always ask me that as if I can't be more than five feet away from her?

The building ache in my chest reminds me of just that: I can't.

"She's inside, sleeping," I lie and turn to Landon. "I'm going for a walk, can you make sure she's okay?" He nods.

"Where are you going?" my father's voice calls as I walk past them.

"Out," I snap and walk faster.

BY THE TIME I reach a stop sign a few roads over, I realize I have no fucking idea where I'm going or even how to get back to where I came from. I just know I've been walking for a while, and that all of these roads are deceptively windy.

I officially hate this place.

It didn't seem so bad while I was watching Tessa's hair blow lightly in the wind, her eyes focused on the shining water, her lips turned up in a small, satisfied smile. She looked so relaxed, like the calm waves far from the shore, steady and undisturbed until our boat intruded on their peace. Now behind us, the water roars, whipping up onto the sides of our boat in an angry way. Soon they'll go back to their resting state, until another boat comes along to disturb their ease.

A girl's voice interrupts the image of Tessa's sun-kissed skin. "Are you lost or something?"

When I turn around, I'm surprised to find a girl, around my age, I think. Her brown hair is as long as Tessa's. She's alone out here at night. I look around us. There's nothing, only an empty gravel road and forest.

"Are you?" I reply, taking notice of her long skirt.

She smiles at me and walks closer. She must be lacking brain cells to be out here in the middle of nowhere asking a complete stranger that looks like me if he's lost.

"No. I'm escaping," she says, tucking her hair behind her ear.

"You're running away? At, like, age twenty?" She better keep her ass moving down this street, then. The last thing I need is some angry father looking for his overdressed teenage daughter.

"No." She laughs. "I'm home from college visiting my parents, and they were boring me to death."

"Oh, good for you. I hope your freedom trail finds you at Shangri-la," I reply and begin to walk away from her.

"You're going the wrong way," she calls out.

"Don't care," I say.

And then I groan when I hear her footsteps crunching against the gravel behind me.

chapter twenty-eight

TESSA

I'm so exhausted, just plain tired of dealing with fight after fight with Hardin. I'm not sure what to do now, where to go from here. I've been following him down the path we've been on for months now, and I'm not sure we're actually going anywhere. We're both just as lost as we were at the start.

"Tessa?" Landon's voice carries through the room and out to the balcony.

"Out here," I reply, thankful that I put on a pair of shorts and a sweatshirt. Hardin always teases me when I do that, but it's comfortable at times like this, not too hot but not too cold.

"Hey," he says, coming out and sitting in the chair next to mine.

"Hey." I glance over at him before staring back at the water.

"Are you okay?"

I take a moment to think over his question: Am I okay? *No.* Will I be? *Yes.*

"Yeah, this time I think I am." I bring my knees to my chest and wrap my arms around them.

"Do you want to talk about it?"

"No. I don't want to ruin the trip with all my drama. I'm fine, really."

"Okay, just know if you want to talk, I'll listen."

"I know." I look over at him, and he gives me a reassuring smile. I don't know what I'm going to do without him.

His eyes go wide, and he points over at something. "Are those . . . ?"

I look over to where he's staring.

"Oh God!" I jump from my seat and grab the red panties that are floating in the hot tub and shove them into the front pocket of my sweatshirt.

Landon bites down on his bottom lip to stifle his laugh, but I can't keep mine in. We both burst into laughter—his genuine, mine out of humiliation. But I'll take this laughter with Landon over my usual postfight crying with Hardin any day.

chapter twenty-nine

HARDIN

I'm growing more and more sick of seeing nothing but gravel and trees while roaming around this small town. The strange girl is still following behind me, and my fight with Tess is still weighing down on me.

"Are you going to follow me around this entire town?" I ask the pestering girl.

"No, I'm going back to my parents' cabin."

"Well, go to their cabin alone."

"You aren't very polite," she hums.

"Really?" I roll my eyes even though she can't see my face. "I've been told civility is one of my strongest attributes."

"Someone lied to you," she says and giggles behind me.

I kick at a rock, for once glad for Tessa's cleanliness, since if she hadn't made me take my shoes off at the door of the cabin, I'd be stuck wearing Landon's sneakers. Not a good look. Plus, I'm almost certain his feet are much smaller than mine.

"So where are you from?" she asks.

I ignore her and continue on my trek. I think I'm supposed to turn left at the next stop sign. I sure as hell hope so.

"England?"

"Yup," I say. Then figure I might as well ask. "Which way?"

I turn and see her point to the right. Of course, I was wrong.

Her eyes are an icy blue, and her skirt drags across the gravel below her feet. She reminds me of Tessa . . . well, the Tessa I was first introduced to. My Tessa no longer wears hideous things like that. She has also learned a new vocabulary; all credit for that goes to me for making her cuss my ass out on a wide range of occasions.

"Are you here with your parents, too?" Her voice is low, sweet even.

"No . . . Well, sort of."

"They are sort of your parents?" She smiles; her use of "they are" instead of the contraction "they're" reminds me of Tess, too.

I look over to the girl again to make sure she's actually there and this isn't some freaky *Christmas Carol*–type shit where she's an apparition that has come to teach me some sort of lesson.

"They're my family, and my girlfriend. I have a girlfriend, by the way," I warn her. I don't see this girl being interested in someone like me, but then again I once thought the same about Tessa.

"Okay . . ." she says,

"Okay." I pick up my pace, wanting to create some space between us. I turn right, and she does, too. Both of us move onto the grass as a truck passes us by, and she catches up again.

"Where is she, then? Your girlfriend?" she asks.

"Sleeping." It makes sense to use the same lie I told my father and Karen.

"Hmm . . ."

"Hmm, what?" I look at her.

"Nothing." She stares forward.

"You've already followed me halfway back. If you have something to say, then say it," I say irritably.

She twists something in her hands, looking down. "I was just thinking that you seem like you're trying to escape from something or hide . . . I don't know, never mind."

"I'm not hiding; she told me to get the fuck out, so I did." What the hell does this wannabe Tessa know anyway?

She looks up at me. "Why did she kick you out?"

"Are you always this nosy?"

She smiles. "Yeah, I am," she says with a nod.

"I hate nosy people."

Except Tessa, of course. No matter how much I love her, sometimes I want to tape her mouth shut following one of her interrogations. She's literally the most intrusive human being I've ever met.

I'm lying, really. I love her pestering behavior; I used to hate it, but I get it now. I want to know all about her, too . . . what she's thinking, what she's doing, what she wants. I realize, to my fucking horror, that I ask more questions now than she does.

"So, are you going to tell me?" the girl presses.

"What's your name?" I ask her, avoiding her question.

"Lillian," she says and drops whatever was in her hand.

"I'm Hardin."

She tucks her hair behind her ear. "Tell me about your girlfriend."

"Why?"

"It seems like you're upset, and who better to talk to than a stranger?"

I don't want to talk to her; she's eerily similar to Tessa, and it's making me uneasy. "I don't think it's a good idea."

The sun has disappeared early here, and the sky is nearly black.

"And keeping it in is?" she asks sensibly. Too sensibly.

"Look, you seem . . . nice and all, but I don't know you and you don't know me, so this conversation isn't going to happen."

She frowns. Then sighs. "Fine."

Finally, I can see the familiar sloped roof of my father's cabin in the distance. "Well, this is me," I say by way of dismissing myself.

"Really? Wait . . . your dad is Ken, isn't he?" She slaps her small hand against her forehead.

"Yeah?" I say, surprised.

We both stop walking at the end of the driveway. "I'm an idiot, of course! With the accents, how did I not think of it earlier." She laughs.

"I don't get it." I look down at her.

"Your dad and my dad are friends, they went to college together or something. I just spent the last hour listening to them tell stories of their glory days."

"Oh, that's ironic." I half smile. I don't feel as uncomfortable around the girl as I did a few minutes ago.

She smiles brightly. "So really we aren't strangers after all."

chapter thirty

TESSA

Cookies," Landon and I answer in unison.

"Cookies it is, then." Karen smiles and opens the cabinet.

Karen never stops, she's always baking, roasting, toasting. Not that I'm complaining; her cooking is incredible.

"It's dark out now. I hope he doesn't get lost out there," Ken says. Landon just shrugs like *That's Hardin*.

Hardin has been gone for nearly three hours, and I'm trying my best not to panic. I know he's okay; if something were to ever happen to him, I would know. I don't know how to explain it, but I know deep down that I would just know.

So something harming him is not what I'm worried about. I'm worried that his frustration will just become an excuse to find some local bar. As much as I wanted him to get away from me, it would kill me to see him stumble through the door and smell liquor on his breath. I just needed my space, time to think and cool down. I haven't gotten around to the thinking part; I've been avoiding it at all costs.

"I was thinking we could all get in the Jacuzzi tonight or maybe in the morning?" Karen suggests.

Landon spits his soda back into his cup, and I look away quickly, biting the inside of my cheek. The memory of Landon spotting my floating panties is much too fresh, and I can feel the heat in my cheeks.

"Karen, honey, I don't think they want to get in the Jacuzzi with us." Ken laughs and Karen smiles, realizing that it would be a little awkward maybe.

"I guess you're right." She laughs and starts separating the cookie dough into small balls. She scrunches her nose. "I hate this premade stuff."

I'm sure that for Karen, premade cookie dough is awful, but for me, it's heaven. Especially now, when I feel like I could snap at any moment.

Landon and I were in the middle of a discussion about Dakota and their soon-to-be apartment when his mother and Ken finally checked in on us. They mentioned that they ran into Hardin as he was leaving. Apparently he told them that I was asleep, so I did my best to go along with his lie, saying that I had only woken up when Landon came in.

I've been wondering where Hardin is and when he will return since the moment he left. Part of me doesn't want to see him at all, but part of me, a much bigger part, needs to know that he isn't doing anything that will further jeopardize our already fragile relationship. I'm still extremely angry at his interfering with my move to Seattle, and I have no idea what the hell I'm going to do about it.

chapter thirty-one

HARDIN

You sabotaged her getting an apartment?" Lillian asks, her jaw falling open.

"I told you it was fucked up," I remind her.

Another pair of headlights flashes by us as we walk to her parents' cabin. I had every intention of going back to my father's, but Lillian has proven herself to be a decent listener so far. So when she asked me to walk her back to her cabin and finish our discussion, I accepted. My absence will give Tessa some time to cool down and hopefully be ready to talk by the time I return.

"You didn't tell me what level of messed up it was. I don't blame her for being mad at you," the girl says, of course ready to take Tessa's side.

I can't imagine what she'd think of me if she knew about all the shit I've put Tessa through in the past six months.

"Well, what are you going to do about it?" she asks, opening the front door to her parents' cabin. She gestures for me to come in, like it was a foregone conclusion that I would.

Once I step inside, I see it's very extravagant. Even bigger than my father's. Fucking rich people.

"They should be upstairs," she says as we walk inside.

"Who should be upstairs?" a woman's voice questions, and Lillian grimaces before turning around to the woman I assume is her mum. She looks just like her, the only difference between them being age. "Who's this?" she asks.

Just then, a middle-aged man wearing a polo shirt and khakis walks into the living room.

Great; fucking great. I should've just stuck to walking Lillian home. I wonder how Tessa would feel if she knew I was here. Would she mind? She's pretty mad at me anyway, and she has a history of being jealous of Molly. Still, this girl isn't Molly; she's nothing like her.

"Mom, Dad, this is Hardin, Ken's son."

A huge grin appears on the man's face. "I was wondering if I'd get to meet you!" he exclaims with a posh British accent. Well, that explains how he would know my father from university.

He walks over and pats my shoulder. I take a step back, causing him to frown slightly, although he also kind of seems to have expected this reaction from me. My father must have warned him about me. I almost laugh at the thought.

"Honey," he says, turning to his wife. "This is Trish's son."

"You know my mum?" I ask him before also turning to his wife.

"Yeah, I knew your mom back before she was your mom," the woman says with a smile. "We were all friends, the five of us," she adds.

"Five?" I ask.

Lillian's dad looks at her. "Now, honey."

"Anyway, you look just like her! Only you have your father's eyes. I haven't seen her since I moved back to America. How is she?" she asks.

"She's good, she's getting married soon."

"Really?" she squeals. "Tell her congratulations from me, that is just so great to hear."

"Okay," I respond. These people smile too damn much. It's like being in a room with three Karens, only much more annoying and much less charming. "Well, I'm going to get going," I tell Lillian, figuring this has been awkward enough.

"No, no. You don't have to go—we'll go upstairs," Lillian's father says, then wraps his arm around his wife's waist and leads her away.

Lillian watches them go, then looks up at me. "Sorry, they are . . ."

"Fake?" I answer for her. I can sense the bullshit behind the man's bleached white smile.

"Yes, very." She laughs and goes over and sits on the couch.

I stand awkwardly by the door.

"Will your girlfriend mind if you're here?" she asks me.

"I don't know, probably." I groan, running exasperated fingers through my hair.

"Would you want her to do the same thing? How would you feel if she was hanging out with a guy, one she just met?" As soon as the words leave her lips, anger swells in my chest.

"I'd be seeing red," I growl.

"Thought so." She smirks and pats the couch next to her.

I take a deep breath and stride over to sit on the opposite side of the couch from her. I'm not sure how to read her; she's rude as hell and a little annoying.

"You're the jealous type, then?" she asks, eyes wide.

"I guess so." I shrug.

"I bet your girlfriend wouldn't like it much if you kissed me." She moves closer, and I jump up from the couch. I'm halfway to the door before she begins to laugh.

"What the hell?" I try to keep my voice down.

"I was just messing with you. I'm not interested, trust me." She smiles. "And it's a relief to know that you aren't either. Now sit."

She may have a lot of the same traits as Tessa but she isn't as sweet . . . nor as innocent. I sit down on the chair across from the couch. I don't know this chick enough to trust her. I'm only here because I don't want to face what's back at my dad's cabin. And Lillian, despite being a stranger, is a neutral third party, unlike

Landon, who happens to be Tessa's best friend. It's sort of nice to have someone to talk to who doesn't have a reason to judge me. And hell, she's a little nutty, so she's more likely to get where I'm coming from.

"Now tell me what is in Seattle that you aren't willing to face for her?"

"It's not anything specific. I do have some bad history there, but it's more than that. It's the fact that she'll be thriving," I respond, knowing how fucking insane I sound. But I don't give a fuck; this girl stalked me for an hour, so if anyone is insane, it's her.

"And that's a bad thing?"

"No. I want her to thrive, of course. I just want to be a part of it." I sigh, missing Tessa desperately even though it's only been a few hours. The fact that she's so angry with me makes me miss her even more.

"So you refuse to go to Seattle with her because you want to be involved in her life? It doesn't make sense," she says, stating the obvious.

"I know you don't get it, she doesn't either, but she's the only thing I have. Literally, she's the only thing in my life that I give a shit about, and I can't lose her. I'd have nothing without her."

Why am I telling her this shit?

"I know I sound fucking pathetic."

"No, you don't." She gives me a sympathetic smile, and I look away. The last thing I want is sympathy.

The light on the staircase shuts off, and I look back at Lillian. "Should I go?" I ask.

"No, I'm sure my father is ecstatic that I brought you home," she says, no sarcasm in her voice.

"Why is that?"

"Well, ever since I introduced them to Riley, he's been hoping we would break up."

"He doesn't like him or some shit?"

"Her."

"What?"

"He doesn't like her," she says, and I almost smile at her.

I feel bad for her father not accepting her relationship, but I have to admit I'm extremely relieved.

chapter thirty-two

TESSA

Landon's been explaining that since their apartment is so close to campus, they can walk there easily every day. No need to drive, and he won't even have to take the subway on a daily basis.

"Well, I'm just glad you won't be driving in that massive city. Thank goodness," Karen says, putting her hand on her son's shoulder.

He shakes his head. "I'm a fine driver, better than Tessa," he teases.

"I'm not that bad, better than Hardin," I remark.

"*There's* something to brag about," Landon says playfully.

"And it's not *your* driving I'm worried about. It's those insane taxis!" Karen says, like a mother hen.

I grab a cookie off the plate on the counter and look at the front door again. I've been watching it, waiting for Hardin to return. My anger has been slowly shifting to concern as the minutes tick by.

"Okay, thanks for letting me know. I'll see you tomorrow," Ken says into his phone as he joins us in the kitchen.

"Who was that?"

"Max. Hardin's at their cabin with Lillian," he says, and my stomach drops.

"Lillian?" I can't stop myself from asking.

"Max's daughter; she's about your age."

Why would Hardin be at the neighbors' cabin with their daughter? Does he know her? Has he dated her?

"He'll be back soon, I'm sure." Ken frowns, and when he looks at me, I get the feeling he hadn't considered my reaction to this information before he said it. That he seems uncomfortable makes me even more uncomfortable.

"Yeah," I choke, standing from the stool at the counter. "I'm just . . . I'm going to go to bed," I tell them, trying to hold myself together. I can feel my anger resurfacing, and I need to get away from them before it boils over.

"I'll come up with you," Landon offers.

"No, I'm okay, really. I had an early morning, we all did, and it's getting late," I assure him, and he nods even though I can tell he isn't buying it.

As I reach the stairs I hear him say, "He's a damn idiot."

Yes, Landon. Yes, he is.

I CLOSE THE BALCONY DOORS before walking over to the dresser to change into my pajamas. With my mind racing, I'm finding it difficult to focus on clothing. Nothing appeals as a substitute for Hardin's worn clothing, and I refuse to wear the white T-shirt resting on the arm of the chair. I need to be able to sleep in my own damn clothes. I give up after rummaging through the drawer and decide to settle for the shorts and sweatshirt that I have on, and lie down on the bed.

Who is this mystery girl that Hardin's with? Ironically, I'm more upset about my apartment in Seattle than I am about her. If he wants to jeopardize our relationship by cheating, that's his choice. Yes, it would tear what's left of me into pieces, and I don't think I would ever recover, but I'm not going to focus on it.

For the life of me I can't picture it. I can't picture him actually cheating on me. Despite all of the things he's done in the past, I just don't see it. Not after his letter, not after his pleading for my forgiveness. Yes, he's controlling, too controlling, and he doesn't know when to stop interfering with my life, but the intentions behind his actions are more about keeping me near him than trying to escape, like cheating would be.

Even after I've spent an hour staring at the ceiling and counting the beams of stained wood lining the sloped surface, the throb of resentment toward Hardin hasn't let up.

I don't know if I'm ready to talk to him just yet, but I know I won't be able to sleep until I hear him return. The longer he's gone, the stronger the twist of jealousy grows in my chest. I can't help but notice the double standard here. If I was out with a guy, Hardin would lose it and probably try to burn down the woods surrounding the place. I want to laugh at the ridiculous thought, but I just don't have it in me. Instead I close my eyes again, begging sleep to come.

chapter thirty-three

HARDIN

Do you want a drink?" Lillian asks.

"Sure." I shrug and glance at the clock.

She gets up and goes over to a silver bar cart. Looking at the bottles it contains, she selects one and shows it to me quickly, like she's Vanna White or something. Pulling the top off of a bottle of brandy that I'm sure cost more than the massive television hanging on the wall, she looks back at me with mock sympathy. "You can't be a coward forever, you know."

"Shut up."

"You're so much like her." She giggles.

"Like Tessa? No, I'm not. And how would you know?"

"No, not Tessa. Riley."

"How's that?"

Lillian pours the dark liquor into a curved glass and places it in my hand before sitting back down on the couch.

"Where's your drink?" I ask.

She gives a regal shake of the head. "I don't drink."

Of course she doesn't. I really shouldn't be drinking, but the slightly sweet, intense aroma of the brandy pushes the nagging reminder away.

"Are you going to tell me how I'm like her or not?" I look at her expectantly.

"You just are; she has that brooding, angry-at-the-world thing going on, too." She makes an exaggerated emo face and crosses her legs under her.

"Well, maybe she has something to be angry about," I say, defending her girlfriend without even knowing her, then gulp down half the glass of liquor. It's strong, aged to perfection, and I can feel the burn down to the soles of my boots.

Lillian doesn't reply. Instead she purses her lips and stares at the wall behind me, deep in thought.

"I'm not into this whole Dr. Phil, you-talk-I-talk, 'Kumbaya' shit," I tell her, and she nods.

"I'm not expecting 'Kumbaya,' but I think you should at least come up with a plan to apologize to Tamara."

"Her name is Tessa," I snap, annoyed suddenly by her small mistake.

She smiles and pulls her brown hair to one shoulder. "Tessa, sorry. I have a cousin named Tamara, and it was in my head, I guess."

"What makes you assume I'll be apologizing, anyway?" I click my tongue against the roof of my mouth while waiting for her response.

"You're kidding, right? You owe her an apology!" she says loudly. "You need to at least tell her you'll go to Seattle with her."

I groan. "I'm *not* going to Seattle, for fuck's sake." *What is it with Tessa and fucking Tessa Number Two and pestering me over Seattle?*

"Well, then I hope she goes without you," she says curtly.

I look at her, this girl who I thought might understand. "What did you say?" I put the brandy glass down on the table quickly, sloshing brown liquid onto its white surface.

Lillian arches one brow. "I said I hope she does go, because you tried to mess up her apartment deal and still aren't willing to move with her."

"Good thing I don't give a fuck what you think." I stand to leave. I know she's right, but I'm over this bullshit.

"Yes, you do, you just won't admit it. I have come to learn

that the people who pretend to care the least actually care the most."

I pick the glass back up and finish it off before heading toward the door. "You don't know shit about me," I say through my teeth.

Lillian gets up and pads over to me casually. "Yes, I do. Like I said, you're just like Riley."

"Well, I feel sorry for her because she has to put up . . ." I begin to lash out at the girl but stop myself. She hasn't done anything wrong; she's actually been trying to help me and doesn't deserve my anger.

I sigh. "Sorry, okay?" I walk back into the living room, plopping myself back onto the couch.

"See, apologizing isn't so hard, is it?" Lillian smiles and goes over to the silver bar, bringing the brandy over to where I sit.

"You obviously need another drink." She smiles and grabs my empty glass.

AFTER MY THIRD GLASS, I mumble, "Tessa hates when I drink."

"Are you a mean drunk?"

"No," I say reflexively. But seeing that she's really interested, I ponder the question some more and reconsider. "Sometimes."

"Hmm . . ."

"Why don't you drink?" I ask.

"I don't know, I just don't."

"Does your boyf . . ." I begin but correct myself, "girlfriend drink?"

She nods. "Yes, sometimes. Not as much as before."

"Oh." This Riley and I may have more in common than I thought.

"Lillian?" her father calls out, and then I hear the staircase creak.

I sit up and move away from her out of instinct, and she turns her attention to him. "Yes, Father?"

"It's nearly one in the morning. I think it's time your company heads out," he says.

One in the morning? *Holy shit.*

"Okay." She nods and looks back to me. "He seems to forget I'm an adult," she whispers, annoyance clear in her voice.

"I need to go anyway. Tessa's going to kill me," I gripe. When I stand, my legs aren't as steady under me as they should be.

"You're welcome to come back tomorrow, Hardin," my father's friend says as I reach the door.

"Just apologize and consider Seattle," Lillian reminds me.

But I'm determined to ignore her, and I walk out the door, down the steps, and onto the paved driveway. I would really love to know what her dad does for a living; he's obviously rich as fuck.

It's pitch-black out here. Literally, I can barely see my hand as I wave it idiotically in front of my face. When I reach the end of the driveway, the lights outside my father's cabin come into view, and they guide me to to his driveway and up the porch steps.

The screen door creaks when I open it, and I curse at it. The last thing I need is my father waking up and smelling the brandy on my breath. Then again, he may want some himself.

My inner Tessa immediately scolds me for the cynical thought, and I pinch the bridge of my nose, shaking my head to get her out.

I nearly knock over a lamp trying to pull my boots off of my feet. I grip the corner of the wall to steady myself and finally manage to place my boots next to Tessa's shoes. My palms begin to sweat as I take the staircase as slowly as possible. I'm not drunk, but I am quite buzzed, and I know she's going to be even more upset than she was before. She was downright cheesed the fuck off earlier, and now that I've stayed out this long—and have been drinking—she's going to lose it. I'm actually a little . . . afraid of her right now. She was so mad earlier, cursing at me and ordering me away.

The door to the room we're sharing opens with a small squeak, and I try to be as quiet as possible and guide myself through the dark room without waking her.

No such luck.

The lamp on the nightstand switches on, and Tessa's impassive glare is focused on me.

"Sorry . . . I didn't want to wake you," I apologize.

A frown forms on her full lips. "I wasn't asleep," she states, and my chest begins to tighten.

"I know it's late, I'm sorry," I say, my words running together.

She squints. "Have you been drinking?"

Despite her expression, her eyes are bright. The way the soft light of the lamp hits her face makes me want to reach across the bed and touch her.

"Yes," I say and wait for the fury of my very own Lyssa.

She sighs and brings her hands to her forehead to brush the loose tendrils that have escaped her ponytail. She doesn't seem to be alarmed or surprised by my state.

Thirty seconds later, I'm still waiting on the rage.

But nothing.

She's just sitting there on the bed, leaning back on her arms, staring at me with despondent eyes while I stand awkwardly in the center of the room.

"Are you going to say anything?" I finally ask, hoping to break this haunting silence.

"No, I'm not."

"Huh?"

"I'm exhausted and you're drunk; there's really nothing for me to say," she says without emotion.

I'm always nervously anticipating her to finally snap, to finally get to the point where she's tired of putting up with my shit, and honestly, I'm scared to fucking death that this may be it.

"I'm not drunk, I only had three drinks. You know that's not shit to me," I say and sit on the edge of the bed. A chill runs down my spine when she moves closer to the headboard to get away from me.

"Where were you?" Her voice is soft.

"Next door."

She continues to stare at me, expecting more information.

"I was with this girl Lillian, her dad went to college with mine and we were talking, one thing led to another and—"

"Oh God." Tessa's eyes snap shut, and her hands move to cover her ears as she pulls her knees up to her chest.

I reach across, taking both her wrists in one hand and gently pushing them down to her lap. "No, no, not like that. *Fuck*. We were talking about *you*," I tell her, then wait for her normal eye rolling and signs of disbelief at anything I tell her.

She opens her eyes and looks up. "What about me?"

"Just this Seattle shit."

"You talked to her about Seattle, but you won't talk to me?"

Tessa's voice isn't angry, just curious, and I'm really fucking confused. It's not like I wanted to talk to the girl, she practically fucking forced me, but in a way I guess I'm sort of glad she did.

"It's not like that—you made me leave," I remind the girl in front of me with Tessa's face but none of her normal attitude.

"And you were with her this entire time?" Her lip trembles, and she presses her teeth into it.

"No, I went for a walk and ran into her." I reach across to move her unruly hair away from her cheek, and she doesn't pull away. Her skin is hot to my touch, and her cheeks look as if they're glowing in the muted light. She leans into my palm, and her eyes flutter closed as I rub my thumb along her cheekbone. "She's a lot like you."

This isn't how I expected this to go. I expected World War Fucking Tessa by now.

"You like her, then?" she asks, gray eyes opening slightly to meet mine.

"Yeah, she's okay." I shrug, and she closes her eyes again.

I'm thrown off by her calm behavior, and that mixed with the aged brandy makes for one confused Hardin.

"I'm tired," she says and reaches up to remove my hand from her cheek.

"You're not mad?" I question. Something is nagging at the back of my mind, but it just won't surface. Fucking liquor.

"I'm just tired," she answers and lies back against the pillows.

Okay . . .

Warning bells . . . No, fucking *tornado sirens* go off in my mind at the lack of emotion in her voice. There's something she's not saying. And I want her to just say it.

But as she falls back asleep—or at least feigns it—and I realize I have to choose to ignore the silent signals for tonight. It's late. If I push her too hard, she'll make me leave again, and I can't have that. I can't sleep without her, and I'm thankful she's even fucking letting me near her after the shit with Sandra. I'm also thankful the liquor is making me so drowsy that I won't be up all night worrying about what's stewing inside of Tessa's brain.

chapter thirty-four

TESSA

The morning light sweeps over the room as the sun rises in the distance. My eyes move from the uncovered balcony doors to my stomach, where Hardin's arm is draped over my body. His full lips are parted, soft purrs sounding from between them. I don't know whether I should shove him off the bed or brush his brown hair back from his forehead and press my lips against the reddened skin.

I'm angry, so damn angry at Hardin for everything that happened last night. He had the audacity to return to the cabin at one thirty in the morning, and just like I feared, his breath was laced with liquor. Yet another strand in this tangled web. Then there's this girl, a girl like me, whom he spent hours upon hours with. He said they were just talking—and it's not that I don't believe that they were only talking. It's the fact that Hardin refuses to discuss Seattle or anything remotely related to Seattle with me, but he seems to be able to talk to her.

I don't know what to think, and I'm sick of thinking all the damn time. There's always some problem to fix, some argument to be gotten through. And I'm tired. Tired of all of it. I love Hardin more than I can comprehend, but I don't know how much longer I can do this. I can't worry about him coming home drunk every time we have a problem. I wanted to scream at him, throw a pillow at his face, and tell him how big of a jerk he is, but I'm finally beginning to realize that you can only fight with someone over the same thing so many times before you're burned out.

I don't know what to do about him not coming to Seattle, but I do know that lying here in this bed isn't of any help to me. I lift Hardin's arm and wriggle out from under his weight, gently placing his arm across the pillow next to him. He groans in his slumber, but thankfully he only stirs and doesn't wake.

I grab my phone from the bedside table and quietly pad to the balcony doors. They open with minimal noise, and I let out a relieved sigh before closing them behind me. The air is much cooler than yesterday; granted, it's only seven in the morning.

Phone in hand, I begin to ponder my living situation in Seattle, which at this point is nonexistent. My transfer to Seattle is becoming more of a hassle than I ever anticipated, and honestly, at times it seems more of a hassle than it's worth. I immediately scold myself for entertaining the thought. That's exactly what Hardin is trying to do—he's trying to make it as difficult for me to move as he possibly can, hoping that I'll give up on doing what I want to do and stay with him.

Well, that's just not going to happen.

I open the browser on my phone and wait impatiently for Google to load. I stare at the small screen, waiting for the annoying circle to stop going round and round. Frustrated at the slow response on my ancient phone, I tread back into the bedroom and grab Hardin's off of the chair, then go back out to the balcony.

If he wakes up and finds me on his phone, he'll be angry. But I'm not going through his calls or texts. I'm only using his internet.

Yeah, she's okay. His words about this Lillian girl play through my mind as I try to search for apartments in Seattle.

I shake my head, disposing of the memory and instead admiring a luxury apartment that I wish I could afford. I scroll to the next, a smaller one-bedroom in a duplex. I don't feel comfortable in a duplex; I like the idea of someone having to go through a lobby to get to my door, especially since it appears that I'll be alone in Seattle. I swipe my finger across the screen a few more times before finally finding a one-bedroom in a midsize high-rise. It's over my budget, but not by much. If I have to go without being able to buy groceries until I get settled in, I will.

I enter the phone number into my phone and continue to browse through the listings. Impossible thoughts of searching for an apartment alongside Hardin's haunt me. The two of us would be sitting on the bed, me cross-legged, Hardin with his long legs stretched out in front of him and his back against the headboard. I would show him apartment after apartment and he'd roll his eyes and complain about the process of apartment hunting, but I'd catch him smiling, with his eyes focused on my lips. He'd tell me how cute I am when I'm flustered before taking the laptop from me and assuring me he'd find the place for us.

That would be too simple, though. Too easy. Everything in my life was simple and easy until six months ago. My mother helped me with my dorm, and I had everything sorted and in order before I even arrived at Washington Central.

My mother . . . I can't help but miss her. She has no idea that I've reunited with my father. She'd be so angry if she knew. I know she would.

Before I can talk myself out of it, I'm dialing her number.

"Hello?" she answers smoothly.

"Mother?"

"Who else would it be?"

I'm already regretting this phone call. "How are you?" I ask quietly.

She sighs. "I'm good. I've been a little busy with everything going on." Pots and pans clank in the background.

"What's going on?" *Does she know about my father?* I quickly decide that if she doesn't, now isn't the time to tell her.

"Nothing specific, really. I've been working a lot of overtime, and we got a new pastor—oh, and Ruth passed away."

"Ruth Porter?"

"Yes, I was going to call you," she says, her cold voice warming slightly.

Noah's grandmother Ruth was one of the sweetest women I've ever had the pleasure of meeting. She was always so kind, and next to Karen, she made the best chocolate chip cookies on the planet.

"How's Noah doing?" I dare to ask. He was very close with his grandmother, and I know this has to be hard for him. I never had the chance to get close to any of my grandparents; my father's parents passed away before I was old enough to remember, and my mother's parents were not the type of people to allow anyone to get close to them.

"He's taking it pretty hard. You should call him, Tessa."

"I . . ." I begin to tell her that I can't call him, but I stop myself. Why can't I call him? I can and I will. "I will . . . I'll call him right now."

"Really?" The surprise is evident in her voice. "Well, at least wait until after nine," she advises, and I can't help but smile at her tone. I know she's smiling on the other end of the line. "How is school going?"

"I'm leaving Monday for Seattle," I confess, and I hear something clatter to the ground.

"What?"

"I told you, remember?" *I did, didn't I?*

"No, you didn't. You mentioned that your company was moving there, but you never told me that you were leaving for certain."

"I'm sorry, I've just been so busy with Seattle and Hardin."

Her voice is incredibly controlled when she asks, "He's going with you?"

"I'm . . . I don't know." I sigh.

"Are you okay? You sound upset."

"I'm okay," I lie.

"I know we haven't been on the best of terms lately, but I'm still your mother, Tessa. You can talk to me if something is going on in your life."

"I'm fine, really; I'm just stressed over this move and transferring to a new campus."

"Oh, that? You'll do great there—you'd excel at any campus. You can excel anywhere," she says with assurance.

"I know, but I'm already so used to this campus, and I got to know a few of the professors and I have friends . . . a few friends." I don't really have friends that I will miss terribly, save Landon. And maybe Steph . . . but mostly only Landon.

"Tessa, this is what we've been working toward for years, and look at you now—in such a short period of time you've accomplished it. You should be proud of yourself."

I'm surprised by her words, and my mind rushes to process them. "Thank you," I mutter.

"Tell me as soon as you move into your place in Seattle so I can come visit, since you obviously won't be coming home anytime soon," she says.

"I will." I ignore her harsh tone.

"I'll have to call you back. I have to get ready for work. Make sure you don't forget to call Noah."

"I know, I'm going to call him in a couple hours."

As I hang up, a movement on the balcony catches my attention and I look up to see Hardin. He's dressed now, in his normal black T-shirt and black jeans. His feet are bare, and his eyes are focused on me.

"Who was that?" he asks.

"My mother," I respond and pull my knees up to my chest in the chair.

"Why did she call?" He grabs the back of the empty chair, and it squeaks as he pulls it closer to me before sitting down.

"I called her," I answer without looking at him.

"Why is my phone out here?" He grabs it from my lap and scans it.

"I was using the internet."

"Oh," he says as if he doesn't believe me.

If he doesn't have anything to hide, why would he care?

"Who were you talking about when you said you were going to call him?" he asks, sitting on the edge of the hot tub.

I look over at him. "Noah," I respond drily.

His eyes narrow. "Like hell you are."

"Well, I am."

"Why do you need to talk to him?" He places his hands on his knees and leans forward. "You don't."

"So you can spend hours with someone else and come back drunk, but—"

"He's your *ex-boyfriend,*" he interrupts.

"And how do I know she isn't one of your ex-girlfriends?"

"Because I don't have any ex-girlfriends, remember?"

I huff in frustration; my earlier resolve has now faded, and I'm getting angry again. "Okay, all the girls you *fucked around with*, then. In any case," I continue, my voice low and clear, "you don't get to tell me who I am allowed to call. Ex-boyfriend or not."

"I thought you weren't mad at me."

I sigh, staring out onto the water and away from his piercing green eyes. "I'm not, I'm really not. You did exactly what I expected you to do."

"Which was . . . ?"

"Running off for hours, then returning with liquor on your breath."

"You told me to leave."

"That doesn't make it okay that you came back drunk."

"And here it is!" he groans. "I knew you wouldn't stay quiet like you did last night."

"Stay quiet? See, that's your problem; you expect me to stay quiet. I'm over it."

"Over what?" He leans toward me, his face too close to mine.

"This . . ." I wave my hand dramatically and rise to my feet. "I'm just over all of it. You go ahead and do whatever the hell you want, but you can find someone else to sit here beside you and not take note of your antics and remain quiet—because I'm not doing it anymore." I turn away from him.

He jumps to his feet and hooks his fingers around my arm to gently pull me back. "Stop," he orders. One large hand spreads across my waist while the other goes to my arm. I think about twisting free, but then he pulls me to his chest. "Stop fighting me—you're not going anywhere."

His lips press into a hard line as I pull my arm from his grasp.

"Let me go, and I'll sit down," I huff. I don't want to give in, but I also refuse to ruin anyone else's time on this trip. If I go downstairs, Hardin will surely follow, and we'll end up staging a big blowout in front of his family.

He swiftly lets go of me, and I plop myself into the chair again. He sits back down across from me and stares at me expectantly with his elbows on his thighs.

"What?" I snap.

"So you're leaving me, then?" he whispers, which softens my harsh demeanor a little.

"If you mean leaving to Seattle, yes."

"Monday?"

"Yes, Monday. I've gone over this with you again and again. I know you thought that little stunt you pulled would discourage me," I say, seething, "but it didn't, and nothing you can do will."

"Nothing?" He looks up at me through his thick lashes.

I'll marry you, he told me while he was drunk. Does he mean it now? As much as I want to ask him right here, right now, I can't. I don't think I'm ready for his sober answer.

"Hardin, what is it in Seattle that you're so eager to avoid?" I ask instead.

His eyes dart away from mine. "Nothing important."

"Hardin, I swear, if there's something that you've kept from me, I will never speak to you again," I say, and mean it. "I've had enough of this shit, honestly."

"It's nothing, Tessa. I have some old friends there that I don't particularly care for because they're part of my old life."

" 'Old life'?"

"My life before you: the drinking, the parties, fucking every girl that passed my way," he says. When I cringe, he mumbles "Sorry" but continues. "There's no big secret, just bad memories. But that's not why I don't want to go, anyway."

I wait for him to get to the heart of the matter, but he doesn't say anything else. "Okay, then tell me why. Because I don't get it."

His face is devoid of any emotion as he looks into my eyes. "Why do you need an explanation? I don't want to go and I don't want you to go without me."

"Well, that's not enough of an explanation. I'm going," I say and shake my head. "And you know what? I don't want you to come with me anymore."

"What?" His eyes darken.

"I don't want you to come." I stay as calm as possible and stand up from the chair. I'm proud of myself for having this discussion without yelling. "You've tried to ruin this for me—this has been my dream since I can remember, and you tried to ruin it for me. You've turned something that I should be looking forward to into something that I can barely stand. I should be excited and ready to go meet my dreams. But instead you've made sure I have nowhere to live and no support system at all. So no, I don't want you to go."

His mouth opens and closes before he stands and paces across the wooden deck. "You . . ." he begins, but then stops himself, looking like he's reconsidering his thoughts.

But being Hardin, things never change, and he chooses the harder, uglier path instead. "You . . . you know what, Tessa? No one gives a *fuck* about Seattle except someone like you. Who the hell grows up planning on moving to *Seattle fucking Washington*. *Real* ambitious," he growls. He takes in a deep, violent breath. "And in case you forgot, I'm the only reason you have that opportunity to begin with. You think anyone else is getting a paid fucking internship as a freshman in college? Fuck, no! Most people struggle to get a paid internship even after they graduate."

"That's not even close to the fucking point here." I roll my eyes at him and the nerve he has.

"Then what is the point, you ungrateful—"

I take a step toward him, and my hand flies at him before I really register what I'm doing.

But Hardin's too quick and grabs me by the wrist, stopping me only inches from his cheek.

"Don't," he warns. His voice is rough, laced with anger, and I wish he hadn't stopped me from slapping him. His minty breath fans across my cheeks as he tries to control his temper.

Bring it on, Hardin, my thoughts challenge. I'm not intimidated by his harsh breathing or his foul words. I can give them back to him in spades.

"You don't get to talk to people like that without consequences." My words come out low, threatening even.

"Consequences?" He stares down at me with burning eyes. "I've known nothing in my life but consequences."

I hate the way he's taking credit for my internship, I hate the way he pushes when I pull and I push when he pulls. I hate the way he drives my anger to grow so strong that I would try to slap him, and I hate the way I feel as if I'm losing control of something I'm not sure I've ever held. I look up at him, his hand still holding my wrist, using only enough pressure to keep me from attempting to slap him again, and he looks hurt, in a dangerous way. There's a challenge behind his eyes that makes my stomach turn.

He brings my hand to his chest, his eyes never leaving mine, and says, "You know nothing of consequences."

Then he walks away from me, that look still in his eyes, and my hand drops down to my side.

chapter thirty-five

HARDIN

Who the fuck does she think she is? She thinks just because I don't want to go to Seattle with her that she can say shit like this to me? She doesn't want me to fucking go?

She fucking uninvited me to Seattle, and she's the one trying to slap me? I don't fucking think so. I was only seeing red as I spoke, and her trying to hit me surprised me—a lot. I left her with wide eyes, her pupils blown in rage, but I had to get as far from that bullshit as I could.

I find myself at the small coffee shop in town. The coffee tastes like tar, and the weird-ass muffin I got is even worse. I hate this bullshit small town and its lack of every goddamn thing.

I tear three sugar packets at once and dump them into the disgusting coffee, stirring it with a plastic spoon. It's too early for this shit.

"Good morning," a familiar voice greets. Not the voice I wanted to hear, though.

"Why are you here?" I roll my eyes and ask Lillian as she comes around from behind me.

"Well, *you* obviously aren't a morning person," she says saccharinely and takes the seat in front of me.

"Go away," I huff and look around the small café. A line has formed nearly to the door, and almost all of the tables are full. I should probably do everyone in line a favor and tell them to find a fucking Starbucks, because this place blows.

She eyes me. "You didn't apologize, did you."

"God, you are so damn nosy." I pinch the bridge of my nose, and she smiles.

"Are you going to finish that?" She gestures to the rock-hard muffin in front of me.

I slide it over to her, and she tears off a piece. "I wouldn't eat that," I warn, but she does anyway.

"It's not that bad," she lies. I can tell she wants to spit it out, but instead she swallows it down. "So are you going to tell me why you didn't apologize to Tamara?"

"Her fucking name is Tessa, if you call her—"

"Whoa, calm down. Joke, joke! I was just messing with you." She giggles, proud of her annoying self.

"Ha. Ha." I down the rest of my coffee.

"Anyway, why didn't you?"

"I don't know."

"Yes, you do," she presses.

"Why do you care, anyway?" I lean toward her, and she sits back in the chair.

"I don't know . . . because you seem to love her, and you're my friend."

"Your *friend*? I don't even know you, and you sure as hell don't know me," I declare.

Her neutral expression falters for a moment, and she blinks her eyes slowly. If she cries, I'm going to punch someone. I can't handle this much drama this early in the fucking morning.

"Look, you're cool and all. But this"—I gesture back and forth between her body and mine—"isn't a friendship. I don't have friendships."

She tilts her head to the side. "You don't have any friends? Not even one?"

"No, I have people I party with and Tessa."

"You should have friends; at least one."

"What would be the point of you and me being friends? We're only here until tomorrow afternoon."

She shrugs. "We could be friends until then."

"You obviously don't have any friends either."

"Not many. Riley doesn't seem to like them."

"And? Why does that matter?"

"Because I don't want to start a fight with her, so I just don't hang out with them much."

"Sorry, but Riley sounds like a bitch."

"Don't say that about her." Lillian's cheeks flush, and for the first time since I met her she's exhibiting an emotion besides calmness or omniscience.

I play with my cup smoothly, kind of glad to get a rise out of her. "Just saying. I wouldn't let someone tell me who I can and can't be friends with."

"So you're telling me that Tessa has friends she hangs out with besides you?" She raises her brow, and I look away to think about her question.

She has friends . . . she has Landon. "Yes."

"You don't count."

"No, not me. Landon."

"Landon is your stepbrother; he doesn't count."

Steph is sort of Tessa's friend but not really, and Zed . . . not a problem anymore. "She has me," I say.

She smirks. "That's exactly what I thought."

"What does it matter? Once we get away from here, and start over, she can make new friends. We can make new friends together."

"Sure. The problem is that you aren't going to the same place," she reminds me.

"She'll come with me. I know it doesn't seem like it, but you don't know her. I do, and I know she can't live without me."

Lillian looks up at me with thoughtful eyes. "You know, there's a big difference between not being able to live without someone and loving them."

This chick doesn't even know what she's talking about—she makes no sense. "I don't want to talk about her anymore; if we're going to be friends, I need to know about you and Regan."

"Riley," she says sharply.

I chuckle lightly. "Annoying, isn't it?"

Lillian glowers playfully at me, but then tells me all about how she met her girlfriend. They were partnered up together for Lillian's freshman orientation. Riley had been rude at first but later made a move on her, surprising both of them. Apparently this Riley has a jealous streak and a temper. Sounds familiar.

"Most of our fights stem from her jealousy. She's always afraid that I'll stray from her. I don't know why, because she's the one always getting attention from everyone, male and female, and she's dated both." She sighs. "So it's sort of like everyone's fair game."

"You haven't?"

"No, I've never dated a guy." She crinkles her nose. "Well, once in eighth grade, because I felt like I had to. My friends were hassling me for never having a boyfriend."

"Why didn't you just tell them?" I ask her.

"It's not that simple."

"It should be."

She smiles. "Yes, it should be. But it's not. Anyway, I've never dated anyone except Riley and one other girl." Then her smile disappears. "Riley's dated a lot."

THE REST OF MY MORNING and the entire afternoon is spent this way, listening to this girl's problems. I don't mind as much as I thought, though. It's nice to know I'm not the only one with these types of issues. Lillian reminds me a lot of Tessa and Landon. If they were morphed into one person, it would certainly be Lillian. I hate to admit it, but I don't mind her company too much. She's an outsider, like me, but she doesn't judge me, because she barely knows me. Strangers come and go, in and out of the coffee shop, and each time a blonde steps in, I can't help but look up, hoping it will be *my* blond stranger.

A funny little tune starts to play. "That would be my dad calling . . ." Lillian says and looks down at her phone. "Shit, it's almost five," she says, panicked. "We need to go. Well, I need to go. I still don't have anything to wear tonight."

"For what?" I ask her when she stands up.

"Dinner. You knew we're going to dinner with your parents, didn't you?"

"Karen isn't my . . ." I begin but decide to let it go. She knows.

I get up and follow her down the block to a small clothing store filled with colorful dresses and gaudy jewelry. It smells like mothballs and salt water.

"There's nothing to choose from," she groans, holding up a bright pink frilly dress.

"That's hideous," I tell her, and she nods, hanging it back up.

I can't help but think of what Tessa is doing right now. Is she wondering where I am? I'm sure she assumes that I'm with Lillian, which is true, but she doesn't have anything to worry about. She knows this.

Wait . . . no, she doesn't. I haven't told her about Lillian's girlfriend.

"Tessa doesn't know you're gay," I blurt as she shows me a black beaded dress.

She looks at me smoothly and just sweeps her hand across the dress again, kind of like she did with the brandy bottle last night.

"I'm not giving you fashion advice here, so stop trying," I groan.

She rolls her eyes. "So why didn't you tell her?"

I poke at this feather necklace thing. "I don't know, I didn't think about it."

"Well, I'm oh-so-flattered that my orientation was so unnnotable to you," she says with feigned gratitude and a spread hand at her neck. "But you really should tell her." She smiles. "No wonder she almost backhanded you."

I knew I shouldn't have told her about the slap.

"Shut up. I'll tell her . . ." Although it might work in my favor not to, actually. "Maybe," I add.

Lillian rolls her eyes, again. She rolls her eyes almost as much as Tessa does.

"She's difficult, and I know what I'm doing, okay?" I think I do, at least. I know exactly how to push her buttons to get what I want.

"You need to dress up tonight; the place we're going is disgustingly fancy," she warns me while eyeing the dress with a twist of the hanger.

"Hell no, I'm not. What makes you think I'm going, anyway?"

"Why not? You want to make the missus a little less pissed off, don't you?"

The sound of her words throws me off for a moment. " 'The missus'? Don't call her that."

She slaps a white button-up against my chest. "Just wear a nice shirt at least, otherwise my dad will give you shit about it all night," she says and steps into the dressing room.

A few minutes later she comes out in the black dress. It looks good on her—she's hot and all—but I immediately start fantasizing about how Tessa would look in it. It would be much tighter: Tessa's boobs are much bigger than Lillian's, Tessa's hips are a little wider, so she would fill the dress much better.

"It's not as ugly as the rest of the shit in here," I half compliment, and she closes the curtain with yet another eye roll and a middle finger.

chapter thirty-six

TESSA

I stare into the long mirror and ask Landon, "Are you sure this looks okay?"

"Yes, it's fine," he says with a smile. "Can we try to remember that I'm a guy, though?"

I sigh, then chuckle. "I know. I'm sorry. It's not my fault you're my only friend."

The dark sparkly dress feels odd against my skin; the material is hard, and the small beads scratch me a little when I move. The small clothing boutique in town didn't have much to choose from, and I surely wasn't going to pick the hot-pink dress made entirely of tulle. I need something to wear to this dreaded dinner tonight, and Hardin's suggestion that I wear jeans isn't going to work.

"Do you think he'll even come back before it's time to leave?" I ask Landon.

Hardin took off, as always, after our fight and hasn't been back since. He hasn't called or texted either. He's probably with the mystery girl with whom he loves to discuss our problems. You know, the girl he can talk to better than he can talk to his own girlfriend. In his anger, I wouldn't be surprised if he did something with her to spite me.

No . . . he wouldn't.

"I don't know, honestly," Landon says. "I hope he does. My mom will be disappointed if he doesn't."

"Yeah." I push another pin into my bun and grab my mascara off of the bathroom counter.

"He'll come around, he's just stubborn."

"I don't know if *we* will, though." I sweep the small brush across my lashes. "I'm reaching my breaking point, I can feel it. You know what I felt last night when he told me he was with another girl?"

"What?" He stares blankly at me.

"I think this is just the end of the turbulent love story." I try to make a joke, but it falls flat.

"It's weird hearing you say that, you of all people," he says. "How are you feeling?"

"A little angry, but that's it. It's like I'm numb to it now, to all of it. I just don't have it in me to keep doing this over and over. I'm beginning to think he's a lost cause, and that breaks my heart," I say, forbidding myself from crying.

"Nobody's a lost cause. They just think they are, so they don't even bother to try sometimes."

"Are you guys ready?" Karen's voice calls from the living room, and Landon assures her that we'll be down any minute. I slide on my new pair of black heels with straps at the ankles. Unfortunately, they're as uncomfortable as they look. It's times like this that I miss wearing Toms every day.

Hardin still hasn't returned by the time we pile into the car. "We can't wait any longer," Ken says through a disappointed frown.

"It's fine, we can bring him something back," Karen sweetly offers, knowing that's not the solution but trying her best to calm her husband's irritation.

Landon looks over at me, and I offer a smile to assure him that I'm fine. He tries to distract me the whole drive talking about various students we know, making little jokes about how they are in class. Especially some of the ones in the religion course.

As Ken pulls up to our destination, I see that the restaurant is exquisite. The building is a massive log cabin, big enough to be a lodge, and the inside contradicts the woodsy feel of the exterior. It's modern and sleek, black and white everywhere, with gray accents along the walls and floor. The lighting is right on the verge of being too dark, but it adds to the atmosphere. Unexpectedly, my dress is the brightest thing in the room; when the light hits the glittering beads, they shine like diamonds in the dark, which everyone seems to notice.

"Scott," I hear Ken tell the beautiful woman behind the rostrum.

"The rest of your party is already here." She smiles, her perfect teeth white nearly to the point of blinding.

"Party?" I turn to Landon, and he shrugs.

We follow the woman to a table in the corner of the room. I hate the way everyone seems to be staring at me because of this dress. I should have gone with the hot-pink monstrosity; it would have attracted less attention. A middle-aged man knocks over his drink as we walk by, and Landon pulls me closer to his side as we pass the creep. The dress isn't inappropriate; it rests just above my knees. The problem is that it was made for someone with a much smaller bust than me, causing the built-in bra to act as a push-up, giving me maximum cleavage.

"It's about time you joined us," an unfamiliar male voice says, and I peer around Karen to look for the source.

A man, who I assume is Ken's friend, stands to shake his hand. My eyes move to his right, where his wife is smiling, greeting Karen. Next to her is a young girl—*the* girl, I sense on instinct—and my stomach drops. She's beautiful, extremely beautiful.

And she's wearing the exact same dress as I am.

Of course.

I can see the bright blue of her eyes from here, and when she smiles at me, she's even more beautiful. I'm so distracted by my growing jealousy that I almost fail to notice that Hardin is sitting right next to her, dressed in a white button-down shirt.

chapter thirty-seven

HARDIN

Oh my God . . ." Lillian whispers loudly. I'm broken from my thoughts of my earlier fight with Tessa and look up to see what she's gaping at.

Tessa.

In a dress . . . that fucking dress that I was imagining her in. And it makes her already big chest look . . . *fuck*. I blink rapidly, trying to collect myself before she reaches the table. For a moment I'm convinced that I'm hallucinating; it looks even sexier than I imagined. Every guy she passes turns to look at her; one even knocks over his drink. I grip the edge of the table waiting for the asshole to speak to her. If he does, I swear to fuck—

"*That's* Tessa? Oh my God." Lillian is practically panting.

"Stop staring at her," I warn, and she laughs.

The man who knocked over his drink leans away from his wife as his eyes follow my girl.

"Chill," Lillian says, gently touching my hands. My scarred knuckles are now white from my tight grip on the table.

Landon pulls Tessa close to him and away from the married asshole; she smiles up at him, and he pulls her even closer as they walk. *What the fuck was that?*

Tessa stands behind Landon as Lillian's parents and Karen and Ken go through the normal I'm-so-fucking-classy-because-I-shake-your-hand-even-though-I-saw-you-last-night shit. Before I know it, Tessa's eyes find Lillian, and they widen and lower. She's jealous.

Good. I was hoping she'd be.

chapter thirty-eight

TESSA

Panic courses through me at the sight of Hardin sitting next to this girl—he doesn't even acknowledge my presence as I take the seat next to Landon, on the other side of the table from him.

"Hello, and who might you be?" Ken's friend asks with a smile. I can tell by his tone that he's one of those men that think they are better than everyone else in the room.

"Hi, I'm Tessa," I say, then smile curtly and nod. "Landon's friend."

My eyes dart to Hardin, whose lips press into a thin line. Well, he's clearly entertaining the man's daughter, so why ruin their fun?

"It's great to meet you, Tessa. I'm Max, and this is Denise." He gestures to the woman beside him.

"It's nice to meet you," Denise says. "The two of you are an adorable couple."

Hardin starts coughing. Or choking. I don't want to look at him and see which . . . but I can't help it. When I do, his eyes are narrow, glaring at me.

Landon laughs. "Oh, we aren't together." He looks at Hardin, like he expects him to say something.

Of course he doesn't. The girl looks slightly lost and a little uncomfortable. Good. Hardin leans into her and says something into her ear, and she smiles at him before shaking her head. *What the hell is happening?*

"I'm Lillian; it's nice to meet you," she introduces herself with a friendly smile.

Bitch.

"You, too," I manage to say in return. My heart is hammering in my chest, and I can barely see straight. If we weren't at the table with Hardin's family and Ken's friends, I would throw a drink in Hardin's face, and with his eyes stinging, he wouldn't have a chance to stop me from slapping him this time. A menu is placed in front of each of us, and I wait as one of the empty glasses in front of me is filled with water. Ken and Max begin to talk about the oddness of having to choose between tap and bottled water.

"Do you know what you want?" Landon asks quietly a few moments later. I know he's trying to distract me from Hardin and his new friend.

"I . . . I don't know," I whisper and look over the fancy handwritten menu. I can't imagine eating right now; my stomach won't stop turning, and I can't seem to control my breathing.

"Do you want to go?" he says into my ear. I glance across the table at Hardin, whose eyes meet mine before he turns back to Lillian.

Yes. I want to get the hell out of here and tell Hardin to never speak to me again.

"No. I'm not going anywhere," I say and sit up higher, straightening my back against the chair.

"Good." Landon praises me as a handsome server arrives at our table.

"We'll have a bottle of your best white wine," Ken's friend tells him, and he nods. Just as he begins to walk away, Max calls after him.

"We weren't finished yet," he says. Max orders a list of appetizers. I've never heard of any of the dishes he's chosen, but I don't suspect I'll be eating much of them anyway.

I try desperately not to look across the table at Hardin, but it's hard, so damn hard. Why would he come here with her? He's dressed up, too; if he doesn't have jeans on under the table, I think what's left of my heart will shatter. It takes me an hour of begging to get Hardin dressed in anything other than black jeans and a T-shirt, yet here he is next to this girl in a white button-down.

"I'll give you a few minutes to look over the menu, and if you have any questions about the dishes, my name is Robert," the server says. His eyes meet mine, and his mouth opens slightly before he looks away quickly, only to look back at me. It's this dress and the damn cleavage. I offer a small, awkward smile, and he returns it, red creeping up his neck and spreading to his cheeks.

I expect him to look at Hardin, but then I remember that due to the way we're seated, it's Landon and I that look like a couple, and Hardin's with Lillian. My stomach flips again.

"Hey, man. Take our order, or go," Hardin says, interrupting my thoughts.

"S-sorry," Robert stammers and leaves the table in haste.

All eyes move to Hardin, mostly showing disapproval of his behavior. Karen looks embarrassed; Ken, too.

"Don't worry, he'll be back. It's his job," Max says with a shrug. He *would* think Hardin's behavior was acceptable.

I scowl at Hardin, but he doesn't seem to care, he's too infatuated by those damn blue eyes. As I watch him with her I feel like he's a stranger to me, as if I'm intruding on some private moment shared between a loving couple. The thought causes bile to rise in my throat. I swallow it down, and I'm thankful when the server, Robert, returns with the wine and ice buckets, this time bringing another server along, likely for moral support. Or protection.

Hardin watches him the entire time, and I roll my eyes at his audacity: glaring at the poor guy when here *he* is, acting as if he doesn't know me at all.

Nervously, Robert fills my glass to the brim, and I quietly thank him. He smiles less shyly this time and moves to fill

Landon's. I've never seen Landon drink except at Ken and Karen's wedding, and even then he only had one glass of champagne. If I wasn't so distraught over Hardin's behavior, I'd turn down the wine and not drink in front of Ken and Karen, but I've had a long day, and without the wine I don't think I be able to make it through this dinner.

Ken covers the top of his glass and says, "No, thank you," when Robert comes his way.

I look up at Hardin to make sure he isn't readying a snide remark about his father, but once again he's talking quietly to Lillian.

I'm so confused right now—why is he doing this? Yes, we were fighting, but this is too much.

Taking a big sip, I find that the wine is cool and crisp and deliciously sweet on my tongue. I'm tempted to just gulp it all down, but I have to pace myself. The last thing I need is to get drunk and emotional in front of everyone. Hardin doesn't decline the wine, but Lillian does. He rolls his eyes at her, teasing her, and I force my eyes away from them before I turn into a puddle of tears on the beautifully stained hardwood floor.

". . . MAX WAS SCALING THE WALL—he was so drunk that he had to be pulled down by campus security!" Ken says, and everyone at our table laughs.

Everyone except Hardin, of course.

I twirl my fork around my pasta and take another bite. I focus on how delicious the freshly made noodles are, and how they look wound around the tines of the fork. Otherwise I'd have to focus on Hardin.

"I think you have an admirer," Denise says to me. I look up and follow her eyes to Robert, who is clearing the dishes from the table beside us, his eyes on me.

"Don't pay him too much attention; just a waiter wanting what he can't have," Max states with a sly smile, surprising me with his callousness.

"Dad." Lillian glares at her father.

But he just gives her a smile before cutting into his steak. "Sorry, sweetie, I'm only stating the truth . . . A girl as beautiful as Tessa here shouldn't be looking at anyone working in hospitality."

If only he'd stopped there, but oblivious—or immune to—our discomfort, Max continues his degrading remarks until I finally drop my fork onto my plate with a clatter.

"Don't," Hardin says to me, speaking to me for the first time since I arrived.

Shocked, I look at him, then back to Max, weighing my options. He's being a jerk, and I've had almost an entire glass of wine. I should probably keep my mouth shut, like Hardin said.

"You can't talk about people like that." Lillian looks at her father and he shrugs.

"Fine, fine," he grumbles, waving his knife a little and chewing on his steak. "Far be it from me to upset anyone."

Beside him, his wife looks embarrassed as she wipes the corners of her mouth with a cloth napkin.

"I'm going to need more wine," I tell Landon, and he smiles, sliding his half-empty glass over to me. I smile at the gesture. "I'll wait for *Robert* to come back to the table. Thank you, though."

I can feel Hardin's eyes on me as I search the restaurant. I don't see the server's blond hair, so I reach over, grab the bottle myself, and fill my glass. I half expect Max to make a comment about my manners, but he refrains. Hardin is staring coolly across the room, and Lillian is talking to her mother. I'm in my own world, a hallucination in which Hardin is sitting next to me, his hand on my thigh, and he leans in to make some cheeky comment that makes me laugh and blush feverishly.

My head is a little fuzzy as I clear all of the food off my plate and finish off my second glass of wine. Landon is in conversation with Max and Ken about sports, of course. I stare at the printed tablecloth, trying to find faces or pictures inside the black and white swirls. I find a cluster that resembles an *H*, and my finger traces the pattern repeatedly. Suddenly I stop and look up quickly, paranoid that he may have seen me tracing the letter.

But Hardin isn't paying attention to me; his eyes are only for her.

"I need some air," I tell Landon and stand. My chair screeches against the wooden floor, and Hardin looks up from his conversation momentarily, but then he catches himself and pretends to have only been looking for his water before he returns to talking to this new girl of his.

chapter thirty-nine

TESSA

My heels clacking loudly on the hardwood, I concentrate on making it to the back door of the restaurant through my alcohol haze. If we were closer to home, I'd leave right now, pack my bags for Seattle, and stay in a hotel until I found an apartment.

I am so sick of Hardin doing this kind of shit to me—it's painful and embarrassing, and it's breaking me down. *He's* breaking me down, and he knows it. That's exactly why he's doing it. He's said as much before: he does these things because he knows they'll get to me.

When I push through the door—briefly hoping it won't set off an alarm or something—the chill night air envelops me. It's calming, blanketing me in something other than the stale air and awkward tension of dull dinner companions.

I rest my elbows on a rock ledge and look out into the woods. It's dark, nearly pitch-black out there. The restaurant is nestled right in the middle of a wooded area, creating a secluded atmosphere. It works, and would be wonderful, but it's not ideal for me right now, when I already feel trapped.

"Are you all right?" a voice sounds from behind me.

When I turn, Robert is standing in the doorway, a stack of plates in one hand.

"Um, yeah, I just needed to breathe," I say.

"Oh, it's a little cold out here." He smiles. His smile is polite and actually very endearing.

I give a smile back. "Yeah, a little."

Both of us stand in silence. It's slightly awkward, but I don't mind. Nothing is as awkward as sitting at that table.

A few seconds later he speaks up. "I haven't seen you around here before." He gently places the plates on an empty table and walks closer to me. He leans his elbows on the ledge only a few feet away.

"I'm visiting. I've never been here before."

"You should visit in the summer. February is the worst time to come. Well, except for November and December . . . maybe even January." His cheeks flush as he stammers, "Y-you get what I mean." Then he lets out a little chucklelike sound.

Trying not to giggle at him and his red cheeks, I say, "I bet it's beautiful in the summer."

"Yeah, you are." His eyes widen. "I mean *it* is. *It* is beautiful," he corrects himself, and runs his hand over his face.

I force my lips together in an attempt not to laugh at him, but I can't help it. A small giggle escapes, causing him to look even more horrified than before.

"Do you live here?" I ask, trying to sidestep his embarrassment. His company is refreshing; it's nice to be around someone who's not so intimidating. Hardin owns every room he's in, and his presence is overwhelming half the time.

That calms him a tiny bit. "Yeah, born and raised. And you?"

"I go to WCU. I'll be starting at the Seattle campus next week." I feel like I've been waiting so long to say those words.

"Wow, Seattle. Impressive!"

He smiles and I laugh again. "Sorry, wine makes me laugh a lot," I blurt, and he looks over at me with a grin.

"Well, I'm glad it's not me that you're laughing at." His eyes roam my face, and I turn away. He looks back to the restaurant. "You should get back inside before your boyfriend comes looking for you."

I turn around to look in through the windows into the elegant space. Hardin's head is still turned toward Lillian.

"Trust me, no one is coming to look for me," I say with a sigh, and my bottom lip quivers as my heart betrays me, sinking lower and lower.

"He looks pretty lost without you," Robert tries to reassure me.

I spy Landon looking around the room, with nobody to talk to. "Oh! That's not my boyfriend. Mine is the one across the table—the one with the tattoos." I watch as Robert looks at Hardin and Lillian and confusion sweeps over his soft features. Swirls of black ink peek out from the top of Hardin's collared dress shirt. I love the way white looks on him; I love being able to see the hint of ink under the light-colored fabric.

"Um, does he *know* he's your boyfriend?" Robert asks, raising his eyebrow.

I tear my eyes away from Hardin as he smirks, a deep smirk, the kind of smirk that shows his dimples, the kind of smirk that is usually given only to me. "I'm beginning to wonder the same thing."

I bring my hands to my face and shake my head. "It's complicated," I groan.

Hold yourself together, don't fall into his game. Not this time.

Robert shrugs. "Well, who better to talk about your problems with than a stranger?"

We both gaze at the table that I'm missing from. No one except Landon seems to even notice.

"Don't you have to work?" I ask, hoping that he doesn't. Robert is young, older than me, but he can't be any older than twenty-three at the most.

He seems fully confident as he smiles and says, "Yeah, but I have it in good with the owner," seeming to be telling himself a joke that I'm not included in.

"Oh."

"So, if that's your boyfriend, who's the girl with him?"

"Her name is Lillian." I can hear the venom in my own voice. "I don't know her, neither does he . . . well, he didn't, but apparently now he does."

Robert's eyes meet mine. "So he brought her here to make you jealous?"

"I don't know; it's not working. Well, I *am* jealous—I mean, look at her. She's wearing the same dress as I am, and she looks way better in it."

"No; no, she doesn't," he says quietly, and I smile, thanking him.

"We were getting along fine until yesterday. Well, fine for us. And then we got in a fight this morning—but we always fight. I mean, we fight all the time, so I don't know what it is about this fight that's so different, but it is. It's different; it doesn't feel like the rest of our fights, and now he's ignoring me the way he used to when we first met." I realize that I've been speaking more to myself than to this stranger with curious blue eyes. "I sound insane, I know I do. It's the wine."

The corners of his lips turn into a smile, and he shakes his head. "No, not insane at all. " Robert smiles, which brings a little laugh out of me. With a nod at my table, he says, "He's looking at you."

My head snaps up to look. Sure enough, Hardin's eyes are on me and my new shrink, eyes that burn into me and make me literally flinch at their intensity.

"You should probably go inside," I warn him. I'm expecting Hardin to get up from the table at any time, to rush out here and throw Robert over the deck and into the woods.

He doesn't, though. He remains still, his fingers wrapped around the stem of a wineglass as he looks at me one last time before lifting his free hand and resting it across the back of Lillian's chair. *Oh God.* My chest tightens at his callous action.

"I'm sorry," Robert says.

I'd almost forgotten he was next to me.

"It's fine, really. I should be used to it. I've been playing these games with him for six months now." I cringe at the truth, cursing myself for not learning my lesson after one month, or two, or three—yet here I am outside with a stranger watching as Hardin shamelessly flirts with another girl. "I don't know why I'm telling you all of this. I'm sorry."

"Hey, I'm the one who asked," he kindly reminds me. "And we've got plenty more wine, if you want some." His smile is kind and playful.

"I certainly will need more." I nod and turn away from the window. "Do you get this a lot? Half-drunk girls whining about their boyfriends?"

He chuckles. "No, actually, it's usually rich old men complaining that their steak isn't medium rare."

"Like the guy at my table, the one in the red tie." I gesture to Max. "God, he's a jerk."

Robert nods in agreement. "Yeah, he is. No offense, but anyone who sends a salad back because it has 'too many olives' is a jerk by definition."

We both laugh, and I cover my mouth with the back of my hand, then worry that the laughter will bring some of my tears out.

"Right! He's so serious, too, like he gave us this massive speech on his well-considered reasoning about olives after that." I deepen my voice to try to mimic the annoying girl's annoying father. "'Too many olives overpowers the delicate yet earthy taste of the arugula.'"

Robert bursts out laughing, doubling over. Hands on his knees, he looks up, and asks in a voice much closer to Max's than mine was, "'Could I have four? Three just will not do, and five is far too many—it simply does *not* balance the flavor palate!'"

I lose myself in laughter to the point that my stomach is

aching. I don't know how long it lasts, but I hear a door open suddenly, and Robert and I both instinctively stop and look up . . . to see Hardin standing in the doorway.

I stand up straight, smoothing my dress. I can't help but feel like I was doing something wrong, even though I know that I wasn't.

"Am I interrupting something?" Hardin barks, commanding all attention.

"Yes," I respond, my voice coming out as clear as I was hoping. My breath is still staccato from laughing so hard, my head is swimming from the wine, and my heart is aching over Hardin.

Hardin looks to Robert. "Apparently."

Robert's face still holds a smile, his eyes alight with humor as Hardin tries his best to intimidate him. But he doesn't falter, he doesn't even blink. Even *he* has had enough of Hardin's shit—and he's *trained* to always be nice. But here, out of earshot of the rest of the diners, he doesn't seem to have a problem showing his amusement at Hardin's absurd attitude.

"What do you want?" I ask Hardin. When he turns to me, his mouth is pressed in a hard line.

"Get inside," he demands, but I shake my head. "Tessa, don't play these games with me. Let's go."

He reaches for my arm, but I yank it away and stand my ground. "I said no. *You* go back inside—I'm sure your friend misses you," I hiss.

"You . . ." Hardin looks back to Robert. "You should really be the one to go inside. Our drinks are in need of refilling," he says, then snaps his fingers in the most insulting way possible.

"I'm off, actually. But I'm sure you can charm someone else into taking care of your drinks," Robert says with a shrug.

Hardin's stance falters momentarily; he's not used to anyone talking back to him, especially not strangers.

"Okay, let me rephrase this . . ." He steps toward Robert. "Get the fuck away from her. Get inside and find something fucking *else* to do before I grab you by that fucking ridiculous collar and bash your head against that ledge."

"Hardin!" I reproach him, stepping between the two of them.

But Robert seems unfazed. "Go ahead," he says slowly, confidently. "But you should know that this is a very small town. My dad's the sheriff, Grandpa's the judge, and Uncle's the one they locked up for assault and battery. So if you want to take your chances bashing my head in"—he shrugs—"go for it."

My mouth is wide open, and I can't seem to close it. Hardin's glare is murderous, and he seems to be weighing his options as he looks back and forth between Robert, me, and the inside of the restaurant.

"Let's go," he says again to me at last.

"I'm not going," I tell him, backing away. But I do turn to Robert and say, "Can you give us a minute, please?"

He nods slowly, giving Hardin one last glare before walking back inside.

"So what, you're going to fuck the waiter now?" Hardin grimaces, and I step back even farther, willing myself not to break under his stare.

"Would you just stop, already? We both know how this will go. You'll keep insulting me. I'll walk away. You'll come after me and tell me you won't be rude anymore. We'll go back to the cabin and sleep together." I roll my eyes, and he looks absolutely lost.

In his usual Hardin way, he collects himself rapidly. Throwing his head back in laughter, he simply says, "Wrong," and steps back toward the door. "I won't be doing that. It seems you've forgotten how it really goes: you throw a fit over something I say, you walk away, and I only come after you so I can fuck you. And you . . ." he adds with a sinister glare, "you always let me."

My mouth falls open in horror, and my hands move to my stomach to hold my body together after his splintering words.

"Why?" I gasp, the cold air nowhere to be found as I try to catch my breath.

"I don't know. Because you can't stay away. Probably because I fuck you better than anyone else ever would." His tone is clipped and cruel.

"Why . . . now?" I correct my earlier question. "What I meant was, why are you doing this now? Is it because I won't go to England with you?"

"Yes and no."

"I won't give up Seattle for you, so you turn on me?" My eyes are burning, but I will not cry. "You show up with *her*"—I gesture toward Lillian at the table—"and say all these hateful things to me? I thought we were past this. What happened to you not being able to live without me? What happened to you trying your best to treat me the way you should?"

He looks away from me, and for a moment, a barely recognizable moment, I see a deeper emotion behind his hateful glare.

"There is a big difference between not being able to live without someone and loving them," he says.

And like that, he walks away, whatever was left of my respect for him following in his wake.

chapter forty

HARDIN

I wanted to hurt her, to make her feel like shit, the way that I felt when I looked up from the table to see her laughing. She was fucking laughing when she should have been sitting across from me vying for my attention. It was like she didn't give a fuck about me getting close to Lillian. She was too focused on the fucking waiter and whatever the hell he was saying.

So my mind began sifting through hateful thoughts, trying to pick one that was sure to break her down. Lillian's statement from this morning popped in, and it warmed my anger, so I said it before I could stop myself. *There is a big difference between not being able to live without someone and loving them.*

I almost want to take them back . . . almost. She deserves them, she really does. She shouldn't have said that she didn't want me to go to Seattle with her. She said I turned on her; I didn't turn on her. I'm here for her, on her side. She's the one trying to leave me every damn chance she gets.

"I'm leaving," I announce when I reach the table. Six sets of eyes look up, and Landon rolls his before looking over to the door. "She's outside," I tell him sarcastically. He can go out there and put on fucking kid gloves for her—I'm sure as hell not going to.

"What did you do now?" he has the nerve to ask me in front of everyone.

I glare at him. "Mind your own fucking business."

"Hardin," my father warns. Not *him*, too—everyone is fucking against me, apparently. If my father wants to start shit with me, I fucking dare him.

"I'll go, too," Lillian says, standing.

"No," I snap, but she ignores me and follows me as I make my way through the restaurant and out the front door.

"What the heck happened?" she asks when we get outside.

Without breaking my stride, I shout over my shoulder, "She was out there with that fucking guy, that's what happened."

"Then what? What did she say when you told her that I'm not a threat?" She stumbles slightly in her high heels, but I don't stop to help her as I try to decide where the hell I'm actually going. I knew I should have fucking driven my own car here, but no, Tessa had to get her way. *Big surprise there.*

"I didn't tell her."

"Why not? Do you know what she's probably thinking right now?"

"I don't give a shit what she thinks. I hope she's thinking that I'm going to fuck you."

She stops walking. "Why? If you love her, why would you want her to think that?"

Oh, lovely, now Lillian is turning on me, too. I turn to face her. "Because she needs to learn that—"

She holds up one hand. "Stop. Just stop there, because she doesn't need to 'learn' anything. It seems to me that you're the one who needs to be learning something—what did you say to the poor girl?"

"I said what you said to me this morning about there being a difference between not being able to live without someone and loving them," I tell her.

She shakes her head in confusion. "You said that to her, as in *you* can't live without her but don't love her?"

"Yes—did I not just tell you that?" Tessa Number Two needs to just go away, because she's getting on my last fucking nerve just like Tessa the Original.

"Wow," she says, and laughs.

She's laughing at me, too? "What? What's so funny?" I nearly yell.

"You are so *clueless*," she mocks me. "When I said that to you this morning, I wasn't referring to you, I was talking about her. I meant that just because you think she can't live without you doesn't mean that she's in love with you."

"What?"

"You assume that you have her so wrapped around your finger that she won't leave you because she can't live without you, when in reality it seems like you have her trapped and *that's* why she won't leave you: not because she loves you, but because you've made her feel that she can't be without you."

"No . . . she loves me." I know she does, and that's why she'll be following me out here any moment now.

Lillian throws her arms wide. "*Does* she? Why would she, when you do things to hurt her on purpose?"

I've had enough of this shit. "You're in no position to be giving anyone a goddamned lecture." I throw my hands in the air as wildly as she just did. "Your girlfriend is probably fucking someone else right now while you're here trying to play couples therapist between Tessa and me," I growl.

Lillian's eyes widen, and she takes a step back from me . . . the way Tessa did only minutes ago. Her blue eyes begin to water, shining in the darkness. She shakes her head and starts to walk back toward the restaurant parking lot.

"Where are you going?" I call to her through the wind.

"Back inside. Tessa may be stupid enough to put up with your crap, but I'm not."

For a moment I almost follow this girl who I thought was my . . . *friend*? I don't know, but I felt like I could trust her despite only knowing her for two days.

Fuck that: I'm not following anyone. Tessa or Tessa Number Two. They can both go to hell—I don't need either of them.

chapter forty-one

TESSA

My chest is aching, my throat is dry, and my head is spinning. Hardin basically just told me that he doesn't love me and that he chases me just so he can sleep with me. The worst thing about the things he said to me is that I know he didn't mean them. I know he loves me—he does. In his own way, he loves me more than anything. He's shown me that time and time again in the last six months. But he's also shown me that he'll stop at nothing to hurt me, to make me feel weak just because his ego is bruised. If he loved me the way he should, he wouldn't purposely hurt me.

He couldn't have meant that he only wants sex from me. He doesn't really see me as a toy, does he? With him, truth and lies slide back and forth as easily as his moods. He couldn't have meant it. But he said it with such conviction; he didn't even blink. I honestly don't know anymore. Through all of the fights, tears, holes in our walls, I have always held on to the small certainty that he loves me.

Without that, we have nothing. And without him, I have nothing. The irrational and flaring tempers we both have, mixed with our young ages, are becoming too much to handle.

There's a difference between not being able to live without someone and loving them—the words slice through me again.

The air in this place is too stale, too thick and consuming, and the laughter of the customers is growing sinister. I look for an exit. Glass doors leading to a balcony are closed; I open them and welcome the cool air. I sit there, staring out into the darkness, enjoying the quiet of the night and my own slowing mind.

I don't notice the door to the deck opening until Robert is next to me. "Brought you something," he says and holds up the bottle of wine, waggling it playfully. He dips his shoulder to one side, and a grin spreads across his handsome face.

I surprise myself by smiling, a real smile, despite the fact that on the inside I'm screaming, huddled in a corner crying.

"Pity wine?" I question, holding my hands out for the white-labeled bottle. I recognize it as the same wine Max ordered earlier; it must have cost a fortune.

He grins, placing the wine in my hands. "What other type of wine is there?" The bottle is cold, but my hands are nearly numb from the February air.

"Glasses." He smiles, dipping his hands into the deep pockets of his apron. "I couldn't fit actual wineglasses, so I grabbed these." He hands me a small Styrofoam cup, and I hold it up while he uncorks the bottle.

"Thank you." The wine fills the cup, and I bring it to my lips the moment he pulls away.

"We can go inside, you know? There are a few sections that are closed down already, so we can sit there," Robert says, then takes a sip.

"I don't know." I sigh, shifting my gaze to the table.

"He left," he says, the sympathy obvious in his voice. "So did she," he adds. "Do you want to talk about it?"

"No, not really." I shrug. "Tell me about this wine." I grasp for a neutral, nondepressing subject.

"This guy? Okay, well, it's, um, old and aged to perfection?" He laughs and I join him. "I'm good at drinking it, though, not so much studying it."

"Okay, not the wine, then," I say. Tipping my cup back, I finish the rest as quickly as possible.

"Um," he says, looking behind me. My stomach drops at his nervous expression, and I hope Hardin isn't back to spit more venom at me. When I turn around, Lillian is standing in the doorway, seemingly unsure whether to come out or not.

"What do you want?" I ask her. I'm trying to control my jealousy, but the wine coursing through me doesn't work in favor of manners. Robert grabs my empty cup just as the wind knocks it over, and begins to refill it. I get the feeling he's trying to keep himself busy to avoid whatever dramatic or awkward situation lies ahead.

"Can I talk to you?" Lillian asks.

"What is there for us to talk about? Everything is pretty clear to me." I take a big gulp from my cup, letting the cold wine fill my mouth.

Unexpectedly, she doesn't respond to my attitude. She just walks over to us and says flatly, "I'm gay."

What? If Robert's clear blue eyes hadn't been focused on me, I'd have spit the wine back into my cup. I look from him to her and swallow slowly.

"It's true. I have a girlfriend. Hardin and I are only friends." She frowns. "If you would even call us that."

I know that look. He must have just told her off.

"Then why . . ." I start. *Is she being honest?* "But you guys were all over each other."

"No, he was being a little . . . *touchy-feely*, I guess you'd say, like when he put his arm around my chair. But he was only doing it to make you jealous."

"Why would he do that? On purpose?" I ask. But I know the answer: to hurt me, of course.

"I told him to tell you. I'm sorry if you thought something was going on between us. It's not. I'm in a relationship, with a *girl*."

I roll my eyes and hold my cup out to Robert for more wine. "You seemed pretty comfortable going along with it," I remark harshly.

With honest, pleading eyes, she says, "That wasn't my intention. I wasn't really paying attention to what he was doing. I'm really sorry if you were hurt in all this."

I'm fumbling for reasons to tell this girl off, but I can't come up with any. Lillian being gay is a huge relief to me, and I wish that I'd known sooner, but it really doesn't change much with Hardin. If anything, it makes his behavior worse, because he was purposely trying to make me jealous and then upped the ante by saying the most hateful things he could think of to me. Watching him flirt with her didn't hurt nearly as bad as hearing him tell me that he didn't love me.

Robert fills my glass, and I take a small sip while watching Lillian. "So what changed your mind and made you tell me? He went off on you, didn't he?"

She half smiles, then sits down at the table with us. "Yeah, he did."

"He's good at that," I say and she nods. I can tell she's slightly nervous, and I keep reminding myself that she isn't the problem here, Hardin is.

"Do you have any more cups?" I ask Robert, and he nods, giving me a proud smile. My stomach flutters lightly; from the wine, I'm sure.

"Not in my pocket, but I can grab another from inside," he offers politely. "We should go inside, anyway; your lips are turning blue."

I look up at him, and my gaze goes to his lips. They're full and pink; they look so soft. Why am I staring at his lips? This is what wine does to me. I want to be staring at Hardin's lips, but he only uses them to yell at me lately, it seems.

"Is he inside?" I ask Lillian, and she shakes her head. "Okay, let's go in, then. I have to save Landon from that table, anyway, especially from that Max guy," I say without thinking, then quickly look at Lillian. "Shit, sorry,"

She surprises me by laughing. "It's fine, trust me. I know my dad's an asshole."

I don't respond. She may not be a threat to my relationship with Hardin, but that doesn't mean that I like her, even if she does seem kind of sweet.

"Are we going inside or . . ." Robert rocks on the heels of his black dress shoes.

"Yeah." I gulp down the rest of my wine and head inside. "I'll get Landon. Are you sure you can drink here? In your uniform?" I ask my new friend. I don't want him to get in trouble. My head is fuzzy, and the thought of him getting arrested by his father makes me giggle.

"What?" he asks, his eyes searching my face.

"Nothing," I lie.

Heading inside, Lillian and I walk over to our party's table. I put my hands on the back of Landon's chair, and he turns to look up at me.

"You okay?" he asks quietly while Lillian speaks to her parents.

I shrug. "Yeah, sort of." I wouldn't be if I wasn't borderline drunk from downing several cups of wine. "Do you want to hang out with us? We're going to hang out here and have some wine . . . some more wine." I smile.

"Who? Her, too?" Landon glances across the table at Lillian.

"Yeah, she's . . . well, she's okay." I don't want to blurt out the girl's personal business in front of everyone.

"I told Ken that I'd watch the game with them at Max's cabin, but if you want me to stay here, I will."

"No . . ." I do want him to stay, but I don't want him to alter his plans for me. "It's okay. I just thought you might want to get away from them," I whisper, and he smiles.

"I do, but Ken's excited for me to come because Max likes the opposing team. I think he thinks it'll be funny to watch us give each other crap or something." Then he leans in closer so only I can hear him. "Are you sure about hanging out with that guy? He seems nice, but Hardin will probably try to murder him."

"I think he can hold his own," I assure him. "Have fun watching the game." I lean down and press my lips against Landon's cheek.

I jerk away quickly and cover my mouth. "I'm sorry. I have no idea why . . ."

"It's okay." Landon laughs.

I look around the table and I'm relieved to see that everyone seems to be in engaged in conversation. Thankfully my embarrassing show of affection went unnoticed.

"Be careful, okay, Tessa? And call me if you need me."

"I will. And if you get bored, come back here."

"Will do." He smiles. I know he won't get bored watching the game with Ken. He loves spending time with the only father figure in his life, something that Hardin doesn't share the same enthusiasm for.

"Dad, I'm an adult," I hear Lillian huff from across the table.

Max shakes his head once with authority. "There is absolutely no need for you to be out running the streets here; you'll go back to the cabin with us. That's final." It's obvious that he's one of those men who love to have complete control over everyone in his life. The nasty smirk on his hard face confirms it.

"Fine," his frustrated daughter responds. She looks to her mother, but the woman stays silent. If I had another glass of wine, I would call the jerk out, but I don't want to upset Ken and Karen.

"Tessa, are you coming back with us?" Karen asks.

"No, I'm going to stay here for a little while, if that's okay?" I hope she doesn't mind. I watch as she looks to Lillian and then behind me to where Robert stands in the distance. I get the feeling she has no clue about Lillian's sexual orientation, and she's annoyed by the way Hardin was behaving with her. I love Karen.

"That's fine with us; you have fun." She smiles approvingly.

"Okay." I return her smile and walk away from the table without saying goodbye to Max and his wife.

"We're good to go; she's not allowed to stay," I tell Robert when I reach him.

"Not allowed?"

"Her father is a jerk. I'm sort of glad, though, because I'm not sure how I feel about her. She reminds me of someone. I can't quite put my finger on who . . ." I let the thought trail off as I follow Robert to an empty section of the restaurant. A few tables sit in the closed-off area, bare save for unlit votive candles and salt and pepper shakers.

As we sit, Zed's mutilated face flashes through my mind. I ask Robert, "Are you sure you're okay with hanging out with me? Hardin may come back, and he has a tendency to assault people . . ."

Robert pulls a chair out for me and laughs. "I'm sure," he answers.

Taking the seat across from me, he refills our Styrofoam cups with white wine, and we toast, the cups' soft material bending slightly and lacking that clink of glassware. Nice and cozy, unlike the rest of this hard-edged restaurant.

chapter forty-two

HARDIN

I've called every damn taxi company between here and college trying to get a ride back home. No one accepted, of course, because of the distance. I could take a bus, but public transportation really isn't my thing. I remember the way I used to cringe when Steph would mention Tessa taking the bus to the mall or to Target. Even when I disliked Tessa . . . well, when I thought I did . . . I'd still panic at the thought of her sitting alone on the bus with a bunch of fucking creeps.

Everything has changed since then, since those days when I'd tease and taunt Tessa just to get a rise out of her. Her face when I left her on the balcony of the restaurant . . . maybe it hasn't changed at all. I haven't changed.

I'm torturing the girl I love. That's exactly what I'm doing, and I can't seem to stop. This isn't all my fault, though—it's her fault, too. She keeps pushing me to go to Seattle, and I've made it clear that I'm not giving in on that. Instead of battling me, she should just pack her shit and come to England with me. I'm not staying here whether I'm expelled or not—I'm bored in America, and it's been nothing but shit for me. I'm sick of seeing my dad all the time; I'm sick of everything here.

"Watch where you're going, dick," a female voice says in the darkness, startling me.

I sidestep the figure before I run into her. "You watch where *you're* going," I fire back, without stopping. *Why the hell is this chick out here in front of Max's cabin, anyway?*

"*Excuse* me?" she says, and I turn around to look at her just as the motion-sensor light clicks on from the cabin's porch. I get a good look at her: brown skin, curly hair, ripped jeans, biker boots.

"Let me guess: Riley, right?" I roll my eyes at the girl in front of me.

She puts a hand on her hip. "And who the hell are you?"

"Yep, Riley. If you're looking for Lillian, she isn't here."

"Where is she? And how do you know that I'm looking for her?" the feisty girl challenges.

"Because I just fucked her."

She tenses up, lowering her head so darkness overtakes her features. "What did you just say?" she says and steps forward.

I tilt my head to the side and stare at her. "Christ, I'm just fucking with you. She's at the restaurant down the road with her parents."

Riley raises her head and stops. "Okay, and how do you know her?"

"Met her yesterday. Her dad went to college with mine, I guess. Does she know you're here?"

"No, I've been trying to get hold of her," she says and gestures at the woods surrounding us. "But since she's out in the middle of fucking nowhere, she hasn't been answering. Probably her shit-sucker of a dad keeping her from talking."

I sigh. "Yeah, he is that. Is he even going to let you see her?"

She scowls at me. "Aren't you nosy as hell?" But then she smirks proudly. "Yeah, he will. He's a dick, but he's even more of a pussy, and he's afraid of me."

Headlights flash out in the darkness, and I step onto the grass. "That's them," I tell her.

Shortly, the car pulls into the driveway and comes to a halt. Lillian practically jumps out the door and into Riley's arms.

"How did you get here?" she practically squeals.

"I drove," her girlfriend answers drily.

"How did you find me? I haven't had service all week." She nuzzles into her girlfriend's neck, and I watch as Riley's tough-girl exterior begins to crack. Her hand moves up and down against Lillian's back lovingly.

"It's a small place, baby. It wasn't too hard." She pulls back a little to look at Lillian's face. "Is your dad going to give me shit for coming?"

"No. Well, maybe. But you know he won't make you leave."

I force out a cough, feeling awkward standing there watching this reunion. "Okay, well, I'm going to go," I say and begin to walk off.

"Bye," Riley says. Lillian doesn't say anything.

After a few minutes, I reach the gate to my father's cabin and walk up the driveway. Tessa will be here any minute, and I want to be inside before the SUV pulls into the driveway. She'll be crying, I'm sure, and I'll have to come up with an apology to make her stop and listen to me.

I barely make it to the porch when Karen and Lillian's mother step out of the car. "Where is everyone else?" I ask her, my eyes searching for Tess.

"Oh, well, your dad and Landon rode back with Max to watch some game on television."

"Where's Tessa?" Panic rises in my chest.

"She's back at the restaurant."

"What?" *What the fuck.* This isn't how it's supposed to go.

"She's with him, isn't she?" I ask the two women, even though I already know the answer. She's with the blond asshole with the sheriff for a father.

"Yeah, she is," Karen says, and if I wasn't stuck out in the middle of nowhere with her, I'd cuss her out for the small smile she's trying to hide.

chapter forty-three

TESSA

So that's basically the story of my life," Robert ends with a grin. His smile is warm and honest—almost childlike, but in the most endearing way.

"That was . . . interesting." I reach for the wine bottle on the table and lift it to fill my glass. Nothing comes out.

"Liar," he teases, and I burst into wine-induced giggles. His life story was short and sweet. Not plain really, not exciting, just normal. He grew up with both parents: his mother the schoolteacher, his father the sheriff. After graduating from the small college two towns away, he decided to go to medical school. He's only working here now because he's on the wait list to get into the medical program at the University of Washington. Well, that and he makes pretty good money working at the most expensive restaurant around.

"You should have gone to WCU instead," I tell him, and he shakes his head. He stands up from the table and puts his index finger in the air to pause our conversation. I sit back in the chair while I wait for him to return. I rest my head against the wooden chair and look up. The ceiling in this small section is painted with clouds, castles, and cherubs. The figure directly above me is sleeping, with pink staining her cheeks and blond curly hair topping her head. Her small white wings lay almost flat in slumber. Next to her, a boy—at least I assume it's a boy—stares at her, watching her with his black wings spread behind him.

Hardin.

"No way," Robert says suddenly, interrupting my thoughts. "Even if I wanted to, they don't offer the program I need. Plus, the medical program is part of the main campus in Seattle. At WCU, your Seattle campus is much smaller." When I lift my head up, I see he has a new bottle of wine in his hands.

"Have you been there? To the campus?" I ask him, eager to learn more about my new location. I'm even more eager to stop staring at creepy images of baby angels on the ceiling.

"Yeah, only once. It's small but it's nice."

"I'm supposed to be there on Monday, and I have nowhere to live." I laugh. I know my poor planning shouldn't be funny, but right now it feels that way.

"This Monday? As in today is Thursday and Monday is right around the corner?"

"Yep." I nod.

"What about the dorms?" he asks as he uncorks the bottle.

Living in the dorms never crossed my mind, not even once. I had assumed . . . well, hoped . . . that Hardin would be accompanying me, so they weren't on my radar.

"I don't want to live on campus, especially now that I know how it feels to live on my own."

He nods and starts pouring. "True, once you get a taste of freedom, you can't go back."

"So true. If Hardin went to Seattle . . ." I stop myself. "Never mind."

"So were you guys planning on trying the long-distance thing?"

"No, it would never work," I say, feeling an ache rise in my chest. "The short-distance thing barely even works for us." I need to change the subject before I end up a blubbering mess. "Blubbering," what a strange word.

"Blubbering," I say while pinching my lips between my thumb and index finger.

"Entertaining yourself?" Robert smiles and places a full cup of wine before me. I nod, still laughing. "I have to say, this is the most fun I've had at work in a while."

"Me, too," I agree. "Well, if I worked here." I'm making no sense at all. "I don't drink often—well, more now than I ever did before—but not enough to have built a tolerance, so I get drunk pret-ty fast," I sing, lifting my cup in front of my face.

"I'm the same. I'm not much of a drinker, but when a beautiful girl is having a bad night, I make an exception," he says bravely, but then flushes terribly. "I just meant . . . ahh . . ." He covers his face with his hands. "I don't seem to have a filter around you."

I reach across the table and lower his hands from his face; he flinches slightly, and when he looks up at me his blue eyes are so clear.

"It's like I can tell what you're thinking," I say aloud, without a thought.

"Maybe you can," he whispers in response, and his tongue darts out to wet his lips.

I know he wants to kiss me; I can read it on his face. I can see it in his honest eyes. Hardin's eyes are so guarded all the time I have to struggle to be able to read him, and even then I've never been able to read him the way I want to, the way I need to. I lean closer to Robert, the small table still between us as he leans forward, too.

"If I didn't love him so much, I'd kiss you," I quietly say, not pulling back but not moving any closer. As drunk as I am, and as angry as I am at Hardin, I can't do it. I can't kiss this other guy. I want to, but I can't.

The left corner of his mouth lifts into a crooked smile. "And if I didn't know how much you love him, I'd let you."

"Okay . . ." I'm not sure what else to say, and I'm drunk and awkward, and I don't know how to act around anyone other than

Hardin and Zed, but in a way those two are similar. Robert isn't like anyone I've ever met. Except Landon. Landon is sweet and kind, and my mind is racing from the almost-kiss with someone who is not Hardin.

"I'm sorry." I sit back down on the chair, and he does the same.

"Don't be. I'd much rather you not kiss me than kiss me and regret it."

"You're strange," I tell him. I wish I'd chosen a different word, but it's too late now. "In a good way," I correct myself.

"So are you." He chuckles. "When I first saw you in that dress, I thought you were going to be some snobby rich girl with no personality at all."

"Well, sorry. I'm surely not rich." I laugh.

"Or snobby," he adds.

"My personality isn't too bad." I shrug.

"It will do," he teases with a smile.

"You're awfully nice."

"Why wouldn't I be?"

"I don't know." I start poking at my cup. "Sorry, I know I sound like an idiot."

He looks puzzled for a moment, then says, "You don't sound like an idiot. And you don't have to keep apologizing."

"What do you mean?" I ask. I'm vaguely aware that I have now picked apart the rim of the Styrofoam cup; small pieces of white litter the table in front of me.

"You keep apologizing for everything you say. You've said 'sorry' at least ten times in the last hour. You haven't done anything wrong, so you don't have anything to apologize for."

I'm embarrassed by his words, but his eyes are so kind and his voice doesn't hold even a sliver of annoyance or judgment. "I'm sorry . . ." I say again reflexively. "See! I don't know why I do that." I smooth a loose lock of hair behind my ear.

"I can guess, but I won't. Just know that you shouldn't have to," he states simply.

I take a deep breath and let it out. It's relaxing to have a conversation with someone without worrying about upsetting them the entire time.

"Anyway, tell me more about your new job in Seattle," he says, and I'm thankful for the subject change.

chapter forty-four

HARDIN

"Where do you *think* I'm going?" I yell up the walk at Karen, tossing my hands in the air out of frustration.

She walks partway back down the porch steps, then says, "I don't mean to butt in, Hardin, but don't you think you should leave her be . . . for once? I really don't want to upset you, but I don't think anything good will come out of you going down there and causing a scene. I know you want to see her, but—"

"You don't know anything," I snap, and my father's wife pulls her head back a little.

"I'm sorry, Hardin, but I think you need to leave her be for tonight," she says, like she's my mother.

"Oh, why? So she can fucking cheat on me?" Frustrated fingers tug at the roots of my hair. Tessa's already had one glass—one and a half glasses, to be exact—at dinner, and Lord knows she can't handle alcohol.

"If that's what you think of her . . ." Karen begins but stops herself. "Never mind, go on, then—like always." She looks at Max's wife once, then adjusts her knee-length dress. "Just be careful, dear," she says with a forced smile and goes up the stairs with her friend.

That headache gone, I continue on with my original plan and march toward the restaurant. I'll drag Tessa out of there—not literally, of course, but she *will* come with me. This whole thing is bullshit, and it's all because I forgot to put on a fucking condom. That's what started this whole spiraling mess we're in. I could have called Sandra earlier and corrected the apartment shit, or I could have found Tessa another place to live . . . but that wouldn't work either. Seattle can't happen. It's taking longer to convince Tessa than I imagined it would, and now it's all even more complicated.

I'm still shocked that she didn't get out of the car with Karen and whatever Lillian's mum's name is. I was positive that she'd be upset and ready to talk to me. It's that waiter—what kind of influence did he manage to have on her that would make her stay at the restaurant instead of coming with me? What did she see in him?

Needing to collect my thoughts for a minute, I stop and sit down on one of the large rocks decorating the edge of the yard. Maybe barging in there isn't the best idea. Maybe I should get Landon to go inside and get her. She listens to him much more than she does me. But then I curse at my stupid idea because I know he won't go for it, and, taking his mum's side, he'll make me look weak and tell me to leave her alone.

I can't, though. Sitting on this cold-ass rock for twenty minutes has made it worse, not better. All I can think about is the way she stepped back away from me on the deck and how she was so carefree laughing with him.

What will I say to her? He seems like the kind of asshole who'll try to stop me from making her leave. I won't have to hit him; if I yell enough, she'll come with me to avoid a fight. I hope. She hasn't done what I predicted so far tonight.

This is all so juvenile: my behavior, my manipulation of her feelings. I know it—I just don't know what to do about it. I love her—*fuck*, do I love that girl. But I'm running out of ways to keep her close to me.

In reality it seems like you have her trapped, and that's *why she won't leave you: not because she loves you, but because you've made her feel that she can't be without you.*

Lillian's words play like a broken record through my mind as I get up and head past the end of the driveway. It's cold as fuck outside now, and this stupid shirt is too thin. Tessa didn't bring a jacket to dinner with her, and that dress—that *dress*—is skimpy and she'll definitely be cold. I should probably grab her a jacket . . .

What if he offers her his jacket? Jealousy courses through me, and I ball my fists at the thought.

. . . you have her trapped, and that's *why she won't leave you: not because she loves you . . .*

Fucking Tessa Number Two and her bullshit psychotherapy. She doesn't even know what she's talking about. Tessa does love me. I see it in her blue-gray eyes every time she looks at me. I feel it on her fingertips as she traces over the ink stained into my skin. I feel it when her lips touch mine. I know the difference between love and being trapped, between love and being addicted.

I swallow the slight panic that threatens to overtake me again. She loves me. She does. Tessa loves me. If she didn't, I wouldn't know how to handle it. I couldn't. I need her to love me and be there for me. I've never let anyone get as close to me as she is; she's the only person that I know will always love me unconditionally. Even my mum gets sick of my shit sometimes, but Tessa always forgives me, and no matter what I do she's always there for me when I need her. That stubborn, obnoxious, uncompromising girl is my entire world.

"What are you doing, creep?" I hear from the darkness.

"You have *got* to be fucking kidding me," I groan and turn to find Riley walking down the driveway of Max's cabin. I need to be paying more attention. I didn't even notice her coming toward me.

"You're the one out here stalking the damn driveway," she fires back.

"Where's Lillian?"

"Not your concern. Where's Tessa?" she says with a smirk. Lillian must have told her about our fight. *Lovely.*

"Not your concern. Why are you out here?"

"Why are *you*?" Riley clearly has an attitude problem.

"Do you have to be such a bitch?"

She nods exaggeratedly a few times. "Yeah. I do, actually." I figured she'd chew my head off for calling her a bitch, but she doesn't seem to mind; I'm sure she knows she is. "And I'm out here because Lillian just fell asleep. And between *her* dad, *your* dad, and your dorky-ass brother, I'm ready to puke."

"So what, you thought you'd walk around in the dark in the middle of February?"

"I'm wearing a coat." She tugs at the bottom of her garment to prove her point. "I'm going to find that bar I passed while I was driving up here."

"Why don't you drive, then?"

"Because I want to *drink*. And do I look like someone who wants to spend their weekend in jail?" she scoffs, walking past me. She looks back without stopping. "Where're you going?"

"To get Tessa; she's hanging out with . . . never mind." I'm sick of telling people my fucking business.

Now Riley does stop. "You're an asshole for not telling her that Lil is gay."

"Of course she told you," I say.

"She tells me everything. That was a major dick move."

"It's a long story."

"You won't move to Seattle with Tessa, and now"—she flips her hair over her shoulder—"she's probably giving that blond dude a blow job in the bathroom of—"

I step toward her, anger boiling in my veins. "Shut the fuck up. *Now*. Don't you fucking dare say shit like that to me." I have to remember that even though she has a mouth like mine, she is a female and I would never take it there.

Unfazed by my outburst, she replies calmly, "Don't like that much, do you? Maybe you'd do best to remember that next time you make some snarky-ass comment about fucking my girlfriend."

My breathing falters, deep and out of control. I can't stop thinking about Tessa's full lips touching him. I tug at my hair again and turn in a circle.

"It's driving you crazy, isn't it? Her being with him?"

"You really need to stop taunting me," I warn her, and she shrugs.

"I know it is. Look, I probably shouldn't have said that, but you were a dick first, remember?" When I don't respond, she continues. "Let's call a truce here. I'll buy you a drink, and you can cry over Tessa while I brag about how good Lillian is with her tongue." She walks over to me and tugs at my sleeve, trying to drag me across the street. I can see the cheesy multicolored lantern lights on top of the tin roof of the small bar from here.

I jerk my arm away from her. "I need to get Tessa."

"*One* drink, and then I'll come with you as backup." Riley's words mimic my thoughts from a few minutes ago.

"Why? Why do you want to hang out with me?" I make eye contact with her, and she shrugs again.

"I don't, really. But I'm bored, and you're out here. Besides, Lil seems to care about you for some reason that I don't get." She runs her eyes up and down my body. "I really don't get it, but she likes you, as a *friend*," Riley says, with as much emphasis on the word "friend" as possible. "So yeah, I would like to impress her by pretending that I give a shit about your doomed relationship."

"Doomed?" I begin to follow her down the road.

"Out of all the shit that I just said, you chose that to comment on?" She shakes her head. "You're worse than me."

She laughs and I stay quiet. The obnoxious girl grabs hold of my shirt again and leads me down the road. I'm too busy thinking to push her off.

How can she think we are doomed when she doesn't even know me, know us?

We aren't doomed.

I know we aren't. I'm damned, but she's not. She will save me. She always does.

chapter forty-five

TESSA

Yikes, it dropped at least ten degrees out here," Robert says to me as we step out the door. The cold air smacks me, and I wrap my arms around myself trying to stay warm. He looks over at me with a little frown. "I wish I had a jacket to offer you . . . I also wish I could offer to drive you back, but I've been drinking." With a playfully horrified look, he adds, "Guess I'm not very gentlemanly tonight."

"It's okay, really," I say with a smile. "I'm pretty drunk, so I'm warm . . . That makes no sense." I giggle and follow him down the sidewalk in front of the restaurant. "Although, I should have worn different shoes."

"We could trade?" he jokes.

I gently push against his shoulder, and he smiles for what has to be the hundredth time tonight. "Your shoes look more comfortable than Hardin's; his boots are so heavy and he always leaves them by the door, so I . . . never mind." Embarrassed by what I just started talking about, I shake my head to stop myself.

"I'm more of a sneaker guy," Robert says, letting me know it's okay.

"Me, too. Well, not a *guy*." Again I laugh. My head is swimming from the wine, and my mouth seems to let out every single thought that crosses my mind, nonsensical and all. "Do you know which way the cabins are?"

He reaches over to steady me as I almost walk into a parking block. "Which cabins? This whole town is full of them."

"Um, well, there's a street with a small sign and then like three or four more cabins, then another street?" I try to remember the drive to the restaurant from Ken and Karen's place, but none of it makes sense.

"That doesn't give me much to go on"—he chuckles—"but we can walk until we find it?"

"Okay, but if we don't find it within twenty minutes, I'm going to a hotel." I groan, dreading the walk and the discussion Hardin and I are sure to have when I arrive. And by "discussion," I mean full-on, knock-down, drag-out verbal brawl. Especially when he finds out that I've been drinking with Robert.

Suddenly I turn to look at him as we walk through the dark. "Do you ever get sick of people telling you what to do all the time?"

"No one really does, but if they did, I would."

"You're lucky. I feel like someone's always telling me what to do, where to go, who to talk to, where to live." I let out a breath and watch it turn to steam in the cold air. "It's getting on my nerves."

"I'm sure it is."

I look up at the stars for a moment. "I want to do something about it, but I just don't know what that is."

"Maybe Seattle will help you."

"Maybe . . . I want to do something now, though, like run away or cuss someone out."

"Cuss someone out?" He laughs and halts to bend down to lace his shoe. I stop walking a few feet ahead of him and look around at my surroundings. Now that my mind is racing with all the possibilities of potential reckless behaviors, I can't stop it.

"Yeah, cuss out someone in particular."

"You probably should take it slow. I know cussing someone out is pretty wild and all, but maybe start with something a little lighter," he says. It takes me a moment to comprehend that he's teasing me, but once I do, I see the humor in it.

"I mean it, though. Right now I just feel like doing something . . . crazy?" I pull my top lip between my teeth, pondering the idea.

"It's the wine—it's pretty strong, and you drank a load in a short amount of time."

We both laugh again and I can't seem to stop. The only things that bring me back to normalcy are the canteen-style lanterns hanging from a small building nearby.

"That's our bar," Robert informs me with a nod toward it.

"It's so small!" I exclaim.

"Well, it doesn't have to be huge when it's the only one in the town. It's a load of fun. The bartenders dance on the bar and everything."

"Like Coyote Ugly?"

His smile brightens. "Yes, only these women are all over forty and have a bit more clothing on."

His smile is infectious, and I know what we're doing next.

chapter forty-six

HARDIN

"No, I told you one drink. I meant one drink." I roll my eyes and push the ice around the empty glass with my finger.

"Whatever." She waves down the bartender and orders two more drinks.

"I said I didn't—"

"No one said it's for you," she says with a condescending look. "Sometimes a girl needs a backup."

"Well, you have fun. I'm going to get Tessa now." I get up from the bar stool, but she grabs hold of my shirt. Again. "Stop touching me."

"Dude, stop being a dick. I said I would come; just let me finish these drinks. Do you even know what you're going to say to her, or are you planning to go all caveman style?"

"No." I sit back down. I really haven't thought about what it is I'm going to say. I don't need to say anything except *Let's fucking go*. "What would you say?" I dare to ask.

"Well, first of all"—she pauses to give the bartender two fives and pulls the glasses near her—"Lillian wouldn't be down at some restaurant with another girl . . . or guy, without me." She takes a big drink out of one glass and looks at me. "I would have burned that shit to the ground already."

I really don't like her tone much. "Yet you tell *me* to come and have a drink before I go?"

She shrugs. "I didn't say my way was right. I'm just saying."

"This is bullshit. You are bullshit. I'm going."

As I take a couple steps toward the door, the headache-inducing country music playing in the small bar gradually gets louder and louder, and I know what's coming. I shouldn't have even come to this shitty bar in the first place. I should've gone straight to find Tessa instead. The patrons inside all start cheering, and I turn to see two of the middle-aged bartenders climb onto the bar top.

This is so damn awkward. Entertaining, but still fucking weird.

"You're going to miss the show!" Riley cackles.

I'm about to say something, but I hear a sound behind me, and once again, I sense what's coming. As I turn, my mouth dries and my blood begins to boil instantly. Because as I do, Tessa stumbles in through the door of the little roadhouse. With *him*.

Rather than rushing him like I'd like to do, I step back to the bar and say to the back of Riley's head, "She's here, with him. That's her."

Riley takes her eyes off the old women on the bar and turns. Her jaw drops. "Holy shit, she's hot."

I glare at her. "Stop. Don't look at her like that."

"Lillian said she was pretty, but, fuck, look at her big ti—"

"Don't finish that sentence." I stare at Tessa. She *is* fucking hot, I know this, but more importantly she's drunk and she's laughing as she navigates through the high-topped tables. She chooses an empty one close to the bathroom and takes a seat.

"I'm going over there," I tell Riley. I don't have a fucking clue why I'm telling her anything, but part of me sort of wants to know what she'd do if she were in my shoes. I know Tessa is upset with me for a whole list of shit, and I don't exactly want to add anything else to it. She doesn't have any right to be mad at me, anyway—she's the one hanging out with a random-ass guy from dinner, and now she comes stumbling in here drunk and laughing. With him.

"Why don't you just wait . . . you know, watch her for a little bit," Riley suggests.

"What a fucking stupid idea—why would I watch her hang all over that douche bag? She's mine, and . . ."

Riley looks up at me with curious eyes. "Does she throw a fit when you call her yours?"

"No. She likes it, I think." At least she once told me she did: *"Yours, Hardin, yours," she moaned into my neck as I shifted my hips, burying myself deeper inside of her.*

"Lill gets so pissed off when I say that. She thinks I'm claiming her as property or something," Riley says next to me, but all I can focus on is Tessa. The way she gathers her long hair in one hand and moves it to one shoulder. My anger is rising, my annoyance is growing, and my focus is blurring. How does she not know that I'm here? I can always tell when she enters a room; it's like the air changes and my body can literally feel hers coming near. She's too busy paying attention to him; he's probably telling her the proper way to pour water into a damn glass.

Still looking at my girl, I say, "Well, Tess *is* mine, so I don't care what she thinks about being claimed."

"Spoken like a true asshole," Riley says and looks over at Tessa. "You have to compromise, though. If she's anything like Lillian, she'll get sick of it and you'll end up with an ultimatum."

"What?" I tear my eyes away from Tessa for a moment, and it's torture.

"Lillian got sick of my shit and left me. She"—she lifts her glass toward Tessa—"will do the same thing if you don't listen to what she wants sometimes."

It's amazing how much cooler Lillian is than her girlfriend. "Okay, you don't know anything about our relationship, so you don't know what you're talking about." I look back at Tessa, who is now sitting alone at the table fiddling with a stray lock of hair and moving her shoulders to the music. After a second, I locate her waiter friend at the end of the bar, and my nerves calm slightly because of the distance between them.

"Look, man," Riley says. "I don't have to know the details. I've spent the last . . . almost hour with you. I know that you're a dumb-ass and she's a needy . . ." When I open my mouth to cuss her out, she just continues: "Lillian is, too, so don't get all pissy over it. She's needy, and you know it. But you know what the best part about having a needy girlfriend is?" She gives a wicked smile. "Besides the frequent sex, of course . . ."

"Get to the point." I roll my eyes and look back to Tessa. Her cheeks are red and her eyes are wide in amusement as she watches the women finishing up their dance on the bar. Any second she'll see me standing here.

"The best part is that they need us, just not in the way you expect them to need you, though. They need us to be there for them sometimes, too. Lillian was always so caught up in trying to save . . . me or whatever the hell she was doing . . . that her needs weren't being met. I mean, I didn't even acknowledge her birthday. I didn't do shit for her. I *thought* I was, though, because I was around her and sometimes telling her that I love her, but it wasn't enough."

An unwelcome chill travels down my spine. I watch as Riley finishes the rest of her first drink. "But she's with you now, right?"

"Yeah, but only because I showed her that she can depend on me and that I'm not the same bitch I was when she met me." She looks over at Tessa, then back to me. "You know that saying all the stupid girls are always posting online? I think it's like, 'While you're making . . . if you don't' . . . fuck. I can't remember, but basically it says treat your girl well or someone else will."

"I don't treat her bad." *Not all the time, at least.*

She barks out a disbelieving little laugh. "Dude, just own it. Look, I'm no saint. I still don't treat Lillian the way I should, but I own that shit. You are in some hard-core denial if you're sitting here thinking you don't treat her like shit—if you didn't, she wouldn't be sitting over there with that douche, who happens to be the exact opposite of you and pretty damn hot."

I can't even argue with her; she's right, for the most part. I don't treat Tessa like shit all the time, only when she does something to get me going. Like right now.

And earlier.

"She's looking," Riley tells me, and my blood runs cold. I turn my head slowly in Tessa's direction.

Her eyes are focused on mine—blazing—and I swear I see a hint of red in them as she looks at Riley and then back to me. She doesn't move, she doesn't even blink. Her stare turns from surprised to primal in an instant, and I'm taken aback by the murderous glare directed our way.

"She's so pissed." Riley laughs next to me, and it takes everything in me not to pour her backup drink over her head.

Instead, I mumble, "Shut up," grab the drink, and walk toward Tessa.

Her douchey waiter is still at the end of the bar by the time I reach her.

"Whoa, I never thought I'd find you here, in a bar, drinking with another girl. Surprise, surprise," she quips with a sarcastic smile.

"Why are you here?" I ask, stepping closer to her.

She leans away. "Why are *you*?"

"Tessa," I warn, and she rolls her eyes.

"Not tonight, Hardin, not happening." She climbs off of the tall chair and pulls her dress down.

"Don't walk away from me." My words come out as a command, but I know they're really a plea. I reach for her arm, but she pulls away.

"Why not? That's what you always do to me." She glares at Riley again. "We're both here with other people."

I shake my head. "Fuck, no. That's Lillian's girlfriend."

Her shoulders instantly relax. "Oh." She looks into my eyes and pulls her bottom lip between her teeth.

"We need to leave now."

"So go."

"You and I," I clarify.

"I'm not going anywhere except somewhere fun, more fun than this place, since you're here and you're always stopping my fun. You're like the fun police." She smiles at her own stupid joke and continues. "That's exactly what you are! You're the fun police. I should really get you a badge made and you can wear it all around—you know, to stop everyone's fun," she rambles and bursts into full-on giggles.

Christ, she's fucking wasted.

"How much did you drink?" I yell over the music. I thought it was going to die down, but apparently the elderly dancers have been goaded into an encore.

She shrugs. "I don't know. A few, and this one, too." She takes the cup from my hand before I can stop her, sets it on the table, and hoists herself back onto the chair.

"Don't drink that. You're obviously smashed."

"What's that sound?" She puts her hand to her ear. "Is that the siren of the fun police I hear? *Wah, wah, wah*." For a second she pouts like a child, then laughs. "Go away if you're going to be a fun-sucker." Tessa lifts the glass to her mouth and takes three large gulps. She's swallowed half the drink in seconds.

"You're going to get sick," I say.

"Blah, blah, blah," she mocks, tilting her head back and forth with each word. She looks past me, and a small smirk plays on her lips. "You know Robert, right?"

I look to my side to find the asshole is standing next to me with a drink in each hand.

"Nice to see you again," Robert says, then half smiles. His eyes are bloodshot. He's drunk, too.

Did he take advantage of her? Did he kiss her?

I take a deep breath. *His father is the sheriff. His father is the sheriff. His father is the sheriff.*

His father is the fucking sheriff of this shithole of a town.

I look back at Tessa and say over my shoulder, "Go away."

Tessa rolls her eyes. I forgot how ballsy she becomes when she has liquor in her veins. "Don't go," she says, challenging me, and he sits down at the table. "Don't you have company to entertain?" she taunts.

"No, I don't. Let's go home." I'm barely controlling my temper. If this were any other night, Robert's face would be imprinted on the table by now.

"That cabin isn't home; we're hours from home." She finishes off the drink she stole from me. Then she gives me a look that somehow manages to mix loathing, drunk-flippancy, and indifference. "Actually, as of Monday, I don't have a home anyway, thanks to you."

chapter forty-seven

TESSA

Hardin's nostrils flare as he tries to control his temper. I glance over at Robert, who looks slightly uncomfortable, though not in the least bit intimidated by Hardin.

"If you're purposely trying to make me angry, it's working," Hardin says.

"I'm not, I just don't want to go." And right as the music cuts off, I practically yell, "I want to drink and be young and have fun!"

Everyone turns to me. I'm not sure what to do with all the attention, so I awkwardly wave my hand in the air. Someone gives a hoot of approval, and half the bar raises their glasses in salute and then goes back to talking. The music resumes, and Robert laughs. Hardin glowers.

"You've obviously had enough to drink," he says, eyeing the now half-empty glass that Robert brought to me.

"News flash, Hardin: I'm an adult," I remark in a childish tone.

"Dammit, Tessa."

"Maybe I should go . . ." Robert stands.

"Obviously," Hardin replies at the same time that I say "No."

But then, looking around us, I let out a sigh. As much as I was enjoying my evening with Robert, I know that Hardin will stand here the entire time making rude remarks, threats, whatever he has to do to make him leave. It's better if he does go.

"I'm sorry. I'll go and you can stay," I tell Robert.

He shakes his head with understanding. "No, no—don't

worry about it. I had a long day, anyway." He's so calm and easy-going about everything. It's really refreshing.

"I'll walk you out," I tell him. I'm not sure if I'll ever see him again, and he's been so kind to me tonight.

"No, you won't," Hardin chimes in, but I ignore him and follow Robert toward the door of the small bar. When I look back at the table, Hardin is leaning against it with his eyes closed. I hope he's taking deep breaths in and out, because I'm in no mood for his crap tonight.

Once we get outside, I turn to Robert. "I really am sorry. I didn't know he was here. I was just trying to have a fun night."

Robert smiles and slouches a little to better meet my eyes. "Remember when I said to stop to apologizing for everything?" He reaches into his pocket and pulls out a small pad and pen. "I'm not expecting anything, but if someday you're bored and alone in Seattle, give me a call. Or not. It's up to you if you want to or not." He writes something down, then hands it to me.

"Okay." I don't want to make any promises that I can't keep, so I just smile and tuck the small paper into the top of my dress. "Sorry!" I squeak when I realize that I basically just fondled myself in front of him.

"Stop saying sorry!" He laughs. "And especially not for *that*!" He looks at the entrance to the bar, then out at the dark, dark night. "Well, I better go. It was nice to meet you; maybe we'll see one another again?"

I nod and smile as he walks down the sidewalk.

"It's cold out here," Hardin's voice says behind me, scaring the shit out of me.

I huff and walk past him back into the bar. The table that I was sitting at is now taken by a bald man and his supersized mug of beer. I grab my purse off the stool next to him, and he just gives me a dead-eyed look. Or rather, gives my breasts one.

Hardin is behind me. Again. "Let's just go, please."

I step over to the bar area. "Can I just get two feet of space? I don't even want to be around you right now. You said some pretty hateful things to me," I remind him.

"You know I didn't mean them," he answers, defending himself, attempting to make eye contact with me. I'm not falling for it.

"That doesn't mean you can say them." I look over at the girl—Lillian's girlfriend—who's watching Hardin and me from the bar. "I don't want to talk about it right now. I was having a nice night, and you aren't ruining it."

Hardin steps in between us. "So you don't want me here?" His eyes flash with hurt, and something in their green depths makes me backtrack.

"I'm not saying that, but if you're going to tell me that you don't love me or how you use me for sex again, then you need to go. Or I will." I'm trying my hardest to keep my bubbly, giggly attitude instead of sinking down and letting the pain and frustration take over.

"You are the one who started all this shit when you came here with him—drunk, might I add . . ." he begins.

I sigh. "Here we go." Hardin is the king of double standards. His latest one is walking toward us now.

"Jesus, would you two shut up. We're in a public place." The beautiful girl that Hardin was sitting with interrupts us.

"Not now," Hardin snaps at her.

"Come on, Hardin's obsession. Let's take a seat at the bar," she says, ignoring him.

Sitting at a table toward the back of the bar and having a drink brought to me is one thing; sitting at the bar top and ordering my own is another. "I'm not old enough," I inform her.

"Oh, please. With that dress on, you'll get a drink." She stares at my chest, and I pull the front up slightly.

"If I get kicked out, it's your fault," I tell her, and she tips her head back in laughter.

"I'll bail you out of jail." She winks, and Hardin stiffens next to me. He watches her with warning in his eyes, and I can't help but laugh. He tried to make me jealous with Lillian all night, and now he's jealous of Lillian's girlfriend winking at me.

All of this juvenile back-and-forth—he's jealous, I'm jealous, the old lady at the bar is jealous, everyone is jealous—it's annoying. Slightly entertaining, especially now, but still annoying.

"My name is Riley, by the way." She takes a seat at the end of the bar. "I'm sure your rude-ass boyfriend isn't planning on introducing us."

I glance back at Hardin, expecting him to cuss her out, but he only rolls his eyes, which is pretty restrained for him. He tries to sit at the stool between us, but I grab the back, then place my hand on his arm to help myself get up onto it. I know I shouldn't be touching him, but I want to sit here and enjoy my last night of this minivacation-turned-disaster. Hardin has scared away my new friend, and Landon is probably already asleep by now. I don't have any other options except sitting alone in the room back at the cabin. This seems better.

"What can I get you?" a copper-haired bartender in a jean jacket asks me.

"We'll have three shots of Jack. Chill them first," Riley answers for me.

The woman scans my face for a few seconds, and my heart begins to race. "Coming up," she says finally, and pulls three shot glasses from under the bar and places them in front of us.

"I wasn't going to drink. I only had one before you came," Hardin leans over and says into my ear.

"Drink what you want; I am," I say without looking at him. Still, I silently pray that he doesn't get too drunk. I never know how he'll act.

"I can see that," he says by way of scolding me.

I look at him with scorn, but end up staring at his mouth instead. Sometimes I just sit and stare at the slow movements of his lips when he talks; it's one of my favorite things to do.

Perhaps noticing I've softened somewhat, he asks, "Are you upset with me still?"

"Yes, very."

"Then why are you acting like you aren't?" His lips move even slower. I really need to find out the name of that wine. It was really good.

"I already told you, I want to have fun," I repeat. "Are *you* mad at me?"

"I always am," he replies.

I laugh a little. "Isn't that the truth."

"What did you say?"

"Nothing." I smile innocently and watch him rub the back of his neck with his hand, pinching the top of his shoulders between his thumb and forefinger.

A shot of brown liquor is placed in front of me seconds later, and Riley raises her shot glass to Hardin and me. "Here's to dysfunctional, borderline-psychotic relationships." She smirks and tilts her head back to take her shot.

Hardin followers her lead.

I take a deep breath before welcoming the cool burn of whiskey down my throat.

"ONE MORE!" Riley cheers, sliding another shot in front of me.

"I dunno if I can," I slur. "I've never b-been this drunk, never never."

The whiskey has officially taken over my mind, set up camp, and doesn't appear to be leaving anytime soon. Hardin is up to five shots, I lost count of mine after three, and I'm pretty sure Riley should be heaving on the floor from alcohol poisoning by now.

"I feel like this whiskey tastes good," I remark, dipping my tongue into the chilled shot.

Next to me, Hardin laughs, and I lean into his shoulder and put my hand on his thigh. His eyes immediately follow my hand, and I quickly pull it away. I shouldn't be acting like nothing happened earlier—I know I shouldn't, but it's easier said than done. Especially when I can barely think straight and Hardin looks so good in his white button-down shirt. I'll deal with our problems tomorrow.

"See, all you needed was a little whiskey to loosen up." Riley slams her empty shot glass on the bar top, and I giggle.

"What?" she barks.

"You and Hardin are the same." I cover my mouth to conceal my obnoxious giggles.

"No we aren't," Hardin says, speaking at that slower pace he resorts to when he's intoxicated. So does Riley.

"Yes—you are! It's like a mirror." I laugh. "Does Lillian know you're here?" I swing my head to the side and ask her.

"Nope. She's asleep for now." She licks her lips. "But I fully intend on waking her up when I return."

The music starts to increase in volume again, and I watch the copper-haired woman climb onto the bar for probably the fourth time tonight.

"Again?" Hardin scrunches his nose, and I laugh.

"I think it's funny." I think everything is funny right now.

"I think it's lame, and it interrupts me every thirty minutes," he gripes.

"You should go up there." Riley nudges me.

"Up where?"

"The bar, you should dance on the bar."

I shake my head and laugh. And blush. "No way!"

"Come on—you've been whining about being young and having fun, or whatever the hell you were going on and on about. Now's your chance. Dance on the bar."

"I can't dance." It's true. I've only danced, excluding slow dancing, once, and that was at the nightclub in Seattle.

"No one will notice—they're all even more wasted than you." She raises a brow, challenging me.

"No fucking way," Hardin says.

Through my drunken haze I remember one thing: I'm sure as hell done letting him tell me what I can and can't do.

Without a word, I reach down and unfasten the horribly uncomfortable straps around my ankles and let my high heels drop to the floor.

Hardin's eyes are wide as I climb on top of the stool, then onto the bar. "What are you doing?" He stands and looks behind us as the few patrons left in the bar begin to cheer. "Tess . . ."

The song gets louder, and the woman who has been serving us drinks smiles wickedly at me and takes my hand. "Do you know any line dances, honey?" she yells

I shake my head, suddenly unsure of myself.

"I'll teach you!" she yells.

What the hell was I thinking? I just wanted to prove a point to Hardin, and look where it got me—on top of a bar getting ready to attempt a dance . . . of some kind. I'm not even sure what a line dance is, exactly. If I'd known I was going to be up here, I would have planned it out better and paid more attention to the women when they were dancing earlier.

chapter forty-eight

HARDIN

Riley's looking up at Tessa standing in front of her on the bar. "Damn, I didn't think she would actually do it!" she calls.

Neither did I, but then again, she seems determined to push my buttons tonight.

Riley looks at me, her face aglow. "She's quite the wild child."

"No . . . she's not," I quietly disagree. Tessa looks mortified, obviously second-guessing her impulsive decision. "I'm going to help her down." I begin to lift my hand up, but Riley smacks it down.

"Let her do it, man."

I look at Tessa again. The woman who made our drinks is speaking to her, but I can't make out what she's saying. This is absolute bullshit, her dancing on a bar in a short-ass dress. If I was to lean onto the bar, I could see up her dress, as can anyone else at the bar. It occurs to me that Riley probably already is. I glance down the bar both ways, take note that neither of the greasy men at the opposite end are eyeing her. Yet.

Tessa watches the woman next to her, her brows furrowed in concentration—completely the opposite of her sudden need to be "wild." She follows the movements of the old gal and kicks out one of her legs, then the other, followed by a swift movement of her hips.

"Sit down and enjoy the show," Riley says next to me, sliding over one of her backup drinks.

I'm drunk—too drunk—but my mind is clear as I watch Tessa

begin to move, really fucking move. Her hands go to her hips, and she finally smiles, no longer caring that she has the full attention of almost everyone in the bar. Her eyes meet mine, and she fumbles her dance moves momentarily before collecting herself and directing her eyes to the back of the room.

"Hot, isn't it?" Riley smiles next to me as she brings her glass to her lips.

Yes, obviously, watching Tessa on the bar is hot as hell, but it's also infuriating and unexpected. The first thought that comes to mind is: *Fuck, this is hot*. The second thought is that I shouldn't be so engrossed in it and should be irritated at her constant need to defy me. But I can't think straight because of that first thought and the fact that she's dancing right in front of me.

The way her dress is riding up her thighs, the way she's holding her hair back in one hand and laughing while trying to keep up with the woman next to her . . . I love to see her this way, so carefree. I don't see her laugh like that very often. A thin layer of sweat has coated her body, making her glow under the spotlights. I shift uncomfortably and pull the ridiculous dress shirt I'm wearing down in the front a little.

"Uh-oh," Riley says.

"What?" I snap out of my trance and follow her eyes down the bar. Two men at the end of the bar are gawking at Tessa, and by gawking I mean their fucking eyes are bulging worse than my fucking dick right now.

I look back up at Tessa, and her dress is dangerously high on her thighs; each time she kicks her legs out in front of her, it goes a little higher.

That's enough of this shit.

"Easy, killer," Riley says. "The song will be over in . . ." And then she raises her hand and waves it as the music fades.

chapter forty-nine

TESSA

Hardin's hand reaches for mine to aid me, and I'm surprised. By the way he was scowling and pouting the entire time I was dancing, I thought he'd be yelling by now. Or worse, I was half expecting him to climb up and drag me off the bar, then start a brawl with all the customers.

"See, no one noticed that you're a shitty dancer!" Riley laughs, and I sit down on the cool bar top.

"That was actually so much fun!" I yell, and once again the music stops. I laugh and jump down from the bar, Hardin's arm wrapped protectively around me until I'm steady enough for him to retreat.

"You should get up there next time!" I say into Hardin's ear, and he shakes his head.

"No," he says solemnly.

"Don't pout, it's not cute." I reach out and touch his lips. It *is* cute, though, the way his bottom lip sticks out. His eyes shine at the contact, and my pulse quickens. I already feel high from the adrenaline that came from dancing on the bar top, something I never in my life thought I would do. As much fun as it was, I know I'll never do it again. Hardin sits down on the bar stool, and I stay standing between him and Riley, next to my empty stool.

"You love it." He smiles, my fingers still pressed against his lips.

"Your lips?" I say with a smirk.

He shakes his head. He's playful yet very serious at the same time, and it's intoxicating, he's intoxicating, and I'm highly intoxicated. This should be interesting.

"No, pissing me off. You love to piss me off." His tone is dry.

"No. You just get pissed off too easily."

"You were dancing on a bar in front of a roomful of people." His face is mere inches from mine, and his breath is a heady combination of mint and whiskey. "Obviously that would get to me, Tessa. You're lucky I didn't pull you down, put you over my shoulder, and carry you out of this place."

"Over your shoulder, not your knee?" I tease and stare into his eyes, completely disarming him.

"Wh-what?" he stutters.

I laugh before turning to Riley. "Don't let him fool you, he loved that shit," she whispers to me, and I nod. My stomach tightens at the thought of Hardin watching me, but my mind tries to overrule my dirty thoughts. I should be fuming, I should be ignoring him or yelling at him over sabotaging Seattle for me, again, or for the hurtful words he said to me, but it's nearly impossible to be pissed off when I'm this drunk.

I allow myself to pretend that none of that happened, at least for now, and imagine that Hardin and I are a normal couple out with our friend having a drink. No lies, no dramatic fights, only fun and table dancing.

"I still can't believe I actually did that!" I say to both of them.

"Me either," Hardin grumbles.

"I won't be doing it again, that's for sure." I swipe my hand across my forehead. I'm sweaty and it's hot in the small bar; the air is thick and I need to breathe.

"What's wrong?" he asks.

"Nothing, it's hot." I fan myself with my hand, and he nods once.

"Let's go, then, before you pass out."

"No, I want to stay longer. I'm such having fun. I mean, such a fun time."

"You can't even form a coherent sentence."

"So? Maybe I don't want to. Either you loosen up or you can go."

"You . . ." he begins, but I cover his mouth with my palm.

"Shh . . . for once just shh. Let's have fun." I use my other hand to touch his thigh again, squeezing this time.

"Fine," he says into my hand.

I uncover his mouth, but I keep my hand inches away so I can cover it again if I need to.

"No more dancing on the bar," he says, gently negotiating.

"Fine. No more pouting or scowling," I fire back.

He smiles. "Fine."

"Stop saying 'fine.' " I bite back a grin.

He nods. "Fine."

"You're annoying-ish."

"Annoying-ish? What would your Literature professor say to that kind of grammar?" Hardin's eyes are deep jade, alight with humor, splashed bloodshot from the liquor.

"You're funny sometimes." I lean into him.

He hooks his arm around my waist and brings me between his legs. "Sometimes?" He kisses my hair, and I relax in his grip.

"Yep, only sometimes."

He chuckles and doesn't let me go. I don't think I want him to. I know I should, but I don't. He's drunk and playful, and the alcohol in my system makes me lose sight of all common sense . . . as always.

"Look at the two of you getting along." Riley holds her hands up to us like we're on display.

"She's so annoying," Hardin huffs.

"Twins." I laugh, and he shakes his head at me.

* * *

"LAST CALL!" My new friend calls from behind the bar. In the last hour I have learned that her name is Cami, that she's nearly fifty, and that she just had her first grandchild in December. She shoved some printed pictures in my face, like every grandmother does, and I praised them, telling her how beautiful the child is. Hardin barely glanced at the images. Instead he started mumbling something about trolls, and so I quickly pulled the picture away from him before Cami heard.

I sway from side to side. "One more and I'm so done."

"I don't know how you haven't passed out yet!" Riley exclaims, with obvious admiration.

I do: Hardin has been taking my drinks from me halfway through and finishing them himself.

"*You've* been drinking more than anyone, probababally more than himmm," I slur, pointing to the man at the end of the bar who has literally passed out with his head on the top of the bar. "I wish Lillian could've came with us," I say, and Hardin crinkles his nose.

"I thought you hated her?" he asks, and Riley snaps her head to me.

"I don't hate her," I correct him. "I didn't like her when you were trying to make me jealous by hanging out with her."

Riley tenses, looking at Hardin beside me. "What?"

Shit.

"Don't back away now, darling," she presses.

I'm trapped and drunk and have no idea what the hell to say. I don't want to make her mad, that's for sure.

"Nothing," Hardin says to her and holds up a hand. "I was being a dick and didn't tell Tessa that she was gay. You already know that."

Her shoulders relax. "Oh, okay, then."

Jeez, she's just like him.

"See, nothing happened, so chill out," Hardin says to her.

"I'm chill, trust me," she coos and moves her stool slightly closer to mine. "Nothing wrong with a little jealousy, right?" Riley looks at me with a glint in her drunken gaze. "Have you ever kissed a girl, Tessa?"

My scalp prickles, and I gasp dramatically. "What?"

"Riley, what the—" Hardin says, but she cuts him off.

"I'm only asking a question. Have you ever kissed a girl?"

"No."

"Have you ever thought about it?"

Drunk or not, I feel the embarrassment creeping onto my cheeks. "I—"

"Being with a girl is much better, honestly. They're soft." Her hand moves to my arm. "They know exactly what you want . . . where you want it."

Hardin reaches up and swipes her hand from my skin. "Enough," he growls, and I pull my arm away.

Riley breaks into uncontrollable laughter. "I'm sorry! I'm sorry! I couldn't resist. *He* started it." She nods toward Hardin through her convulsions and then stops to look at him with a big smile. "I warned you earlier not to fuck with me."

I let out a breath, extremely relieved that she was only trying to get a rise out of Hardin. A giggle bursts from my mouth, and Hardin looks mortified, pissed off, and . . . maybe slightly turned on?

"You're paying for the drinks, since you want to be an asshole," Hardin says, pushing the long piece of paper past me and in front of her.

Riley rolls her eyes and reaches into her back pocket, pulling out a card and placing it on top of the receipt. Cami quickly swipes it and goes to attend to the passed-out man at the other end of the bar.

As we get to the door, Riley announces, "Well, we closed down the bar—Lil is going to be *pissed*."

Hardin holds the door for me to walk out. He almost closes it in her face, but I reach out to stop it and give him a hard glare. He laughs and shrugs as if he did nothing wrong, and I can't stop the smile on my face. He's a jerk, but he's my jerk.

Isn't he?

Nothing's for certain, but I sure as hell don't want to think about that while walking back to the cabin at two in the morning.

"Will she still be asleep?" I ask Riley.

"I sure as hell hope so."

I hope everyone in our cabin is asleep, too. The last thing I want is for Ken or Karen to be awake as we stumble through the front door.

"What? Are you afraid she'll scold you or something?" Hardin taunts her.

"No . . . well, yes. I don't want to upset her. I'm already skating on thin ice."

"Why?" I ask nosily.

"Doesn't matter," Hardin says, dismissing me and leaving Riley lost in thought.

The remainder of the walk is spent in near silence. I count my steps and laugh occasionally when I recall my bar-dancing experience.

When we reach Max's cabin, Riley hesitates before departing. "It was . . . nice to meet you," she says. I can't help but laugh at the comical way she scrunches her face, as if the words taste sour coming out of her mouth.

I smile. "You, too; it was fun." For a moment I think about hugging her, but that would be awkward and I get the feeling Hardin wouldn't like it at all.

"Bye," Hardin simply states without stopping.

When we're almost to the cabin, it hits me how tired I am

and how I'm so thankful to be close. My feet are aching, and the harsh fabric of this itchy, uncomfortable dress has surely scratched my skin.

"My feet hurt," I whine.

"Come here, I'll carry you," Hardin offers.

What? I giggle.

He smiles uncertainly. "Why are you looking at me like that?"

"You just offered to carry me."

"And . . ."

"It's just unlike you, that's all." I shrug, and he steps closer, hooks his arm under my legs, and lifts me into his arms.

"I would do anything for you, Tessa. You shouldn't be surprised that I'd carry you up a damn driveway."

I don't speak, I just laugh. Hard. Uncontrollable laughter racks my body. I cover my mouth to stop it, but it doesn't help one bit.

"Why are you laughing?" His face is stone, serious and intimidating.

"I don't know . . . that was just funny," I say.

We reach the porch, and he shifts me slightly so he can turn the knob on the door. "Me telling you that I'd do anything for you is funny?"

"You'll do anything for me—except go to Seattle, marry me, or have children with me?" Even in my drunkenness, the irony is not lost on me.

"Don't start with me; we're too drunk to have this conversation right now."

"Ooooh," I immaturely remark, knowing that he's right.

Hardin shakes his head and walks up the stairs. I latch on to his neck, and he smiles down at me despite his curt behavior.

"Don't drop me," I whisper, and he lets go of me just enough to slide me down his torso. I turn and wrap my legs around his waist, letting out a small yelp as I cling to his body.

"Shh, if I was going to drop you," he threatens, "it would be from the top."

I do my best to look appalled. A wicked grin spreads over his face, and I lean up and stick my tongue out at him, touching the end of his nose with it.

I blame the whiskey.

At the end of the hall, a light clicks on, and Hardin hurries to the room we're sharing. "You woke them up," he says and places me on the bed. I lean down to remove my shoes, rubbing my sore ankles as I drop the monstrous shoes to the floor.

"Your fault," I say and walk past him and open the dresser drawer to dig out something more comfortable to sleep in. "This dress is killing me," I groan, reaching behind me to unzip it. It was much easier to zip it when I was sober.

"Here." Hardin moves behind me and brushes my hand aside. "What the hell?"

"What?"

His fingers trace over my skin, raising goose bumps. "Your skin is red, like the dress left these marks on you." He touches a spot under my shoulder blade and pushes the fabric down my back until it hits the floor.

"It was really uncomfortable," I whine.

"I can see that." He circles me with hungry eyes. "Nothing is supposed to be marking you, except me."

I gulp. He's drunk, playful, and his dark eyes give away exactly what he's thinking.

"Come here." He steps toward me, closing the small gap between us. He's fully dressed, and I'm only in a bra and panties.

I shake my head. "No . . ." I know there's something I have to say to him, I just can't recall what it is. I can barely remember my name when he's looking at me this way.

"Yes," he counters, and I back away.

"I'm not having sex with you."

He grabs me by the arm and pushes his free hand into my hair, gently tugging at it so I'm forced to look up at him. His breath fans across my face, his lips only inches from mine. "And why is that?" he asks.

"Because . . ." My mind scrambles for answers as my subconscious begs for the rest of my clothes to be torn off. "I'm upset with you."

"So? I'm upset with you, too." His lips graze over my skin, trailing along my jawline. My knees are weak, my mind is heavy and cloudy.

I crinkle my brow and ask, "Why would you be? I didn't do anything." My stomach clenches when his hands move to my backside, squeezing and kneading slowly.

"Your little show on the bar was enough to send me to the fucking madhouse, not to mention the fact that you were parading around town with that fucking waiter; you disrespected me in front of everyone by staying with him." His tone is threatening, but his lips are soft as they travel down to my neck. "I want you so bad, I wanted you at that shitty bar. After watching you dance like that, I wanted to take you into the bathroom and fuck you against the wall." He presses himself against me, and I can feel how hard he is.

As much as I want him, I can't allow him to blame everything on me.

"You . . ." I close my eyes, relishing the feeling of his hands on me, his lips on me. "You are the one . . ." I can't form a solid thought, let alone make a sentence. "Stop it."

I grab his hands to stop them from groping me further.

His eyes flash, and he drops his hands to his sides. "You don't want me?"

"Of course I do, I always do. I just . . . I'm supposed to be mad."

"Be mad tomorrow," he says with that evil grin of his.

"I always do that, I need to—"

"Shh . . ." He covers my mouth with his lips and kisses me, hard. My lips part, and he takes full advantage, tugging at my hair once more, dipping his tongue into my mouth, and pulling me as close to his body as possible.

"Touch me," he begs, reaching for my hands. I don't have to be told twice; I want to touch him, and he needs the reassurance. This is the way we deal with things, and as unhealthy as it is, it doesn't feel that way when he's kissing me like this and begging me to put my hands on him.

I fumble for the buttons on his shirt, and he groans impatiently, using both hands to tug at either side of it, popping off the buttons.

"I liked that shirt," I say into his mouth, and he smiles, his lips against mine.

"I hated it."

I push the fabric down past his shoulders and let it fall to the floor. His tongue is slow in my mouth, and I'm melting in his arms at the rough yet incredibly sweet kiss. I feel the anger and frustration behind his lips, but he does his best to hide it. He's always hiding.

"I know you'll leave me soon," he says, moving his lips down to my neck again.

"What?" I pull back a little, surprised by his words, and confused.

My heart aches for him, the liquor making me even more sympathetic toward his feelings. I love him, I love him so much. But he makes me feel so weak, so vulnerable. The moment I allow myself to believe he's worried, sad, or upset in any way, it's like all my emotions shift, only focusing on him and not myself or how I feel.

"I love you so," he whispers, dragging his thumb slowly across my lips. His bare chest and torso look heavenly against his black jeans, and I know I'm at his complete mercy.

"Hardin, what—"

"Let's talk later. I want to feel you." He guides me to the bed, and I try to ignore my mind screaming at me to stop him, not to give in to him. I can't, though. I'm not strong enough to stop myself when his callused hands are running up my thighs, pushing them open slightly, when he's teasing me with an index finger running over my panties.

"Condom," I pant, and his bloodshot eyes meet mine.

"What if we don't use one? What if I come inside of you, you wouldn't be . . ."

But he stops himself, and I'm glad. I don't think I'm prepared for whatever it was he was going to say. He lifts himself off of me, stands to his feet, and saunters over to the suitcase on the floor. I lie back, staring at the ceiling, trying to sift through my drunken thoughts. *Do I really need Seattle? Is Seattle important enough to me to lose Hardin?* The pain that courses through me at the thought is nearly unbearable.

"Are you fucking kidding me?" he says from across the room.

When I sit up, he's staring down at a small piece of paper in his hand.

"What the fuck is this?" he asks as his eyes meet mine.

"What?" I look down at the floor; my dress lies in a pile on the dark hardwood with my shoes. At first I'm a little confused, but then I look down and see my bra lying on the floor. *Shit.* I hop up quickly and attempt to grab the paper from him.

"Don't play stupid with me—you got his *fucking number*?" He gapes, holding the paper above his head so I have no chance of taking it back.

"It wasn't like that, I was mad and he was—"

"Bullshit!" he shouts.

Here we go. I know that look. I still remember the first time I saw that look on his face. He was pushing over the cabinet at his father's house the first time I saw his face twisted in anger this way. "Hardin—"

"Go on, call him. Let him fuck you—because I sure as hell don't want to."

"Don't overreact," I beg. I'm too drunk to get into a screaming match with him.

"*Overreact?* I just found another guy's number in your dress," he hisses through his teeth, jaw clenched in annoyance.

"You aren't innocent here either," I remark as he paces back and forth. "If you're going to yell at me, save your breath. I'm done fighting with you every single day," I say with a sigh.

He points at me angrily. "You do this! You're the one that constantly enrages me; it's your fault that I'm like this, and you know it!"

"No! No, it's not." I struggle to keep my voice down. "You can't blame everything on me. We both make mistakes."

"No, *you* make mistakes. A shit ton of them, and I'm sick of it." He tugs at his hair. "You think I want to be this way? Fuck no, I don't. You do this to me!"

I stay quiet.

"Go on, cry," he says, mocking me.

"I'm not going to cry."

His eyes go wide. "Well, surprise, surprise." He claps his hands in the most degrading way possible.

I laugh. Which stops him.

"Why are you laughing?" He stares at me for a beat. "Answer me."

I shake my head. "You're fucked up. I mean colossally fucked up."

"And you're a selfish bitch. What else is new?" he snaps, and my laughter comes to an abrupt halt.

I rise from the bed without a word, without a tear, and grab a T-shirt and shorts from the drawer. I pull them on hastily as he watches me.

"Where do you think you're going?" he asks.

"Leave me alone."

"No, come here." He reaches for me and I desperately want to slap him, but I know he'll stop me.

"No, get off of me!" I shake my arm from his grip. "I'm done. I'm so done with this back-and-forth. I'm tired and exhausted, and I don't want to do it anymore. You don't love me—you want to possess me, and I won't let you." I look straight into his brilliant green eyes. Straight through them, and say, "You're broken, Hardin, and I can't fix you."

His face falls at the realization of what he's done to me, and to himself, and he stands in front of me with all emotion pulled out of him. His shoulders sink, and his eyes are no longer brilliant as he stares back at me, finally seeing a blank expression mirrored back at him. I have nothing left to say, he has nothing left to break inside of me or himself, and by the way the color has drained from his face, he's finally realized it.

chapter fifty

TESSA

Landon opens the door, rubbing his eyes. He's half dressed, wearing only plaid pants, no shirt or socks.

"Can I sleep in here?" I ask him, and he nods drowsily, not asking any questions. "I'm sorry for waking you up," I whisper to him.

"It's okay," he mumbles, and stumbles back to the bed. "Here, you can have this one, the other is flat." He pushes a fluffy white pillow against my chest.

I smile, hugging the pillow close and sitting on the edge of the bed. "This is why I love you. Well, not the only reason, but one of them."

"Because I gave you the best pillow?" His smile is even more adorable when laced with sleep.

"No, because you're always here for me . . . *and* you have soft pillows." My voice is so slow when I'm drunk . . . it's odd.

Landon lies back on the bed and moves his body over so that there's plenty of room for me on the other side. "Is he going to come in here after you?" he asks quietly.

"I don't think so." The moment of humor that came with Landon and his soft pillows has been replaced by the ache of Hardin and the words we exchanged moments ago.

I lie down on my side and look over at Landon lying next to me. "Remember when you said he isn't a lost cause?" I whisper.

"Yeah."

"Do you really believe that?"

"Yeah, I do." He pauses. "Unless he did something else . . ."

"No, well . . . nothing new, really. I just . . . I don't know if I can do it anymore. We keep moving backward, and we shouldn't be. Every single time I think we're making progress, he becomes that same Hardin I met six months ago. He calls me a selfish bitch, or basically tells me he doesn't love me—and I know he doesn't mean the words, but every syllable crushes me a little more than the last, and I think I'm starting to understand that this really is just the way he is. He can't help it, but he can't change it either."

Landon watches me with thoughtful eyes before his mouth turns to a frown. "He called you a bitch? Tonight?"

I nod, and he sighs heavily, running his hand over his face.

"I was saying hurtful things to him, too." I hiccup. The heavy combination of wine and whiskey is going to haunt me tomorrow, I know it.

"He shouldn't call you out of your name—he's a man and you're a woman. It's never okay, Tessa. Please don't make excuses for him."

"I'm not . . . I just . . ." But that's exactly what I'm doing. I sigh. "I think this is all about Seattle. He went from getting a tattoo for me and telling me that he can't live without me to telling me he only chases me because I fuck him. Oh my gosh! I'm sorry, Landon!" I cover my face with my hands. I cannot believe I just said that in front of him.

"It's okay—you did just fish your underwear out of the hot tub, remember?" He grins, lightening the conversation, and I hope that the relative darkness of the room at least hides my blushing.

"This trip has been a disaster." I shake my head, pressing it against the cool pillow.

"Maybe not; maybe this is what you two needed."

"To break up?"

"No . . . is that what happened?" He lays another pillow next to me.

"I don't know." I bury my face further.

"Is that what you want?" he asks delicately.

"No, but it's what I *should* want. It's not fair to either of us to keep doing this day in and day out. I'm not innocent here either—I always expect too much from him." My mother's flaws have been passed down to me. She expects too much from everyone, too.

Landon shifts a little. "There isn't anything wrong with expecting things from him, especially when the things that you expect from him are reasonable," he replies. "He has to see what he has. You're the best thing that's ever happened to him; he needs to remember that."

"He said that it's my fault . . . that he is the way he is. All I want is for him to be kind to me at least *half* the time, and I want security in our relationship, that's all. It's pathetic, really." I groan, my voice breaks, and I can still taste the whiskey laced with Hardin's mint on my tongue. "Would you go to Seattle if you were me? I can't help but think I should just call it off and stay here, or go with him to England. If he's acting like this because I'm going to Seattle, maybe I should—"

"You can't not go," Landon interrupts. "You've been gushing over Seattle since the day I met you. If Hardin won't go with you, then that's his loss. Besides, I give him a week of you being gone before he shows up at your doorstep. You can't give in on this; he has to know that you're serious this time. You have to let him miss you."

I smile while envisioning Hardin showing up a week after I leave, desperately begging for my forgiveness with lilies in his hand. "I don't even have a doorstep for him to show up on."

"That was him, wasn't it? The reason that woman wasn't calling you back?"

"Yeah."

"I knew it. Realtors don't just not return calls. You have to go. Ken will help you find somewhere to stay until you find a permanent place."

"What if he doesn't come after all? And worse, what if he does come but he's even more angry because he hates it there?"

"Tessa, I'm only saying this because I care about you, okay?" He waits for my response, and I nod. "You'd have to be insane to give up Seattle for someone who loves you more than anything but is only willing to show it half of the time."

I think about Hardin saying that I make all the mistakes, that *I* make him act the way he does. "Do you think he'd be better off without me?" I ask Landon.

He sits up a little and says, "No, heck no! But seeing as I know you don't tell me even half of the messed-up things he says to you, maybe it really isn't going to work." Reaching across the empty space between us, his hand touches my arm and he rubs slowly.

Using the alcohol in my veins as an excuse, I grant myself permission to ignore the fact that Landon, one of the only people who actually had faith in my relationship with Hardin, has just thrown in the towel. "I'm going to feel like hell tomorrow," I say to change the subject before I break the promise that I made with myself not to cry.

"Yeah, you are," he teases. "You smell like a liquor cabinet."

"I met Lillian's girlfriend. She kept giving me shots. Oh, and I danced on a bar."

He gasps gleefully. "You didn't."

"I did. It was so embarrassing. It was Riley's idea."

"She's . . . interesting." Landon smiles and seems to notice his fingertips still running over my skin. He pulls them away and tucks his arm under his head.

"She's the female version of Hardin." I laugh.

"She is! No wonder she sounds so annoying!" he teases, and in a moment of drunken insanity, I glance over to the door, expecting to see Hardin there with a deep scowl after hearing Landon's playful insult.

"You make me forget about everything." My mouth releases the words before my mind can catch up.

"I'm glad." My best friend smiles and grabs the blanket at the foot of the bed. He pulls it up over both of our bodies, and I close my eyes.

Minutes pass in silence, and my mind is putting up a fight as sleep tries to pull me under. Landon's breathing slows, and I have to keep my eyes closed and pretend that it's Hardin breathing next to me or my mind will never surrender.

Hardin's angry scowl and harsh words float through my hazy thoughts as I finally fall asleep: *You're a selfish bitch.*

"NO!"

Hardin's voice startles me awake. It takes a moment to remember that I'm in Landon's room and Hardin is down the hall, alone.

"Get off of her!" His voice echoes down the hallway seconds later.

I'm out of bed and at the door before he even finishes the sentence.

He has to see what he has. He has to know that you're serious this time. You have to let him miss you.

If I go rushing into that room, I know I'll forgive everything. I'll see him feeling vulnerable and afraid, and I'll say whatever he needs to hear to comfort him.

I pick my heart up off of the floor and walk back to the bed. I place the pillow over my head just as another *"No!"* rips through the cabin.

"Tessa . . . are you . . ." Landon whispers.

"No," I reply, my voice cracking at the end. I bite down on the pillow and break my own promise. I begin to cry. Not for myself. The tears are for Hardin, for the boy who doesn't know how to treat the people that he cares about, the boy who has nightmares when I'm not in bed with him, but who tells me that he doesn't love me. The boy who really does need to be reminded how it feels to be alone.

chapter fifty-one

HARDIN

They won't stop, they won't stop touching her. His dirty, wrinkled hands run up her thighs, and she whimpers as the other man fists her ponytail in his hand, pulling her head back, hard.

"Get away from her!" I try to shout at them, but they can't hear me. I try to move but am frozen on the staircase from my childhood. Her gray eyes are wide, afraid, and absolutely fucking lifeless as she looks at me while a purple bruise already begins forming on her cheek.

"You don't love me," she whispers. Her eyes burn into mine as his hand creeps up and wraps around her neck.

What?

"Yes; yes, I do! I do love you, Tess!" I shout, but she doesn't listen.

She shakes her head as he tightens his grip on her and his friend reaches down between her legs.

"No!" I scream one last time before she begins to fade in front of my eyes.

"You don't love me . . ." Her eyes are bloodshot from his assault, and I can't do a damn thing to help her.

"Tess!" *I flail my arm out across the bed to reach for her. The moment I touch her, this panic will go away, taking with it the fucked-up images of those hands wrapped around her neck.*

She's not here.

She didn't come back. I sit up and click on the lamp on the

nightstand and scan the room. My heart is hammering against my rib cage, and my body is drenched in sweat.

She's not here.

A light knock at the door sounds, and I hold my breath as it creaks open. Please be . . .

"Hardin?" Karen's soft voice fills the room. *Fuck.*

"I'm fine," I snap, and she opens the door further.

"If you need anything, please let me—"

"I fucking said I'm fine!" My hand swipes across the nightstand, knocking the lamp to the floor with a hideous crash.

Without a word, Karen leaves the room, closing the door behind her, and I'm left alone in the darkness.

TESSA'S HEAD lies on the counter, cushioned by her crossed arms. She's still in her pajamas, and her hair is in a nest on top of her head. "I just need to take some Tylenol and drink some water," she groans.

Landon sits next to her, spooning cereal into his mouth.

"I'll get you some. Once we get the car packed up, we can head out. Ken is still in bed, though; he had trouble sleeping last night," Karen says.

Tessa looks up at her but stays silent. I know she's thinking, *Did they all hear me screaming like a pathetic little bitch?*

Karen walks over to open a drawer and grabs a couple of foil packets. I watch all three of them, waiting for someone to acknowledge me. No one does.

"I'm going to go pack; thank you so much for the Tylenol." Tessa's voice is soft as she stands up from her seat at the counter. She takes the medication quickly, and when she sets the glass of water back onto the counter, her eyes meet mine, but she quickly looks away.

It's only been one night without her, and already I miss her so much. I can't get the haunting images from my nightmare out of my mind, especially when she walks past me with no emotion at all. Nothing to let me know that I'll be okay.

The dream felt so real, and she's being so cold.

I stand still for a moment debating whether or not to follow her, but my feet decide for me as they scale the stairs. When I enter the room, she's kneeling down, unzipping the suitcase.

"I'm just going to pack everything, then we can go," she says without turning around.

I nod, then realize that she can't see me. "Yeah, okay," I mutter. I don't know what she's thinking, what she's feeling, or what I should say. I'm fucking clueless, as usual.

"I'm sorry," I say too damn loud.

"I know," she replies quickly. Her back is still turned to me as she begins to refold my clothes from the dresser and floor.

"I really am. I didn't mean what I said." I need her to look at me so I can be reassured that my dream was just that.

"I know you didn't. Don't worry about it." She sighs, and I notice the way her shoulders are slumped lower than before.

"Are you sure . . . I said some fucked-up shit." *You're broken, Hardin, and I can't fix you*—that was the worst possible thing she could have said to me. She finally realizes how fucked up I am, and more importantly, she realizes that there's no cure for what's wrong with me. No one can fix me if it isn't her.

"So did I. It's fine. I have a really bad headache; can we talk about something else?"

"Of course." I kick at a piece of the lamp I broke last night. I have to owe my father and Karen at least five fucking lamps by now.

I feel slightly guilty for snapping at Karen last night, but I don't want to bring it up to her first, and she's probably too *polite* and *understanding* to bring it up herself.

"Can you get your stuff from the bathroom, please?" Tessa asks.

The remainder of my time at that damn cabin is spent this way, watching Tessa as she packs our things and cleans up the broken lamp without another word to me, without really looking at me.

chapter fifty-two

TESSA

I'm so thrilled that we got to see Max and Denise again—it's been years!" Karen gushes as Ken starts the SUV. The bags have been placed securely in the back, and I borrowed Landon's headphones to distract myself during the drive.

"It was nice. Lillian has grown so much." Ken appeases Karen with a smile.

"She has. She's such a beautiful girl."

I can't help but roll my eyes. Lillian was nice and all, but after spending hours under the impression that she was interested in Hardin, I'm not sure if I'll ever care for the girl. I'm grateful that the chances of me seeing her again are slim to nonexistent.

"Max hasn't changed over the years," Ken remarks, his voice low and disapproving. At least I'm not the only one who doesn't care for his arrogance and haughty attitude.

"Do you feel any better?" Landon turns around to ask me.

"Not really." I sigh.

He nods. "You can sleep it off during the drive. Do you want a bottle of water?"

"I can get it," Hardin interjects.

Ignoring him, Landon grabs a thing of water from the small cooler on the floor in front of his seat. I thank him quietly and push the earbuds into my ears. My phone freezes repeatedly, so I turn it off and on again, hoping it will work. This drive will be miserable if I can't drown out the tension with music. I don't know why I never did this before the "great depression," when Landon had to show me how to download music.

I smile slightly at the ridiculous nickname I've given those long days without Hardin; I don't know why I'm smiling, given that those were the worst few days of my life. I feel a similar sensation now. I know that time is coming again.

"What's wrong?" Hardin leans down to speak into my ear, and on reflex I jerk away. He frowns and doesn't make a move to touch me again.

"Nothing, my phone is just . . . it's junk." I hold the device in the air.

"What are you trying to do, exactly?"

"Listen to music and hopefully sleep," I whisper.

He takes the phone from my hand and messes with the settings. "If you listened to me and got a new phone, this wouldn't happen," he scolds.

I bite my tongue and stare out the window while he attempts to fix my phone. I don't want a new one, and I don't really have the money to get one right now, anyway. I have an apartment to find, new furniture to buy, bills to pay. The last thing on my mind is paying hundreds of dollars for something I already paid money for recently.

"It's working now, I think. If not, you can just use mine," he says.

Use his? Hardin is voluntarily offering to allow me to use his phone? This is new.

"Thanks," I mutter and scroll through the song list on my phone before choosing. Soon music floods through my ears and enters my thoughts, drowning out my inner turmoil.

Hardin leans his head against the window and closes his eyes, the dark rings beneath them emphasizing his lack of sleep.

A wave of guilt hits me, but I push it back. Within minutes, the calming music coaxes me to sleep.

* * *

"TESSA." Hardin's voice wakes me. "Are you hungry?"

"No," I groan, not wanting to open my eyes.

"You're hungover; you should eat," he says.

Suddenly I realize that I'm feeling the need for something to absorb all that stomach acid. "Fine," I say, giving in. I don't have the energy to put up a fight today, anyway.

Minutes later a sandwich and fries are placed on my lap, and I open my eyes. I pick at the food and lay my head back on the seat after finishing half of it. But my phone has frozen yet again.

Seeing me start to futz with it, Hardin pulls my earbuds out of my phone and plugs them into his. "Here."

"Thanks."

He's already opened the music app for me. A long list appears on the screen, and I scroll through to find anything familiar. I almost give up, but then my eyes move to a folder named *T*. I look over at Hardin, whose eyes, surprisingly, are closed and not watching me. When I tap the folder, all of my favorite music appears, even songs that I've never mentioned to him. He must have seen them on my phone.

Things like these make me question myself. The small, thoughtful gestures that he tries to conceal from me are my favorite things in the entire world. I wish he'd stop hiding them.

WITH A GENTLE NUDGE, it's Karen who wakes me this time. "Wake up, dear."

I look over and see Hardin is asleep; his hand is on the seat between us, his fingers barely touching my leg. Even in his sleep, he gravitates to me.

"Hardin, wake up," I whisper, and his eyes fly open, wide and immediately alert. He rubs them, then scratches his head and stares at me, gauging my expression.

"Are you okay?" he asks quietly, and I nod. I'm trying to avoid any confrontation with him today, but I'm growing nervous at his calm demeanor. It's usually a precursor to a blowup.

We file out of the car, and Hardin walks to the back to retrieve our bags.

Karen wraps her arms around me and hugs me tight. "Tessa, dear, thank you again for coming. It was a lovely time. Please come visit soon, but in the meanwhile, take Seattle by storm." When she pulls away, her eyes are full of tears.

"I'll visit soon, I promise." I hug her again. She has always been so kind and supportive of me, almost like the mother I never had.

"Good luck, Tessa, and let me know if you need anything. I have a lot of connections in Seattle." Ken smiles and awkwardly wraps an arm around my shoulder.

"I'll see you again before I leave for New York, so no hugs for you yet," Landon says, and we both laugh.

"I'll be in the car," Hardin mumbles and walks off, not even saying goodbye to his family.

Watching him go, Ken says to me, "He'll come around, if he knows what's good for him."

I look at Hardin, who is now sitting in the car. "I sure hope so."

"Going back to England isn't good for him. He has too many memories, too many enemies, too many mistakes there. You're what's good for him, you and Seattle," Ken assures me, and I nod. If only Hardin saw it that way.

"Thank you again." I smile at them before joining Hardin in the car.

He doesn't say a word when I get in; he only turns on the radio and raises the volume up high so I know he doesn't want to talk. I wish I knew what went on inside his mind at times like this, when he's so unreadable.

My fingers fiddle with the bracelet he gave me for Christmas, and I stare out the window as the drive continues. By the time we park at the apartment, the tension I feel between us has grown to an unbearable level. It's driving me insane, yet he doesn't seem to be affected at all.

I move to get out, and Hardin's large hand reaches over to stop me. He brings his other hand to my chin and tips my head up so I have to look at him. "I'm sorry. Please don't be upset with me," he says quietly, his mouth inches from mine.

"Okay," I breathe, inhaling his minty scent.

"You're not okay, though, I can tell. You're holding back, and I hate it."

He's right; he always knows exactly what I'm thinking, but yet he's so clueless at the same time. It's a confusing contradiction. "I don't want to fight with you anymore."

"So don't," he states, as if it's that simple.

"I'm trying not to, but so much happened during that trip. I'm still trying to process it all," I admit. It started with me finding out that Hardin sabotaged my apartment and ended with him calling me a selfish bitch.

"I know I ruined the trip."

"It wasn't only you. I shouldn't have spent time with—"

"Don't finish," he interrupts and drops his hand from my chin. "I don't want to hear about it."

"Okay." I glance away from his intense stare, and he puts his hand over mine, squeezing gently.

"Sometimes I . . . well, sometimes I get . . . *fuck*." He sighs and starts again. "Sometimes when I think about us, I start to get paranoid, you know? Like I don't know why you're with me sometimes, so I act out and my mind starts making me believe that it won't work or that I'm losing you, and that's when I say stupid shit. If you could just forget about Seattle, we could be happy finally—no more distractions."

"Seattle isn't a distraction, Hardin," I reply softly.

"It is. You're only pushing it so much to prove a point." It's amazing how his tone can change from soothing to ice in a matter of seconds.

I look out the window. "Can we please stop talking about Seattle? Nothing is changing: you don't want to go, and I do. I'm sick of going around and around about it."

He pulls his hand away, and I turn back to him. "Fine, what do you suggest we do, then? You go to Seattle without me? How long do you think we would last? A week? A month?" His eyes regard me coolly, and I shiver.

"We could make it work if we really wanted to. At least long enough for me to try Seattle and see if it's what I want. If I don't like it, we can go to England."

"No, no, no," he says with a shrug. "If you go to Seattle, we won't be together at all. That will be it."

"What? Why?" I fumble the words and scramble for my next response.

"Because I don't do long distance."

"You also didn't 'do' dating, remember?" I remind him. It's infuriating that I'm basically begging him to stay in a relationship with me when I should be considering leaving him for the way he treats me.

"Look how that's turning out," he says cynically.

"You were literally just apologizing for lashing out at me two minutes ago, and now you're threatening to end our relationship if I go to Seattle without you?" I gape while he nods slowly. "So let me get this straight: you offered to marry me if I don't go, but if I do go, you're breaking up with me?" I wasn't prepared to bring up his offer, but I couldn't stop the words from coming.

"Marry you?" His mouth falls open and his eyes narrow. I knew I shouldn't have mentioned it. "What—"

"You said that if I chose you, you'd marry me. I know you were drunk, but I thought maybe—"

"You thought *what*? That I would *marry* you?" As he speaks these words, all of the air in the car disappears, and breathing proves harder and harder as the seconds pass in silence.

I will not cry in front of this boy. "No, I knew you wouldn't, I just—"

"Then why bring it up? You know how drunk I was and desperate for you to stay—I would have said anything."

My heart sinks at his words, at the scorn in his voice. Like he's blaming me for believing the bullshit that comes out of *his* mouth. I knew insulting me would be his reaction, but a small part of me—the part that still had faith in his love for me—led me to believe that maybe he meant his proposal.

This is déjà vu. I once sat here, in this car seat, while he mocked me and laughed at me for thinking we would begin a relationship. The fact that I'm just as hurt now, actually a lot more hurt than I was then, makes me want to scream.

I don't, though. I sit there, quiet and embarrassed, just like I always do when Hardin does what he always does.

"I love you. I love you more than anything, Tessa, and I don't want to hurt your feelings, okay?"

"Well, you're doing an amazing job," I snap and bite down on the inside of my cheek. "I'm going inside."

He sighs and opens his car door at the same time as I open mine. Going around to the back, he opens the trunk. I'd offer to help him carry the bags, but I really don't feel like interacting with him, and he'd just insist on doing it himself anyway. Because more than anything, Hardin wants to be an island.

We walk through the complex in silence, and the only noise in the elevator is the whir of the machinery pulling us upward.

When we get to our place, Hardin puts his key in the lock, then asks me, "Did you forget to lock the door?"

At first I don't realize what he's asked, but then I recover and reply, "No, you locked it. I remember." I watched him lock the door before we left; I remember how he rolled his eyes and made a joke about me taking too long to get ready.

"That's weird," he says, and steps inside. His eyes scan the room like he's searching for something.

"Do you think—" I start.

"Someone was in here," he answers, becoming instantly alert as he presses his mouth into a hard line.

I begin to panic. "Are you sure? It doesn't look like anything is missing." I walk toward the hallway but he quickly pulls me back.

"Don't go in there until I look around," he commands.

I want to tell him to stay put, that I will check, but it's silly, really: the idea of me protecting him, when in reality he'd be the one protecting me. I nod, and a chill creeps down my spine. *What if someone really is inside? Who would come into our apartment when we aren't here and* not *steal the giant flat-screen television I can still see hanging on the wall in the living room?*

Hardin disappears into our bedroom, and I hold my breath until I hear his voice again.

"It's clear." He reappears from the bedroom, and I let out a deep breath.

"Are you sure someone was here?"

"Yes, but I don't know why they didn't take anything . . ."

"Me either." My eyes scan the room, and I notice the difference. The small stack of books on the nightstand next to Hardin's side of the bed has been moved. I especially remember the highlighted book I gave him being on top, because it made me smile knowing that he was reading it over again.

"It was your fucking dad!" he suddenly shouts.

"What?" If I'm honest, the thought was already planted in my mind, but I didn't want to be the one say it.

"It had to be him! Who else would know we were gone and come into our home but not steal shit? Only him, that stupid, drunk motherfucker!"

"Hardin!"

"Call him, right now," he demands.

I reach for my phone in my back pocket but then freeze. "He doesn't have a phone."

Hardin throws his hands up like it's the worst thing he's ever heard. "Oh yeah, of course not. He's fucking broke and homeless."

"Stop it," I say with a glare. "Just because you think it may have been him doesn't mean you can say things like that in front of me!"

"Fine." He lowers his arms and makes a sweeping gesture to escort me out. "Let's go find him, then."

I walk over to our landline. "No! We should just call the police and report it, not go on a manhunt for my father."

"Call the police and say what? That your drug-addict father broke into our apartment but didn't steal anything?"

I stop in my tracks and turn to face him. I can practically *feel* my temper flaring through my eyes. "Drug addict?"

He blinks rapidly and takes a step toward me. "I meant drunk . . ." He doesn't look at me. He's lying.

"Tell me why you said drug addict," I demand.

He shakes his head, running his hands over his hair. He looks at me, then down at the floor. "It's just an assumption, okay?"

"And why would you assume that?" My eyes burn and my throat aches at the thought. *Hardin and his brilliant assumptions.*

"I don't know, maybe because that guy who showed up to pick him up looked like your everyday meth addict." He looks up at me with softness in his eyes. "Did you see the guy's arms?"

I remember the man scratching his forearms, but he was wearing long sleeves. "My father is not a drug addict . . ." I say slowly, unsure if I believe the words that are coming out of my mouth, but knowing that I'm not ready to face the possibility.

"You don't even know him. I wasn't even going to say anything." He steps toward me again, but I back away.

My bottom lip trembles, and I can't look at him any longer. "You don't know him either. And if you weren't going to say anything, then why did you?"

He shrugs. "I don't know."

My headache has now intensified, and I'm so exhausted that I feel like I could pass out at any moment. "What was the point of saying it, then?"

"I said it because it just came out, and he broke into our fucking apartment."

"You don't know that." He wouldn't. *Would he?*

"Fine, Tessa, you go ahead and pretend that your dad—who, may I remind you, *is a drunk*—is perfectly innocent here."

His nerve is outstanding, as always. He is calling my father out for drinking? Hardin Scott is calling someone out for their drinking, when he gets so drunk that he can barely remember anything the next day?

"You're a drunk, too!" I say and then instantly cover my mouth.

"What did you say?" Any trace of sympathy drops from his face. He eyes me like a predator, starts circling me.

I feel bad, but I can see he's just trying to scare me into staying quiet. He's so unaware of himself and how he is. "If you think about it, you are. You only drink when you're upset or angry; you don't know when to stop drinking; and you're a mean drunk. You break things and get into fights—"

"I'm not a fucking drunk. I had stopped drinking altogether until you came along."

"You can't blame me for everything, Hardin." I ignore the way my mind is reminding me that I, too, have been turning to wine when I'm upset or angry.

"I'm not blaming you for the drinking, Tessa," he says pretty loudly.

"Two more days and neither of us will have to worry about any of this!" I stalk out into the living room, and he follows.

"Would you just stop and listen to me?" he says in a tone that's electric, but at least it's not yelling. "You know I don't want you to leave me."

"Yeah, well, you do a pretty good job at showing me otherwise."

"What is that supposed to mean? I tell you how much I love you on a constant!"

I see the flicker of doubt cross his face as he shouts the words to me; he knows that he doesn't show his love for me enough. "You don't even believe that yourself. I can tell."

"Tell me this, then: you think you can find someone else to put up with your shit? Your constant whining and bitching, your annoying need to have everything in order, and your attitude?" He waves his hands in the air in front of him.

I laugh. I laugh right in Hardin's face; even with my hand covering my mouth, I can't stop. "My attitude? *My* attitude? You are constantly disrespecting me—you're borderline emotionally abusive, obsessive, suffocating, and rude. You came into my life, turned it upside down, and you expect me to bow down to you because you have this idea of yourself that is complete bullshit. You act like you're this tough guy who doesn't give a crap about anyone but himself, yet you can't even sleep without me! I look past every single one of your flaws, but I will not stand around and let you talk to me like that."

I pace back and forth across the concrete floor, and he watches my every move. I feel slightly guilty for yelling at him this way, but all it takes is remembering the words he just said to me to refuel my anger toward him. "And by the way, I may be a lot to handle sometimes, but that's because I'm so busy worrying about you and everyone else around me, and trying not to piss you off, that I forget about myself. So excuse *me* if I annoy you, or bitch at you when you're constantly lashing out at me for *no damn reason*!"

Hardin's expression is grave. His hands are in fists at his sides, and his cheeks are a deep red. "I don't know what else to do, okay? You know that I haven't ever done this before, you knew going into this that I'd be a challenge. You have no right to bitch about it now."

" 'No right to bitch about it'? This is my life, too, and I can bitch about it if I fucking want to," I say with a snort. He can't be serious. For a second, I thought the expression on his face meant he'd apologize for the way he treats me, but I should have known better. The problem with Hardin is that when he's good, he's *so* good, so sweet and honest that I love him so; but when he's bad, he's the most hateful person I have ever, and will ever, encounter.

I walk back into the bedroom and open the suitcase, tossing my clothes into a pile inside of it.

"Where are you going?" he asks me.

"I don't know," I answer truthfully. *Away from you, I know that.*

"You know what your problem is, Theresa? Your problem is that you read too many damn novels and you forget that they're all bullshit. There are no Darcys, there are only Wickhams and Alec d'Urbervilles, so wake up and stop expecting me to be some goddamned literary hero—because it's not going to fucking happen!"

His words wrap around me and seep into my every pore. This

is it. "This is exactly why we will never work. I have tried and tried with you until I'm blue in the face, I have forgiven you for the disgusting things you have done to me—and to others—yet you still do this to me. Actually, I do this to myself. I'm not a victim, I'm just a stupid girl who loves you too much—yet still I mean nothing to you. Once I leave on Monday, your life will go back to normal. You'll still be the same Hardin who doesn't give a shit about anyone, and I will be the one who is in pain and can barely function—but I did that to myself. I let myself get wrapped up in you, wrapped around your finger, knowing that it would end this way. I thought that when we were separated before, you'd see that you're better off with me than alone, but that's the thing, Hardin. You aren't better off with me. You're better off alone. You'll always be alone. Even if you find another naïve girl who's willing to give everything up for you, including herself, she, too, will grow tired of the back-and-forth and leave you just the way I . . ."

Hardin stares at me. His eyes are bloodshot, his hands are shaking, and I know he's about to lose it. "Go on, Tessa! Tell me that you're leaving me. Better yet, don't. Just pack your shit and get out."

"Stop trying to hold yourself together," I tell him, angry, but also pleading inside. "You're trying not to break, but you know you want to. If you'd just let yourself show me how you really feel—"

"You know nothing of how I really feel. *Leave!*" His voice catches at the end, and I want nothing more than to wrap my arms around him and tell him I would never leave him.

But I can't.

"All you have to do is tell me. Please, Hardin, just tell me that you'll try, really try this time." I'm begging him; I don't know what else to do. I don't want to leave him, even though I know I have to.

He stands there, only a few feet away from me, and I can see him shutting down. Every glimmer of light that my Hardin holds is disappearing slowly, burning out into darkness, and taking the man I love further and further away from me. When he finally tears his eyes away from me and crosses his arms in front of his chest, I can see the way that he's gone now; I've lost him.

"I don't want to try anymore. I am who I am, and if that's not good enough, then you know where the door is."

"That's what you want, then? You're not even willing to try? If I leave, this time it'll be for good. I know you don't believe me because I always say it—but it's true. Just tell me you're only acting this way because you're panicking over me going to Seattle."

Staring at the wall behind me, he simply says, "I'm sure you can find somewhere to stay until Monday."

When I don't respond, he turns on his heel and leaves the room. I stand in place, shocked that he hasn't came back to put up more of a fight. Minutes pass before I finally pick up the pieces of me that he has shattered and pack my bags for the last time.

chapter fifty-three

HARDIN

My mouth keeps saying shit that my mind doesn't want it to say, but it's like I have absolutely no control over it. Obviously I don't want her to leave. I want to pull her into my arms and kiss her hair. I want to tell her that I'll do anything for her, that I'll change for her and love her until I die. Instead, I walk out and leave her standing alone.

I hear her rustling around the bedroom. I know I should go in there and stop her from packing, but what's the point, really? She's leaving Monday, anyway; she may as well leave now. I'm still astounded that she brought up trying a long-distance relationship. It would never work, her being hours away from me, only calling once or twice a day, not sleeping in the same bed. I couldn't do it.

At least if our relationship is terminated, I won't feel guilty for drinking and doing whatever the hell I choose to do . . . But who am I kidding—it's not even that I want to do anything else. I'd rather sit on the couch and have her force me to watch *Friends* over and over than spend one minute doing something without her.

Moments later, Tessa appears in the hallway dragging two suitcases behind her. Her purse is slung over her shoulder, and her face is pale. "I don't think I forgot anything except some books, but I'll just get new copies," she says in a low, shaky voice.

This is it—this is the moment I've feared since the day I met this girl. She's leaving me, and here I am, doing nothing to stop her. I can't stop her; she was always meant to do things greater than me, be with someone better than me. I knew that from the start. I was just hoping that somehow I would be wrong, as always.

Instead of all that, I simply say, "Okay."

"Okay." She gulps and squares her shoulders. When she reaches the door, she raises her arm to grab her keys from the hook, and her purse slides down her shoulder. I don't know what's wrong with me; I should stop her, or help her, but I can't.

Tessa looks back at me. "Well, that's it, then. All the fighting, the crying, the lovemaking, the laughs—everything—it was all for nothing," she says softly. No anger tints her words. Just a blank . . . blank neutrality.

I nod, unable to speak. If I *could* speak, I would make this one hundred times harder on both of us. I know it.

She shakes her head and opens the door, holding it open with her foot so she can drag the suitcases behind her.

Once she's through the door, she looks over at me and says so quietly that it's barely audible, "I will always love you. I hope you know that."

Stop talking, Tessa. Please.

"And someone else will, too, hopefully as much as I do."

"Shh," I gently coax. I can't listen to this.

"You won't always be alone. I know I said that, but if you just get some help or something, learn to control your anger, you could find some—"

I swallow the bile rising in my throat and step to the doorway. "Go, just go," I say, and shut the door in her face. Even through its thick wood, I can hear her sharp intake of breath.

I just slammed the door in her face—*what the fuck is wrong with me?*

I begin to panic, and let the pain course through me. I held it for so long, barely controlled, until she walked away. My fingers go to my hair, my knees hit the concrete floor, and I simply don't know what to do with myself. I'm officially the world's largest fuckup, and there's nothing I can do about it. It sounds so simple: just go to Seattle with her and live happily ever after, but it's not that damn simple. Everything will be different there: she'll be absorbed in her internship and new classes; she'll make new friends, experience new things—better things—and forget about me. She won't need me anymore. I wipe at the tears pooling in my eyes.

What? For the first time I realize just how selfish I am. "Make new friends"? What's so bad about her making new friends and experiencing new things? I would be there, right next to her, experiencing them, too. Why did I go to such lengths to keep her from Seattle instead of embracing this opportunity for her? This opportunity to prove that I could be part of something she wanted. That's all she asked of me, and I couldn't fucking deliver.

If I call her right now, she'll turn the car around and I can pack my shit and find us somewhere, anywhere, to live in Seattle . . .

No, she won't, she won't turn around. She gave me the chance to stop her, and I didn't even try. She even tried to make me feel better while I was watching every ounce of faith she had in me die right in front of my eyes. I should have been comforting her, but instead I slammed the door in her face.

You won't always be alone, she said. She's wrong: I will be, but she won't. She'll find someone to love her the way that I couldn't. No one will ever love that girl more than me, but perhaps they can show her how it *feels* to be loved, how it feels to have someone love you despite all the shit you put them through, the way she was always there for me, always.

And she deserves to have that. Thinking about the fact that getting what she deserves means being with someone else makes it hard for me to breathe. But this is the way it should be. I should have let her go a long time ago instead of sinking my claws further into her and making her waste her time on me.

I'm divided. Half of me knows she'll come back to me tonight, maybe tomorrow, and forgive me. But the other half of me knows she really is done trying to fix me.

SOMETIME LATER, I pull myself up from the floor and pad into the bedroom. When I get there, I nearly collapse again. The bracelet I had made for her sits on top of a piece of paper, alongside her e-reader and a copy of *Wuthering Heights*. I pick up the bracelet, twirl the infinity heart charm between my fingers, and look at the matching tattoo on my wrist.

Why would she leave this here? It was a gift from me to her, at a time when I was desperate to show my love for her. I needed her love and forgiveness, and she gave it to me. To my horror, the piece of paper under the bracelet is the handwritten letter that I wrote her. As I unfold it and read it over, my chest is slowly ripped open and its contents are tossed onto the hard floor. Memories flood my fucked-up mind: the first time I told her that I loved her, then took it back; the date with the blond girl that I tried to replace her with; the way I felt when I saw her standing in the doorway after reading the letter. I continue reading.

> *You love me when you shouldn't, and I need you. I have always needed you and always will. When you left me just last week it nearly killed me, I was lost. So completely lost without you. I went on a date with someone last week. I wasn't going to tell you, but I can't stand to chance losing you again.*

My fingers tremble, and I nearly tear the flimsy paper trying to hold it still enough to read.

> *I know you can do better than me. I'm not romantic, I won't ever write you poetry or sing you a song.*

I'm not even kind.

I can't promise that I won't hurt you again, but I can swear that I will love you until the day that I die. I'm a terrible person, and I don't deserve you, but I hope that you'll allow me the chance to restore your faith in me. I am sorry for all the pain I have caused you, and I understand if you can't forgive me.

She did forgive me, though. She's always forgiven me for my wrongs, but not this time. I was supposed to be restoring her faith in me, yet I continued to hurt her over and over again. My hands work quickly, tearing the pathetic confession into pieces. Falling, they swirl around before settling into a scattered pattern on the cold concrete.

See—I destroy everything! I know how much that damn thing meant to her, and I turned it into a pile of shit.

"No! No, no, no!" I scurry to the ground and frantically try to gather the pieces and restore the page. But there are too many little bits—none of them line up, and I keep dropping them back onto the floor and watching them float here and there. This must be how she felt trying to put me back together. I stand and kick my boot at the pile of scraps I've gathered before quickly bending down and picking them up again and putting them in a pile on the desk. Covering them with a book so they can't blow away, I see I've grabbed *Pride and Prejudice*, of fucking course.

I lie back on the bed and wait for the sound of the door clicking open, signaling her return.

I must wait there for hours and hours, but the click never comes.

chapter fifty-four

TESSA

I lie to Steph. I don't want to tell anyone about my relationship problems, especially right now, when I haven't had a chance to process what just happened. And that's exactly why I called Steph: Landon is too close to the situation, and I don't want to trouble him again. I have no other options, which is what happens when you have exactly one friend and they happen to be your boyfriend's stepbrother.

Well, ex-boyfriend, now . . .

So when Steph sounds concerned on the phone, I tell her, "No, no. I'm fine. I just . . . Hardin is . . . he's out of town with his father, and he locked me out, so I need somewhere to stay until he comes home Monday."

"Sounds like Hardin," she says, and I feel relieved that my lie has worked. "Okay, come on over. Same room as before—it'll be just like old times!" she goes on cheerily, and I try to muster a little laugh.

Great. Old times.

"I'm supposed to be going to the mall with Tristan later, but you can hang out here if you want, or come along. It's up to you."

"I have a lot to do to get ready for Seattle, so I'll just hang around the room, if that's all right."

"Sure, sure." Then she adds, "I hope you're ready for your party tomorrow night!"

"Party?" I question.

Oh yeah . . . the party. I've been so preoccupied with everything that I forgot about the party Steph planned for my going away. As with Hardin's "birthday party," I'm pretty sure his crew would be hanging out and drinking regardless of whether I showed up or not, but she seems like she really wants me to go, and since I'm asking her this big favor, I want to be nice.

"One last time, come on! I know Hardin probably said no, but—"

"Hardin doesn't decide what I do," I remind her, and she laughs.

"I know! I'm just saying, we won't ever see each other again. I'm moving and so are you," she whines.

"Okay, let me think about it. I'm on my way over now," I say. But instead of heading straight to her dorm, I drive around a bit. I have to make sure I'll be able to hold myself together in front of her; no crying at all. *No crying. No crying.* I bite down on my cheek again to stop myself from giving in to the tears.

Luckily I'm used to the pain by now. I'm practically numb to it.

By the time I get to Steph's room, she's in the process of getting dressed. She's pulling a red dress down over some black fishnet stockings when she opens the door with a smile.

"I've missed you!" she squeals and pulls me in for a hug.

I nearly lose it, but I hold firm. "I missed you, too, even though it hasn't been that long." I smile and she nods. It feels like ages ago that Hardin and I met her at the tattoo shop, not a mere week.

"Guess so. It seems like it, though." She grabs a pair of knee-high boots from her closet and sits down on the bed. "I shouldn't be gone too long. Make yourself at home . . . but don't clean anything!" she says, noticing the way my eyes are scanning the messy room.

"I wasn't going to!" I lie.

"You so were! And you probably still will." She laughs, and I try to force myself to do the same. It doesn't work, and I end up making a noise between a snort and a cough, though fortunately she doesn't call me out on it.

"I already told everyone you'd be there, by the way. They were excited!" she adds right as she walks out of the room and shuts the door. I open my mouth to protest, but she's already gone.

This room brings back too many memories. I hate it, but love it at the same time. My old side is still empty, although Steph has covered the bed in clothes and shopping bags. I run my fingers along the footboard, remembering the first time Hardin slept in the small bed with me.

I can't wait to get away from this campus—from this entire town and all the people in it. I've had nothing but heartbreak since the day I arrived at WCU, and I wish I'd never come in the first place.

Even the wall reminds me of Hardin and the time he tossed my notes around the room, making me want to slap him, until he kissed me, hard, up against it. My fingers move to my lips, tracing the shape of them, and they tremble at the thought of never kissing him again.

I don't think I can stay in this room tonight. My mind will be reeling the entire time; memories will be haunting me, playing behind my eyes each time they close.

Needing to find something to do to keep myself distracted, I take out my laptop and try to search for somewhere to live in Seattle. Just as I suspected, it's a lost cause. The only apartment that I can find is a thirty-minute drive from Vance Publishing's new office, and it's slightly over my budget. I save the phone number in my cell anyway.

After another hour of searching, I end up swallowing my pride and call Kimberly. I didn't want to ask her if I could stay with her and Christian, but Hardin has left me no choice. Being Kimberly, of course, she happily obliges, emphasizing how delighted they'll be to host me at their new house in Seattle and bragging a little that it's even bigger than what they're in now.

I promise her that I won't stay longer than two weeks, hoping to buy myself enough time to find an affordable apartment that doesn't come with bars across the windows. Suddenly I realize that with all the Hardin drama I've been dealing with, I'd almost forgotten about the mess at the apartment and the fact that someone broke into it while we were gone. I'd like to think it wasn't my father, but I just don't know if I can believe that. If it *was* him, he didn't steal anything; maybe he just needed a place to stay for the night and he didn't have anywhere else to go. I pray that Hardin doesn't hunt him down and accuse him of the break-in. What would be the point? Still, I probably should try to find him first, but it's getting late, and honestly, I'm a little afraid to be on that side of town alone.

I WAKE UP when Steph stumbles into the room around midnight, tripping over her own feet as she falls onto her bed. I don't remember falling asleep at the desk, and my neck aches when I lift up my head. When I run my hands over it, it hurts worse than before.

"Don't forget your party tomorrow," she mumbles and passes out almost immediately.

I walk over and take her boots off her feet while she begins to snore, quietly thanking her for being a good friend to me and letting me stay in her room with only an hour's warning.

She groans and says something incoherent before rolling over and snoring again.

I'VE BEEN LYING in my old bed reading all day. I don't want to go anywhere or talk to anyone, and I especially don't want to run into Hardin, though I doubt I would. He has no reason to be anywhere near here, but I'm paranoid and heartbroken and don't want to take any chances.

Steph doesn't wake up until after four in the afternoon.

"I'm going to order pizza—do you want some?" she asks, wiping last night's heavy eyeliner from her eyes with a small napkin from her purse.

"Yes, please." My stomach growls, reminding me that I haven't eaten once today.

Steph and I spend the next two hours eating and talking about her upcoming move to Louisiana, and how Tristan's parents are less than pleased with him transferring schools because of her.

"I'm sure they'll come around—they liked you, right?" I encourage her.

"Yeah, sort of. But his family is obsessed with WCU and something like legacy blah blah blah." She rolls her eyes, and I laugh, not wanting to explain to her what it means to families to continue a legacy.

"So, the party. Do you know what you're wearing yet?" she asks, smiling wickedly. "Or do you want to borrow something of mine for old times' sake?"

I shake my head. "I can't believe I'm even agreeing to this after . . ." I almost mention Hardin, but I redirect. ". . . after all the times you've forced me to come to these parties in the past."

"But it's the last one. Plus, you know you won't find anyone even remotely as cool as us to hang with at the Seattle campus." She bats her long false lashes at me, and I groan.

"I remember when I first saw you. I opened the door to this room and nearly had a heart attack. No offense." I smile, and she returns it. "You said the parties were big, and my mother nearly passed out. She wanted me to switch rooms, but I wouldn't . . ."

"Good thing you didn't or you wouldn't be dating Hardin," she says with a smirk, then looks away from me. For a moment I fantasize what it would have been like if I had changed rooms and never seen him again. Despite everything we've been through, I would never want to take any of it back.

"Enough reminiscing—let's get ready!" she cheers, clapping her hands in front of my face before she grabs me by the arms and drags me off the bed.

"NOW I REMEMBER why I hated communal showers," I groan, while towel-drying my hair.

"They aren't so bad." Steph laughs, and I roll my eyes, thinking about the shower at the apartment. Every single thing reminds me of Hardin, and I'm doing my best to keep this fake smile going, but inside I'm burning.

Finally, my makeup applied and hair curled, Steph helps zip me into the yellow-and-black dress that I bought just recently. The only thing keeping me standing and present right now is the hope that the party may in fact be fun and I can have at least two hours of peace.

Tristan arrives a little after eight to pick us up; Steph refuses to let me drive, because she plans on having me drink until I can't see straight. Which is an idea I think I like. If I can't see straight, then I can't see Hardin's dimpled smile or scowl before me every time I open my eyes. Still, it won't stop me imagining him when my eyes are closed.

"Where's Hardin tonight?" Nate asks from the passenger seat, and I panic momentarily.

"Gone. Out of town with his father," I lie.

"Aren't you two leaving Monday for Seattle?"

"Yeah, that's the plan." I feel my palms beginning to sweat. I hate lying and I'm terrible at it.

Nate turns around and offers me a sweet smile. "Well, good luck to both of you. Wish I could've seen him before he left."

The burn increases. "Thanks, Nate. I'll let him know you said that."

When we pull up to the frat house, I immediately regret my decision to come. I knew this was a bad idea, but I wasn't thinking clearly and felt I needed a distraction. This isn't a distraction, however. This is one big reminder of everything I've been through and everything I've subsequently lost.

It's almost humorous, the way I regret coming here every single time but somehow always end up at this damn frat house.

"Showtime," Steph says and hooks her arm through mine with a wild smile.

For a second her eyes brighten, and I can't help but feel as if there's something else behind her choice of words.

chapter fifty-five

HARDIN

When I knock on the door to my father's office, I feel nauseous. I can't believe it's come to this, to me seeking him out for advice. I just need someone to listen to me, someone who knows how I feel, or close to it.

His voice sounds from inside the room. "Come in, dear." I hesitate before entering, knowing this is going to be uncomfortable but necessary. I sit down in the chair in front of his large desk, watching his expression change from expectant to surprised.

A little laugh escapes his mouth. "Sorry, I thought you were Karen." But then, seeing my mood, he stops, watching me carefully.

I nod, then look away. "I don't know why I'm here, but I don't know where else to go." I lay my head in my hands, and my father takes a seat on the edge of his mahogany desk.

"I'm glad you came to me," he says quietly, gauging my reaction.

"I wouldn't exactly say I came to you," I remind him. I did in fact come to him, but I don't want him thinking this is some big revelation or some shit, even though it sort of maybe is. I watch as he gulps and nods slowly, his eyes moving everywhere in the room except to me.

"You don't have to be nervous; I'm not going to throw a fit or break anything. I don't have the energy." I stare at the rows of plaques on the wall behind him.

When he doesn't respond, I let out a sigh.

Of course *that* seems to prompt him, that sign of my defeat, and he says, "Do you want to tell me what happened?"

"No. I don't," I say and look at the books along his wall.

"Okay . . ."

I sigh, feeling the inevitability of this moment. "I don't want to, but I'm going to, I guess."

My father looks puzzled for a moment, and his brown eyes widen, taking me in, watching me carefully, waiting for the catch, I'm sure.

"Believe me," I say. "If I had anyone else to go to, I wouldn't be here, but Landon is a biased asshole and always takes her side." I know this isn't even half true, but I don't want Landon's advice right now. More than that, I don't want to admit to him what a dick I've been and the shit I've said to Tessa over the last few days. His opinion doesn't really matter to me, but for some reason it matters more than anyone else's, save Tessa's, of course.

My father gives me a pained smile. "I know that, son."

"Good."

I don't know where to start, and honestly, I'm still not sure what brought me here. I had every intention of going to a bar to have a drink, but somehow I ended up pulling into my father's . . . no, my *dad's* driveway. The way Tessa only says "mother" and "father" instead of "mom" or "dad" used to drive me insane; but now it's crept into my speech, too. He's lucky I'm even referring to him as "father" or "dad" instead of "Ken" or "asshole"—as I've done for most of my life.

"Well, as you've probably guessed, Tessa finally left me," I admit, and look up at him. He does his best to keep a neutral expression while he waits for me to continue, but all I add is "And I didn't stop her."

"You're sure she won't be back?" he asks.

"Yes, I'm sure. She gave me multiple opportunities to stop her, and she hasn't tried to call or text in"—I glance at the clock on the wall—"almost twenty-eight hours, and I don't have the slightest clue where she is."

I was expecting her car to be in the driveway when I arrived at Ken and Karen's. I'm sure it's one of the reasons I headed over here to begin with. Where else could she even be? I hope she didn't drive all the way to her mum's house.

"You've done this before, though," my father begins. "The two of you always seem to find a way—"

"Are you listening to me? I said she isn't coming back," I huff, interrupting him.

"I'm listening. I'm just curious as to what makes this time different from the others."

When I glare at him, he's staring impassively at me, and I resist the urge to get up and leave his overdecorated office. "It just is. I don't know how I know that—and you probably think I'm a dumb-ass for even coming here—but I'm tired, Dad. I'm so fucking tired of being this way, and I don't know what to do about it."

Fuck. I sound so desperate and fucking pathetic.

He opens his mouth a little, but he stops himself and doesn't say anything.

"I blame you," I go on. "I really do *blame you*. Because if you'd been around for me, maybe you could have shown me how to . . . I don't know—how to not treat people like shit. If I'd had a man in the house while growing up, maybe I wouldn't be such a shitty person. If I don't find some resolution for Tessa and me, I'm going to end up just like you. Well, you before you became this." I gesture to his sweater vest and perfectly pressed dress slacks. "If I can't find a way to stop hating you, I'll never be able to . . ."

I don't want to finish the sentence in front of him. What I want to say is that if I can't stop hating him, I'll never be able to show her how much I love her and treat her the way I should, the way she deserves.

My unspoken words linger there in the stuffy, wood-paneled

study like a tortured spirit neither one of us knows how to exorcise.

"You're right." He surprises me by agreeing at last.

"I am?"

"Yes, you are. If you'd had a father to guide you and show you how to be a man, you'd be better equipped to handle these things, and life in general. I've blamed myself for your . . ."—I watch as he struggles for the words, and find myself leaning forward a little—"*behavior.* The way you are *is* my fault. It all stems from me and from the mistakes I made. I'll carry the guilt for my sins for the entirety of my life, and for those sins, I am so, so sorry, son." His voice catches at the end, and suddenly I feel . . . I feel . . .

Incredibly nauseous. "Well, that's great, that you can be forgiven, but the result is how I *am* now! What am I supposed to do about it now?" I pick at the torn skin around my fingernails and note that my knuckles are surprisingly not busted, for once. Somehow that takes some of the anger out of me. "There has to be something," I say softly.

"I think you should talk to someone," he suggests.

But his answer feels insufficient, and the anger flares back. *No shit I should talk to someone—you don't fucking say?* I wave my hand into the open space between us. "What are we doing right now? We're talking."

"I'm referring to a professional," he replies calmly. "You're holding on to a lot of anger from your childhood, and unless you find some way to let it go, or at least deal with it in a healthy way, I'm afraid you won't make any progress at all. I can't be the one to give you these tools; I caused you all this pain to begin with, and in your angrier moments you'd doubt what I had to say, even if it was helpful."

"So coming here was a waste of my time, then? There's nothing you can do?" I knew I should've hit the bar. I could be on my second whiskey and Coke by now.

"It wasn't a waste of time. It was a really big step in your efforts to become a better person." He makes eye contact with me again, and I can literally taste the whiskey that I should be drinking right now instead of having this conversation. "She'll be so proud of you," he adds.

Proud? Why the hell would anyone be proud of me? Shocked that I'm here maybe, but proud . . . no.

"She called me a drunk," I confess without thinking.

"Is she right?" he asks, concern clear on his face.

"I don't know. I don't think I am, but I don't know."

"If you don't know if you're a drunk, you may want to find out the answer before it becomes too late."

I study my father's face and can see real fear for me behind his eyes. He has the fear maybe I should have. "Why did you start drinking in the first place?" I probe. I've always wanted to know the answer to that question, but I've never really felt like I could ask.

He sighs, and his hand moves up to smooth his short hair. "Well, your mum and I weren't at the best place at the time, and the downward spiral started when I left one night and got drunk. By 'drunk,' I mean I couldn't even walk home, but I found that I liked the way I felt, immobile or not. It numbed me to all the pain I was feeling, and it became a habit after that. I spent more time at that damned bar across the street than I did with you and her. It got to the point where I couldn't function without the liquor, but I wasn't really functioning *with* it either. It was a losing battle."

I don't remember anything before my father became a drunk; I had always assumed he was like that since before I was born. "What was so painful that you were trying to escape?"

"That's not important. What's important is that I finally woke up one day and got sober."

"After you left us," I remind him.

"Yes, son, after I left you both. You both were better off without me. I was in no position to be a father or a husband. Your mum did an excellent job raising you—I wish she hadn't had to do it alone, but it turned out better than with me around."

Anger churns and heats inside me, and I press my fingers into the armrests of the chair. "But you can be a husband to Karen, and a father to Landon."

There, I said it. I have so much fucking resentment toward this man who was a drunk asshole my entire life—who fucked up my life—but who manages to remarry and take on a new son and new life. Not to mention he's rich now, and we didn't have shit while I was growing up. Karen and Landon have everything that my mum and I should have had.

"I know it seems that way, Hardin, but it's not true. I met Karen two years after I stopped drinking. Landon was already sixteen, and I wasn't trying to be a father figure to him. He didn't grow up with a man in the house either, so he was quick to embrace me. It wasn't my intention to have a new family and 'replace' you—I could never replace you. You never wanted anything to do with me—and I don't blame you for that—but, son, I spent most of my life living in the dark—a blinding, desolate darkness. And Karen was my light, the way Tessa is for you."

My heart nearly stops at the mention of Tessa. I was so lost in reliving my shitty childhood that I was able to stop thinking about her for a moment.

"I couldn't help but be happy and grateful that Karen came into my life, Landon included," Ken continues. "I'd give anything to have a relationship with you the way I do with him; maybe one day that could happen."

I can see that my father is out of breath after his long confession, and I'm left speechless. I've never had this type of conversation with him, or with anyone in my life but Tessa. She always seems to be the exception.

I don't know what to say to him. I don't forgive him for fucking up my life and choosing liquor over my mum, but I meant what I said about trying to forgive him. If I don't, I'll never be able to be normal. Really, I'm not even sure I'll ever be able to be "normal" anyway, but I want to be able to go a week without breaking something, or someone.

The humiliation on Tessa's face when I told her to leave the apartment is clear in my mind. But instead of fighting it like I always do, I embrace it. I need to be reminded of what I did to her—no more hiding from the consequences of my actions.

"You haven't said anything," my dad says, interrupting my thoughts. The image of Tessa's face begins to fade, and though I try to hang on to it, it slips away. The only comfort I have is in knowing that it'll be back to haunt me soon enough.

"I don't really know what the hell to say. This has been a lot for me; I don't know what to think," I admit. The honesty in my words terrifies me, and I wait for him to make shit awkward.

But he doesn't. He just nods in agreement and stands to his feet. "Karen is making a late dinner, if you want to stay."

"No, I'll pass," I groan. I want to go home. The only problem with home is that Tessa isn't there. And that's my own damn fault.

I RAN INTO LANDON in the hallway as I was leaving, but I ignored him and left before he could try to force his unsolicited advice on me. I should've asked him where Tessa was; I'm desperate to know. But I also know myself and that I'd show up wherever she is and try to convince her to leave with me. I need to be with her, wherever she is. Listening to my dad's explanation of why he was such a shitty father to me was a step in the right direction, but I'm not miraculously going to be able to stop being a controlling bastard all of a sudden. And if Tessa is somewhere that I don't want her to be—like with Zed, for example . . .

Is she with Zed? Holy shit, would she be with him? I don't think so, but it's not like I've given her the option of having many friends. And if she isn't with Landon . . .

No, she's not with Zed. She's just not.

I continue to convince myself of this as I ride the elevator up to our apartment. Half of me hopes that whoever the asshole was that broke into our apartment is back now; I could really use an outlet for my mounting anger.

A chill runs down my back and over my entire body. What if Tessa had been home alone when the intruder broke in? The image of her flushed, tearstained face from my nightmares flashes in front of me, and my body goes rigid. If anyone ever tried to hurt her, it would be the last thing they ever fucking did.

I'm such a fucking hypocrite! Here I am, threatening to kill someone for hurting her when that's all I seem capable of doing.

After grabbing some water and looking around the empty apartment for a few minutes, I start to get antsy. To keep myself busy, I sort through Tessa's book collection. She left too many behind, and I know it killed her to do so. Just more evidence of how toxic I am.

A leather notebook hidden between two different editions of *Emma* catches my eye, and I run my fingers along the clasp. Pulling it out, I sift through the pages to find that Tessa's handwriting fills each page. Is this some sort of diary that I didn't know she was keeping?

Introduction to World Religion is written neatly on the first page. I sit down on the bed with the book in my hands and begin to read.

chapter fifty-six

TESSA

Logan calls to me from the other side of the kitchen, but when it's clear I can't hear him, he walks over to me. "It was cool of you to come. I wasn't sure if you were going to!" he says with a big smile.

"I wouldn't miss my own going-away party," I say, tilting the red cup in my shaky hands as a sort of toast.

"I've missed you around here; no one has choked Molly in a while." He laughs and tips his head back, pouring clear liquor straight from the bottle down his throat. He swallows it down, blinks, then clears his throat, shaking his head in a way that makes me cringe at the thought of how bad that had to burn.

"You'll always be my hero for that," he teases and offers the bottle to me.

I shake my head and hold up the half-empty cup in my hand. "I'm sure it won't be long until someone else comes along and does it again." I take a moment to smile at the thought.

"Uh-oh! Speak of the devil," Logan says, his eyes focused behind me.

I don't want to turn around. "Why?" I quietly groan, leaning one elbow on the counter. When Logan playfully offers me the bottle again, I accept it.

"Drink up." He smiles and walks away, leaving me with the bottle.

Molly comes into my line of vision and lifts her red cup to me in greeting. "As sad as I am that you're moving away," she says, her voice deceptively soft and sweet, "I'm glad I won't have to see you again. I'll miss Hardin, though . . . the things that boy can do with his tongue . . ."

I roll my eyes at her while I try to think of a comeback but fail. Jealousy runs like ice through my veins, and I contemplate choking her again, right here, right now.

"Oh, go away," I eventually say, and she laughs. It's a hideous noise, really.

"Oh, come on, Tessa. I was your first enemy at college—that counts for something, right?" She winks and bumps her hip into mine as she walks past me.

This party was a terrible idea; I knew better than to come to this place, especially without Hardin. Steph has disappeared, and while Logan was nice enough to keep me company for a minute, he's since found a more available girl to occupy himself with. When I first see the girl, she's in profile, and she looks preppy and wholesome, but when she turns and I glimpse her from the front, I'm shocked to see that the other half of her face is full of tattoos. *Ouch.* I begin to wonder if they're actually permanent as I pour a little more liquor into my cup. I plan to nurse this drink all night and sip it very slowly. Otherwise the facade that I've been struggling to hold up will crumble and fall, and I'll end up being that annoying drunk girl who cries every time someone looks at her.

I force myself to walk a slow lap around the house in search of Steph's crimson hair, but she's nowhere to be found. When I finally spot Nate's familiar face, I see he, too, is working on some girl, and I don't want to interrupt. I feel so out of place here. Not just because I don't exactly fit in with this crowd, but because I have this feeling that even though this party was labeled as our "going-away party," I don't get the sense that anyone here actually cares if Hardin and I disappear. Perhaps they'd show more interest if Hardin had actually come along with me; he *is* their friend, after all.

After sitting alone at the kitchen counter for nearly an hour, I finally hear Steph's voice exclaim, "There you are!" By this point I've eaten an entire bowl of pretzels, and I'm up to two drinks. I've been debating whether to call a cab or not, but now that Steph has finally surfaced again, I'll try to hang in a little longer. Tristan, Molly, and Dan are behind her, and I do my best to keep a neutral expression.

I miss Hardin.

"I thought you left or something!" I call over the music, distracting myself from thoughts of how wrong it feels to be here without Hardin. For the past hour, I'd been battling myself to stay away from his old bedroom upstairs; I want to go in there so badly, to hide from the uncomfortable mass of people, to reminisce . . . I don't know. I keep finding my gaze gravitating toward the stairs, and it's killing me slowly.

"No way! I got you a drink." Steph smiles and takes the cup that's already in my hand. She replaces it with an identical one filled with pink liquid. "Cherry vodka sour, duh!" she squeals at my confusion, and I force an awkward laugh out while I raise the cup to my lips.

"To your last party with us!" Steph cheers, and multiple strangers lift their cups in the air. Molly looks away as I tilt my head back and allow the sweet cherry flavoring to flood my mouth.

"Talk about good timing," Molly says to Steph, and I turn around quickly. I can't decide if I want the person who's just arrived to be Hardin or not, but my dilemma is settled for me when Zed walks into the kitchen dressed in all black.

My mouth falls open slightly, and I turn back to Steph. "You said he wouldn't be here." The last thing I need right now is another reminder of the mess I've made of my life. I said my goodbyes to Zed already, and I'm not prepared to reopen the wounds that came from being friends with him.

"Sorry," she says with a shrug. "He just showed up. I didn't know." She leans into Tristan.

I give her a look emboldened by alcohol. "Are you sure this party is even for me?" I know I sound ungrateful, but the fact that Steph has invited Zed and Molly really bothers me. If Hardin had come, he'd have lost it for sure when Zed entered the kitchen.

"Of course it is! Look, I'm sorry he's here. I'll tell him to stay away from you," she assures me and begins to walk toward Zed, but I grab her arm.

"No, don't. I don't want to be mean. It's fine."

Zed is in conversation with a blond girl who follows him farther into the kitchen. He's smiling down at her as she laughs, but when he looks up and notices my presence, his smile fades. His eyes dart to Steph and Tristan, but they both avoid his gaze and leave the room with Molly and Dan in tow. Once again I'm left alone.

I watch as Zed leans down and says something in the blonde's ear, after which she smiles and walks away from him.

"Hey." He smiles awkwardly and shifts on his feet when he reaches me.

"Hey." I take another sip from my cup.

"I didn't know you'd be here," we say in unison and then laugh uncomfortably.

He grins and says, "You first."

I'm relieved that he doesn't seem to be holding a grudge against me.

"I was just saying that I had no idea you were coming."

"And I had no idea that you were coming either."

"I thought so. Steph keeps saying that this is some kind of going-away party for me, but I'm positive now that she was just saying it to be nice."

I take another sip. The cherry vodka sour is much stronger than the other two drinks I had. "You . . . you're here with Steph?" he asks, closing the space between us.

"Yeah. Hardin isn't here, if that's what you're wondering."

"No, I . . ." His eyes move to my hand as I place the empty cup on the counter. "What is that?"

"Cherry vodka sour. Ironic, isn't it?" I say, but he doesn't laugh. Which surprises me, given they're his favorite drink. Instead, his face twists in confusion as he looks from my face, back down to the cup, and up to my face again.

"Did Steph give you that?" His tone is serious . . . too serious . . . and my mind is slow.

Too slow. "Yeah . . . so?"

"Fuck." He snatches the cup from the counter. "Stay here," he commands, and I nod slowly. I notice that my head is starting to feel kind of heavy. I try to focus on Zed as he disappears from the kitchen, but I find myself distracted by the way the lights above my head seem to be spinning round and round. The lights are so pretty, so distracting in the way they're dancing on people's heads.

The lights dancing? They do dance . . . I should dance.

No, I should sit down.

I lean into the counter and focus on the warped wall, the way it curves and twists, blending into the lights that shine on people's heads . . . or are they shining on the people who are dancing? Either way it's pretty . . . and disorienting as well . . . and the truth is that I'm not sure what's actually happening.

chapter fifty-seven

HARDIN

Scanning through the pages of the little notebook, I'm having a hard time deciding where to start reading. It's a journal from Tessa's religion class; it took me a minute to figure out what the hell it was, because despite the title on the front, each entry is labeled with a word and a date, most of them having nothing to do with religion. It's also less structured than the essays I've seen Tessa write, a little more stream-of-conscious.

Pain. The word catches my eye, and I begin to read.

Does pain turn people away from their God? If so, how?

Pain can turn anyone away from just about anything. Pain is capable of causing you to do things you would never consider doing, such as blaming God for your unhappiness.

Pain . . . such a simple word, but so packed with meaning. I have come to learn that pain is the strongest emotion one can feel. Unlike every other emotion, it's the only one every human being is guaranteed *to feel at some point in their life, and there is no upside to pain, no positive aspect that can make you look at it from a different perspective . . . there's only the overwhelming sensation of pain itself. Lately I've become very well acquainted with pain—the ache has become nearly unbearable. Sometimes when I'm alone, which is more often than not as of recently, I find myself trying to decide which type of pain is worse. The answer isn't as simple as I thought it would be. The slow and steady-*

aching pain, the type of pain that comes when you've been hurt repeatedly by the same person, yet here you are, here I am, allowing the pain to continue . . . it never ends.

Only in those rare moments when he pulls me to his chest and makes promises that he never seems able to keep does the pain disappear. Just as I get used to the freedom, my freedom from my self-inflicted pain, it returns with another blow.

This doesn't have a damn thing to do with religion; this is about me.

I have decided that the hot, burning, inescapable pain is the worst. This pain comes when you finally begin to relax, you finally breathe, thinking that some issue is yesterday's problem, when in fact it's today's problem, tomorrow's problem, and the problem of every day after that. This pain comes when you pour everything into something, into someone, and they betray you so completely—so seemingly on a whim—that the pain crushes you and you feel as if you're barely breathing, barely holding on to that small fraction of whatever is left inside of you begging you to go on, to not give up.

Fuck.

Sometimes it's faith that people hold on to. Sometimes, if you're lucky enough, you can confide in someone else and trust them to pull you out of the pain before you dwell in it for too long. Pain is one of those hideous places that, once visited, you have to fight your way out, and even when you think you have escaped it, you find that it has permanently marked you. If you're like me, you don't have anyone to depend on, no one to take your hand and assure you that you'll make it through this hell. Instead, you have to lace up your boots, grab your own hand, and pull yourself out.

My eyes move to the date at the top of the page. This was written while I was in England. I shouldn't read any more. I should just put the damn book down and never open it again, but I can't. I have to know what else was written in this book of secrets. I fear this is the closest to her I will fucking get anymore.

I turn to another page labeled *Faith.*

What does faith mean to you? Do you have faith in something higher? Do you believe that faith can bring good things to people's lives?

This should be better; this entry shouldn't twist the knife and worsen the ache in my chest. This one couldn't be related to me.

To me, faith means believing in something other than yourself. I don't believe that any two people can possibly hold the same view on faith, whether their only faith is religion-based or not. I do believe in something higher—I was raised that way. My mother and I went to church every single Sunday, and most Wednesdays, too. I don't go to church now, which I probably should do, but I'm still deciding how I feel about my religious faith now that I'm an adult and no longer obliged to do what my mother expects me to do.

When I think about faith, my mind doesn't automatically go to religion. It probably should, but it just doesn't. It goes to him; everything does. He is my every thought. I'm not entirely sure if that's a good thing, but that's the way it is, and I have faith that it will work out for us in the end. Yes, he's difficult and overprotective, sometimes even controlling . . . okay, he's often controlling, but I have faith in him, that he means well, no matter how frustrating his actions. My relationship with him tests me in ways that I never thought imaginable, but every second is worth it. I truly believe that one day his deep fear of losing me will dissolve and we will embrace our future together; that's all I want. I know he wants it, too, though he would never say so. I have so much faith in that man that I will take every single tear, every single pointless argument . . . I'll take it all just to be around to see him on the day when he's able to have faith in himself.

Meanwhile, I have faith that one day Hardin will say what he feels openly and honestly, finally putting an end to his self-imposed exile from feeling things and dealing with them in the way that he should. That one day he will finally see that he isn't a villain. He tries so hard to be one, but deep down he's really a hero. He's been my hero, my tormentor at times, but mostly my hero. He saved me from myself. I spent my life pretending to be someone I wasn't, and Hardin has shown me that it's okay to be myself. I'm no longer conforming to my mother's idea of who I am and who I'm supposed to be becoming, and I thank him dearly for helping me to get to this point. I believe that one day he will see how truly incredible he is. He's so incredibly perfectly imperfect, and I love him so much for that.

He may not show the heroism inside him the conventional way, but he tries, and that's all I can ask for. I have faith that if he continues to try, he will finally allow himself to be happy. I will continue to have faith in him until he has it in himself.

I close the book and pinch the bridge of my nose in an attempt to control my emotions. Tessa believes in me for no damn reason. I'll never understand why she wasted her time on me in the first place, but reading her unedited thoughts this way twists the knife in my chest, pulls it out, and then impales me with its blade once more.

The realization that Tessa is just like me both frightens and thrills me at the same time. Knowing that everything in her world revolves . . . *revolved* around me makes me happy, even giddy, but when I'm reminded that I fucking blew it, the happiness disappears just as fast as it came. I owe it to her and to myself to be better. I owe it to her to try to let go of my anger.

Oddly enough, I feel as if a weight has been lifted from my shoulders since my awkward conversation with my father. I wouldn't go as far as to say that all the ugly, hurtful memories are forgiven, or that we'll suddenly become pals, watching sports together on TV and shit, but I do hate him less than I did before. I'm more like my father than I care to admit. I've tried to leave Tessa for her own good, but I have yet to be strong enough to do it. So, in a way, he's stronger than me. He actually left and didn't come back. If I had a child with Tessa, and I knew I would fuck up their lives, I would want to leave, too.

Fuck that. The thought of having a child makes me nauseous. I would be the worst possible father, and Tessa really would be better off on her own. I can't even show *her* love the way that I should, let alone a child.

"Enough of that," I say out loud and sigh, rising to my feet. I walk into the kitchen and open a cabinet. The half-empty bottle of vodka on the shelf is calling my name, begging me to open it.

I really am a fucking drunk. I'm hovering over the kitchen counter with a fucking bottle of vodka in my hands. I twist the cap off and bring the bottle to my lips. Just one drink will cause the guilt to go away. With one drink I can force myself to pretend Tessa will be home soon. It's worked before to numb the pain, and it will work again. One drink.

Just as I close my eyes and tilt my head back, I can see Tessa's teary eyes flashing behind mine. I open my eyes, turn on the sink faucet, and pour the vodka down the drain.

chapter fifty-eight

TESSA

Mouths are opening. Lips are moving without sounds. And the music is bouncing off of the walls, rattling my mind.

How long have I been standing here? When did I walk into the kitchen? I don't remember.

"Hey." Dan slides in front of me, and I shudder a little where I'm leaning against the counter. His face is a little off-kilter; I stare harder, trying to bring him into focus.

"Hey . . ." My reply comes soooo slow.

He smiles. "Are you okay?"

I nod. I think I do. "I feel weird, sort of," I admit and scan the room for Zed. I hope he comes back soon.

"What do you mean?"

"I don't know, like I feel . . . odd. Like drunk, but slower, but then I have this energy at the same time." I wave my hand in front of my face . . . I have three hands.

Dan laughs. "You must have had *a lot* to drink."

I nod again. Look at the floor. Watch a girl cross in front of me at a snail's pace. "Is Zed coming back?" I ask him.

Dan looks around. "Where did he go?"

"To find Steph about my drink." I lean farther onto the counter. Probably half of my body's on it at this point. I can't really tell.

"He did? Hmm, I can help you find him." He shrugs. "I think I saw him go upstairs."

"Okay," I say. I don't think I like Dan, but I need to find Zed, because my head is getting heavier and heavier.

I follow slowly behind Dan as he pushes through the crowd and heads toward the stairs. The music is amazingly loud now, and I find my head moving slowly back and forth, back and forth as I climb the steps.

"Is he up here?" I ask Dan.

"Yeah. He just went in here, I think." He nods his head toward the door across the hall.

"That's Hardin's room," I inform him, and he shrugs. "Can I just sit here for a minute? I can't walk anymore, I think." My feet feel heavy, but my mind feels like it's getting sharper, and this makes no sense to me.

"Sure, yeah, you can sit in here." Dan grabs hold of my arm and leads me into Hardin's old room. I stumble to the edge of the bed, and memories seem to take shape and swirl in the air around me: Hardin and me sitting on the bed, the same spot I'm in now. I kissed him for the first time. I was so overwhelmed and confused by my growing need to be close to him. My dark boy. That was the first time I got a glimpse of the softer, kinder Hardin. He didn't stay long, but it was nice to meet him.

"Where's Hardin?" I ask, looking up at Dan.

An expression crosses his face, then disappears as he chuckles. "Oh, Hardin isn't here, and you said you were sure he wasn't coming, remember?" He closes the door and locks it behind him.

What's going on? My mind reels with the possibilities, but my body feels too heavy to move. I want to lie down, but an alarm is screeching through my head telling me to fight it. *Don't lie down! Keep your eyes open!*

"O-open the door," I say and try to stand, but the room begins to spin.

As if on cue, there's a knock at the door. Relief floods over me when Dan unlocks the door and it opens to reveal Steph.

"Steph!" I moan. "He's . . . he's doing something." I don't know how to explain it, but I know he was going to do something.

She looks at Dan, who gives her a sinister smile. Looking back at me, she asks simply, "Doing what?"

"Steph . . ." I call for her again. I need her to help me leave this haunted room.

"Stop whining!" she snaps, and I lose my breath.

"What?" I manage to say.

But Steph just smiles up at Dan while she digs her hand through the bag she's brought in. When I moan again, she stops and glares at me. "God, do you ever shut up? I'm so sick of hearing you bitch and complain all the damn time."

My brain isn't working correctly—Steph can't be saying these things to me.

She rolls her eyes. "Ugh, and that stupid innocent pout—like give it a fucking rest, already." After a couple more seconds of digging, she says, "Found it . . . here," and she hands a small object to Dan.

I almost fade out, but a little beep brings me back to consciousness . . . for at least a few more seconds.

I see a little red light, like a teeny-tiny cherry.

Like the cherry vodka sour. Steph, Dan, Molly, Zed. The party. Oh no.

"What did you do?" I ask her, and she laughs again.

"Didn't I tell you to stop whining? You'll be fine," she groans and walks toward the bed. There's a camera in Dan's hand. The red light shows that it's on.

"G-get away from me," I try to yell, but it comes out a mere whisper. I try to stand to my feet, but I stumble back to the bed. It's soft . . . like quicksand.

"I thought you . . ." I begin.

But Steph puts her hands on my shoulders and pushes me back against the mattress. I can't get back up. "You thought what? I was your friend?" She kneels on the bed, hovering over me. Steph's fingers grip the bottom of my dress and begin to pull it up my thighs. "You were too busy being a whore going back and forth between Zed and Hardin to realize that I've actually always despised you. Don't you think if I really gave a shit about you I would have told you that Hardin was only dating you to win a bet? Don't you think a friend would have warned you?"

She's right, and once again my idiocy is glaringly obvious. The sting of betrayal is multiplied by the fuzziness in my head—and when I look at Steph now, the red-haired devil, her face is twisted, distorted in the most evil way imaginable, and the glow of her dark eyes sends a chill through me.

"Oh, and by the way." She laughs. "I hope you had fun waiting on Hardin to show up on his birthday. Amazing what I can do with one little text. So a video camera must be so much worse, huh?"

I try to fight her off, but it's impossible. She easily removes my fingers from where I've dug them into her arms and continues pulling on my dress. I close my eyes and imagine Hardin bursting through the door to rescue me, my knight in black armor.

"Hardin will find . . . out," I threaten weakly.

"Ha ha, yeah—that's the point. Now stop talking."

Another knock sounds at the door, and again I pointlessly try to push her off of me.

"Close the door—hurry," Dan says, and when I crane my neck toward the door, I'm not surprised to find that Molly has joined us.

"Help me get her dress off," Steph says.

My eyes flutter, and I try to shake my head, but it doesn't work. Nothing works. Dan is going to force himself on me, I know it. This was Steph's plan for this party. It was never meant to be a going-away party for me. It was meant to destroy me. I have no idea why I ever thought she was my friend.

Molly's hair falls onto my face when she climbs onto the bed next to me, and Steph pushes me up and rolls over to get better access to the back of my dress.

"Why-y-y?" My voice is broken, and I'm vaguely aware of the tears on my cheeks, now wetting the sheets on the bed.

"*Why?*" Dan echoes, bringing his face close to mine. "Why? Your asshole boyfriend taped himself fucking my sister—that's why." His warm breath on my face feels like mud.

"Whoa!" Molly says loudly. "I thought you said you were only taking some pictures of her!"

"We are . . . and maybe a little video," Steph responds.

"No way! Hell no, dude—you can't have him rape her!" Molly shouts.

"He's not . . . Jesus. I'm not, like, psychotic. He's just going to touch her and make it look like they're fucking so that when Hardin sees the tape he'll fucking lose it. Just picture his face when he sees his innocent little whore of a girlfriend getting fucked by Dan." Steph laughs. "I thought you were into this," she hisses at Molly. "You said you were."

"I'm into pissing him off, but you can't tape this shit." Molly is whispering, but I can hear her clear as day.

"You sound like her." Steph turns me back over after removing my dress completely.

"Stop," I whimper. Steph rolls her eyes, and Molly looks like she might vomit any second.

"I don't know about this anymore," Molly says, panicked.

Steph grabs her shoulder viciously and points. "Well, there's the door, then. If you're going to be a pussy about it, go downstairs and we'll join you in a few."

Another knock at the door, and I hear Tristan's voice. "Steph, are you in there?" he says through the wood. *Not him, too.*

"Shit," Steph mutters. "Yeah, um, I'm talking to Molly. Be out in a minute!"

I open my mouth to scream, but her hand clamps down over my face to silence me. It's sticky and smells like alcohol.

I try to look at Molly for help, but she turns away. Coward.

"Go downstairs, babe. I'll be right there. She's . . . she's upset. Girl stuff, you know?" she lies, and despite all of this mess, I can't help but be relieved that Tristan seems oblivious to his cruel girlfriend's intentions.

"Okay!" he shouts.

"Come over here," Steph quietly instructs Dan. Then she touches my cheek. "Open your eyes."

They open, barely, and I feel Dan's hand trail up my thigh. Fear shoots through me, and I close them again.

"I'm going downstairs," Molly finally says when Dan brings the small camera in front of his face.

"Fine, lock the door," Steph snaps.

"Move over," Dan says, and the bed shifts under me when Steph climbs off and he takes her place. "You hold it."

I try my hardest to replace Dan's hands with Hardin's in my mind, but it's impossible. Dan's hands are soft, too soft, and I try my hardest to replace them with something, anything. I picture the softest blanket that I had as a child touching my skin . . . The door closes, signaling Molly's exit, and I whimper again.

"He's going to hurt you," I choke, keeping my eyes tightly closed.

"Nah, he won't," Dan replies. "He'll want to make sure no one sees this, so he won't do shit." His fingers trace along the top of my panties, and he whispers to me, "This is the way the world works."

I gather up all the strength I can and try to throw him off me, but I only manage to make the bed shake a little.

Steph laughs some evil sound. "Hardin is a dick, okay?" she yells, putting the camera in my face. "And he's always fucking with people: he fucked with Dan's sister, he fucked with me, he led so many girls on, fucked them, then tossed them aside. Until you, that is. Why he likes you so much will never make any sense to me." Her tone is full of disgust.

"Tessa!" Zed's voice booms from somewhere, and Steph covers my mouth again as I hear pounding at the door.

"Keep quiet," she commands. I try to bite her hand. She reaches over and slaps me across the face, but fortunately I barely feel it.

"Open the fucking door, Steph—let me in!" Zed shouts.

Is he in on this, too? Was Hardin right about him? Is everyone around me trying to hurt me? The thought isn't impossible: nearly everyone I've trusted since coming to college has betrayed me. The names just keep piling up.

"I'll break the door—I'm not fucking around. Go get Tristan!" I hear him yell, and Steph immediately removes her hand from my mouth.

"Wait!" she yells, going to the door. But it's too late. The door bursts opens with a loud crack, and Dan's hand is no longer on me. When I open my eyes, he's backing away from me quickly as Zed strides into the room, his presence filling it.

"What the fuck!" he yells, rushing toward me.

A blanket is thrown over my body by someone as I try to reach for him.

"Help me," I beg him, and pray that he isn't involved in this nightmare. That he can actually hear me.

He stalks toward Steph and grabs the small camera from her hands. "What the hell is wrong with you?" Dropping it to the ground, he stomps on it repeatedly.

"Chill out, dude, it was a joke," she says and crosses her arms in front of her just as Tristan enters the room.

"A *joke*? You put something in her drink and you're up here with a video camera while Dan tries to fucking rape her! That's not a goddamn joke!"

Tristan's mouth falls open. "What?"

Ever the manipulator, Steph points an accusatory finger at Zed and starts crying on command. "Don't listen to him!"

Zed shakes his head. "No, man, it's true. Go ask Jace. She asked him for a benzo—and now look at Tessa! The camera they were using is right there." He points to the ground.

Holding the blanket against me, I try to sit up again. I fail.

"It was a prank. No one was going to hurt her!" Steph says with a fake chuckle that seems meant to hide her maliciousness.

But Tristan looks at his girlfriend in horror. "How could you do that to her? I thought she was your friend!"

"No, no, baby, it's not as bad as it seems—it was Dan's idea!"

Dan throws his arms up, also wanting to avoid blame. "What the fuck! No, it wasn't my idea! It was yours." He points to Steph and looks at Tristan. "She has a fucked-up obsession with Hardin . . . it was her idea."

Shaking his head, Tristan turns to leave the room, but seems to change his mind as he swings his fist through the air, connecting with Dan's jaw. Dan crumples to the floor, and Tristan makes toward the door again. Steph starts after him.

"Get away from me! We're done!" he yells and disappears.

Circling, looking at everyone in the room, she yells, "Thanks a fucking lot!"

I want to laugh at the irony of her planning this horror show, then blaming everyone else when it backfires in her face. And were I not lying here, catching my breath, I *would* laugh.

Zed's face hovers above mine. "Tessa . . . are you okay?"

"No . . ." I admit, feeling dizzier than ever. At first it was only my body that was slow; my mind was clouded only slightly, but now I can feel it becoming more and more affected by the drug.

"I'm sorry I left you alone. I should have known better." After Zed tucks the blanket more tightly around me, one of his arms hooks under my legs and the other settles across my back, and he lifts me from the bed.

He starts carrying me out of the room, but he stops in front of Dan, who is just picking himself up off the floor. "I hope when

Hardin finds out about what you did, he fucking kills you. You deserve it."

I'm slightly aware of all the gasps and whispers going on around me as Zed carries me through the crowded house. I don't care, though. I just want to escape from this place and never look back.

"What the hell?" I recognize Logan's voice.

"Can you go upstairs and get her dress and purse?" Zed asks quietly.

"Yeah, sure, man," Logan responds.

Zed backs through the front door, and cold air hits me, making me shiver. At least, I think I'm shivering, but I can't really tell. Zed tries to tighten the blanket around me, but it keeps slipping. I'm not any help, since I can barely move my arms.

"I'm going to call Hardin as soon as I get you into my truck, okay?" Zed says.

"No, don't," I groan. Hardin will be so mad at me. The last thing I want is to be screamed at when I can barely keep my eyes open.

"Tessa, I really think I should call him."

"Please, no." I begin to cry again. Hardin is the only person I want to see right now, but I don't want to know how he'll react when he finds out what happened. If he had been the one to show up instead of Zed, what would he have done to Dan and Steph? Something that would've landed him in jail, I'm sure.

"Don't tell him," I say again. "None of it, shhh."

"He'll find out anyway. Even with the video destroyed, too many people know what happened."

"No, please."

I hear Zed's frustrated sigh as he shifts my body into one arm so he can pull the passenger door of his truck open.

Logan comes back as Zed places me on the cold seat. "Here's her stuff. Is she okay?" he asks with obvious concern.

"Yeah, I think so. She's on benzo."

"What the hell?"

"It's a long story. Have you ever taken it?" Zed asks.

"Yeah, once, but only half, and I passed out after an hour. You better hope she doesn't start hallucinating. Some people have crazy reactions to that stuff."

"Shit," Zed groans, and I can picture him twisting his lip ring between his fingers.

"Does Hardin know?" Logan asks.

"Not yet . . ."

The two of them continue to discuss me as if I'm not there, but I'm relieved when the heater in the truck finally shifts from blowing cold air to warm.

"I need to get her home," Zed finally says, and within seconds he's in the truck next to me.

Looking at me with a worried expression, Zed says, "If you don't want me to tell him, where do you want to go? You can come to my place, but you know how pissed he'll be when he finds out."

If I could form an actual sentence, I'd tell him about our breakup, but since I can't, I make a sound that is something between a cry and a cough. "Mother," I manage.

"You're sure?"

"Yes . . . no Hardin. Please," I breathe.

He nods, and the truck begins to move down the street. I try to focus on Zed's voice as he talks on the phone, but in my attempts to remain sitting up straight, I lose track of what he's said, and within minutes I'm lying across the seat.

Giving up, I just close my eyes.

chapter fifty-nine

HARDIN

Love is the single most important emotion one can hold. Whether it's your love for God or your love for another, it's the most powerful, overwhelming, incredible experience. The moment when you realize that you are capable of loving someone else more than yourself is quite possibly the most important moment in your life. It was for me, anyway. I love Hardin more than myself, more than anything.

My phone vibrates on the coffee table for the fifth time in the last two minutes. I finally decide to answer it so I can tell her off.

"What the fuck do you want?" I bark into the speaker.

"It's—"

"Spit it out, Molly, I don't have time for your shit."

"It's about Tessa."

I stand to my feet, and the journal falls to the floor. My blood is ice cold. "What the hell are you talking about?"

"She's . . . look, don't freak out, but Steph slipped her something and Dan is—"

"Where are you?"

"The frat house." She barely gets the words out before I hang up the phone, grab my keys, and rush out of the apartment.

* * *

MY HEART IS POUNDING out of my chest the entire drive. Why the fuck did I get an apartment so far from the campus? This is hands down the longest twenty-mile drive of my life.

Steph fucking slipped something to Tessa . . . What the fuck is wrong with her? And Dan—fucking Dan is a dead man if he lays one goddamn finger on her.

I run every single red light and ignore the resulting flashes that indicate I'll be getting at least four tickets in the mail.

It's Tessa . . . Molly's voice plays over and over in my mind until I finally reach the old frat house. I don't bother turning off my car—my car is the least of my concerns right now. Crowds of drunken idiots litter the living room and hallways as I push my way through the downstairs in search for Tessa.

My hands wrap around Nate's collar the moment I see him, and I slam him into the wall without a thought. "Where is she?"

"I don't know! I haven't seen her!" he shouts, and I loosen my grip.

"Where the fuck is Steph?" I demand.

"She's in the backyard—I think—I haven't seen her in a while."

I let go of him with a shove, and he stumbles forward with a glare at me.

I stalk out to the backyard in a panic . . . If Tessa is out there in the cold with Steph and Dan . . .

Steph's red hair is bright in the darkness, and I don't hesitate to grab her collar and lift her from the ground by the back of her leather coat.

She starts swatting her arms behind her. "What the fuck!"

"Where is she?" I growl, keeping my fist full of the leather.

"I don't know—you tell me," she spits, and I turn her around to face me.

"Where the fuck is she?"

"You won't do shit to me."

"I wouldn't doubt me, if I were you. Tell me where the fuck Tessa is—*now!"* I scream in her face.

Steph flinches, and her bravado falters for a moment before she shakes her head. "I don't know where the hell she is, but she's probably passed out by now."

"You're a sick, disgusting bitch. If I were you, I would leave this place before I find Tessa. Once I know she's okay, there won't be anything stopping me from coming after you!" For a moment I consider the idea of hurting Steph, but I know I couldn't actually do it. I can't imagine Tessa's reaction if I laid a hand on a woman, even an evil one like Steph.

I turn on my heel and head inside. I don't have time to play games.

"Where's Dan Heard?" I ask a random blond girl I see sitting alone at the bottom of the stairs.

"Him?" she asks, pointing a painted fingernail toward the top of the stairs.

I don't respond but just run over and take the stairs two at a time. Dan isn't aware of my presence until I've tackled him to the ground, knocking over a couple other people along the way. I flip him over and pin him beneath me, closing my hands around his neck. *Déjà fucking vu.*

"Where the fuck is Tessa?" I tighten my grip.

Dan's face is already turning a nice shade of pink, and he makes a pathetic choking sound instead of answering. I clamp my fingers tighter.

"If you hurt her in any goddamn way, I will beat every last breath from your body," I curse.

He kicks his feet, and I look up at the guy he was standing with.

"Where is Tessa Young?" I ask the kid, who just raises his hands in surrender.

"I don't . . . I don't know her, man. I swear!" the pussy yells, backing away as I continue to strangle his friend.

Dan's face has turned from pink to purple. "Are you ready to tell me?" I ask.

He nods frantically.

"Fucking *talk!*" I shout, letting go of him.

"She's . . . Zed." He manages to mutter along with a strained and hollow-sounding cough the moment I remove my hands from his neck.

"Zed?" My vision goes black as all my fears suddenly materialize. "He put you up to this, didn't he."

"No. Zed didn't have anything to do with it," Molly says, stepping out from one of the rooms along the hallway. "He didn't. I mean, he heard Steph talking about doing something, but I don't think he thought she was serious."

I look at Molly with wild eyes. "Where is she? Where's Tessa?" I ask for the hundredth time. Each second that I don't see her, each moment that I'm not assured of her safety, is another blow to my rapidly dwindling sanity.

"I don't know. I think she left with Zed."

"What did they do to her? Tell me everything—now." I stand to my feet and leave Dan on the ground running his hands over his neck as he tries to catch his breath.

Molly shakes her head. "They didn't do anything; he stopped them before they could."

"He?"

"Zed. I went down and got him and Tristan before anything could happen. Steph was being so fucking crazy, like she was going to have Dan rape Tessa or something. She says she was only going to make it look that way, but I don't know, she was acting like a psycho."

"Rape Tessa?" I choke out. *No.* "Did he . . . touch her?"

"A little," she says sadly and looks at the ground.

I look back down at Dan, who is sitting up now. My boot collides with his cheek, and he drops back to the floor immediately.

"Holy shit! You're going to kill him!" Molly shrieks.

"Like you give a fuck," I snap at her and try to gauge just how hard I would have to kick him to permanently indent his skull. Blood trickles down his cheek and out of the corner of his mouth. Good.

"I don't . . . I don't give a fuck about any of this, actually."

"Then why did you call me? I thought you hate Tessa."

"I do, trust me. But I can't sit there and let someone rape her."

"Well . . ." I almost thank her, but I quickly remember what a bitch she is, so I just nod and walk away to find Tessa.

Why was Zed here in the first place? That motherfucker always seems to show up at the right time—the exact moment that will make me look like an asshole, and now, once again, he has saved her.

Regardless of my extreme jealousy, I'm so fucking relieved to know she's away from Steph and Dan and their fucking sick plan for revenge against me. This whole ordeal is just another reminder that every single bad thing in Tessa's life stems from me. If I hadn't done that shit to Dan's sister, this never would have happened. Now Tessa is fucking drugged and she's with Zed. Who knows what the fuck he'll try to do with her.

This is it—this is what hell feels like. Knowing that she was in this mess because of me. She could have been raped because of me.

Just like in my dreams . . . and I wasn't there to stop her. Just like I wasn't able to stop it from happening to my mum.

I hate this. I hate myself so fucking much. I ruin everything and anyone that comes in contact with me. I'm poison, and she's the slowly eroding seraph, holding on to the last bit of herself that I haven't destroyed.

"Hardin!" Logan meets me at the bottom the stairs.

"Do you know where Tessa and Zed are?" The words taste like acid on my tongue.

"They left about fifteen minutes ago—I assumed they were going back to your place," he responds.

So she didn't tell anyone about our breakup. "Was she . . . was she okay?" I ask him and hold my breath until he responds.

"I don't know, she was pretty out of it. They gave her benzo."

"Fuck." I tug at my hair and walk to the front door. "If you hear from Zed before I find them, call me," I instruct him.

Logan nods in agreement, and I run to my car. Thankfully no one has stolen it. However, someone *has* taken the opportunity to be a dick and pour a beer down my windshield and leave the empty cup on the hood. Fucking assholes.

I give Tessa a call, but end up just muttering into her voicemail, "Answer the phone, please . . . please just answer once."

I know she probably isn't capable of answering right now, but Zed could answer the damn phone for her. The thought of her being so incoherent when I'm not around to protect her sickens me. I smash my hands against the steering wheel and peel out onto the street. This is a fucking disaster, and Tessa is with Zed, of all people. I don't trust him any more than I do Dan or Steph.

That's not entirely true, but I still don't trust him. By the time I get to Zed's apartment, I'm in tears—literal *tears* stain and coat my cheeks, reminding me of how big of a fuckup I really am. I let this happen; I let her get fucking drugged, nearly raped, and humiliated. I should have been there. No one would have dared to try that shit if I *had* been. She was probably so afraid . . .

I lift my T-shirt up to wipe my traitorous eyes and park in front of Zed's apartment. His truck isn't in the lot . . . *Where the fuck is he? Where is she?*

I try to call Tessa, then Zed, then Tessa again, but nobody's picking up. If he does something to her while she's passed out, I will do much worse to him than he could ever imagine.

Where else would she go?

To Landon?

"Hardin?" Landon's sleepy voice comes through the phone, and I press the speakerphone button.

"Is Tessa there?"

He yawns. "No . . . is she supposed to be?"

"No, I can't find her."

"Are you . . ." He stops himself. "Are you okay?"

"Yeah . . . no. I'm not. I can't find Tessa, and I don't know where else to look."

"Does she want to be found?" he asks softly.

Does she? Probably not. But then again, at this point she probably can't even form a coherent thought. These aren't normal circumstances, to put it mildly.

"I'll take your silence as a no, Hardin. My guess is, if she doesn't want to be found, she's at the one place where she knows you won't go."

"Her mother's," I groan, punching my thigh for not thinking of that earlier.

"Oh, now I've done it . . . Are you going there?"

"Yeah." *But would Zed really drive her two hours to take her to her mum's?*

"Do you know how to get there?"

"Not exactly, but I can go by the apartment and get the address."

"I think I have something here that has it written on it . . . she left some transfer paperwork here a while ago. Let me look and call you right back."

"Thanks." I wait impatiently and turn my car around in the nearest empty parking lot. I stare out the window, taking in the darkness, fighting not to let it take me over. I have to focus on seeing Tess, on making sure she's okay.

"Are you going to tell me what's going on?" Landon asks moments later when he calls back.

"Steph . . . you know, the redhead? She drugged Tessa."

Landon gasps. "Wait, what?"

"Yeah, it's a fucked-up situation and I wasn't there to help her so she's with Zed," I tell him.

"Is she okay?" He sounds like he's panicking.

"I don't have a fucking clue."

I wipe my nose on my shirt, and Landon gives me directions to Tessa's childhood home.

Her mum is going to lose her shit when I show up, especially given the situation, but I don't care. I don't have a clue as to what the hell I'm going to do when I arrive, but I have to see her and make sure she's okay.

chapter sixty

TESSA

What happened? Tell me the entire story!" my mother cries out as Zed lifts me out of his truck. His arms around me jar me back into consciousness, and a blooming sense of embarrassment.

"Tessa's old roommate slipped something into her drink, and Tessa asked me to bring her here," Zed tells her half truthfully. I'm relieved that he kept some of the details from her.

"Oh my God! Why would that girl do such a thing?"

"I don't know, Mrs. Young . . . Tessa can explain when she wakes up."

I am awake! I want to scream, but I can't. It's an odd feeling, hearing everything that's going on around me but not being able to participate in the conversation. I can't move or speak, my mind is foggy, and my thoughts are twisted—but I'm strangely aware of everything that is happening. What's happening, though, changes every few minutes: sometimes Zed's voice turns into Hardin's, and I swear I hear Hardin's laughter and see his face when I try to open my eyes. I'm losing it. This drug is making me crazy, and I want it to stop.

Some time passes—I have no idea how much—and I'm placed on what I can tell is the sofa. Slowly, maybe even reluctantly, Zed's arms slide out from underneath me.

"Well, thank you for bringing her here," my mother says. "This is just dreadful. When will she wake up?" Her voice is piercing. My head is spinning slowly.

"I don't know. I think the effects last twelve hours at most. It's been about three already."

"How could she be so stupid?" my mother snaps at Zed, and the word "stupid" echoes in my mind until it fades out.

"Who, Steph?" he asks.

"No, Theresa. How could she be that stupid to associate with those people."

"It wasn't her fault," Zed answers, defending me. "It was supposed to be a going-away party. Tessa thought the girl was her friend."

"Friend? Please! Tessa should know better than to try to be friends with that girl, or any of you, for that matter."

"No disrespect or anything, but you don't know me. I did just drive for two hours to bring your daughter here," Zed politely responds.

My mother sighs, and I focus on the sound of her heels clicking on the tile of the kitchen floor.

"Do you need anything else?" he asks her. The couch, I notice, is much softer than Zed's arms. Hardin's arms are soft but hard at the same time; the way his muscles strain under his skin is something I always loved to watch. My thoughts are blurring again. I hate this constant shift back and forth between clarity and confusion.

From a distance I hear my mother's voice say, "No. Thank you for bringing her. I was rude a moment ago, and I apologize for it."

"I'll get her clothes and stuff from my car real quick, then be on my way."

"Okay." I hear the clicking of her high heels from across the room.

I wait to hear the roar of Zed's truck. It doesn't come, or maybe it did already and I missed it. I'm confused. My head is heavy. I don't know how long I've been lying here, but I'm thirsty. Did Zed leave yet?

"What the hell are *you* doing here?" my mother screams, bringing a sharp edge of clarity to the haze. Though I still don't know what's happening.

"Is she okay?" a panting, ragged voice asks. Hardin.

He's here. Hardin.

Unless it's Zed's voice deceiving me again. No, I know it's Hardin. I can feel him here somehow.

"You aren't coming into this house!" my mother yells. "Did you not hear me! Don't walk past me like you didn't hear me!"

I hear the screen door slam shut, and my mother continues to yell.

And then I think I feel his hand on my cheek.

chapter sixty-one

HARDIN

They couldn't have been here long—I went twenty miles over the speed limit the whole way. The moment I spot Zed's truck in the driveway of the small brick house, I nearly vomit. When he steps out onto the porch, my vision goes red.

Zed walks slowly to his truck as I park on the street, not wanting to block him in, so he can just get the fuck out of here. *What will I say to him? What will I say to her? Will she even be able to hear me?*

"I knew you'd show up here," he says quietly when I appear in front of him.

"Why wouldn't I?" I growl, biting back my rising anger.

"Maybe because this is all your fault."

"Are you fucking serious? It's my fault that Steph is a god-damned psycho?" *Yes; yes, it is.*

"No, it's your fault that you didn't come with Tessa to that party in the first place. You should have seen her face when I busted that door in." He shakes his head as if to rid himself of the memory. My chest tightens. Tessa must not have told him that we aren't together. *Does that mean she's still holding on, the way that I am?*

"I . . . I didn't even know she was going there, so fuck off. Where is she?"

"Inside." He states the obvious with a murderous glare.

"Don't fucking look at me like that—you shouldn't even be here in the first place," I remind him.

"If it wasn't for me, she would have been raped and God knows what else—"

My hands find the collar of his leather jacket, and I push him up against the side of his truck. "No matter how many times you try, no matter how many times you 'save' her, she will never want you. Don't forget that."

I give him one last push and step away. I want to hit him, bust his fucking nose for being such a smug asshole, but Tessa is just inside that house, and seeing her is much more important right now. As I walk past his truck windows I see on his seat Tessa's purse and . . . dress.

She doesn't have clothes on?

"Why is her dress off?" I dare to ask. I yank on the door handle and gather her things into my arms. When he doesn't answer immediately, I glare at him, waiting for his response.

"They took it off of her," he simply remarks, his expression grim.

"Fuck," I murmur and turn to walk up the path to Tessa's mother's house.

As I reach the porch, Carol comes out to block the front door. "What the hell are *you* doing here?"

Her daughter's wounded, and her first thought is to scream at me. Fucking lovely.

"I need to see her." I grab the handle to the screen door. She shakes her head, but moves out of my way. I get the feeling that she knows I'll push right past her.

"You aren't coming into this house!" she shouts.

I ignore her and step around her. "Did you not hear me! Don't walk past me like you didn't hear me!" The screen door slams somewhere behind me as I scan the small living room to find my girl.

And then I freeze momentarily when I see her. She's lying on the couch with her knees bent slightly, her hair like a blond halo around her head, and her eyes closed. Carol continues to harass me, threatening to call the cops, but I don't give a shit. I step over to Tessa, then kneel down so that I'm level with her face. Without thought, I brush a thumb over her cheekbone and cup her flushed cheek in my palm.

"Christ," I curse and watch closely as her chest moves up and down slowly.

"Fuck, Tess, I'm so sorry. This is all my fault," I whisper to her, hoping that she can hear me. She's so beautiful, still and calm, her lips parted slightly, innocence clear on her breathtaking face.

Carol of course jumps into the moment, spewing her anger at me. "You've got that right! This *is* your fault. Now get out of my house before I have you *dragged* out by the police!"

Without turning to her, I say, "Would you just give it a rest? I'm not going anywhere. Go ahead and call the police. Have them show up here this late at night—you'll be the talk of the town, and we all know you don't want that." I know she's glaring at me, throwing daggers in her mind, but I can't look away from the girl in front of me.

"Fine," Carol finally snorts. "You have five minutes."

Her shoes drag against the carpet in the most hideous way. *Why is she so dressed up this late anyway?*

"I hope you can hear me, Tessa," I begin. My words are rushed but my touch is gentle as I caress the soft skin of her cheek. Tears well up in my eyes and fall onto her clear skin. "I'm so sorry. God, I'm so sorry for all of this. I shouldn't have let you walk away in the first place. What was I thinking?

"You would be proud of me, a little, I think. I didn't kill Dan when I found him; I only kicked him in the face . . . oh, and I choked him a little, but he's still breathing." I pause before admitting, "And I almost drank tonight, but I didn't. I couldn't make things even worse between us. I know you think I don't care, but I do, I just don't know how to show you." I stop to examine the way her eyelids flutter at my voice.

"Tessa, can you hear me?" I ask, hopeful.

"Zed?" she barely whispers, and for a moment I swear the devil is messing with my mind.

"No, baby, it's Hardin. I'm Hardin, not Zed." I can't help the irritation that flares in me from hearing his name come so softly from her lips.

"No Hardin." Her eyebrows pull together in confusion, but her eyes stay closed. "Zed?" she repeats, and I drop my hand from her cheek.

When I rise to my feet, her mum is nowhere in sight. I'm surprised she wasn't hovering over my shoulder while I tried to make amends with her daughter.

And then, as if my thoughts conjured her, she bursts back into the room. "Are you finished?" she demands.

I hold one palm up toward her back. "No, I'm not." I want to be—Tessa's calling out for Zed, after all.

Then, meekly, as if admitting that she's not in control of the entire world, her mum asks, "Can you put her in her room for me before you go? She can't just lie on the couch."

"So I'm not allowed here, but . . ." I stop myself, knowing it won't do any good to get into it with this woman for the tenth time since I met her. So I just nod. "Sure, where's the room?"

"Last door on the left," she replies curtly and disappears again. I don't know where Tessa's kindness came from, but it sure as hell wasn't from this woman.

Sighing, I push one arm under Tessa's knees and one under her neck, lifting her gently. A soft groan falls from her lips as I bring her close to my chest. I keep my head down slightly as I carry her down the hall. This house is small, much smaller than I had imagined.

The last door on the left is nearly closed, and when I push it open with my foot, I'm surprised at the nostalgic feelings that well up deep inside me at the sight of a room that I've never been in before. A small bed rests against the far wall, filling nearly half of the tiny bedroom. The desk in the corner is almost the same size as the bed. A teenage Tessa flows through my imagination, the way she must have spent hours and hours sitting at the large desk working on countless homework assignments. Her eyebrows pushed together, her mouth set in a straight overconcentrated line, her hair falling over her eyes, and her hand pushing it back swiftly before pushing the pencil back behind her ear.

Knowing her now, I wouldn't have guessed these pink sheets and this purple duvet would belong to her. They must have been holdovers from back when a younger Tessa went through her Barbie doll phase that she once described as "the best and worst time in her life." I remember her describing how she constantly felt the need to ask her mum things like where Barbie worked, what university she attended, if she would have children one day.

I look down at the adult Tessa in my arms and stifle a laugh as I think about her constant curiosity—one of my most and least favorite things about her now. I yank back the blanket and gently lay her across the bed, making sure that there's only one pillow underneath her head, just the way she sleeps at home.

Home . . . this is not her home anymore. Just like this small house, our apartment was a short stop for her on the way to her dream: Seattle.

The small wooden dresser creaks as I open the top drawer, searching for clothes to place on her half-naked body. The thought of Dan undressing her makes my fists clench around the thin fabric of an old T-shirt from her dresser. I lift Tessa up as gently as I can and drag the shirt over her head. Her hair is messy, and when I attempt to smooth it, it only gets worse. She groans again, and her fingers twitch. She's trying to move, and she can't. I hate this. I swallow the bile in my throat and blink away the thoughts of that shit bag's hands on her.

To be respectful, I look away from her while my hands pull her arms through the small holes and finally she's dressed. Carol is standing in the doorway; a thoughtful yet uptight expression covers her face, and I wonder how long she's been standing there.

chapter sixty-two

TESSA

Just stop! I want to scream at the two of them. I can't keep up with them fighting this way. I can't keep up: time doesn't make sense in this state that I'm in. Everything is out of order. There are slamming doors and my mother and Hardin arguing—and it's all so hard to hear—but mostly there's just darkness dragging me under, pulling hard . . .

At some point I ask Hardin, "Yes, what about Zed? Did you hurt him?" At least, the thoughts are there, and I'm trying my hardest to say them. I'm not sure if they make it out of my mouth or not, if my mouth is coordinated with my mind.

"No, it's Hardin. I'm Hardin, not Zed."

Hardin is here, not Zed. Wait, Zed is here, too. Isn't he?

"No, Hardin, did you hurt Zed?" The darkness is tugging me in the opposite direction of his voice. My mother's voice enters the room and fills it with her authoritarian air, but I can't make out a word. The only clarity I have is in Hardin's voice. Not even his words, but how it sounds, how it moves through me.

At some point, I feel something push under my body. Hardin's arm? I'm not entirely sure, but I'm lifted off of the couch as the familiar minty scent fills my nostrils. Why is he here, and how did he find me?

Only seconds later I'm gently laid back on the bed, then I'm lifted again. I don't want to move. Hardin's shaky hands push a shirt over my head, and I want to scream at him to stop touching me. The last thing I want is to be touched, but the moment Hardin's fingers brush against my skin, the disgusting memory of Dan is erased.

"Touch me again, please. Make it go away," I beg. He doesn't reply. His hands keep touching my head, my neck, my hair, and I try to lift my hand to his, but it's too heavy.

"I love you and I'm so sorry," I hear before my head rests back on the pillow. "I want to take her home."

No, leave me here. Please, I think to myself. But don't go . . .

chapter sixty-three

HARDIN

Carol crosses her arms over her chest. "Not happening."

"I know that," I seethe and wonder just how angry Tessa would be if I cussed her mother out. Leaving her room, her childhood bedroom, is hard enough without hearing the strangled whine that falls from her lips when I cross the threshold into the hallway.

"Where were you tonight while this was happening?" she questions.

"At home."

"Why weren't you there to stop this?"

"What makes you so sure I wasn't a part of it? You're usually quick to blame me for everything wrong in the world."

"Because I know that regardless of your poor choices and your even poorer attitude, you wouldn't let anything like this happen to Tessa if you could help it."

Is that a compliment from her? A backhanded one . . . but, hell, I'll take it, especially considering the circumstances. "Well . . ." I begin.

She holds her hand up to silence me. "I wasn't finished. I don't blame you for everything that's wrong in the world." She gestures to the sleeping, or half-conscious, girl lying on the small bed. "Just *her* world."

"I won't argue with that." I sigh in defeat. I know she's right; there's no denying that I've ruined nearly everything in Tessa's life.

He's been my hero, my tormentor at times, but mostly my hero, she had said in her journal. A hero? I'm far from a fucking hero. I would give anything to be one for her, but I just don't know how to go about it.

"Well, at least we can agree on something." Her full lips turn up in a half smile, but she blinks it away and looks down at her feet. "Well, if that was all you needed, you can go."

"Okay . . ." I take one last look at Tessa and then turn back to her mum, who is staring at me again.

"What are your plans in regard to my daughter?" she asks with some authority, but also maybe a little fear. "I have to know what your long-term intentions are, because every time I turn around, something else is happening with her, and not something good. What do you plan to do with her in Seattle?"

"I'm not going to Seattle with her." The words are thick and heavy on my tongue.

"What?" She begins to walk down the hallway, and I follow her.

"I'm not going. She's going without me."

"As happy as that makes me, may I ask why?" A perfectly arched brow rises, and I look away.

"I'm just not, that's why. It's better for her that I don't go, anyway."

"You sound just like my ex-husband." She swallows. "Sometimes I blame myself for Tessa attaching herself to you. I worry that it's because of the way her father was, before he left us." Her manicured hand lifts up to smooth her hair, and she tries to appear unaffected by her mention of Richard.

"He has nothing to do with her relationship with me; she barely knows him. The few days they've spent together lately shows just that: she doesn't remember enough about him to affect her choice in men."

"Lately?" Carol's eyes widen in surprise, and I watch in horror as the color drains from her face. And any small understanding we had been creating seems to disappear along with it.

Shit. Fuck. Fucking shit. "She . . . um, we ran into him a little over a week ago."

"Richard? He found her?" Her voice breaks, and she places her hand on her neck.

"No, she ran into him."

Her fingers start running nervously over the pearls around her neck. "Where?"

"I don't think I should be telling you any of this."

"*Excuse* me?" Her arms drop, and she stands there gaping in shock.

"If Tessa wanted you to know that she'd seen her dad, she would have told you herself."

"This is more important than your dislike for me, Hardin. Has she been seeing him *often*?" Her gray eyes are now glazed over, threatening to spill tears at any moment, but knowing this woman, she would never in a million years shed a tear in front of anyone, especially me.

I sigh, not wanting to betray Tessa, but reluctant to cause any more shit with her mum. "He stayed with us for a few days."

"She wasn't going to tell me, was she?" Her voice is thin and hoarse while she picks at her red fingernails.

"Probably not. You aren't the easiest person to talk to," I remind her. I wonder if this is a good time to bring up my suspicion about him breaking into the apartment.

"And you are?" She raises her voice, and I step closer. "At least I care about her well-being; that's more than I can say for you!"

I knew the civil conversation between us wouldn't last long. "I care about her more than anyone, even you!" I fire back.

"I am her mother; no one loves her more than I do. The fact that you think you possibly could just shows how demented you really are!" Her shoes click against the floor as she paces back and forth.

"You know what I think? I think that you hate me because I remind you of him. You hate the constant reminder of what you ruined, so you hate me so you don't have to hate yourself . . . but do you want to know something?" I wait for her sarcastic nod before continuing: "You and I are a lot alike, too. More alike than Richard and I, really: we both refuse to take any responsibility for our mistakes. Instead we blame everyone else. We isolate the ones we love and force them—"

"No! You're wrong!" she cries out.

Her tears and histrionics somehow keep me from finishing that thought: that she will spend the rest of her days alone. "No, I'm not wrong. But what I *am* is leaving. Tessa's car is still around school somewhere, so I'll bring it back tomorrow unless you want to make the drive yourself."

Carol wipes at her eyes. "Fine, bring the car. At five tomorrow." She looks up at me through bloodshot eyes and smeared mascara. "That doesn't change anything. I'll never like you."

"And I'll never care if you do." I walk toward the front door, momentarily debating whether I should go back down the hallway, get Tessa, and bring her with me.

"Hardin, despite the way I feel toward you, I do know that you love my daughter. I just want to remind you again that if you love her—truly love her—you will stop interfering in her life. She's not the same girl that I dropped off at that devil school half a year ago."

"I know." As much as I hate this woman, I feel pity for her, because, like me, she'll probably be alone for the rest of her miserable life. "Can you do me a favor?" I ask.

She eyes me suspiciously. "What would that be?"

"Don't tell her that I was here. If she doesn't remember, don't tell her." Tessa is so out of it she probably won't remember a thing. I don't think she even knows that I'm here now.

Carol looks at me, looks through me, and nods. "That I can do."

chapter sixty-four

TESSA

My head is heavy, so heavy, and the light shining through the yellow curtains is bright, too bright.

Yellow curtains? I reopen my eyes to find the familiar yellow curtains of my old bedroom covering the windows. Those curtains always drove us both crazy, but my mother couldn't afford to buy a matching set, so we learned to live with them. And the last twelve hours come flooding back in pieces, broken and jumbled memories that make little sense to me.

Nothing makes sense. It takes seconds, minutes maybe, for my mind to even attempt to comprehend what happened.

Steph's betrayal is my strongest memory from the night, one of the most painful memories I have ever had to experience. How could she do that to me? To anyone? The whole situation is just so wrong, so twisted, and I never saw it coming. I remember the strong sense of relief I felt when she walked into the room, only to slip back into a panic when she admitted she had never been a friend to me after all. Her voice was so clear, despite the state I was in. She put something in my drink to slow me down, or worse, to make me pass out—all so she could get some sort of unwarranted revenge on me and Hardin. I was so afraid last night, and she went from being my safety to being a predator so quickly that I could barely comprehend the shift.

I was drugged, at a party by someone who I thought was my friend. The reality of this hits me hard, and I swipe angrily at the tears soaking my cheeks.

Humiliation replaces the sting of betrayal when I remember Dan and his camera. They took off my dress . . . the small red camera light in the dim room is something I don't think I'll ever forget. They wanted to violate me, tape it, and show it to an audience. I hold my stomach, hoping to not get sick, again.

Every single time I think I may get a break from the constant battle that has become my life, something worse happens. And I keep putting myself in these situations. Steph, of all people? I still can't grasp it. If her reasoning was true, if she did it only because she doesn't like me and she has a thing for Hardin, why didn't she just tell me in the first place? Why did she pretend to be my friend all this time only to set me up? How could she smile in my face and go shopping with me, listen to my secrets and share my worries, only to be planning something like this behind my back?

I sit up slowly, and it's still too fast. My pulse is pounding behind my ears, and I want to rush to the bathroom and force myself to throw up, in case any of the drug remains in my stomach. I don't, though, and instead close my eyes again.

When I wake up again, my head is a little lighter, and I manage to get out of my childhood bed. I don't have any pants on, only a small T-shirt that I don't remember putting on in the first place. My mother must have dressed me . . . but that doesn't seem likely.

The only pajama pants left in my old dresser are uncomfortably tight and too short. I have gained weight since I left for college, but I feel more confortable and confident in my body . . . more now than I ever felt before.

I wobble out of the bedroom, down the hallway, and to the kitchen, where I find my mother leaning against the counter, reading a magazine. Her black dress is smooth and lint-free, her matching heels are high, and her hair is curled into perfect, classic waves. When I glance at the clock on the stove, I see that it's a bit past four in the afternoon.

"How are you feeling?" my mother asks timidly as she turns to face me.

"Terrible," I groan, unable to put on a friendly, much less a brave face.

"I'd imagine, after the night you had."

Here we go . . .

"Have some coffee and some Advil; you'll feel better."

I nod slowly and walk over to the cabinet to grab a coffee mug.

"I have church this evening; I assume you won't be coming along? You missed the morning service," she says in a flat voice.

"No, I'm in no shape to be in church right now." Only my mother would ask me to go to church with her when I just woke up after sleeping off a date-rape drug.

She grabs her handbag from the kitchen table, then turns back to me. "Okay, I'll tell Noah and Mr. and Mrs. Porter you said hello. I'll be home around eight, maybe shortly after."

A pang of guilt hits me at the mention of Noah's name. I still haven't called him since I learned of his grandmother's passing. I know I should have, and I need to. I'll do it after church ends—if I can find my phone, that is.

"How did I get here last night?" I ask, trying to put the pieces of the puzzle together. I remember Zed storming into Hardin's old room and breaking the camera.

"The young man who brought you was named Zed, I believe." She looks back down at her magazine and quietly clears her throat.

"Oh."

I hate this. I hate not knowing. I like to be in control of everything, and last night I wasn't in control of my thoughts or of my body.

My mother puts down the magazine with what sounds like a slap. She looks at me blankly, says, "Call me if you need anything," and walks toward the front door.

"Okay . . ."

Turning, my mother gives one last disapproving glance toward my tight pajamas and leaves the house. "Oh, and go through my closet and find yourself something to wear."

The moment the screen door closes, a flash of Hardin's voice pops into my mind.

This is all my fault, he said. It couldn't have been Hardin—my mind is playing tricks on me. I need to call Zed and thank him for everything. I owe him so much for coming to my aid, for saving me. I'm so grateful to him, and I'll never be able to thank him enough for helping me and driving me all the way here. I can't imagine what would have happened in front of that camera had he not shown up.

Salty tears mix with black coffee for the next half hour. Finally, I force myself from the table and into the bathroom to wash last night's disgusting events from my body. By the time I'm searching in my mother's closet for something without a built-in underwire bra, I feel a good deal better.

"Do you not own any *normal* clothing?" I groan, pushing through hanger after hanger holding cocktail dresses. I'm at the point where I would rather sit naked before I finally find a cream-colored sweater and dark jeans. The jeans fit perfectly, and the sweater is tight on my chest, but I'm grateful to have found anything casual at all, so I'm not going to complain.

Searching the house for my phone and purse, I realize that I don't have a single memory that could point me toward their hiding place. Why can't my mind just clear through the jumbled night and make sense of everything? I'm assuming my car is still parked outside of Steph's dorm; hopefully she hasn't slashed my tires.

I go back into my old bedroom and pull open the desk drawer. My phone sits inside, on top of my small purse. I press the power button and wait for the home screen to appear. I nearly turn it back off when the alert vibrations go on endlessly. Text message after text message, voicemail after voicemail, pop onto the small screen.

Hardin . . . Hardin . . . Zed . . . Hardin . . . unknown . . . Hardin . . . Hardin . . .

My stomach flutters in the most uncomfortable way as I read his name on the screen. He knows; he has to. Someone told him what happened, and that's why he called and text-messaged me so many times. I should call him and at least let him know that I'm okay before he worries himself crazy. Regardless of the state of our relationship, he's probably upset after hearing about what happened . . . "upset" being an understatement, for sure.

I hang up the phone after six rings, just as his voicemail picks up, and head back into my mother's bedroom to attempt to style my hair. The last thing I care about is my appearance right now, but I also don't care for the idea of listening to my mother's insults if I don't make myself look at least decent. Dealing with my appearance also helps to distract me from my anxiety over the scattershot memories of last night that flash into my mind occasionally. I cover the deep circles under my eyes and apply a few swipes of mascara and brush my hair. It's nearly dry now, working in my favor as I rake my fingers through the natural waves. It doesn't look nearly as good as I would like, but I don't have the energy to mess with the frizzy mess any longer than I already have.

The faint sound of someone knocking at the front door draws me out of my daze. *Who could be coming here at this time?* And suddenly my stomach turns at the thought of Hardin being on the other side of the door.

"Tessa?" a familiar voice calls as I hear the door open.

Noah lets himself in, and I see him in the living room. Relief and guilt hit me as I take in his familiar but shaky smile.

"Hey . . ." He nods, shifting from one foot to the other.

Without thinking, I practically throw myself at him, wrapping my arms around his neck. I bury my face in his chest and begin to cry.

His strong arms wrap around me and hold me, keeping both of us from toppling over. "Are you okay?"

"Yes, I'm just . . . No, I'm not." I lift my head from his chest, not wanting to smear my mascara on his tan cardigan.

"Your mom said you were in town." He continues to hold me while I continue to relish the familiarity of him. "So I kind of ducked out before the service ended so I could say hey without everyone around. So what happened?"

"So much, too much to even explain. I'm being so dramatic," I groan and step away from him.

"College still isn't treating you the way you hoped?" he asks with a sympathetic little smile.

I shake my head and gesture for him to follow me into the kitchen, where I make another pot of coffee. "No, not at all. I'm moving to Seattle."

"Your mom told me," he says and sits at the table.

"Are you still thinking of going to WCU in the spring?" I bark out a little laugh. "I wouldn't recommend that school." But trying to make a joke at my own expense fails as tears fill my eyes.

"Yeah, that's the plan. This . . . girl I've been seeing . . . we've been thinking about San Francisco, though. You know how I love California."

I wasn't prepared for that—Noah dating someone. I suppose I should have been, but it feels so weird that all I can think to say is, "Oh?"

Noah's blue eyes shine under the fluorescent kitchen lights. "Yeah, it's been going pretty well. I've been trying to take it in stride, though, you know . . . because of everything."

Not wanting him to finish that thought and make me feel even more guilty about how we broke up, I ask, "Uhm, so how did you two meet?"

"Well, she works at Zooms or something, a store in the mall near you, and—"

"You were in town?" I interrupt him. It feels strange that he didn't tell me, didn't stop by . . . but I get it.

"Yeah, to see Becca. I should have called you or something, but everything was so weird between us . . ."

"I know, it's okay," I assure him and let him finish. That name, Becca, rings a bell . . . but the fragment of memory drops from my mind as he continues.

"Well, anyway, I guess after that, we got pretty close. We had some problems here and there, and I thought I couldn't trust her for a while, but we're doing pretty good now."

Hearing about his woes brings me back to my own, and I sigh. "I feel like I can't trust anyone anymore." When Noah frowns, I hastily add, "Except you. I'm not talking about you. Every single person that I've met since I arrived at that school has lied to me in some way."

Even Hardin. Especially Hardin.

"Is that what happened last night?"

"Sort of . . ." I wonder what my mother told him.

"I knew it had to be something big to bring you home." I nod, and he reaches across the table to clasp my hands in his. "I missed you," he murmurs, sadness clear in his voice.

I look up at him with wide eyes; I can feel the tears coming again. "I'm so sorry that I haven't called about your grandma."

"It's okay, I know you're busy." He leans back against the chair with soft eyes.

"That's not an excuse, I've been so terrible to you."

"You haven't," he lies, shaking his head slowly.

"You know that I have. I've treated you so poorly since I left home, and I'm so sorry. You didn't deserve any of it."

"Stop beating yourself up; I'm okay now," he assures me with a warm smile, but the guilt doesn't subside.

"I still shouldn't have done it."

Then he surprises me with something I wouldn't have expected him to ever ask. "If you could do it all over again, what would you change?"

"The way I went about things. I shouldn't have strung you along and gone behind your back. I've known you half my life and I dropped you so suddenly, it was terrible of me."

"It was," he starts, "but I get it now. We weren't good for each other . . . Well, we were perfect together," he says with a laugh. "But I think that was actually the problem."

The small kitchen feels more spacious now as my guilt begins to dissolve. "You think so?"

"Yeah, I do. I love you, and I'll always love you. I just don't love you the way I always thought I did, and you could never love me the way you love him."

I choke on my breath at his mention of Hardin. He's right, he's so right, but I can't talk about Hardin with Noah. Not right now.

I need to change the subject. "So Becca makes you happy, then?"

"Yeah, she's different than you'd probably expect, but then, Hardin isn't exactly who I expected you to break up with me for." His smile isn't harsh as he chuckles softly. "I guess we both needed something different."

He's right, yet again. "I guess so." I laugh along with him and we continue to lighten the conversation until another knock at the door interrupts us.

"I'll get it," he says, standing to his feet and leaving the small kitchen before I can stop him.

chapter sixty-five

HARDIN

Watching the clock change from minute to minute is slowly murdering me. I'd rather pull my hair out piece by piece than sit here and wait in this goddamned driveway until five. I don't see Tessa's mum's car. There are no cars in the driveway except Tessa's, which I'm sitting in. Landon has parked on the street, having followed me here so I get a lift back. Luckily he cares about Tessa's well-being more than anyone except me, so it didn't take any convincing.

"Go knock on the door, or I will," he threatens through the phone.

"I'm going to! Fuck, give me a second. I don't know if anyone's here."

"Well, if not, leave the keys in the mailbox, and we'll go." That's exactly why I haven't done that already—I want her to be inside. I have to know that she's okay.

"I'm going up now," I say and hang up on my obnoxious stepbrother.

The seventeen steps up to her mum's front door are the worst of my life. I knock on the outer screen door, but I'm not sure if it was loud enough. Fuck it. I knock again, this time much harder. Too hard, too hard. I put my hand down when the flimsy aluminum bends, snapping a couple pieces of wire from the screen. Shit.

The door creaks open, and instead of Tessa, her mum, or anyone else on the fucking planet that I'd rather see, it's Noah.

"You've got to be fucking kidding me," I say.

When he tries to close the door in my face, I stop it with my boot.

"Don't be a dick." I push the door open, and he steps back.

"Why are you here?" he asks, his face etched in a deep scowl. I should be asking him why the fuck *he* is here. Tessa and I haven't been separated three days, and here this asshole is, worming his way back into her life.

"To drop her car off." I look behind him, but I can't see shit. "Is she here?" The entire way here, I told myself that I didn't want her to see me or remember that I was at her house at all last night, but I know I was just bullshitting myself.

"Maybe. Does she know you're coming?" Noah crosses his arms, and it takes every bit of self-control I have not to knock him to the ground, step over him—maybe *on* him—and find her.

"No. I just want to make sure that she's okay. What did she tell you?" I ask him, backing back off of the porch.

"Nothing. She didn't have to. She doesn't have to tell me anything. I know she wouldn't come all the way here if you hadn't done something to her."

I frown. "You're wrong, actually; it wasn't me . . . this time." He looks surprised by my small admission, so I continue—peacefully, for now. "Look, I know you hate me, and you have every reason to, but I *will* see her one way or another, so you can either move out of my way or I'll—"

"Hardin?" Tessa's voice is a small whisper, nearly lost in the breeze, as she appears behind Noah.

"Hey . . ." My feet carry me inside the house, and Noah sensibly moves out of my way. "Are you okay?" I ask, cupping her cheeks in my cold hands.

Her head jerks away—because of the cold, I force myself to believe—and she steps back from me. "Yeah, I'm okay," she lies.

Questions tumble out of my mouth. "Are you sure? How are you feeling? Did you sleep? Does your head ache?"

"Yes, okay, some, yes," she answers, nodding along, but I already forgot what I asked her in the first place.

"Who told you?" she asks me, her cheeks a deep red.

"Molly."

"Molly?"

"Yeah, she called when you were . . . um, in my old room." I can't keep the panic from my voice.

"Oh . . ." She looks past me, focusing on some distant space, her eyebrows drawn together in concentration.

Does she remember that I was here? Do I want her to?

Yes, of course I do. "You're okay, though?"

"Yes."

Noah steps to where we're standing, and with alarm clear in his voice asks, "Tessa, *what* happened?"

Looking back at Tessa, I can tell she doesn't want him to know about everything. I like the idea of that more than I should.

"Nothing, don't worry about it," I answer him so she doesn't have to.

"Was it serious?" he presses.

"I said, don't worry about it," I growl, and he gulps. I turn back to Tessa. "I brought your car," I tell her.

"You did?" she says. "Thanks, I thought Steph would have busted the windshield or something." She sighs, her shoulders slouching further with every word. Her attempt at a joke didn't work for anyone, herself included.

"Why did you go to her, anyway? Out of all people, why her?" I ask her.

She looks at Noah, then back to me. "Noah, can you give us a minute?" she sweetly requests.

He nods and gives me what I assume is supposed to be some kind of warning glare before leaving us alone in the small living room.

"Why her? Tell me, please," I repeat.

"I don't know. I didn't have anywhere else to go, Hardin."

"You could have gone to Landon; you practically have your own bedroom at that house," I point out.

"I don't want to keep dragging your family into it. I've done it enough, and it's not fair to them."

"And you knew I would go there?" When she looks down at her hands, I say, "I wouldn't have."

"Okay," she says sadly.

Fuck, that's not what I meant. "I didn't mean it like that. I meant I was going to give you space."

"Oh," she whispers while picking at her fingernails.

"You're being really quiet."

"I'm just . . . I don't know. It's been a long night and morning." She frowns. I want to walk over and smooth the line between her brows and kiss her pain away.

"No Hardin, Zed," she called out in her barely conscious state.

"I know, do you remember it?" I ask her, not sure if I can bear to listen to her response.

I expect her to tell me to go away or cuss me out even, but she doesn't. Instead she nods and sits down on the couch, gesturing for me to sit on the other side.

chapter sixty-six

HARDIN

I want to move closer to her, to reach for her shaking hand and find a way to erase her memories. I hate that she went through such an ordeal, and I'm once again blown away by her strength. She's sitting up, her back as straight as a board, and ready to talk to me.

"Why did you come here?" she asks quietly.

By way of answer, I ask, "Why is *he* here?" and nod my head toward the kitchen. I just *know* Noah is perched against the wall, listening in to our conversation. I really can't fucking stand him, but given the circumstances, I should probably shut up about it.

Playing with her hands, she says, "He's here to check on me."

"He doesn't need to check on you." That's why I'm here.

"Hardin"—she frowns—"not today. Please."

"Sorry . . ." I inch back, feeling like an even bigger asshole than I did seconds ago.

"Why did you come here?" Tessa asks again.

"To bring your car. You don't want me here, do you?" I haven't once, until now, even considered that possibility. And it burns through me like acid. My being here might only be making things worse for her. The days of her finding solace in me are no longer.

"It's not that . . . I'm just confused."

"About what?"

Her eyes shine under the dim lights of her mum's living room. "You, last night, Steph, everything. Did you know that it was all a game to her, and she really has hated me all this time."

"No, of course I didn't know," I tell her.

"You had no idea that she had any bad feelings toward me?"

Dammit. But I want to be honest, so I say, "Maybe a little, I guess. Molly had mentioned it once or twice, but she didn't elaborate, and I didn't think it was something to this extent—or that Molly even knew what she was talking about."

"Molly? Since when does Molly care about me?"

So black and white. Tessa always wants things to be so black and white, and it makes me shake my head, a little sad that things just can never be so simple. "She doesn't, she hates you still," I tell her and look down. "But she called me after that Applebee's shit, and I was mad. I didn't want her or Steph to ruin things between me and you. I thought Steph was trying to meddle just to be a nosy bitch. I didn't think she was a fucking psycho."

When I look over at Tessa, she's wiping tears from her eyes. I move across the couch to close the space between us, and she recoils. "Hey, it's okay," I say and grab her arm to pull her to my chest. "Shhh . . ." My hand rests over her hair, and after a few seconds of trying to pull away, she gives in.

"I just want to start over. I want to forget about everything that's happened in the last six months," she sobs.

My chest tightens as I nod along, agreeing with her even though I don't want to. I don't want her to want to forget me.

"I hate college. I always looked forward to it, but it's been one mistake after another for me." She pulls at my shirt, bringing herself closer to me. I stay silent, not wanting to make her feel any worse than she's already feeling. I didn't have a fucking clue of what I was walking into when I knocked on the door, but I sure as hell didn't expect to have a crying Tessa in my arms.

"I'm being so dramatic." She pulls away too soon, and for a moment I consider pulling her back to me.

"No. No, you're not. You're being really calm, considering

what happened. Tell me what you remember, don't make me ask again. Please."

"It's all a blur really, it was so . . . strange. I was aware of everything but nothing made any sense. I don't know how to explain it. I couldn't move, but I could feel things." She shudders.

"Feel things? Where did he touch you?" I don't want to know.

"My legs . . . they undressed me."

"Only your legs?" *Please say yes.*

"Yes, I think so. It could have been so much worse, but Zed—" She stops. Takes a breath. "Anyway, the pills made my body so heavy . . . I don't know how to explain it."

I nod. "I know what you mean."

"What?"

Broken memoires of blacking out in bars and stumbling down the streets of London race through my mind. The idea of fun that I once had is completely different from what I consider to be fun now. "I used to take them now and then for fun."

"You did?" Her mouth falls open, and I don't like how her look makes me feel.

"I guess 'fun' isn't really the word," I backtrack. "Not anymore."

She nods and gives me a sweet, relieved smile. She adjusts the collar of her sweater, which I see now is pretty tight on her.

"Where did that come from?" I ask.

"The sweater?" She gives me a wry smile. "It's my mother's . . . can't you tell?" Her fingers tug at the thick fabric.

"I don't know. Noah was at the door, and you're dressed like that . . . I thought I had stepped into a time machine," I tease. Her eyes light up with humor, all sadness momentarily washed away, and she bites down on her lip in an attempt to stop from laughing.

She sniffles and reaches over to the small table to pull a tissue from the floral box. "No. There are no time machines." Tessa shakes her head back and forth slowly while wiping at her nose.

Fuck, even after crying she's so damned beautiful. "I was worried about you," I tell her.

Her smile disappears. *Fuck.*

"This is what confuses me," she says. "You told me you didn't want to try anymore, but here you are telling me that you were worried about me." She stares at me blankly, her lip trembling.

She's right. I don't always say it, but it's true. I spend hours a day worrying about her. Emotion . . . this is what I need from her. I need the reassurance.

But she takes my silence the wrong way. "It's okay, I'm not upset with you. I do appreciate you coming here and bringing my car. It means a lot to me that you did that."

I remain mute on the couch, unable to talk for some time.

"It's nothing," I finally manage to say with a shrug. But I need to say something real, anything.

After watching more of my painful silence for a moment, Tessa goes into polite hostess mode. "How will you get home? Wait . . . how did you even know how to get here?"

Shit. "Landon. He told me."

Her eyes light up again. "Oh, he's here?"

"Yeah, he's outside."

She flushes and rises to her feet. "Oh! I'm keeping you, I'm sorry."

"No, you aren't. He's fine out there waiting," I stammer. *I don't want to leave. Unless you're coming with me.*

"He should have come inside." She glances toward the door.

"He's fine." My voice comes out much too sharp.

"Thank you again for bringing my car . . ." She's trying to dismiss me in a polite way. I know her.

"Do you want me to bring your stuff inside?" I offer.

"No, I'm leaving in the morning, so it's easier to keep it in there."

Why does it surprise me that every single time she opens her mouth, she reminds me that she's going to Seattle? I keep waiting for her to change her mind, but it will never happen.

chapter sixty-seven

TESSA

As Hardin reaches the door, I ask, "What did you do about Dan?"

I want to know more about last night, even if Noah can hear us talking. As we pass him in the hallway, Hardin doesn't so much as look at him. Noah glares, though, unsure of what to do, I assume.

"Dan. You said Molly told you. What did you do?" I know Hardin well enough to know that he went after him. I'm still surprised by Molly's help—I was far from expecting it when she walked into the bedroom last night. I shudder at the memory.

Hardin half smiles. "Nothing too bad."

I didn't kill Dan when I found him; I only kicked him in the face . . .

"You kicked him in the face . . ." I say, trying to dig through the mess in my head.

He raises a brow. "Yeah . . . Did Zed tell you that?"

"I . . . I don't know . . ." I remember hearing the words, I just can't remember who said them.

I'm Hardin, not Zed, Hardin said—his voice in my mind feels so real.

"You were here, weren't you? Last night?" I step toward him. He backs into the wall. "You *were;* I remember it. You said you were going to drink and you didn't . . ."

"I didn't think you remembered," Hardin mutters.

"Why wouldn't you just tell me?" My head aches while I struggle to separate drug-induced dreaming from reality.

"I don't know. I was going to, but then everything got so familiar and you were smiling and I didn't want to ruin it." He shrugs one shoulder, and his eyes focus on the large painting of the golden gates of Heaven on my mother's wall.

"How would you telling me that you drove me home ruin it?"

"I didn't drive you home. Zed did."

I remembered that earlier, sort of. This is so frustrating.

"So you came after? What was I doing?" I want Hardin to help me put together the sequence of events. I can't seem to do it on my own.

"You were lying on the couch; you could barely speak."

"Oh . . ."

"You were calling out for him," he adds quietly, venom laced through his deep voice.

"For who?"

"Zed." His answer is simple, but I can feel the emotion behind it.

"No, I wasn't." That doesn't make sense. "This is so frustrating." I sift through the mental mud and finally find a lump of sense . . . Hardin speaking about Dan, Hardin asking me if I can hear him, me asking him about Zed . . .

"I wanted to know about him, if you had hurt him. I think." The memory is fuzzy, but it's there.

"You said his name more than once; it's okay. You were so out of it." His eyes drop to the carpet and stay there. "I didn't expect you to want me anyway."

"I didn't want him. I may not remember much, but I was afraid. I know myself enough to know that I would only call for you," I admit without thinking.

Why did I just say that? Hardin and I broke up, again. This is our second actual breakup, but it feels like there have been so many more. Maybe because this time I haven't jumped into his arms at the slightest sign of affection from him. This time I left the house and the gifts from Hardin; this time I'm leaving for Seattle in less than twenty-four hours.

"Come here," he says, holding his arms open.

"I can't." I take a page from his book and run my fingers over my hair.

"Yes, you can."

Whenever Hardin is around me, despite the situation, the familiarity of him always seeps into every fiber of my being. We either scream at each other or we smile and tease. There's never any distance, no middle ground between us. It's such a natural thing for me now, an instinct really, to let myself find comfort in his arms, laugh at his stale attitude, and ignore the issues that caused us to be in whatever terrible situation that we're in at the time.

"We aren't together anymore," I say quietly, more to remind myself.

"I know."

"I can't pretend that we are." I pull my bottom lip between my teeth and try not to notice the way his eyes dull at the reminder of our status.

"I'm not asking you to do that. All I'm asking is for you to come here." His arms are still open, still long and inviting, calling for me, pulling me closer and closer.

"And if I do, we'll only fall back into repeating the cycle that we both decided to end."

"Tessa . . ."

"Hardin, please." I back away. This living room is much too small for me to avoid him, and my self-control is faltering.

"Fine." He finally sighs and his hands tug at his hair, his usual sign of frustration.

"We need this, you know that we do. We have to spend some time apart."

"Some time apart?" He looks wounded, pissed off, and I'm a

little afraid of what will come out of his mouth next. I don't want a fight with him, and today isn't the day for him to try to start one.

"Yes, some time alone. We can't get along and everything seems to always be working against us. You said yourself the other day that you were sick of it. You kicked me out of the apartment." I cross my arms in front of my chest.

"Tessa . . . you can't be fucking—" He looks into my eyes and stops midsentence. "How much time?"

"What?"

"How much time apart?"

"I . . ." I didn't expect him to agree. "I don't know."

"A week? A month?" He pushes for specifics.

"I don't know, Hardin. We both need to get ourselves to a better place."

"You're my better place, Tess."

His words swarm through my chest, and I force my eyes to move from his face before I lose whatever resistance I have left. "You're mine, too, you know you are, but you're so angry and I'm always on edge with you. You have to do something about your anger, and I need time to myself."

"So this is my fault, again?" he asks.

"No, it's me, too. I'm too dependent on you. I need to be more independent."

"Since when does any of this matter?" The tone of his voice tells me that he hasn't ever considered my dependency on him a problem.

"Since we had that massive blowup at the apartment a few nights ago. Actually, it started a while ago; Seattle and the argument the other night were just the icing on the cake."

When I finally gather the courage to look up at Hardin, I see that his expression has changed.

"Okay. I get it," he says. "I'm sorry, I know I fuck up a lot. We've already beaten the Seattle thing into the ground, and maybe it's time that I start listening to you more." He reaches for my hand, and I let him take it, momentarily baffled by his newfound agreeability. "I'll give you some space, okay? You've dealt with enough shit in the past twenty-four hours alone. I don't want to be another problem . . . for once."

"Thank you," I respond simply.

"Can you let me know when you get to Seattle? And get some food in your stomach, and rest, please." His green eyes are soft, warm, and comforting.

And I want to ask him to stay, but I know it's not a good idea.

"I will. Thank you . . . Really."

"You don't have to thank me." His hands push into the tight pockets of his black jeans, and his eyes measure my face. "I'll tell Landon you said hello," he says and walks out the door.

I can't help but smile at the way he lingers by Landon's car, staring at my mother's house for a long beat before getting into the passenger seat.

chapter sixty-eight

TESSA

The moment that Landon's car is out of sight, the emptiness weighs heavy on my chest, and I step back from the entryway, letting the door close.

Noah is leaning against the threshold between the living room and kitchen. "Is he gone? " he asks gently.

"Yeah, he's gone." My voice is distant, unfamiliar even to myself.

"I didn't know you guys weren't together."

"We . . . well . . . we're just trying to figure everything out."

"Can you tell me one thing before you change the subject?" His eyes scan my face. "I know that look—you're about to find a reason to."

Even after the months we've been apart, Noah still reads me so well. "What do you want to know?" I ask.

His blue eyes stare into mine. He holds my gaze for a long time, a bravely long time. "If you could go back, would you, Tessa? I heard you say you want to erase the last six months . . . but if you could, would you, really?"

Would I?

I sit down on the couch to ponder his question. Would I take it all back? Erase everything that's happened to me in the last six months? The bet, the endless fights with Hardin, the downward spiral of my relationship with my mother, Steph's betrayal, all the humiliation, everything.

"Yes. In a heartbeat."

Hardin's hand on mine, the way his inked arms wrapped around me, pulling me to his chest. The way he sometimes laughed so hard that his eyes would pinch closed and the sound would fill my ears, my heart, and the entire apartment with such a rare happiness that I felt more alive than I'd ever felt before.

"No. I wouldn't. I couldn't," I say, changing my answer.

Noah shakes his head. "Which is it?" He chuckles and sits on the recliner across from the couch. "I've never known you to be so indecisive."

I shake my head firmly. "I wouldn't erase it."

"You're sure? It's been a bad year for you . . . and I don't even know the half of it."

"I'm sure." I nod a couple of times, then take a seat on the edge of the couch. "I would do some things differently, though, with you."

Noah gives me a slight smile. "Yeah, me, too," he quietly agrees.

"THERESA." A hand grasps my shoulder and shakes me. "Theresa, wake up."

"I'm up." I groan and open my eyes. The living room. I'm in my mother's living room. I kick a blanket off my legs . . . a blanket Noah covered me with when I lay down after we talked a bit more and then started to watch some TV together. Just like old times.

I wriggle out of my mother's grip. "What time is it?"

"Nine p.m. I was going to wake you up earlier." She purses her lips.

It must have been driving her insane to let me sleep the day away. Oddly, the thought amuses me.

"Sorry, I don't even remember falling asleep." I stretch my arms and stand to my feet. "Did Noah leave?" I peer into the kitchen, and I don't see him.

"Yes. Mrs. Porter really wanted to see you, but I told her it wasn't a good time," she says and goes into the kitchen.

I follow her, smelling something cooking. "Thank you." I do wish I'd said a proper goodbye to Noah, especially because I know I'll see him again.

My mother goes to the stove and says over her shoulder, "Hardin brought your car, I see," disapproval coloring her voice. A moment later, she turns from the stove and hands me a plate of lettuce and grilled tomatoes.

I haven't missed her idea of a good meal. But I take the plate from her hand anyway.

"Why didn't you tell me that Hardin came here that night? I remember it now."

She shrugs. "He asked me not to."

Taking a seat at the table, I poke at the "meal" tentatively. "Since when do you care what he wants?" I challenge, nervous about her reaction . . .

"I don't," she says and prepares her own plate. "I didn't mention it because it's in your best interest not to remember."

My fork slips from my fingers and hits the plate with a sharp clink. "Keeping things from me isn't in my best interest," I say. I'm doing my best to keep my voice cool and calm, I really am. To emphasize this, I dab the corners of my mouth with a perfectly folded napkin.

"Theresa, do not take your frustrations out on me," my mother says, joining me at the table. "Whatever that man has done to make you this way is your own fault. Not mine."

The moment her red lips pull into a confident smirk, I stand from the table, throw my napkin onto the plate, and storm out of the room.

"Where are you going, young lady?" she calls.

"To bed. I have to get up at four in the morning, and I have a long drive ahead of me," I yell down the hallway and close the door to my bedroom.

I take a seat on my childhood bed . . . and immediately the light gray walls seem to be closing in on me. I hate this house. I shouldn't, but I do. I hate the way I feel inside it, like I can't breathe without being scolded or corrected. I never realized how caged and controlled I had been my entire life until I had my first taste of freedom with Hardin. I love having pizza for dinner, spending the entire day naked in bed with him. No folded napkins. No curled hair. No hideous yellow curtains.

Before I can stop myself, I'm calling him, and he's answering on the second ring.

"Tess?" he says, out of breath.

"Um, hey," I whisper.

"What's wrong?" he huffs.

"Nothing, are you all right?"

"Come on, Scott. Get back over here," a female voice says in the background.

My heart starts hammering against my rib cage as the possibilities flood my mind. "Oh, you're . . . I'll let you go."

"No, it's fine. She can wait." The background noise gets softer and softer by the second. He must be walking away from whoever she is.

"Really, it's okay. I'll just go, I don't want to . . . interrupt you." Looking at the gray wall nearest my bed, I swear it's crept closer to me. Like it's ready to pounce.

"Okay," he breathes.

What?

"Okay, bye," I say quickly and hang up, holding my hand over my mouth to keep from vomiting on my mother's carpet.

There has to be some sort of logical—

My phone buzzes next to my thigh, Hardin's name clear on the small screen. I answer despite myself.

"I'm not doing what you think I'm doing . . . I didn't even realize how it sounded," he immediately states. I can hear a harsh wind blowing around him, muffling his voice.

"It's okay, really."

"No, Tess, it wouldn't be," he says, calling me out. "If I was with someone else right now, that wouldn't be okay, so stop acting like it would be."

I lie back on the bed, admitting to myself that he's right. "I didn't think you were doing anything," I half lie. I somehow knew he wasn't, but my imagination . . . it took me there still.

"Good, maybe you finally trust me."

"Maybe."

"Which would be much more relevant if you hadn't left me." His tone is sharp.

"Hardin . . ."

He sighs. "Why did you call? Is your mum being a bitch?"

"No, don't call her that." I roll my eyes. "Well . . . she kind of is being one, but it's nothing big. I'm just . . . I don't know why I called, really."

"Well . . ." He pauses, and I hear a car door shut. "Do you want to talk or something?"

"Is that okay? Can we?" I ask him. Only hours ago I was telling him that I needed to be more independent, yet here I am, calling him the moment I'm upset.

"Sure."

"Where are you, anyway?" I need to keep the conversation as neutral as possible . . . not that it's ever possible to keep things between Hardin and me neutral.

"A gym."

I almost laugh. "A gym? You don't go to the gym." Hardin is

one of the few people to be blessed with an incredible body without ever having to work out. His naturally large build is perfect, tall with broad shoulders, even though he claims that he was lanky and thin as a young teenager. His muscles are hard but not too defined; his body is the perfect mixture of soft and hard.

"I know. She was kicking my ass. I was genuinely embarrassed."

"Who?" I say a little forcefully. *Calm down, Tessa, it's obviously the woman whose voice you heard.*

"Oh, the trainer. I decided to use that kickboxing shit you got me for my birthday."

"Really?" The thought of Hardin kickboxing makes me think about things that I shouldn't be thinking about. Like him sweating . . .

"Yeah," he says, a little shyly.

I shake my head to try to cast out the image of him shirtless. "How was it?"

"Okay, I guess. I prefer a different type of exercise. But on the plus side, I'm a lot less tense than I was a few hours ago."

I narrow my eyes at his response even though he can't see me.

My fingers trace the flower-print fabric of the comforter. "Do you think you'll go again?" I finally feel like I can breathe as Hardin begins to tell me about how awkward the first half hour of his session was, how he kept cursing at the woman until she slapped him across the back of his head, repeatedly, which, in turn made him respect her and stop being such a jerk to her.

"Wait." I finally speak. "Are you still there?"

"No, I'm home now."

"You just . . . left? Did you tell her?"

"No, why would I?" he asks, as if people acted like him all the time.

I like the idea that he dropped what he was doing just to talk to me on the phone. I shouldn't, but I do. Which warms me, but also makes me sigh and say, "We aren't doing a very good job on this space thing."

"We never do." I can picture his smirk even though he's speaking from more than a hundred miles away.

"I know, but—"

"This is our version of space. You didn't get in the car and drive here. You only called."

"I guess so . . ." I allow myself to agree with his twisted logic. In a way, though, he's right. I don't know yet if it's a good or a bad thing.

"Is Noah still there?"

"No, he left hours ago."

"Good."

I'm looking at the darkness beyond the ugly curtains of my room when Hardin laughs and says, "Talking on the phone is so fucking weird."

"Why?" I ask.

"I don't know. We've been talking for over an hour."

I pull my phone from my ear to check the time, and sure enough, he's right. "It doesn't seem that long," I say.

"I know, I never talk to anyone on the phone. Except when you call me to bother me about bringing something home, or a few calls to my friends, but they never last longer than like two minutes."

"Really?"

"Yeah, why would I? I was never into the teenage dating shit; all my friends used to spend hours on the phone listening to their girlfriends go on about nail polish or whatever the fuck girls talk about for hours on end." He laughs lightly, and I frown a little at the reminder that Hardin never got the chance to be a normal teenager.

"You didn't miss out on much," I assure him.

"Who did you used to talk to for hours? Noah?" Spitefulness is clear in his question.

"No, I never did that talking-for-hours thing either. I was busy shoving my nose into novels." Perhaps I was never a true teenager either.

"Well, I'm glad you were a nerd, then," he says, making my stomach flutter.

"Theresa!" I'm snapped back into reality as my mother repeatedly calls for me.

"Oh, is it past your bedtime?" Hardin teases. Our relationship, nonrelationship, giving-each-other-space-but-talking-on-the-phone thing, has become even more confusing within the last hour.

"Shut up," I respond and cover the receiver long enough to tell my mother I'll be right out. "I need to see what she wants."

"You're really going tomorrow?"

"Yeah, I am."

After a moment of silence, he says, "Okay, well, be safe . . . I guess."

"I can call you in the morning?" My voice is shaky as I offer.

"No, we probably shouldn't do this again," he says, and my chest tightens. "Well, not often, anyway. It doesn't make sense to talk all the time if we aren't going to be together."

"Okay." My response sounds small, defeated.

"Good night, Tessa," he says, and then the line goes dead.

He's right—I know he is. But knowing that doesn't make it hurt any less. I shouldn't even have called him in the first place.

chapter sixty-nine

TESSA

It's fifteen minutes until five o'clock in the morning, and for once my mother isn't dressed for going out. She's wearing a silk pajama suit and has her robe wrapped around her, matching slippers covering her feet. My hair is still damp from my shower, but I've taken the time to apply some makeup and decent clothing.

My mother studies me. "You have everything you need, correct?"

"Yes, everything I have is in my car," I say.

"Okay, be sure to get gas before you leave town."

"I'll be fine, Mother."

"I know. I'm only trying to help."

"I know you are." I open my arms to hug her goodbye, and when she gives me a stiff little embrace, I pull back and decide to pour myself a cup of coffee for the road. That small, silly hope still nags at me, the foolish part of me that wishes so badly that headlights will appear in the darkness, Hardin will climb out of the car, bags in hand, and tell me that he's ready to go to Seattle with me.

But that foolish part of me is just that: foolish.

At ten minutes after five, I give my mother one last hug and climb into the car, which fortunately I had the foresight to warm up with the heater on. Kimberly and Christian's address is programmed into the GPS on my phone. It keeps closing down and recalculating, and I haven't even left the driveway. I really do need a new phone. If Hardin were here, he'd remind me repeatedly that this is another reason to get an iPhone.

But Hardin's not here.

THE DRIVE IS LONG. I'm just at the beginning of my adventure, and already a thick cloud of unease is forming within me. Each small town that I pass makes me feel more and more out of place, and I wonder if Seattle will feel even worse. Will I settle in there, or will I run back to the main WCU campus, or even to my mother's place?

When I check the clock on my dashboard, I see it's only been an hour. Although, as I think about it, the hour did pass pretty quickly, which, in an odd way, makes my mind begin to feel lighter.

When I look again, twenty minutes have passed in a blink. The farther I get from everything, the lighter my mind feels. I'm not controlled by panicked thoughts as I drive down the dark and unfamiliar roads. I focus on my future. The future that no one can take from me, that no one can make me give up. I stop frequently for coffee, snacks, and just to breathe in the morning air. When the sun finally comes up halfway through my drive, I focus on the bright yellow and orange light it casts and the way the colors blend together, making a beautiful, bright new beginning to the day. My mood lightens with the sky, and I find myself singing along to Taylor Swift and tapping my fingers on the steering wheel as she talks about "trouble walking in"—and I laugh at the irony of the lyrics.

As I pass the sign welcoming me to the City of Seattle, my stomach fills with butterflies, the good kind. I'm doing this. Theresa Young is now officially in Seattle, making a life for herself at an age when most of her friends are still trying to figure out what they want to do with their lives.

I did it. I didn't repeat my mother's mistakes and rely on other people to carve my future for me. I had help, obviously—and I'm grateful for it—but it's up to me now to take it all to the next level. I have an amazing internship, a sassy friend and her loving fiancé, and a car full of my belongings.

I don't have an apartment . . . I don't have anything except my books, the few boxes in my backseat, and my job.

But it will work out.

It will. It has to.

I will be happy in Seattle . . . it'll be just like I had always imagined it to be. It will.

Every single mile drags on and on . . . every second is filled with memories, goodbyes, and doubts.

KIMBERLY AND CHRISTIAN'S HOUSE is even larger than I had expected from Kimberly's description. I'm nervous and intimated by the driveway alone. Trees line the property, the hedges around the house are well manicured, and the air smells of some flower I don't quite recognize. I park behind Kimberly's car and take a deep breath before climbing out. The large wooden door is crested with a large *V*—and I'm giggling at the arrogance of such a decoration when Kimberly opens the door.

She raises her eyebrow to me and follows my eyes to the door she's just opened. "We didn't put that there! I swear: the last family that lived here was named Vermon!"

"I didn't say anything," I inform her with a shrug.

"I know what you're thinking; it's hideous. Christian is a proud man, but even he wouldn't do such a thing." She taps the letter with her red fingernail, and I laugh again as she ushers me inside. "How was the drive? Come in, come in, it's cold out there."

I follow her into the foyer and welcome the warm air and sweet smell of a fireplace.

"It was okay . . . long," I tell her.

"I hope I never have to make that drive again." She scrunches up her nose. "Christian's at the office. I took the day off to make sure you get settled in. Smith will be home from school in a few hours."

"Thank you again for letting me stay. I promise I won't be here longer than two weeks."

"Don't stress yourself; you're finally in Seattle." She beams, and at last it hits me: *I AM in Seattle!*

chapter seventy

HARDIN

"How was the kickboxing yesterday?" Landon asks, his voice strained, his face contorted into a stupid-looking expression of physical effort as he lifts yet another bag of mulch. When he drops it into place, he puts his hands on his hips and says with a dramatic eye roll, "You could help, you know."

"I know," I say from the chair I'm sitting on and prop my feet up on one of the wooden shelves inside Karen's greenhouse. "Kickboxing was okay. The trainer was a woman, so that was fucking lame."

"Why? Because she kicked your butt?"

"You mean my *ass*? And no, she did not."

"What made you go, anyway? I told Tess not to buy you that pass to the gym, because you wouldn't use it."

Annoyance flares in my chest at the way he called her "Tess." I don't like it one fucking bit. *It's only Landon*, I remind myself. Of all the shit I have to worry about right now, Landon is the least of my concerns.

"Because I was enraged, and I felt like I was going to break everything in that goddamned apartment. So when I noticed the voucher as I was pulling out all of the drawers in the dresser, I grabbed it, put my shoes on, and took off."

"You pulled out all the drawers? Tessa's going to kill you . . ." He shakes his head and finally takes a seat on the stack of mulch bags. I don't know why he agreed to help his mum move all this shit around, anyway.

"She won't see it. . . it's not her place anymore," I remind him, trying to keep the edge out of my voice.

He looks at me guiltily. "Sorry."

"Yeah." I sigh; I don't even have a witty comeback.

"It's hard for me to feel bad for you when you could be there with her," Landon says after a few beats of silence.

"Fuck you." I lean my head back against the wall, and I can feel him staring at me.

"It doesn't make sense," he adds.

"Not to you."

"Or her. Or anyone."

"I don't have to explain myself to anyone," I snap.

"Then why are you even here?"

Instead of answering him, I look around the greenhouse, unsure of what I'm doing in this place myself. "I don't have anywhere else to go."

Does he think that I don't miss her every fucking second? That I wouldn't much rather be with her than standing here talking to him?

He gives me a sideways look. "What about your friends?"

"You mean the one who fucking drugged Tessa? Or the other one who set me up in order to tell her about the bet." I start counting them on my fingers to add to the dramatic effect. "Or you could mean the one who is constantly trying to get into her pants. Shall I go on?"

"Guess not. Though I could have told you that your friends sucked," he says in an annoying tone. "So what are you going to do?"

Deciding that keeping the peace is better than murdering him, I just shrug. "Exactly what I'm doing now."

"So you're going to hang out with me and mope around?"

"I'm not moping. I'm doing what you told me to do and *bettering myself*," I mock, using air quotes. "Have you talked to her since she left?" I ask.

"Yeah, she texted me this morning to tell me she arrived."

"She's at Vance's, isn't she?"

"Why don't you find out for yourself?"

Fuck, Landon is annoying. "I know she is. Where else would she be?"

"With that Trevor guy," Landon is quick to suggest. And his smirk makes me reconsider the stay of execution I had just granted him. If I tackled him, it wouldn't hurt much; he's only about three feet off the ground anyway. It probably wouldn't even leave a bruise . . .

"I forgot about fucking Trevor," I groan, rubbing harshly at my temples. Trevor is almost as infuriating as Zed. Only, I believe that Trevor does actually have good intentions when it comes to Tessa, which only upsets me even more. It makes him more dangerous.

"So what's next in Project Self-Improvement?" Landon smiles, but it fades quickly and his expression turns serious. "I'm really proud of you for doing this, you know. It's nice to see you actually trying for once, instead of making an effort for an hour, then going back to the way you were the moment she forgives you. It'll mean a lot to her to see you really following through on these changes."

I drop my feet and rock in the chair slightly. Talking like this is stirring something up in me. "Don't try to lecture me. I haven't done shit yet; it's only been a day." A long, miserable, lonely day.

Landon's eyes go wide in sympathy. "No, I'm serious. You didn't turn to alcohol and you haven't gotten into a fight, you haven't been arrested, and I know you came to talk to your dad."

My mouth drops open. "He *told* you?" That fucker.

"No, he didn't tell me. I live here, and I saw your car."

"Oh . . ."

"I think you talking to him really would mean a lot to Tessa," he continues.

"Would you just stop?" I say, imploring him with a quick

hunch of my shoulders. "*Fuck*. You're not my shrink. Stop acting like you're better than me and I'm some damaged fucking animal that you need to—"

"Why can't you just graciously accept a compliment?" Landon says over me. "I never said I was better than you. All I'm trying to do is be there for you as a friend. You don't have anyone—you said it yourself, and now that you let Tessa move to Seattle, you don't have a single person to give you moral support." He stares at me but I look away. "You have to stop pushing people away, Hardin. I know you don't like me—you hate me because you think I'm somewhat responsible for some of the issues you have with your dad, but I care deeply for Tessa and you, whether you want to hear that or not."

"I don't want to hear it," I fire back at him. Why does he always have to say shit like this? I came here to . . . I don't know, talk to him. Not to *talk* to him . . . not to have him tell me how much he cares about me.

And why would he care about me, anyway? I've been nothing but an asshole to him since the day I met him, but I don't hate him. Does he really think that I do?

"Well, that's one of those things you need to work on." He stands to his feet and walks out of the greenhouse, leaving me alone.

"Fuck." I kick my foot out in front of me, and it collides with the wooden shelving unit. A crack sounds through the room, and I jump to my feet. "No, no, no!"

I try to catch the flower boxes, clay pots, and random shit before they crash to the floor. Within seconds, all of it—the *pieces* of all of it—is on the floor. This isn't fucking happening. I didn't even mean to break this shit, and here I am with a pile of dirt, flowers, and cracked pots at my feet.

Maybe I can clean some of this shit up before Karen . . .

"Oh my," I hear her gasp, and I turn to the doorway to see her standing there, a little trowel in her hand.

Fuuuck.

"I didn't mean to knock them down, I swear. I kicked my foot out and accidentally broke the shelf—and all this shit started falling down, and I tried to catch it!" I frantically explain as Karen rushes over to a pile of broken pottery.

Her hands sift through the rubble, trying to piece together a blue flowerpot that has no chance of ever becoming one again. She doesn't say anything, but I hear her sniffle, and she lifts her arm to wipe her cheeks with her dirt-covered hands.

After a few seconds, she says, "I've had this pot since I was a little girl. It was the first pot I ever used for transplanting a cutting."

"I . . ." I don't know what to say to her. Of all the shit I've broken, this time it truly was an accident. I feel like complete shit.

"This and my china were the only things of my grandmother's that I had left," she cries.

The china. The china that I smashed into a million pieces.

"Karen, I'm sorry. I—"

"It's okay, Hardin." She sighs, tossing the pieces of the flowerpot back into the pile of dirt.

But it's not okay, I can see it in her brown eyes. I can see how hurt she is, and I'm surprised by the heaviness of the guilt I feel pressing on my chest at the sight of the sadness in her eyes. She stares at the shattered pot for a few more seconds, and I watch her silently. I try to imagine Karen as a young girl, big brown eyes and a kind soul even at that point. I bet she was one of those girls who was nice to everyone, even the assholes like me. I think about her grandmother, probably nice like her, giving her something that Karen felt was important enough to keep safe all these years. I've never had anything in my life that wasn't destroyed.

"I'm going to finish dinner. It'll be ready soon," she says at last.

Then, with a wipe of her eyes, she leaves the greenhouse the same way her son left only minutes ago.

chapter seventy-one

TESSA

There's no denying Smith and his adorable little way of walking around, looking at things, greeting you with a formal handshake, and then drilling you with questions as you try to do chores. So when I'm putting away my clothes and he waddles in and asks me in a quiet voice, "Where's your Hardin?" I can't really be upset.

It makes me a bit sad to have to say that I left him back at WCU, but the cuteness of this little kid eases some of that pain.

"And where's WCU?" he asks.

I do my best to smile. "It's a long way away."

Smith bats his beautiful green eyes. "Is he coming?"

"I don't think so. Um, you like Hardin, don't you, Smith?" I laugh and push the sleeves of my old maroon dress over a hanger and place it inside the closet.

"Sort of. He's funny."

"Hey, I'm funny, too!" I tease, but he only smiles a shy smile.

"Not really," he answers bluntly.

Which only makes me laugh harder. "Hardin thinks that I'm funny," I lie.

"He does?" Smith follows my actions and begins to help me unpack and refold my clothes.

"Yes, he won't admit it, though."

"Why?"

"I don't know." I shrug. Probably because I'm not very funny, and when I try to be funny, it's even worse.

"Well, tell your Hardin to come here and live, like you," he says very matter-of-factly. Like a little king issuing an edict.

My chest tightens at the sweet little boy's words. "I'll tell him. You don't have to fold those," I tell him, reaching for a blue shirt in his small hands.

"I like to fold." He hides the shirt back behind him, and what can I do but nod?

"You'll make a good husband one day," I tell him, and smile. His dimples show when he smiles back. At least he seems to like me a little more than he did before.

"I don't want to be husband," he says, scrunching up his nose, and I roll my eyes at this five-year-old who speaks exactly like a grown man.

"You'll change your mind one day," I tease.

"Nope." And with that he ends the conversation, and we finish with my clothes in silence.

My first day in Seattle is coming to a close, and tomorrow will be my first day at the new office. I'm extremely nervous and anxious about it. I don't care for new things; in fact, they terrify me. I like to be in control of every situation and enter new environments with a solid plan. I haven't had time to plan much about this move, save enrolling into my new classes, and honestly, I'm not looking forward to them as much as I should be. Somewhere in the middle of my scolding myself, Smith has disappeared, leaving a perfectly folded pile of clothing on the bed.

I need to get out and see Seattle tomorrow after work. I need to be reminded of what I loved so much about this city, because right now, in this strange bedroom, hours away from everything I've ever known, it just feels so . . . lonely.

chapter seventy-two

HARDIN

I watch Logan down the entire pint of beer, foamy head and all. Put the glass on the table and wipe his mouth. "Steph's a psycho. No one knew she was going to do that to Tessa," he says. And then burps.

"Dan knew. And if I find out that anyone else did . . ." I warn him.

He looks at me solemnly and nods. "No one else knew. Well . . . not that I know of. But you know no one tells me shit anyway." A tall brunette appears at his side, and he slides his arm around her. "Nate and Chelsea will be here soon," he says to her.

"A couples night," I groan. "Time for me to go." I move to stand, but Logan stops me.

"It's not a couples night. Tristan is single now, and Nate isn't dating Chelsea: they're just fucking."

I don't know why I came here anyway, but Landon would barely speak to me, and Karen looked so sad at dinner I just couldn't sit there at the table any longer.

"Let me guess: Zed will be here, too?"

Logan shakes his head. "I don't think so. I think he was even more pissed than you about the shit that went down, because he hasn't spoken to any of us since then."

"*No one* is more pissed than me," I say through my teeth. Hanging out with my old friends isn't helping me "better myself." It's only making me annoyed. How dare anyone say that Zed cares more about Tessa than I do.

Logan waves his hand in the air. "I didn't mean it like that . . . my bad. Have a beer and chill out." He looks around for the bartender.

I look over and see that Nate, she-who-must-be-Chelsea, and Tristan are walking across the floor of the small bar toward us.

"I don't want a fucking beer," I say quietly, trying to control my attitude. Logan is only trying to help, but he's annoying me. Everyone is annoying me. Everything is annoying me.

Tristan smacks me on the shoulder. "Long time no see," he tries to joke, but it's only awkward, and neither of us even cracks a smile. "I'm sorry about the shit that Steph did—I had no idea what she was up to, honest," he finally says, making it even more awkward.

"I don't want to talk about it," I say forcefully, closing the conversation.

While the small group of my friends drinks and talks about shit that I give absolutely no fuck about, I find myself thinking about Tessa. *What is she doing right now? Does she like Seattle? Does she feel as uncomfortable at Vance's house as I suspect she does? Are Christian and Kimberly being nice to her?*

Of course they are; Kimberly and Christian are always nice. So really, I'm just avoiding the big question: Does Tessa miss me the way I miss her?

"Are you going to have one?" Nate interrupts my thoughts and waves a shot glass in front of my face.

"No, I'm good." I gesture to my soda on the table, and he shrugs before tipping his head back to take the shot.

This is the last thing I want to be doing right now. This adolescent, drinking-until-they-throw-up-or-black-out shit may be good enough for them, but it's not for me. They haven't had the luxury of having someone's voice nagging in the back of their mind, telling them to be better, to do more with their lives. They haven't had anyone love them enough to make them want to be better.

I want to be good for you, Tess, I once told her. What a great job I've done so far.

"I'm going," I announce, but no one even notices as I stand from my seat and leave. I've made up my mind that I will no longer waste my time hanging out at bars with people who really don't give a shit about me. I have nothing against most of them, but in all actuality none of them really know me or care enough to. They only liked the drunk, rowdy, fucking-random-girls me. I was only another prop at one of their massive parties. They don't know shit about me—they didn't even know that my father is the fucking chancellor at our college. I'm sure they don't know what a chancellor does either.

No one knows me the way she does, no one has ever even cared to get to know me the way Tessa does. She always asks the most intrusive and random questions: *"What are you thinking?" "Why do you like that show?" "What do you think that man across the room is thinking right now?" "What is your first memory?"*

I always acted as if her need to know everything was obnoxious, but really it made me feel . . . special . . . or like someone cared about me enough to want to know the answers to these ridiculous questions. I don't know why my mind won't connect with itself; one half is telling me to get over myself and take my pathetic ass to Seattle, knock down Vance's door, and promise to never let her leave again. It's not that easy, though. There's a bigger, stronger, other part of me, the half that always wins, telling me how fucked up I am. I'm so fucked up, and all I do is ruin every fucking thing in my life and everyone else's, so I would be doing Tessa a favor by leaving her alone. That's the only side I can believe, especially without her here to tell me that I'm wrong. Especially since it's always proven to be true in the past.

Landon's plan for me to become a better person sounds good on paper, but then what? I'm supposed to believe that I can actually stay that way forever? I'm supposed to believe that I'll be good enough for her just because I decide not to down a bottle of vodka when I got mad?

This would be so much easier if I wasn't willing to admit how much of a fuckup I am. I don't know what I'm going to do, but the question's not going to be settled right now. For tonight, I'm going to go inside my apartment and watch Tessa's favorite television shows—the worst shows, which are full of ridiculous plot lines and horrible acting. I'll probably even pretend that she's there explaining every scene to me, even though I'm watching it right next to her, and I clearly understand what is going on. I love when she does that. It's annoying, but I love how passionate she is about the smallest details. Like who is wearing a red coat and harassing those obnoxious pretty little lying girls.

As I step off of the elevator, I continue to plan my night. I'll end up watching that shit, then eating, take a shower, probably get myself off while picturing Tessa's mouth around me, and I'll do my best not to do anything stupid. Maybe I'll clean up the mess I made yesterday even.

I stop in front of my apartment door and look back down the hall. Why the fuck is the door cracked open? Is Tessa back, or did someone break in again? I'm not sure which answer would make me angrier.

"Tessa?" I push the door open with my foot, and my stomach drops to the floor at the sight of her father slumped over, covered in blood.

"What the fuck?" I shout and slam the door closed.

"Watch out," Richard groans, and my eyes follow his to the hallway, where, over his shoulder, I catch sight of something moving.

A man's there, hovering over him. I square my shoulders and am ready to charge if need be.

But then I realize it's Richard's friend . . . Chad, I think his name is. "What the hell happened to him, and why the fuck are you here?" I ask him.

"I was hoping to see the girl, but you'll do," he sneers.

My blood boils at the way this vile man refers to my Tessa. "Get the fuck out and take him with you." I gesture to the piece of shit that brought this man to my apartment. His blood is making a mess on my floor.

Chad rolls his shoulders and twists his head back and forth. I can tell he's trying to be calm but is feeling agitated. "The problem with that is he owes me a lot of money, and he doesn't have a way to pay it," he says, his dirty fingernails scratching at the small red dots on his arms.

Fucking junkie.

I hold up a flat hand. "Not my fucking problem. I'm not going to tell you again to leave, and I'm sure as hell not giving you any money."

But Chad only smirks. "You don't know who you're talking to, kid!" He kicks Richard just below his rib cage. A pathetic whine falls from Richard's lips as he slides down onto the floor and doesn't get up.

I am *not* in the mood to deal with fucking drug addicts breaking into my apartment. "I don't give a fuck about you, or him. You're sadly mistaken if you think I'm afraid of you," I growl.

What the fuck else could possibly happen this week?

No, wait. I don't want to know the answer to that.

I step toward Chad, and he backs away, just like I knew he would. "Maybe to be nice, I *will* say it once more: get out or I'll call the cops. And while we wait for them to show up and save you, I'll be beating the shit out of you with the baseball bat I keep handy in case some dumb fuck tries to pull shit like this." I move toward the hall closet and grab the weapon from where it leans against the wall, lifting it slowly to prove my point.

"If I leave without the money he owes me, whatever I do to him is on you. His blood will be on your hands."

"I don't give a fuck what you do to him," I say. But then I'm suddenly unsure of whether I actually mean that.

"Sure," he says and looks around the living room.

"How fucking much money?" I say.

"Five hundred."

"I'm not giving you five hundred dollars." I know how Tessa will feel when she learns that my suspicions about her father being an addict are true, and this makes me want to throw the wallet in Chad's face and give him everything I have just to get rid of him. I hate knowing that I was right about her father; at this point she only half believes me, but soon she's going to have to realize the whole truth. I just wish this all would go away, Dick included. "I don't have that kind of cash on me."

"Two hundred?" he asks. I can practically see his addiction begging me through his eyes.

"Fine." I can't believe I'm actually giving money to this junkie who has broken into my apartment and beaten Tessa's dad to a pulp. I don't even have two hundred in cash. What am I supposed to do—take the creep with me to the ATM? This is such fucking bullshit.

Who the fuck comes home to this shit?

Me. That's fucking who.

For her. Only for her.

I pull my wallet from my pocket and toss the eighty dollars I just pulled from the bank at him and walk into the bedroom, bat still in hand. I grab the watch my father and Karen bought me for Christmas and throw it at him. For such a skeletal wreck of a human, Chad snatches it out of the air pretty deftly. He must really want it . . . or what he can trade it for.

"That watch is worth more than five hundred. Now get the

fuck out," I say. But I don't want him to leave, really, I want him to try to come at me so I can bust his head open.

Chad laughs, then coughs, then laughs again. "Until next time, Rick," he threatens and walks out the door.

I follow him and point the bat at him, saying, "And, Chad? If I see you again, I *will* kill you."

Then I slam the door on his ugly face.

chapter seventy-three

HARDIN

I nudge Richard's thigh with my boot. I'm beyond mad, and this whole mess is his damn fault.

"I'm sorry," he groans, attempting to lift himself up from the floor; within seconds he winces and slides back onto the hardwood. The last thing I want to do is lift his pathetic ass up off of the floor, but at this point I'm not sure what else to do with him.

"I'll put you in the chair, but you aren't sitting on my couch, not until you take a shower."

"Okay," he mutters and closes his eyes as I bend down to lift him. He's not as heavy as I expected him to be, especially for his height.

I drag him over to a kitchen chair, and as soon as I sit him down, he bends over, wrapping his arms around his torso.

"What now? What am I supposed to do with you now?" I ask him quietly.

What would Tessa do if she was here? Knowing her, she'd run him a hot bath and make him something to eat. I'm not doing either of those things.

"Take me back," he suggests. His shaky fingers lift the neckline of his torn T-shirt, something of mine that Tessa let him keep. Has he been wearing it since he left here? He wipes the blood from his mouth, lazily smearing it down his chin and into the mess of thick hair there.

"Back where?" I say. Maybe I should've called the police when I first entered the apartment, maybe I shouldn't have given

Chad that watch . . . I wasn't thinking properly at the time, all I could think about was keeping Tessa out of this.

But of course she's completely out of it already . . . she's so far away.

"Why did you bring him here? If Tessa had been here . . ." My voice trails off.

"She moved out. I knew she wouldn't be here," he strains to say.

I know it's hard for him to speak, but I need answers and my patience is running thin. "Did you come here a few days ago, too?"

"I did. I only came to eat and sh-shower," Richard pants.

"You came all the way here just to eat and shower?"

"Yeah, I took the bus the first time. But Chad"—he takes a breath and howls in pain before shifting his weight—"he offered to bring me here, but then he turned on me as soon as we got inside."

"How the fuck did you get in?"

"I took Tessie's spare key."

He took it . . . or she gave it to him? I wonder.

He nods toward the sink. "From the drawer."

"So let me get this straight, you stole a key to my apartment and thought you could just come here whenever the hell you wanted to take a shower. *Then* you bring Chad the Charming Junkie to my house, and he beats your ass in my living room because you owe him money?" How did I end up in the middle of an episode of *Intervention*?

"No one was home. I didn't think it mattered."

"You didn't think—that's the problem! What if Tessa had been the one to come here? Do you even care how she'd feel if she saw you like this?" I'm completely out of my element here. My first instinct is to drag this old fool out of our—out of *my* apartment and leave him bleeding in the hallway. I can't do that, though, because

I happen to be desperately in love with his daughter, and by doing it, all I'd accomplish would be to hurt her even more than I already have. Isn't love just fucking awesome?

"Well, what should we do now?" I scratch ay my chin. "Should I take you to a hospital?"

"I don't need a hospital, just a bandage or two. Can you call Tessie for me and tell her I'm sorry?"

I dismiss his suggestion with a sweep of the arm. "No, I will not. She isn't going to know about this. I don't want her worrying about this shit."

"Okay," he agrees and shifts on the chair again.

"How long have you been using?" I ask him.

He swallows. "I don't," he says meekly.

"Don't lie to me, I'm not a fucking idiot. Just tell me."

He looks deep in thought, distracted. "About a year, but I've been trying so hard to stop since the day I ran into Tessie."

"She's going to be heartbroken—you know that, don't you?" I hope he does. And I certainly have no problem reminding him multiple times if he ever happens to forget.

"I know, I'm going to get better for her," he claims.

Aren't we all . . .

"Well, you may want to hurry your rehabilitation along, because if she saw you now . . ." I don't finish the sentence. I'm debating whether or not to call her and ask her what the hell I'm supposed to do with her dad, but I know that's not the answer. She doesn't need to be bothered with this, not right now. Not while she's trying to turn her dreams into reality.

"I'm going to my room. Feel free to take a shower, eat, or whatever you were planning on doing before I came home and interrupted you." I saunter out of the kitchen and into the bedroom. I close the door behind me and lean against it. This has been the longest twenty-four hours of my life.

chapter seventy-four

TESSA

I can't keep the ridiculous grin off of my face as Kimberly and Christian show me my new office. The walls are a clean white, the trim and door are dark gray, and the desk and bookcases are black, sleek, and modern. The size of the room is the same as my first office, but the view here is incredible; breathtaking, really. The new Vance Publishing office is located in the center of downtown Seattle; the city below is thriving, constantly moving, constantly developing, and here I am, right in the center of it all.

"This is amazing—thank you so much!" I say, with probably more enthusiasm than most people would consider to be professional.

"Everything you need is within walking distance—coffee, any cuisine you could possibly crave, it's all here." Christian proudly stares down at the city and wraps his arm around his fiancée's waist.

"Stop bragging, would you?" Kimberly teases, and he plants a soft kiss to her forehead.

"Well, we'll leave you be. Now, get to work," Christian playfully scolds me. Kimberly grabs him by his tie and practically drags him out of the office.

I arrange the things in my desk the way I like them and read a little, but by lunchtime I've sent at least ten pictures of my office to Landon . . . and to Hardin. I knew that Hardin wouldn't respond, but I couldn't help myself. I wanted him to see the view—maybe it would make him change his mind about moving here? I'm only making excuses for my momentary lapse in judgment in sending him the pictures. But I miss him—there, I said it. I miss him terribly, and I was hoping for a response from him, even a simple text. Something. But nothing came.

Landon sent an excited response to each of the pictures, even when I sent a cheesy one of me holding a coffee mug with VANCE PUBLISHING printed on the side.

The more I dwell on my impulsive decision to send those pictures to Hardin, the more I regret it. What if he takes them the wrong way? He does have a tendency to do that. He may see them as a reminder of the fact that I'm moving on; he may even think that I'm trying to rub this whole thing in his face. That truly wasn't my intention, and I can only hope that he doesn't take it that way.

Maybe I should send another message to explain myself, I think. Or tell him that I sent the pictures accidentally. I don't know which would be more believable.

Neither, I'm sure. I'm overthinking this; after all, they're only pictures. And I can't be fully responsible for how he chooses to interpret them. I can't be fully responsible for his emotions like that.

When I walk into the break room on my floor, I find Trevor sitting at one of the square tables with a tablet in front of him.

"Welcome to Seattle," he says, his blue eyes beaming bright.

"Hey." I return his enthusiasm with a smile and swipe my debit card through the slot on the massive vending machine. I press a few small numbered buttons and am rewarded with a sleeve of peanut butter crackers. I'm too nervous to be hungry, and I'll go out for lunch tomorrow after I've had a chance to explore the area.

"How do you like Seattle so far?" Trevor asks.

I look to him for permission, and when he nods, I slide into the chair across from him. "I haven't seen much yet. I only arrived yesterday, but I love this new building."

Two women enter the room and smile at Trevor; one of them turns to smile at me, and I give her a small wave. They begin to talk with each other, and then the shorter woman, who has black hair, pulls open the refrigerator and takes out a microwavable meal while her friend picks at her fingernails.

"You should explore, then; there are so many things to do here. It's a beautiful city," Trevor declares as I munch absent-mindedly on a cracker. "The Space Needle, the Pacific Science Center, art museums, you name it."

"I do want to see the Space Needle, and Pike Place Market," I say. But I'm beginning to feel uneasy, because every time I glance over at the women, I can tell that they're both looking at me and talking quietly.

I'm quite paranoid today.

"You should. Have you decided where you're staying yet?" he asks, swiping his index finger across the screen to close the window on his tablet, giving me his full attention.

"I'm actually at Kimberly and Christian's house for right now . . . only for a week or two until I can find my own place." The urgency in my voice is embarrassing. I hate that I have to stay with them, because Hardin ruined my chance to rent the only apartment I could find. I want to live on my own and not worry about being a burden to anyone.

"I could ask around and see if there are any vacancies in my building," Trevor offers. He adjusts his tie and smoothes the silver fabric down before running his hands over the lapels of his suit.

"Thanks, but I'm not sure your building would be in my price range," I softly remind him. He's the head of finance, and I'm an intern—a decently paid intern, but I'm sure that I can't even afford to rent the Dumpster behind his building.

He flushes. "Okay," he says, realizing the massive difference between our incomes. "I can still ask around and see if anyone knows of any places."

"Thank you." I smile a convincing smile. "I'm sure Seattle will feel more like home once I actually have a home."

"I agree; it's going to take some time, but I know you'll love it here." His crooked grin is warm and welcoming.

"Do you have any plans after work?" I ask before I can stop myself.

"I do," he says, his soft voice fumbling. "But I can cancel them."

"No, no. It's fine, I was just thinking that since you know the city, you could show me around, but if you already have plans, don't worry about it." I hope that I can make some friends here in Seattle.

"I'd love to show you around. I was just going jogging, that's all."

"Jogging?" My nose crinkles. "What for?"

"For fun."

"That doesn't sound like much fun." I laugh, and he shakes his head in amused displeasure.

"I usually go every day after work. I'm still getting to know the city, too, and it's a good way to learn the layout. You should come along one day."

"I don't know . . ." The idea doesn't sound appealing.

"We could walk instead." He chuckles. "I live in Ballard; it's a pretty cool neighborhood."

"I've heard of Ballard, actually," I say, remembering browsing through page after page on sites showing the neighborhoods of Seattle. "Okay, yeah. Let's walk around Ballard, then." I close my hands in front of me and rest them on my lap.

I can't help but think how Hardin would feel about this. He despises Trevor, and he's already having a hard enough time with our "space" arrangement. Not that he's said this, but I'd like to think that he is. Regardless of how much space is put between Hardin and me, literal or metaphorical, I only see Trevor as a friend. The last thing on my mind is being romantic with someone, especially anyone other than Hardin.

"Okay, then." He smiles, clearly surprised that I've agreed to come along. "My lunch hour is over, so I have to get back to my office, but I'll text you my address, or we can go straight from work if you want."

"Let's just go straight from here—I'm wearing reasonable shoes." I point down to my flats, mentally patting myself on the back for not wearing heels today.

"Sounds good. I'll meet you at your office at five?" he says and stands up.

"Yes, that's fine." I get up, too, and toss the crackers wrapper into the trash can.

"We all know why she got the job anyway," I hear one of the women say behind me.

When, out of curiosity, I look over to where they're sitting, they both quickly get quiet and stare down at the table. I can't help but feel that they were talking about me.

So much for making friends in Seattle.

"All those two do is gossip, ignore them," Trevor says, placing his hand between my shoulder blades and guiding me out of the break room.

When I get back to my office, I reach into my desk drawer and pull out my cell phone. Two missed calls, both from Hardin.

Should I call him back right now? *He called twice, so maybe something is wrong. I should*, I think, by way of bargaining with myself.

He answers on the first ring, and hurriedly says, "Why didn't you answer when I called you?"

"Is something wrong?" I stand up from my chair in a slight panic.

"No. Nothing's wrong," he breathes. I can picture the exact way his pink lips move as he says the simple words "Why did you send those pictures?"

I look around my office, worried about upsetting him. "I was just excited about my office, and I wanted you to see it. I hope you didn't think I was trying to be mean about it and brag. I'm sorry for—"

"No, I was just confused," he coolly interjects, then goes silent.

After a few seconds, I say, "I won't send any more, I shouldn't even have sent those." I lean my forehead against the office window and stare down at the streets of the city.

"Don't worry, it's fine . . . how is it there? Do you like the place?" Hardin's voice is somber, and I want to smooth away the frown that I know is marring his face right now.

"It's lovely here."

He calls me out, I knew he would: "You didn't answer the question."

"I like it here," I say softly.

"You sound absolutely ecstatic."

"I really do like it, I'm just . . . adjusting. That's all. What's happening back there?" I ask in order to keep the conversation going. I'm not ready to get off the phone with him just yet.

"Nothing," he quickly responds.

"Is this awkward for you? I know you said you didn't want to talk on the phone, but you called me, so I was just—"

"No, it's not awkward," he interrupts. "It's never awkward with us, and I only meant I don't think we should talk for hours every day if we aren't going to be together, because that doesn't make any sense and it's only going to torture me."

"So you do want to talk to me, then?" I ask because I'm pathetic and I need to hear him say the words.

"Yes, of course I do."

A car horn honks in the background, and I think he must be driving. "So what, then? We're going to chat on the phone, like friends?" he asks, no anger in his voice at all, only curiosity.

"I don't know, maybe we could try that?" This separation feels so different from the last; this time we separated on good terms, and it wasn't a clean break. I'm not ready to decide if a clean break from Hardin is what I actually need, so I push the thought back, file it away, and promise to visit it later.

"It won't work."

"I don't want us to ignore one another and not speak again, but I haven't changed my mind about the space thing," I tell him.

"Fine, tell me about Seattle, then," he finally says into the receiver.

chapter seventy-five

TESSA

After I spend half an afternoon on the phone with Hardin and getting close to no actual work done, my first day at the new office is over, and I wait patiently for Trevor just outside my door.

Hardin was so calm earlier, and he sounded so clear, as if he was focused on something. Standing here in the corridor, I can't contain my happiness that we're still communicating; it's so much better now that we're no longer avoiding each other. Deep down, I know that it won't continue to be this easy, talking this way, teasing myself with small doses of Hardin when in reality I want him, all of him, all the time. I want him here with me, holding me, kissing me, making me laugh.

This must be what denial feels like.

I'm fine with that for now. It feels pretty good, compared to my other option: sadness.

I sigh and rest my head against the wall as I continue to wait. I'm beginning to wish that I hadn't asked Trevor if he was free after work. I'd rather be at Kimberly's house, talking on the phone to Hardin. I wish he had just come here; he could be the one meeting me instead. He could have an office close to mine; he could come by my office multiple times a day, and in between those times, I could make excuses to go to his. I'm sure Christian would give Hardin a job if he wanted one. He's made it clear that he wanted Hardin to work for him again a couple of times.

We could spend our lunch hour together, maybe even re-create some of the memories we shared at the old office. I begin picturing Hardin behind me, me bent down over the top of my desk, my hair wrapped tightly around his fist—

"Sorry I'm a little late, my meeting ran over." Trevor interrupts my reverie, and I jump in both surprise and embarrassment.

"Oh, um, it's okay. I was just"—I tuck my hair behind my ear and swallow—"waiting."

If only he knew what I was thinking; thank goodness he doesn't have a clue. I'm not sure where those thoughts even came from.

He inclines his head the other way, peering down the empty hallway. "Are you ready to go?"

"Yes."

We make small talk as we walk through the building. Nearly everyone has left for the day, leaving the office quiet. Trevor tells me about his brother's new job in Ohio and how he went shopping for a new suit to wear to our coworker Krystal's wedding next month. Idly, I wonder just how many suits Trevor owns.

Once we get to our cars, I follow Trevor's BMW as he drives through the crowded city, and we finally arrive in the small neighborhood of Ballard. According to the blogs I was reading before my move, it's one of the hippest neighborhoods in Seattle. Coffee shops, vegan restaurants, and hipster bars line the narrow streets. I pull my car into the parking garage beneath Trevor's building and laugh to myself while remembering that he offered to help me find an apartment in this pricey place.

Trevor smiles, gesturing to his suit. "I just need to change, obviously."

Once we get to his apartment and he wanders off, I nosily glance around his expansive living room. Pictures of family and articles clipped from newspapers and magazines fill the frames on his mantel; an intricate display piece made from melted and molded wine bottles takes up the entire coffee table. Not a trace of dust has been allowed to collect in any of the corners. I'm impressed.

"Ready!" Trevor announces, stepping out of his bedroom and zipping up a red sweatshirt. It always catches me off guard to see him dressed so casually—it's such a vast difference from how he looks normally.

After walking two blocks from his building, both of us are shivering and shaking.

"Are you hungry, Tessa? We can grab something to eat." White puffs of cold air follow his words.

I nod eagerly. My stomach growls in hunger, reminding me of just how insufficient a package of peanut butter crackers is for lunch.

I tell Trevor to choose a restaurant he likes, and we end up at a small Italian grill only feet away from where we were just walking. The sweet smell of garlic fills my senses, and my mouth waters as we're escorted to a small booth in the back.

chapter seventy-six

HARDIN

"You look much more . . . *hygienic* now," I tell Richard as he steps out of the bathroom wiping his freshly shaven face with a white towel.

"I haven't shaved my face in months," he responds, rubbing the smooth skin on his chin.

"You don't say." I roll my eyes, and he grants me half a smile.

"Thanks again for letting me stay here . . ." His deep voice trails off.

"It's not permanent, so don't thank me. I'm still not cool with this whole situation." I take another bite of the pizza I ordered for myself . . . and ended up sharing with Richard. I need to find a way to take some of the pressure off of Tessa. She has too much going on lately, and if I can help her in any way by handling this mess with her father, I will.

"I know it. I'm surprised you haven't thrown me out yet," he says with a laugh. As if that's something to make a joke about. I stare at him. His eyes look too large for his face, with dark rings showing through his white skin.

I sigh. "So am I," I admit with annoyance.

Richard quivers while I stare at him—not from intimidation, but from a lack of whatever the hell drug it is that he's used to taking.

I want to know if he brought any drugs into our apartment while he was staying here just last week. However, if I ask him and he says yes, I'll lose my temper and he'll be out of my apartment within seconds. For Tessa's sake, and for mine, I rise to my feet and leave the living room with my empty plate in hand. The stack of dirty dishes in the sink has managed to double in size, and loading the dishwasher is the last thing I want to do at the moment.

"Do the dishes as payment!" I call to Richard.

I hear his deep laughter from the hallway, and he walks into the kitchen just as I reach the bedroom door and close it.

I want to call Tessa again, just to hear her voice. I want to know about the rest of her day . . . What does she plan to do after work? Did she stare at her phone with a stupid-ass grin on her face after we hung up earlier, like I did?

Probably not.

I now know that all my past sins are finally catching up to me—that's why Tessa was given to me. A merciless punishment disguised as a beautiful reward. Having her for months just to have her taken from me, yet still dangling in front of my face by means of casual phone calls. I don't know how much longer it will be until I succumb to my fate and finally allow myself to break out of this denial.

Denial, that's exactly what this is.

It doesn't have to be, though. I can change the outcome of all this. I can be who she needs me to be without dragging her down to my hell again.

Fuck this, I'm calling her.

Her phone rings and rings, yet she doesn't pick up. It's almost six—she should be done with work and back at her place. Where the hell else would she go? While debating whether or not to call Christian, I push my feet into my gym shoes, lazily tie them, and shove my arms through my jacket.

I know she'll be upset—*beyond* mad, surely—if I call him, but I've already called her six times, and she hasn't answered once.

I groan and run my fingers over my unwashed hair. This giving-each-other-space shit is really fucking irritating me.

"I'm going out," I tell my unwanted houseguest. He nods, unable to speak due to the handful of potato chips that he's shoveling into his mouth. At least the sink is free of dishes now.

Where the fuck am I even supposed to go?

Within minutes, my car is parked in the lot behind the small gym. I don't know what being here will accomplish or if this shit will help me, but right now I'm growing more and more irritated at Tessa, and all I can think about doing is cussing her out or driving to Seattle to find her. I don't need to do either of those things . . . they'd only make things worse.

chapter seventy-seven

TESSA

By the time my plate is clear, I'm practically twitching in my seat. The moment we ordered our meals I realized that I left my phone in my car, and it's driving me more insane than it should. No one really calls me much. However, I can't help but think that maybe Hardin has, or at least sent me a text message. I'm trying my best to listen to Trevor while he talks about an article in the *Times* he read, trying not to think of Hardin and the possibility that he may have called, but I can't help it. I'm distracted during the entire dinner and am positive that Trevor notices; he's just too kind to call me out on it.

"Don't you agree?" Trevor's voice pulls me from my thoughts.

I scramble through the last few seconds of conversation, trying to remember what he could be talking about. The article was about health care . . . I think.

"Yeah, I do," I lie. I have no clue if I agree or not, but I do wish the server would hurry and bring our check.

As if on cue, the young man places a small booklet on our table, and Trevor hastily pulls out his wallet.

"I can . . ." I begin.

But he slides several bills inside, and the server disappears back into the restaurant kitchen. "It's on me."

I quietly thank him and glance at the large stone clock hanging just above the door. It's past seven; we've been in the restaurant for over an hour. I let out a breath of relief when Trevor says, "Well," claps his hands, and stands.

On the way back to his place, we pass a small coffee shop, and Trevor raises his brow, a silent invitation.

"Maybe another night this week?" I offer with a smile.

"Sounds like a plan." The corner of his mouth rises into his famous half smile, and we continue the trek to his building.

With a quick goodbye and a friendly hug, I climb into my car and immediately reach for my phone. I'm frazzled with anxiety and desperation, but I shove those feelings back into the darkness. Nine missed calls, every single one from Hardin.

I call him back immediately, only to get his voicemail. The drive from Trevor's apartment to Kimberly's house is long and tedious. The traffic in Seattle is terrible, bumper-to-bumper and noisy. Honking horns, small cars whipping from lane to lane—it's pretty overwhelming, and by the time I pull into the driveway, I have a massive headache.

When I step through the front door, I see Kimberly seated on the white leather couch, a glass of wine in her hand. "How was your day?" she asks and leans over to place her drink onto the glass table in front of her.

"Good. But the traffic in this city is *unreal*," I groan and plop down on the crimson chair next to the window. "My head is killing me."

"Yeah, it is. Have some wine for your headache." She stands up and walks across the living room.

Before I can protest, she pours the bubbling white wine into a long-stemmed glass and brings it to me. Taking a little sip, I find it's cool and crisp, sweet on my tongue.

"Thank you," I say with a smile and take bigger sip.

"So . . . you were with Trevor, right?" Kimberly is so nosy . . . in the sweetest way.

"Yes, we had a friendly dinner. As friends," I say innocently.

"Maybe you could try answering again and use the word

'friend' a few more times," she teases, and I can't help but laugh.

"I'm just trying to make it clear that we're only . . . uh . . . friends."

Her brown eyes shine with curiosity. "Does Hardin know you were being *friends* with Trevor?"

"No, but I plan on telling him as soon as I speak to him. He doesn't care for Trevor, for some reason."

She nods. "I can't blame him. Trevor could be a model, if he wasn't so shy. Have you seen those blue eyes of his?" She exaggerates her words by fanning her face with her free hand, and we both giggle like schoolgirls.

"Don't you mean *green* eyes, love?" Christian says as he suddenly appears in the foyer, causing me to nearly drop my glass of wine onto the hardwood floor.

Kim smiles at him. "Of course I do."

But he just shakes his head and gives us both a sly smile. "I suppose I could be a model as well," he comments with a wink. For my part, I'm relieved that he isn't upset. Hardin would have flipped the table over if he caught me speaking about Trevor the way Kimberly was.

Christian sits down on the couch next to Kimberly, and she climbs into his lap. "And how's Hardin doing? You've spoken to him, I assume?" he asks.

I look away. "Yes, a little. He's good."

"Stubborn, he is. I'm still offended that he hasn't taken me up on my offer, given his situation."

Christian smiles into Kim's neck and kisses her softly just beneath her ear. These two clearly have no issue with public displays of affection. I try to look away again, but I can't.

Wait . . .

"What offer?" I ask, my surprise obvious.

"Why, the job I offered him—I told you about it, didn't I? I wish he'd come out here. I mean, he only has, what, one semester left, and he'll be graduating early, no?"

What? Why didn't I know about this? This is the first I've heard about Hardin graduating early. But I respond, "Erm, yeah . . . I believe so."

Christian wraps his arms around Kimberly and rocks her a little. "He's practically a genius, that boy. If he had applied himself a little more, his GPA would be a perfect four."

"He really is very smart . . ." I agree. And it's true. Hardin's mind never ceases to surprise and intrigue me. It's one of the things that I love most about him.

"Quite the writer, too," he says and steals a sip of Kimberly's wine. "I don't know why he decided to stop. I was looking forward to reading more of his work." Christian sighs while Kimberly undoes the silver tie around his neck.

I'm overwhelmed by this information. Hardin . . . writing? I remember him briefly mentioning that he used to dabble a little in it during his freshman year of college, but he never went into detail. Every time I brought it up in conversation, he'd change the subject or pooh-pooh the idea, giving me the impression that it wasn't very important to him.

"Yeah." I finish off my wine and stand, pointing to the bottle. "May I?"

Kimberly nods. "Of course, have as much as you please. We have an entire cellarful," she says with a sweet smile.

Three glasses of white wine later, my headache has evaporated and my curiosity has grown geometrically. I wait for Christian to bring up Hardin's writing or the job offer again, but he doesn't. He dives into a full-blown business discussion about how he has been in talks with a media group to expand Vance Publishing's in-house film and television efforts. As interesting as it is, I want to get to my room and try to call Hardin again. When an appropriate opening presents itself, I wish them a both a good night and excuse myself to rush off to my temporary bedroom.

"Take the bottle with you!" Kimberly calls to me just as I pass the table where the half-full wine bottle rests.

I nod, thanking her, and do just that.

chapter seventy-eight

HARDIN

I walk into the apartment, my legs still sore from kicking the hell out of that bag at the gym. Grabbing a water bottle from the fridge, I try to ignore the sleeping man on my couch. It's for her, I remind myself. All for her. I gulp down half of the bottle, dig my phone out of my gym bag, and turn on the power. Just as I try to call her, her name pops up on my screen.

"Hello?" I answer as I pull my sweat-soaked T-shirt over my head and toss it to the floor.

"Hi" is all she says.

Her response is short. Too short. I want to talk to her. I need her to want to talk to me.

I kick at my shirt, then pick it up, knowing that if she could see me, she'd scowl at me for being such a slob. "What are you up to?"

"I went out exploring the city," she answers calmly. "I tried to call you back, but it went to your voicemail." The sound of her voice soothes my temper.

"I went back to that gym." I lie back on the bed, wishing she were here with me, her head on my chest, instead of in Seattle.

"You did? That's great!" she says, then adds, "I'm taking my shoes off."

"Okay . . ."

She giggles. "I don't know why I told you that."

"Are you drunk?" I sit up, using one elbow to hold my weight.

"I've had some wine," she admits. I should have caught that immediately.

"With who?"

"Kimberly, and Mr. Vance . . . Christian, I mean."

"Oh." I don't know how I feel about her going out drinking in a foreign city, but I know it's not the time to bring that up.

"He says you're an amazing writer," she says, accusation clear in her voice. *Fuck.*

"Why would he say that?" I reply. My heart pounds.

"I don't know. Why won't you write anymore?" Her voice is full of wine and curiosity.

"I don't know. But I don't want to talk about me. I want to talk about you and Seattle and why you've been avoiding me."

"Well, he also said you're graduating next semester," she says, ignoring my words.

Christian obviously has no idea how to mind his own damned business. "Yeah, so?"

"I didn't know that," Tessa says. I hear her shuffling around, and she groans, clearly irritated.

"I wasn't hiding it from you, it just didn't come up. You have a long time before you graduate, so it doesn't matter anyway. It's not like I was going to go anywhere."

"Hang on," she says into the phone. What the hell is she doing? How much wine has she drunk?

After listening to her mumble incomprehensibly and futz around, I finally ask, "What are you doing?"

"What? Oh, my hair was caught in my shirt buttons. Sorry, I was listening, I promise."

"Why were you grilling your boss about me, anyway?"

"He brought you up. You know, since he offered you a job a couple of times and you refused, you were a *topic*," she says with emphasis.

"Old news." I don't exactly remember mentioning the offer,

but I wasn't purposely keeping it from her. "My intentions concerning Seattle have always been clear."

"You can say that again," she says, and I can practically see her rolling her eyes . . . again.

I change the subject. "You didn't answer when I called you. I called so many times."

"I know, I left my phone in the car at Trevor's . . ." She stops midsentence.

I stand from the bed and pace across the room. I fucking *knew* it.

"He was only showing me around as friends, that's it." She's quick to defend herself.

"You didn't answer my calls because you were with *fucking Trevor*?" I growl, my pulse quickening with each beat of the silence that meets my question.

Then she snaps: "Don't you fight with me over Trevor, he's only a friend, and you're the one who isn't here. You don't choose my friends, do you understand?"

"Tessa . . ." I warn.

"Hardin Allen Scott!" she exclaims, and bursts into laughter.

"Why are you laughing?" I ask, but I can't help the smile that takes over my face. Fuck, I'm pathetic.

"I . . . don't know!"

The sound of her laughter resonates through my ears and travels straight down to my heart, warming my chest.

"You should put the wine down," I tease, wishing I could see her roll her eyes in response to my scolding her.

"*Make* me," she challenges, her voice thick and playful.

"If I was there, I would—you can be damned sure of that."

"What else would you do if you were here?" she asks me.

I drop back onto my bed. Is she taking this where I think she is? I never know with her, especially when she's been drinking.

"Theresa Lynn Young—are you trying to have phone sex with me?" I taunt her.

Immediately she coughs violently—choking on a gulp of wine, I assume. "What! No! I . . . I was just asking!" she squeals.

"Sure, you can deny it now," I joke, laughing at her horrified tone.

"Unless . . . is that something *you* want to do?" she whispers.

"You're serious?" The thought alone makes my cock twitch.

"Maybe . . . I don't know. Are you mad about Trevor?" The tone of her voice is much more intoxicating to me than any amount of wine I could consume.

Hell yes I'm irritated that she was with him, but that's not what I want to discuss right now. I hear her gulp loudly, followed by the soft clink of a glass. "I don't give a shit about fucking Trevor right now," I lie. Then I command, "Don't chug the wine." I know her too well. "You'll get sick."

I hear a couple of loud gulps come through the phone. "You can't boss me around long distance." She's chugging the wine again, to build up her nerve, I'm sure.

"I can boss you around from any distance, baby." I grin, running my fingers over my lips.

"Can I tell you something?" she asks quietly.

"Please do."

"I was thinking about you today, and when you came to my office that first time . . ."

"You were thinking about me fucking you when you were with him?" I ask her, praying she says yes.

"At the time, I was waiting for him."

"Tell me more about it, tell me what you were thinking," I press.

This is so fucking confusing. Every time I'm talking to her I feel as if we aren't "taking a break," that everything is the same as it's always been. The only difference at the moment is that I can't physically see her, or touch her. Fuck, I want to touch her, run my tongue across her smooth skin . . .

"I was thinking about how . . ." she starts, but then takes another drink.

"Don't be embarrassed." I coax her to continue.

"That I liked it, and it made me want to do it again."

"With who?" I ask, just to hear her say it.

"You, only you."

"Good," I say with a smooth grin. "You're still mine, even though you're making me give you space; you're still only for me—you know that, don't you?" I ask her in the most gentle way I possibly can.

"I know," she says. My chest swells, and I welcome the flood of relief that comes along with her words. "Are you mine?" she asks in a voice filled with much more confidence than it had moments ago.

"Yes, always."

I don't have a choice. I haven't since the day I met you, I want to add, but I stay quiet, nervously awaiting her response.

"Good," Tessa says with authority. "Now, tell me what you would do if you were here, and don't leave out any details."

chapter seventy-nine

TESSA

My thoughts are slightly hazy, and my head feels full and heavy, but in the best way. I'm grinning from ear to ear, intoxicated from the wine and Hardin's thick voice. I love this playful side of Hardin, and if he wants to play, I'll play.

"Oh no," he says with that cool tone of his. "You tell me what you'd want me to do first."

I take a pull straight from the bottle. "I already did," I say.

"Chug some more wine; you only seem to tell me what you want when you've been drinking."

"Fine." I run my index finger along the cool wooden bed frame. "I want you to bend me over this bed here . . . and take me the way you did on that desk." Instead of embarrassment, I only feel the warm flush of heat trailing up my neck to my cheeks.

Hardin curses under his breath; I know that he didn't actually expect me to answer more graphically. "Then?" he asks quietly.

"Well . . ." I start, pausing to take another long swig to gain confidence. Hardin and I have never done this before. He's sent me a few racy text messages, but this . . . this is different.

"Just say it, don't be shy now."

"You would hold me by the hips, the way you always do, and I'd cling to the sheets to try and keep myself stable. Your fingers would dig into me, leaving marks in their wake . . ." I clench my thighs together when I hear his breathing hitch through the line.

"Touch yourself," he says, and I quickly look around the

room, momentarily forgetting that no one can hear our private conversation.

"What? No," I harshly whisper, cupping the phone.

"Yes."

"I'm not doing that . . . here. They'll hear me." If I were talking to anyone other than Hardin in this way, I'd be completely horrified, wine or not.

"No, they won't. Do it. You want to, I can tell."

How can he?

Do I want to?

"Just lie back on the bed, close your eyes, spread your legs, and I'll tell you what to do," he says smoothly. As silken as his words are, they come through as a full-on command.

"But I—"

"Do it." The authority in his voice makes me squirm while my mind and my hormones battle it out. I can't deny that the idea of Hardin coaxing me through this over the phone, naming the dirty things he would do to me, raises the temperature of the room at least ten degrees.

"Okay, now that you've submitted, " he begins without my actually having said anything, "tell me when you are down to only your panties."

Oh . . . But I quietly pad over to the door and turn the lock between my fingers. Kimberly and Christian's room, as well as Smith's, is on the upper level of the house, but as far as I know, they could still be on the first floor with me. I listen closely for movement, and when I hear a door shut above me, I feel better.

I hurry and grab the wine bottle, finishing it off. The heat inside of me has turned from a small flicker to a blazing inferno, and I try not to overthink the fact that I'm stepping out of my pants and climbing onto the bed, wearing only a thin cotton shirt and panties.

"Still with me?" Hardin asks, an evil smirk surely on his face.

"Yes, I'm . . . I'm preparing." I can't believe I'm really doing this.

"Stop overthinking it. You'll thank me after."

"Stop knowing everything that I'm thinking," I tease, hoping that he's right.

"You remember what I showed you, right?"

I nod, forgetting that he can't see me.

"I'll take nervous silence as a yes. Good. So, just press your fingers where you did last time . . ."

chapter eighty

HARDIN

I hear Tessa gasp, and I know she's followed my instructions. I can picture it perfectly, her lying on the bed, legs spread open. *Holy fuck.*

"God, I wish I was there right now, to watch you," I groan, trying to ignore the blood rushing straight to my dick.

"You like that, don't you—to watch me?" she gasps through the line.

"Yeah, fuck yeah, I do. And you like to be watched, I can tell."

"I do, just like the way you like it when I pull your hair."

Reflexively, my hand goes between my legs. Images of her writhing underneath my tongue, her fingers tugging my hair as she moans my name, fill my mind, and I press my palm against myself. Only Tessa can make me this hard this quickly.

Her moans are quiet, too quiet. She needs more encouragement.

"Faster, Tess, move your fingers in a circle, faster. Imagine I'm there, it's me, and my fingers are circling you, making you feel so fucking good, making you come," I say, keeping my voice down in case my annoying houseguest happens to be in the hall.

"Oh my," she pants and moans again.

"My tongue, too, baby, swirling against your skin, my sinful lips pressed against you, sucking, biting, teasing." I slide my gym shorts down and begin to stroke myself gently. I close my eyes and focus on her soft pants, pleas, and moans.

"Do what I'm doing—touch yourself," she whispers, and I'm

gifted with the image of her back arching off the mattress as she pleasures herself.

"Already am," I mutter, and she whimpers. *Fuck, I want to see her.*

"Talk to me, again," Tessa begs. I fucking love the way her innocence disappears in these moments . . . she always loves to hear such filthy things.

"I want to fuck you. No—I want to lay you back on the bed, and make love to you, hard and fast, so powerfully that you're screaming my name as I thrust deeper and deeper—"

"I'm . . ." she moans low in her throat. And her breath catches.

"Come on, baby, let go. I want to hear you." I stop speaking when I hear her come, soft whimpers and whines as she bites into the pillow, or the mattress. I have no fucking clue, but the image sends me over the edge, and I spill into my boxers with a strangled groan of her name.

Our matched breathing is the only sound on the line for seconds or minutes, I can't keep track.

"That was . . ." she begins, panting and out of breath.

I open my eyes and rest my elbows on the desk in front of me. My chest moves up and down as I try to catch my own breath. "Yeah."

"I need a moment." She giggles. A slow smile tugs at the corners of my mouth, and then she adds, "And here I thought we had done close to everything."

"Oh, there are plenty of other things I want to do to you. However, alas, we have to be in the same city to do them."

"Come here, then," she says quickly.

I put the phone on speaker and examine my hand, front and back. "You said you didn't want me there. We need space, remember?"

"I know," she says a little sadly. "We do need space . . . and this seems to be working for us. Don't you think?"

"No," I lie. But I know she's right: I've been trying to be better for her, and I'm afraid that if she's quick to forgive me again, I'll slip and lose the motivation. If we . . . *when* we find our way back to each other, I want it to be different, for her. I want it to be permanent so I can show her that the pattern—the "endless cycle," as she calls it—will end.

"I do miss you, so much," she says. I know she loves me, but each time I'm given a sliver of reassurance, it's like a weight's been lifted from my chest.

"I miss you, too." More than anything.

"Don't say 'too.' It sounds like you're just agreeing with me," she says sarcastically, and my small smile grows, overtaking my entire being.

"You can't use my ideas; way to be original," I playfully scold her and she laughs.

"Can, too," she childishly fires back. If she were here, I'd be greeted with her tongue sticking out at me in mock defiance.

"God, you're feisty tonight." I roll off the bed; I need a shower.

"That I am."

"And incredibly daring. Who knew I could convince you to get yourself off over the phone?" I chuckle and walk into the hallway.

"Hardin!" she squeals in horror, like I knew she would. "And by the way, you should know by now that you can get me to do just about anything."

"If only that were true . . ." I murmur. If it was, she would be here now.

In the hallway, the floor is cold on my bare feet, and I wince. But when I hear a voice start to speak, I drop my phone to the ground.

"Sorry, man," Richard says close to me. "It was getting a little warm in here earlier, so I—"

He stops when he sees me scramble to pick up my phone, but it's too late.

"Who was that?" I hear Tessa exclaim through the speaker on my phone. The drowsy, relaxed girl she'd been so recently is gone, and she's on high alert. "Hardin, who *was that*?" she asks more forcefully.

Fuck. I mouth a quick "way to fucking go" to her father and grab the phone, removing it from speaker and hurrying to the bathroom. "It's—" I begin.

"Was that my father?"

I want to lie to her, but that would be fucking stupid, and I'm trying not to be so damn stupid anymore. "Yeah, it was," I say, and wait for her to scream into the receiver.

"Why is he there?" she questions.

"I . . . well . . ."

"Are you letting him stay with you?" She releases me from the panic of having to find the right words to say in order to explain this fucked-up situation.

"Something like that."

"I'm confused."

"So am I," I admit.

"For how long? And why didn't you tell me?"

"I'm sorry . . . it's only been like two days."

The next thing I hear is the sound of water running in a tub, so she must be feeling okay to start that up. But still she asks, "Why did he come there in the first place?"

I can't bring myself to tell her the whole truth, not right now. "He doesn't have anywhere else to go, I guess." I start the shower myself as she sighs.

"Okay . . ."

"Are you mad?" I ask.

"No, I'm not mad. I'm confused . . ." she says, her voice full of wonder. "I can't believe you're actually allowing him to stay at your apartment."

"Neither can I."

The small bathroom fills with a thick cloud of steam, and I wipe the mirror with my palm. I look like a fucking ghost, a shell, really. Under my eyes, dark rings have already appeared from my lack of sleep. The only thing that gives me life is Tess's voice coming through the line.

"It means a lot to me, Hardin," she finally says.

"It does?" This is going much, much better than I expected.

"Yes, of course it does."

I feel giddy all of the sudden, like a puppy that's been rewarded with a treat from its owner . . . and surprisingly, I'm perfectly fucking okay with that.

"Good." I don't know what else to say to her. I feel slightly guilty for not telling her about her father's . . . habits, but this isn't the time, and over the phone isn't the way.

"Wait . . . so my father was there when you were . . . *you know*?" she whispers, and a small roar sounds on the other line. She must have turned on the fan in the bathroom to drown out her voice.

"Well, he wasn't in the room; I'm not into that type of thing," I tease, to lighten the mood, and she responds with a giggle.

"You probably are," she jokes.

"Nope, that's one of the very few things I'm not into, believe it or not," I say with a smile. "I will never share you, baby. Not even with your father."

I can't help but laugh as she makes a sound of disgust.

"You're sick!"

"Sure am," I fire back, and she giggles. The wine has made her adventurous and heightened her sense of humor. Me? Well, I have no damn excuse for this ridiculous grin on my face.

"I need to take a shower; I'm standing here with come all over me." I step put of my boxers.

"Me, too," she says. "Not the part about being covered with . . . you know, but I'm pretty messy and in need of a shower, too."

"Okay . . . so I guess we should get off . . ."

"We did already." She laughs, proud of her terrible attempt at a joke.

"Ha ha," I tease. But then I rush out my "Have a good night, Tessa."

"You, too," she says, lingering on the line, and I end the call before she can.

Hot water cascades down my body. I still haven't fully recovered from her touching herself while we were on the phone. It's not only a huge fucking turn-on; it's . . . more than that. It shows that she still trusts me, she still trusts me enough to expose herself to me. Lost in my thoughts, I push the hard bar of soap across my tattooed skin. It's hard to imagine that only two weeks ago, we stood in this shower together . . .

"I think this one is my favorite." She touched a tattoo and peered up at me through wet lashes.

"Why is that? I hate that one." I glanced down at her small fingers trailing over the large flower etched near my elbow.

"I don't know; it's sort of beautiful the way you have a flower surrounded by all of this darkness." Her finger moved over the haunting design of a withered skull just below.

"I never thought of it that way." I pressed my thumb under her chin to bring her eyes to mine. "You always see the light in me . . . How is that possible when there isn't any?"

"There's plenty. And you'll see it, too. Someday." She smiled and stood on her toes to press her lips against the corner of my mouth. Water rushed between our lips, and she smiled again before pulling away.

"I hope you're right," I whispered into the stream of water, so quietly that she didn't hear me.

The memory haunts me, replaying as I try to wash it away. It's not that I don't want to remember her, because I do. Tessa is my every thought—she always is. It's only the memories and times when she gave me too much praise, when she tried to convince me that I'm better than I really am, that drive me mad.

I wish I could see myself the way she sees me. I wish I could believe her when she says that I'm good for her. But how can that be true when I'm so fucked up?

It means a lot to me, Hardin, she said only minutes ago.

Maybe if I keep doing what I'm doing now and stay away from shit that could get me in trouble, I can continue to do things that mean a lot to her. I can make her happy instead of miserable, and maybe, just maybe, I could see some of the light in myself that she claims to see.

Maybe there is hope for us after all.

chapter eighty-one

TESSA

I can't help the anxiety that fills me as I drive through the campus. The WCU Seattle campus is not as small as Ken had made it out to be, and all the roads in Seattle seem intent on curving and going up and down hills.

I prepared as best I could to ensure that everything would go as planned today. I left two hours early to be sure to make it to my first class on time. Half of that time was spent sitting in traffic, listening to talk radio. I'd never understood that whole fad until this morning, when a distraught woman called in and told the story of her best friend betraying her by sleeping with her husband. And the two of them running off together, taking her cat, Mazzy, with them. Through her tears, she held on to a certain amount of her dignity . . . Well, about as much as someone calling in to a radio station to relate her own tale of woe possibly could. I found myself sucked right into her dramatic story, and in the end I got the sense that even she knew she was better off without that guy.

By the time I stop by the administration building and retrieve my student identification card and parking pass, I have only thirty minutes before my class. My nerves are stretched to the limit, and I can't shake my anxiety over possibly being late to my first class. Luckily, I find the student parking lot easily, and it's near to where my class is, so I make it with fifteen minutes to spare.

As I take my seat in the front row, I can't help but feel a sense of loneliness. There was no meeting Landon at the coffee shop before class, and he's not in the seat next to mine now as I sit in this classroom remembering my first half year of college.

The classroom fills with students, and I begin to regret my decision when I notice that besides me and one other female, the entire class is guys. I thought I'd sandwich this course—which I didn't really want to take—between some others this semester, but overall I just wish I hadn't decided to take political science at all.

A handsome boy with light brown skin sits down in the empty chair next to me, and I try not to stare at him. His white button-up shirt is crisp and perfectly ironed at the seams, and he's wearing a tie. He looks like a politician, bright white smile and all.

He notices me looking at him and grins. "Can I help you with something?" he asks, his voice full of both authority and charm.

Yeah, he's certainly going to be a politician one day.

"No, s-sorry," I stammer, not meeting his eyes.

When class starts, I avoid looking at him and instead focus on taking notes, reading over the syllabus repeatedly, and looking at my map of the campus until class is dismissed.

My next class, art history, is much better. I feel more comfortable surrounded by a casual crowd of art students. A boy with blue hair sits next to me and introduces himself as Michael. As the teacher has us all go around and introduce ourselves, I find that I'm the only English major in the room. But everyone is friendly, and Michael has quite a sense of humor, making jokes throughout class and keeping everyone entertained, including our instructor.

Creative writing is last, and most certainly the most enjoyable. I'm lost in the process of writing down my thoughts on paper, and it's freeing, entertaining, and I love it. When my professor releases us, it feels as if only ten minutes have passed.

The rest of my week comes and goes in this fashion. I oscillate between feeling like I'm finding my way around more easily and thinking I'm just as confused as ever. But most of all, I feel as if I'm constantly waiting for something that never comes.

BY THE TIME Friday evening arrives, I'm exhausted and my entire body is tense. This week has been challenging, both in good ways and bad. I miss the familiarity of the old campus and having Landon there with me. I miss Hardin meeting me between classes, and I even miss Zed and the glowing flowers that fill the environmental studies building.

Zed. I haven't spoken to him once since he rescued me from Steph and Dan at the party and drove me all the way to my mother's house. He saved me from being thoroughly violated and humiliated, and I haven't even thanked him. I put down my political science textbook and reach for my phone.

"Hello?" Zed's voice sounds so foreign, despite the fact that it's been no more than a week since I've heard it.

"Zed? Hi, it's Tessa." I chew on the inside of my cheek and wait for his response.

"Um, hey."

I take a deep breath and know that I have to say what I called to say. "Listen, I'm so sorry for not calling you to thank you sooner. Everything has happened so fast this week, and I think part of me was trying not to think about what happened. And I know that's not a good excuse . . . so, I'm a jerk, and I'm sorry, and—" The words are rushing out of my mouth so quickly I can barely process what I'm saying, but he interrupts me before I finish.

"It's all right, I know you had a lot going on."

"I still should have called you, especially after what you did for me. I can't tell you how thankful I am that you were at that party," I say, desperate for him to understand how much gratitude I feel toward him. I shiver at the recollection of Dan's fingertips trailing up my thigh. "If you hadn't shown up, God only knows what they would've done to me . . ."

"Hey," he says to silence me, but gently. "I stopped them before anything could happen, Tessa. Try not to think about it. And you definitely don't have to thank me for anything."

"But I do! And I can't help how much it hurts me that Steph would do what she did. I never did anything to hurt her, or any of you—"

"Please don't include me with them," Zed says, clearly a little insulted.

"No, no, I'm so sorry—I didn't mean to say that you were involved. I just meant your group of friends." I apologize for the way my mouth has been moving before my mind has approved the words.

"'S'okay," he mumbles. "Anyway, we aren't much of a group anymore. Tristan is leaving for New Orleans early—in a few days, actually—and I haven't seen Steph on campus all week."

"Oh . . ." I pause and look around this room I'm staying in, in this massive, somewhat alien house. "Zed, I'm also sorry for accusing you of texting me from Hardin's phone. Steph admitted that it was her during the . . . Dan *incident*." I smile, to try and counteract the shiver that person's name induces.

He lets out a little breath that might also be a chuckle. "I have to admit, I did appear to be the most likely candidate to have done that," he replies sweetly. "So . . . how's everything?"

"Seattle is . . . different," I say.

"You're there? I thought maybe since Hardin was at your mom's house—"

"No, I'm here." I interrupt him before he can tell me how he, too, expected me to stay for Hardin.

"Have you made any new friends?"

"What do you think?" I smile and reach across the bed to grab my half-empty glass of water.

"You will soon." He laughs, and I join him.

"I doubt it." I think of the two women who were gossiping in the break room at Vance. Each time I saw them this week, they seemed to be laughing to themselves, and I can't help but think they were laughing at me. "I really am sorry it took me so long to call."

"Tessa, it's okay—stop apologizing. You do that too much."

"Sorry," I say and lightly smack my palm against my forehead. Both that waiter, Robert, and Zed have said that I apologize too much. Maybe they're right.

"Do you think you'll come visit anytime soon? Or are we still . . . not able to be friends?" he asks softly.

"We can be friends," I remark. "But I have no clue when I'll be able to come visit." Truthfully, I'd been wanting to go back home this weekend. I miss Hardin and the traffic-less streets further east.

But wait—why did I just call it home? I only lived there six months.

And then I realize: Hardin. It's because of Hardin. Wherever he is will always feel like home to me.

"Well, that's too bad. Maybe I'll make a trip to Seattle soon. I have some friends there," Zed says. "Would that be okay?" he asks after a few seconds.

"Oh, yeah! Of course."

"Okay." He laughs. "I'm flying down to Florida to see my parents this weekend—I'm running late for my flight, actually—but maybe I could try next weekend or something?"

"Yeah, sure. Just let me know. Have fun in Florida," I say just before I hang up. I put the phone down on my stack of notes, and mere seconds later it vibrates.

Hardin's name appears on the screen, and taking a deep breath and ignoring the flutter in my chest, I answer.

"What are you doing?" he asks immediately.

"Um, nothing."

"Where are you?"

"Kim and Christian's house. Where are *you*?" I sarcastically respond.

"Home," he says matter-of-factly. "Where else would I be?"

"I don't know . . . the gym?" Hardin has been consistently going to the gym, every day, all week.

"I just left there. Now I'm home."

"How was it, Captain Brevity?"

"Same," he curtly remarks.

"Is something wrong?" I ask him.

"No. I'm fine. How was your day?" He's quick to change the subject, and I wonder why, but I don't want to push him, not with the phone call to Zed weighing on my chest already.

"It was okay. Long, I guess. I still don't like my political science class," I groan.

"I told you to drop it already. You can take another class for your social science elective," he reminds me.

I lie back on my bed. "I know . . . I'll be okay."

"Are you staying in tonight?" he asks, warning clear in his voice.

"Yeah, I'm already in my pajamas."

"Good," he says, which makes me roll my eyes.

"I called Zed, just a few minutes ago," I blurt. Might as well get it over with. Silence looms on the line, and I wait patiently for Hardin's breathing to slow.

"You *what*?" he says sharply.

"I called him to thank him for . . . last weekend."

"Why, though? I thought we were . . ." I can hear him barely controlling his anger as he breathes heavily into the receiver. "Tessa, I thought we were working on our problems."

"We are, but I owed it to him. If he hadn't shown up when he did—"

"I know!" Hardin snaps, like he's trying to keep something at bay.

I don't want to argue with him, but I can't expect anything to change if I keep things from him. "He said he was thinking about visiting," I say.

"He's not coming there. End of discussion."

"Hardin . . ."

"Tessa, no. He isn't. I'm doing my best here, okay? I'm trying really fucking hard not to lose my shit right now, so the least you can do is help me out on this."

I sigh in defeat. "Okay." Spending time with Zed can't possibly end well for anyone, Zed included. I can't lead him on again. It's not fair to him, and I don't think he and I will ever be able to have a strictly platonic relationship, not in Hardin's eyes, or, really, in Zed's own.

"Thank you. Now, if it were always that easy to get you to comply . . ."

What? "I will *never* just comply, Hardin, that's—"

"Easy, easy, I'm just teasing. No need to get all testy," he says quickly. "Anything else I should know about while you're at it?"

"No."

"Good. Now, tell me what's been happening on that shitty radio station you've become obsessed with."

And as I go into detail about a woman who was looking for her long-lost love from high school while she was pregnant with her neighbor's child, the lurid details of the story, and the scandal that ensues, have me animated and laughing. By the time I mention the cat, Mazzy, I'm laughing hysterically. I tell him how it would be hard to be in love with one man while pregnant with another man's child, and he doesn't agree. Of course, he believes the man and woman brought the scandal upon themselves, and teases me for getting so involved in talk radio. Hardin laughs along with my story, and I close my eyes and pretend that he's lying next to me.

chapter eighty-two

HARDIN

I'm sorry!" Richard says with a ragged breath. A layer of sweat has coated his entire body as he wipes his vomit from his chin. I lean against the doorframe and debate whether or not to walk away, leaving him in his own filth.

He's been doing this all day, vomiting, shaking, sweating, whining.

"It will be out of my system soo—"

He leans back over the toilet and expels more vomit, like a geyser. Fucking great. At least he made it to the toilet this time.

"Hope so," I say and leave the bathroom. I open the window in the kitchen, allowing the cold breeze to waft in, and grab a clean glass from the cabinet. The sink creaks as I turn the faucet to fill the glass, and I shake my head.

What the hell am I supposed to do with him? He's detoxing all over my goddamn bathroom. With one last sigh, I take the glass of water and a sleeve of crackers into the bathroom and place them on the rim of the sink.

I tap his shoulder. "Eat these."

He nods in acknowledgment—or from delirium tremens and/or withdrawal. His skin is so pale and clammy, it reminds me of clay. I don't actually think eating crackers will help him, but the possibility is there.

"Thanks," he finally groans, and I leave him alone again to vomit all over my bathroom.

This bedroom—my bedroom—isn't the same without her.

The bed is never made correctly when I climb into it at night. I've tried time and time again to tuck the corners of the sheet under the mattress the way Tessa does, but it's just not possible. My clothes, clean and dirty, are scattered across the floor, empty water bottles and soda cans clutter the end tables, and it's cold. The heat is on, but the room is just . . . cold.

I send her one last text message to wish her good night and close my eyes, praying for a dreamless sleep . . . for once.

"Tessa?" I call from the hallway, announcing that I'm home. The apartment is quiet; only soft sounds fill the air. Is Tessa on the phone with someone?

"Tessa!" I call again and turn the bedroom doorknob. The sight that greets my eyes stops me dead in my tracks. Tessa is sprawled out on the white duvet, her blond hair matted to her forehead with sweat, the fingers of one hand gripping the headboard and a fistful of raven hair in the other. As she rocks her hips, I can feel ice replacing the hot blood pumping through my veins.

Zed's head is buried between her creamy thighs. His hands roam her body.

I try to move toward them to grab him by his throat and throw him against the wall, but my feet are frozen to the ground. I try to scream at them, but my mouth refuses to open.

"Oh, Zed," Tessa moans. I cover my ears with my hands, but it doesn't help—her voice travels straight to my brain; there's no escaping it.

"You're so beautiful," he coos, and she moans again. One of his hands travels up to her chest, and he runs his fingertips over her while his mouth is pressed against her.

I'm frozen.

They don't see me; they haven't even noticed that I'm in the room. Tessa calls out his name once more, and when his head lifts from between her thighs, he finally sees me. He keeps eye contact with me while his lips run up her body, to her jaw, nipping along the way. My eyes won't leave their naked bodies, and my insides have been ripped from my body and tossed onto the cold floor. I can't bear to watch this, but I'm forced to do so anyway.

"I love you," he says to her while smirking at me.

"I love you, too," Tessa whimpers. She rakes her nails down his tattooed back as he thrusts into her. Finally, my voice comes as I scream, silencing their moans.

"Fuck!" I scream out, and grab the glass from the nightstand. With a crash, it shatters against the wall.

chapter eighty-three

HARDIN

I'm pacing back and forth across the floor, furious fingers tugging at my sweat-soaked hair, all the clothes and books I'm stepping on registering vividly on the soles of my bare feet.

"Hardin? Are you okay?" Tessa's voice is thick with sleep. I'm so glad she answered. I need her to be here with me, even through a telephone line.

"I . . . I don't know," I croak into the phone.

"What's wrong?"

"Are you in bed?" I ask her.

"Yes, it's three in the morning. Where else would I be? What's wrong, Hardin?"

"I just can't sleep, that's all," I admit, staring into the darkness of our—my—room.

"Oh . . ." She lets out a long breath of relief. "I was worried for a second."

"Did you talk to Zed again?" I ask her.

"What? No, I haven't talked to him since I told you about him wanting to visit."

"Call him and tell him that he can't." I sound like a lunatic, but I don't give a shit.

"I'm not calling him this late, what's gotten into you?"

She's being so defensive . . . though I suppose I can't blame her. "Nothing, Tessa. Never mind." I sigh.

"Hardin, what's going on?" she asks, clearly worried.

"Nothing, just . . . nothing." I hang up the phone and press down on the power button until the screen turns black.

chapter eighty-four

TESSA

"You're not staying in your pajamas the entire day again, are you?" Kimberly asks the next morning when she sees me sitting at the kitchen counter.

I spoon a mouthful of granola into my mouth, so I'm unable to answer her. Because that's exactly what I plan to do today. I didn't sleep well after Hardin's phone call. He has since sent a few text messages, none of them mentioning his odd behavior last night. I want to call him, but the way he hung up so quickly makes me think better of it. Besides, I haven't paid much attention to Kimberly since I arrived. Most of my free time has been spent talking on the phone with Hardin or doing my first round of assignments for my new classes. The least I can do is chat with her over breakfast.

"You never wear clothes," Smith chimes in, and I nearly spit the granola out onto the table.

"Yes, I do," I reply, my mouth still full.

"You're right, Smith, she doesn't." Kimberly cackles, and I roll my eyes at her.

At that moment Christian enters the room and places a kiss against her temple. Smith smiles at his father and soon-to-be stepmother before looking back to me.

"Pajamas are more comfortable," I tell him, and he nods in agreement. His green eyes look down at himself, taking in his Spider-Man print pajamas. "Do you like Spider-Man?" I ask, wanting to start a conversation that isn't about me.

His small fingers pick at his toast. "No."

"No? You're wearing those," I reply and point to his clothing.

"She bought them." He nods toward Kim. Then he whispers, "Don't tell her I hate them; she'll cry."

I laugh. Smith is five going on twenty.

"I won't," I promise him, and we finish the meal in comfortable silence.

chapter eighty-five

HARDIN

Landon shakes the moisture from his hat onto the floor and rests his closed umbrella against the wall in an exaggerated and theatrical way. He wants me to see what an "effort" he's making to help me out.

"Well, what was so urgent that I had to come here in the freezing rain?" he asks, half smug, half concerned. Looking at my bare chest, he adds, "You know, the thing that I actually put *clothes* on for and ran over to help out with. So what is it?"

I wave toward Richard, who's spread out on the couch, asleep. "Him."

Landon leans to one side to look around me. "Who is that?" he asks. Then, straightening, he looks at me with a gaping mouth. "Wait . . . Is that Tessa's father?"

I roll my eyes at his question. "No, it's another random, homeless fuck that I let sleep on my couch. It's what all the hipsters are doing nowadays."

He ignores my sarcasm. "Why is he here? Does Tessa know?"

"Yes, she knows. However, she doesn't know that he's been going through withdrawal for the last five days and vomiting all over the damn place."

Richard groans in his sleep, and I grab Landon by the sleeve of his plaid shirt and pull him into the hallway.

This is clearly a little out of my stepbrother's league. "Withdrawal?" he asks. "From, like, *drugs*?"

"Yes. And alcohol."

He seems to ponder this for a second. "He hasn't found your liquor yet?" he asks, then raises a brow at me. "Or has he already consumed it?"

"I don't have any liquor here anymore, dick."

He peers back around the corner to the sleeping man perched on my couch. "I still don't see how I fit into this."

"You're going to babysit him," I inform him, and he immediately takes a step back.

"No way!" He tries to whisper, but his voice comes out much more like a hushed scream.

"Chill." I pat his shoulder. "It's only for one night."

"No way. I'm not staying here with him. I don't even know him!"

"Neither do I," I counter.

"You know him better than I do; he would be your father-in-law someday if you weren't such an idiot." Landon's words hit me harder than they should. Father-in-law? The title sounds odd when I repeat it in my mind . . . while I'm staring at this gross lump of man on my couch.

"I want to see her," I plead.

"Who . . . Tess?"

"Yes, Tes-*sa*," I correct him. "Who else?"

Landon starts playing with his fingers like a nervous child. "Well, why can't she come here? I don't think it's a good idea for me to stay with him."

"Don't be such a pussy, he's not dangerous or anything," I say. "Just make sure he doesn't leave the apartment. There's plenty of food and water here."

"You sound like you're talking about a dog . . ." Landon remarks.

I rub my temples in annoyance. "Dude might as well be at this point. Are you going to help me or not?"

He glares at me, and I add, "For Tessa?" It's a low blow, but I know it will work.

After a second he breaks, and nods. "One night only," he agrees, and I turn away from him to hide my smile.

I don't know how Tessa will react to me ignoring our "space" agreement, but it's only one night. One short night with her is what I need right now. I need *her*. Phone calls and text messages are sufficient enough during the week, but after that nightmare I had, I need to see her more than anything. I need to confirm the fact that her body holds no marks that were put on it by anyone other than myself.

"Does she know you're coming?" Landon asks me as he follows me into the bedroom, where I search the floor for a T-shirt to pull over my bare torso.

"She will once I arrive, won't she?"

"She told me about you two on the phone."

She did? That's really unlike her.

"Why would she tell you about us getting off over the phone . . . ?" I wonder.

Landon's eyes go wide. "Whoa! What! What! I wasn't . . . Oh God," he groans. He tries to cover his ears, but it's too late. His cheeks turn a deep red, and my laughter fills the bedroom.

"You have to be more specific when you're talking about Tessa and me, don't you know that by now?" I grin, relishing the memory of her moans coming through the line.

"Apparently I do." He scowls and regroups. "I meant that you two have been talking a lot on the phone."

"And . . . ? "

"Does she seem happy to you?"

My smile disappears. "Why do you ask?"

Worry spreads over his features. "I'm just wondering. I'm a little worried about her. She doesn't seem as excited and happy about Seattle as I assumed she'd be."

"I don't know." I rub my hand over the back of my neck. "She doesn't sound happy, it's true, but I can't tell if it's because I'm an asshole or because she doesn't like Seattle as much as she thought she would," I answer truthfully.

"I hope it's the first. I want her to be happy there," Landon says.

"So do I, sort of," I say.

Landon kicks a dirty pair of black jeans out from under his foot.

"Hey, I was going to wear those," I snap and bend down to grab them.

"Don't you have any clean clothes?"

"Not at the moment."

"Have you done any laundry at all since she left?"

"Yes . . ." I lie.

"Uh-huh." He points to the stain on my black T-shirt. Mustard, maybe?

"Shit." I pull the shirt off and toss it back onto the floor. "I don't have shit to wear." I pull out the bottom drawer of the dresser and let out a relieved breath when I spot a stack of clean black T-shirts in the back.

"What about these?" Landon points to a pair of dark blue jeans hanging in the closet.

"No."

"Why not? You never wear anything other than black jeans."

"Exactly," I retort.

"Well, the only pair of pants you seem to have to wear is dirty, so—"

"I have *five* pairs," I correct him. "They just happen to be the same exact style." With a huff, I reach past him into the closet and pull the blue jeans off of the hanger. I hate these fucking things. My mum bought them for me for Christmas, and I vowed to never wear them, yet here I am. For true love or something. She'd probably swoon.

"They're a little . . . *snug*." Landon bites down on his bottom lip to keep from laughing.

"Fuck off," I say and raise my middle finger, then finish shoving shit into my bag.

Twenty minutes later we're back in the living room, Richard is still asleep, Landon is still making obnoxious remarks about my fucking tight jeans, and I'm ready to go see Tessa in Seattle.

"What should I tell him when he wakes up?" he asks.

"Whatever you want. It would be quite funny if you fucked with him for a little while. You could pretend you're me or that you don't know why he's there." I laugh. "He would be so confused."

Landon doesn't see the humor in my idea, and he basically pushes me out the door. "Be careful driving, the roads are slick," he warns.

"Gotcha." I hoist my bag over my shoulder and leave before he can make another mushy-ass remark.

DURING THE DRIVE, I can't help but think about my nightmare. It was so clear, so fucking vivid. I could hear Tessa moaning that asshole's name; I could even hear her nails running along his skin.

I turn the radio up to drown out my thoughts, but it doesn't work. I decide to think of *her* instead, of memories of us together, to stop the images from haunting me. Otherwise this will be the longest drive of my entire life.

"Look how cute those babies are!" Tessa had squealed while pointing to a platoon of squirming little beings. Well, only two babies, actually. But still.

"Yeah, yeah. So cute." I rolled my eyes and dragged her along through the store.

"They even have matching bows in their hair." She was smiling so big, and her voice did that weird high-pitched thing that women

do when they're around small children and some hormone or other kicks in.

"Yep," I said and continued behind her down the narrow aisles at Conner's. She'd been searching for some specific cheese she needed to make our dinner that night. But babies overtook her brain.

"Admit that they were cute." She beamed up at me, and I shook my head in defiance. "Come on, Hardin, you know they were cute. Just say it."

"They. Were. Cute . . ." I responded flatly, and she pressed her mouth into a hard line while she crossed her arms over her chest like a petulant child herself.

"Maybe you'll turn out to be one of those people who only thinks their own kids are cute," she said, and I watched as a dawning recognition quickly stole her smile away. "That is, if you ever want kids." she added somberly, making me want to kiss away the frown on her beautiful face.

"Sure, maybe. Too bad I don't want them, though," I said, trying to drill the statement permanently into her head.

"I know . . ." she said softly. Soon thereafter, she found the item she was so avidly searching for and dropped it into the basket with a dull thud.

Her smile still hadn't returned by the time we were waiting in the checkout line. I looked down and gently nudged with my elbow. "Hey."

When she looked up at me, her eyes were dim, and she was obviously waiting for me to speak.

"I know we agreed not to talk about kids anymore . . ." I started as she focused her eyes on the floor. "Hey," I repeated and set the basket on the floor next to my boot. "Look at me." Both of my hands covered her cheeks, and I pressed my forehead against hers.

"It's okay. I wasn't really thinking when I said that," she admitted with a shrug.

I watched as she glanced around the small market, taking in our surroundings, and I could practically see her wondering why I was touching her this way in public.

"Well then, let's agree again not to bring up children. It does nothing but cause problems between us," I said and gave her a quick kiss to her lips, followed by another. My lips lingered on hers, and her small hands pushed into the pockets of my jacket.

"I love you, Hardin," she said when Grumpy Gloria, the cashier we'd laughed about many times, cleared her throat.

"I love you, Tess. I will love you enough that you won't even need children," I promised her.

She turned away from me—to hide her frown, I know. But right then I didn't care, because I figured the question was settled, and I'd gotten what I wanted.

As I continue to drive, I begin to wonder: Has there ever been a time in my life when I wasn't a selfish prick?

chapter eighty-six

TESSA

As I'm plodding from my room to the couch with a copy of *Wuthering Heights* in hand, Kimberly says with a beautiful wide smile, "You're in a funk, Tessa, and as your friend and mentor, it's my responsibility to get you out of it." Her blond hair is straight and glossy, and her makeup is too perfect. She's one of those women that other women love to hate.

"*Mentor?* Really?" I giggle, and she rolls her heavily shadowed eyes.

"Okay, maybe not so much of a mentor. But a friend," she corrects herself.

"I'm not in a funk. I just have a lot of course work to do, and I just don't feel like going anywhere tonight," I say.

"You are nineteen, girl—act like it! When I was nineteen, I was out all the time. I barely showed up for any of my classes. I dated boys . . . many, many, boys." Her heel taps on the concrete floor.

"Did you, now?" Christian cuts in as he enters the room. He's unwrapping some sort of tape from around his hands.

"None as wonderful as you, of course." Kim winks at him, and he laughs.

He grins. "That's what I get for dating such a young woman. I have to compete with still-fresh memories of college-age men." His green eyes shine with humor.

"Hey, I'm not that much younger than you," she says with a smack to his chest.

"Twelve years," he points out.

Kimberly rolls her eyes. "Yes, but you're a young soul. Unlike Tessa here, who behaves as if she's forty."

"Sure, honey." He tosses the used tape into a wastepaper basket. "Now, go on and enlighten the girl about how *not* to behave during college." He gives her one last smile, smacks her on her ass, and disappears, leaving her grinning from ear to ear.

"I love that man so much," she tells me, and I nod along, because I know it's true. "I really wanted you to come along with us tonight. Christian and his partners just opened a new jazz club downtown. It's beautiful, and I'm sure you'd have an amazing time."

"Christian owns a jazz club?" I ask.

"He invested in it, so he didn't actually do any work," she whispers with a sly smile. "They have guest musicians on Saturdays, sort of an open-mic-type thing."

I shrug. "Maybe next weekend?" The last thing I want to do right now is get dressed and go out to any type of club.

"Fine, next weekend: I'm holding you to that. Smith doesn't want to come either. I've tried to convince him, but you know how he is. He lectured me on how jazz is nothing, compared to classical music." She laughs. "So his sitter will be here in a few hours."

"I can watch him," I offer. "I'll be here, anyway."

"No, honey, you don't have to."

"I know, but I want to."

"Well, it would be kinda great, and so much easier. He doesn't like the sitter, for some reason."

"He doesn't like me either." I laugh.

"True, but he talks to you more than he does to most people." She looks down at the engagement ring on her finger and then up to Smith's school portrait hanging over the mantel. "He's such a sweet boy . . . just very guarded," she says quietly, almost as an afterthought.

A doorbell sounds, breaking the moment.

Kimberly looks at me quizzically. "Now, who the heck would be coming here in the middle of the afternoon?" she asks, as if I could possibly know the answer.

I stand there, looking at a really cute picture of Smith on the wall. He's such a serious little kid. Like a little engineer or mathematician, almost.

"Well . . . well . . . well . . . Look who it is!" Kimberly calls from the door. When I turn to see what she's talking about, my mouth falls open.

"Hardin!" His name falls from my lips without a single thought, and an immediate surge of adrenaline at the sight of him propels me across the room. My socks make me slide on the hardwood floor, nearly causing me to fall on my face. Once I'm steady enough to continue, I latch myself on to him, hugging him tighter than maybe I ever have before.

chapter eighty-seven

HARDIN

I nearly have a goddamned heart attack when Tessa stumbles and starts to fall, but she quickly collects herself and hurls herself into my arms.

This is sure as hell not the reaction I had expected.

I thought I would be granted with an uncomfortable "hello" and a smile that didn't meet her eyes. But man, was I wrong. Very wrong. Tessa tightens her arms around my neck, and I bury my head in her hair. The sweet scent of her shampoo fills my senses, and I'm momentarily overwhelmed by her presence, warm and welcoming, in my arms.

"Hi," I finally say, and she glances up at me.

"You're freezing," she remarks. Her hands move to my cheeks, instantly heating them.

"It's freezing rain out there, and it's worse back home . . . my home, I mean," I correct myself. Her eyes quickly dart to the floor before looking back up at me.

"What are you doing here?" she practically whispers to me, trying her best to shield the question from our company.

"I called Christian on the way up," I inform Kimberly, who continues to faux-glare at me, a smirk playing on her painted lips.

Couldn't stay away, could you? she mouths to me behind Tessa's back. That woman is the biggest ballbuster around; I'm not sure how Christian puts up with her, and willingly at that.

"You can stay in the room across from Tessa's, she can show you," Kimberly announces and then disappears.

I detach myself from Tessa and give her a little smile.

"I—I'm sorry!" Tessa stutters, looking around the room and blushing. "I don't know why I did that. I-it's just nice to see a familiar face."

"It's good to see you, too," I tell her, trying to free her of her embarrassment. It's not like I let go because I *didn't* want to hold her. Her lack of confidence always has her interpret things in negative ways.

"I slipped on the floor," she blurts out, then flushes again as I bite down on the inside of my cheek, trying my best not to laugh at her.

"Yeah, I saw it." I can't help the small chuckle that escapes from me, and she shakes her head, laughing at herself.

"Are you really staying?" she asks.

"Yes, if that's okay with you?"

Her eyes are bright and a lighter shade of blue-gray than usual. Her hair is down, slightly wavy and unstyled. Not a trace of makeup mars her complexion, and she looks absolutely fucking perfect. The number of hours that I've spent picturing her face in front of me did not adequately prepare me for the moment when I'm finally able to look at her again. My mind can't possibly catch all of her, all the details . . . the freckle just below her neckline, the curve of her lips, the brilliance of her eyes—it's fucking impossible.

Her T-shirt hangs loose on her body, and those hideous fluffy cloud pants cover her legs. She keeps adjusting her shirt, tugging it down, playing with the collar; she's the only girl I've ever seen who can manage to wear these ugly-ass clothes to bed but somehow still look so damn sexy. Through the white shirt, I can see her black bra . . . she's wearing that black lace one that I love. I wonder if she's aware that I can see right through her shirt . . .

"What changed your mind? And where's the rest of your

stuff?" Tessa asks as she leads me down the hallway. "Everyone else's rooms are upstairs," she informs me, unaware of my perverted thoughts. Or maybe she's not . . .

"This is all I brought. It's only for one night," I tell her, and she stops in front of me.

"You're only staying one night?" she says, her eyes searching my face.

"Yeah, what did you think? That I was moving here?" Of course she did. She always has too much faith in me.

"No." She looks away. "I don't know, I thought a little longer than that, though." And now this is where it gets awkward. I knew it would.

"Here's the room." She opens the door for me, but I don't step inside.

"Your room is just across the hall?" My voice breaks, and I sound like a damned fool.

"Yeah," she mutters, looking down at her fingers.

"Cool," I remark dumbly. "You're sure it's okay that I'm here, right?"

"Yes, of course. You know I missed you."

The excitement on her face seems to vanish as the memory of my previous actions—being an asshole in general, and refusing to come to Seattle specifically—looms unspoken over our heads. I'll never forget the way she ran to me, literally, when she saw me at the door; there was such emotion on her face, so much longing, and I felt it, too, more than she did. I've been insane without her.

"Yeah, but the last time that we saw one another in that apartment I was basically kicking you out." I watch her face change as my words remind her of what took place. I can literally see the fucking wall rising up between us as she gives me a fake smile. "I don't know why I brought that up," I say and wipe my wrist across my forehead.

Her eyes move to another room; her room. Then turning to the door we're standing in front of, she says, "You can put your stuff in here."

Grabbing my bag from me, she heads inside and unzips it on the bed. I watch as she pulls the wadded-up T-shirts and boxers out of the bag and scrunches her nose.

"Are these clean?" she asks.

I shake my head. "The boxers are."

She holds the bag at arm's length. "I don't even want to know what the apartment looks like."

The corners of her mouth lift into a smug smile. "Good thing you won't ever see it again, then," I tease her. Her smile fades.

What a shitty joke—*what the fuck is wrong with me?*

"I didn't mean it that way," I say quickly, desperate to recover from my poor choice of words.

"It's fine. Relax, okay?" Her voice is gentle. "It's only me, Hardin."

"I know." I take a deep breath and continue, "It just feels like it's been so fucking long, and we're in that weird middle, half-relationship shit that we are really shitty at. And we haven't seen each other, and I've just missed you, and I hope you missed me, too." *Wow, I really said that all way too fast.*

She smiles. "I did."

"You did what?" I press for the exact words.

"I missed you. I told you that every day we've talked."

"I know." I step closer to her. "I just wanted to hear it again." I reach out and tuck her hair behind her ears, using both hands, and she leans into me.

"When did *you* get here?" a small voice suddenly says, and Tessa jumps away from me.

Great. Just fucking great.

And there's Smith, standing in the doorway of Tessa's new bedroom.

"Just now," I reply, hoping that he'll leave the room so I can continue what almost was started moments ago.

"Why did you come?" he asks and enters the room.

I point to Tessa, who is now more than five feet away from me, pulling my clothes out of my bag and gathering them in her arms. "I came to see her."

"Oh," he quietly replies, staring down at his feet.

"Do you not want me here?" I inquire.

"I don't mind," he says with a shrug, and I smile at him.

"Good, because I wouldn't have left if you did."

"I know." Smith smiles back and leaves Tessa and me alone. Thank fucking God.

"He likes you," Tessa says.

"He's okay." I shrug, and she laughs.

"You like him, too," she accuses.

"No, I don't. I said simply: He's *okay*."

She rolls her eyes. "Suuuuure."

She's right, I do sort of like him. More than any other five-year-old that I've ever met, at least.

"I'm watching him tonight while Kim and Christian go to a club opening," she says.

"Why aren't you going along?"

"I don't know, I just didn't want to."

"Hmm." I pinch my lips between my fingers to hide my smile from her. I'm thrilled that she didn't want to go out, and I find myself hoping that she'd planned on spending her evening talking to me on the phone.

Tessa gives me a weird look. "You can go if you'd like; you don't have to stay in with me."

I give her an indignant look. "What? I didn't drive all this way to go out to some shitty club without you. You don't want me to stay with you?"

Her eyes meet mine, and she presses my clothes to her chest. "Yes, of course I want you to stay."

"Good, because I wouldn't have left if you didn't," I joke.

She doesn't smile the way Smith did, but she does roll her eyes, which is just as cute.

"Where are you going?" I ask when I notice her inching toward the door with my things.

She gives me a look that's both funny and sultry. "To do your laundry," she says, and disappears into the hall.

chapter eighty-eight

TESSA

My thoughts are racing as I start the washing machine. Hardin came here, to Seattle—and I didn't have to ask or beg him. He came of his own accord. Even if it's only for one night, it means so much to me, and I hope that it will turn out to be a step in the right direction for us. I'm still so conflicted when it comes to our relationship . . . We always have so many problems, so many pointless fights. We're such different people, and I'm at a point now where I'm not sure it will ever work.

But right now, now that he's here with me, I want nothing more than to try this long-distance half relationship/half friendship, and see where it takes us.

"I knew he'd show up," Kimberly says from behind me.

When I turn around, I see her leaning against the doorframe of the laundry room. "I didn't," I tell her.

She gives me an oh-please look. "You had to know he would. I've never seen a couple like the two of you."

I sigh. "We aren't exactly a couple . . ."

"You ran into his arms like something out of a movie. He's been here for less than fifteen minutes, and you're already doing his laundry." She nods to the machine.

"Well, his clothes are filthy," I say, ignoring the first part of her remark.

"You two just can't stay away from one another; it's really something to watch. I do wish you were coming out tonight so you could get dressed up and show him what he's missing by not being here in Seattle with you." She winks and then leaves me alone in the laundry room.

She's right about Hardin and me not being able to stay away from each other. It's always been that way, since the day I met him. Even when I tried to convince myself that I didn't want him, I couldn't ignore the fluttering I felt inside me every time we ran into each other.

Back then, Hardin always seemed to appear wherever I was . . . Granted, I did go to his fraternity house every chance I could. I hated it there, but something inside me drew me to the place, knowing that if I went, I would see him. I didn't admit it then, not even to myself, but I longed for his company, even when he was being cruel to me. The memories feel so ancient and almost dreamlike as I recall the way he used to stare at me during class, then roll his eyes when I said hello.

The washing machine makes a random little beep, bringing me back to reality, and I hurry down the hallway to the guest room that has been designated as Hardin's for the night. The room is empty; Hardin's empty bag is still on the bed, but he's nowhere to be found. I walk across the hall and find him standing over the desk in my room. His fingertips are tracing the cover of one of my notebooks.

"What are you doing in here?" I ask.

"I just wanted to see where you're . . . living now. I wanted to see your room."

"Oh." I notice the way his brows pull together when he calls it "my room."

"Is this for a class?" he asks, holding up the black leather notebook.

"It's for creative writing." I nod at him. "Did you read it?" I can't help but feel a little nervous at the thought that he may have. I've only completed one assignment so far, but like everything else in my life, it ended up relating to him.

"A little."

"It's just an assignment," I say, fumbling to explain myself. "We were asked to do a freestyle essay as the first assignment and—"

"It's good, really good," he says, praising me, and places the book back on the desk for a moment before picking it up again and opening it to the first page. " 'Who I am.' " He reads the first line out loud.

"Please don't," I beg.

He gives me a questioning little smirk. "Since when are you shy about showing your schoolwork?"

"I'm not. It's just . . . that piece is personal. I'm not even sure if I want to turn it in."

"I read your religion journal," he says—and my heart stops.

"What?" I pray that I heard him wrong. *He wouldn't. He couldn't have read it . . .*

"I read it. You left it at the apartment, and I found it."

This is humiliating. I stand in silence while Hardin stares at me from across the room. Those were private thoughts that I never expected anyone to read, except my professor, maybe. I'm mortified that Hardin pored over my deepest thoughts.

"You weren't supposed to read those. Why would you?" I ask, trying not to look at him.

"Every entry was about me," he says by way of defending himself.

"That's not the point, Hardin." My stomach is in my throat, making it hard to breathe. "I was going through a really bad time, and those were private thoughts for my journal. You were never meant to—"

"They were really good, Tess. So good. It hurt me to read the way you were feeling, but the words, what you had to say—it was perfect."

I know he's trying to compliment me, but it only embarrasses me further.

"How would you feel if I read something you wrote to express your feelings in a private way?" I ignore the compliments from him about my writing. His eyes flash with panic, and I tilt my head in confusion. "What?"

"Nothing," is all he says, shaking his head.

chapter eighty-nine

HARDIN

The look in her eyes almost makes me stop, but I have to be honest, and I want her to know how interesting I found her writing. "I've read it at least ten times," I admit.

Her wide eyes don't meet mine, but her lips part slightly and she replies, "You have?"

"Don't be ashamed. It's only me, remember?" I smile at her, and she steps closer to me.

"I know, but I probably sounded so pathetic. I wasn't thinking clearly when I was writing them."

I press my fingers against her lips to silence her. "No, you didn't. They were brilliant."

"I . . ." She tries to speak beneath my fingers, and I press them harder.

"Are you done yet?" I grin at her, and she nods. Slowly, I remove my fingers from her lips, and her tongue darts out to wet them. I can't help but stare.

"I have to kiss you," I whisper, our faces mere inches apart. Her eyes look into mine, and she swallows loudly before licking her lips again.

"Okay," she whispers back to me. Her hands are greedy as she wraps her fists around the fabric of my shirt. She pulls me closer, her breathing heavy.

Just before our lips can connect, a knock sounds at the bedroom door. "Tessa?" Kimberly's high-pitched voice calls through the half-open door.

"Get rid of her," I whisper, and Tessa backs away from me.

First the kid, now his mom. We might as well invite Vance to join as well.

"We're leaving in a few minutes," Kimberly says without coming in.

Good for you. Now get the fuck out of here . . .

"Okay—I'll be right out," Tessa responds, and my irritation grows.

"Thanks, hon," Kimberly says and walks off, humming some pop song.

"I shouldn't have even fucking—" I begin.

When Tessa looks over at me, I stop myself from finishing my rude remark. It wasn't true, anyway . . . nothing could keep me from wanting to be here right now.

"I have to go out there now, to watch Smith. If you want to stay in here, you can."

"No, I want to be wherever you are," I tell her, and she smiles.

Fuck, I want to kiss her. I've missed her so much, and she says she's missed me, too . . . Why doesn't she just . . . Her hands wrap around the top of my black T-shirt, and she presses her lips against mine. I feel as if someone has plugged me into an electrical outlet, every fiber of me igniting and buzzing. Her tongue enters my mouth, pressing and caressing, and I wrap my hands around her hips.

I pull her across the room until my feet hit the footboard of the bed. I lie back, and she falls gently on top of me. Wrapping her body into my arms, I turn us over so her body is under mine. I can feel her pulse hammering under my lips as they slide down her neckline and back up to the sweet spot just under her ear. Gasps and quiet moans are my reward. Slowly, I begin what I know are torturing movements, grinding my hips against hers, pressing her into the mattress. Tessa's fingers move to touch the heated skin under my T-shirt, and her nails rake down my back. As I bring her earlobe between my lips—

The image of Zed thrusting into her flashes through my mind, and I'm on my feet within seconds.

"What's wrong?" she asks. Her lips are deep pink and swollen from my gentle assault.

"I-it's, it's nothing. We should . . . um . . . go out there. Take care of the little shit," I respond frantically.

"Hardin," she presses.

"Tessa, let it go. It's nothing." Oh, you know, just that I dreamed of Zed fucking you practically through to the other side of our mattress, and now I can't stop picturing it.

"Okay." She lifts herself from the bed and wipes her hands against the soft material of her pajamas.

I close my eyes for a moment, trying to rid my mind of the disgusting images. If that poser asshole interrupts another second of my time with Tessa, I'll break every bone in his goddamned body.

chapter ninety

TESSA

After too many kisses for Smith's liking, Kimberly and Vance finally leave. Each of the three times they reminded us they were only a phone call away in case there's trouble, Hardin and Smith rolled their eyes dramatically. When she pointed to the list of emergency numbers on the kitchen counter, they shared a little, cute look of disbelief.

"What do you want to watch?" I ask Smith once their car is out of sight.

He shrugs from where he's sitting on the couch and looks up at Hardin, who looks down at the kid like he's an amusing little ferret or something.

"Okay . . . What about a game—do you want to play a game or something?" I suggest when neither of them speaks.

"No," Smith replies.

"I think he just wants to go back to his room and do whatever the hell he was doing before Kim dragged him out here," Hardin says, and Smith nods curtly in agreement.

"Well . . . okay, then. You can go back to your room, Smith. Hardin and I will be out here if you need anything. I'll be ordering dinner soon," I tell him.

"Can you come with me, Hardin?" Smith asks in the softest tone possible.

"To your room? No, I'm good."

Without a word, Smith climbs down from the couch and

walks over to the stairs. I shoot a glare at Hardin, and he shrugs his shoulders. "What?"

"Go to his room with him," I whisper.

"I don't want to go to his room. I want to be out here with you," he says matter-of-factly. As much as I want Hardin to stay with me, I feel bad for Smith.

"Come on." I nod to the blond boy as he slowly ascends the steps. "He's lonely."

"Dammit, fine." Hardin groans and sulks across the living room to follow Smith up the stairs. I'm still a little bothered by his odd reaction to our kiss in the bedroom. I thought it was going great—better than great—but he climbed off me so abruptly that I thought he'd been injured. Maybe after being away from me for so long he doesn't feel the same? Maybe he's not as attracted to me . . . sexually, as he once was. I know that I'm dressed in baggy pajamas, but he never had a problem with them before.

Unable to come up with any reasonable explanation for his behavior, instead of letting my imagination run wild, I grab the small stack of takeout pamphlets that Kimberly left for us so we could figure out what to order for dinner. I decide on pizza, and grab my phone before going into the laundry room. I place Hardin's clothes in the dryer and sit on the bench in the center of the room. I call for the pizza and wait while watching the machine turn around and around.

chapter ninety-one

HARDIN

As Smith walks around his bedroom, I stand in the doorway and take a mental inventory of all the shit this kid has. Man, he's spoiled as hell.

"What do you want to do?" I ask the kid as I step into the room.

"I don't know." He stares at the wall. His blond hair is combed to one side so perfectly it's almost creepy.

"Then why did you want me to come up here?"

"I don't know," the little shit repeats. Stubborn little fucker.

"Okay . . . well, this isn't going anywhere . . ." I trail off.

"Are you living here now, too, with your girl?" Smith suddenly blurts.

"No, only visiting for tonight," I say and look away from the kid.

"Why?" His eyes home in on me. I can feel them without even glancing his way.

"Because I don't want to live here." I do, though. Sort of.

"Why? You don't like her?" he questions.

"Yes. I like her." I laugh. "I just . . . I don't know. Why do you always ask me so many questions?"

"I don't know," he responds simply and pulls some sort of train set from under his bed.

"Don't you have any friends you can play with?" I ask the boy.

"No."

That doesn't seem right. He's an all-right kid. "Why not?"

He shrugs and disconnects a piece of the train track. His small hands disconnect another piece, and he switches the metal out with two new tracks from a box at the end of his bed.

"I'm sure you can make friends at school."

"No, I can't."

"Are the kids assholes to you or something?" I ask him. I don't bother to correct my language. Vance has the mouth of a fucking sailor, and I'm sure his son has heard worse.

"Sometimes." He twists the edges of some type of wire and connects a small train car to it. The wire sparks in his hands, but he doesn't flinch. Within seconds, the train begins to move around the track, starting slowly and then gradually picking up speed.

"What was that, that you just did?" I ask him.

"Made it go faster; it was really slow."

"No wonder you don't have any friends." I laugh, but then I catch myself. Shit. He's just sitting there, staring at his train. "I just meant because you're so smart; sometimes smart people are terrible at being social, and no one likes them. Like Tessa, for example—she's too smart sometimes, and it makes people feel uncomfortable."

"Okay . . ." He looks over and begins staring at me, and I can't help but feel bad for him. I'm shit at giving advice, and I don't know why I even tried.

I know what it's like to grow up not having any friends. As a child, I never had a single one until I hit puberty and started drinking, smoking pot, and hanging out with shitty people. They weren't actually my friends, anyway—they only liked me because I did whatever the fuck I wanted to do, and that was "cool" to them. They didn't enjoy reading the way that I did; they only enjoyed partying.

I was always that angry little boy in the corner whom no one talked to because they were afraid of me. To this day, that hasn't changed much, really . . .

But I met Tessa; she's the only person who genuinely gives a fuck about me. She's afraid of me sometimes, too, though. Images from Christmas and red wine splattered across her white cardigan bring my thoughts to life. I suspect that Landon cares for me, too, I guess. But that's still a weird situation with him, and I'm pretty sure he only cares because of Tessa. She tends to have that power over people.

Me, especially.

chapter ninety-two

TESSA

Is your pizza good?" I ask Smith from across the table.

He looks up at me, mouth full, and nods his head yes. His small hands are holding a fork and knife to cut into his meal. This doesn't surprise me.

When his plate is clear, he stands from the table and walks his dishes to the dishwasher, placing them inside. "I'm going to retire for the night. I'm ready for bed," the little scientist announces.

Hardin shakes his head in amusement over the maturity of the kid.

I stand up and ask, "Do you need anything? Water, or to be walked to your room?"

But he declines and grabs his blanket from the couch before heading up to his bedroom.

I watch Smith disappear upstairs, then sit back down and realize that Hardin has spoken less than ten words to me in the last hour. He's kept his distance, and I can't help but find myself comparing his behavior tonight to the way he spoke during our phone calls this week. A small part of me wishes we were on the phone now instead of sitting silently on the couch.

"I have to piss," he announces, then heads off as I surf through the channels on the flat-screen TV.

Moments later Kimberly and Christian come through the front door, followed by another couple. A tall blond woman dressed in a short gold dress saunters across the hardwood floor. I take one glance at her sky-high heels, and my ankles start to ache for her. She gives me a smile and a wave as she follows Kimberly through the foyer and into the living room. Hardin appears in the hallway but doesn't make a move to enter the room.

"Sasha, this is Tessa and Hardin," Kimberly kindly introduces us.

"It's nice to meet you." I smile, hating that I didn't put on better-looking pajamas.

"You, too," Sasha responds, but she's looking directly to Hardin, who looks back at her for a moment but doesn't otherwise greet her or come fully into the living room.

"Sasha is a friend of Christian's business partner," Kimberly informs us.

Well, informs *me,* because Hardin isn't paying them any attention, having fixed his eyes on the wildlife program I ended up landing on.

"And this is Max, who does business with Christian."

The man, who had been joking and laughing with Christian, steps around from behind Sasha, and when I finally get a look at him, I'm surprised to see Ken's friend from college, that girl Lillian's father.

"Max," I repeat, discreetly staring at Hardin and trying to draw his attention to the familiar face in front of us.

Catching on, Kimberly looks back and forth between Max and me. "You two have met before?"

"Only once, at Sand Point," I respond.

Max's dark eyes are intimidating, and he has an overpowering presence that immediately claims the room as his, but his cold features do soften slightly at my reminder.

"Ah, yes. You're Hardin Scott's . . . friend," he says, drawing the last word out with a smile.

"Actually, she's . . ." Hardin starts, finally joining us in the living room.

I watch in annoyance as Sasha's eyes follow Hardin's every movement as he crosses the room. She adjusts the golden straps of her dress and licks her lips. I couldn't be more irritated with myself for wearing these damn cloud pants if I tried. Hardin's eyes flicker to her, and I watch as they slowly rake down her body, taking in her tall yet curvy frame, before his attention turns to Max.

"She's not just a friend," Hardin finishes just as Max's hand darts out for a quick and awkward handshake.

"I see." The older man smiles. "Well, either way, she's a lovely girl."

"She is," Hardin mutters. I can sense his annoyance at Max's presence.

Kimberly, the perfect hostess as always, walks over to the bar and gathers glasses for their guests. She politely takes drink orders while I try not to stare at Sasha as she introduces herself to Hardin for the second time. He gives her a brisk nod and sits down on the couch. A pang of disappointment hits me when he leaves a large space between us. Why do I feel so clingy all of a sudden? Is it because Sasha is so beautiful, or is it the way that Hardin's eyes traveled down her body, or how weird he's been all night?

"How's Lillian?" I ask to break the awkwardness and the tension and the aching jealousy that's stirring inside of me.

"She's fine. She's been busy with university," he coolly states.

Kimberly hands him a glass of brown liquor, and he gulps half of it down within seconds.

He raises his brow to Christian. "Bourbon?"

"Only the best," Christian responds with a grin.

"You should call Lillian up sometime. You'd be a good influence on her." Max's eyes move to Hardin.

"I don't think she needs any influence," I retort. I didn't

care much for Lillian, due to my jealousy, but I feel a strong need to defend her against her father. I can't help but think that he's referring to her sexual orientation, and that bothers me immensely.

"Oh, I beg to differ." He smiles a bleached-white smile, and I sink back against the couch cushions. This whole exchange has been uncomfortable. Max is charming and rich, but I can't ignore the darkness that lurks within his deep brown eyes and the hidden malice in his wide smile.

Why is he here with Sasha, anyway? He's a married man, and by the short cut of her dress and the way she smiles at him, they don't appear to be only on "friend"-ly terms.

"Lillian is our regular sitter!" Kimberly chimes in.

"Small world." Hardin rolls his eyes so as to appear as uninterested as possible, but I know he's fuming.

"It is, isn't it." Max grins at Hardin. His British accent is thicker than either Hardin's or Christian's, and not nearly as pleasant to listen to.

"Tessa, go upstairs," Hardin quietly instructs me. Max and Kimberly both look at him, making it known that they heard his command.

This situation is even more awkward now than it was only seconds ago. Now that everyone's heard Hardin tell me to go upstairs, I definitely don't want to oblige. However, I know Hardin, and know that he'll make sure I get upstairs, whether he has to carry me or not.

"I think she should stay and have some wine, or a shot of this bourbon. It's aged and very good," Kimberly says as she rises to her feet and pads over to the little bar. "Which will it be?" She smiles, clearly defying Hardin.

He glares at her and presses his lips into a thin, hard line. I want to laugh at the way Kimberly is challenging Hardin, or leave the room—preferably both—but Max is watching our exchange with more curiosity than seems necessary, and I stay put.

"I'll have a glass of wine," I say.

Kimberly nods, pours the white liquid into a long-stemmed glass, and brings it to me.

The space between Hardin and me seems to be growing by the second, and I can practically see the heat rolling off him in small waves. I take a small sip of the crisp wine, and Max finally looks away from me.

Hardin is staring at the wall. His mood has drastically changed since we kissed, and that really worries me. I thought he'd be excited, happy, and most of all, I thought he'd be turned on and want more, the way he always does, the way I do.

"Do you two live here, in Seattle?" Sasha asks Hardin.

I take another sip of wine. I've been drinking a lot lately.

"I don't." He doesn't look at her as he answers.

"Hmm, where is it that you live?"

"*Not* in Seattle."

If this conversation were happening in any other circumstance, I would scold him for being so rude, but right now I'm happy that he is. Sasha frowns and leans against Max. He looks at me before gently guiding her in the opposite direction.

I already know you're having an affair, so don't play coy now.

Sasha stays quiet, and Kimberly looks to Christian for help to turn the conversation to more pleasant matters. "Well . . ." Christian clears his throat. "The club opening was great; who knew we'd have such a turnout?"

"It was brilliant, that band . . . I can't recall the name, but the last one . . ." Max begins.

"The Reford something . . . ?" Kimberly suggests.

"No, that wasn't it, love." Christian chuckles, and Kimberly walks over to sit on his lap.

"Well, whoever they are, we need to get them booked for next weekend, too," Max says.

Within minutes of the start of their business talk, Hardin turns and disappears down the hallway . . .

"He's usually more polite," Kimberly tells Sasha.

"No, he's not. But we wouldn't have him any other way." Christian laughs, and the rest of the room joins in.

"I'm going to . . ." I begin.

"Go on." Kimberly waves me off, and I give a small good night wave to the guests. By the time I reach the end of the hallway, Hardin is already in the guest room and has closed the door. I hesitate outside of the room for a moment before turning the knob and pushing the door open. When I finally enter, Hardin is pacing back and forth across the length of the room.

"Is something wrong?" I ask him.

"No."

"Are you sure, because you've been weird ever since—"

"I'm fine. I'm just irritated." He sits down at the edge of the bed and rubs his palms against the knees of his jeans.

I love his new jeans. I recognize them from our—*his*—closet at the apartment. Trish got them for him for Christmas, and he hated them.

"And why's that?" I quietly ask, making sure to keep my voice from traveling down the hall and into the living room.

"Max is a prick," Hardin booms. He clearly doesn't care if he's heard.

Laughing, I whisper, "Yeah, he is."

"He was just asking for me to lose my shit when he was being rude to you," he breaths.

"He wasn't being rude to me, specifically. I think that's just his personality." I shrug my shoulders, a gesture that doesn't really calm Hardin.

"Well, either way, I don't fucking like him, and it's annoying that we have one night together and it's with a full house." Hardin brushes his hair back from his forehead and grabs a pillow to lie back on.

"I know." I agree. I hope Max and his mistress leave soon. "I hate that he's cheating on his wife. Denise seemed so nice."

"I don't give a shit about that, really. I just don't like him," Hardin says.

I'm a little surprised by his immediate brushing off such a betrayal. "Don't you feel bad for her? Even a little bit? I'm sure she has no idea about Sasha."

He waves his hand in the air and then tucks his arm behind his head. "I'm sure she knows. Max is an asshole. She can't be that stupid."

I picture Max's wife sitting in a mansion in the hills somewhere, wearing an expensive dress, full hair and makeup, waiting for her unfaithful husband to return home. The thought saddens me, and the best I can hope for is that she has a "friend," too.

The thought surprises me that I would wish for her to do the same thing back to him, but her husband is in the wrong here, and though I barely know her, I want her to find *some* happiness, even if it's not exactly the best decision.

"Either way, it's still wrong," I insist.

"Yeah, but that's marriage for you. Cheating, lying, so on and so on."

"That's not always the case."

"Nine times out of ten." He shrugs. I hate the way he views marriage so negatively.

"No, that's not true." I cross my arms over my chest.

"You're going to argue with me over marriage, again? I don't think we should go there," he warns. His eyes meet mine, and he takes a deep breath.

I want to battle this out with him, tell him that he's wrong and change his view on marriage, but I know it's pointless. Hardin made up his mind about such things long before he met me.

"You're right, we shouldn't talk about this. Especially when you're already wound up."

"I'm not wound up," he scoffs.

"Okay." I roll my eyes at him, and he rises to his feet.

"Stop rolling your eyes at me," he snaps.

I can't help but roll my eyes, again.

"Tessa . . ." he growls.

I stand still, unmoving and unwavering. He has no reason to be short with me. Max's being a pompous jerk is in no way my fault. This is a typical Hardin Scott tantrum, and I'm not caving this time.

"You're only here for one night, remember?" I remind him and watch as the hardness and energy slip from his features. He continues to watch me, though, expecting a fight. I'm not giving him one.

"Dammit, you're right. I'm sorry," he finally sighs, impressing me with this sudden change in his mood and his ability to calm himself down. "Come here." He opens his arms, the way Hardin always does, and I walk into them, the way I haven't for so long. He doesn't say anything; he only wraps his arms around me and rests his chin on top of my head. His scent is overpowering, his breathing has slowed since his little hissy fit, and he is warm, so warm. Seconds, or maybe minutes later, he pulls away from me and presses his thumb under my chin.

"I'm sorry for being a dick. I don't know what my problem was. Max just bugs the shit out of me, or maybe it was the babysitting, or that obnoxious Stacey. I don't know, but I'm sorry."

"Sasha." I correct him with a smile.

"Same thing—a whore is a whore is a whore."

"Hardin!" I gently swat at his chest. The muscles underneath feel harder than I remember. He's been working out daily . . . briefly, my thoughts travel to what he looks like under his black T-shirt, and I wonder if his body has changed since I last laid eyes on it.

"Just saying." He shrugs and brushes his fingertips over the soft line of my jaw. "I really am sorry. I don't want to ruin my time with you. Forgive me?"

His cheeks flush, and his voice is so soft, and his fingertips are gently scraping against my skin, and it feels so good. My eyes flutter closed as he traces the outline of my lips with his thumb.

"Answer me," he softly presses.

"I always do, don't I?" I say with a breath. I rest both of my hands on his hips, my thumbs pressing into the bare skin under his T-shirt. I expect to feel his lips on mine, but when I open my eyes, his guard has been drawn up. I hesitate, but ask, "Is something wrong?"

"I had . . ." He stops midsentence. "I have a headache."

"Do you need something? I can ask Kim if—"

"No, not her. I think I just need to sleep or something. It's late, anyway."

My heart sinks at his words. What is going on with him, and why doesn't he want to kiss me again? Only moments ago he told me that he didn't want to ruin our short time together, yet now he wants to go to sleep?

I sigh out a quiet "Okay." I'm not going to beg Hardin to stay awake and spend time with me. I'm embarrassed by his rejection, and honestly I do need a moment alone without his minty breath fanning across my cheeks and his green eyes piercing into mine, clouding the smidge of judgment I have left.

Still, I linger a little, waiting for him to ask if he can sleep in my room or vice versa.

He doesn't. "I'll see you in the morning, then?" he asks.

"Yeah, sure." I leave the room before I embarrass myself further and lock my bedroom door behind me. Pathetically, I pad back across the room and unlock the door, hoping that maybe, just maybe, he will come through it.

chapter ninety-three

HARDIN

Fuck.

Fuck.

I have been containing my anger, for the most part at least, all week. It's becoming harder and harder to do so when Zed keeps creeping his way into my head, and it's driving me fucking mad. I know I'm batshit crazy for obsessing over this, and I have no doubt Tessa would agree if I told her why I'm so wound up. It's not only Zed, it's Max and his mocking tone with Tessa, his whore and her gawking at me, Kimberly challenging me when I told Tessa to go upstairs—it's all one big fucking annoyance, and my control is slipping. I can feel my nerves being tightened to the brink of snapping, and the only way to relax them is to punch something or bury myself into Tessa and forget about everything; but I can't even fucking do that. I should be sinking myself inside of her right now, over and over until the goddamned sun comes up, to make up for the last week of hell without her touch.

Leave it to me to fuck this night up. I'm sure she's not surprised, though. It's what I do without fail, every time.

I lie down on the bed and stare back and forth between the ceiling and the clock. Eventually it's two in the morning. The annoying voices from the living room halted over an hour ago, and I was glad to hear the sounds of fawning goodbyes and then Vance and Kim's footsteps coming up the stairs.

From across the hall, I feel it. I feel the pull, the fucking magnetic charge, drawing me to Tessa and begging me to be at her side. Ignoring the overwhelming electricity, I climb out of the bed and change into the clean black shorts that Tessa has folded and placed on the dresser. I know Vance has a gym in this massive house somewhere. I need to find it before I lose what's left of my fucking mind.

chapter ninety-four

TESSA

I can't sleep. I've tried to close my eyes and block out the world, leave the chaos and stress of the mess that is my love life, but I can't. It's impossible. It's impossible to fight the irresistible power that draws me to Hardin's room, that begs me to be near him. He's being so distant, and I have to know why. I have to know if he's behaving this way because of something I did, or because of something I didn't do. I have to know that it had nothing to do with Sasha and her tiny gold dress, or Hardin losing interest in me.

I have to know.

Hesitantly, I climb out of the bed and tug on the small cord to bring the lamp to life. I pull the thin band from around my wrist and gather my hair into my hands, pulling it into a ponytail. As quietly as possible, I tiptoe across the hall and slowly turn the handle on the guest room door. It opens with a low creak, and I'm surprised to find the lamp on and the bed empty. A pile of black sheets and blankets are pushed against the edge of the bed, but Hardin isn't in the room.

My heart sinks at the thought that he's left Seattle and gone back home—to his home. I know things were awkward between us, but we should be able to talk about whatever it happens to be that is weighing on Hardin's mind. Scanning the room, I'm relieved to see his bag still on the floor, the piles of clean and folded clothes knocked over, but at least still there.

I've loved seeing the changes in Hardin since his arrival only hours ago. He's been sweeter, calmer, and he actually apologized to me without me having to pull the words from him. Regardless of the fact that he's being cold and distant right now, I can't ignore the changes that a week apart seems to have made and the positive impact that the distance between us has had on him.

I quietly pad down the hallway in search of him. The house is dark, the only light coming from small night-lights lined along the floor of the halls. The bathrooms, living room, and kitchen are empty, and I don't hear a single noise coming from upstairs. He has to be upstairs, though . . . maybe he's in the library?

I keep my fingers crossed that I don't wake anyone during my search, and just as I close the door to the dark and empty library, I see a thin line of light creeping from the door at the end of the long corridor. During my brief stay here, I haven't made it to this part of the house, though I think Kimberly had vaguely indicated that this is where the theater and the gym are. Apparently, Christian spends hours in the gym.

The door is unlocked, and I push it open with ease. I feel a momentary spark of worry as I entertain the idea that it's Christian, not Hardin, who's in the room. That would be incredibly awkward, and I pray it isn't the case.

All four walls of the room are mirrored from floor to ceiling and lined with large, intimidating machines, a treadmill being the only recognizable one. Weights and more weights cover the far wall, and most of the floor is padded. My eyes move to the mirrored walls, and my insides liquefy at the sight of them. Hardin—four Hardins, actually—are reflected in the mirrors. He's shirtless, and his movements are aggressively quick. His hands are wrapped in the same black tape that I've seen on Christian's each day this week.

Hardin's back is to me, his hard muscles straining under pale skin as he lifts his foot to kick the large black bag hanging from the ceiling. His fist strikes out next; a loud thud follows his movement, and he repeats it with the other fist. I watch as he continues to punch and kick the bag; he looks so angry, and hot, and sweaty, and I can barely think straight as I watch him.

With swift movements, he hits with his left leg, then his right, and then both fists smash into the bag with such fluidity, it's incredible to watch. His skin is shining and covered in sweat, and his chest and stomach look slightly different than before, more defined. He simply looks . . . larger. The metal chain attached to the ceiling looks like it's going to snap from the force of Hardin's aggression. My mouth is dry, and my thoughts are sluggish as I watch him and listen to the angry groans that escape as he begins using only his fists against the bag.

I don't know if it's the soft moan that falls from my lips at watching him, or if he somehow felt my presence, but he suddenly stops. The bag continues to sway on its chain, and while keeping his eyes on me, Hardin reaches out one hand to stop it.

I don't want to be the first to speak, but he gives me no choice as he continues to stare at me with wide and angry eyes.

"Hey," I say, my voice hoarse and tiny.

His chest rises and falls rapidly. "Hi," he says, panting.

"What, um"—I try to contain myself—"what are you doing?"

"Couldn't sleep," he breathes heavily. "What're *you* doing up?" He gathers his black T-shirt from the floor and wipes the moisture from his face. I gulp. I can't seem to find the strength to look away from his sweat-soaked body.

"Um, same as you. Couldn't sleep." I smile weakly, and my eyes flicker to his toned torso, the muscles moving in sync with his hard breaths.

He nods; his eyes don't meet mine, and I can't help but ask, "Did I do something? If I did, we could just talk about it and work it out."

"No, you didn't do anything."

"Then tell me what's wrong, please, Hardin. I need to know what's going on." I gather as much confidence as I can manage.

"Do you . . . never mind." The ounce of confidence I had slips away under his stare.

"Do I what?" He sits down on a long black cushion, which I think is some sort of weight bench. After wiping the T-shirt over his face again, he wraps it around his head, restraining his dampened mess of hair.

The impromptu headband is oddly endearing and very attractive, so much so that I find myself fumbling for words. "I'm just beginning to wonder if maybe, possibly, you . . . you're starting to not like me as much as you did." The question sounded much better inside of my head. When said out loud, it sounds pathetic and needy.

"What?" He drops his hands onto his knees. "What are you talking about?"

"Are you still as attracted to me . . . physically?" I ask. I wouldn't feel so ashamed or insecure if he hadn't rejected me earlier tonight. That, and if Ms. Long Legs Short Dress hadn't been fawning over him right in front of me. Not to mention the way his eyes lingered as they slowly took in her body . . .

"What . . . where is this coming from?" As his chest rises and falls, the sparrows inked just under his collarbone appear to be fluttering along with his breathing.

"Well . . ." Although I take a few steps farther into the room, I make sure to leave a few feet between Hardin and me. "Earlier . . . when we were kissing . . . you stopped, and you've barely touched me since, and then you just up and went to bed."

"You actually think that I'm not attracted to you anymore?" He opens his mouth to continue but suddenly closes it again and sits silently.

"It *has* crossed my mind," I admit. The padded flooring has suddenly become fascinating as I stare down at it.

"That is fucking insane," he begins. "Look at me." My eyes

meet his, and he sighs deeply before continuing. "I can't begin to fathom why you would ever consider the notion that I'm not attracted to you, Tessa." He seems to think over his response and adds, "Well, I guess I can see why you would think that because of how I acted earlier, but it's not true; that literally could not be further from the fucking truth."

The ache in my chest slowly begins to dissolve. "Then what is it?"

"You're going to think I'm fucking morbid."

Oh no.

"Why? Tell me, please," I beg him. I watch as frustrated fingers run over the slight stubble on his chin; it's barely there, probably only a day's worth of not shaving.

"Just hear me out before you get mad, okay?"

I nod slowly, an action that completely contradicts the paranoid thoughts that are beginning to flutter through me.

"I had this dream, well, nightmare, actually . . ."

My chest tightens, and I pray that it's not as bad as he's making it out to be. Half of me is relieved that he's upset over a nightmare, not an actual event, but the other half aches for him. He's been alone all week, and it hurts to know that his nightmares have returned.

"Go on," I gently encourage him.

"About you . . . and Zed."

Oh boy. "What do you mean?" I ask.

"He was at our—*my*—apartment, and I came home to find him in between your legs. You were moaning his name and—"

"Okay, okay, I get it," I say, raising a hand to stop him.

The pained expression on his face compels me to keep my hand up for a few seconds to keep him silent, but then he says, "No, let me tell you."

I'm extremely uncomfortable about having to listen to Hardin talk about Zed and me in bed, but if he feels like he needs to tell me—if telling me will help him work it out—I'll bite my tongue and listen.

"He was on top of you, fucking you, in our bed. You said that you loved him." He grimaces.

All of this tension and all of Hardin's strange and awkward behavior since he came to Seattle stemmed from a dream he had about me and Zed? At least this helps explain his middle-of-the-night demand last night that I call Zed and take back the invitation to visit me in Seattle that I agreed to.

As I stare across the room at the green-eyed, grief-stricken man with his face resting on his hands, my earlier paranoia and frustration dissolve like sugar on my tongue.

chapter ninety-five

HARDIN

When my name escapes her lips, it comes out on a breath, soft, her tongue caressing the word. As if in saying that one word she's summed up all of her feelings for me, all of the times I've touched her, all of the times she's proved that she loves me—even if part of me still can't believe it.

Tessa walks closer, and I can see the sympathetic look in her eyes. "Why didn't you just tell me earlier?" she asks.

I look down and pick at the thick tape wrapped around my hands.

"It was only a dream. You know something like that would never actually happen," she says.

When I look up at her, the pressure in my eyes, in my chest, is unrelenting. "It's stuck in my head—I can't stop it from replaying it. He was fucking taunting me the entire time, smirking as he fucked you."

Tessa's small hands quickly move to cover her ears, and she crinkles her nose in displeasure. Then, looking up at me, she drops her arms slowly. "Why do you think you had that dream?"

"I don't know, probably because you agreed to let him visit you here."

"I didn't know what else to say, and we were . . . well, we still are, in that weird place," she mutters.

"I don't want him near you. I know it's fucked up, but I don't give a shit. Honestly, Zed is the line for me; it will always be that way. No amount of kickboxing will change that. Weird place or not, you are only for me. Not just sexually, but entirely. I can't stand you being in any sort of emotional relationship with that guy."

"He hasn't been near me since he took me to my mother's house . . . that night," she reminds me.

But the panic burning inside of me doesn't budge. I look down, breathe in and out deeply to try to calm myself down a little.

"But"—she takes a step closer, though she remains just out of reach—"if it will make you stop thinking these things, I'll tell him not to visit."

My eyes dart to her beautiful face. "You will?" I expected more of a fight from her.

"Yes, I will. I don't want it weighing on you like this." With nervous eyes, she looks down at my chest and back up to my face.

"Come here." I lift one bandaged hand to beckon her.

Because her feet are moving too slowly, I lean up and grab hold of her arm, wrapping my hand around her elbow to bring her to me more quickly.

My breathing has yet to return to normal. I have all this adrenaline rushing through my body. I couldn't help but beat the shit out of that damn bag, but my hands and feet are aching—I still haven't released all of my anger. There's something inside my head, just sitting in the back of my mind, nagging at me, not allowing me to release my grudge against Zed.

That is, until her lips are on mine. She surprises me by pushing her tongue into my mouth and wrapping her small hands into my sweat-soaked hair, tugging hard, pulling the rolled-up T-shirt from around my head and tossing it onto the floor.

"Tessa . . ." I gently push against her chest and remove my mouth from hers. As I sit down on the weight bench, I see her eyes narrow at me.

She doesn't speak as she moves to stand in front of me. "I

won't put up with you rejecting me because of a dream, Hardin. If you don't want me, then that's fine, but this is bullshit," she says through her teeth.

As twisted as it is, her anger stirs something inside of me, causing my blood to flow straight to my dick. I've wanted this woman since the last time I was inside of her, and now here she is, wanting me—and getting frustrated that I'm stopping her from taking what she wants.

Hearing her come over the phone would never be good enough; I need to feel it.

A war is being fought within me. With the wild energy still pumping through my veins like fire, I finally say, "I can't help it, Tessa, I know it doesn't make sense—"

"Fuck me, then," she says, and my mouth falls open. "You should just fuck me until you forget about that dream, because you're here for one night, and I've missed you, but you're too stuck on imagining me with Zed to even give me the attention that I want."

"The attention that you want?" I can't help the harshness of my tone as I hear her ridiculous and untrue words. She has no idea how many times I've fucked my own hand, pretending it was her, imagining her voice in my ear telling me how much she needs me, how much she loves me.

"Yes, Hardin. That. I. Want."

"What is it exactly that you want?" I ask her. Her gaze is hard and slightly unnerving.

"I want you to spend time with me without obsessing over Zed, I want you to touch me and kiss me without pulling away. *That,* Hardin, is what I want." She scowls and places her hands on her hips. "I want you to touch me—only you," she adds, relaxing her stance by a fraction.

Her words, reassuring and flattering, begin to push the paranoid thoughts from my mind, and I begin to realize just how stupid this whole ordeal we're going through really is. She's mine, not his. He's sitting alone somewhere, and I'm here with her—and she wants me. I can't keep my eyes off her pouty lips, her angry glare, the soft curve of her tits just under the thin white T-shirt. The T-shirt that should be, but isn't, one of mine. Which is another result of my stubbornness.

Tessa closes the remaining distance between us, and my somewhat shy—yet *very fucking dirty*—girl is looking at me, expecting a reply as her hand moves to my shoulder and pushes me back just enough for her to climb onto my lap.

Fuck this. I don't give a shit about some stupid fucking dream or our stupid fucking rule about distance. All I want is her and me, me and her: Tessa and the mess that is fucking Hardin.

Her lips find their way to my neck, and my fingertips press into her hips. No matter how many times I imagined it throughout the week, no fantasy will ever compare to her tongue skimming across my damp collarbone and up to that fucking spot just under my ear.

"Lock the door," I instruct as her teeth softly sink into my skin and she grinds her hips down against me. I'm rock fucking hard against her ridiculous fluffy fucking pants, and I need her *now.*

I ignore the aching throb between my legs as she climbs off me and hurries across the room to do as I said. I don't waste a goddamn second when she returns. Her pants are pushed down her thighs, and her black panties follow, pooling around her ankles on the padded floor.

"I've been tortured all week, thinking about how you look when you're like this," I groan, my eyes drinking in every fucking detail of her half-naked body. "So beautiful," I say with awe.

When she pulls her T-shirt over her head, I can't help but lean forward and kiss the curve of her wide hips. A slow shiver rakes through her, and she reaches behind her back to unclasp her bra.

Holy fuck. Out of all the times I have made love to her, I can't remember ever feeling this feverish. Even the times when she woke me up by wrapping her mouth around my cock, I never felt this fucking animalistic.

I reach for her, taking one of her breasts into my mouth and one in my hand. Her hands move to my shoulders to keep her steady as I pucker my lips around her soft skin.

"Oh God," she moans, her nails digging into my shoulder, and I suck harder. "Lower, please."

She attempts to guide my head down with a gentle push, so I use my teeth against her, to tease her. I run my fingertips along the underside of both of her breasts, slow and torturous . . . this is what she gets for being so fucking tempting and teasing.

Her hips move forward, and I slide my body down slightly so that my mouth is at the perfect height to press against the swollen bud of nerve endings between her thighs. With a soft moan, she encourages me to go further, and my lips wrap around her, sucking and savoring the wetness already gathered there. She's so warm and so fucking sweet.

"Your fingers haven't quite satisfied you, have they?" I pull away to ask her. She breathes a deep breath, her blue-gray eyes watching me as I tilt my head and run my tongue along her pubic bone.

"Don't tease me," she whines, tugging at my hair again.

"Did you touch yourself off again this week, after our chat on the phone?" I taunt her. She squirms and gasps when my tongue lands exactly where she wants it.

"No."

"You're lying." I call her out. I can tell by the redness creeping from her neckline to her cheeks and the way her eyes flicker away to the mirrored wall that she's not telling the truth. She *has* gotten herself off since our time on the phone . . . and the thought of her lying there, her legs spread open, her fingers moving over herself, her finding such pleasure from what I taught her . . . it makes me groan against her hot skin.

"Only once," she lies again.

"That's too bad." I completely pull away from her.

"Three times, okay?" Tessa admits, embarrassment clear in her voice.

"What were you thinking about? What was it that made you come?" I ask with a smirk.

"You, only you." Her eyes are hopeful, needy.

Her admission thrills me, and I want to please her now more than ever before. I know that I can make her come in less than a minute using only my tongue, but I don't want that. With one last kiss to the apex of her thighs, I pull away and stand. Tessa is completely naked, and the mirrors . . . *fuck,* the mirrors reflect her perfect body all around me, multiplying those luscious curves of hers ten-fold. Her smooth skin surrounds me, making me tug my shorts and boxers down to my ankles with only one hand. I begin to pull at the tape wrapped around my knuckles, but her hand quickly darts out to stop me.

"No, leave it," Tessa requests, a flicker of darker lust sparking in her eyes. So she likes the tape . . . or maybe watching me work out . . . or the mirrors . . .

I do as she says and press my body against hers, my mouth claiming hers, and I pull her down to the padded floor with me.

Her hands run across my bare chest, and her eyes darken to a smoky gray. "Your body is different now."

"I've only been working out for a week." I roll her naked body so that's she pinned underneath mine.

"But I can tell . . ." Her tongue runs across her full lips so slowly that I don't hesitate to press myself against her, letting her know just how fucking hard I am. She's so smooth and so goddamn wet against me, one small movement, and I'll finally be inside her.

Then it hits me.

"I don't have a fucking condom in here," I curse and bury my face in her shoulder.

She lets out a frustrated groan but presses her nails into me, pulling me closer. "I need you," she moans, flicking her tongue across my mouth.

I press against the warm, soaked flesh and slowly fill her.

"But . . ." I begin to try to remind her of the risks, but her eyes flutter closed, and sensation overwhelms me as I flex my hips to get deeper, as deep inside her as I possibly can.

"Fuck, I've missed you," I moan. I can't get over just how fucking warm and soft she feels without the barrier of a condom. All of my common sense has been erased; all the warnings that I've given to myself and to her have vanished. I only need a few seconds, a few more thrusts into her eagerly waiting body, and I'll stop.

I lift myself by stretching my arms below me, straightening them to gain leverage. I want to look at her while I'm moving in and out of her. Her head is lifted off the padded floor, and she's staring at the spot where our flushed bodies are connected.

"Look into the mirror," I say. I'll stop after three more . . . okay, four. I can't help but continue to move as she turns her head to watch us in the mirrored wall. Her body looks so soft and perfect, and fucking clean, compared to the black stains covering mine. We are pure passion personified, devil and angel, and I've never been more madly fucking in love with her.

"I knew you liked watching, even if it's only by your own self, I fucking knew it."

Her fingers press into the bottom of my spine, pulling me closer and deeper, and fuck, I have to stop now, I feel the pressure building from the bottom of my spine to my groin as I reveal one of her kinks. I have to stop . . .

I slowly pull out of her, letting both of us enjoy the lingering moment of pleasure. Her whines are quickly cut short when my fingers slide into her with ease. "I'm going to make you come now and then take you to your bed," I promise her, and she smiles a dazed smile before looking back into the mirror, watching me.

"Quiet, baby, you'll wake the others," I whisper against her. I love the noises she makes, the way she moans my name, but the last thing I need is one of the cock-blocking Vances knocking at the door.

Within seconds, I feel her tighten around my fingers. I nip and suck at the nerve endings above her entrance, and she tugs at my hair, continuing to watch me fuck her with my fingers until she comes, gasping and panting my name repeatedly.

chapter ninety-six

TESSA

Hardin's mouth leaves a trail of moisture up my stomach and along my chest before he finally places a soft kiss on my temple. I lie there on the floor next to him, trying to catch my breath and relive the events leading up to this moment. I had every intention of having a serious conversation with him about his—no, *our*—lack of communication, but watching him angrily assault that punching bag had me gasping and moaning his name within minutes.

I lean up onto my elbow and look down at him. "I want to reciprocate."

"Be my guest." He grins, his lips coated with my moisture.

I move quickly, taking him into my mouth before he catches a single breath.

"Fuck," he groans. The sensual noise causes my mouth to fall open too far, and he slips out, down across my tongue. Hardin bucks his hips off the floor to meet my lips again, pressing himself inside my mouth again.

"Please, Tess," he begs.

I can taste myself on him, but I barely notice it as he moans my name.

"I'm not . . . fuck, I'm not going to last long," he pants, and I speed up. All too soon he tugs my hair and lifts my head back.

"I'm going to come in your mouth, then take you to the bed and fuck you again." He runs his thumb over my lips, and playfully, I bite down gently on the pad of his finger. His head falls back, and his grip on my hair tightens as I work my mouth on him.

I can feel his cock twitching, his legs stiffening as he gets closer. "Fuck, Tessa . . . so good, baby," he groans as his warmth fills my mouth. I take it all, swallowing all he has to give. Standing to my feet, I wipe at my lips with one finger.

"Get dressed," he commands, tossing my bra to me.

As Hardin and I hastily get dressed, I catch him staring at me time and time again. Not that it comes as all that much of a surprise . . . I haven't stopped staring at him either.

"Ready?" he asks.

I nod, and Hardin turns the lights off, closes the door behind us as if nothing happened in that room, and leads me down the hallway. We walk in comfortable silence, a vast difference from the tension between us earlier. When we reach the part of the hallway just outside my bedroom, he stops me by gently grabbing hold of my elbow.

"I should have told you about that nightmare instead of distancing myself from you," he says. The dim night-lights along the floor cast just enough light onto his face to allow me to see the pure honesty and softness behind his eyes.

"We both just need to learn to communicate."

"You're so much more understanding than I deserve you to be," he whispers and lifts my hand to his face. His lips press against each of my knuckles, and my knees nearly buckle at the touching gesture.

Hardin opens the door and takes my hand in his as he leads me to the bed.

chapter ninety-seven

TESSA

Hardin's hands are still covered in rough black tape, yet they feel so tender wrapped around mine.

"I hope I haven't worn you out." He grins, brushing his taped knuckles across my cheekbone.

"No." The majority of the tension that I was feeling in my body has been released by his fingers. However, the not-so-subtle ache for him is still there. It always is.

"This is okay, right? I mean, you wanted space . . . and this isn't exactly space." His arms wrap around me as we hesitantly stand in front of the bed.

"We still need space, but this is what I want right now," I explain. I'm sure this doesn't make much sense to Hardin, because really, it doesn't make much sense to me, especially now, when his overwhelming presence is right here in front of me.

"Me, too," he breathes and dips his head down to my neck. "This is what's good for us . . . to be close this way," he whispers. His arms tighten around my body, and he uses his knees to guide us onto the bed as his lips gently suck on my tingling skin. I can feel him growing hard against my leg; he's ready to go again, and so am I.

"I've missed you so fucking much . . . I've missed your body," he hisses. His hands travel under my thin cotton T-shirt, and he pulls it up over my head. My ponytail catches on the neckline, but Hardin gently untangles my hair, and his fingers reach behind me to pull the band out, letting my hair fall against the mattress beneath me. He gently presses his lips to my forehead; his mood has changed since he ravished me at the gym. He was rough there, sexy and commanding. But now he's being my Hardin, the soft and gentle man hiding inside of a tough exterior.

"The way your pulse"—his lips hover inches from mine, and his fingers press against the tender beating in my neck as he breathes—"goes fucking crazy when I touch you, especially here"—his free hand slides down over my stomach and into the front of my pajama pants.

"You're always so ready for me." He groans, running his middle finger up and down. I feel my skin catch fire—it's a steady burn instead of an explosion, as fits his gentle touch. Hardin removes his hand, then brings his finger to his lips. "So sweet," he says, and his wet tongue slowly darts out to cover the tip of his finger.

He knows exactly what he's doing to me. He knows how much his dirty words affect me and how much they make me want him. He knows, and he's doing a damn good job at making me burn with desire from the inside out.

chapter ninety-eight

HARDIN

I know exactly what I'm doing to her. I know how much she loves my filthy mouth, and when I look down at her, she doesn't even bother to conceal it.

"You're being such a good girl," I say with a dark smile, eliciting a moan from her without so much as a touch to her flaming skin.

"Tell me what you want," I whisper into her ear. I can practically hear her erratic pulse under her skin. I'm driving her crazy, and I fucking love it.

"You," she says, desperately, vaguely.

"I want it slow. I want you to feel every single moment that you were away from me."

I tug on her pajamas and give her a commanding look. Without a word she nods and pulls them down. Then I press my thumb into her thin cotton panties, tearing them from her body. Her eyes are wide and dark, her lips pink and swollen. The force of my movement pulls her into me, and she wraps both of her small hands around my arms, hooking them with her beautiful little fingers.

"Grab the condom," she reminds me.

Fuck, it's across the hall in the room that no one could have possibly expected me to actually stay in, with Tessa only meters away. Curiously, however, the nightstand was stocked with condoms upon my arrival.

"*You* grab the condom." I playfully fight back, knowing there's no chance in hell I'm having her scurry across the hallway half dressed. I gently push my hands under her back and unsnap her bra, then slide the black straps down before tossing the whole contraption onto the floor behind us.

"Cond—" she starts to remind me.

But her own sharp intake of breath interrupts the thought as I suck on her newly exposed nipples. She's so sensitive to my touch, and I want to savor every second of her.

"Shh . . ." I silence her by biting down on the sensitive flesh.

But after a moment, I do climb to my feet. I don't waste my time getting dressed. At least I'm wearing boxers; even if I wasn't, I sure as hell wouldn't be wasting my time putting clothes on right now.

I return to the room, four condoms in hand . . . I'm a little ambitious and overprepared, but with the way Tessa is behaving tonight, we may need the entire drawerful.

"I missed you," she sweetly remarks, a shy smile covering her face. And then there's a flash of embarrassment in her eyes when she realizes she's said the words aloud.

"And I you," I reply, which sounds as cheesy as I expected it to.

Without any further Hallmark statements, I move to join her on the bed again. She's sitting up, completely topless, with her back against the headboard and her knees slightly bent. She's completely naked; only the cream satin sheets drape over the top of her thighs, blending in with her creamy skin.

I have to control myself at the sight. I have to stop myself from literally diving onto the bed, ripping the sheets away from her, and taking what is mine. I want tonight . . . well . . . morning now, to go smoothly, and I don't want to rush it.

Smiling, I stare at the woman on the bed. She's staring back at me, her eyes soft and warm, her cheeks painted a deep pink. When I join her on the bed, eager hands move straight to the lining of my boxers, tugging them down my thighs. Her feet finish the job, and she gathers me in her hand, squeezing gently.

"Christ," I hiss, momentarily losing my focus on everything except her touch. She begins to slowly pump, her small wrist twisting slightly as it moves up and down, and I fucking love the way she knows exactly how to touch me. As she lays herself down, her hand keeps a steady rhythm, and I give her the condom, silently instructing her what to do next.

She bites her lip and quickly obliges. As the latex rolls down me, I silently curse at her, and myself, for never following through with the birth-control plan. The feeling of skin on skin with her is heavenly, and now that I've felt it, I crave more and more.

She's quick to climb on top of me and straddle my waist, my dick only a breath away from slipping inside her.

"Wait . . ." I stop her by gently wrapping my hands around her hips and laying her back down beside me on the bed.

Confusion flashes in her beautiful eyes. "What's wrong?"

"Nothing . . . I just want to kiss you a little more first," I assure her and cup my hand around the nape of her neck to bring her face closer to mine. My mouth covers hers, and I hover over her body, forcing myself to take this slow. With her naked body pressed against mine, I take a moment to appreciate that after all the shit I've put her through, she's still here, she's always fucking here, and it's about goddamned time I make it worth her while. I support my weight with one arm and lie on top of her, parting her legs with my knee.

"I love you . . . so much. You still know that, don't you?" I ask her between strokes of my tongue over hers.

She nods, but for a dreadful moment, Zed's face appears in my mind. His confession of love for my Tessa, and her thankful acceptance of it. "I love you, too," she had moaned in her sleep. A slow shiver travels through me, and I pause.

Noticing my hesitation, she pushes her fingers into my unruly hair and takes possession of my mouth with hers.

"Come back to me," she begs.

That's all it takes.

Everything fades except for the softness of her body underneath mine, the wetness between her legs as I slowly push into her. The feeling is exquisite. No matter how many times I've taken her, it won't ever be enough.

"I love you." She repeats the words. I wrap one arm under her so our bodies are pressed as closely together as possible. I lick my dry lips and bury my head in her neck again, whispering dirty things into her ear and moving to kiss her every time she moans my name.

I feel the buildup of pressure rising from my spine, igniting every fucking vertebra. Tessa's fingernails dig into my back, across my shoulder blades, as if she's reaching for the words inked across my skin. The words meant for her, and only her.

"I never wish to be parted from you from this day on," it says. And I'm going to do everything I have to do in order to keep my permanent promise.

I lean up to look at her. One hand still rests under her back; the other travels up her torso and across both of her breasts, and rests just below her throat.

"Tell me how it feels," I say with a grunt. I'm barely holding on to the pleasure that is coursing though me. I want to keep it there for both of us, to make it last longer. I want to create this space that we can both inhabit.

My movements quicken, and she moves one of her hands down to fist the bedsheets. Every sinful twist of my hips, every violent thrust into her waiting body, intensifies and further seals the power she has over me.

"So good, Hardin . . . so good . . ." Her voice is thick and hoarse, and I swallow the rest of her moans like the greedy bastard I am. I feel her body begin to go rigid, and I can't wait any longer. With a soft cry of her name, I spill into the condom with slow and sloppy thrusts before collapsing, barely breathing, next to her.

I reach over and pull her body to mine, and when I open my eyes, a sheer layer of sweat covers her silky skin, her eyes are open, and she's staring at the ceiling fan.

"You okay?" I ask her. I know I was a little rough toward the end, but I also know how much she loves that shit.

"Yeah, of course." She leans over to plant a kiss on my bare chest and climbs out of the bed. I groan in disappointment when she pulls her white T-shirt down over her head, covering her body.

"Here's your headband." She smiles, proud of her corny remark, and she tosses the sweat-dampened T-shirt I wrapped around my head in the gym onto the bed. I roll the fabric up and wrap it around my head again just to get a reaction out of her.

"You don't like it?" I ask, and she giggles.

"I do, actually." Tessa is really putting on a show as she bends down to pick up her black panties from the floor and shimmies them up her thighs. That she isn't wearing a bra is wonderfully apparent as she shakes her body.

"Good. It's easier this way." I point to the contraption on my head.

I really need a fucking haircut, but Steph's friend, a lavender-haired chick named Mads, has always been the one to cut it. My blood begins to boil at the thought of Steph. *That stupid fucking . . .*

"Earth to Hardin!" Tessa's voice brings me out of my hateful thoughts.

I snap my head up. "Sorry."

Back in her pajamas, Tessa snuggles up next to me and, strangely, grabs the remote to the TV and starts flipping around trying to find something to watch. I'm a little dazed, so the cooldown feels comfortable, but after a few minutes I realize she's sighed quite a few times. And when I look over at her, there's a deep scowl on her face, like finding a program to watch is more frustrating than it should be.

"Something wrong?" I ask her.

"No," she lies.

"Tell me now," I press, and she lets out a quick breath.

"It's nothing . . . I'm just a little . . ." Her cheeks flush. "Wound up."

"Wound up? You should be anything but wound up after that." I pull back a little and look at her.

"I didn't . . . you know, I—I didn't," she stutters. Her shyness never fails to surprise me. One minute she's moaning into my ear to fuck her harder, faster, deeper, and the next she can't form a sentence.

"Spill it," I demand.

"I didn't finish."

"What?" I choke. *Had I really been that consumed by my own pleasure that I didn't notice when she didn't come?*

"You stopped right before . . ." she quietly explains.

"Why didn't you say something? Come here, then." I tug at her shirt to lift it over her head.

"What are you going to do?" she asks, excitement laced in her tone.

"Shh . . ." I don't know what I want to do . . . I want to make love to her again, but I need a little more time to refuel.

Wait—got it.

"We're going to do something that we've only done once." I smirk at her, and her eyes widen. "Because, you know, practice makes perfect."

"What's that?" And just like that, her excitement has been replaced by nervousness.

I lie back on my elbows and beckon to her to come to me.

"I don't get it," she says.

"Come here; put your thighs here." I tap the empty space on both sides of my head.

"What?"

"Tessa, come here, and then spread your thighs over my face, so I can get you off right and proper," I explain slowly and clearly.

"Oh," she squeaks. I see the hesitation in her eyes, and I reach over to turn the lamp off. I want her to be as comfortable as possible. Despite the darkness, I can still make out the soft planes of her body, the fullness of her chest, the sexy curve of her hips.

Tessa removes her panties, and within seconds she's following my instructions and kneeling over me.

"This is quite the view I have here," I tease her, and my vision disappears. She's pulled my T-shirt down over my eyes.

"Well, this is much hotter, actually." I smile against her thighs. She smacks me playfully on the head in response. "Really, though . . . it's really fucking hot," I add.

I hear her laugh in the darkness, and I bring my hands to her hips, guiding her movements. Once my tongue touches her, she begins to move her hips on her own, tugging at my hair and whispering my name until she loses herself in the pleasure I'm giving her.

chapter ninety-nine

TESSA

I come back to reality, slowly, unwillingly, but happy Hardin's lying next to me.

"Hey." He smiles, kissing me on my lips.

I laugh—it's a lazy sound, not wanting to move. My body is slightly sore, but in the best way.

"I wish you weren't leaving tomorrow," I whisper while running my fingertips over one of the branches on his tattoo. The tree is dark, haunting and intricate. I wonder: If Hardin were getting this tattoo now, would he get the dead tree again? Or would there be just a few leaves on the branches, now that he's happier, more lively?

"Me, too," he answers simply.

I can't mask the desperation behind my plea when I say "Then don't."

Hardin's fingers spread across my back, and he presses my naked body closer to his. "I don't want to, but I know you're only saying that because I just made you come repeatedly."

A horrified scoff falls from my lips. "That's not true!" Hardin's body shakes gently with an amused chuckle. "It really isn't the only reason . . . Maybe we could be with each other on the weekends for a little while and see where it goes from there?"

"You expect me to drive here every weekend?"

"Not every one. I'll come there, too." I tilt to my head to look into his eyes. "It's working for us so far."

"Tessa . . ." He sighs, "I already told you how I felt about the long-distance shit." My eyes flicker to the ceiling fan slowly spinning around and around in the dimness of the room. Rachel is pouring marinara sauce into Monica's handbag on the television screen.

"Yes, yet here you are," I challenge him.

He sighs and tugs gently at the ends of my hair, forcing me to look at him once more. "Touché."

"Well, I think there's some sort of compromise that can be reached here, don't you?"

"What's your offer?" he asks softly, briefly closing his eyes to take a deep breath.

"I don't know exactly . . . give me a moment," I say.

What exactly *am* I offering him? It's in the best interest of both of our sanities to stay somewhat distant from each other for now. As much as my heart forgets all the terrible things that Hardin and I have been through in the past, my brain won't allow me to give up all of my remaining dignity.

I am in Seattle, following my dream, alone, with no apartment because of Hardin's possessive nature and the unwillingness of both of us to compromise over even the most trivial details.

"I don't know, really," I finally say when I can't come up with a solid suggestion.

"Well, do you want me around still? Just for the weekends, at least?" he asks. His fingers twist and twirl my hair.

"Yes."

"Every weekend?"

"Mostly." I smile.

"Do you want to talk on the phone each day like we did this week?"

"Yes." I loved the simple way Hardin and I spoke on the phone, neither of us even noticing the minutes and hours as they ticked by.

"So everything will be the same as it was this week, then. I don't know about that," he says.

"Why not?" It's seemed to work for him so far, so why would he object to continuing the same way?

"Because, Tessa, you're here in Seattle without me, and we aren't actually together, you could see someone else or meet someone—"

"Hardin." I lift myself onto my elbow to look down at him. His eyes bore into mine, and a lock of my unruly blond hair falls onto his face. Without breaking eye contact or even so much as a blink, his fingers move to tuck the fallen hair back behind my ear. "I'm not planning on seeing or meeting anyone else. All I want out of this is some independence and for both of us to be able to communicate."

"Why is it so important to you to be independent all of a sudden?" he asks. His thumb and forefinger glide across the shell of my ear, sending a shiver down my spine. If he's trying to distract me, he's succeeding.

Despite his gentle touch and burning jade eyes, I continue in my quest to make him understand where I'm coming from. "It's not a sudden thing. I've mentioned this to you before. I also hadn't noticed just how dependent on you I was until recently, and I don't like it. I don't like being that way."

"I do," he says quietly.

"I know you do, but I don't," I say, refusing to allow the confidence in my voice to falter. A part of me pats myself on the back, then rolls her eyes at me because she isn't buying it.

"Well, how do I play into this independent shit?"

"Just keep doing what you're doing now. I have to be able to make decisions without thinking about having your permission or what you would think about them."

"You definitely don't think about having my permission now, or you wouldn't do half the shit you do."

I don't want to have a fight. "Hardin," I warn him. "This is important to me. I need to be able to think for myself. We should be partners . . . equals, neither of us should hold more . . . *power* than the other." I struggle to find the words, sifting through my mind for a better way to explain what I want . . . what I need. I have to do this. This is part of who I am, or who I want to be. I'm working hard to find myself, to find out who I am on my own, with or without Hardin.

"Equals? Power? *You* obviously have more power here. I mean, come on."

"It's not only for me . . . it's been good for you, too. You know it has."

"I guess so, but what does that say about us that we can only get along if we're in different cities?" he asks . . . putting into words the question that's been nagging at me since he arrived.

"Well, we'll figure that out later."

"Sure." He stubbornly rolls his eyes but softens the reaction by kissing my forehead.

"Remember what you said about there being a difference between loving someone and not being able to live without them?" I ask.

"I don't ever want to hear that statement again, really."

I swipe his damp hair off of his forehead. "You're the one who said it," I remind him. My fingertips graze along the outline of his nose, down to his swollen lips. "I've been thinking about it so much since then," I admit.

Hardin groans in annoyance. "Why?"

"Because you said it for a reason, didn't you?"

"Out of anger, that's all. I didn't have a clue what it even meant. I was just being a dick."

"Well, either way, I keep thinking about it." I gently tap on the tip of his nose.

"Well, I wish you wouldn't, because there's no difference

between the two." His words fall slowly between us, his tone thoughtful.

"How so?"

He gives me a small smile. "I can't live without you *and* I love you: they go hand in hand. If I could live without you, I wouldn't be as in love with you as I am, and I clearly cannot be far from you."

"I'll say." I bite back the giggle that's threatening to emerge.

He notices my lightness. "I know you aren't talking about me . . . You nearly busted your ass running to tackle me when I arrived." Even in the darkness of the room, I can see his bright, widening smile, and my breath catches as I take in the raw beauty of him. When he behaves this way, unguarded and natural, there's nothing better in my world.

"I knew you were going to torture me for that!" I swat at his bare chest, and his hand flies up to catch my wrist between his long fingers.

"Are you trying to get rough with me again? Look what happened last time." He lifts his head off the mattress, and the heat begins to spread down my body, resting between my already sore thighs.

"Can you stay one more day?" I dodge his remark about being rough. I need to know if I'm going to have more time with him tomorrow so we can spend the remainder of the morning hours . . . well . . . getting rough. "Please," I add, snuggling my head into the crook of his neck.

"Fine," he says. I can feel his jaw move as he smiles against my forehead. "But only if you blindfold me again."

In one quick motion, he wraps his arms around my back and flips my body under his, and seconds later we're lost in each other . . . again and again . . .

chapter one hundred

HARDIN

Kimberly is sitting at the breakfast bar when I walk into the kitchen. Her face is free of makeup, and her hair is pulled back away from her face. I don't think I've ever seen her without a shit ton of crap on her face, and for Vance's sake I contemplate hiding the shit from her because she looks much better without it.

"Well, look who's finally awake," she says in a chipper tone.

"Yeah, yeah." I groan and walk straight past her to the coffee machine nestled in the corner of the dark granite countertop.

"What time are you leaving?" she asks while picking at a bowl of lettuce.

"Not until tomorrow, if that's okay. Or do you want me out now?" I fill a mug with the black liquid and turn to face her.

"Of course you can stay." She grins. "As long as you aren't being an asshole to Tessa."

"Actually, I'm not." I roll my eyes as Vance enters the room. "You need to get a tighter leash on this one, perhaps even a muzzle," I tell him.

A deep bellowing laugh comes from her fiancé just as Kimberly raises her middle finger to me.

"So classy," I taunt her.

"You're in an awfully cheery mood." Christian grins wickedly, and Kimberly shoots him a glare.

What the hell is that about?

"Wonder why that is?" he adds, and she elbows him.

"Christian . . ." she scolds, and he shakes his head. His hand lifts in defense to block her from repeating the playful assault.

"Probably because he's *missed* Tessa," Kimberly suggests and eyes Christian as he circles around the oversized island to grab a banana from the fruit basket.

His eyes twinkle in amusement as he pulls down the peel of a banana. "I heard midnight workouts will do that."

My blood turns cold. "What did you say?"

"Calm down . . . he shut the camera off before the good stuff," Kimberly assures me.

Camera?

Fuck. Of fucking course this asshole would have a camera in his gym . . . Hell, every main access room is probably equipped with security cameras. He's always been more paranoid behind that slick demeanor than he lets on.

"What did you see?" I growl, trying to keep my pulsing anger at bay.

"Nothing. Only that Tessa came into the room; he knew better than to continue . . ." Kimberly bites back a grin, and relief floods through me. I was too caught up in the moment, caught up in Tessa, to think about shit like security cams.

I scowl at Vance. "Why were you even watching the footage? That's pretty fucking creepy that you were watching me work out."

"Don't flatter yourself. I was checking the kitchen monitor, because it had a short; the gym just happened to be playing alongside it at the time."

"Sure," I say, stretching the word out.

"Hardin's staying another night; that's fine, right?" Kim asks him.

"Of course it's fine. I don't know why your ass isn't here to stay anyway. You know I'll pay you more than Bolthouse."

"You didn't the first time—that was the problem," I remind him with a smug grin.

"That's because you were only a freshman in college at the time. You were lucky to have a paid internship, let alone an actual job, without a degree." He shrugs, trying to dismiss my argument.

I cross my arms in defense. "Bolthouse disagrees with you."

"They are twats. Need I remind you that in the last year alone, Vance Publishing has surpassed them by a huge margin. I've expanded here to Seattle, and I plan on opening a New York office by next year."

"Is there a point to all this bragging?" I ask.

"Yes. Point is, Vance is better, bigger, and happens to be where she's working." He doesn't have to say Tessa's name for me to feel the weight of his words. "You'll be graduating after this semester; don't make an impulsive decision now that will impact the entirety of your career before it even begins." He takes a quick bite of the fruit in his hand, and I scowl at him, trying to think of a sharp reply.

I can't seem to come up with one. "Bolthouse has an office in London."

He looks at me in mocking disbelief. "Who's going back to London? You?" He doesn't hide the sarcasm in his voice.

"Possibly. I had planned on it and still am."

"Yeah, so did I." He glances at his future wife. "You'll never go back to live there, just as I won't either."

Kimberly flushes and gushes at his words, and I come to the conclusion that they're the most obnoxious couple I've ever encountered. It's like you can see how much they love each other just by watching them interact. It's annoying and uncomfortable.

"Point proven." Christian snickers.

"I didn't agree with you," I snap.

"Yes," Kimberly butts in, like the ballbuster she is. "But you didn't disagree either."

Without another word, I take my coffee mug and my balls as far away from Kimberly as I can get them.

chapter one hundred and one

TESSA

The morning arrives much too quickly, and when I wake up, I'm alone in the bed. The empty side of the mattress still bears the imprint of Hardin's body, so he must have gotten up only a few minutes ago.

Right on cue, he enters the room quietly, coffee mug in hand.

"Good morning," he says when he notices that I'm awake.

"Morning." My throat is tight and dry. Images of Hardin moving in and out of my mouth with furious thrusts makes my insides tighten.

"Are you feeling okay?" He places the steaming mug of coffee on the dresser and walks over to the bed. He sits down next to me on the edge of the mattress. "Answer me," he calmly adds when I take too long to respond.

"Yeah, just sore." I stretch my arms and legs out in front of me. Yes . . . definitely sore. "Where did you go?"

"I went to get some coffee, and I had to call Landon to tell him I won't be home today," he tells me. "If you still want me to stay, that is."

"I do." I nod at him. "But why do you have to tell Landon?"

Hardin runs his hand over his hair, and his eyes concentrate on reading my expression. I get the feeling that I'm missing something here.

"Answer me," I say, using his own words back at him.

"He's babysitting your dad."

"Why?" *Why would my father need a babysitter?*

"Your dad's trying to get sober, that's why. And I'm not stupid enough to leave him at that apartment by himself."

"You have liquor there, don't you?"

"No, I tossed it. Just drop this, okay?" His tone is no longer gentle; it's urgent, and he's clearly on edge.

"I'm not going to just drop it. Is there something that I should know? Because I feel like I'm being left out of the loop here, again." I cross my arms over my chest and he takes a deep, dramatic breath, his eyes closing with the gesture.

"Yes, there is something that you don't know about, but I'm begging you to just trust me, okay?"

"How bad?" I ask; the possibilities terrify me.

"Just trust me, okay?"

"Trust you to do what?"

"Trust that I will take care of all of this shit so that by the time I tell you what happened, it won't matter anymore. You have enough shit going on right now; please, just trust me on this. Let me do this for you, and let it go," he urges.

The initial paranoia and panic that always come with these types of situations flutter through me, and I'm moments away from snatching Hardin's phone from him and calling Landon myself. The look on Hardin's face, though, stops me. He's pleading for me to trust him on this, trust that he'll be able to fix whatever it is that's going on; and to tell the truth, as much as I want to know, I don't think I can handle another problem on my already full plate.

"Okay." I sigh.

His brows furrow, and he cocks his head to the side. "Really?" He's astounded by how easy it was to persuade me to back off, I'm sure.

"Yes. I'll do my best not to worry about the situation with my dad as long as you can promise me that it's better for me not to know."

He nods. "I promise."

I believe him, mostly.

"Fine." I finalize the agreement with the word and try my best to push my obsessive need to know what's happening to the back of my mind. I need to trust Hardin with this. I need to trust him of my own resolve. If I can't trust him with this, how can I entertain a future for us at all?

I sigh, and Hardin smiles at my acquiescence.

chapter one hundred and two

TESSA

"Looks like I'll be filling out these thank-you cards to the guests who made last night's club opening such a big success," Kimberly says with a wry grin and a wave of an envelope when I enter the kitchen. "What are the two of you planning for today?"

A look at the stack of cards she's already addressed, and the pile she's still working on, makes me wonder just how many businesses Christian has invested in, if all those people she's writing to were "partners" of some sort. The size of this house alone has to mean he has more enterprises going on than just Vance Publishing and a single jazz club.

"I'm not sure. We'll figure it out when Hardin gets out of the shower," I tell her, and slide a fresh stack of small envelopes across the granite countertop.

I had to force Hardin into the bathroom to take a shower alone; he was still irritated with me for locking him out of the bathroom while I took mine. No matter how many times I tried to explain to him how awkward I'd feel if the Vances knew we were showering together in their home, he'd give me a weird little look and argue that we'd done much worse in their house than shower together over the past twelve hours.

I stood my ground despite his pleading. The events in the gym were motivated by pure lust and were entirely unplanned. The love we made in my bedroom isn't an issue, because it's my bedroom for now, and I'm an adult having consensual sex with my . . . whatever it is that Hardin is to me right now. The shower thing, however, makes me feel differently.

Being the stubborn man he is, Hardin still didn't agree, which led to me asking him to get me a glass of water from the kitchen. I pouted, and he fell for it. The moment he left the room, I jetted down the hall to the bathroom, locking the door behind me and ignoring his annoyed demands for me to let him in.

"You should make him take you sightseeing," Kimberly tells me. "Maybe throwing yourselves into the culture of the city will help him with his decision to move here with you."

This kind of weighty conversation is not something that I want to deal with right now. "So . . . Sasha seemed nice," I say, to not-so-covertly move the conversation away from my relationship issues.

Kimberly snorts. "Sasha? Nice? Not so much."

"She knows that Max is married, doesn't she?"

"Of course she does." She licks her lips. "But does she care? No, not at all. She likes his money and the expensive jewelry that comes along with seeing him. She could care less about his wife and daughter." The disapproval in Kim's voice is heavy, and I'm relieved to find that we're in agreement on this subject.

"Max is a jerk, but I'm still surprised that he'd have the nerve to bring her around other people. I mean, doesn't he care if Denise or Lillian find out about her?"

"I suspect that Denise already knows. With a guy like Max, there have been plenty of other Sashas over the years, and poor Lillian already despises her father, so it wouldn't make any difference if she knew."

"That's so sad; they've been married since college, right?" I don't know how much Kimberly knows about Max and his family, but given her gossiping ways, I'm sure it's not nothing.

"They married right out of college—it was quite the scandal." Kimberly's eyes light up with the thrill of spilling such a juicy story to my unknowing ears. "Apparently, Max was set to marry someone else, some woman whose family was close with his. It was basically a business deal. Max's father came from old money; I think that's at least part of why Max is such an asshole. Denise was heartbroken when he told her of his plan to marry another woman." Kimberly speaks as if she was actually present at the time all this was happening, instead of just passing along gossip. Maybe, though, that's what gossips always feel like?

She takes a sip of water before continuing. "Anyway, after graduation, Max rebelled against his father and literally left the woman waiting at the altar. On the very day of the wedding, he showed up at Trish and Ken's place in his tuxedo and waited outside the door until Denise came out. That same night, the five of them bribed a pastor, using a fancy bottle of scotch and the little bit of cash in their pockets. Denise and Max were married just before midnight, and she was pregnant with Lillian a few weeks later."

My brain has a hard time picturing Max as a lovesick young man, rushing through the streets of London in a tuxedo, tracking down the woman he loved. The same woman that he now repeatedly betrays by hopping into bed with the likes of Sasha.

"I don't mean to intrude, but was Christian's . . ." I'm unsure what to call her. "I mean, Smith's mother, was she . . ."

With an understanding smile, Kimberly ends my awkward fumbling. "Rose came along many years later. Christian was always the fifth wheel with the two couples. Once he and Ken stopped speaking and Christian came to America . . . that's when Christian met Rose."

"How long were they married?" I search Kimberly's face for signs of discomfort. I don't want to intrude, but I can't help being fascinated by the history of this group of friends. I hope that Kimberly knows me well enough by now not to be surprised by how many questions I'm prone to ask.

"Only two years. They'd only been dating a few months before she got sick." Her voice cracks, and she swallows, tears brimming in her eyes. "He married her anyway . . . She was taken down the aisle . . . in a wheelchair . . . by her father, who insisted on doing it. Halfway to the altar, Christian stepped down and pushed her the rest of the way." Kimberly breaks into sobs, and I brush away the tears that are falling from my eyes.

"I'm sorry," she says with a wan smile. "I haven't told this story in a long time, and it just makes me so emotional." She reaches across the countertop to pull a wad of tissues from a box and passes one to me. "Just thinking about it always shows me that behind his smart mouth and brilliant mind, there is an incredible loving man."

She looks at me, then down at the stacks of envelopes. "Shit, I got tears on the cards!" she exclaims, recovering quickly.

I want to ask her more questions about Rose and Smith, Ken and Trish in their college days, but I don't want to push her.

"He loved Rose, and she healed him, even in her dying days. He only loved one woman his entire life, and she finally broke him of that."

The story, as lovely as it is, only confuses me further. Who was this woman that Christian loved, and why did he need healing after this?

Kimberly blows her nose and looks up. I turn to the doorway, where Hardin awkwardly glances back and forth between Kimberly and me, taking in the scene unfolding in the kitchen.

"Well, I obviously showed up at the wrong time," he says.

I can't help but smile at how we must look, crying for no apparent reason, two massive stacks of cards and envelopes sitting in front of us on the countertop.

Hardin's hair is wet from his shower, and his face is freshly shaven. He looks incredible in a plain black T-shirt and jeans.

He's wearing nothing on his feet except socks, and his expression is wary as he silently beckons me to him.

"Should I expect you two for dinner tonight?" Kimberly asks as I cross the room to stand at Hardin's side.

"Yes," I respond at the same time that Hardin says "No."

Kim laughs and shakes her head. "Well, text me when you two come to an agreement."

A FEW MINUTES LATER, as Hardin and I reach the front door, Christian suddenly pops out from a side room, sporting a huge grin. "It's freezing outside. Where's your coat, boy?"

"First off, I don't need a coat. Second, don't call me boy." Hardin rolls his eyes.

Christian pulls a heavy navy-blue pea coat from the rack next to the door. "Here, wear this. It's like a damn heater in and of itself."

"Hell no," Hardin scoffs, and I can't help but laugh.

"Don't be an idiot; it's twenty degrees outside. Your lady may need you to keep her warm," Christian teases, and Hardin's eyes assess my thick purple sweater, purple coat, and purple beanie, which he hasn't stopped teasing me about since I pushed it onto my head. I wore this same outfit the night that he took me ice skating, and he teased me then, too. Some things never change.

"Fine," Hardin grumbles and pushes his long arms into the coat. I'm not surprised to find that he pulls off the look; even the large bronze buttons that line the front of the jacket somehow assume a masculine edge when mixed with Hardin's simple style. His new jeans, which I have grown really fond of, and his plain black T-shirt, black boots, and now this coat, make him look like he was plucked straight from the pages of a magazine. It's simply not fair the way he looks so effortlessly perfect.

"Stare much?"

I jump slightly at Hardin's words. In turn, I'm granted a smirk and a warm hand wrapped around mine.

Just then, Kimberly rushes through the living room and into the foyer, followed by Smith, calling, "Wait! Smith wants to ask you something." She looks down at her soon-to-be stepson with a loving smile. "Go ahead, sweetie."

The blond boy looks directly at Hardin. "Can you take a picture for my school thing?"

"What?" Hardin's face slightly pales, and he looks at me. I know how he feels about being photographed.

"It's sort of a collage he's doing. He said he wants your picture, too," Kimberly tells Hardin, and I look over to him, pleading with him not to deny the boy who clearly idolizes him.

"Um, sure?" Hardin shifts on his heels and looks at Smith. "Can Tessa be in the picture, too?"

Smith shrugs. "I guess so."

I smile at him, but he doesn't seem to notice. Hardin shoots me a he-likes-me-more-than-you-and-I don't-even-have-to-try look, and I discreetly elbow him as we walk into the living room. I pull the beanie from my head and use the band on my wrist to pull my hair back for the picture. Hardin's beauty is so unforced and natural; all he has to do is stand there with his uncomfortable frown on his face, and he looks perfect.

"I'll take it quickly," Kimberly says.

Hardin moves closer to me and lazily hooks his arm around my waist. I give my best smile while he attempts to smile without showing his teeth. I nudge him, and his smile brightens just in time for Kimberly to take the shot.

"Thank you." I can see that she's genuinely pleased.

"Let's go," Hardin says, and I nod, giving Smith a small wave before following Hardin through the foyer to the front door.

"That was so nice of you," I tell him.

"Whatever." He smiles and covers my mouth with his. I hear

the small click of a camera and pull away from him to find Kimberly with the camera again held to her face. Hardin turns his head to hide in my hair, and she takes another shot.

"Enough, shit." He groans and drags me out the door. "What is with this family and their videos and pictures," he rambles on, and I close the heavy door behind me.

"Videos?" I ask.

"Never mind."

The cold air whips around us, and I quickly put my hair down and pull my hat back over my head.

"We'll take your car and get an oil change first," Hardin says over the howling wind. I dig into the front pockets of my coat to retrieve my keys to give to him, but he shakes his head and dangles his key chain in front of my face. It's now furnished with one key bearing a familiar green band.

"You didn't take your key back when you left all your gifts," he says.

"Oh . . ." My mind fills with the memory of leaving my most precious possessions in a pile on the bed we once shared. "I'd like those things back soon, if that's okay."

Hardin climbs into the car without another glance my way, mumbling over his shoulder, "Um, yeah. Sure."

Once we're inside the car, Hardin turns the heat all the way up and reaches across to grab my hand. He rests both of our hands on my thigh, and his fingers trace a thoughtful pattern over my wrist, where the bracelet would normally rest.

"I hate that you left it there . . . It should be here." He presses against the base of my wrist.

"I know." My voice is barely a whisper. I miss that bracelet every day; my e-reader, too. I want the letter he wrote me back as well. I want to be able to read it over and over.

"Maybe you can bring them when you come back next weekend?" I ask, hopeful.

"Yeah, sure," he says, but his eyes stay focused on the road.

"Why are we getting an oil change, anyway?" I ask him. We finally make it out of the long driveway and turn onto the residential road.

"You need one." He gestures toward the small sticker on the windshield.

"Okay . . ."

"What?" He glowers at me.

"Nothing. It's just an odd thing to do, to take someone's car to get an oil change."

"I've been the only one taking your car for an oil change for months; why would it surprise you now?"

He's right; he's always the one to take my care for any type of maintenance it may need, and sometimes I suspect he's being paranoid and has things fixed or replaced that don't need to be.

"I don't know. I guess I forget that we were a normal couple sometimes," I admit, fidgeting in my seat.

"Explain."

"It's hard to remember the small, normal things like oil changes or the time you let me braid your hair." I smile at the memory. "When we always seem to be going through some sort of crisis."

"First of all . . ."—he smirks—"don't ever mention that hair-braiding fiasco again. You know damned well that the only reason I let that happen was because you bribed me with head and cookies." He gently squeezes my thigh, and a rush of heat flares under my skin. "Second, I guess you're right in a way. It would be nice if your memories of me weren't tainted by my constant habit of fucking everything up."

"It's not only you; we both made mistakes," I correct him. Hardin's mistakes usually caused much more damage than mine, but I'm not innocent either. We need to stop blaming ourselves or each other and try to reach some sort of middle ground—

together. That can't happen if Hardin continues to beat himself up over every mistake he's made in the past. He has to find a way to forgive himself . . . so he can move on and be the person I know he really wants to be.

"*You* didn't," he retorts, fighting back.

"Instead of the two of us going back and forth over who made mistakes and who didn't, let's decide what we're going to do with our day after the oil change."

"You'll get an iPhone," he says.

"How many times do I have to tell you that I don't want an iPhone . . . ?" I grumble. My phone is slow, yes, but iPhones are expensive and complicated—two things I can't afford to add to my life right now.

"Everyone wants an iPhone. You're just one of those people who don't want to give in to the trend." He looks over at me, and I see his dimples pucker evilly. "That's why you were still wearing floor-length skirts in college." Finding himself absolutely hilarious, he fills the car with his laughter.

I playfully scowl at his overused dig. "I can't afford one right now anyway. I have to save my money for an apartment and groceries. You know, the *necessities.*" I roll my eyes, but smile back at him to soften the blow.

"Imagine the things we could do if you had an iPhone, too. There'd be even more ways for us to communicate, and you know I'd get it for you, so don't mention the money again."

"What I can imagine is doing things like tracking my phone so you could see where I go," I tease, ignoring his overpowering need to buy me things.

"No, like we could video-chat."

"Why would we do that?"

He looks at me as if I've grown another set of eyes and shakes his head. "Because, imagine being able to see me each day on your shiny new iPhone screen."

Images of phone sex and video chats immediately spring into mind, and I shamelessly run through shots of Hardin touching himself on the screen. *What is wrong with me?*

My cheeks heat, and I can't help but glance at his lap.

With one finger under my chin, Hardin tilts my face up to look at him. "You're thinking about it . . . going over all the dirty shit I could do to you via iPhone."

"No, I'm not." Holding tight to my stubborn refusal to get a new cell phone, I change the subject. "My new office is nice . . . the view is incredible."

"Is it?" Hardin's tone immediately turns somber.

"Yes, and the view from the lunchroom is even better. Trevor's office has—" I stop myself from finishing the sentence, but it's too late. Hardin is already glaring at me, expecting me to finish.

"No, no. Continue."

"Trevor's office has the best view," I tell him, my voice coming out much more clear and steady than I'm feeling on the inside.

"Just how often are you *in* his office, Tessa?" Hardin's eyes flicker to me and then back to the road.

"I've been there twice this week. We have lunch together."

"You *what*?" Hardin snaps. I knew I should have waited until after dinner to bring up Trevor. Or not brought him up at all. I shouldn't even have mentioned his name.

"I have lunch with him, usually," I admit. Unfortunately for me, at that moment my car is stopped at a red light, leaving me no choice but to be at the receiving end of Hardin's glare.

"Every day?"

"Yes . . ."

"Is there a reason behind it?"

"He's the only person I know that has the same lunch hour as me. Kimberly's so busy helping Christian that she hasn't even been taking a lunch hour." Both of my hands move in front of my face to aid in my explanation.

"So have your lunch hour changed." The light turns green, but Hardin doesn't step on the gas pedal until an angry horn sounds from behind us in the line of traffic.

"I'm not having my lunch hour changed. Trevor is my co-worker, end of story."

"Well," Hardin breathes, "I would prefer you not to eat lunch with *fucking Trevor.* I can't stand him."

Laughing, I reach down onto my lap and place my hand on top of Hardin's. "You're being irrationally jealous, and it happens that there's no one else for me to have lunch with, especially when the other two women that share the same lunch hour have been mean to me all week."

He glances sideways at me while switching lanes smoothly. "What do you mean, they've been mean to you?"

"They haven't been mean exactly. I don't know, maybe I'm just paranoid."

"What happened? Tell me," he urges.

"It's nothing serious, I just get the feeling that they don't like me for some reason. I always catch the two of them laughing or whispering while staring at me. Trevor said they like to gossip, and I swear I heard them say something about how I got the job."

"They said *what*?" Hardin sneers. His knuckles are white as he grips the steering wheel.

"They made a comment, something like 'we know how she got the job anyway.'"

"Did you say something to them? Or to Christian?"

"No, I don't want to cause any problems. I've only been there a week, and I don't want to run and tattle on them like a school-girl."

"Fuck that. You need to tell those women to fuck off, or I'll tell Christian myself. What are their names? I may know them."

"It's not that big of a deal," I say, trying to deactivate the bomb I've clearly assembled myself. "Every office has a set of catty women. The ones in mine just happen to have targeted *me.* I don't want this to be a thing; I just want to blend in there and maybe even make some friends."

"Not likely to happen if you continue to let them act like bitches and hang out with fucking Trevor all day." He licks his lips and takes a deep breath.

I take an equally deep breath and look at him, debating whether or not to defend Trevor.

Fuck it.

"Trevor is the only person there that makes any type of effort to be kind to me, and I already know him. That's why I spend my lunch hour with him." I stare out the window and watch my favorite city in the world pass by as I wait for the bomb to explode.

When Hardin doesn't respond, I look over at him and his laser stare at the road ahead, then add, "I really miss Landon."

"He misses you, too. So does your dad."

I sigh. "I want to know how he is, but if I ask one question, it'll lead to thirty. You know how I am." Worry blooms inside my chest, and I do my best to push it back down and lock it away.

"I do know, that's why I won't answer them."

"How's Karen? And your father? Is it sad that I miss those two more than I miss my own parents?" I ask.

"No, considering who your parents are." He scrunches his nose. "To answer your question, they're good, I guess. I don't really pay attention."

"I hope this place starts to feel like home soon," I say without thinking and sink back into the leather seat.

"You don't seem to like Seattle so far, so what the hell are you doing here?" Hardin pulls my car into the lot of a small building. Plastered on the front is a massive yellow sign promising fifteen-minute oil changes and friendly service.

I don't know how to answer him. I'm afraid to share my fears and doubts about my recent move with Hardin. Not because I don't trust him, but because I don't want him to use them as an opening to push me to leave Seattle. I could really use a big pep talk right now, but, frankly, would settle for silence over the "I told you so" I'm most likely to hear from Hardin.

"It's not that I don't like it here, I'm just not used to it yet. It's only been one week, and I'm used to my routine and Landon, and you," I explain.

"I'll pull into the line and meet you inside," Hardin tells me without a word regarding my response.

With a nod, I climb out of the car and hurry out of the cold and into the small mechanic shop. The scent of burned rubber and stale coffee fills the waiting room. I'm staring at a framed photograph of an old-fashioned car when I feel Hardin's hand come to rest on the small of my back.

"It shouldn't be too long." He takes my hand in his and leads me to the dusty leather couch in the center of the room.

Twenty minutes later, he's on his feet, pacing back and forth across the black-and-white-tiled flooring. A bell chimes through the room, signaling that someone has joined us.

"The sign outside says fifteen-minute oil change," Hardin snaps at the young man wearing oil-stained coveralls.

"Yeah, it does." The man shrugs. The cigarette tucked behind his ear falls down onto the counter, and he quickly retrieves it with a gloved hand.

"Are you shitting me?" Hardin growls, his patience clearly grown thin.

"It's almost done," the mechanic assures him before exiting the waiting room just as abruptly as he entered. I don't blame him.

I turn to Hardin and rise to my feet. "It's fine; we aren't in a hurry."

"He's wasting my time with you. I have less than twenty-four hours with you, and he's fucking wasting it."

"It's fine." I walk across the tile floor to stand in front of him. "We're here together." I push my hands into the pockets of Christian's coat, and he presses his lips into a tight line to keep his frown from turning into a smile.

"If they aren't done within ten minutes, I'm not paying for this shit," he threatens, and I shake my head at him and bury my head in his chest.

"Don't apologize to that guy for me either." He reaches under my chin with his thumb and lifts my head to look into my eyes. "I know you're planning to." He places a soft kiss against my lips, and I find myself hungry and anxious for more.

The topics of discussion in the car have proven to be sore spots for us in the past, yet we made the entire drive here without a major blowup. I'm surprisingly giddy over that, or maybe it's Hardin's warm arms wrapping around my waist, or his usual minty scent laced with Christian's cologne that he borrowed.

Whatever it is, I'm aware of the fact that we're the only people waiting in the small shop, and I'm surprised by Hardin's affectionateness as he kisses me again; this time his lips press much harder and his tongue swipes out to meet mine. My hands find their way into his hair, and I tug gently at the ends, making him groan and tighten his grip on my waist. He brings my body flush to his, his mouth still claiming mine, until the shrill sound of a bell goes off, making me jump away from him and smooth my hand over my beanie out of nervousness alone.

"Aaaaaall done," the cigarette-toting man from minutes ago announces.

"About time," Hardin rudely remarks and pulls his wallet from his back pocket, shooting me a warning glare when I do the same.

chapter one hundred and three

HARDIN

He wasn't staring at me," she says, trying to convince me as we finally reach her car, which I was forced to park in the farthest possible spot away from the restaurant.

"He was panting over his lasagna. There was a line of drool hanging from his chin to prove it." The man's eyes were glued to Tessa the entire time that I tried to enjoy our overpriced, over-sauced pasta plate.

I want to press it further, but I decide against it. She didn't even notice the man's attention; she was too busy smiling and talking with me to give him a second glance. Her smiles are bright and honest, her patience with my annoyed remarks about waiting too long for a table was remarkable, and she seems to always find a way to touch me. A hand on mine, a soft brush of her fingers over my arm, her soft hand brushing the mop of hair off my forehead; she's constantly touching me, and I feel like a fucking kid on Christmas. If I were to know how being excited on Christmas as a child actually felt.

I turn the heat in the car to the highest setting, wanting to get her warmed up as quickly as possible. Her nose and cheeks are an adorable shade of red, and I can't help but lean over and run my cold hand across her quivering lips.

"Well, it's a shame that he'll be paying so much for drool-filled lasagna then, huh?" She giggles, and I lean over to silence her corny remark by pressing my mouth to hers.

"Come here," I groan. I gently pull her onto my lap by the sleeves of her purple jacket. She doesn't protest; instead, she climbs over the small barrier of armrests and onto my lap. Her mouth is steady on mine, and I possessively stake my claim by pulling her body as close to mine as the awkward design of this small car will allow. She gasps when I pull the lever on the seat to cause it to lie back, and her body falls onto mine.

"I'm still sore," she tells me, and I gently pull away from her.

"I just wanted to kiss you," I tell her. It's true. Not that I would turn down making love to her in the front seat of her car, but it wasn't on my mind at the time.

"I want to, though," she shyly admits, turning her head slightly to hide from my view.

"We can go home . . . well, to your place—"

"Why not here?"

"Hello? Tessa?" I wave my hand in front of her face, and she looks up at me, bewildered. "Have you seen Tessa around anywhere, because this hormone-addled, sex-crazed woman wiggling in my lap is certainly not her," I tease, and she catches on, finally.

"I'm not sex-crazed." She pouts, pushing out her lower lip, and I lean up to catch it between my teeth. Her hips move against me, and I scan the parking lot. The sun has begun to set already, the thick air and cloudy skies making it appear to be even later than it actually is. The parking lot is nearly full of cars, though, and the last thing I want is someone catching us fucking in public.

She pulls her mouth from mine and trails her lips down the column of my neck. "I'm stressed, and you've been gone, and I love you." Despite the blasting heat pouring from the vents, a shiver rakes down my spine, and she reaches between us to palm me through my jeans. "So maybe I'm a little hormonal, it's almost . . . you know, that time." She whispers the last two words as if they're a dirty secret.

"Oh, now I get it." I grin, concocting vulgar jokes in my mind to tease her with the entire week, the way I always do.

She reads my mind. "Don't say a word," she scolds, gently squeezing and kneading my cock while her mouth moves against my neck.

"Then stop doing that before I come in my pants. I've already done that too many times since I met you."

"Yeah, you have." She bites down on my flesh, and my hips betray me by lifting to meet her torturous swirling movements.

"Let's go back . . . If someone sees you like this, riding me in the middle of the parking lot, I'd have to kill them."

Thoughtfully, Tessa glances around the parking lot, surveying the surroundings, and I watch as the realization of our location sinks in. "Fine." She pouts again and climbs back into the passenger seat.

"Look how the tables have turned." I wince as her hand cups me again and squeezes.

She sweetly smiles as if she didn't just make a mild attempt to castrate me. "Just drive."

"I'll run every red light so I can get you home and give you your fix," I tease her.

She rolls her eyes and rests her head against the window.

By the time we reach the next red light, she's fast asleep. I reach over to make sure she's still warm; tiny drops of sweat bead her forehead in her sleep, making me cut the heat off immediately. Deciding to enjoy the soft noises of her muted slumber, I take the long way back to Vance's house.

* * *

I GENTLY SHAKE her shoulder to wake her. "Tessa, we're back."

Her eyes pop open, and she blinks rapidly to assess her location. "It's already so late?" she asks, glancing at the clock on her dashboard.

"There was traffic," I say.

Truth is, I drove around the city, trying to find whatever it is that has her so captivated. It was a lost cause. I couldn't find it through the freezing air. Or the bumper-to-bumper traffic. Or the drawbridge causing that traffic. The only thing that made sense to me was the sleeping girl in my car. Despite the hundreds of buildings that line and light up the skyline, she's the only thing that could make this city worth a damn.

"I'm still so tired . . . I think I ate too much." She half smiles and pushes me away when I offer to carry her to her room.

She lumbers like a zombie through Vance's house, and the moment her head hits the pillow, she's asleep again. I carefully undress her and pull the duvet over her half-naked body, laying my worn T-shirt next to her head in hopes that she'll pull it on when she wakes.

I stare over at her. Her lips are parted slightly, and her arms are wrapped around one of mine like she's holding a soft pillow instead of a hard arm. It can't be comfortable for her, but she's sound asleep, holding on to me as if she's afraid I'll disappear.

I think, maybe, if I continue to not be a fuckup during the week, I'll be rewarded with times like this every weekend, and that's enough for me to hold on to until she can see how devoted I am to improving myself for her.

"HOW MANY TIMES are you going to call me?" I bark through the line. My phone has been buzzing all night and morning with my mum's name flashing on the screen. Tessa keeps waking up and, in turn, waking me up. I swear I put the damn thing on silent the last time.

"You should have answered! I have something important to talk to you about." Her voice is soft, and I can't remember the last time I spoke to her.

"Get to it, then," I groan and instinctively lean up to turn the lamp on. The light from the small lamp is much too bright for this early hour, so I tug the string and return the room to its original state of darkness.

"Well, here goes . . ." She lets out a deep breath. "Mike and I are going to be married." She squeals into the phone, and I move the device from my ear for a moment to save my hearing.

"Okay . . ." I say, expecting more.

"Aren't you surprised?" she questions, obviously disappointed in my reaction.

"He told me he was going to ask you, and I figured you'd say yes. What is there to be surprised about?"

"He told you?"

"Yeah," I say, looking at the dark, rectangular shapes of some photos hanging on the wall.

"Well, what do you think about it?"

"Does it matter?" I ask her.

"Of course it matters, Hardin." My mum sighs, and I sit up fully. Tessa stirs in her sleep and reaches for me.

"I don't care either way. I was a little surprised, but what do I care if you get married?" I whisper, wrapping my legs around Tessa's smooth legs.

"I'm not asking for your permission. I just wanted to see how you felt about the whole thing so I could tell you the reason I've been calling you all morning."

"I'm fine with it, now tell me."

"As you know, Mike thought it would be a good idea to sell the house."

"And?"

"Well, it's sold. The new owners won't be moving in until next month, until after the wedding."

"Next month?" I rub my temples with my index finger. I knew I shouldn't have picked up the damn phone this early.

"We were going to wait until next year, but neither of us is getting any younger, and with Mike's son going off to university, there's no better time than now. It should start warming up in the next few months, but we don't want to wait. It may be chilly, but it won't be unbearable. You'll come, won't you? And bring Tessa?"

"So the wedding is next month, or in two weeks?" My brain doesn't function this fucking early.

"Two weeks!" she responds with glee.

"I don't think I can . . ." I trail off. It's not that I don't want to join the joyous festivities of a requited love and all that shit, but I don't want to go all the way to England, and I know Tessa isn't going to come along on such short notice, especially given the state of our relationship right now.

"Why not? I'll ask her myself if I—"

"No, you won't." I cut her off. Realizing that I'm being a little harsh, I backtrack. "She doesn't even have a passport." It's an excuse, but a truthful one.

"She can get one within two weeks if they expedite it."

I sigh. "I don't know, Mum, give me a little time to think about it. It's seven in the damn morning." I groan and end the call, then realize I didn't even say congratulations. Fuck. Well, it's not like she expected it from me necessarily.

From down the hall, I hear someone scavenging through fucking cabinets. I pull the thick duvet over my head to drown out the noise of slamming and the obnoxious beeping of a dishwasher, but the noises don't abate. The cacophony continues until I guess I just fall asleep in spite of it.

chapter
one hundred and four

HARDIN

It's a little past eight, and I can see through the living room to the kitchen, where Tessa is fully dressed, eating breakfast with Kimberly.

Shit, it's Monday already. She has to go to work, and I have to drive back to school. I'll miss today's classes, but I couldn't care less. I'll have my diploma in less than two months.

"Are you going to wake him up?" Kimberly asks Tessa just as I walk in.

"I'm up." I groan, still groggy from sleep. I slept more peacefully last night than I have all week. My first night here we were up nearly the entire night.

"Hey." Tessa's smile lights up the dim room, and Kimberly covertly slides off the high stool she's sitting on and leaves us alone. Which means she's set a new record for not annoying me.

"How long have you been up?" I ask Tessa.

"Two hours. Christian said I could have an extra hour, since you weren't awake."

"You should have woken me up earlier." My eyes greedily rake down her body. She's dressed in a deep red button-down shirt tucked into a solid black, knee-length pencil skirt. The material hugs her hips in a way that makes me want to bend her over the stool, push her skirt up to reveal her panties—lace panties, perhaps—and take her right here, right now . . .

She calls me out from my thoughts. "What?"

The front door closes, and I'm relieved that we're finally alone in the massive house.

"Nothing," I lie and walk over to the half-full coffeepot. "You'd think they'd have a Keurig, rich bastards."

Tessa laughs at my remark. "I'm glad they don't. I hate those things." She leans on her elbows on the kitchen island, and her hair falls down to frame her face.

"Me, too." I glance around the spacious kitchen and back to Tessa's chest as she stands up straight. "What time do you have to leave?" I ask. She crosses her arms in front of her chest, blocking my view.

"Twenty minutes."

"Dammit." I sigh, and we both bring our coffee mugs to our mouths at the same time.

"You should have woken me up. Tell Vance you're not coming in."

"No!" She blows at the steaming cup of coffee in her hand.

"Yes."

"No," she says with a firm voice. "I can't take advantage of my personal relationship with him like that." Her choice of words sends an unwelcome annoyance through me.

"It's not a 'personal relationship.' You're staying here because you're friends with Kimberly, and ultimately because I introduced you to Vance in the first place," I remind her, fully aware of just how annoyed she gets when I bring this up with her.

Her blue-gray eyes roll back dramatically, and she strides across the rich hardwood flooring, her heels clicking loudly as she passes me. My fingers hook around her elbow, halting her dramatic exit.

I pull her to my chest and press my lips against the base of her throat. "Where do you think you're going?"

"To my room to grab my bag," she says. But the heavy rising

and falling of her chest completely contradicts her cool tone and cooler gaze.

"Tell him you need more time," I demand, barely brushing my lips over the flushed skin below her neck. She tries to appear unaffected by my touch, but I know better. I know her body better than she does.

"No." She makes a minimal effort to pull away, just to be able to tell herself that she did. "I don't want to take advantage of him. They're already letting me stay here for free."

I'm not budging. "I'll call him, then," I say. He doesn't need her at the office today. He already has her three days a week. I need her more than Vance Publishing does.

"Hardin . . ." She reaches for my hand before I can dig into my pocket to retrieve my cell phone. "I'll call Kim." She frowns, and I'm surprised and very grateful that she gave in so quickly.

chapter one hundred and five

TESSA

Kim. Hey, it's Tessa. I was—"

"Go ahead." She cuts me off. "I already told Christian you probably wouldn't be in today."

"I'm sorry for asking. I—"

"Tessa, it's fine. We get it." The sincerity in her voice makes me smile despite my annoyance with Hardin. It's nice to finally have a female friend. The weight of Steph's betrayal is something I'm having a hard time lifting from my chest. I look around my temporary bedroom and remind myself that I'm hours away from her, from that campus, from all the friends I thought I had made during my first semester at college, all of them fakes. This is my life now. Seattle is where I belong, and I'll never have to see Steph or any of them again.

"Thank you so much," I tell her.

"You don't have to thank me. Just remember that all the main rooms in the house are under surveillance." Kimberly laughs. "I'm sure that after the gym incident you wouldn't forget that."

My eyes dart up to Hardin as he enters the bedroom.

His expectant grin and the way those dark blue jeans hang low on his hips distract me from Kimberly's words. I have to scramble to remember what she said only seconds ago.

The gym? Oh God. My blood runs cold, and Hardin stalks toward me.

"Um, yeah," I mumble, holding my hand up to stop Hardin from coming any closer.

"Have fun." Kimberly ends the call.

"They have cameras in the gym! They saw us!" I say, panicking.

Hardin shrugs as if it's no big deal. "They turned them off before they saw anything."

"Hardin! They know we . . . you know, in their *gym*!" My hands fly through the air in front of me. "I'm so mortified!" I cover my face with my hands, but Hardin quickly removes them.

"They didn't see anything. I spoke to them already. Calm down. Don't you think I would've lost my shit if he'd actually seen anything on tape?"

I relax, slightly. He's right; he would've been much more upset than he appears to be right now, but that doesn't mean that I'm not completely humiliated by the fact that they *know,* even if they did stop the tape.

But wait, what does "tape" even mean here—everything's digital. And they could have just said *they stopped the cameras but really all they did was just look away . . .*

"The footage . . . it's not saved anywhere or anything, right?" I can't help but ask the question. My fingertip traces over the small cross tattoo on Hardin's hand.

Hardin lowers his eyes at me defensively. "What is that supposed to mean?"

Hardin's . . . old hobbies flash through my mind. "That's not what I meant," I say quickly. Maybe too quickly.

"You sure?" he asks. I watch as his features harden and his eyes fill with guilt. "I mean, how would you know what I was worried you were thinking about if you hadn't already been thinking about it yourself?"

"Don't," I say strongly and close the small space between us.

"Don't what?" he asks.

I can read his thoughts in this moment; I can see him reliving the terrible things he has done. "Don't do that; don't go back there."

"I can't help it." He rubs his hand down his face in a slow yet frenzied motion. "Is that what you were thinking? That I knew about the tape, and that I let him watch it?"

"*What? No!* I would never think that," I say honestly. "I only connected the tape from the gym to . . . to what happened before when you said something. It just *reminded* me of that—I never thought you were doing that now." My fingers wrap around the tattered neckline of his black T-shirt. "I know you would never show anyone a tape of me." I stare into his eyes, willing him to believe me.

"If anyone ever did something like that to you . . ." He takes a long pause and a deep breath. "I don't know what I would do to them, even if it was Vance," he grimly admits. Hardin's temper is something I've grown very familiar with over the last six months.

I stand on my tiptoes so I can look him in the eyes. "It won't happen."

"Something terrible almost did, though, only last week with Steph and Dan." A shudder shakes his shoulders, and I desperately search for the right thing to say to him to pull him out of this dark place.

"Nothing happened." The irony of my being the one to comfort him now, when the trauma was actually something that happened to me, isn't lost on me; but this role reversal speaks true to the nature of our relationship and Hardin's need to blame himself for things he can't control. Just like his mother, just like me. I can see this now.

"If he had been inside you . . ."

The words bring back vague flashes of memory from that night, images of Dan's fingers running up my thigh, of Steph pulling at my dress.

"I don't want to discuss the hypothetical." I lean into him, and his arms wrap around my waist, caging me, protecting me from bad memories and nonexistent threats.

He glowers. "We've barely discussed it at all."

"I don't want to. We talked about it enough at my mother's house, and this is not how I want to spend my newly cleared afternoon." I give him the best smile I can manage in a failed attempt to lighten the mood.

"I couldn't bear anyone hurting you like that. I hate the thought of him violating you. It makes me murderous—all I see is red. I can't handle it." Hardin's angry expression has not lightened, only intensified. His green eyes burn into mine, and the rough grip of his fingers tightens on the span of my hips.

"Let's not talk about it, then. I want you to try and forget it, like I have." I caress his back with my fingers, gently begging him to forget the whole thing. It won't do either of us any good to harp on it. It was terrible and disgusting, but I won't let it rule me. "I love you—I love you so, so much."

His mouth catches mine, and I wrap my fingers around his arms, pulling him closer to me.

Between breaths, I say, "So focus on me, Hardin. Only on m—"

I'm interrupted by the pressure of his mouth on mine again, possessing me, proving his commitment to both me and himself. His tongue is hard, pushing through my lips to massage mine. Hardin's fingertips dig into my hips even further, and I whimper as his hands glide up my stomach to my chest. He cups my breasts, and I push into his body harder, filling his greedy hands.

"Show me that it's only me," he whispers into my mouth, and I know exactly what he wants, what he needs.

I drop to my knees in front of him and hastily tug at the lone button on his jeans. The zipper proves to be more of a problem, and I briefly consider ripping the jagged metal lining and destroying it altogether. However, I can't bring myself to do this, considering how hot he looks in the tight blue jeans. My fingertips slowly graze over the light dusting of hair leading from his navel to the waistband of his boxers, and he groans impatiently.

"Please," he begs, "no teasing."

I give a small nod and pull down his boxers, letting them pool at his calves atop the bunched-up jeans. Hardin groans once more, this time much louder, much more primal, and I take him into my mouth. Slow movements and flicks of my tongue say the things that I try to instill in his paranoid mind, reassuring him that these acts of pleasure are different from anything someone could force me into.

I love him. I'm aware that what I'm doing now may not be the healthiest way to handle his anger and anxiety, but my need for him is stronger than my moral compass, which, at the moment, is smugly waving a self-help book in front of my face.

"I fucking love that I'm the only man who has had your mouth," he groans as I use one hand to take what my mouth cannot. "Those lips have only been wrapped around me." A quick movement of his hips makes me gag, and he reaches down to run his thumb along my forehead. "Look at me," he instructs.

And I happily comply. I'm enjoying this just as much as he is. I always do. I love the way his eyelids fall closed with each long stroke of my tongue against him. I love the way he grunts and groans when I add more suction.

"Fuck, you know exactly . . ." His head rolls back, and I can feel the muscles in his legs tightening under my hand, which I've rested on him to steady myself. "I'm the only man who you'll ever be on your knees in front of . . ."

I press my thighs together to relieve some of the tension his filthy mouth arouses in me. Hardin uses one hand to steady himself against the wall as my mouth brings him closer and closer to his high. I keep my eyes on his, knowing that it drives him absolutely crazy to watch me as I enjoy pleasuring him so much. His free hand moves down from the top of my head to my mouth, and he runs the pad of his thumb across my top lip, moving in and out of my mouth at a quickening pace.

"Fuck, Tess." His body goes rigid as he tells me how good it feels, how much he loves me, while he climbs closer to release. I take all of him, moaning while he's filling my mouth—and he groans, emptying himself on my tongue. I keep sucking, milking every drop of his release as he softly rubs my cheek with his thumb.

I lean into his touch, reveling in its tenderness, and he gently helps me to my feet. The moment I'm standing next to him, he's pulling me into his arms, hugging me in an intimate gesture that almost overwhelms me.

"I'm sorry for dragging all that shit up," he whispers into my hair.

"Shh," I whisper back, not wanting to backtrack to the dark conversation we left behind only minutes ago.

"Bend over the bed, baby," Hardin says, and it takes me a moment to register his words. He doesn't give me an opportunity to respond before he's gently pushing his palm against the small of my back, guiding me to the edge of the mattress. His hands grip my thighs, pushing my skirt up my legs until my entire behind is bared to him.

I want him so badly that it physically hurts. An ache that only he can soothe. As I move to step out of my shoes, he presses his palm against my back again.

"No, leave them on," he growls.

I groan as my panties are pushed to the side and he slides a finger inside of me. He steps closer, his legs nearly touching mine, his cock softly teasing the back of my legs.

"So soft, baby, so warm." He adds another finger, and I groan, leaning all my weight onto my elbows on the mattress. My back arches when he finds a rhythm, steadily entering me, dragging his long fingers into and out of me.

"Your sounds are so sexy, Tess," he coos, closing the gap between our bodies so I feel his hard cock pressing against me.

"Please, Hardin." I groan, needing him now. Within seconds he fills me in the way that only he has and only he ever will. I lust for him, but it's nothing compared to the overwhelming, all-consuming, judgment-altering love that I have for him, and I know deep down—deep in the depth of me that only he and I can see—that it will always be only him.

LATER, AS WE'RE LYING IN BED, Hardin whines, "I don't want to go," and in a very un-Hardin-like gesture, he leans his head down and buries it in my shoulder, wrapping his arms and legs around my body. His thick hair tickles my skin. I try to tame it with my fingers, but there is simply too much of it.

"I need a haircut," he announces, as if answering my thoughts.

"I like it this way." I gently tug at the damp strands.

"You wouldn't tell me if you didn't," he says, calling me out. He's right, but only because I couldn't imagine a hairstyle on Hardin that wouldn't flatter him. Still, I do happen to love his hair this length.

"Your phone is ringing again," I point out, and he lifts his head to shoot me a glare. "Something could be wrong with my father, and I'm trying my best not to freak out, and I really want to trust you, so please just answer it," I rattle out.

"If it's something with your father, Landon can handle it, Tessa."

"Hardin, you know how hard it is for me not—?"

"Tessa," he says to silence me, but then he climbs off the bed and retrieves the vibrating phone from the desk.

"See, it's my mum." He holds the screen up so the word "Trish" is clear from where he stands. I really wish he'd listen to me and change her entry to "Mom" in his phone, but he refuses. Baby steps, I remind myself.

"Answer it! It could be an emergency." I climb off the bed and try to grab the phone from his quick hands.

"She's fine. She's been pestering me all morning." Hardin childishly holds the phone up over my head.

"About what?" I ask him and watch as he turns the power off on the device.

"Nothing important. You know how annoying she can be."

"She's not annoying," I say in Trish's defense. She's very sweet, and I love her sense of humor. Something which her son could use more of.

"You're just as annoying as she is; I knew you would say that." He grins. His long fingers reach out to tuck my hair behind my ears.

I give him a fake evil eye. "You're being awfully charming today. Aside from calling me annoying just now, of course." I'm not complaining, but given our history, I'm afraid that this behavior will disappear when our blissful weekend has ended.

"Would you prefer me to be an asshole?" He raises a brow.

I smile, enjoying his playful behavior, no matter how briefly it lasts.

chapter one hundred and six

HARDIN

As if the long-ass drive through the freezing rain wasn't pleasant enough, when I get back to my apartment, I'm bombarded with a disturbing image of Tessa's dad sprawled out on my couch, wearing my clothes. My cotton pajama pants and black T-shirt are way too tight on him, and I can literally taste the bagel Tessa fed me this morning rising in the back of my throat, just begging to be regurgitated onto the concrete floor.

"How is Tessie doing?" Richard asks me the moment I walk in the door.

"Why are you wearing my clothes, again?" I groan, not necessarily expecting an answer from the man but knowing I'm going to get one anyway.

"I only have that one shirt you gave me, and I couldn't get the smell out of it," he replies, rising to his feet.

"Where's Landon?"

"Landon's in the kitchen." My stepbrother's voice carries into the living room from behind me. A moment later he joins us, a dish towel in his hands. Drops of soap fall to the floor, and I scowl at him for not making Richard do the damn dishes.

"So how is she?" he asks.

"She's good. Fuck. In case anyone was wondering, I'm good, too," I gripe.

The apartment is much cleaner than it was when I left it. The stacks of shitty manuscripts that I had planned to throw away are now gone, the tower of empty water bottles I had built on the coffee table is nowhere to be seen, and even the dust mound that I've grown used to watching grow has disappeared from the corners of the television stand.

"What the fuck happened in here?" I ask both of them. My patience is wearing too thin, given that I've only been in this apartment for a couple of minutes.

"If you mean what happened, as in why did we clean the place—" Landon begins, but I cut him off.

"Where's all my shit?" I pace across the floor. "Did I ask either of you to touch any of my shit?" My fingers move to pinch the bridge of my nose, and I take a deep breath in an attempt to control my sudden anger. Why would they just clean my fucking apartment without asking me first?

I look back and forth between the two of them before stalking off to my bedroom.

"Someone's in a mood," I hear Richard remark just as I reach the door.

"Just ignore him . . . he misses her," Landon quickly says.

As a fuck-you to both of them, I slam the door as loudly as possible.

Landon is right. I know he is. I could feel it as I drove away from that damned city, away from her. I could feel every single tendon and muscle in my body tighten the farther I got from her. Every single fucking mile widened the gaping hole inside of me. A hole that only she can fill.

Cursing at every asshole on the highway helped maintain my temper at a slow burn, but it wasn't going to suffice for long. I should have stayed in Seattle a few more hours, convinced her to take the week off and come home with me. With the way she was dressed, I shouldn't have given her a choice.

The more I sink into my thoughts, the more I find myself

visualizing her half-naked body. Her skirt was bunched up around her waist, creating the sexiest sight. As I rocked into her repeatedly, she promised not to forget me during the long week ahead and told me how much she loved me.

The more I think about the way she kissed me and then kissed me again, the more agitated I become.

My need for her is stronger than it's ever been. It's lust and love melted together—no, the need I have for her goes much deeper than lust. The way we're connected while making love is indescribable, the sounds she makes, the way I'm reminded that I'm the only man who has ever made her feel that way. I love her and she loves me, end of fucking story.

"Hey," I say into the receiver, having called her before I even realized what I was doing.

"Hey. Is something wrong?" she asks.

"No." I look around my bedroom. My newly tidied bedroom. "Yes."

"What's wrong? Are you home?"

No, it's not home. You're not here. "Yeah, and your fucking dad and Landon are on my last fucking nerve."

She lets out a little chuckle. "It's been, what, like probably ten minutes you've been home. What did they do already?"

"They cleaned the entire apartment, moved all my shit around. I can't find anything." I wish there was a dirty shirt on the floor or something I could kick.

"What're you looking for?" she asks, but in the background I hear another voice on her end.

It takes everything I have not to ask her who the hell she's with. "Nothing specific," I admit. "But what I'm saying is that if I did want to find something, I wouldn't be able to."

She laughs. "So you're mad that they cleaned up the apartment and you can't find something you're not even looking for?"

"Yeah," I say with a grin. I'm being a fucking baby, and I

know it. She knows it, too, but instead of chastising me, she giggles.

"You should go to the gym."

"I should drive back to Seattle and fuck you over your bed. Again," I fire back. She gasps, and the sound resonates deep inside me, making the need for her stronger.

"Um, yeah," she whispers.

"Who's with you?" I lasted about forty seconds there. Progress.

"Trevor and Kim," she replies slowly.

"You've got to be kidding me." Fucking Trevor is always around. He's becoming more of a nuisance than Zed, and that's saying a fucking lot.

"*Har*-din . . ." I can tell she's uncomfortable, and she doesn't want to explain herself in front of them.

"Ther-*esa.*"

"I'm going to go to my room for a minute." She politely excuses herself, and while I listen to her breathing, I grow more and more impatient.

"Why is fucking Trevor at your house?" I say, sounding more like a lunatic than I'd planned on.

"This isn't *my* house," she reminds me.

"Yeah, well, you live there and—"

She interrupts me. "You should go to the gym; you're obviously wound up." I can hear the concern in her voice, and the silence that follows proves her point. "Please, Hardin."

There's no way I can say no to her. "I'll call you when I get back," I agree and hang up the phone.

I CAN'T SAY that I *didn't* see fucking Trevor's fucking annoying, model-fucking-like face imprinted on the black bag as I kicked, punched, kicked, punched for two hours straight. But I also can't say that it helped, not really. I'm still . . . just revved up. I don't even know why I'm annoyed except that Tessa isn't here and I'm not there.

Fuck, this is going to be a long week.

A text from Tessa is waiting for me when I reach my car. I hadn't expected to work out for so long, but I clearly needed it.

Been trying to stay awake but I'm worn out ;) her message reads. I'm thankful for the darkness outside that conceals the stupid-ass grin on my face from her corny innuendo. She's so damn endearing without even trying.

I nearly ignore a message from Landon reminding me that I'm running low on groceries. I haven't bought actual groceries for myself since . . . ever. When I lived in the frat house I just ate the shit that other people bought.

However, Tessa may be upset if she finds out I'm not feeding her dad, and Landon won't hesitate to tattle on me . . .

Somehow I find myself pulling into Target instead of Conner's for groceries. Tessa is clearly influencing me without even being here. She spends just as much time at Conner's as she does at Target, even though she can go on for hours explaining to me why Target is much better than any other store. She even expresses this while we're *in* the middle of Conner's. It annoys the shit out me, but I've learned to nod at the exact right moments to make her think I'm listening and partly agreeing with her.

Just as I toss a box of Frosted Flakes into a shopping cart, a flash of red hair appears at the end of the aisle. I know it's Steph before she turns around. Her skanky thigh-high black boots with red laces are a dead giveaway.

Quickly, I go over the two options here. One, I can walk over and remind her what a stupid *fucking* . . .

She turns to face me before I can go over the second option, which I probably would have preferred.

"Hardin! Wait!" Steph's voice sounds loud when I turn on

my heel and leave the cart in the middle of the aisle. Regardless of the hard workout I just completed, there's no way that I could possibly control myself around Steph. No fucking way.

I can hear the heavy thud of her boots against the laminate floor as she follows me despite my obvious attempt at avoiding her.

"Listen to me!" she yells when she gets right behind me. When I stop walking, she collides with my back and falls to the floor.

I spin and growl at her. "What the fuck do you want?"

She quickly scrambles to her feet. I notice that her black dress is now dusted white from the dirty floor.

"I thought you were in Seattle."

"I am, just not at the moment," I lie. I'm not sure what possessed me to even try to keep a front up with her, but it's too late to backtrack now.

"I know you hate me now," she begins.

"First smart thought you've had in a while," I snap out, then get a good look at her. Her green eyes are nearly nonexistent what with the thick lines of black circling them. She looks like shit.

"I'm not in the mood for your crap," I warn her.

"You never have been." She smiles.

I clench my fists at my sides. "I don't have shit to say to you, and you know how I get when I don't want to be bothered."

"You're *threatening* me? *Really?*" She raises her arms in front of her, then drops them back down. I stay quiet as images of a barely conscious Tessa swarm my mind. I need to get away from Steph. I would never hurt her physically, but I know all the shit to say to cut her much deeper than anything she could imagine. It's one of my many talents.

"She isn't good for you," Steph has the nerve to say.

I can't help but laugh at the audacity of this bitch. "You aren't stupid enough to try to discuss this with me."

But Steph has never been anything if not sure of herself. Full of herself. "You know it's true. She isn't enough for you, and you're never going to be enough for her." The heat inside me turns from a simmer to a raging boil as she continues: "You're going to get bored with her prudish behavior, and you know it. You're probably already bored."

"Prudish?" I bark another laugh. She doesn't know the Tessa who likes to be fucked in front of a mirror and fucks herself on my fingers until she screams my name.

Steph nods. "And she'll get over this bad-boy fetish she's got with you and marry a banker or some shit. You can't be stupid enough to think she's in this for the long run. I know you saw how she was with Noah, that douche bag made of cardigans. They were like the poster couple for people who belong together, and you know it. You can't compete with that."

"And what? You're implying that you and I would be better?" My voice comes out sounding much less demanding than I planned. She's prying at my biggest insecurities, and I'm trying my best not to falter.

She rolls her raccoon eyes. "No, of course not."

"I know you don't want me—you never did. My point is, I care about you," she says. I look away from her to scan the empty aisles. "I know you don't *want* to believe me, and I know you want to wring my neck for messing with your Virgin Mary, but in that dark heart of yours, you know what I'm saying is true."

I bite the inside of my cheek at the nickname that my so-called friends branded Tessa with early on.

"Deep down, you know it won't work. She's too silver spoon for you. You're covered in ink, and it's only a matter of time before she's sick of being embarrassed to be seen with you."

"She's not embarrassed to be seen with me." I take a step toward the redheaded harpy.

"You know she is. She even told me she was when you two first started dating. I'm sure that hasn't changed." She smiles; her nose ring glistens under the lighting, and I cringe at the memory of her hands touching me, making me come.

I swallow back bile and speak. "You're trying to manipulate me—because that's all you have to work with—and I'm not buying it." I push past her.

She croaks out a gross little laugh. "If you were enough for her, then why did she run to Zed so many times? You know what people were saying."

I stop dead in my tracks. I remember Tessa coming back from that lunch with Steph. She was so upset after she left Applebee's the day that Steph brought Molly along, and the two of them hinted to Tessa that there were rumors going around that she fucked Zed. I was enraged enough to call Molly and warn her not to fucking try to come between Tessa and me. Steph obviously didn't get the message, even though it was her I needed to worry about the entire time.

"You made up those rumors," I accuse.

"No . . . Zed's roommate did. He's the one who heard her moaning his name and heard Zed's bed smacking against the wall while he was trying to sleep. Annoying, right?" Steph's malevolent grin snaps every bit of self-control I've managed to hang on to since Tessa left for Seattle.

I need to walk away now. I need to walk away now.

"Zed said she was nice and tight, though, and apparently she does this . . . like, thing with her hips or something. Oh, and that freckle . . . you know the one." Her black nails tap against her chin.

I can't handle it.

"Shut up!" I cover my ears with my hands. "Shut the fuck up!" I scream through the aisle, and Steph backs away, still grinning.

"Believe me or not." She shrugs. "I don't care, but you know it's a waste of time. She's a waste of time."

She sneers, disappearing just as my fist connects with metal shelving.

chapter one hundred and seven

HARDIN

Boxes fall from the shelves and tumble onto the floor in a blur. I connect with the metal again, leaving a thick red stain behind. The familiar sting of splitting flesh across my knuckles only heightens the rush of my adrenaline, pushing me further into my rage. It's almost soothing, the relief of allowing myself to express my anger in the way I've always been used to. I don't have to stop myself. I don't have to overthink my actions. I can surrender to the anger, let it spill out, allow it to pull me under.

"What are you doing! Someone come help!" a woman yells.

When I snap my head her way, she takes a step backward into the wide opening at the aisle's end, and I notice a little blond-haired girl clinging to her skirt. The woman's eyes are wide with fear and caution.

When the little girl's bright blue eyes meet mine, I can't look away. The innocence in their depths is being stolen with every angry breath that leaves my body. I break the hold of the girl's gaze and look toward the mess I've made in the aisle. Disappointment replaces rage in an instant, and the realization that I'm destroying shit in the middle of a Target hits me hard. If the cops arrive before I can get out of here, I'm fucked.

With one last look toward the little girl in her floor-length dress and sparkling shoes, I rush down the aisle and toward the front of the store. Avoiding the chaos that is brewing around me, I cross from aisle to aisle, staying as much out of sight as possible.

I can't think clearly. Not a single thought makes sense to me.

Tessa didn't fuck Zed.

She didn't.

She couldn't have.

I would know if she did. Someone would have told me.

She would have told me. She's the only person I know who doesn't lie to me.

I burst outside, and the winter air is unforgiving as it bites at my skin. I keep my eyes focused on my car, which is parked toward the back of the lot, thankful to be shielded by the darkness of the night.

"Fuck!" I scream once I reach my car. My boot collides with my bumper and the grinding noise of metal bending out of place ratchets up my feeling of frustration.

"She's only been with me!" I say out loud, then hop inside the car.

I'm pushing the key into the ignition just as two police cars pull into the parking lot with lights blazing and sirens howling. I pull out of the space slowly to avoid any unwanted attention and watch as they park on the curb and rush inside like a murder has been committed.

The moment I make it out of the parking lot, relief floods through me. If I'd been arrested at Target, Tessa would have flipped shit on me.

Tessa . . . and Zed.

I know better than to believe Steph's bullshit lies about Tessa fucking him. I know she didn't. I know that I'm the only man who has ever been inside of her, the only one who has ever made her come. Not him.

Not fucking anyone. Only me.

I shake my head to rid myself of the vision of the two of them, her fingers wrapped around his arms as he pushes into her. Fuck, not this again.

I literally can't think straight. I can't see straight. I should have wrapped my hands around Steph's neck and . . .

No, I can't allow myself to finish the thought. She got exactly what she wanted out of me, and that makes me even angrier. She knew exactly what she was doing when she mentioned Zed; she was purposely taunting me, trying to make me snap, and it worked. She knew she was pulling the pin from a grenade and walking away. But I'm not a grenade—I should be able to control myself.

I immediately call Tessa, but she doesn't pick up. Her phone rings . . . and rings . . . and rings. She did tell me that she was going to sleep, but I know damn well that her phone is always on vibrate and that woman can't sleep through shit.

"Come on, Tess, pick up the phone," I groan and toss my cell onto the passenger seat. I need to get as far away from Target as possible before the cops check the parking-lot cameras and get my plate number or some shit.

The freeway is a fucking nightmare, and I keep trying to call Tessa. If she doesn't get back to me within the hour, I'm calling Christian.

I should have stayed in Seattle another night. Hell, I should have *moved* there in the fucking first place. All of my reasons for not wanting to go seem so fucking pointless now. All of the fears I had, and still have, are only being kept alive by the distance between where she lives and where I live.

"Deep down you know it won't work."

"You're covered in ink, and it's only a matter of time before she's sick of being embarrassed to be seen with you."

"Bad-boy fetish."

"Marry a banker or some shit."

Steph's voice pierces my ears over and over again. I'm going insane—I'm literally losing my fucking mind on this wide-open road. All the efforts that I made all week mean nothing now. The two days that I spent with Tessa have been ruined by that viper.

Is all of this worth it? Is all of this constant trying worth it? Will I always have to stop myself from saying or doing the wrong shit? And if I do continue this potential transformation, will she really love me after, or just feel like she finished some kind of project for a psych class?

After all this, will there be enough of me left for her to love? Will I even be the same man that she fell in love with, or is this her way of transforming me into someone she wishes I could be—someone she will tire of?

Is she trying to make me more like him . . . more like Noah?

"You can't compete with that . . ." Steph is right. I can't compete with Noah and the simple relationship Tessa shared with him. She never had to worry about anything when she was with him. They were good together. Good and simple.

He isn't broken the way that I am.

I remember the days when I used to sit in my room and wait hours for Steph to tell me when Tessa returned after she'd spent some time with him. I interfered as much as I could and, surprisingly enough, it worked out for me. She chose me over him, over the boy she grew up loving.

The idea of Tessa telling Noah she loves him makes me sick to my stomach.

"Bad-boy fetish . . ." I'm more than a fetish to Tessa. I have to be. I've fucked more than my share of girls who were only looking to frighten their daddies, but Tessa isn't one of them. She's put up with enough shit from me to prove that.

My thoughts are jumbled and frantic, and I can't keep up with them.

Why am I letting Steph get inside my head? I shouldn't have

listened to a word that bitch said. Now that I have, though, I can't get her words out of me. I wipe my bloody and busted knuckles across the legs of my blue jeans and park the car.

When I look up, I find myself parked in the lot at Blind Bob's. I've driven all the way here without so much as a thought about it. I shouldn't go inside . . . but I can't stop myself.

And behind the bar, I see an old . . . friend. Carly. Carly, wearing minimal clothing and deep red lipstick.

"Well . . . well . . . well . . ." She grins at me.

"Save it." I groan and slide onto a bar stool directly in front of her.

"Not a chance." She shakes her head, her blond ponytail whipping back and forth. "The last time I served you, it spiraled into one big drama-fest, and I have neither the time nor the patience for a repeat performance tonight."

The last time I was here, I got so shit-faced that Carly forced me to spend the night on her couch, which only led to a huge misunderstanding with Tessa, who got into a car accident that day because of me. Because of the shit I bring into her otherwise clean life.

"Your job is to get me a drink when I order one." I point at the bottle of dark whiskey on the shelf behind her.

"There's a sign right there that states otherwise." She leans her elbows onto the bar top, and I sit back on my bar stool, creating as much space between us as possible.

The small WE HAVE THE RIGHT TO REFUSE SERVICE TO ANYONE is taped to the wall, and I can't help but laugh.

"Easy on the ice, I don't want it watered down." I ignore another of her eye rolls as she pushes herself up and grabs an empty glass.

A thick stream of dark liquor pours into my glass, and Steph's voice replays again and again in my brain. This is the only way to rid myself of her accusations and lies.

Carly's voice breaks me from my daze. "She's calling."

Glancing down, I see the picture that I snapped while Tessa was asleep this morning; it's flashing on my phone's screen.

"Fuck." I instinctively push the glass away, spilling its freshly poured contents onto the bar top. I ignore Carly's high-pitched cursing and leave the bar just as quickly as I arrived.

Outside, I swipe my thumb across the screen. "Tess."

"Hardin!" she says, panicked. "Are you okay?"

"I called you so many times." I let out a breath of relief at the sound of her voice through the small speaker.

"I know, I'm sorry. I was asleep. Are you okay? Where are you?"

"Blind Bob's," I admit. There's no use in lying—she always finds out the truth one way or another.

"Oh . . ." she barely whispers.

"I ordered a drink." I may as well tell her everything.

"Only one?"

"Yes, and I didn't get the chance to even taste it before you called." I can't decide how I feel about that. Her voice is my lifeline, but I can feel a thread of something calling me back to the bar as well.

"That's good, then," she says. "Are you leaving there?"

"Yes, right now." I pull the handle on my car door and climb into the driver's seat.

After a few beats, Tessa asks, "Why'd you go there? It's okay that you did . . . I'm just wondering why."

"I saw Steph."

She gasps. "What happened? Did you . . . did anything happen?"

"I didn't hurt her, if that's what you mean." I turn on my car but keep it in park. I want to talk to Tessa without the distraction of driving. "She said some shit to me that really . . . it really set me off. I lost my temper in Target."

"Are you okay? Wait, I thought you hated Target."

"Out of all the things . . ." I begin.

"Sorry. I'm half asleep." I can hear the smile in her voice, but it's quickly replaced by worry. "Are you okay? What did she say?"

"She said that you fucked Zed," I tell her. I don't want to repeat the other shit she said about Tessa and me not being good for each other.

"*What?* You know that's not true. Hardin, I swear nothing happened between us that you don't already—"

I tap a finger on the windshield, watching my fingerprints accumulate. "She said his roommate heard you."

"You don't believe her, right? You couldn't possibly believe her, Hardin; you know me—you know I would have told you if anyone else had touched me—" Her voice cracks, and my chest aches.

"Shhh . . ." I shouldn't have let her go on about it for so long. I should have told her that I knew it wasn't true, but being the selfish bastard that I am, I needed to hear her say it.

"What else did she say?" She's crying.

"Just bullshit. About you and Zed. And she played on every fear and insecurity that I have about us."

"Is that why you went to the bar?" There's no judgment in Tessa's voice, only an understanding that I wasn't expecting.

"I guess so." I sigh. "She knew things. About your body . . . things that only I should know." A shiver rakes down my spine.

"She was my roommate. She saw me change any number of times, not to mention she's the one who undressed me that night," she says with a sniffle.

Anger ripples through me again. The thought of Tessa, unable to move while Steph forcefully undressed her . . .

"Don't cry, please. I can't bear it, not when you're hours away," I beg her.

Now that Tessa's soft voice is on the line, Steph's words seem to hold no truth, and the madness—the pure fucking madness—that I felt only minutes ago has dissolved.

"Let's talk about something else while I drive home." I shift my car into reverse and put Tessa on speakerphone.

"Okay, yeah . . ." she says, then hums a little while she thinks. "Um, Kimberly and Christian invited me to join them at their club this weekend."

"You aren't going."

"If you would let me finish," she scolds me. "But since you will hopefully be here, and I knew you wouldn't come along, we agreed on me going Wednesday night instead."

"What kind of club is open on a Wednesday?" I glance into my rearview mirror, answering my own question. "I'm going," I say.

"Why? You don't like clubs, remember?"

I roll my eyes. "I'll go with you this weekend. I don't want you to go Wednesday."

"I'm going on Wednesday. We can go again this weekend if you'd like, but I already told Kimberly that I'm coming, and there's no reason that I shouldn't."

"I would rather you not go," I say through my teeth. I'm already on edge, and she's testing me. "Or I can come Wednesday, too," I offer, trying my best to be reasonable.

"You don't have to drive all the way here on Wednesday when you'll already be coming for the weekend.

"You don't want to be seen with me?" The words are out before I can stop them.

"What?" I hear the click of her lamp turning on in the background. "Why would you say that? You know it's not true. Don't let Steph in your head. That's what this is about, isn't it?"

I pull into the parking lot of the apartment and park the car before I respond. Tessa waits in silence for an explanation. Finally I sigh. "No. I don't know."

"We have to learn to fight together, not against one another. It shouldn't be Steph versus you versus me. We have to be in this together," she continues.

"That's not what I'm doing . . ."

She's right. She's always fucking right. "I'll come on Wednesday and stay until Sunday."

"I have classes and work."

"It sounds like you don't want me to come." My paranoia seeps through my already broken confidence.

"Of course I do. You know I do."

I savor the words; fuck, I miss her so much.

"Are you home yet?" Tessa asks just as I turn off the ignition.

"Yes, I just got here."

"I miss you."

The sadness in her voice stops me in my tracks. "I miss you too, baby. I'm sorry—I'm going crazy without you, Tess."

"I am, too." She sighs, and it makes me want to apologize again.

"I'm a dumb-ass for not coming to Seattle with you in the first place."

Coughing sounds through the speaker. "What?"

"You heard me. I'm not repeating it."

"Fine." She finally stops coughing as I step onto the elevator. "I know I couldn't have heard you correctly anyway."

"Anyway, what do you want me to do about Steph and Dan?" I change the subject.

"What *can* you do?" she quietly asks.

"You don't want me to answer that."

"Nothing, then, just leave them be."

"She's probably going to tell everyone about tonight and continue to spread the rumor about you and Zed."

"I don't live there anymore. It's okay," Tessa says, trying to convince me. But I know how much a rumor like this will hurt her feelings, whether she admits it or not.

"I don't want to leave it alone," I confess.

"I don't want you getting in any trouble over them."

"Fine," I say, and then we exchange our good nights. She's not going to agree to my ideas on how to stop Steph, so I'll just drop it. I unlock the door to my apartment and walk in to find Richard sprawled out asleep on the couch. Jerry Springer's voice fills the entire apartment. I turn the television off and go straight to my bedroom.

chapter
one hundred and eight

HARDIN

The entire morning I'm dead on my feet. I don't remember walking into my first class, and I begin to wonder why I even bother.

When I walk past the administration building, Nate and Logan are standing at the bottom of the steps. I pull my hood up and pass them by without a word. I have to get the hell away from this place.

In a split-second decision, I turn back around and take the steep flight of stairs up to the front of the building. My father's secretary greets me with the fakest smile I've seen in a while.

"Can I help you?"

"I'm here to see Ken Scott."

"Do you have an appointment?" the woman sweetly asks, knowing damn well that I don't. Knowing damn well who I am.

"Obviously not. Is my father in there or not?" I gesture to the thick wooden door in front of me. The fogged glass in the center of it makes it hard to tell if he's inside.

"He's in there, but he's on a conference call at the moment. If you have a seat, I'll—"

I walk past her desk and go straight to his door. When I turn the knob and push it open, my father's head turns my way, and he calmly raises a finger to ask me to give him a moment.

Being the polite gentleman that I am, I roll my eyes and take a seat in front of his desk.

After another minute or so, my father returns the phone to its base and rises to his feet to greet me. "I wasn't expecting you."

"I wasn't expecting to be here," I admit.

"Is something wrong?" His eyes move to his closed door behind me and back to my face.

"I have a question." I rest my hands on his almost maroon cherrywood desk and look up at him. Dark patches of stubble are visible on his face, making it obvious that he hasn't shaved in a few days, and his white button-down shirt is slightly wrinkled at the cuffs. I don't think I've seen him wearing a wrinkled shirt since I moved to America. This is a man who comes to breakfast in a sweater vest and pressed khakis.

"I'm listening," my father says.

The tension between us is abundant, but even so, I have to struggle to remember the searing hate that I once felt toward this man. I don't know how to feel about him now. I don't think I'll ever be able to forgive him completely, but holding on to all that anger toward him simply takes too much fucking energy. We'll never have the relationship that he has with my stepbrother, but it's sort of nice to know that when I need something from him, he usually tries his best to help. The majority of the time, his help doesn't get me anywhere, but the effort is appreciated, somewhat.

"How hard do you think it will be for me to transfer to the Seattle campus?"

His brow rises dramatically. "Really?"

"Yes. I don't want your opinion, I want an answer." I make it clear that my sudden change of mind isn't open for discussion.

He eyes me thoughtfully before answering. "Well, it would set your graduation back. You're better off staying at my campus for the remainder of this semester. By the time you apply to transfer, register, and move to Seattle, it wouldn't be worth the hassle and time . . . *logistically* speaking."

I sit back against the leather chair and stare at him. "Couldn't you help speed the process along?"

"Yes, but it would still put off your graduation date."

"So basically I have to stay here."

"You don't have to"—he rubs the dark stubble on his chin—"but it makes more sense for now. You're so close."

"I'm not attending that ceremony," I remind him.

"I had hoped you changed your mind." My father sighs, and I look away.

"Well, I haven't, so . . ."

"It's a very important day for you. The last three years of your life—"

"I don't give a shit. I don't want to go. I'm fine with having my diploma mailed to me. I'm not going, end of discussion." My eyes travel up the wall behind him to focus on the frames hanging heavily on the dark brown walls of his office. The white-framed certificates and diplomas mark his achievements, and I can tell by the way he proudly stares up at them that they mean more to him than they ever would to me.

"I'm sorry to hear that." He continues to stare at the frames. "I won't ask again." My father frowns.

"Why is it so important to you for me to go?" I dare to ask.

The hostility between us has thickened, and the air has grown heavier, but my father's features soften tremendously as the moments of silence between us go by.

"Because"—he draws in a long breath—"there was a time, a long time, when I wasn't sure . . ."—another pause—"how you would turn out."

"Meaning?"

"Are you sure you have time to talk right now?" His eyes move to my busted knuckles and bloodstained jeans. I know he really means: *Are you sure you're mentally stable enough to talk right now?*

I knew I should have changed my jeans. I didn't feel like doing much of anything this morning. I literally rolled out of bed and drove to campus.

"I want to know," I sternly reply.

He nods. "There was a time when I didn't think you'd even graduate high school, you know, given the trouble you always got into."

Flashes of bar fights, burglarized convenience stores, crying half-naked girls, complaining neighbors, and one very disappointed mother play before my eyes. "I know," I agree. "Technically, I'm still into trouble."

My father gives me a look that says he's not at all pleased to hear me being a little flippant over what was a substantial headache for him. "Not nearly as much," he says. "Not since . . . her," he adds softly.

"She causes most of my trouble." I rub the back of my neck with my hand, knowing I'm full of shit.

"I wouldn't say that." His brown eyes narrow, and his fingers play with the top button of his vest. Both of us sit in silence for a beat, unsure what to say. "I have so much guilt, Hardin. If you hadn't made it through high school and gone to college, I don't know what I would've done."

"Nothing—you would have been living your perfect life here," I snap.

He flinches as if I've slapped him. "That's not true. I only want the best for you. I didn't always show it, and I know that, but your future is very important to me."

"Is that why you had me accepted into WCU in the first place?" We've never discussed the fact that I know he used his position to get me into this damn school. I know he did. I didn't do shit in high school, and my transcripts prove it.

"That, and the fact that your mother was at her breaking

point with you. I wanted you to come here so I could get to know you. You aren't the same boy you were when I left."

"If you wanted to know me, you should have stuck around longer. And drunk less." Fragments of memories that I've tried so hard to forget push their way into my mind. "You left, and I never had the chance to just be a boy."

I used to occasionally wonder how it felt to be a happy child with a strong and loving family. While my mum worked from sunup to sundown, I would sit in the living room alone, just staring at the dingy and slanted walls for hours. I would make myself some shitty meal that was barely edible and imagine that I was sitting at a table full of people who loved me. They would laugh and ask how my day went. When I'd get into a fight at school, I'd sometimes wish I had a father around to either pat me on the back or bust my ass for starting trouble.

Things got much easier for me as I grew up. Once I was a teenager and I realized I could hurt people, everything was easier. I could get back at my mum for leaving me alone while she worked by calling her by her first name and denying her the simple joy of hearing her only child say "I love you."

I could get back at my father by not speaking to him. I had one goal: to make everyone around me as miserable as I felt; that way, I would finally fit in. I used sex and lies to hurt girls, and made a game of it. That backfired when my mum's friend spent too much time around me; her marriage was ruined, along with her dignity, and my mum was heartbroken that her fourteen-year-old son had done such a thing.

Ken looks like he catches on, as if he knows exactly what I'm thinking. "I know that, and I'm sorry for all the things you were subjected to because of me."

"I don't want to talk about this anymore." I push the chair back and stand up.

My father stays seated, and I can't help the thrill of power that I get from standing over him this way. I feel so . . . above him in every way possible. He's haunted by his guilt and regrets, and I'm finally coming to terms with mine.

"So much happened that you wouldn't understand. I wish I could tell you, but it wouldn't change anything."

"I said I don't want to talk about it anymore. I've already had a shitty day, and this is too much. I get it; you regret leaving us and all that shit. I'm over it," I lie, and he nods. It's not a full-on lie, really. I'm much closer to being over it than I've ever been before.

When I reach the door, a thought pops into my mind, and I turn around to face him. "My mum's getting married. Did you know that?" I ask out of curiosity.

From his blank stare and the way his brows lower, it's clear that he had no fucking clue.

"To Mike . . . you know, the neighbor guy?"

"Oh." He frowns.

"In two weeks."

"That soon?"

"Yeah." I nod. "Is that a problem or something?"

"No, not at all. I'm just a little surprised, that's all."

"Yeah; me, too." I lean my shoulder against the doorframe and watch as my father's expression transforms from sullen to relieved.

"Will you be attending?"

"No."

Ken Scott rises to his feet and walks around his massive desk to stand in front of me. I have to admit, I'm slightly intimidated. Not by him, of course, but by the raw emotion in his eyes when he says, "You have to go, Hardin. It will break her heart if you don't. Especially because she knows that you attended my wedding to Karen."

"Yeah, well, we both know why I attended yours. I didn't

have a choice, and your wedding wasn't halfway across the damn planet."

"It might as well have been, given how we never really talked. You have to go. Tessa knows about it?"

Fuck. I hadn't considered this.

"No, and you don't need to tell her either. Or Landon; he won't keep his mouth shut if he knows."

"Is there a reason that you're hiding it from her?" he asks, judgment filling his voice.

"It's not that I'm hiding it. I just don't want her to worry about going. She doesn't even have a passport. She's never even left the state of Washington."

"You know she'll want to go. Tessa loves England."

"She's never even been there!" I raise my voice and take a deep breath in an attempt to calm myself down. It drives me insane the way he acts as if she's his own daughter, as if he knows her better than I do.

"I won't say anything," he says, raising his hands slightly as if to placate me.

I'm glad he doesn't press the topic. I've done enough talking already, and I'm fucking exhausted. I got absolutely no sleep last night after I got off of the phone with Tessa. My nightmares came back full fucking force, and I made myself stay awake after I woke up dry-heaving for the third time.

"You should go by and see Karen soon. She was asking about you last night," he says just before I walk out of his office.

"Um, yeah," I mumble and close the door behind me.

chapter one hundred and nine

TESSA

In class, the guy I've determined is a future politician leans over and whispers to me, "Who did you vote for in the election?"

I feel slightly uncomfortable around my new classmate. He's charming, too charming, and his dressy clothes and brown skin make for a very distracting sight. He's not attractive in the same way that Hardin is, but he's certainly attractive, and he knows it.

"I didn't," I reply. "I wasn't old enough to vote."

He laughs. "Right."

I didn't really want to talk with him, but in the last few minutes of class our professor instructed us to talk among ourselves while he took a phone call. I'm relieved when the clock strikes ten and it's time to go.

The future politician's attempt to continue making small talk with me as we exit the classroom fails miserably, and after a few seconds he dismisses himself and walks the other way.

I've been distracted all morning. I haven't been able to stop thinking about what Steph must have said to Hardin to get him so worked up. I know he believed me about the rumors about Zed, but whatever else it was that she said to him bothered him enough that he didn't want to repeat it.

I hate Steph. I hate her for what she did to me and for getting into Hardin's head and hurting him—by using me, in a way.

By the time I make it to my art history class, I've planned ten different scenarios of how to murder that horrible girl in my mind.

I sit next to Michael, the blue-haired boy from the first class with the good sense of humor, and spend the entire hour of art history laughing at his jokes, which is a good distraction from my homicidal thoughts.

At last the day's over, and I'm heading to my car. Right as I reach it and start to climb in, my phone starts vibrating. I expect it to be Hardin, but looking down, I see it's not. I have three text messages, two of which just showed up.

I decide to read my mother's first: Call me. We need to talk.

Next is Zed's. I take a deep breath before pressing the small envelope-shaped button. I'll be in Seattle Thurs-Sat. Let me know when you're free :)

I rub my temples, grateful that I saved Kimberly's message for last. Nothing she has to say could possibly be as stressful as telling Zed that I take back my offer of seeing him or having a conversation with my mother. Did you know Loverboy is going to London next weekend?

I spoke too soon.

England? Why would Hardin be going to England? Is he moving there after he graduates? I reread her text message . . .

Next weekend!

I rest my forehead against the steering wheel of my car and close my eyes. My first instinct is to call him and ask him why he's hiding the trip from me. I stop myself from doing that because this is the perfect opportunity for me to try not to jump to conclusions without asking him first. There is a chance, a small one, that Kimberly is mistaken and Hardin isn't going to England next weekend.

My chest tightens at the thought of him still wanting to move back there. I'm still trying to convince myself that I'll be enough to keep him here.

chapter one hundred and ten

HARDIN

It feels like ages since I've been at this place. I'd been driving around for the last hour, going over the possible outcomes of my coming here. After formulating a mental list of pros and cons—something I never, ever do—I shut my car off and step into the cold afternoon air.

I'm assuming he's home; if not, I just wasted my entire afternoon, and I'll be even more irritated than I already am. I glance around the parking lot and find his truck near the front. The brown apartment building is set just off of the street, and a rusty staircase leads up to the second floor, where his place is. With each stomp of my boot against the metal staircase, I run through the reasons why I'm here in the first place.

Just as I reach apartment C, my phone vibrates in my back pocket. It's either Tessa or my mum, neither of whom I want to speak with right now. If I talk to Tessa, I'll be thrown off my plan. And my mum will just annoy me with her wedding talk.

I knock on the door. Within seconds Zed answers, wearing only drawstring pants. His feet are bare, and I notice the intricate clockwork-and-gear tattoo that he showed me before has spread further across his stomach. He must have gotten more of it done after he tried to get with my fucking girl.

Zed doesn't greet me. Instead, he just stares at me from the doorway, a look of obvious shock and suspicion on his face.

"We need to talk," I finally say and push past him to enter his apartment.

"Should I call the cops?" he asks in that dry tone he gets.

I take a seat on his worn leather couch and stare up at him. "That depends on whether you cooperate or not."

Dark hair covers his jawline and frames his mouth. It feels like months have passed since I saw him outside Tessa's mum's house instead of only ten or so days.

He sighs and leans his back against the wall on the opposite side of his small living room. "Well, get to it, then."

"You know this is about Tessa."

"I figured as much." He frowns and crosses his tattooed arms.

"You aren't going to Seattle."

He raises a thick brow before he smiles. "I am, though. I've already made the plans."

What the fuck? Why would he be going to Seattle? He's making this much harder than it needs to be, and I'm beginning to kick myself in the ass for thinking this conversation would end in any way except him leaving on a stretcher.

"The thing is . . ." I breathe in a deep breath to keep myself calm and stick to the plan. "You aren't going to Seattle."

"I'm visiting my friends there," he answers, challenging me.

"Bullshit. I know exactly what you're doing," I bite back.

"I'm staying with some friends in Seattle, but in case you were wondering, she did invite me to visit her."

The moment the words leave his mouth, I'm on my feet. "Don't push me—I'm trying to do this the right way. You have no reason to visit her. She's mine."

He raises one brow. "Do you realize how that sounds? Saying she's yours like she's your property?"

"I don't give a fuck how it sounds; it's true." I take another step toward him. The air between us has shifted from tense to downright primal. Both of us are trying to stake a claim here, and I'm not backing down.

"If she's *yours,* then why aren't you in Seattle *with her*?" he presses.

"I'm graduating after this semester, that's why." *Why am I even answering his questions?* I came here to talk, not to listen and "engage in dialogue," as a professor of mine used to say. I'll be damned if he tries to turn this shit on me. "Me not being there is irrelevant. You won't be seeing her while you're there."

"That's for her to decide, don't you think?"

"If I thought that, I wouldn't be here, would I?" My fists tighten at my sides, and I look away from him to stare at the stack of science textbooks on his coffee table. "Why won't you just leave her alone? Is this because of what I did to—"

"No," he interrupts smoothly. "It has nothing to do with that. I care about Tessa, just like you. But unlike you, I treat her the way she deserves to be treated."

"You know nothing about how I treat her," I growl.

"Yeah, man, I actually do. How many times has she run to me crying because of something you did or said? Too many." He points a finger at me. "All you do is hurt her, and you know it."

"You don't even know her, first of all, and secondly, don't you think it's a little pathetic of you to keep pining after someone you'll never have? How many times have we had this conversation, about how many girls?"

He eyes me carefully, taking in my anger, but not really biting on my pointing out his history with girls. "No"—his tongue darts out to wet his lips—"it's not pathetic. It's genius, actually. With Tessa, I'll be waiting in the background for the day when you fuck up again—which is inevitable—and when you do, I'll be there for her."

"You are a fucking—" I step back across the room to put as much space between his body and mine before his head ends up going through his wall. "What will it take, then? Do you want her to tell you herself that she doesn't want you around? I thought she already did that, yet here you are . . ."

"You're the one in my apartment."

"Goddammit, Zed!" I shout. "Why can't you just fucking stop? You know what she means to me, and you're always trying to get in the way. Find someone else to toy with. There are plenty of whores around campus."

" 'Whores'?" He repeats the word, mocking me.

"You know I didn't mean Tessa," I growl, struggling to keep my fists at my sides.

"If she meant so much to you, you wouldn't have done half the shit you did. Does she know that you fucked Molly while you were chasing her around?"

"Yes, she knows that. I told her."

"And she didn't mind?" His voice is the complete opposite of mine. He's so collected and calm, while I'm struggling mightily to keep the lid on my boiling anger.

"She knows that it meant nothing to me, and that it was before everything." I glare at him, trying to focus again. "But I didn't come here to discuss my relationship."

"Okay, why, exactly, *did* you come, then?"

He's such a smug bastard.

"To let you know that you aren't going to see her in Seattle. I thought we could discuss it in a more . . ."—I search for the right words—"civilized manner."

"Civilized? Sorry, but I find it hard to believe that you came here with 'enlightened' intentions," he scoffs, pointing to the bump on the bridge of his nose.

I close my eyes momentarily and envision his nose busted and bleeding, snapping under the metal casing when I slammed his head against it. The memory of the sound heightens my already buzzing adrenaline. "This is civilized for me! I came here to talk, not to fight—however, if you won't stay away from her, I don't have any other options." I widen my stance a little.

"Than what?" Zed asks.

"What?"

"Than *what*? We've been down this road before. There are only so many times that you can assault me before you get yourself arrested. And this time I *will* follow through on pressing charges."

He makes a valid point. Which only makes me madder. I hate the fact that I can't do a fucking thing about it, except literally murder him, which isn't an option . . . at this point at least.

I take a couple of breaths and try to relax my muscles. I have to offer my last option. One that I didn't want to have to rely on, but he's not giving me much room here. "I came here thinking we could come to some sort of agreement," I say.

He tilts his head to the side in the cockiest way possible. "What type of agreement? Is it another bet?"

"You're really pushing me . . ." I say through my teeth. "Tell me what it'll take for you to leave her alone. What can I give you to make you go away? Name it, and it's yours."

Zed stares at me, blinking rapidly, as if I've grown another head.

"Well, come on, now. Every man has a price," I murmur drily. It infuriates me that I have to negotiate with someone like him, but there's nothing else I can do to make him go away.

"Let her see me again, one more time," he suggests. "I'll be in Seattle on Thursday."

"No. Absolutely not." *Is he fucking stupid?*

"I'm not asking your permission here. I'm trying to make you feel more comfortable with it."

"It's not happening. You two have no reason to spend time together; she isn't available to you—or any other man—and she never will be."

"There you go, getting all possessive." He rolls his eyes, and

I wonder what Tessa would say if she could see this side of him, the only side I've ever known. What would I be as her man if I weren't possessive, if I was okay sharing her with someone?

I bite my tongue while Zed stares at the ceiling as if he's deliberating his next words. This is such fucking bullshit, pure and utter fucking bullshit. My head is spinning, and I'm honestly beginning to wonder just how much longer I can keep my cool.

Finally, Zed looks at me, a smirk slowly overtaking his features. Then he says simply, "Your car."

My mouth falls open at his audacity, and I can't help but laugh. "No fucking way!" I take two steps toward him. "I'm not giving you my fucking car. Are you out of your fucking mind?" My hands fly into the air.

"Sorry, then; looks like we can't come to an agreement after all." His eyes glitter through their thick lashes, and he rubs his fingers over his beard.

Images from my nightmare float through my head, him thrusting into her, making her come . . .

I shake my head to get rid of them.

Then I dig my keys out of my pocket and toss them onto the coffee table between us.

He gapes, bending down to retrieve the key chain. "You're serious?" He studies the keys, turning them over in his palm a few times before looking back up at me. "I was fucking with you!"

He tosses me the keys, but I don't catch them in time; they land only inches from the toe of my boot.

"I'll back off . . . fuck. I didn't expect you to actually give me your keys." He laughs, mocking me. "I'm not as big an asshole as *you*."

I glower at him. "You weren't giving me many options."

"We were friends once, remember?" Zed remarks.

I stay silent as we both remember how everything used to be, before all of this shit, before I actually gave a fuck about anything . . . before her. His eyes have shifted, his shoulders have tensed along with the air after his question.

It's hard to recall those supposed days. "I was too shit-faced to remember."

"You know that isn't true!" he exclaims, raising his voice. "You stopped drinking after—"

"I didn't come here to take a walk down memory lane with you. Are you going to back off or not?" I look at him. He's different somehow, harder.

He shrugs. "Sure, yeah."

But that was too easy . . . "I'm serious."

"So am I," he says with a wave of his hand at me.

"This means absolutely no contact with her. None," I remind him again.

"She's going to wonder why. I texted her earlier today."

I choose to ignore this. "Tell her you don't want to be friends with her anymore."

"I don't want to hurt her feelings like that," he says.

"I don't give a fuck about hurting her feelings. You need to make it clear that you aren't going to be pining after her anymore." The momentary calm I felt has ceased, and my temper is rising again. The possibility that Tessa's feelings would somehow be hurt by Zed not wanting to be friends with her drives me fucking crazy.

I walk toward the door, knowing myself well enough that I won't make it another five minutes in this musty apartment. I'm pretty damn proud of myself for remaining peaceful this long in a room with Zed after all the shit he's done to interfere with my relationship.

As my hand touches the rusted doorknob, he says, "I'll do what I have to do for now, but it still isn't going to change the outcome of all this."

"You're right. It won't." I agree with him, knowing that he means the exact opposite of what I do.

Before his fucking mouth can utter another word, I get out of his apartment and walk down the staircase as quickly as possible.

BY THE TIME I pull into my father's driveway, the sun is setting, and I still haven't been able to reach Tessa, each call going straight to voicemail. I've even called Christian twice, but he's yet to answer or return my calls.

Tessa's going to be mad that I went to Zed's apartment; she feels something for him that I'm never going to understand or tolerate. After today, I pray that I won't have to worry about him any longer. Unless she clings to him . . .

No. I stop myself from doubting her. I know Steph was feeding me bullshit, and it seeped into every insecure crack in my stone facade. If Zed had actually fucked Tessa, he'd have used this afternoon as the perfect opportunity to throw it in my face.

I walk into my father's house without knocking and search the downstairs for Karen or Landon. Karen is in the kitchen, standing over the stove with a wire whisk in her hand. She turns and greets me with a warm smile but also with troubled, tired eyes. An unfamiliar feeling of guilt spreads through me as I remember the planter I accidentally broke in her greenhouse.

"Hi, Hardin. Are you looking for Landon?" she asks, placing the whisk on a plate and wiping her hands on the bottom of her strawberry-print apron.

"I . . . I don't know, really," I admit. What *am* I doing here?

How pathetic is my life right now, that I find comfort in coming to this house, of all places? I know it's because of the memories that were created when I was here with Tessa.

"He's upstairs, on the phone with Dakota."

Something about Karen's tone throws me off.

"Is . . ." I'm not very good at interacting with people besides Tessa, and I'm particularly bad at dealing with other people's emotions. "Is he having a bad day or something?" I ask, sounding like a dumb-ass.

"I think so. He's having a hard time, I think. He hasn't spoken to me about anything, but he seems upset lately."

"Yeah . . ." I say, but I haven't noticed anything different about my stepbrother's mood. Then again, I've been too busy forcing him to babysit Richard to notice.

"When does he leave for New York again?"

"Three weeks." She tries to hide the pain in her voice that comes along with the words but fails miserably.

"Oh." I'm growing more and more uncomfortable by the minute. "Well, I'm going to go . . ."

"Don't you want to stay for dinner?" she asks eagerly.

"Uh, no. I'm okay."

Between the talk with my father this morning, the time I spent with Zed, and now this awkward shit with Karen, I'm on overload. I can't take the chance that something is actually wrong with Landon. I won't be able to deal with him being all emotional and shit, not today. I already have to go home to a recovering drug addict and an empty fucking bed.

chapter one hundred and eleven

TESSA

Kimberly is waiting in the kitchen for me when I arrive home from school. Two wineglasses, one full, one empty, sit in front of her, letting me know that she took my silence as confirmation that I, in fact, didn't know about Hardin's plan to fly to England.

She offers me a sympathetic smile when I drop my bag on the floor and sit on the stool next to her. "Hey, girl."

I swing my head dramatically to face her. "Hey."

"You didn't know?" Her blond hair is expertly curled today, resting perfectly on her shoulders. Her black, bow-shaped earrings glitter under the bright lighting.

"Nope. Didn't tell me." I sigh, reaching for the full glass of wine in front of her.

She laughs and grabs the bottle to fill the empty glass that was originally intended for me. "Christian said Hardin hasn't given Trish a definite answer yet. I shouldn't have said anything until I knew, but I had a feeling he wouldn't have mentioned the wedding to you."

I quickly swallow the white wine in my mouth before I spit it out. *"Wedding?"* I hurry to take another sip before I have to speak again. A wild thought shoots through me . . . that Hardin's going back to get married. Like an arranged marriage; they do those in England, don't they?

No, I know they *don't.* But the horrible thought electrifies me while I wait for Kimberly's next words. Am I drunk already?

"His mom's getting married. She called Christian this morning to invite us."

I quickly look down at the dark granite. "That's news to me."

Hardin's mother is getting married in two weeks, yet he didn't mention it to me at all. Then I remember . . . when he was being weird earlier.

"*That's* why she was calling so much!"

Kimberly looks at me with wide, questioning eyes as she takes a sip of her wine.

"What should I do?" I ask her. "Just pretend that I don't know? Hardin and I have been communicating so much better lately . . ." I trail off. I know that it's only been a week of improvement, but it's been one amazing week for me. I feel like we've made more progress in the last seven or so days than we have in the last seven months. Hardin and I both have been talking through issues that previously would have turned into massive fights, yet here I am being transported back in time to when he kept things from me.

I always find out. Doesn't he know this by now?

"Do you want to go?" she asks.

"I couldn't, even if I were invited." I rest my cheek against my hand.

Kimberly moves her stool to the side and grips the edges of mine to turn it to face her. "I asked if you *want* to go," she corrects me, a hint of wine on her breath.

"It would be lovely, but I—"

"Then you should *go!* I'll bring you as a guest, if I have to. I'm sure Hardin's mom would love you there. Christian says she absolutely adores you."

Despite my mood over Hardin's secrecy, her words thrill me. I absolutely adore Trish.

"I can't go, I don't have a passport," I say. And I could never afford a plane ticket on such short notice.

She waves off my objection. "Those can be expedited."

"I don't know . . ." I say. The butterflies I'm feeling in my belly at the mention of England make me want to rush down the hall to my computer and research how to get a passport—but the unwelcome knowledge of Hardin's purposely keeping the wedding from me forces me to stay in my seat.

"Don't doubt it. Trish would love to have you come along, and Lord knows Hardin could use a push toward commitment." She sips on her wine, leaving a deep red print of her full lips on the rim of the glass.

I'm sure he has his reasons for not telling me. If he's going, he probably doesn't want me to tag along all the way to England. I know his past haunts him, and crazy as it sounds, his demons could easily be stalking the streets of London and find us both.

"Hardin doesn't work that way," I say. "The more I push, the harder he pulls."

"Well then . . ." She moves her red-toed high heel and gently taps her foot against mine. "You need to dig your heels in the damn dirt and not let him pull you anymore."

I seize on her words and save them to analyze later, when I'm not under her watchful gaze. "Hardin doesn't like weddings."

"Everyone likes weddings."

"Not Hardin. He thoroughly hates them and the entire concept of marriage," I tell her and watch with a peculiar amusement as her eyes widen and she carefully places her wineglass back onto the countertop.

"So . . . then, what . . . I mean . . ." She blinks. "I don't even have anything to say, and that's really saying something!" Kimberly bursts out laughing.

I can't help but laugh along. "Yeah, tell me about it."

Kimberly's laugh is contagious, regardless of my mood, and

I love that about her. Certainly, she can be excessively nosy at times, and I don't always feel comfortable with the way she speaks about Hardin, but her openness and honesty happen to be the things I love the most about her. She tells it like it is, and she's very easy to read. There's not a layer of guile there, unlike so many people I've met of late.

"So you'll what? Just date forever?" she asks.

"I said the same thing." I can't help but giggle. Maybe it's the glass of wine I finished, or the fact that Hardin's refusal of any type of permanent commitment had slipped my mind in the last week . . . I don't know, but it feels good to laugh with Kim.

"What about your children? You don't mind having them out of wedlock?"

"Children!" I laugh again. "He doesn't want any children."

"This just keeps getting better and better." She rolls her eyes and picks up her glass to finish it off.

"He says that now, but I'm hoping . . ." I don't finish the wish. It's too desperate sounding when said out loud.

Kimberly winks. "Ahh—gotcha," she says knowingly, and I'm thankful when she changes the subject to this redhead in the office, Carine, who has a crush on Trevor. And when she describes a hypothetical sexual encounter between the two of them as being like watching lobsters awkwardly bumping into each other, I start laughing all over again.

BY THE TIME I get to my room, it's past nine o'clock. I purposely powered off my cell phone so that I could have a few uninterrupted hours with Kimberly. I told her about Hardin's plan to come to Seattle on Wednesday instead of Friday, and she laughed, telling me she knew he wouldn't stay gone long.

My hair is still damp from a shower, and I've been taking my time picking out my outfit for work tomorrow. I'm stalling, and I know it. I'm sure that when I turn on my phone, I'll have to deal with Hardin, and confront him, or not, about the wedding. In a perfect world, I'd just casually bring it up, and Hardin would invite me, explaining that he waited to ask because he was trying to think of the right way to convince me to come. But this isn't a perfect world, and I'm growing more anxious by the second. It hurts me to know that whatever Steph said to him bothered him so much that he's back to keeping things from me. I hate her. I love Hardin so much, and I just want him to see that nothing she, or anyone else, says will ever change that.

Hesitantly, I take my phone out of my bag and power it back on. I have to call my mother back and text Zed, but I want to talk to Hardin first. The notifications on the top of my small screen appear, and the envelope icon flashes, text message after text message appearing, all from Hardin. Before I read any of them, I just call.

He answers on the first ring. "Tessa, what the hell!"

"Have you tried to call?" I ask timidly, as innocently as I can, trying to keep the mood as calm as possible.

"Have I tried to call? You're joking, right? I've been calling you nonstop for the last three hours," he huffs. "I even called Christian."

"What?" I say, but then, not wanting things to escalate, I follow up quickly with "I was just hanging out with Kim."

"Where?" he immediately demands.

"Here, at the house," I say and begin to fold my dirty clothes and place them in the hamper; I figure I'll do a load of laundry before I go to bed.

"Well, next time you really need . . ." He lets out a groan of frustration, and his voice softens as he begins again: "Maybe next time you could just send me a text or something if you're going to have your phone off." He releases a big breath, then adds, "You know how I get."

I appreciate the change in his tone and the fact that he stopped himself from saying whatever it was he had originally planned to say, which I'd rather not find out. Unfortunately, the small buzz I got from the wine has mostly disappeared, and the revelation of Hardin's plans to go to England rests heavily on my chest.

"How was your day today?" I ask him, hoping that if I give him an opportunity to bring the wedding up, he will.

He sighs. "It was . . . well, long."

"Mine, too." I don't know what to say to him without coming out and asking point-blank. "Zed texted me today."

"Did he?" Hardin's voice is calm, but I can detect a note of harshness that would usually intimidate me.

"Yeah, this afternoon. He says he's coming to Seattle on Thursday."

"And what did you say back to him?"

"Nothing yet."

"Why are you telling me this?" Hardin asks.

"Because, I want us to be open with one another. No more secrets, no more *hiding* things." I emphasize the last part of the sentence, hoping it will elicit the truth from him.

"Well . . . thanks for telling me. I appreciate it," he says. And then says nothing more.

Seriously?

"Yeah, so . . . is there anything you want to tell me?" I ask, still clinging to the dwindling hope that he'll reciprocate my honesty.

"Um, I talked to my dad today."

"Really? About what?" Thank goodness, I knew he would come around.

"Transferring to the Seattle campus."

"Really!" The word comes out sounding more like a squeal than I intended, and Hardin's deep laugh resonates through the line.

"Yeah, but he says it will postpone my graduation, so it wouldn't make sense to move, this late in the semester."

"Oh." I feel myself pouting. I hesitate a moment before asking, "But after graduation?"

"Yeah, sure."

"Yeah sure? That's it? That easy?" The smile that overcomes me crowds out everything else. I wish he were here; I'd grab him by his T-shirt and kiss him, hard.

Then he says, "I mean, why stall the inevitable?"

My smile fades. "You're speaking like moving to Seattle is a jail sentence."

He stays quiet.

"Hardin?"

"I don't think of it like that. I'm just annoyed by the whole thing—all this time has been wasted, and it frustrates me."

"I get that," I say. His words aren't elegant, but they mean he's missing me. My head is still spinning from his agreeing to finally move to Seattle to be with me. We've been battling over this issue for months, and he's suddenly given in without so much as a final fight. "So, Seattle it is, then? Are you sure?" I have to ask again.

"Yeah. I'm ready to start fresh somewhere, may as well be Seattle."

I hug my arms around my body in excitement. "No England, then?" I give him one last chance to bring up the wedding.

"Nope. No England."

I've already won the Great Battle of Seattle, so when the niggling irritation about the wedding flares up again, I don't push my guy any further tonight. Whatever's going on with that, I'm going to get what I want: Hardin in Seattle, with me.

chapter one hundred and twelve

TESSA

When my alarm sounds the next morning, I'm exhausted. I barely slept at all. I spent hours tossing and turning, always on the brink of sleep but never achieving it.

I don't know if it was the excitement over Hardin agreeing to move to Seattle, or if it was the looming discussion we're bound to have about England, but either way, I got no sleep, and now I look like hell. Dark shadows aren't as easy to hide with concealer as the cosmetics companies would have you believe, and my unruly hair looks as if I stuck my finger into a light socket. Apparently the joy I felt about him moving here couldn't completely eliminate the underlying anxiety about his lying by omission.

I take Kimberly up on her offer to ride to work together this morning, buying myself a few extra minutes to apply another coat of mascara while she recklessly whips in and out of lanes on the freeway. She reminds me of Hardin, cursing at nearly every car and honking more often than any reasonable person needs to do.

Hardin hasn't mentioned whether or not he's still planning on coming to Seattle today. When I asked him just before we got off the phone last night, he told me he'd let me know in the morning. It's close to nine now, and I haven't heard from him. I can't shake the feeling that something is happening within him, something that if not handled properly will cause us more turmoil. I know Steph got to him; I can tell by the way he's doubting everything

I say. He's keeping things from me again, and I'm terrified of the problems this could lead to.

"Maybe you should go back this weekend instead of having him coming to you," Kimberly suggests between cursing out a semi and a MINI.

"It's that obvious?" I ask, lifting my cheek from the cold window.

"Yes, very obvious."

"Sorry, I'm being such a downer." I sigh.

Going back this weekend isn't a bad idea. I miss Landon terribly, and it would be nice to see my father again.

"You are." She grins at me. "But that's nothing a little coffee and some red lipstick won't fix."

When I nod my agreement, she quickly exits the highway, makes a U-turn in the middle of a busy intersection, and says, "I know a great little coffee shop nearby."

BY LUNCHTIME, my morning blues have disappeared, although I still haven't heard from Hardin. I texted him twice but ultimately stopped myself from calling him. Trevor is waiting for me at an empty table in the break room, two plates of pasta in front of him.

"They sent double my order, so I figured I'd save you from a microwave meal for at least one day." He smiles, sliding a packet of plastic eating utensils across the table.

The pasta tastes as savory as it smells. The delicious Alfredo sauce reminds me that I skipped breakfast this morning, and I flush when a small moan falls from my mouth as I take my first bite.

"Good, huh?" Trevor beams, wiping his thumb across the corner of his mouth to capture a drop of the creamy sauce. He brings his thumb to his mouth, and I can't help but think how odd the causal gesture looks on a man who's wearing a suit.

"Mmm . . ." I can barely answer, because I'm too busy shoving noodles in my face.

"I'm glad . . ." Trevor's deep blue eyes dart away from mine, and he shifts in his seat.

"Is everything all right?" I ask him.

"Yeah . . . I . . . well . . . I wanted to talk to you about something."

And like that, I begin to ask myself if the double meal wasn't in fact purposely ordered.

"Okay . . ." I respond, hoping this isn't going to be too awkward.

"It may be a little awkward."

Great. "Go on," I say with an encouraging smile.

"Okay . . . here goes." He pauses and runs his fingertip over a silver cuff link. "Carine has asked me to attend Krystal's wedding with her."

I take the opportunity to shovel a forkful of pasta into my mouth so I don't have to speak just yet. Really, I'm not sure why he's telling me this, or what I'm supposed to say. I nod, pushing him to continue, and try not to laugh thinking the funny Carine imitation Kimberly was doing yesterday.

"And I was wondering if there was any reason that I should say no to her," Trevor says. He pauses to look at me like he expects a response.

I'm positive that the choking sound I make frightens him, but when he shoots me a look of concern, I hold up one finger and continue chewing, thoroughly, then swallow rather dramatically before responding. "I don't see any reason for it."

I hope that's the end of that. But when he goes on to say "What I mean is . . ." all I can hope is that he magically guesses that I, in fact, know exactly what he means and will just sort of let that sentence trail off without further explanation.

No such luck.

"I know you're on and off with Hardin, and I also know this is one of those 'off' times, so I just wanted to be sure before I accept her proposal that I can give her my full affection. Without distractions."

I'm not sure what to say, so I quietly ask, "Am I a distraction?"

I feel so uncomfortable, but Trevor is so sweet, and his cheeks have turned such a deep shade of red, that I feel an overwhelming urge to comfort him at the same time.

"Yes, you have been since you came to Vance," he says, rushing the words out. "I don't mean that in a bad way; it's just that I've been waiting in the background, and I wanted my intentions to be clear before I explored the possibility of a relationship with someone else."

My very own Mr. Collins sits in front of me—a much more handsome version, of course—and I feel just as awkward and embarrassed for him as Elizabeth Bennett did in *Pride and Prejudice.*

"Trevor, I'm sorry I—"

"It's okay, really." The sincerity in his eyes is almost overwhelming. "I get it. I just wanted to confirm it one last time." He pokes at his pasta a little, then adds, "I guess the last few times hadn't done it for me." He laughs quietly, a nervous laugh, and I join in sympathetically.

"She's lucky to have you as a date to the wedding," I say, hoping to numb the embarrassment I know he feels. I shouldn't have compared him to Mr. Collins; he's not nearly as aggressive or obnoxious. I take a long drink of water, hoping that will end things.

"Thank you," he says, but then he adds with a little smile, "Maybe now Hardin will stop calling me 'fucking Trevor.' "

I smack my hand against my mouth to stop the water from spewing from my mouth. I swallow quickly, then say, "I didn't know you knew about that!" My horrified laugh fills the small room.

"Yeah, I've noticed." Trevor's eyes shine with humor, and I'm so relieved that we can share a laugh, as friends, with no confusion.

My momentary bliss is cut short when Trevor's smile disappears, and I turn around to follow his gaze to the doorway.

"It smells so good in here!" one of the gossips says to the other as she enters. I feel petty for the level of dislike I feel for them, but I can't help it.

"We should go," Trevor whispers, eyeing the shorter woman.

I stare back at him, puzzled, but get to my feet and toss the empty Styrofoam box into the trash can.

"You look stunning today, Tessa," the taller of the two says. I can't read her expression, but I'm positive that she's mocking me. I know I look like hell today.

"Um, thank you."

"It's such a small world, you know? Is Hardin still working for Bolthouse?"

My purse slips off of my shoulder, and I quickly grab the leather strap before it hits the floor. *She knows Hardin?*

"Yup, still is," I say and straighten my back in an attempt to appear completely unfazed at the mention of his name.

"Tell him I said hey, would you?" She smirks, and with that, she turns on her heel and disappears, along with her evil sidekick.

"What the hell was that?" I ask Trevor after checking the hall to be sure the two aren't lurking around nearby. "Did you know they were going to say something to me?"

"I wasn't sure, but I suspected it. I overheard them talking about you."

"What about me? They don't even know me."

He's uncomfortable again. Trevor is easier to read than anyone I've ever met. "It wasn't about you, exactly . . ."

"They were talking about Hardin, weren't they?" I ask and he nods, confirming my suspicion. "What exactly did they say?"

Trevor tucks the corners of his bright red tie into his suit. "I . . . I don't really want to repeat it. You should ask him."

Given Trevor's reluctance, I suddenly shiver at the thought that Hardin may have slept with one of them, or both. They aren't much older than I am: twenty-five at the most, and, I have to admit, both beautiful—in an over-the-top, too-much-spray-tan way, but attractive all the same.

The walk back to my office is long, and a strong feeling of jealousy starts gnawing at me. If I don't ask Hardin about the woman, I think I'll go insane.

The moment I get to my office, I call him. I need to know if he's coming here tonight, and I need some reassurance.

Zed's name flashes across my phone screen before I can bring up Hardin's name in my contacts list. I flinch a little, but decide I might as well do this now.

"Hey," I say. But I sound "off"—too excited, too fake.

"Hey, Tessa, how's it going?" Zed asks. It feels like it's been so long since I've heard his smooth voice even though that isn't the case.

"It's . . . going." I lay my forehead against the cool surface of my desk.

"Sounds rough."

"It's okay, just a lot going on."

"Well, that's why I called you, actually. I know I said I was going to be in town Thursday, but I've had a change of plans."

"Oh?" Relief washes over me. I look up at the ceiling and let out a breath I didn't realize I was holding. "Well, it's okay. Next time it'll work—"

"No, I mean I'm actually in Seattle right now," he says, and instantly my heart rate skyrockets. "I got in last night; had a hell of a drive. I'm only a few blocks away from your office, actually. I won't bother you there or anything, but maybe we could grab some dinner or something when you're done for the day?"

"Um . . ." I glance at the clock. It's fifteen minutes past two, and Hardin still hasn't responded to my messages. "I don't know if that's good for me, actually. I think Hardin is coming in tonight," I admit.

First Trevor, now Zed. Did the extra mascara this morning bring along some weird juju with it or something?

"Are you sure?" Zed asks. "I saw him out yesterday . . . it was pretty late."

What? Hardin and I got off the phone around eleven last night. Could he have gone out again after we got off the phone? Has he been spending time with his crew of so-called friends again?

"I don't know," I say and dramatically hit my head against my desk, too gently to do any damage but hard enough that I know Zed can hear through the line.

"It's only dinner. Then I'll let you get to whatever plans you have," he coaxes. "It'll be nice to see a familiar face, yeah?" I can picture his smile now, the one that I adore so much.

So I ask, "I rode in to work today with someone, so I don't have my car. Could you pick me up at five?" And when he happily agrees, I'm both thrilled and terrified.

chapter one hundred and thirteen

TESSA

Five minutes before five o'clock I try to call Hardin, but he doesn't pick up. Where has he been all day? Was Zed right when he said that Hardin was out late? It's possible that he's on his way to Seattle and is planning to surprise me, but really, what are the odds of that? My meeting with Zed has been weighing on my chest since the moment I agreed to it. I know Hardin hates our friendship. He hates it so much that it haunts him in his dreams, and here I am, fueling that hatred.

I don't bother to check my hair or touch up my makeup before taking the elevator down to the lobby, studiously ignoring Kimberly's critical gaze. I probably shouldn't have informed her of my plans. Through the plate-glass windows, Zed's truck is visible, and is a beautiful sight for me, and I can't ignore the excitement I feel to see a familiar face. I'd rather it be Hardin's, but Zed's here, and Hardin isn't.

Zed climbs out of his truck to greet me as soon as I step out of the building. His smile grows as I walk across the sidewalk, and I see that his face is now covered by dark hair. Dressed in black jeans and a gray long-sleeve shirt, he looks as handsome as ever, and I look like death.

"Hey." He smiles, opening his arms for a hug.

Uncertainty floods through me, but the need to be polite pushes me into his waiting arms.

"It's been a while," he says into my hair.

I nod in agreement and ask, "How was your drive?" as I pull back from the embrace.

He blows out a breath. "Long. But I got to listen to some pretty good music on the way."

He opens the passenger door for me, and I hurry to get inside and out of the cold air. The cab of his truck is warm and smells like him.

"What made you decide to come today instead of tomorrow?" I ask, to begin the conversation as Zed hesitantly pulls into traffic.

"It was just . . . a change of mind, nothing, really." His eyes dart back and forth between the rearview and the side mirrors.

"Driving in the city is intimidating," I say to him.

"Yes. Very." He smiles, still focused on the road.

"Do you know where you want to grab dinner? I haven't done much exploring yet, so I don't know where the best spots are."

I check my phone; nothing from Hardin. So I pull up some restaurant options on an app, and after a couple minutes, Zed and I decide on a small Mongolian Style grill.

I GO WITH the chicken and vegetables and watch in awe as the chef prepares the food in front of us. I've never been to a place like this before, and Zed finds that amusing. We're seated in the very back of the small restaurant, Zed sitting across from me, and we're both too quiet for it to be comfortable.

"Is something wrong?" I ask him while picking at my food.

Zed's eyes are soft and full of worry. "I don't know if I should even bring it up . . . You seem like you've got so much going on already, and I want you to have a nice time."

"I'm fine. Tell me whatever it is that you need to." I brace myself for the unknown blow I'm sure is about to land.

"Hardin came to my place yesterday."

"What?" I can't hide the surprise in my voice. Why would Hardin do that? And if he did, how is it that Zed is sitting here without any bruises or missing limbs? "What did he want?" I ask.

"To tell me to stay away from you," he promptly answers.

When I mentioned Zed's text message to Hardin last night, he seemed so indifferent about the situation. "What time?" I ask, hoping it was after we talked about not keeping things from each other.

"Afternoon, around three."

I let out an exasperated breath. Sometimes Hardin has no boundaries, and his list of offenses is growing by the second.

I rub my temples, my appetite having disappeared. "What did he say, exactly?"

"That he didn't care how I did it, or if I hurt your feelings, just that I needed to stay away. He was being so calm, it was kinda freaky." He stabs his fork at a piece of broccoli and pops it into his mouth.

"And you came here anyway?"

"Yes, I did."

The testosterone-fueled battle between the two of them is wearing me out, and I'm on the sidelines, trying to keep the peace but failing. "Why?"

His golden eyes meet mine. "Because his threats aren't going to work on me anymore. He can't tell me who to be friends with, which is something I hope you feel the same way about."

I'm beyond irritated that Hardin went to Zed's apartment like that. I'm even more irritated that he didn't say anything to me about it, and that he wanted Zed to hurt my feelings and end our friendship while keeping his role in the whole exchange hidden.

"I feel the same about Hardin controlling who I'm friends with." As the words leave my mouth, Zed's eyes fill with triumph, which also bothers me. "But, I also think he has good reasons for not wanting us to be friends. Don't you?"

Zed shakes his head amicably. "Yes and no. I won't hide my feelings for you, but you know that I don't push them onto you. I told you that I'll take what you can give me, and if friendship is all I can get, I'll live with it."

"I know you don't push." I choose to respond only to half of his statement. Zed never pushes me to do anything, and he never tries to force me into anything, but I hate the way he talks about Hardin.

"Can you say the same for him?" Zed challenges, looking at me intensely.

The urge to defend Hardin makes me say, "No. I can't. I know how he is, but that's just who he is."

"You're always so quick to defend him. I don't get it."

"You don't have to get it," I say harshly.

"Really?" Zed says quietly and frowns.

"Yes." I straighten my back and sit up as tall as I can manage.

"It doesn't bother you how possessive he is? He tells you who you can be friends with . . ."

"It does bother me but—"

"You let him do it."

"Did you come all the way to Seattle to remind me that Hardin is controlling?"

Zed opens his mouth to speak but closes it.

"What?" I push him.

"He has a claim on you, and I'm worried about you. You seem so stressed out."

I sigh in defeat. I *am* stressed, too stressed, but fighting with Zed isn't going to help anything. It's only intensifying my frustration. "I'm not going to make excuses for him, but you don't know anything about our relationship. You don't see how he is with me. You don't understand him the way that I do."

I push my plate away and notice that the couple at the next table over has turned their attention on us. Lowering my voice, I say, "I don't want to fight with you, Zed. I'm exhausted, and I was really looking forward to spending this time with you."

He leans back in his chair. "I'm being such a jerk, aren't I." he says with sad eyes. "I'm sorry, Tessa. I would blame the drive . . . but that's not an excuse. I'm sorry."

"It's okay, I didn't mean to snap at you. I don't know what's gotten into me." My period is due any day now—that must be why I'm so on edge.

"It's my fault, really." He reaches across the table and squeezes my hand.

Tension still fills the air, and I can't stop thinking of Hardin, but I'd like to have a nice time, so I ask, "How is everything else going?"

Zed dives into stories about his family and how warm Florida was the last time he visited. The conversation between us reverts to its normal, easy, meandering flow, and the tension evaporates, allowing me to finish my meal.

After we're done eating and are heading to the exit, Zed asks, "Do you have more plans for the night?"

"Yes, I'm going to Christian's jazz club. It just opened."

"Christian?" Zed questions.

"Oh, my boss. That's who I'm staying with."

His brow rises. "You're staying with your boss?"

"Yes, but he went to college with Hardin's father and he's a longtime friend of Ken and Karen," I explain. It hasn't occurred to me that Zed doesn't know any of the details about my life. Although he picked me up after Christian's surprise engagement party for Kimberly, he doesn't know anything about them.

"Oh, so that's how you got a paid internship, then?"

Ouch. "Yes." I admit.

"Well, it's awesome either way."

"Thanks." I stare out the window and pull my cell phone from my purse. Still nothing. "What else do you plan on doing while you're in Seattle?" I ask in the middle of trying to explain which roads to take to get us to Christian and Kimberly's house. I give up after a few minutes and type the address into my phone. The screen freezes, and the power shuts off twice before the device finally cooperates.

"I'm not sure. I'm going to see what my friends are up to. Maybe we could meet up again later tonight? Or before I leave on Saturday?"

"That could be cool. I'll let you know," I say.

"When will Hardin be here?" The venomous undertone to his question doesn't go unnoticed.

I glance at my phone again, this time out of habit. "I'm not sure, maybe tonight."

"Are you guys together right now? I know we said we wouldn't talk about it anymore, but I'm confused."

"So am I," I admit. "We've been putting some space between us lately."

"Is that working?"

"Yes." Until the last few days when Hardin started to pull away from me.

"That's good, then."

I have to know what thought is running through his mind. I can see it churning behind his eyes. "What?"

"Nothing. You don't want to hear it."

"Yes, I do." I know I'll regret it, but that doesn't stop my curiosity.

"I just don't see any space. You're in Seattle, staying with friends of his family, one of whom is also your boss. Even from miles away, he's controlling you, trying to end the few friendships that you have. And when he's not doing that, he's coming to Seattle to visit. That doesn't seem like much space to me."

I haven't thought about my living arrangement from that perspective until now. Is that another reason why Hardin sabotaged my getting an apartment? So that if I still decided to go to Seattle, I could be under the watchful eyes of his family's friends?

I shake my head to escape the thought. "It's working for us. I know it doesn't make sense to you, but it's working for us. I know—"

"He tried to pay me off to stay away from you," Zed interjects.

"What?"

"Yeah, he was threatening me, and he told me to make him an offer. He told me to find another 'whore on campus' to toy with."

Whore?

Zed shrugs nonchalantly. "He said that no one else will ever have you, and he was awfully proud of himself that you stuck around even after he told you about sleeping with Molly after the two of you started hanging out."

The mention of Hardin and Molly stings—Zed knew it would. And that's exactly why he said it.

"We've already dealt with that. I don't want to talk about Hardin and Molly," I say through gritted teeth.

"I just want you to know what you're dealing with. He's not the same person when you're not around."

"That's not a bad thing," I retort, fighting back. "You don't know him." I'm relieved when we pull onto the access road and into the outskirts of the city, signaling that we're less than five minutes away from Christian's place. The sooner this car ride is over, the better.

"You don't either, not really," he says. "You spend all of your time fighting with him."

"What's your goal here, Zed?" I ask. I hate the direction our conversation has taken, but I don't know how to bring it back to neutral territory.

"Nothing. I just thought that after all this time and all the shit he puts you through, you'd see the truth."

A thought strikes me. "Did you tell him you were coming here?"

"No."

"You're not fighting fair here," I say, calling him out.

"Neither is he." He sighs, desperately trying to keep his voice down. "Look, I know you'll defend him until you're blue in the face, but you can't blame me for wanting to have what he has. I want to be the one you're defending, I want to be the one that you trust, even though you shouldn't. I'm always there for you when he isn't." He rubs his hand over his facial hair and takes another breath. "I'm not fighting fair, but neither is he. He hasn't from the beginning. Sometimes I swear the only reason he's so attached to you is because he knows that I have feelings for you, too."

This is exactly why Zed and I will never be able to have a friendship. Regardless of his sweetness and understanding, it will never work. He hasn't given up, and I suppose there's honor in that. However, I can't give him what he wants from me, and I don't want to feel like I have to explain my relationship with Hardin every time I see him. He's been there for me, it's true, but only because I allowed him to be.

I say, "I don't know if I have enough left of me to give to you, even as a friend."

Zed looks over at me with an even expression. "That's because he's drained you."

I stay silent and stare out the window at the pine trees lining the road. I don't like the tension I'm feeling right now, and I'm fighting back some tears when I hear Zed mutter, "I didn't want tonight to end up this way. Now you'll probably never want to see me again."

I point out the window. "It's this driveway."

An awkward and tense silence fills the cab of the truck until the massive house comes into view. When I look over at him, Zed is staring wide-eyed at Christian's place.

"This is even bigger than the other house, the one I picked you up from before," he points out, trying to ease the tension.

In an effort to do the same, I begin to tell him about the gym, the spacious kitchen, the way Christian can control what's going on in parts of the house with his iPhone.

And then my heart leaps into my throat.

Hardin's car is parked just behind Kimberly's sleek Audi. Zed spots it at the same time that I do, but he doesn't appear to be affected by it. I can feel the color draining from my face as I say, "I better get inside."

As we park, Zed says, "Again, I'm sorry, Tessa. Please don't go inside upset with me. You have enough going on, I shouldn't have made you feel any worse."

He offers to come inside to be sure everything is okay, but I brush it off. I know Hardin will be pissed—beyond pissed—but I'm the one who created this mess, so I need to be held responsible for cleaning it up.

"It's okay," I reassure him with a fake smile and climb out of his truck with a promise to text him when I can.

I'm aware of my slow strides as I walk to the door, but I don't make an effort to move faster. I'm trying to go over what I should say, whether or not I should be angry with Hardin or apologize for seeing Zed again, when the door opens.

Hardin steps out wearing his dark blue jeans and a plain black T-shirt. Despite the fact that it has only been two days since I last saw him, my pulse quickens and I ache to be closer to him. I've missed him so much in the few days that we've been apart.

His face is set in stone, and his icy gaze follows Zed's old truck as it disappears from view. "Hardin, I—"

"Get inside," he scolds me.

"Don't tell—" I begin.

"It's cold; come inside." Hardin's eyes are blazing, and the heat in them keeps me from arguing. He surprises me by gently resting his hand on the small of my back as he leads me inside the house, past where Kimberly and Smith are playing some card game in the living room, and into my bedroom without a word.

Calmly, he closes the door behind him and turns the lock. Then he looks down at me, and my heart nearly bursts when he asks, "Why?"

"Hardin, nothing happened, I swear. He said there was a change of plans, and I was so relieved, because I thought he wasn't coming, but instead he said that he'd arrived a day early and wanted to grab dinner." I shrug, partly to calm myself down. "I didn't know how to say no."

"You never do," he spits, holding my gaze.

"I know you went to his apartment yesterday. Why didn't you tell me?"

"Because you didn't need to know." His breathing is harsh, barely controlled.

"You don't get to decide what I need to know," I challenge him. "You can't keep things from me. I know about your mother's wedding, too!" I blurt.

"I knew how you would react." He throws his hands up, trying to defend himself.

I roll my eyes, stomping toward him. "Bullshit."

He doesn't even flinch. The veins in his arms are visible under the rare spots of white skin, soft blue laced with the black ink. His fists are tightly balled. "One thing at a time."

"I will be friends with who I want to be friends with—and you won't keep going behind my back, acting like a child throwing a damn tempter tantrum," I warn him.

"You said you wouldn't go near him again."

"I know. I didn't get it before, but after spending time with him today, I made my own choice not to be friends with him. It's not because of you."

I can see him flinch in surprise a little at that, but he maintains his dark intensity. "Why's that?"

I look away, a little ashamed. "Because I know he's a trigger for you, and I shouldn't keep pushing you by seeing him. I know how much it would hurt me if you saw Molly . . . or any other female, for that matter. That being said, you don't get to control my friendships, but I can't lie and say that I wouldn't feel the same way if I were you."

He crosses his arms and breathes out roughly. "Why now? What did he do to make you suddenly change your mind?"

"Nothing. He didn't do anything to me. I just shouldn't have taken this long to get it. We have to be equals—neither of us can hold the power."

I can tell by the glow in his green eyes that he wants to say more, but instead he just nods. "Come here." He opens his arms for me the way he always does, and I'm quick to wrap myself in them.

"How did you know that I was with him?" I press my cheek against his chest. His minty scent invades my senses, pushing out all thoughts of Zed.

"Kimberly told me," he says into my hair.

I frown. "She really doesn't know how to keep her mouth shut."

"You weren't going to tell me?" His thumb presses under my chin and lifts my head up.

"Yes, I was, but I'd rather have told you myself." I suppose that I'm grateful for Kimberly's honesty; it's hypocritical of me to only want her to be honest with me and not with Hardin. "Why didn't you come find us?" I ask. I assumed if he knew that I was with Zed, that's exactly what he would have done.

"Because," he breathes, staring into my eyes, "you kept going on about the cycle, and I wanted to break it."

My heart swells at his honest and thoughtful answer. He really is trying, and it means so much to me.

"I'm still mad," he adds.

"I know." I touch his cheek with my fingertips, and his arms tighten around me. "I'm pissed, too. You didn't tell me about the wedding, and I want to know why."

"Not tonight," he warns.

"Yes, tonight. You got to say your piece about Zed, and now it's my turn."

"Tessa . . ." His lips compress into a hard line.

"Hardin . . ."

"You're infuriating." He releases me and paces across the floor, putting a distance between us that I can't stand.

"So are you!" I fire back, following his movements to get closer to him.

"I don't want to talk about the fucking wedding right now; I'm already livid and barely controlling myself as it is. Don't push me, okay?"

"Fine!" I say loudly, but give in. Not because I'm afraid of what he'll say, but because I just spent two and a half hours with Zed, and I know Hardin's anger is only serving to mask the anxiety and pain I've caused him by doing so.

chapter
one hundred and fourteen

TESSA

I pull open my dresser drawer and dig out clean panties and a matching bra. "I'm going to go shower. Kimberly wants to leave at eight, and it's already seven," I tell Hardin, who's sitting on the edge of my bed with his elbows resting on his knees.

"You're still going?" he scoffs.

"Yes. I told you before, remember? That was the whole reason you wanted to come here, so I didn't have to go alone."

"That's not the only reason I came," he says defensively. I raise a speculative brow at him, and he rolls his eyes. "I didn't say it's not *a* reason, but it's not the only one."

"You still want to come, right?" I ask, dangling my underwear suggestively.

This is rewarded with a slight smirk. "No, I never wanted to come, but if you're going, so am I."

I give him a wide smile, but when I leave the room, he doesn't follow. Which surprises me. I find myself kind of wishing he would this time. I don't know where we stand at the moment. I know he's pissed about Zed, and I'm upset that he's hiding things from me again, but overall I'm thrilled that he's here, and I don't want to waste our time fighting.

I wrap a towel around my hair since I don't have the time to wash and dry it before we leave. The hot water relieves some of the tension in my shoulders and back but doesn't do much to clear my head. I need to work myself into a better mood within the hour. Hardin will be brooding all night, I'm sure. I want us to have a nice time out with Kimberly and Christian—I don't want any awkward silence or public fighting. I want us to get along, and I want to be in a happy mood, both of us. I haven't had a Seattle nightlife experience since I moved here, and I want my first to be as fun as possible. My guilt regarding Zed refuses to subside, but I'm relieved when my irritation and irrational thoughts slide down the drain along with the scalding water and suds of soap.

The moment I shut off the shower, Hardin knocks at the door. I wrap a towel around myself and take a deep breath before answering. "I'll be ready in ten minutes. I need to try to do something with my hair," I say, and when I look into the mirror, there's Hardin standing behind me.

He squints at the frizzy mess on my head. "What's wrong with it now?"

"It's out of control." I laugh. "It won't take long."

"You're wearing *that*?" He eyes the uncomfortable black dress, which is hanging on the shower curtain, since I was trying to de-wrinkle it a bit. The last time I wore it, at the "family vacation," it led to a disastrous night . . . well, week.

"Yes, Kimberly said there's a dress code."

"What kind of dress code?" Hardin looks down to his stained jeans and black T-shirt.

I shrug and smile to myself, imagining Kimberly telling Hardin to change his outfit.

"I'm not changing," he tells me, and I shrug again.

Hardin's eyes don't leave my reflection in the mirror the entire time that I put on my makeup and wrestle with a flatiron and my hair. The steam from the shower has made it curl in a terrible way; there's just no hope for it. I end up pulling it back into a low bun. At least my makeup actually looks really good. An even exchange for such a bad hair day.

"Are you staying until Sunday?" I ask him as I put on my underwear and step into my dress. I want to make sure the tension between us is under control, and we don't spend the entire night arguing.

"Yes, why?" Hardin coolly responds.

"I was thinking that instead of spending Friday here in Seattle, we could go back and I could see Landon and Karen. Your father, too."

"What about yours?"

"Oh yeah . . ." I had momentarily forgotten about my father staying with Hardin. "I've been trying really hard not to think about that situation until you can tell me more about it."

"I don't know if it's a good idea . . ."

"Why not?" I ask. I miss Landon so much.

Hardin rubs the back of his neck with his hand. "I don't know . . . All this shit with Steph and Zed . . ."

"Hardin, I'm not going to see Zed again, and unless Steph shows up at the apartment or your father's house, I won't be seeing her either."

"I still don't think you should go."

"You have to lighten up a little bit." I sigh, resetting the bun in my hair.

"Lighten up?" he says derisively, as if the idea has never occurred to him.

"Yes, lighten up. You can't control everything."

His head snaps up. "I 'can't control everything'? This is coming from *you*, of all people?"

I laugh. "I'm just saying. I'm giving you the Zed thing because I know it's wrong, but you can't keep me from the entire town because you're worried that I might see him or some unpleasant girl."

"Are you done?" Hardin asks, leaning against the sink.

"With the argument or my hair?" I smirk at him.

"You're annoying." He smiles back at me and slaps my behind as I move around him to exit the bathroom.

I'm glad he's being somewhat playful. That bodes well for the night.

As we cross the hallway to my room, Christian calls up from the living room, "Hardin—you here still? You coming to listen to some jazz? It's not heavy metal or whatever, but . . ."

I don't hear the rest of his words because I'm busy laughing at the impromptu Christian Vance impersonation Hardin is doing. Pushing his chest lightly, I say, "Go see him. I'll be right out."

Back in my room, I grab my purse and check my cell phone. I have got to call my mother soon; I keep putting it off, and she won't stop calling. I have a message from Zed as well.

Please don't be upset with me about tonight. I was a jerk and I didn't mean to be. Sorry.

I delete the message and stick my phone back into my purse. My friendship with Zed has to end now. I've been leading him on for too long, and every time I say goodbye to him I end up backtracking and make the situation worse by seeing him again. It's not fair to him or to Hardin. Hardin and I have enough problems as it is. It bothers me as a woman that Hardin tries to forbid me from seeing Zed, but I can't deny that I'm being a huge hypocrite if I continue hanging out with him. I would never want Hardin to be friends with Molly and spend time with her alone—the thought itself makes me nauseous. Zed has made his feelings for me very clear, and it's not fair to anyone if I let the situation with him linger and tacitly encourage him. Zed is kind to me, and he's been there for me a lot, but I hate the way that I always feel like I have to explain myself to him and defend my relationship.

Enjoying the fantasy of a great night out with my guy, I descend the stairs . . . and am surprised that when I enter the living room, Hardin is standing there with his hands in his hair, looking exasperated.

"Hell no!" he huffs, backing away from Christian.

"Bloodstained jeans and that dirty shirt aren't appropriate attire in the club, regardless of your connections to the owner," Christian says, pushing some sort of black fabric to Hardin's chest.

"I'm not going, then." Hardin pouts, letting the garment fall to the floor at Christian's feet.

"Don't be a baby, just put the damn shirt on."

"If I wear the shirt, I'm keeping the jeans on," Hardin says, negotiating, and looking to me for support.

"Didn't you bring any clothes that don't have blood on them?" Christian smiles, then bends down to pick up the shirt.

"You can wear your black jeans, Hardin," I suggest in an effort to mediate between the two men.

"Fine, give me the fucking shirt, then." Hardin snatches the shirt from Christian's hands and lifts his middle finger to him as he stalks down the hallway.

"Maybe a haircut, too," Christian shouts after him teasingly, and I can't help but laugh.

"Oh, would you leave him alone already. I won't stop him from giving you a black eye," Kimberly jokes.

"Yeah . . . yeah . . ." Christian pulls her into his arms and kisses her mouth.

I turn away just as the doorbell rings.

"That will be Lillian!" Kim announces while wiggling out of Christian's embrace.

Hardin walks out into the living room as Lillian comes through the front door. "Why is she here?" he groans. He's put on the black button-down shirt, which doesn't look bad on him.

"Don't be mean. She babysits Smith, and she's your friend, remember?" I say. My first impression of Lillian wasn't a good one, but I've grown to like the girl, even though I haven't seen her since we got home from the Vacation from Hell.

"No, she's not."

"Tessa! Hardin!" Lillian exclaims, her bright blue eyes beaming and her smile bright. I'm thankful that she's not wearing the same dress I am, like she was the first time I met her, at the restaurant in Sand Point.

"Hey." I smile back, and Hardin curtly nods.

"You look great," she compliments, looking me up and down.

"Thanks—so do you." She's dressed in a simple cardigan and khaki pants.

"Okay, if you both are done . . ." Hardin complains.

"Nice to see you, too, Hardin." Lillian rolls her eyes at him, and he slightly softens, offering her a half smile.

Meanwhile, Kimberly is rushing around the living room, putting on her heels and checking her makeup in the large mirror above the couch. "Smith is upstairs. We shouldn't be gone any later than midnight."

"Ready, love?" Christian asks her. And when she nods yes, he spreads his arms wide and gestures to the door.

"We're driving separately," Hardin announces.

"Why? We have a driver for tonight," Christian says.

"I want to drive myself in case we want to leave."

Christian shrugs. "Suit yourself."

As we head out, I get a better look at Hardin's shirt, which is not unlike the one he usually wears when he's forced to dress up. The difference here, however, is that this shirt is covered with a faint, barely noticeable animal print . . .

"Don't say a word," Hardin warns me when he notices me staring.

"I'm not." I bite my lip, and he groans.

"It's hideous," he says, and I giggle the entire way to the car.

THE JAZZ CLUB is centrally located in downtown Seattle. The streets are full of people, as if it were a Saturday night instead of

Wednesday. We wait inside Hardin's car until a sleek black town car pulls up next to us and Kimberly and Christian step out.

"Rich bastard," Hardin says, squeezing my thigh before we get out ourselves.

With a brisk smile, the bald bouncer unhooks the velvet rope from the silver stand and lets us by. Moments later, Kimberly is leading us through the dark club, showing off various features of the place while Christian wanders off by himself. Blocks of gray stone serve as tables, and there are groups of black couches accented with white cushions. The only color in the entire club comes from the bouquets of red roses that are sitting atop each massive stone. The soft music playing through the club is relaxing yet stimulating at the same time.

"Fancy." Hardin rolls his eyes. He looks painfully beautiful under the dim lights. Christian's printed button-down shirt paired with the black jeans make for a deadly attack on my libido.

"It's nice, right?" Kimberly turns around, beaming.

"Sure, sure," Hardin replies. The moment we get near the crowded tables, Hardin's arm wraps around my hips, pulling me closer to him as we walk.

"Christian is in the VIP section. We have it to ourselves," Kimberly informs us.

We walk to the back of the club, and a satin curtain is pulled open to reveal a moderate-sized space with more black curtains serving as walls. Four couches form the perimeter of the room, and a large stone rests in the center, covered with bottles of alcohol, a bowl of ice, and various finger foods.

I'm so distracted I almost miss seeing Max sitting on one of the couches, across from Christian.

Great. Max rubs me the wrong way, and I know Hardin doesn't care for him either. Hardin's arm tightens around me again, and he shoots a glare toward Christian.

Kimberly smiles, ever the perfect hostess. "Nice to see you again, Max."

Max grins. "You, too, dear." He takes her hand in his and lifts it to his lips.

"Excuse me." A woman's voice sounds behind me. Hardin and I step to the side, and Sasha prances through the small space. Her intimidating height and barely-there white dress help her claim the entire room.

"Great," Hardin says, echoing my thought from seconds ago. He's about as happy to see her as I am to see Max.

"Sasha." Kimberly tries to appear pleased to see the woman but fails. One of the flaws of Kim's genuine openness and honesty is that it's hard for her to hide her emotions.

Sasha smiles warmly at her and takes a seat on the couch, next to Max. His dark eyes meet mine as if he's asking me for permission to sit with his mistress. I look away as Hardin guides me to the couch directly across from them. Kimberly takes a seat on Christian's lap and leans forward to grab a bottle of champagne.

"What do you think of the place, Theresa?" Max asks with his smooth, heavy accent.

"Um." I stutter at the use of my full name. "I-it's nice."

"Would you two like some champagne?" Kimberly offers.

Hardin answers for me. "I wouldn't, but Tessa would."

I lean into his shoulder. "If you aren't drinking, I probably shouldn't either."

"Go ahead, I don't mind. I just don't want any."

I smile at Kim. "I'm okay; thank you, though."

Hardin frowns and takes a full glass from the table. "You should have some, you've had a long day."

"You only want me to drink so I don't ask you questions," I whisper, rolling my eyes as I do so.

"No." He smiles, amused. "I just want you to have a nice time out. That's what you wanted, right?"

"I don't have to drink to have a nice time." When I glance around the room, I can see that none of our company is paying any attention to our conversation.

"I never said that you did. I'm only saying, your friend is offering you free champagne that probably cost more than your entire outfit and mine put together." His fingertips dance along the nape of my neck. "So why not enjoy a glass?"

"Good point." I lean into him again, and he hands me the long-stemmed glass. "But I'm only having one," I say.

Thirty minutes later I've just polished off my second glass and am contemplating a third in an attempt to not feel uncomfortable while I watch Sasha parading around the small space. She claims she just wants to dance, but if that were truly the case, she could go out to the public area of the club and dance there.

Attention whore.

I cover my mouth as if I've said the words out loud.

"What?" Hardin, I can see, is bored. Very bored. I can tell by the way he's staring at the black curtain and his hand is dragging lazily up and down my back.

I shake my head in a silent response. I shouldn't be thinking those things about the woman when I don't even know her. All I know about her is that she's sleeping with a married man . . .

That's probably enough to know. I can't help but dislike her.

"Can we go now?" Hardin whispers into my neck and brings his other hand to my thigh.

"Just a little longer," I say to him. I'm not necessarily bored, but I would rather be spending one-on-one time with Hardin than avoiding eye contact with Sasha or her nearly exposed underwear.

"Tessa, come dance . . . ?" Kimberly suggests, and Hardin tenses.

My thoughts flash back to the last time I went out to a nightclub with Kimberly. I danced with a guy just to spite Hardin, even though he was miles away. I was so heartbroken then, so sad, that I could barely think straight. That guy ended up kissing me, and I ended up completely molesting Hardin in my hotel room after he found Trevor there. It was a huge misunderstanding, but when I think back, the night ended pretty well for me.

"I don't really dance, remember?" I say.

"Well, come do a lap or something." She smiles. "You look like you're falling asleep."

"Okay, a lap," I agree and rise to my feet. "Are you coming?" I ask Hardin, who shakes his head.

"She'll be fine; we'll only be gone a minute," Kimberly assures him.

He doesn't look pleased about her stealing me away, but doesn't try to stop her. He's trying to show me that he can lighten up, and I love him for it.

"If you lose her, don't bother coming back," he says.

Kimberly bursts into laughter and drags me through the curtains and into the crowded club.

chapter one hundred and fifteen

HARDIN

Max sidles up to me and asks, "Where do you suppose she took Theresa off to?"

"*Tessa,*" I correct him. How the fuck does he even know her name is Theresa? Okay, maybe it's a little obvious that's her full name, but I don't like his saying it.

"Tessa." He smiles and takes a long sip of champagne. "She's a lovely girl."

I reach for a bottled water from the table and ignore his prodding. I have no interest in talking to the man. I should've gone with Tessa and Kimberly, wherever they went. I try to show Tessa that I can "lighten up," and this is where it gets me. Sitting next to this guy in a club with shitty music.

"I'll be back in a second; the band just arrived," Christian informs us. He tucks his cell phone into his dress slacks and wanders off. Max stands and follows him, giving his date instructions to enjoy herself, to have more champagne.

They aren't seriously leaving me alone in here with this chick . . .

"Looks like it's just us two," this Stacey Whomever chick says to me, confirming that yes, that's exactly what they just did.

"Mm . . ." I spin the plastic cap of a water bottle across the stone table.

"So what do you think of the place? Max says it's been packed every night since the opening." She smiles at me. I pretend not to notice when she tugs at the bottom of her tiny dress to expose her cleavage . . . or lack thereof.

"It only opened a few days ago. Of course it's been packed."

"Even so, it's a nice place." She uncrosses her legs and crosses them again.

Could she be any more desperate? At this point I can't even tell if she's actually trying to come on to me or if she's just so accustomed to being a whore that it's all automatic.

She leans across the table between us. "Do you want to dance? There's room in here." Her long fingernails brush against my sleeve, and I jerk away.

"Are you out of your fucking mind?" I move to the other end of the couch. This time last year I would have taken her desperate ass into the bathroom and fucked her brains out. Now the thought makes me want to vomit on her white dress.

"What? I only asked to dance."

"Maybe dance with your married boyfriend," I snap and reach to push the curtain back, hoping to see Tessa.

"Don't be so quick to judge me. You don't even know me."

"I know enough."

"Yeah, well, I know some stuff about you, too, so if I were you, I'd watch it."

"Do you, now?" I laugh.

She narrows her eyes at me, trying to intimidate me, I'm sure. "Yes, I do."

"If you knew shit about me, you would know better than to be threatening me right now," I warn her.

She lifts a champagne flute and gives me a little salute. "You're exactly like they say . . ."

Which is my cue to leave. I push through the curtains to go find Tessa so we can get the hell out of here.

Exactly like *who* says? Who does she think she is? Christian is lucky that I promised Tessa a nice night. Otherwise, Max would have to answer for his whore's mouth.

I circle the club in search of Tessa's sparkling dress and Kimberly's bright blond hair. I'm thankful that this is not the type of place where everyone is swaying around on a dance floor; most of the patrons are seated at tables, making my search that much easier. Finally, I find them standing at the main bar, talking to Christian, Max, and some other guy. Tessa's back is toward me, but I can tell by her posture that she's nervous. Seconds later, another guy joins them, and as I get closer, the first man starts to look more and more familiar to me.

"Hardin! There you are." Kimberly reaches out her arm to touch my shoulder, but I dodge her and move to Tessa. When she turns to me, her blue-gray eyes are wary as they lead my gaze to the guest.

"Hardin, this is my teacher from World Religion, Professor Soto," she says, smiling politely.

Are you fucking kidding me? Does everyone end up making their way to Seattle?

"Jonah," he corrects her. He pushes his hand into the space between us for a handshake that I'm too thrown off to deny.

chapter
one hundred and sixteen

HARDIN

Tessa's professor smiles, checking her out fairly subtly as he does so. But I see it clearly.

"Nice to see you again," he says, but I can't tell if he's talking to me or Tessa, really, the way he moves about to the music.

"Professor Soto lives in Seattle now," Tessa informs me.

"Convenient," I say under my breath. Tessa hears me and gently nudges me with her elbow, and I wrap my arm around her waist.

Jonah's eyes briefly note where I've placed my arm, then move back up to her face. *She's taken, dick.*

"Yeah, I transferred to the Seattle campus a couple weeks ago. I applied for a job a few months back and finally got it. My band was ready for a move anyway," he tells us with an attitude that indicates he thinks we should care about any of this.

"The Reckless Few will be playing here tonight, and every other night, if we can talk them into it," Christian boasts. Jonah smiles and looks down at his boots.

"I think that might be possible," he says, looking back up with a smile. Finishing his drink in one motion, he says, "Well, we better get ready to play."

"Yeah. Don't let us keep you." Christian pats Soto on the back, and the professor turns to give Tessa one last smile before pushing through the small crowd toward the stage.

"The band is incredible; wait until you hear them!" Vance claps his hands together once before he wraps his arms around Kimberly and leads her to a table in front of the stage.

I've already heard them; they are *not* incredible.

Tessa turns to me with nervous eyes. "He's nice. Remember, he gave you a character witness when you were about to be expelled?"

"No, I don't recall anything about him, actually. Except for the fact that he seems to like you and is mysteriously living in Seattle now, teaching at your fucking campus."

"You heard him say that he applied there months ago . . . and he does not like me."

"He does."

"You think everyone likes me," she fires back. She can't possibly be naive enough to assume that this guy has good intentions.

"Shall we make a list, then? There's Zed, fucking Trevor, that dickhead of a waiter . . . who am I missing? Oh, and now we can add your creepy professor, who was just eyeing you like you were dessert." I look to where that dick is on the little bandstand, walking about with an attitude that's both self-important and fake-casual.

"Zed is the only person on that list that counts. Trevor is very sweet, and he never meant any harm. I'll probably never see Robert again, and Soto is not a stalker."

One word in that spiel doesn't sit well with me. " 'Probably'?"

"I *obviously* won't see him again. You're the one I'm with, okay?" She pushes one of her hands into mine, and I relax. I need to make sure I burned or flushed that damned waiter's phone number, just in case.

"I still think this asshole is a stalker." I nod toward the stage at the douche bag in his leather jacket. I may need to talk to my father just to make sure he isn't as shady as I think he is. Tessa would approach a lion with fucking kid gloves—she's no good at judging character.

She proves my point when she beams up at me, smiling like an idiot because of the champagne running through her veins. She's actually here with me after all the shit I've put her through . . .

"I thought this was a jazz club, but his band is more—" Tessa begins to try and take my mind off the seemingly endless list of men who want her affection.

"Shitty?" I interrupt her.

She swats my arm. "No, just not jazz music. They are more . . . like the Fray, sort of."

"The Fray? Don't go insulting your favorite band, now." The only thing I remember about the professor's band is that they fucking suck.

She bumps her shoulder against my arm. "And yours."

"Not quite."

"Don't act like you don't like them; I know you do." She squeezes my hand, and I shake my head, not denying it, really, but I'm not going to admit it either.

I stare back and forth between the wall and Tessa's tits while waiting for the godforsaken band to set up.

"Can we just go now?" I ask.

"One song." Tessa's cheeks are flushed, and her eyes are wide and glossy. She takes another drink. Her hands run over her dress, tugging it down and up at once.

"Can I at least sit down?" I nod toward line of empty stools at the bar.

I take Tessa's hand in my own and pull her to the bar. I sit on the last stool, closest to the wall and farthest from the crowd.

"What are you having?" a young man with a goatee and a fake-ass Italian accent asks us.

"A glass of champagne and a water," I say as Tessa moves to stand between my legs. I rest one hand on the small of her back, the beads of her dress rough against my palm.

"We only sell champagne by the bottle, sir." The bartender gives me an apologetic smile as if he's sure I couldn't afford a bottle of his fucking champagne.

"A bottle will be fine." Vance's voice sounds next to me, and the bartender nods, looking back and forth between the two of us.

"She'll have it chilled," I cockily remark.

The kid nods again and scurries away to fetch the bottle. *Dick.*

"Stop babysitting us," I tell Vance. Tessa scowls at me, but I ignore her.

He rolls his eyes like the sarcastic twit he is. "I'm clearly not babysitting you. She's underage."

"Yeah, yeah," I say. Someone calls his name, and he pats my shoulder before walking off.

A few moments later, the bartender pops a bottle of champagne open and pours the bubbling liquid into a glass for Tessa. She politely thanks him, and he responds with a smile even more artificial than his accent. His little pantomime of cool is killing me.

She brings the glass to her lips and rests her back against my chest. "It's so good."

Just then, two men walk by and give her a quick glance. She notices; I know she does, because she leans further into me and lays her head against my shoulder.

"There's Sasha," she says over the sound of Professor Stalker's guitar being tested on the sound equipment. The tall blonde is searching the room, either for her boyfriend or a random dude to nail.

"Who cares?" I gently grip her elbow and turn her to face me.

"I don't like her," she quietly states.

"No one does."

"You don't?" she asks.

Is she insane? "Why would I?"

"I don't know." Her eyes move to my mouth. "Because she's pretty."

"So?"

"I don't know . . . I'm just being weird." She shakes her head in an attempt to get rid of the resentment that is clear on her face.

"Are you jealous, 'Theresa'?"

"No." She pouts.

"You shouldn't be." I open my legs further and pull her against me again. *"That's* not what I want." I move my eyes to her nearly exposed chest. "You are." I trace the line of her cleavage with my index finger as if we aren't in a crowded club.

"Only for my boobs." She whispers the last word.

"Obviously." I chuckle, teasing her.

"I knew it." Tessa pretends to be offended but smiles over the rim of her glass.

"Yeah, well, now that the truth is out, you can let me fuck them," I say, much too loud.

Champagne spurts out of her mouth and onto my shirt and lap.

"Sorry!" she squeals, reaching for the napkin bin on the bar. She dabs the napkin across this fucking horrendous monstrosity of a shirt and then moves to wipe at my crotch.

I grab her wrist and take the napkin from her. "I wouldn't do that."

"Oh." Her flush spreads down her neckline.

One of the band members makes their introduction into the microphone, and I try my best not to heave when the eardrum assault begins. Tessa watches intently as they roll from one song to another, and I continue to keep her glass full.

I'm thankful for the way we're sitting. Well, the way I'm sitting. She's standing between my legs, her back toward me, but I can see her face when I slightly lean back against the bar behind me. The low red lighting in the place, the champagne, and her being . . . her, makes her glow. It's impossible not to watch her smile and stare at the stage. I can't even be jealous, because she's just that . . . beautiful.

As if she can read my mind, she turns around and gives me an eager smile. I love seeing her this way, so carefree . . . so young. I need to make her feel this way more often.

"They are good, right?" She nods along to the slow yet edgy sound.

I shrug. "No." They aren't terrible, but they sure as hell aren't good.

"Shurrrr." She exaggerates the word and turns back around. Moments later, her hips begin to sway along to the whining voice of the lead singer. *Fuck.*

I move my hand down to the curve of her hip, and she backs into me, still moving. The tempo of the song speeds up, and Tessa does the same. *Holy fuck.*

We've done a lot of shit . . . I've done a lot of shit, but I've never had anyone dance on me this way. I've had girls and even a few strippers give me a lap dance, but not like this. This is slow, intoxicating . . . and achingly fucking hot. My other hand moves to her other hip, and she turns slightly to place her glass on the bar top. With her hands empty, she gives me a salacious smile and looks back to the stage. She lifts up one hand and runs her small fingers through my hair and places the other hand on top of mine.

"Keep going," I beg.

"You sure?" She tugs at the roots of my hair.

It's hard to believe that this seductive girl, wearing a short, black dress, swaying her hips, and tugging my hair, is the same girl who spits her champagne when I talk about fucking her chest. She's such a turn-on.

"Yes, fuck," I breathe and lift a hand up to the nape of her neck, bringing her ear to my mouth. "Move against me . . ." I squeeze her hip. "Closer."

She does just that. I'm thankful for my height as I sit on the bar stool, the perfect height for her ass to move against me, hitting the exact spot that aches for her.

I pull my attention from her, only for a second, to scan our surroundings. I don't want anyone else watching her dance.

"You're so sexy right now," I say against the shell of her ear. "Dancing this way, in public . . . for me and only me." I swear I hear her moan through the music, and that's all I can take. I turn her around and push my hand under her skirt.

"Hardin." She groans when I slide her panties to the side.

"No one is paying any attention. Even if they were, they can't see," I assure her. I wouldn't be doing this if I thought anyone could possibly witness it.

"You liked putting on that show, didn't you?" I say. She can't deny it, she's soaking.

She doesn't respond; she only rests her head on my shoulder and pulls at the bottom of my shirt, fisting it in her hand like she normally would do our sheets. I pump in and out of her, trying to match the haunting melody of the song. Almost instantly, her legs are stiffening, and she's coming on my fingers. She hums, letting me know just how much pleasure I'm bringing her. She leans in further, her mouth sucking at the base of my neck. Her hips rock into me, keeping a steady beat with my fingers pumping in and out of her wet pussy. Her moans are drowned out by the music and the voices around us, and her nails could possibly be breaking the skin on my stomach.

"I'm going to," she groans into my neck.

"I know, baby. Come for me. Right here, Tessa. Come." I gently persuade her.

She nods, biting down on the tendon in my neck, and I feel

my cock pulsing, pressing against the front of my jeans. All of her weight rests on me as she orgasms, and I hold her up. She's panting, absolutely flushing, glowing under the lights, when she lifts her head.

"Car or bathroom?" she asks when I bring my fingers to my lips, sucking her sweetness from them.

"Car," I reply hastily, and she downs the last of her champagne. Vance can pay for that shit; I don't have time to hunt down the bartender.

Tessa takes my hand and drags me toward the door. She's eager, and I'm hard as fuck from her seduction game at the bar.

"Is that . . . ? " Tessa stops in her tracks near the front of the club. Black hair, styled to stick up wildly, peeks through the crowd. I would have sworn my paranoia was causing me to hallucinate if she hadn't seen him, too.

"Why the fuck is *he* here? Did you tell him you were coming to the club?" I hiss. I've kept my cool all night, only to have it sabotaged by this asshole.

"No! Of course not!" Tessa exclaims, defending herself. I can tell by her wide eyes that she's being honest.

Zed spots us, and a mischievous frown takes over his face. Being the fucking instigator that he is, he walks over to where we're standing.

"What are you doing here?" I ask him as he approaches.

"Same thing as you." He rolls his shoulders and looks at Tessa. I fight the urge to pull the top of her dress up and knock his teeth out.

"How did you know she was here?" I ask him.

Tessa tugs at my arm and looks back and forth between Zed and me.

"I didn't. I'm here to watch the band." A man with the same tanned skin as Zed joins us.

"You should go," I tell the two of them.

"Hardin, please," Tessa whines behind me.

"Don't," I whisper to her. I've had enough of Zed and his shit.

"Hey . . ." The man moves to stand between us. "They're doing another set. Let's go tell them we're here."

"You know Soto?" Tessa asks. *Dammit, Tessa.*

"Yeah, we do," the stranger says.

I can practically see the conspiracy theories floating through her mind about how these people know each other, but just wanting to be away from Zed, I take her by the arm and guide us to the door.

"See you around," Zed says, giving Tessa his best I'm-a-lost-fucking-puppy-and-I-want-you-to-feel-bad-for-me-and-love-me-because-I'm-a-pathetic-fuck smile before following the other guy toward the stage.

I rush out the door and into the cold air. Tessa follows closely behind, insisting, "I didn't know he was coming here! I swear."

I unlock the car and open the passenger door for her. "I know, I know," I say to silence her. I'm trying my best to talk myself down from going back inside. "Drop it. Please. I don't want to ruin the night." I walk around to the other side of the car and slide in next to her.

"Okay," she agrees, nodding.

"Thank you." I sigh. I slip the key into the ignition, and Tessa puts her hand on my cheek to turn my head toward her.

"I really appreciate you making such an effort tonight. I know it's hard for you, but it means the world to me." As she utters her words of praise, I smile against her palm.

"Okay."

"I mean it. I love you, Hardin. So much."

I tell her how much I love her while she climbs across the console and straddles my lap. Her hands are quick to undo my jeans and tug them down just enough . . . her mouth is quick against my neck, and she pulls at my shirt, popping the top two buttons off in a rushed attempt to gain access to my chest. I push her dress up to expose her tight little body to me, and she digs into my back pocket to retrieve the condom that I suspected I would need.

"I only want you, always," she reassures me, calming my racing mind as she slides the condom onto me. I grip her hips and help lift her body. In the small space of the car it feels closer, deeper, as she lowers herself onto me. As I fill her, completely and possessively, a low hiss escapes my mouth. She covers my lips, swallowing my moans as she moves her hips slowly, the way she did in the club.

"It's so fucking deep this way," I say, taking her bun in my hand and tugging gently to force her to look at me.

"So *good,"* she groans, taking me inside her, feeling every inch of me. One of her hands moves to my hair while the other rests at the base of my throat. She's so fucking sexy this way, when alcohol is laced with adrenaline and she's full of hunger and need—need for me, for my body, for this raw passionate connection that only we share. She couldn't find this with anyone else, and neither could I. I have everything I need here with her, and she can't ever leave me.

"Fuck, I love you," I breathe into her mouth as she tugs at my hair and her fingers tighten on my neck. It's not uncomfortable, it's fairly light pressure, but it's driving me fucking insane.

"I love you," she gasps when I lift my hips to meet her, thrusting harder than before. I stare at her and revel in the sensation of her flexing her hips. The slow building of pleasure begins at the base of my spine, and I can feel Tessa tensing as I continue to aid her by lifting my hips with each thrust.

She has got to get on the pill. I need to feel her skin-to-skin again.

"I can't wait to be inside you without a condom . . ." I say into her neck.

"Keep going," she urges me. She loves my dirty mouth.

"I want you to feel me come inside you . . ." I suck at the salty skin of her collarbone, tasting the thin layer of sweat there. "You'll fucking love it, won't you? Me marking you that way?" The thought alone pushes me over the edge.

"I'm almost . . ." she moans, and with one harsh tug at my hair, we ride out our highs together, panting, and moaning, and messy, and us.

I help her off of my lap and roll down the window while she adjusts her dress.

"What are you—" she begins, and I toss the condom out the window. "You did not just throw a dirty condom out of the window! What if Christian sees it?"

I smile evilly at her. "I'm sure it won't be the only condom he finds in this lot."

Her hands fumble with my zipper, helping me dress again so I can drive. "Maybe not." She scrunches her nose and looks out the window as I put the car into gear.

"It smells like sex in here," she adds and bursts into laughter.

I nod and listen to her hum along to every single fucking song on the radio as we drive back to Vance's place. I almost tease her for it, but it's actually sort of a lovely sound, especially after listening to that shitty-shitty band play.

Lovely sound? I'm even starting to talk like her.

"I'm going to have to physically remove my eardrums after tonight," I remark as she carries on. She sticks her tongue out at me like a child and sings even louder.

I TAKE TESSA' S HAND in mine to steady her as we walk up to the driveway en route to the front door. The way she's acting, I'm guessing most of that champagne finally hit her liver.

"What if we're locked out?" she asks with a giggle when we reach the driveway.

"The babysitter is here," I remind her.

"Oh yeah! Lillian . . ." She smiles. "She's so nice."

I grin at the level of her intoxication. "I thought you didn't like her."

"I do, now that I know she doesn't like you the way you led me to believe she did."

I touch her lips. "Don't pout. She's a lot like you . . . only more annoying."

"Excuse me?" She hiccups. "That wasn't very nice of you to make me jealous of her."

"It worked, didn't it?" I reply smugly as we reach the door.

Lillian is seated alone on the couch when we enter the house. I take a moment to pull the front of Tessa's dress up a little. She rolls her eyes at me.

Seeing us, Lillian stands to her feet. "How was it?"

"It was so, *so* much fun! The band was great!" Tessa beams.

"She's wasted," I inform Lillian.

She laughs. "I can see that." After a pause, she says, "Smith is asleep. He almost had a conversation with me tonight."

"Good for you," I say and lead Tessa toward the hall.

My drunk girlfriend waves at Lillian. "It was nice seeing you!"

I don't know if I should tell Lillian to leave now or wait until Vance shows up, so I don't say anything. Besides, let her deal with that little robot kid if he wakes up.

When we get to Tessa's room, I close the door behind us, and she immediately plops onto the bed. "Can you take this off?" She points to her dress. "It's so itchy."

"Yeah, stand up." I help her out of her dress, and she thanks me with a kiss on the tip of my nose. It's a simple gesture, but it catches me off guard, and I smile at her.

"I'm so glad you're here with me," she says.

"Are you?"

She nods and undoes the remainder of the buttons left on

Christian's shirt. Her hands push the garment down my arms, and she folds it neatly before walking to the hamper. I'll never understand why she folds dirty clothes, but I'm used to it by now.

"Yes, very. Seattle isn't as great as I thought," she finally admits.

Then come back with me, I want to say.

"Why not?" I say instead.

"I don't know. It's just not." She frowns, and I'm surprised that instead of wanting to hear how miserable she is here, I want to change the subject. Landon and I both suspected she felt this way; but still it makes me feel bad that it's not exactly what she'd wanted. I should take her out tomorrow during the day to cheer her up.

"You could move to England," I say.

She glares at me with red cheeks and champagne-glazed eyes. "You won't take me there for a wedding, but you want me to move there," she says, calling me out.

"We'll talk about it later," I say, hoping she'll drop it right now.

"Yeah . . . yeah . . . always later." She walks back to sit on the bed but misses completely. Her body rolls onto the floor, and she bursts into a fit of laughter.

"Christ, Tessa." I grab hold of her hand and help her to her feet, my heart pounding in my chest.

"I'm fine." She laughs and sits down on the bed, pulling me with her.

"I gave you too much champagne."

"Yep, you did." She smiles and pushes my shoulders back until I'm flat on the mattress.

"Are you okay? Do you feel sick?"

She rests her head against my chest. "Stop parenting me, I'm fine." I bite my tongue instead of mouthing off to her.

"What do you want to do?" she asks quietly.

"What?"

"I'm bored." She looks up at me with that look. Tessa lifts herself up and stares down at me, eyes wild.

"What would you like to do, drunk ass?"

"Pull your hair." She grins and pulls her bottom lip between her teeth in the most sinful way.

chapter
one hundred and seventeen

HARDIN

"Can't sleep?" Christian turns on the overhead light and joins me in the kitchen.

"Tessa needed some water," I tell him. I push the refrigerator door closed, but he stops it with his hand.

"Kim, too. The price of drinking too much champagne," he says from behind me.

Tessa's endless giggles and insatiable appetite for pleasure have worn me out. I'm convinced she'll be vomiting soon if she doesn't drink some water. Visions of her tonight, lying back on the bed, her legs spread for me as I brought her to orgasm using both my fingers and my tongue, flash through my mind. She was amazing, as she always was when she rode my cock until I emptied myself into a condom.

"Yeah, Tessa's a mess." I bite back a smile while remembering her tumble off the bed.

"So . . . England next weekend, then?" He changes the subject.

"Nah, I'm not going."

"This is your mum's wedding we're talking about."

"And? It's not her first, probably won't be the last," I say.

To say I'm completely shocked when his hand reaches out and knocks the bottled water from my hand would be an understatement.

"What the fuck?" I exclaim and bend down to grab the bottle.

When I stand back up, Vance's eyes are focused on me, and the look in them is intense. "You have no right to speak of your mum that way."

"What does it matter to you? I don't want to go, and I'm not going to."

"Give me a reason, a real one," he challenges me.

What the fuck is his problem? "I don't need to give anyone a reason. I just don't want to go to a stupid wedding. I've already been dragged to one this season, and that was enough for me."

"Fine. I've already sent in for Tessa's passport, so I assume you'll be fine without her while she enjoys visiting England for the first time as Kim's companion?"

I drop the bottle to the floor. It can stay there this time.

"You what?" I stare at him. He's fucking with me—he has to be.

He leans against the island and crosses his arms. "I sent in her application and paid for it the moment I found out about the wedding. She'll have to go downtown to finalize it and get her picture taken, but I've done the rest."

I'm fuming. I can feel myself heating up. "Why would you even do that? That's not even *legal.*" Like I give a fuck if it's legal . . .

"Because I knew you'd be a stubborn asshole about the entire thing, and I also knew that she was the only shot I had to get you to go. This is important to your mum, and she's been worried that you won't go."

"She's right to be worried. You two think you can use Tessa to bully me into going to fucking England? Fuck both you and my mum." I open his refrigerator to grab another bottle of water just to be a dick, but he kicks it closed with his foot.

"Look, I know you've had a shit life, okay? So did I, so I get it. But you won't be talking to me the way you talk to your parents."

"Then stop trying to meddle in my goddamned life the way they do."

"I'm not meddling. You know damn well that Tessa would love to go to that wedding, and you also know that you'll feel like an asshole if you deprive her of the opportunity for your own selfish reasons. You may as well get over being mad at me and thank me for making your week much easier."

I stare at him for a few moments to take in what he is saying. He's half right: I've already started to feel bad for not wanting to go to the wedding. The only reason being that I know how much Tessa would love to go. She's already pouted about it enough tonight, and it's been wearing on my mind.

"I'll take your silence as a thank-you." Vance smirks, and I roll my eyes.

"I don't want this to become a thing."

"What? The wedding?"

"Yeah. How can I take her to another wedding and watch her eyes get all doelike and watery only to have to remind her that she won't ever have that?"

Christian's fingers tap against his chin. "Ahh, I see." His smile grows. "That's what this is about, then? You don't want her getting any ideas?"

"No. She already has the ideas. The woman's mind is full of ideas—that's the problem."

"Why would it be a problem? You don't want her to make an honest man out of you?" Though he's taunting me, I'm glad to see that he isn't holding a grudge against me for my rude remarks only minutes ago. This is why I sort of like Vance: he's not as touchy as my father.

"Because it's not going to happen, and she's one of those crazy women who bring the shit up like a month after dating. She literally broke up with me because I said I wouldn't marry her. She's batshit crazy sometimes."

Vance chuckles and takes a sip of the water meant for his Kimberly. Tessa is waiting on me to bring her water, too; I need to tie this conversation up. It's already been too long, too personal, for my liking.

"Consider yourself lucky that she wants that with you. You aren't exactly the easiest guy to be around. And if anyone knows that, it's her."

I begin to ask him what the fuck he even knows about my relationship, but then I quickly remember that he's engaged to the biggest mouth in Seattle. Scratch that, the entire state of Washington . . . perhaps even the entire United States of—

"Am I right?" He interrupts my thoughts about his obnoxious woman.

"Yes, but still. It's ridiculous to think about marriage at all, especially when she's not even twenty."

"This is coming from the man who doesn't want her more than three feet away from him at any given time?"

"Asshole," I gripe.

"It's true."

"Doesn't mean you're not an asshole."

"Perhaps. I do find it amusing, though, that you don't intend on marrying her but you can't seem to control your temper or anxiety when it comes to losing her."

"What's that supposed to mean?" I don't think I want to know the answer to this question, but it's too late now.

Vance's eyes meet mine. "Your anxiety . . . it's at its highest when you're worried about her leaving you or when another man pays any attention to her."

"Who says I have anxie—"

But the stubborn goat ignores me and continues on. "You know what helps a hell of a lot when it comes to both of those things?"

"What's that?"

"A ring." He holds up his hand and touches the bare finger where a wedding band will soon rest.

"Oh my fuck—she's gotten to you, too! What did she do, pay you off?" I laugh at the idea. It's not exactly too far-fetched, considering Tessa's obsession with marriage and her charm.

"No, you twat!" He throws the cap of the water bottle at me. "It's the truth. Imagine being able to say she's yours and have it be true. Now it's only words, an empty boast to other men who will want her—and trust me, they will—but when Tessa's your wife, it's real. That's when it's fucking real, and it couldn't be more satisfying, especially for overly paranoid men like you and me."

My mouth is dry by the end of his speech, and I want to high-tail it out of this excessively bright kitchen. "That's a load of shit." The words rush from my mouth.

He walks over and opens a cabinet while talking. "Have you ever watched that show *Sex and the City*?"

"No."

"*Sex in the City, Sex and the City*—I don't remember."

"No, no, and no," I respond.

"Kim watches it all the time; she has every season on DVD." Christian tears open a box of cookies.

It's two in the morning. Tessa is waiting for me, and here I am talking about some shit show. "Okay?"

"There's this episode where the women are talking about how you only get two great loves in your life—"

"Okay . . . okay. This is getting too fucking weird," I say, turning to go. "Tessa is waiting for me."

"I know . . . I know . . . let me finish really quick. I'll sum it up for you in the most masculine way possible."

I turn back to find him looking at me expectantly, so I nod hesitantly.

"So they were saying that you only get two great loves in your entire life. My point is . . . well, I have sort of lost my point, but I know that Tessa's your great love."

I'm lost. "You said we get two?"

"Well, for you, the other is your own self." He snorts. "I thought that was obvious."

I raise a brow. "And yours were who? Bigmouth and Smith's mum?"

"Watch it . . ." he warns.

"Sorry, Kimberly and Rose." I roll my eyes again. "They were yours? You better hope those broads on that show were wrong."

"Uhh, yes. Those two were m-mine," he stutters. An emotion flashes across his face, but it disappears before I can really nail down what it was.

Tipping the water bottle to him, I say, "Well, now that you've made no point whatsoever, I'm going to bed."

"Yeah . . ." he says, slightly flustered. "I don't even know what I'm going on about. I drank too much tonight."

"Yeah . . . okay." I leave him alone in the kitchen. I don't know what the hell that was all about, but it was odd seeing the one and only Christian Vance at a loss for words.

By the time I get back to the room, Tessa is asleep on her side. Her hands are resting under her cheek, and her knees are tucked up against her body.

I flick the light off and set her water bottle on the nightstand before climbing into bed behind her. Her naked body is warm to my touch, and I can't help but shiver as the tracing of my fingertips causes small goose bumps to rise on her skin. They comfort me, reminding me that my touch, even in her sleep, awakens something in her.

"Hey," she whispers sleepily.

I jump slightly at her voice and nuzzle my head in her neck, pulling her closer to me. "We're going to England next weekend," I tell her.

She quickly turns her head to look behind her. The room is pretty dark, but there's enough moonlight for me to see the shock on her face. "What?"

"England. Next weekend. You and me."

"But—"

"No. You're going. And I know you want to go, so don't try to argue about it."

"You don't have—"

"Theresa. Let it go." I press my hand over her mouth, and she uses her teeth to softly nip at the skin of my palm. "Are you going to be a good girl and keep quiet if I move my hand?" I tease her, thinking back to her earlier accusation that I was parenting her.

She nods her head, and I let her go. She lifts herself up onto her elbow and turns to face me. I can't possibly hold a conversation with her when she's naked and feisty.

"But I don't have a passport!" she cries out, and I hide my smile. I knew she wasn't done.

"It's already in the works. We'll figure the rest out tomorrow."

"But—"

"Theresa . . ."

"Two times in one minute? Uh-oh." She grins.

"You're never drinking champagne again." I push her messy hair away from her eyes and trace the shape of her bottom lip with my thumb.

"You certainly weren't complaining earlier when I was—"

I silence her drunken mouth by pressing my lips against hers. I love her so much, so fucking much that it frightens me to think about losing her.

Do I really want to mix her—my potential future, the only shot I have at a decent one—with my wicked past?

chapter one hundred and eighteen

TESSA

When I wake up, Hardin isn't draped over me, and the room is too bright even when I close my eyes again. Keeping them closed, I groan, "What time is it?"

My head is throbbing, and even though I know I'm lying down, my body feels like it's swaying back and forth.

"Noon," Hardin's deep voice says from across the room.

"Noon! I missed my first two classes!" I try to sit up, but my head spins. I fall back onto the mattress with a whimper.

"You're fine; go back to sleep."

"No! I can't miss any more classes, Hardin. I just started classes at this campus, and I can't begin this way." I begin to panic. "I'm going to be so behind."

"I'm sure you'll be fine," Hardin says with a shrug, crossing the room to sit on the bed. "You probably already have the assignments completed anyway."

He knows me too well. "That's not the point. The point is that I missed the lecture, and it makes me look bad."

"To whom?" Hardin asks. I know he is mocking me.

"To my professors, my classmates."

"Tessa, I love you, but come on. Your classmates couldn't give less of a fuck if you're there or not. They probably didn't even notice. Your professors, yeah, because you're a suck-up and they like the ego boosts your fawning gives them. But your classmates don't care, and if they do, then so what? Their opinion doesn't fucking matter."

"I guess." I close my eyes and try to see his point. I hate being late, missing classes, sleeping until noon. "I'm not a suck-up," I add.

"How are you feeling?" I feel the mattress shift, and when I open my eyes he's lying next to me.

"Like I had too much to drink last night." My skull is ready to explode.

"You certainly did." He nods several times, very seriously. "How's your ass feeling?" His hand grips my behind, and I wince.

"We didn't . . ." *I wasn't* that *intoxicated . . . was I?*

"No." He chuckles, kneading the skin with his hand. His eyes meet mine. "Not yet."

I gulp.

"Only if you want to. You've turned into a fucking vixen, so I assumed that would be next on your list."

Me, a vixen?

"Don't look so frightened, it was only a suggestion." He smiles at me.

I can't decide how I feel about doing that . . . and I certainly can't keep up or process this type of conversation right now.

But my curiosity gets the best of me.

"Have you . . ." I don't know how to ask the question—this is one of the few things we've never discussed; him saying dirty things about doing it to me in the heat of the moment doesn't count. "Have *you* done that before?"

I search his face for the answer.

"No, actually, I haven't."

"Oh." I'm too aware of his fingers tapping along the bare skin where the line of my panties would be, were I wearing any. The fact that Hardin has never experienced that before makes me want to do it, sort of.

"What are you thinking? I see those wheels turning." He nudges my nose with his, and I smile under his stare.

"I like that you haven't done . . . it before . . ."

"Why?" His brow raises, and I hide my face.

"I don't know." I'm suddenly shy. I don't want to sound insecure or start a fight. I already have a hangover.

"Tell me," he demands softly.

"I don't know. It would just be nice to be your first for something."

He lifts himself up on his elbow and looks down at me. "What do you mean?"

"I just mean that you've done a lot of stuff . . . you know, sexually . . ." I quietly explain. "And I haven't given you any new experiences."

He eyes me carefully, as if he's afraid to reply. "That's not true."

"It is, though." I'm pouting again.

"Like hell it is. That's bullshit, and you know it." His voice is practically a growl, and he's scowling deeply.

"Don't snap at me—how do you think I feel that you haven't been with only me?" I say. The reminder doesn't come as often as it once did, but when it does, it stings terribly.

He winces and gently tugs at both of my arms to pull me to sit up next to him. "Come here." I feel myself being lifted onto his lap; his half-naked body is warm and welcoming underneath my completely bare skin.

"I didn't think of it that way," he says into my shoulder, making me shudder. "If you had been with anyone else, I wouldn't be with you now."

My head snaps back to look at him. "Excuse me?"

"You heard me." He kisses the curve of my shoulder.

"That's not a very nice thing to say." I'm used to Hardin's unfiltered mouth, but these words surprise me. He can't mean them.

"I never claimed to be nice."

I shift my body on his lap and ignore the groan deep in his throat. "You're being serious?"

"Very." He nods.

"So you're telling me if I hadn't been a virgin, you wouldn't have dated me?" This topic isn't one we typically discuss, and I'm nervous to find out where it will lead.

His eyes narrow as he regards my expression before muttering, "That's exactly what I'm saying. If you recall, I didn't really want to date you anyway." He grins, but I scowl.

I press my feet to the floor to lift myself off of his lap, but he holds me in place. "Don't pout," he coaxes and attempts to press his lips against mine, but I quickly turn my head.

I glare at him. "Maybe you *shouldn't* have dated me, then." I feel overly sensitive, and my feelings are hurt.

I add gasoline to the fire and wait for the explosion: "Maybe you should have just ended it after you won the bet."

I stare into his green eyes, waiting for a reaction. Still, it doesn't come. He throws his back in laughter, and my favorite sound fills the room.

"Don't be such a baby," Hardin says and hugs me tighter, taking both of my wrists in one hand to prevent me from wiggling off his lap. "Just because I didn't want to date you in the beginning doesn't mean that I'm not glad I am."

"It's still not nice to say, and you said you wouldn't be with me now if I'd been with someone else. So if I had slept with Noah before I met you, you wouldn't have dated me?"

He flinches at the words. "No. I wouldn't have. We wouldn't have been in that . . . situation . . . if you weren't a virgin." He's treading lightly now. Good.

" 'Situation,' " I repeat, still irritated. It comes out harsher than I intended.

"Yes, situation." He abruptly turns me around and lays me

back against the mattress. He moves his body on top of mine and pins my wrists up over my head using only one hand and his knees to push open my thighs. "I wouldn't be able to stand it if you'd been touched by another man. I know it's fucking crazy, but that's the damn truth, whether you want to hear it or not."

His breath is warm against my face, coming out in hot puffs. Momentarily I forget why I'm annoyed with him. He's being honest, I'll give him that, but it's an obnoxious double standard that he's describing.

"Whatever."

" 'Whatever'?" He chuckles, tightening his hand around my wrists. He flexes his hips, pressing his boxer-clad body between my thighs. "Stop being ridiculous, you know how I am." I feel so exposed right now, and his dominating behavior is turning me on more than it should.

He continues. "And you know you've given me new experiences. I've never loved anyone, romantically, or even family, really . . ." His eyes drift off to ponder what I guess is a painful memory, but then he quickly returns to me. "And I've never lived with anyone. I never gave a fuck about losing anyone before, but when it comes to you, I wouldn't survive it. That's a new experience." His lips ghost over mine. "Is that enough 'new experience' for you?"

I nod, and he smiles. If I lift my head up just a centimeter, my lips will touch his. He seems to read my thoughts and pulls his head back a bit. "And don't throw that bet shit in my face again," he threatens, rubbing himself against me. A treacherous moan escapes his mouth, and his eyes darken. "Got it?"

"Sure." I defiantly roll my eyes at him, and he frees my wrists, running his hand down my body, stopping on my hip and squeezing gently.

"You're being a brat today." He draws circles on my hip, putting more weight on my body.

I feel like a brat today; I'm hungover and hormonal. "You're being an ass, so I guess we're even," I fire back.

He bites the inside of his cheek, then dips his head down to me. Hardin's lips are warm as he kisses me along my jawline, sending a direct line of electricity to my groin. I wrap my legs around his waist and close the small space that's left between our bodies.

"I've only loved you," he reminds me again, soothing the small ache from his earlier words. His lips reach the base of my neck, and one of his hands cups my breast while he uses the other to hold his body up. "I'll always only love you."

I don't speak. I don't want to ruin this moment. I love when he's candid about his feelings for me, and for once I can see this all in a new light. Steph, Molly, and half of the dang campus of WCU may have fooled around with Hardin, but none of them, not one single girl, has ever gotten to hear him say "I love you." They haven't had, and will never have, the privilege of knowing him, the real him, the way that I do. They have no idea how wonderful and incredibly brilliant he is. They don't get to hear him laugh and watch his eyes screw shut and his dimples pop. They'll never get to hear the snippets of his life or hear the conviction in his voice when he swears that he loves me more than breathing. And for that, I pity them.

"I've only loved you," I tell him in return. The love I had for Noah wasn't anything beyond family. I know that now. I love Hardin in that all-consuming, incredible way that I know, deep down, I will never feel again.

I feel Hardin's hand move to his boxers. He tugs them down, and I use my feet to help him get rid of them. In a gentle motion, he slides into me, crying out as he plunges through the slick opening.

"Again," he begs.

"I've only loved you," I repeat.

"Fucking Christ, Tess, I love you so much." The words are a raw confession as they push through his gritted mouth.

"I will always only love you," I promise him. I send a silent prayer that we'll find a way to work through all of our problems, because I know what I just said is true. It will always be him. Even if something drove us apart.

Hardin's thrusts are deep, filling and claiming me as he bites and sucks at the skin on my neck with his warm, wet mouth.

"I can feel you, every single inch . . . you're so fucking warm . . ." he groans, making it known that he hasn't put a condom on. Even through the euphoric trance, warning bells go off in my head. I blink the sensation away and revel in the feeling of Hardin's strong muscles straining under my hands as I run my hands over his broad shoulders and inked arms.

"You have to put one on," I say, though my actions are the opposite of my words; I tighten my legs around his waist, drawing him deeper. My stomach begins to coil, tightening . . .

"I . . . can't stop . . ." His pace quickens, and I think I'll snap in two if he stops now.

"Don't, then." We're both insane, not thinking clearly, but I can't stop raking my nails down his back, encouraging him.

"Fuck, come, Tessa," he instructs me as if I have a choice. As I reach the brink of orgasm, I'm afraid I may pass out from the amount of pleasure I feel when his teeth graze across my chest, tugging, marking me there. With another groan of my name and a declaration of his love for me, Hardin halts his movements, and he pulls himself out of me, releasing himself onto the bare skin of my stomach. I watch in awe as he touches himself, marking me in the most possessive way while never breaking eye contact.

He collapses onto me, shaking and out of breath. We lie in silence, neither of us needing to speak to know what the other is thinking.

* * *

"WHERE DO YOU want to go?" I ask him. I don't even want to leave the bed, but Hardin offering to take me out in Seattle, during the day, is something that hasn't happened in the past, and I'm not sure if or when it will happen again.

"I don't give a shit, really. Maybe, like, shopping?" His eyes roam my face. "Do you need to go shopping? Or want to?"

"I don't really need anything . . ." I answer. When I look up and see how nervous he looks lying there next to me, I backtrack. "Yeah, sure. Shopping is fine."

He's making such an effort. Simple things that couples usually do are completely out of Hardin's comfort zone. I smile at him, remembering the night he took me ice skating to prove that he could, in fact, be a regular boyfriend.

It was so much fun, and he was so charming and playful, much like he's been the past week and a half. I don't want a "regular" boyfriend—I want Hardin, with his crude humor and sour attitude, to take me on simple dates every once in a while and make me feel secure enough in our relationship that the downs will be washed away by the ups.

"Cool." He shifts uncomfortably.

"I just need to brush my teeth and tie my hair back."

"And maybe get dressed." He cups the overly sensitive area between my thighs. Hardin has already used one of his shirts to wipe me clean, something he used to do all the time.

"Right. Maybe I should rinse off in the shower." I gulp, wondering if Hardin and I will go another round before we leave. Frankly, I don't know if either of us could handle it.

I stand up from the bed and wince. I knew I was going to be starting my period any day now; why did it have to come right now, of all days? I suppose it works in my favor, though, since it'll be gone by the time we leave for England.

Leave for England . . . it doesn't seem real.

"What?" Hardin says with a questioning look.

"I'm . . . it's that time . . ." I look away from him, knowing that he's had an entire month to store up his jokes.

"Hmm . . . and what time is that?" He smirks, looking at his bare wrist as if there's a watch there.

"Don't . . ." I whine, pressing my thighs together so I can hurry and put on enough clothes to make it to the bathroom.

"Would you look at that? A hangover and a bloody attitude!" he taunts.

"Your jokes are terrible." I pull his T-shirt over my head and catch the languid smile he shoots at me as he takes in the sight of me wearing his shirt again.

"Terrible, huh?" His green eyes dance with amusement. "Maybe so terrible that you want to pull the plug on them?"

I hurry and exit the room while he's still laughing to himself.

chapter
one hundred and nineteen

HARDIN

I didn't even know you two were here. I thought Tessa had classes today," Kimberly says to me when I enter the kitchen. Why is she even here?

"She wasn't feeling well," I reply. "Aren't you supposed to be at work . . . or is staying home another perk of fucking your boss?"

"Actually, I don't feel well either, you ass." She tosses a wadded-up piece of paper at me but misses.

"You and Tessa should really learn how to hold your champagne," I tell her.

She flips me off.

The microwave sounds, and she pulls out a plastic bowl filled with something that looks and smells like cat food, then sits down at the countertop. She inhales forkful after forkful. I lift my fingers to safeguard my nose.

"That smells like pure shit," I remark.

"Where's Tessa? She'll shut you up."

"Wouldn't count on it." I grin. I have sort of come to like taunting Vance's fiancée. She has a thick skin, and she's obnoxious enough that I'm provided with plenty of ammunition.

"Wouldn't count on what?" Tessa joins us in the kitchen dressed in a sweatshirt, tight jeans, and those slipper things she swears are shoes. Really, they're nothing but overpriced cloth wrapped around a piece of cardboard, using the pretense of charity to rip off stupid consumers. She disagrees, of course, so I've learned to keep this opinion to myself.

"Nothing." I dig my hands into my pockets to fight the urge to nudge Kimberly's smug ass off the stool.

"He's mouthing off, nothing new." Kim takes another bite of her cat food.

"Let's go, she's annoying," I say just loud enough for Kim to hear.

"Be nice," Tessa scolds me. I take her hand in mine and lead her out of the house.

When we get into the car, Tessa shoves a handful of plugs into my glove compartment. An idea strikes me. "You need to get on birth control," I tell her. I've been so careless lately, and now that I've felt her without a condom, there's no going back.

"I know. I keep meaning to make a doctor's appointment, but it's hard to get an appointment with student insurance."

"Sure, sure."

"Maybe later this week I can get in. I need to do it soon; you're careless lately," she says.

"Careless? Me?" I scoff, trying not to panic. "You're the one that keeps catching me off guard, and I can't think straight."

"Oh please!" She giggles and leans her head back against the headrest.

"Hey, if you want to ruin your life by having a child, go for it, but you sure as hell aren't taking me down with you." I squeeze her thigh, and she frowns. "What?"

"Nothing," she lies, faking a smile.

"Tell me, now."

"Children are something we shouldn't discuss, remember?"

"I agree . . . So let's cut out the middleman and get your ass on birth control so we don't have to ever talk or worry about children again."

"I'll find a clinic to go to today so that your future isn't in jeopardy," she flatly remarks.

I've made her upset, but there really isn't a nice way for me to tell her that she needs to get on birth control if she's going to be fucking me multiple times a day whenever we're near each other.

After making a few phone calls, she announces, "I have an appointment Monday."

"Good." I run my hand over my hair before placing it back onto her thigh.

I turn on the radio and follow the directions on my phone to the nearest mall.

BY THE TIME we've walked around the mall once, I'm bored out of my mind with Seattle. The only thing keeping me entertained is Tessa. Even when she's quiet, I can read her thoughts just by watching her expressions. I watch her watch people as they rush through the mall. She frowns when an angry mother swats her child's ass in the middle of a store, and I guide her out before the scene—and her reaction to it—get out of hand. We have lunch at a quiet pizza parlor, and Tessa fills the entire meal with talk about a new book series she's been thinking about reading. I know how judgmental she can be about modern novels, so this surprises and intrigues me.

"I'll have to download them when I get my e-reader back from you," she says, swiping a napkin across her mouth. "I can't wait to have my bracelet back, too. And the letter."

I force myself not to panic and shove almost an entire piece of pizza into my mouth so I'm unable to respond. I can't tell her I destroyed it, so I'm really grateful when she moves to another subject.

The day ends with Tessa falling asleep in the car. She's made a habit of that lately, and for some reason, I love it. I take the long way back to the house, just like I did the last time.

TESSA'S ALARM didn't wake me, and neither did she. I'm less than pleased that I didn't get to see her before she left this morning, especially since she'll be gone all day. When I glance at the clock on the wall, it shows almost noon; at least she'll be taking lunch soon.

I dress quickly and leave the house for the new Vance Publishing branch office. It's strange to think that I could be working there with her, the two of us driving to work together each morning, making the drive back home together . . . we could actually live together again.

Space, Hardin, she wants space. I laugh at the idea; we aren't giving each other any space, really—only three days a week, tops. What we're doing is just making seeing each other more of a pain in the ass, with the excessive driving and distance.

When I get inside the building, I find that the Seattle office is fucking outrageously lavish. It's much bigger than the shit office I worked at. I don't miss working in a stuffy cubicle, that's for damned sure, but this place is nice. Vance wouldn't allow me to work from home. It was Brent, my boss at Bolthouse, that recommended I do my work for him from my living room in order to "keep the peace." It works out perfectly for me, even more so now that Tessa's in Seattle, so joke is on those overly sensitive fucks in the office.

I'm surprised when I don't get lost in this maze of a fucking building.

When I reach the reception area, Kimberly beams at me from behind her desk. "Hello. How may I help you?" she says with emphasis, showing me her ability to remain professional.

"Where's Tessa?"

"In her office," she says, dropping the facade.

"And that is . . ." I lean against the wall and wait for her to show me to Tessa.

"Down the hall. Her name is on the plate outside." She glances back to her computer screen, dismissing me. Rude.

What exactly does Vance pay her to do? Whatever it is, it must be worth it for him to be able to fuck her on a constant and keep him nearby during the day. I shake my head, ridding it of the images of the two of them.

"Thanks for your help," I gripe and head down the long narrow hallway.

When I reach Tessa's office, I open the door without knocking. The room is empty. I reach into my pocket and grab my phone to call her; seconds later I hear a rattling noise and see her phone vibrating on her desk. *Where the hell is she?*

I go down the hallway in search of her. I know Zed is in town, and that has me seeing red. I swear to fucking . . .

"Hardin Scott?" a woman's voice asks from behind me as I turn and enter what looks like a small break room.

I turn around to find a familiar face. "Um . . . hey?" I can't remember where I've seen her before, but I know that I have. Realization hits me when she's joined by another woman. You've got to be fucking kidding me. The universe is playing a sick fucking joke on me, and it's pissing me the fuck off.

Tabitha grins at me. "Well . . . well . . . well . . ."

Tessa's tales of woe about two bitchy office bullies make so much more sense now.

Since clearly neither of us is going to stand on ceremony, I just say, "You're the one giving Tessa shit, aren't you." If I had any idea that Tabitha had transferred to the Seattle office, I'd have known instantly that she was the bitch in question. She was known for that back when I worked for Vance, and I'm sure she hasn't changed.

"What? Me?" She flips her hair over her shoulder and smiles.

She looks different . . . unnatural, really. The little minion who's following in her wake has the same orange shade to her skin . . . they should stop bathing in food coloring, perhaps.

"Cut the shit. Don't mess with her; she's trying to adjust to a new city, and you two aren't going to ruin it for her by being a assholes to her for no reason."

"I haven't even done anything! I was joking anyway." Flashes of her sucking my dick in a bathroom stall flash through my mind, and I swallow the uneasy feeling that comes with the unwelcome memory.

"Don't do it anymore," I warn her. "I'm not fucking around. Don't even speak to her."

"Jesus, you're still as cheery as ever, I see. I won't mess with her anymore. I wouldn't want you telling Mr. Vance on me and getting me fired like you did Sam—"

"That wasn't my fault."

"Yes, it was!" she whispers dramatically, "As soon as her man found out what you two were doing . . . what you did . . . she was mysteriously let go the very same week." Tabitha was easy, so damn easy, and so was Samantha. The moment that I found out who Samantha's boyfriend was, she began to appeal to me. But once I got between her legs, I wanted nothing to do with her. That little game of mine caused me a lot of shit and drama that I'd rather not be reminded of, and I sure as hell don't want Tessa mixed up in this catty shit.

"You don't know half of what really happened, so keep your mouth shut. Leave Tessa alone, and your job will stay yours." Truthfully, I may have had a little something to do with Vance letting Samantha go, but her working there was causing me too many problems. She was only a freshman in college, working part-time, as a copy girl.

"Speak of the spoiled little devil," the short minion remarks and nods her head toward the door of the small break room.

Tessa is smiling and laughing as she enters. And right behind her, dressed in one of his little suits and ties, is fucking Trevor, smiling and laughing along with her.

The little twat spots me first and touches Tessa's arm to draw her attention to me. It takes every ounce of my self-control not to snap him in two. When she sees me from across the room, her face lights up, her smile widens, and she rushes over. Only when she reaches me does she notice Tabitha standing next to me.

"Hey," she says, unsure now, nervous.

"Bye, Tabitha." I wave the snooty woman off. She whispers something to her friend, and the two of them leave the room.

"Bye, Trevor," I say quietly enough that only Tessa hears.

"Stop it!" She swats my arm in the pestering way that she always does.

"Hello, Hardin," Trevor greets me, ever so politely. His arm twitches at his side, like he's trying to decide whether or not to offer his hand for a shake. I hope for his sake that he doesn't. I won't accept it.

"Hi," I say curtly.

"What are you doing here?" Tessa asks. She looks out into the hallway for the two women that just left. I know what she's really asking: *How do you know them, and what did they say?*

"Tabitha won't be a problem anymore."

She gapes, her eyes wide. "What did you do?"

I shrug. "Nothing, I just told her what you should have—to fuck off."

Tessa smiles at fucking Trevor, and he sits down at one of the tables, trying not to look at the two of us. I find his discomfort pretty damn amusing.

"Did you have lunch already?" I ask. She shakes her head. "Let's get you something to eat, then." I give the eavesdropper a fuck-you glare and lead Tessa out of the room and down the hallway.

"The place next door has really good tacos," she says.

It turns out she's wrong. The tacos are shit, but she devours her plate and most of mine. Afterward, she flushes and blames her appetite on her hormones; when she threatens to "shove a tampon down my throat" if I make one more joke about her period, I just laugh.

"I still want to go back tomorrow to see everyone and get my stuff," she says, washing down the spicy salsa she just finished with some water.

"Don't you think going to England next weekend is enough traveling?" I say, trying to derail her plans.

"No. I want to see Landon. I miss him so much."

An unwarranted pang of jealousy hits me, but I brush it off. He *is* her only friend, save annoying-ass Kimberly.

"He'll still be there when we get back from England . . ."

"Hardin, please." She looks up at me, not asking for permission like she sometimes does. This time she's asking for my cooperation, and I can tell by the gleam in her eye that she's going back to see Landon whether I want her to or not.

"Fine. Fuck," I groan.

This can't possibly go well. I look across the table at her, and she's smiling proudly, I don't know if she's proud of herself for winning this argument or proud of me for giving in, but she looks so beautiful. So relaxed.

"I like that you came here today." She takes my hand as we walk down the busy street. Why are there so many people in Seattle?

"You do?" I figured as much, but I had a little anxiety that she might be angry at me for showing up unannounced, not that I would have given a shit, but still.

"Yes." She blinks up at me, stopping in the middle of a swarm of rushing bodies. "I almost . . ." She trails off without finishing.

"You almost what?" I stop her attempt at walking farther and pull her to the wall beside a jewelry store. The sun reflects off the enormous diamond rings on display in the window, and I lead her a few feet down the brick wall to get away from the glare.

"It's silly." She pulls her bottom lip between her teeth and stares at the cement. "But I feel like I can breathe for the first time in months."

"Is that a good thing or . . ." I start to ask, tilting her chin so she has no choice but to look at my face.

"Yes, it's a good thing. I feel like for once everything is working out. I know it hasn't been for long, but this is the most functional we have ever been. We've only had a handful of arguments, and we communicated our way through them. I'm proud of us."

Her comment amuses me, because we still argue and banter constantly. It's not only a handful of arguments, but she's right: we've been talking our way through things. I love that we argue, and I think she does, too. We're totally different people—we couldn't be more different, really—and getting along with her all the time would be boring as hell. I couldn't live without her constant need to correct me or her nagging about my mess-making. She's annoying as hell, but I wouldn't change a fucking thing about her. Except her need to be in Seattle.

"Functional is highly overrated, baby." To prove my point, I lift her by the thighs, wrapping her legs around my waist, and kiss her against the wall right in the middle of one of the busiest streets in Seattle.

chapter one hundred and twenty

TESSA

How much longer?" Hardin complains from the passenger seat.

"Less than five minutes; we just passed Conner's." I know he's well aware of how short the distance is from here to the apartment; it's just that he can't keep himself from complaining. Hardin drove most of the way until I finally persuaded him to let me finish the trip. His eyes were nearly closing, and I knew he needed a break. My point was proven when he stretched his arm across the center console, holding me as best he could while I was driving, and fell asleep almost instantly.

"Landon is still there, right? You talked to him?" I ask. I'm beyond excited to see my best friend. It's been far too long, and I miss his kind words of wisdom and never-faltering smile.

"Yes, for the tenth time," Hardin replies, clearly annoyed. He's been anxious the entire drive, even though he won't admit it. He shrugs it off like he's annoyed because of the distance, but I get the feeling there's something else behind his frustration. I'm not entirely sure that I want to discover what it is.

When I pull into the parking lot of the apartment building that I used to call home, my stomach turns, and my nervousness begins to creep to the surface.

"It'll be fine." Hardin's reassuring words surprise me as we enter the front door.

The small elevator feels so alien as it rises up the building. It feels as if so much more than only three weeks have passed. Hardin keeps his hand over mine until we reach the door, where he slides the key into the lock and pushes it open.

Landon jumps to his feet from the couch and strides across the room with the brightest smile I've seen him wear in the seven months since we became friends. His arms wrap around my back, and he hugs me, welcoming me, and making me aware of just how much I've missed him. Before I know it, I'm sobbing and heaving deep breaths into my friend's chest.

I'm not sure why I'm crying so much. I've just missed Landon terribly, and his warm reaction to my return made me emotional.

"Can her old man get a turn?" I hear my father say from somewhere a little ways off.

Landon starts to back away, but Hardin says, "In a moment," and nods toward Landon, assessing my mental state.

I launch myself at Landon again, and his familiar arms wrap around my back again. "I missed you so much," I tell him.

His shoulders visibly relax, and he unwraps his arms from my body. When I go to hug my father, Landon stays nearby, his smile still bright and loving as ever. Looking at my father, I realize that he must have known that I'd be coming to visit. It looks like he's wearing Landon's clothes and they're tight on his body. I notice that his face is clean-shaven.

"Look at you!" I exclaim with a smile. "No beard!"

He whoops a loud laugh and hugs me tighter. "Yeah, no more beard for me," he says.

"How was the drive?" Landon asks, shoving his hands into the pockets of his navy-colored slacks.

"Shit," Hardin says at the exact moment I say, "Good."

Landon and my father both laugh, Hardin looks annoyed, and I'm just happy to be home . . . with my best friend and the closest relative that I'm in contact with. Which only reminds me that I have to call my mother, which I keep putting off.

"I'm going to put your bag in the bedroom," Hardin announces, leaving the three of us to continue our welcoming. I watch as he disappears into the room we once shared. His shoulders are set low, and I want to follow after him, but I don't.

"I've missed you too much, Tessie. How's Seattle treating you?" my father asks. It's odd to look at him now, wearing one of Landon's collared shirts and dress slacks, with no hair on his face. He looks like a completely different man. The bags under his eyes have gotten puffier, though, and I notice the way his hands are slightly shaking at his sides.

"It's good, I'm still getting used to it," I tell him.

He smiles. "That's good to hear."

Landon steps closer to me as my father takes a seat on the edge of the couch. He turns his back away from my father as if he wants to keep our conversation private. "It feels like you've been gone for months," he says, holding my gaze as he speaks.

He looks tired, too . . . maybe from staying at the apartment with my father? I don't know, but I want to find out.

"It does, I feel like time is strange in Seattle—how *is* everything? I feel like we've barely talked." It's true. I haven't called Landon as often as I should have, and he must've been really busy dealing with his last semester at Washington Central. If less than three weeks is this tough, how will I be able to bear him moving all the way to New York?

"I knew you'd be busy, everything's okay," he says. His eyes dart to the wall, and I sigh. Why do I feel like I'm missing something obvious?

"Are you sure?" I glance back and forth between my best friend and my father, taking in Landon's drained expression.

"Yeah, we'll talk about it later," he says, waving my concern off. "Now tell me about Seattle!" The dim light that was in his eyes intensifies into a bright burn of happiness, the happiness that I have missed so much.

"It's okay . . ." I trail off, and his forehead creases in a frown. "Really, it's okay. Much better now that Hardin is visiting more."

"So much for space, huh?" he playfully teases, nudging my shoulder with the palm of his hand. "You two have the strangest definition of breaking up."

I roll my eyes, agreeing, but I say, "It's been really nice having him there. I'm still as confused as ever, but Seattle feels more like the Seattle of my dreams when Hardin is there with me."

"I'm happy to hear it." Landon smiles, his gaze shifting as Hardin walks up and stands next to me.

Looking around, I say to the three of them, "This place is in much better condition than I thought it would be."

"We've been cleaning it while Hardin was in Seattle," my father says, and I laugh, reminded of Hardin's grumpy complaint that the two of them were messing with his things.

I look back at the well-organized foyer, remembering the very first time I stepped through the door with Hardin. I fell in love instantly with the old-fashioned charm of the place: the exposed brick wall was so enchanting, and I was beyond impressed by the expansive book shelving covering the far wall. The concrete flooring added to the personality of the apartment, unique and beautiful. I couldn't believe that Hardin had chosen the most perfect space, suiting both of us in a way I didn't think was possible. It wasn't extravagant, not in the slightest, but it was so beautiful and so thoughtfully laid out. I remember how nervous he was that I wouldn't like it. I was nervous, too, though. I thought he was insane for wanting to me live with him so soon into our back-and-forth relationship—and I now know that my apprehensiveness was very well justified; Hardin had used this apartment as a trap. He thought that I'd be forced to stay with him after I found out about the wager he'd made with his group of friends. In a way, it worked, and I don't particularly love that part of our past, but I wouldn't change it now.

Despite the memories of our happy first days here, for some reason I still can't shake the unsettling rustling that I feel in my stomach. I feel like a stranger here now. The once-charming brick wall has been stained by bloody knuckles too many times to count, the books on those shelves have been witness to too many screaming matches, the pages have soaked up too many tears in the aftermath of our endless fighting, and the image of Hardin crumpled on his knees in front of me is so strong it's practically imprinted into the floor. This place is no longer the treasure to me that it once was, and these walls now hold memories of sadness and betrayal, not only Hardin's, but Steph's as well.

"What's wrong?" Hardin asks the moment my expression turns melancholy.

"Nothing, I'm fine," I tell him. I want to shake off the unpleasant memories lodging in my mind, taking away from these moments of happiness at being reunited with Landon and my father after the lonely weeks I've endured in Seattle.

"I'm not buying it," Hardin huffs, but drops it and walks into the kitchen. After a second, his voice travels into the living room. "Is there no food in the place?"

"Ahh, here it goes. It had been so nice and quiet," my father whispers to Landon, and they share a friendly laugh. I'm so thankful to have Landon in my life and to have what seems to be a budding relationship with my father, though it seems that Hardin and Landon both know him better than I do.

"I'll be back in just a minute," I say.

I want to change out of this heavy sweatshirt; it's too warm in the small apartment, and I feel my lungs yearning for a fresh breath as the moments pass. I need to read Hardin's letter again; it's my favorite thing in the entire world. It's much more than a thing to me; it expresses his love and passion in a way that his mouth never could. I've read it so many times that I have it memorized, but I need to physically touch it again. Once I hold the tattered and worn pages between my fingers, all the anxiety I'm feeling will be replaced by his thoughtful words, and I'll be able to breathe again and enjoy my weekend here.

I search the top of the dresser and each drawer before moving along to the desk. My fingers push through piles of paper clips and pens to no avail. *But where else could he have placed it?*

I find my e-reader and the bracelet resting on top of my religion journal, but the letter is nowhere to be found. After placing the bracelet on the desk, I move to the closet and search through the empty shoe box that Hardin uses to store his work files during the week. I lift the lid to find it empty except one single piece of paper, which, I'm sad to see, is not the letter. *What is this, though?* Hardin's handwriting is scribbled across it from top to bottom, and if I wasn't so worried about my letter, I would stop to check it out. It's really weird that this paper is randomly here. I make a mental note to come back and read the scribbles on that page and put the lid back onto the box and store it back where I found it.

Worrying that I may have overlooked the letter in the drawer, I march back to the dresser. What if Hardin threw it away?

No, he wouldn't; he knows how much that letter means to me. He'd never do that. I pull my old journal out once more, turn it upside down, and shake it, hoping the letter will fall out. I'm beginning to panic, until a flicker of white catches my attention. It's a shred of paper, twirling through the air between my journal and the floor. I reach down and pick it up just as it lands on the floor.

I recognize the words immediately—they're practically etched into my mind. It's only half a sentence, almost too small to read, but the ink-smeared words are clearly written in Hardin's handwriting. My stomach drops. I stare at the fragment of paper, and the realization hits me. I just know that he did, in fact, destroy it. I begin to weep and let the shred slip from my shaking fingers and fall back to the floor. My heart is instantly broken, and I begin to wonder just how much one heart can bear.

chapter one hundred and twenty-one

HARDIN

You're free to go." I release Landon from his babysitting duties.

"I'm not going, she just got here," he replies, challenging me. I guess he's one of the biggest reasons, if not the only reason, that she wanted to come to this damned place at all.

"Fine," I huff and lower my voice. "How was he while I was gone?" I quietly ask.

"He was good; he's less shaky, and he hasn't thrown up since yesterday morning."

"Fucking junkie." I run my hands over my hair. "Fuck."

"Calm down, it's all going to work out," my stepbrother assures me.

I ignore his words of wisdom and leave him in the kitchen to find Tessa. When I reach the bedroom door, I hear a strangled sob coming from inside. I take a quick step forward to find her with both hands cupped over her mouth, her blue eyes bloodshot and full of tears as they stare down at the floor. One more step is all it takes for me to spot what it is that she's looking at. Fuck.

Fuck.

"Tess?" I had planned on coming up with a plan to fix the problem that I created by ripping up that damned letter, but I just haven't had the chance yet. I was going to find the pieces that were left and try to tape them back together . . . or at least tell Tessa what I did before she found out on her own. Too late now.

"Tess, I'm sorry!" The apology tumbles out as tears roll down her tearstained cheeks.

"Why did you—" she sobs, unable to finish the sentence. My heart constricts in my chest. For a brief moment, I'm convinced that I'm hurting worse than she is.

"I was so mad after you left me," I begin to explain, walking over to her, but she backs away. I don't blame her. "I wasn't thinking properly, and it was there, on the bed, where you left it."

She doesn't speak or look away from me.

"I am so sorry, I swear it!" I frantically proclaim.

"I . . ." She chokes, furiously wiping at her cheeks. "I . . . just need a minute, okay?" Her eyes close, and a few more tears escape from under her fluttering eyelids.

I want to give her a minute like she asked, but I'm selfishly afraid that she'll grow more and more hurt as time passes and decide she doesn't want to see me.

"I'm not going to leave the room," I say. She has both her hands pressed over her mouth, but even so, I hear her let out a muffled cry. The sound cuts straight through me.

"Please," she begs through her pain. I knew she'd be hurt when she found out about me destroying that letter, but what I didn't expect was for it to hurt me so much.

"No, I won't." I refuse to leave her in here alone to cry over my mistakes, again. How many times has that happened in this apartment?

She looks away from me and sits down at the foot of the bed, her shaky hands clasped on her lap, her eyes half closed, and her lips quivering as she tries to calm herself down. I ignore the push of her hand against my chest when I drop to my knees in front of her and wrap my arms around her body.

After a few exhausted efforts to push me away, she finally gives in and allows me to comfort her.

"I'm so sorry, baby," I repeat; I don't know if I've ever meant those words so sincerely before.

"I loved that letter," she says, crying into my shoulder. "It meant so much to me."

"I know it did. I'm so sorry." I don't even try to defend myself, because I'm a fucking idiot, and I knew how much that thing meant to her. I gently push her back by her shoulders and take her tearstained cheeks between my hands and lower my voice. "I don't know what to say except I'm sorry."

Finally she opens her mouth to speak. "I won't say it's okay, because it's not . . ." Her eyes are red-rimmed and already swollen from her sobbing.

"I know." I bow my head, dropping my hands from her face.

Moments later I feel her fingers press under my chin, tilting my face up to look at her, the way I usually do to her.

"I'm upset . . . devastated, really," she says. "But there's nothing I can do about it, and I don't want to sit here and cry all weekend, and I certainly don't want you backtracking and beating yourself up over it." She's trying her hardest to talk herself up, pretending that it doesn't bother her the way that I know it does.

I let out a breath that I didn't realize I was holding. "I'll make it up to you, somehow." When she doesn't answer, I press a little. "Okay?"

She wipes at her eyes, her makeup smearing under her fingertips. Her silence is making me uneasy. I'd rather be screamed at than have her cry like this.

"Tess, please talk to me. Do you want me to take you back to Seattle?" Even if she says yes, I sure as hell won't do it, but the offer is tossed between us before I can think it through.

"No." She shakes her head. "I'm fine."

With a sigh, she stands, sidestepping my body as she exits the bedroom. I get to my feet and follow her. She closes the bathroom door, and I go back into the bedroom to grab her small bag. I know her—she'll want to fix that black-smudged mess underneath her eyes.

I tap on the bathroom door, and she opens it slightly, just enough for me to shove the small bag through. "Thanks," she says, her voice small, defeated.

I've already ruined her weekend, and it's barely started.

"My mom and your dad want you to bring Tessa by the house tomorrow," Landon calls from the end of the hall.

"And . . ."

"I'm just saying. My mom misses Tessa."

"So . . . your mum can see her some other time." Then I realize this might get Tessa's mind off that damned letter. "You know what? *Fine,"* I say before he can get his response out. "I'll take her by tomorrow."

My stepbrother tilts his head. "Is she crying?"

"She's . . . it's not really any of your business, is it?" I snap.

"You've been back here for less than twenty minutes, and she's already locked herself in the bathroom," he says, crossing his arms.

"This isn't the time to start shit with me, Landon," I growl. "I'm already at the point of explosion; the last thing I need is you butting your damn nose in where it doesn't belong."

But he just rolls his eyes in a very Tessa-like way. "Oh, so I'm only allowed to butt in when it involves doing a favor for you?"

What the fuck is his problem, and why do I keep referring to him as my stepbrother? "Fuck off."

"She's probably already overwhelmed, so the two of us need to stop this before she lets herself out of that bathroom." He's trying to reason with me.

"Fine, then stop talking shit to me," I say.

Before he can respond, the bathroom door clicks open, and

Tessa, looking put together but very exhausted, shuffles into the hallway, worry on her face. "What's going on?"

"Nothing. Landon is going to order pizza, and we're all going to spend the remainder of the night as one big happy family." I glance at him. "Isn't that right?"

"Yes," he agrees—for Tessa's sake, I know. I miss the days when Landon wouldn't smart off to me. They were few and far between, but he's grown ballsier as the months have dragged on. Or maybe I've grown weaker . . . I haven't a damn clue, but I don't like the shift.

Tessa lets out a little sigh. I need her to smile, I need to know she can get over this. So I say, "I'm going to take you by my father's house tomorrow; maybe Karen can share some recipes or some shit with you?"

Her eyes lighten, and she grins, finally. "Recipes or 'some shit'?" She chews on the corner of her bottom lip to keep from grinning further. The pressure in my chest dissolves.

"Yeah, or some shit." I smile back at her and lead her to the living room, where we are set to enjoy a torturous night of entertaining Richard and Landon.

RICHARD IS LYING across the span of the couch. Landon is in the chair. And Tessa and I are sitting on the floor.

"Can you pass me another supreme?" Richard asks for the third time since we started this hideous movie. I look at Tessa and Landon, who, of course, are completely fascinated by the email love affair that's going on between Meg Ryan and Tom Hanks. If this were a modern movie, they would have fucked after the first email, not waited until the last scene to even kiss. Hell, they would have been on one of those hookup apps and maybe only known each other by screen names. How depressing is that?

"Here," I groan, sliding the pizza box to Richard. He's already taking up the entire couch, and now he's interrupting me every ten minutes for more fucking pizza.

"This last part used to make your mom cry every time she saw it." Richard's hand reaches out and squeezes Tessa's shoulder. I try my best not to scoot between them or bat his hand away. If she had any idea what her father has been doing the last week, if she had watched the drugs leave his system in a mess of vomit and convulsing withdrawals, she'd push his hand away herself and then sanitize her shoulder.

"Really?" Tess looks up at her father with glossy eyes.

"Yes. I still remember you two watching it every time it was on. More around the holidays, of course."

"Was that—" I begin but halt my vicious words before I utter them.

"What?" Tessa asks me.

"Was that . . . um, dog supposed to be there?" I dumbly ask. It makes no sense, but Tessa, being Tessa, goes into full discussion mode about the last scene of the movie and that the dog, Barkley or Brinkley, I believe she said his name is, is essential to the success of the movie.

Blah, blah, blah . . .

A knock at the door stops Tessa's explanation and Landon gets up to answer.

"I got it," I say and push past him. This is my fucking place, after all.

I don't bother to look through the peephole, but once I pull the door open, I wish that I had.

"Where's he?" the foul-smelling junkie asks.

I step out into the hallway and close the door behind me. Tessa will *not* be bothered by this shit. "What the fuck are you doing here?" I hiss.

"I'm just here to see my buddy, that's all." Chad's teeth are even browner than before, and his facial hair is matted to his skin. He can only be in his thirties, but he possesses the face of a man pushing fifty. The watch my father got me is hanging from his filthy wrist.

"He's not coming out here, and no one is giving you anything, so I suggest you take your ass back where you came from before I bash your face against that railing," I say matter-of-factly and point toward the metal bar in front of the hallway fire extinguisher. "Then, while you're bleeding out, I'll call the police and have you arrested for possession and trespassing." I know he has drugs on him, the fucking asshole.

His eyes focus in on me, and I take a step toward him. "I wouldn't test my patience, not tonight," I warn.

His mouth opens just as the door to the apartment opens behind me. Fucking hell.

"What's going on?" Tessa asks, moving in front of me.

I instinctively jerk her back, and she asks again. "Nothing, Chad here was just leaving." I stare at Chad, so help him God, if he fucking—

Tessa's eyes narrow in on the shiny object dangling from his thin wrist. "Is that your watch?"

"What? No—" I begin to lie, but she already knows. She isn't stupid enough to think it's coincidence that this drug-addict fuck has the same exact expensive-ass watch as I do.

"Hardin . . ." She glares at me. "So what, you've been hanging out with this guy or something?" She crosses her arms and puts more distance between us.

"No!" I half shout. Why would that be the conclusion she draws from this little scene?

I'm conflicted between calling her father out and defending myself or making up yet another lie. "I'm not friends with him, he's leaving." I shoot Chad one more warning.

This time he takes it and backs away down the hall. I suppose it's only Landon who isn't intimidated by me anymore. Maybe I haven't lost my edge after all.

"Who's there?" Richard joins us in the hallway.

"That man . . . Chad," Tessa answers, inquisition clear in her tone.

"Oh . . ." Richard pales and looks helplessly at me.

"I need to know what's going on." Tessa is getting upset. I shouldn't have let her come back here. I saw it on her face the moment she stepped into this damned place.

"Landon!" Tessa calls for her best friend, and I look at her father. Landon will tell her everything; he won't lie to her face the way I have so many times.

"Your dad owed him money, and I gave him that watch for payment," I admit. She gasps and turns to Richard.

"You owed him money for what? Hardin's father gave him that watch as a gift!" she shouts.

Okay . . . this isn't exactly the reaction I was expecting. She's more focused on the stupid watch than the whole your-father-owed-this-creep-money aspect.

"I'm sorry, Tessie. I didn't have any money, and Hardin—"

Before I realize what she's doing, she's halfway to the elevator. *What the fuck!*

I panic, running after her, but she slides into the steel cage just before I reach her. Those doors move with torturous slowness any other time, yet when she's escaping from me, they close instantly.

"Goddammit, Tessa!" I pound my fist once against the metal. Does this place even have a staircase? When I look back down the hall, Landon and Richard are both staring blankly, unmoving. Thanks for the fucking help, assholes.

I move quickly and find the staircase, taking two stairs at a time to get to the bottom. I reach the lobby and glance around for Tessa. When I don't see her, I begin to panic again. Chad could have friends with him . . . they could approach Tessa or hurt her . . .

The elevator opens with a ding, and Tessa steps out of it; the most determined face imaginable covers her features, until she spots me.

"Are you out of your fucking mind?" I shout at her, my voice filling the lobby.

"He's giving that damn watch back, Hardin!" she shouts back. She stalks toward the glass doors, and I wrap my arm around her waist, yanking her back against my chest.

"Get off of me!" She claws at my arms, but I don't relent.

"You can't just chase after him. What're you thinking?"

She keeps fighting me.

"If you don't stop moving, I will literally carry your ass back up to the apartment. Now listen to me," I say.

"He can't have that watch, Hardin! Your father gave it to you, and it meant a lot to him and to you—"

"That watch didn't mean shit to me," I say.

"Yes, it did. You'll never admit it, but it did. I know it." Her eyes are watering again. Fuck, this weekend is going to be hell.

"No, it didn't . . ."

Did it?

Her hands stop moving, and she settles down slightly. I gently coax her back toward the elevator, her drug-dealer-chasing mission aborted, much to her chagrin.

"It's not fair to you that he took that watch because of some stupid bar tab my father ran up! How much freaking alcohol does one consume that they actually owe people money?" Her temper is flaring, and I'm torn between thinking it's amusing and feeling terrible for what I have to tell her.

"It wasn't alcohol, Tess." I watch as she tilts her head to the side, looking anywhere and everywhere but at my eyes.

"Hardin, I know my father and his drinking—don't make

excuses for him." Her chest is moving up and down at an unhealthy pace.

"Tessa, Tessa, you have to calm down."

"Then tell me what's going on, Hardin!"

I don't know what else to say. I'm sorry—sorry that I couldn't shield her from her fuckup of a father, just like I couldn't shield my mother from the devastation of mine. So I do something rather alien for me. I say something brutally honest. "It's not alcohol. It's drugs."

Tessa's reaction seems at first like no reaction at all. But after a second, she shakes her head and says, "No, he's not . . . He's not doing drugs."

Quickly she steps into the elevator and punches the button for our floor. I jump on right after her, but she just stares into space as the doors close us in.

chapter one hundred and twenty-two

TESSA

As Hardin and I walk back into the apartment, it feels like the air has become stale and awkward.

"Are you okay?" Landon asks when Hardin closes the door behind him.

"Yeah," I state simply, lying.

I'm confused, hurt, angry, and exhausted. It's only been a few hours since we arrived, and already I'm ready to go back to Seattle. Any thought I had of wanting to live here again vanished somewhere during the silent walk from the elevator to the apartment door.

"Tessie . . . I didn't mean for any of this to happen," my father says as he follows me into the kitchen. I need a glass of water; my head is throbbing.

"I don't want to talk about it." The sink creaks when I pull at the faucet, and I wait patiently for the glass to fill.

"I think we should at least talk—"

"Please . . ." I turn to face him. I don't want to talk. I don't want to hear the hideous truth, or some well-intentioned lie. I only want to go back to when I was cautiously excited about trying out a relationship with my father that I never had as a child. I know that Hardin has no reason to lie about my father's addictions, but perhaps he's somehow mistaken.

"Tessie . . ." my father pleads.

"She said she doesn't want to talk about it," Hardin insists, suddenly appearing in the room. He walks farther into the kitchen and stands between my father and me. I'm thankful for his intrusion this time, but I'm slightly worried over the quick movements of his chest as his breaths become more shallow and labored. I'm grateful when my father sighs in defeat and leaves me alone with Hardin in the kitchen.

"Thank you." I sag against the counter and take another drink of the lukewarm tap water.

A worried line forms along Hardin's forehead, and he doesn't attempt to hide his deep scowl. His fingers press against his temples, and he leans against the opposite counter. "I shouldn't have let you come here; I knew this would happen."

"I'm fine."

"You always say that."

"Because I always have to be. Otherwise, when the next disaster occurs, I won't be prepared." The adrenaline coursing through me only minutes ago has disappeared, evaporated along with the hope that for once, something could go right for an entire weekend. I don't regret coming here, because I've missed Landon so much and I wanted to pick up my letter, e-reader, and bracelet. My heart still aches over the letter; it doesn't seem rational for an object to hold such significance to me, but it does. It was the first time Hardin had ever been so open with me—no more hiding, no more secrets about his past, all of his cards were on the table—and I didn't have to force the confessions from him. The thought that he put into writing it and the way his hands shook as he held it out to me will always remain in my mind. I'm not upset with him, really; I wish he hadn't destroyed it, but I know his temper, and I'm the one who left it here, somehow sensing that he probably would destroy it. I won't allow myself to dwell on it anymore, though it still hurts to think about the shred of paper that was left; that small piece could never hold all of the emotion packed into the words he had scribbled across the page.

"I hate that it's like that for you," Hardin quietly says.

"Me, too." I sigh in agreement. The pained look on his face makes me add, "It's not your fault."

"Like hell it isn't." Exasperated fingers push through the wave of his hair. "I'm the one who ripped up that damn letter, I drove you here, and I thought I could keep your father's habits from you. I thought that asshole Chad was gone for good when I gave him my watch for the money your dad owed."

I stare at Hardin, who's always so wound up, and I want to hug him. He gave away something of his; regardless of his claims to have no attachment to the object, he gave it up in an attempt to dig my father out of the hole he created for himself. God, I love him.

"I'm very grateful to have you," I tell him. His shoulders straighten, and his head quickly lifts to look at me.

"I don't know why. I create nearly every disaster in your life."

"No, I'm equally to blame," I assure him. I wish he thought more of himself; if only he could see himself the way that I do. "The indifference of the universe does a lot, too."

"You're lying"—he stares at me with expectant eyes—"but I'll take it."

I stare at the wall in silence, my brain running over a thousand thoughts per minute.

"I'm still angry that you ran after him like a fucking madman, though," Hardin scolds me. I don't blame him; it wasn't smart. But I also somehow knew he'd run after me in my ridiculous attempt to chase Chad down and take the watch back from him. What the heck was I thinking?

I was thinking that the watch represented the beginning of a new relationship between Hardin and his father. Hardin said he hated that watch, and he refused to wear it, claiming it was outrageous. He's unaware of the times I passed the bedroom to see him staring at it in its box. Once he even had the watch resting in his open palm, examining it closely, as if it might burn or heal him. His expression was ambivalent when he tossed it carelessly back into the oversize black box.

"My adrenaline got the best of me." I shrug, trying to hide the gentle tremor shaking through me at the thought of actually catching up to the hideous man.

I had a bad feeling about him the first time he came to pick my father up from the apartment, but I was unaware of the possibility that he'd return. Out of all the suspicions I held relating to what exactly was happening here, slimy men selling drugs and being paid in watches was never a thought. This obviously was what Hardin referred to as "taking care of it without me having to worry about it." If I had just kept my behind in the apartment, I could still be blissfully ignorant of the entire situation. I could still see my father in a decent light.

"Well, I don't care much for your adrenaline, then. It obviously cuts off the oxygen to your damn brain," Hardin huffs, glaring at the refrigerator beside me.

"Should we start the next movie?" My father's voice sounds from the living room. I shoot a sudden panicked look toward Hardin, and he opens his mouth to answer for me.

"In a minute," he replies, his tone harsh.

Hardin looks down at me, his height and irritated expression overpowering me. "You don't have to go out there and fake some bullshit conversation with them if you don't want to. I'd dare either of them to say shit to you about it."

The idea of watching a movie with my father does not sound the least bit appealing, but I don't want things to be awkward, and I don't want Landon to go just yet.

"I know." I sigh.

"You're in denial, and I get that, but you're going to need to face the music sooner or later." His words are harsh, but his eyes are sympathetic as he gazes down at me. I feel the heat of his fingers trail down the back of both of my arms.

"I'll take later—for now," I plead with him, and he nods, not approving but accepting my denial. For now.

"Go on and go in there, then. I'll be in in a minute." He tilts his head toward the living room.

"Okay; can you make some popcorn?" I smile up at him, trying my best to convince him that my heart isn't hammering against my rib cage and my palms aren't sweating.

"You're pushing it . . ." A playful smile tugs at the corners of his mouth while he pushes me out of the kitchen. "Go on."

When I enter the dimly lit living room, my father is sitting in his usual spot on the couch and Landon is standing, leaning against the dark brick wall. My father's hands are on his lap; he's picking at the skin on his fingertips, a habit I had as a child until my mother forced me to give it up. Now I know where it came from.

My father lifts dark eyes from his lap to peer up at me, and a chill runs over me. I can't decipher whether it's the lighting or my mind playing tricks on me, but his eyes are nearly black, and it's making me nauseous. Is he really taking drugs? If so, how much and what kind? My knowledge of drugs consists of having watched a few episodes of *Intervention* with Hardin. I cringed and covered my eyes when the addicts would push the needles into their skin or smoke the frothy liquid off of a spoon. I could barely stand to watch them destroy themselves and everyone around them, while Hardin went on about not feeling an ounce of pity for the "fucking junkies."

Is my father really one of them?

"I'll understand if you want me to go . . ." My father's voice doesn't match the look in his haunted eyes. It's small, weak, and broken. My chest aches.

"No, it's okay." I swallow and sit down on the floor to wait for Hardin to join us. I hear the quiet popping of the kernels, and the aroma of popping corn has already filled the apartment.

"I'll tell you anything you want to—"

"It's okay, really," I assure my father with a smile. *Where is Hardin?*

My silent question is answered only moments later when he strides into the living room, a bag of popcorn in one hand and my glass of water in the other. He sits down next to me on the floor without a word and places the bag on my lap.

"It's a little burned, but still edible," he quietly remarks. His eyes move straight to the television screen, and I know he's holding back many thoughts. I squeeze his hand to thank him for keeping them that way. I don't think I'd be able to handle anything else tonight.

The popcorn is delicious and buttery. Hardin gripes when I offer Landon and my father some. I suspect that's why they refuse it.

"What bullshit are we watching now?" Hardin asks.

"*Sleepless in Seattle,*" I answer with a grin.

His eyes roll. "*Really?* Isn't that like an older version of what we just watched!"

I can't help but be amused. "It's a lovely movie."

"Sure." He looks at me, but his eyes don't stay on mine as long as usual. He uses his sweatshirt to wipe the greasy butter off his fingers. I cringe and make a mental note to soak the shirt longer than usual tomorrow before I wash it.

"Is something wrong? This movie isn't that bad," I whisper to him. My father is finishing off the remainder of the pizza, and Landon has taken his seat back on the recliner.

"No." He still doesn't look at me. I don't want to comment on his odd behavior; everyone's already on edge from tonight's events.

The movie distracts me from myself and my vicious mind long enough to laugh with Landon and my father. Hardin stares at the screen, his shoulders stiff again and his mind miles away. I desperately want to ask him what's wrong so that I can fix it, but I know that it's best to leave him be for now. Instead, I snuggle against his chest with my knees bent beneath me and one arm wrapped around his lean torso. He surprises me by pulling me closer and planting a soft kiss on my hair.

"I love you," he whispers. I'm nearly convinced that I'm hearing voices until I look up into his expectant green eyes.

"I love you," I reply softly. I take a few moments to stare at him, just to take in how beautiful he is. He drives me insane, as I do him, but he loves me, and his calm behavior tonight is just another indication of that. No matter how forced the behavior is, he *is* trying, and in that I find solace, a steady certainty that even in the middle of the brewing storm, he will be my anchor. I once feared that he would take me under; now I don't even mind if he does.

A heavy knock at the door jolts me from Hardin's lap. I've somehow migrated there in my near slumber, and he unwraps his arms from around me and gently places me on the floor so he can stand up. I study his face, looking for anger, or shock, but instead he looks . . . worried?

"You're not moving," he says to me. I nod in agreement. I don't want to face Chad again.

"We should just call the police, otherwise he'll never stop coming here." I groan, wondering how this apartment could have changed so drastically in the last few weeks. The panic rises into my chest again, and when I look up to gauge my father and Landon's reactions to the intruder, I see that they're both asleep. The television is set on the menu screen for the pay-per-view; we must have all actually drifted off to sleep without realizing it.

"No," I hear Hardin say. I rise onto my knees when he reaches the door. What If Chad isn't alone? Will he try to hurt Hardin? I stand up and head toward the couch to wake my father.

I barely register the heavy click of high heels across the hard flooring, so when I turn my head and see my mother, in all her tight-red-dress, curled-hair, and red-lipsticked glory, I'm shocked. Her beautiful face is set in a deep scowl as her darkening eyes meet mine.

"What are you—" I begin. I glance at Hardin; and he's calm . . . *expectant* almost . . .

He allows her to storm past him and stalk toward me.

"You *called* her?" My voice squeaks as the puzzle pieces click into place. He looks away from me. How could he call her? He knows firsthand how my mother is; why on earth would he bring her into this?

"You have been avoiding my calls, Theresa," she snaps. "And now I find out that your father is here! At this apartment, and he's on drugs!" She storms past me, too, and goes straight for the kill. Her fire-engine-red manicured fingers grip my father's arm, and she yanks his sleeping body off of the couch. He topples to the floor.

"Get up, Richard!" she booms, and I flinch at the harshness in her voice.

My father scrambles up to a sitting position quickly, using his palms to support his body weight, and shakes his head. His eyes nearly pop out of his skull as he takes in the woman in front of him. I watch as he blinks rapidly and stumbles to his feet.

"Carol?" His voice is even smaller than mine.

"How dare you!" She waves a finger in his face, and he backs away from her only to have his legs hit the couch, causing him to fall back. He looks terrified, and I don't blame him.

Landon stirs in the chair and opens his eyes; his expression mimics my father's, confused and terrified.

"Theresa, go to your bedroom," my mother demands.

What? "No, I will not," I counter. Why did Hardin have to call her? Everything would have been okay. I'd have a way to move on from my father, probably.

"She's not a child anymore, Carol," my father says.

My mother's cheeks puff, and her chest rises, and I know what's coming next. "Don't you dare speak of her as if you know her at all! As if you have any claim on her!"

"I'm trying to make up for lost time—" My father is holding his ground pretty decently for a man who has just been awoken by his angry ex-wife screaming in his face. I don't know what to make of the scene unfolding in front of me. There's something in my father's voice, something in his tone as he steps closer to my mother, gaining confidence that almost looks familiar. I can't quite put my finger on it.

"Lost time! You don't get to make up for lost time! Now I hear you're taking drugs?"

"I'm not anymore!" he yells back at her. I want to cower behind Hardin, but right now I don't know whose side he's actually on. Landon's eyes are focused on me, Hardin's on my father and mother.

"Wanna go?" Landon mouths silently from across the room. I shake my head, silently declining, but hoping that my eyes can convey how thankful I am for his offer.

"Anymore? Anymore!" My mother must have worn her heaviest heels. I'm beginning to wonder if they'll leave dents in the floor as she stomps across it.

"Yes, anymore! Look, I'm not perfect, okay?" His hands move over his short hair, and I freeze. The gesture is so familiar, it's uncanny.

"Not perfect! Ha!" She laughs, her white teeth shining through the dim room. I want to turn a light on but can't bring myself to move. I don't know how to feel or what to think as I watch my parents scream at each other in the middle of the living room. I'm convinced this apartment is cursed; it has to be. "Not perfect is fine; doing drugs and dragging your daughter down the same path is deplorable!"

"I'm not dragging her down any path! I'm trying my hardest to make up for what I did to her . . . and to you!"

"No! You're not! Your coming back around will only confuse her more! She's already messed her life up enough!"

"She hasn't messed up her life," Hardin interrupts. My mother shoots him a fiery glare before turning her attention back to my father.

"This is your fault, Richard Young! All of this! If it weren't for you, Theresa wouldn't be in this toxic relationship with this boy!" She waves her hand toward Hardin. I knew it would only be a matter of time before she started in on him. "She never had a male example to show her how a woman should be treated; that's why she's shacked up here with him! Unmarried, living in sin, and Lord only knows what he's doing! He's probably taking the drugs with you!"

I recoil, my blood instantly boils, and the raging need to defend Hardin surfaces. "Don't you dare bring Hardin into this! He's been taking care of my father and providing him with somewhere to live to keep him off of the streets!" I hate the way my choice of words resembles my mother's.

Hardin crosses the room and stands beside me. I know he's going to warn me to stay out of it.

"It's true, Carol. He's a good man, and he loves her more than I've ever seen a man love a woman," my father chimes in. My mother's fists ball at her sides, and her perfectly blushed cheeks flare a deep red.

"Don't you dare defend him! All of this—she waves one clenched fist through the thick air—"is because of him! She should be in Seattle, creating a life for herself, finding herself a suitable man . . ."

I can barely hear anything over the blood rushing and pumping through my head. In the midst of all of this, I feel terrible for Landon, who has kindly retreated to the bedroom to leave us alone, and for Hardin, who is, yet again, being used as my mother's scapegoat.

"She *is* living in Seattle, she's here visiting her father. I told you that on the phone." Hardin's voice breaks through the chaos; it's barely controlled, and it sends a shiver over my body, raising the small hairs on my arms.

"Don't think that just because you called me we're suddenly friends," she snaps. Hardin jerks me back by my arm, and I glare up at him, puzzled. I hadn't even realized that I started toward her until he stopped me.

"Judgmental as always. You'll never change, you're still the same woman you were all those years ago." My father shakes his head in disapproval. I'm thankful that he's on Hardin's side.

"Judgmental? Are you aware that this boy, the one you're defending, weaseled his way between your daughter's legs to win money in a bet he made with his friends?" My mother's voice is cold—smug, even.

All of the air leaves the room, and I'm choking, gasping for a simple breath.

"That's right! He was bragging around campus about his conquest. So don't you defend him to me," she hisses. My father's eyes are wide. I can see the stormy currents gathering behind them as he looks at Hardin.

"What? Is this true?" My father is choking for breath, too.

"It's not important! We've already passed it," I tell him.

"See, she went and found herself someone exactly like you. Let us pray that he doesn't get her pregnant and leave when times get tough."

I can't listen anymore. I can't let Hardin be dragged through the mud by both of my parents. This is a disaster.

"And not to mention just three weekends ago, a man dropped her at my house unconscious because of his"—she points to Hardin—"friends! They nearly had their way with her!"

The reminder of that night pains me, but it's the way my mother is blaming Hardin that bothers me the most. What happened that night was in no way his fault, and she knows it.

"You son of a bitch!" my father says through his teeth.

"Don't," Hardin calmly warns him. I pray that he listens.

"You had me fooled! Here I was thinking you just had a bad rep, some tattoos, and an attitude! I could deal with that. I'm the same way. But you *used* my daughter!" My father dashes toward Hardin, and I stand in front of him.

My brain hasn't had a chance to catch up with my mouth. "Stop it! Both of you!" I scream. "If you want to go to war over your past, that's your choice, but you won't bring Hardin into it! He called you for a reason, Mother, and yet here you are throwing him under the bus out of anger. This is his place, not either of yours. Both of you can get the hell out!" My eyes burn, as if they're begging me to shed the warm tears, but I refuse.

My mother and father both halt; they look at me, then at each other. "Sort your crap out or leave; we'll be in the bedroom." I wrap my fingers around Hardin's, and I try to pull him behind me.

He hesitates for a moment before using his long legs to step in front of me and lead me down the hallway, still grasping my hand. His grip is tight, nearly unbearably so, but I stay quiet. I'm still in shock from my mother's arrival and blowup; too much pressure on my hand is the least of my concerns.

I push the door closed behind me just in time to muffle the shouting voices of my parents down the hall. Suddenly I'm nine again, running through the backyard of my mother's house to my haven, the small greenhouse. I could always hear the shouting, no matter how loud Noah attempted to be in order to mute the unpleasant noise.

"I wish you hadn't called her." I break from my memories and look up at Hardin. Landon is sitting at the desk, making a point not to stare at us.

"You needed her. You were in denial." His voice is gravelly.

"She made things worse; she told him about what you did."

"It made sense at the time to call her. I was trying to help you."

The look in his eyes tells me he really thought it might work. "I know," I say with a sigh. I wish he'd run the idea past me first, but I know he was doing what he thought was right.

"Damned if I do, damned if I don't." He shakes his head and plops down on the bed. Looking up at me with real anguish, he says, "We'll always be reminded of that shit—you know that, don't you?"

He's shutting down; I can feel it just as surely as I can see it happening in front of me.

"No, that's not true." There's at least some truth to my words in that once everyone we know finds out about the bet, it'll become old news to them all. I shudder at the thought of Kimberly and Christian finding out, but everyone else around us now knows the humiliating truth.

"Yes, it is! You know it is!" Hardin raises his voice and paces across the floor. "It's never going to go away, every time we fucking turn around, someone is throwing it in your face, reminding you of what a fuckup I am!" His fist collides with the top of the desk before I can stop him. The wood splinters, and Landon jumps to his feet.

"Don't do this! Don't let her get to you, please!" I grab a fistful of his black sweatshirt, stopping him from beginning another assault on the already broken wood. He jerks away, but I don't let up. I grab both sleeves this time, and he turns around, fuming.

"Aren't you tired of this shit? Aren't you tired of the constant fight? If you would just let me go, your life would be much easier!" Hardin's words come out clipped and loud, and each syllable cuts deep. He always does this; he always goes for self-destruction. I won't allow it this time.

"Stop that! You know that I don't want easy and loveless." I gather his face between my hands and force him to look at me.

"Both of you, listen to me," Landon interrupts. Hardin doesn't look at him; he keeps his furious gaze on me. My best friend, Hardin's stepbrother, walks across the room to stand only feet away from us.

"You guys can't do this again. Hardin, you can't let people get into your head like that; Tessa's is the only opinion that matters. Let hers be the only voice in your head," he tells us.

It's as if the black rings around Hardin's eyes visibly shrink as he takes in the words. "And Tess . . ." Landon sighs. "You don't need to feel guilty and try to convince Hardin that you want to be with him; you staying around through everything should be proof enough."

Landon has a point, but I'm not sure if Hardin will see it through his anger and pain.

"Tessa needs you to comfort her right now. Her parents are screaming at each other in there, so be here for her—don't make this about you," Landon tells his stepbrother. Something in his words seems to click in Hardin's mind, and he nods, tilting his head down to press his forehead against mine, his harsh breathing slowing with each breath.

"I'm sorry . . ." he whispers.

"I'm going to go home now." Landon looks away from us, seemingly uncomfortable with witnessing the intimacy between Hardin and me. "I'll let my mom know you'll be by."

I move away from Hardin to wrap my arms around Landon's neck. "Thank you for everything. I'm so glad you were here," I say into his chest. His arms tightly hug me, and this time Hardin doesn't pull me away. When I step out of the embrace, Landon leaves the room, and I look back at Hardin. He's examining his bloody knuckles, a sight that was beginning to turn into a distant memory; now I'm seeing it again as the thick blood drips onto the floor.

"About what Landon said," Hardin says, wiping his bloodied hand on the bottom of his sweatshirt. "When he said yours should be the only voice in my head. I want that." When he looks up at me again, his expression is haunted. "I want that so fucking bad. I can't seem to shake them . . . Steph, Zed, now your mum and dad."

"We'll figure it out, we will," I promise him.

"Theresa!" My mother's voice resounds from outside the door. I had been too wrapped up in Hardin to notice that the noise in the living room had dissipated. "Theresa, I'm coming in."

The door opens on the last word, and I stand behind Hardin. This seems to be a pattern.

"We need to talk about this, all of this." She eyes Hardin and me with equal intensity. Hardin's head turns, and he looks down at me, raising an eyebrow for approval.

"I don't think there's much to discuss," I say from behind my shield.

"There's plenty to discuss. I'm sorry for my behavior tonight. I lost my mind when I saw your father here, after all these years. Please give me a little time to explain. Please." The word "please" sounds foreign coming from my mother's lips.

Hardin steps away, exposing me to her. "I'm going to go clean this up." He lifts his battered hand in the air and exits the room before I can stop him.

"Sit down, we have a lot to discuss." My mother runs her palms down the front of her dress and pushes her thick blond waves to one side before she sits down on the edge of the bed.

chapter one hundred and twenty-three

HARDIN

The cold water blasts from the faucet onto my torn flesh. I stare down at the sink, watching as the red-stained water swirls around the metal drain.

Again? This shit happened again? Of course it did; it was only a matter of time.

I leave the bathroom door open so I can easily access the room across the hall if I hear any screaming. I have no fucking idea what I was thinking when I called that bitch. I shouldn't call her that . . . but she is one, so . . . bitch it is. At least I'm not saying it in front of Tessa. When I called her, I could only think of Tessa's blank expression and naive remarks, saying things like "he's not doing drugs" as she tried to convince herself of what was obviously not true. I knew she'd come undone at any moment, and for some stupid fucking reason I thought her mum being here could possibly be of help.

This is precisely why I don't try to help people. I have no experience in it. I'm pretty damn excellent at fucking shit up, but I'm no savior.

A flash of movement in the mirror catches my eye, and I look up to see Richard's reflection staring back at me. He's leaning against the narrow doorframe, his expression wary.

"What? Did you come to try and shank me or something?" I say flatly.

He sighs and runs his hands over his clean-shaven face. "No, not this time."

I scoff, half wishing that he would try and come at me. I'm certainly wound up enough for a brawl, or two.

"Why didn't either of you tell me?" Richard asks, obviously referring to the bet.

Is he fucking serious?

"Why would I tell you? And you sure as hell aren't stupid enough to believe Tessa would tell her father—her *absentee* father—some shit like that." I turn the faucet off and grab a towel to apply pressure to my knuckles; they've stopped bleeding, for the most part. I should learn to switch hands, punch with my right from now on.

"I don't know . . . I feel blindsided, I thought you two were just opposites attracting, but now . . ."

"I'm not asking for your approval. Nor do I need it." I walk past him and hurry down the hallway. I go and grab the bag of burned popcorn that still rests on the floor.

"Let hers be the only voice in your head." Landon's words echo through my mind. I wish it were that easy, and maybe it will be one day . . . I sure as hell hope so.

"I know you don't; I just want to understand all this shit. As her dad, I feel obligated to beat your ass." He shakes his head.

"Right," I say, wanting to remind him again that he hasn't been her father for over nine years.

"Carol was a lot like Tessa when she was young," he says, following me into the kitchen.

I recoil, and the bag nearly slips from my fingers. "No, she wasn't."

There is no way in hell that this could be true. Honestly, I used to think Tessa was just like that prudish, bitchy woman, but now that I actually know her, I'm sure that it couldn't be further from the truth. Her struggle to appear perfect is certainly the result of having the woman as her mother, but otherwise Tessa is nothing like her.

"It's true. She wasn't quite as nice, but she wasn't always . . ." He trails off, grabbing a bottled water from my fridge.

"A bitch?" I finish his sentence for him. His eyes dart down the empty hallway as if he's afraid she's going to appear and toss him around again. I'd like to see that happen, actually . . .

"She was always smiling . . . Her smile was something else. All the men wanted her, but she was mine." He grins at the memory. I didn't sign up for this shit . . . I'm no fucking counselor. Tessa's mum is hot as hell, but she's got a constant stick up her ass that someone needs to remove, or maybe the complete opposite . . .

"Okay . . ." I don't get the point here.

"She had so much ambition and compassion then. It's really fucked up, because Tessa's grandma was just like Carol, if not worse." He laughs at the thought, but I cringe. "Her parents hated, I mean *hated* me. They never hid it, either. They wanted her to marry a stockbroker, a lawyer—anyone except me. I hated them, too; may they rest in peace." He looks up at the ceiling. As fucked up as it is to say, I'm grateful that Tessa's grandparents aren't around to judge me.

"Well, obviously you two shouldn't have been married, then." I close the lid on the trash can, where I've just dropped the bag of popcorn, and lean my elbows on the counter. I'm frustrated with Richard and his stupid fucking habits, which are upsetting to Tessa. I want to kick his ass out and send him right back onto the streets, but he's almost become like a piece of furniture in this apartment. He's like an old couch that smells like shit and always creaks when you sit down on it, and it's uncomfortable as shit, but for some reason you can't throw it away. That's Richard.

His face falls, and he says softly, "We weren't married."

I tilt my head slightly out of confusion. *What? I know Tessa told me that they were . . .*

"Tessa doesn't know. No one does. We were never married legally. We had a wedding to please her parents, but we never filed the paperwork. I didn't want it."

"Why?" But maybe a more important question is, why am I so interested in this shit? Minutes ago I was imagining slamming Richard's head through the drywall; now I'm participating in gossip like a fucking teenage girl. I should be listening at the door of my bedroom, making sure Tessa's mum isn't filling her head with bullshit to try to take her away from me.

"Because marriage wasn't for me"—he scratches his head—"or so I thought. We did everything as a married couple; she took my last name. I'm not quite sure how she pulled that off—I think it was like she thought that by doing it, I'd finally consent or something, but no one knew the sacrifices she made for my selfishness."

I wonder how Tessa would feel about this information . . . she's so obsessed with the idea of marriage. Would this diminish her obsession, or fuel it?

"Over the years, she grew tired of my behavior. We fought like cats and dogs, and let me tell you, that woman was relentless, but I took it from her. Once she stopped fighting me, that's when I knew it was over. I watched the fire slowly die out in her over the years." Looking at his eyes, I can see he's removed himself from this room and launched himself into the past. "Every single night she would be waiting at the dinner table, her and Tessie both in dresses and hairpins, only for me to stumble in and complain about the burned edges of lasagna. Half the time I'd pass out before the fork hit my mouth, and every night ended with a fight . . . I can't remember the half of it." A visible shudder passes over him.

A vision of a very young Tessa, all dressed up at the table, waiting excitedly to see her father after a long day, only to have him crush her, makes me want to reach out and strangle the man.

"I don't want to hear another word," I warn him, meaning it.

"I'll stop now." I can see the embarrassment plastered on his face. "I just wanted you to know that Carol wasn't always like this. I did it to her. I made her the bitter, angry woman she is today. You don't want history to repeat itself, do you?"

chapter
one hundred and twenty-four

TESSA

My mother and I sit in silence. My mind is reeling, and my heart is pounding as I watch her tuck a lock of thick blond hair behind her ear. She's calm and collected—not overwhelmed the way I am.

"Why would you let your father come here? After all this time. I can understand you wanting to see him more after running into him on the street, but not allowing him to move in," she finally says.

"I didn't allow him to move in; I don't live here anymore. Hardin let him stay out of kindness, kindness that you misinterpreted and threw in his face." I don't hide my disgust about the way she treated him.

My mother—everyone—will always misunderstand Hardin, and why I love him. It doesn't matter, though, because I don't need them to.

"He called you because he thought you would be there for me." I sigh, mentally deciding which way I want to steer the conversation before she bulldozes me into acquiescence in her typical Carol Young fashion.

My mother's blue eyes are somber, cast to the ground. "Why do you turn against everyone to defend that boy, after all he has done to you? He's put you through so much, Theresa."

"He's worth the defending, Mother. That's why."

"But—"

"He *is.* I won't keep having this discussion with you. I told you before, if you can't accept him, then I can't have a relationship with you. Hardin and I are a package deal, whether you like it or not."

"I once thought that about your father." I do my best not to flinch when she lifts her hand to smooth the front of my hair.

"Hardin is nothing like my father."

A light laugh sounds from her painted lips. "Yes, oh yes, he is. He is like him in so many ways."

"You can leave if you're going to say those things."

"Calm down." She repeats the smoothing action on my hair. I'm torn between being irritated by the patronizing gesture and being comforted by the decent memories it brings. "I want to tell you a story."

I'll admit I'm intrigued by her words, though I'm skeptical of her motives. She never told me stories about my father while I was growing up, so this ought to be interesting. "Nothing you say will change my mind about Hardin," I tell her.

The corners of her mouth turn up slightly as she declares, "Your father and I never married."

"What?" I sit up straight on the bed, crossing my legs beneath me. *What does she mean, they never married?* Yes, they did, I've seen the pictures. My mother's lace gown was exquisite, despite the fact that her belly was slightly swollen, and my father's suit wasn't tailored properly, it hung off him like a potato sack. I used to love to look through those albums and admire the way my mother's cheeks glowed as my father looked down at her as if she were the only person in his world. I remember the awful scene that ensued one day when my mother found me looking through them; after that, she hid them away, and I never saw them again.

"It's true." She sighs. I can tell that this disclosure is humiliating for her. Her hands are shaking when she says, "We had a wedding, but your father never wanted to be married. I knew that, I knew that if I hadn't gotten pregnant with you, he'd have left me much sooner. Your grandparents pushed the marriage on him. You see, your father and I could never get along, not even for a day. It was exciting in the beginning, thrilling even"—the blue of her eyes is lost in the memory—"but as you will come to see, there's only so much that one person can take. As the nights came and went and the years passed, I prayed to God every night that he would change for me, for you. I prayed that one night, he'd walk through that front door with a bouquet of roses in his hand instead of liquor on his breath." She leans back and crosses her arms in front of her chest. Bracelets that she can't afford hang from her wrists, a tribute to her excessive need to look stylish.

My mother's confession has left me silent. She's never been one for open discussion, especially when the topic is my father. The sympathy that I suddenly find myself feeling for this cold woman brings me to tears.

"Stop that," she scolds me before continuing: "Every woman hopes to be the one to reform her man, but that's all it is: false hope. I don't want you going down the same path that I did. I want more for you." I feel nauseous. "That is why I raised you to be able to get out of that small town and make a life for yourself."

"I'm not—" I begin to defend myself, but she raises her hand to silence me.

"We had our good days, too, Theresa. Your father was funny and charming—she smiles—"and he was trying his best to be what I needed him to be, but his true self overpowered that, and he became frustrated with me and with the life we shared for all those years. He turned to liquor, and it was never the same. I know you remember." Her voice is haunted, and I can hear the vulnerability in her tone and see it shining in her eyes, but she recovers quickly. My mother has never been fond of weakness.

I'm once again taken back to the screaming, the breaking of

dishes, even the occasional "these bruises on my arms are from gardening," and feel my stomach get tied up in knots.

"Can you honestly look me in the eyes and tell me that you have a future with this boy?" she asks as the silence ticks on.

I can't respond. I know the future that I want with Hardin. Whether he'll be willing to give it to me is the question.

"I wasn't always like this, Theresa." She gently dabs both index fingers under her eyes. "I used to love life, I was always excited about the future . . . and look at me now. You may think I'm a horrible person for wanting to protect you from my fate, but I'm only doing what's necessary to keep you from repeating my history. I don't want this for you . . ." I struggle to picture a young Carol, happy and excited about each new day. I can count the times that I've heard the woman laugh in the last five years on one hand.

"It's not the same, Mother." I force myself to say the words.

"Theresa, you cannot deny the similarities."

"There are some, yes," I admit, more to myself than to her, "but I refuse to believe that history is repeating itself. Hardin has already changed so much."

"If you have to change him, why even bother?" Her voice is calm now as she looks around the bedroom that once was mine.

"I haven't changed him, he's changed himself. He's still the same man; all the things that I love about him are there, only he has learned to handle things differently and has become a better version of himself."

"I saw his bloody hand," she points out.

I shrug. "He has a temper." A massive one, but I won't go along with her putting him down. She needs to understand that I'm on his side, and that from now on, to get to him she has to go through me.

"So did your father."

I stand. "Hardin would never purposely hurt me. He isn't perfect, Mother, but neither are you. Neither am I." I'm amazed at my own confidence as I cross my arms and match her glare.

"It's more than his temper . . . Think of what he's done to you. He humiliated you; you had to find another campus."

I don't have the energy to argue with her statement, mostly because it holds a lot of truth. I'd always wanted to move to Seattle, but my bad experience this first year at school gave me the extra push that I needed.

"He's covered in tattoos . . . though at least he removed those hideous piercings." Her face twists in disgust.

"You're not perfect either, Mother," I repeat. "The pearls around your neck hide your scars, just as Hardin's tattoos hide his."

My mother's eyes quickly flick over to me, and I can clearly see the words repeating in her mind. It's finally happened; I've finally made a breakthrough in dealing with her.

"I'm sorry for what my father did to you, I really am, but Hardin isn't my father." I sit back down next to her, and dare to place my hand over hers. Her skin is cold under my palm, but to my surprise, she doesn't pull away. "And I'm not you," I add as gently as possible.

"You will be if you don't get as far away from him as you can."

I remove my hand from hers and take a deep breath to stay calm. "You don't have to approve of my relationship, but you have to respect it. If you can't," I say, struggling to stay confident, "then *you and I* will never be able to have a relationship."

She slowly shakes her head from side to side. I know she was expecting me to give in to her, to agree that Hardin and I could never work. She was wrong.

"You cannot give me that type of ultimatum."

"Yes, I can. I need as much support as possible, and I am beyond exhausted with battling against the world."

"If you feel as if you're battling alone, perhaps it's time to change sides." She raises an accusatory brow at me. I stand again.

"I'm not battling alone, stop doing that. Stop it," I hiss. I'm trying my best to be patient with her, but my resolve is wearing as thin, as this night is long.

"I'm never going to like him," my mother says, and I know she means every word.

"You don't have to like him, but you won't be spreading our business to anyone else, including my father. That was incredibly wrong of you to tell him about the bet, and not in the least justified."

"Your father had the right to know what he has caused."

She doesn't get it! She still doesn't understand. My head is going to explode any moment; I can feel the pressure building in my neck. "Hardin is trying his hardest for me, but until now he's never known any better," I tell her.

She doesn't say a word. She doesn't even look at me.

"That's it, then? You're going to take the second option?" I ask.

She stares at me, silent, the wheels of her mind turning and turning behind her heavily shaded eyes. She has no color left in her cheeks, despite the rosy blush she clearly swept across her cheekbones before she arrived. At last she mutters, "I'll try to respect your relationship. I will try."

"Thank you," I say, but really I don't know what to make of this . . . truce with my mother. I'm not naive enough to believe what she's promised until she proves it, but it still feels pretty good to have one of the heavy stones lifted from my back.

"What will you do about your father?" We both stand; she towers over me in her four-inch heels.

"I don't know." I've been too distracted by the topic of Hardin to focus on my father.

"You should make him leave; he has no business being here clouding your mind and filling it with lies."

"He's done no such thing," I fire back. Every time I believe we've made any type of progress, she uses her sharp heel to kick me back down.

"He has! He has strangers showing up here, shaking him down for money! Hardin told me all of it."

Why would he do that? I understand his concern, but my mother hasn't helped the situation one bit. "I'm not going to kick him out. This isn't my place, and he has nowhere else to go."

My mother's eyes close, and she shakes her head at me for the tenth time in the last twenty minutes. "You have to stop trying to fix people, Theresa. You will spend your entire life doing it, but then you'll have nothing left of yourself, even if you succeed in changing them."

"Tessa?" Hardin's voice calls from outside the bedroom. He opens the door before I respond, and his eyes immediately scan my face for signs of distress.

"You okay?" he asks, ignoring my mother's presence completely.

"Yeah." I gravitate toward him but avoid throwing my arms around him, for my mother's sake. The poor woman has already been dragged through twenty years of memories.

"I was just leaving." My mother runs her palms down her dress, stopping at the hem and then repeating the action, a frown settling on her face.

"Good," Hardin rudely remarks, quick to protect me.

I look up at him, my eyes pleading with him for silence. He rolls his eyes but doesn't say another word as my mother strides by us and marches down the hall. The obnoxious clicking of her heels sends me into a full migraine.

I take his hand and follow in silence. My father attempts to speak to my mother, but she brushes him off.

"You didn't wear a coat?" he unexpectedly asks her.

Just as puzzled as I am, she mumbles "no" and turns to me.

"I'll call you tomorrow . . . Answer this time?" It's a question instead of a demand, which is some sort of progress.

"Yes." I nod.

She doesn't say goodbye. I knew she wouldn't.

"That woman drives me flippin' crazy!" my father shouts when the door closes, his hands flying into the air in exasperation.

"We're going to bed. If anyone else knocks at the damn door, don't answer it," Hardin grumbles and leads me back to the bedroom.

I'm beyond exhausted. I can barely stand on my feet.

"What did she say?" Hardin lifts his sweatshirt over his head and tosses it at me. I detect a flicker of uncertainty as he waits for me to collect it from the floor.

Despite the greasy butter and blood smeared on the black fabric, I gladly remove my own shirt, along with my bra, and pull it over my head. I breathe in the familiar scent of him, which aides in calming my nerves. "More than she's said in my entire life," I admit. My mind is still reeling.

"Did any of it change your mind?" He looks at me, panic and fear filling his eyes. I get the feeling my father must have had a similar talk with him, and wonder if my father holds the same grudge against my mother as she holds against him or if he admits that he's to blame for the turmoil in both of their lives.

"No." I pull my loose pants down my legs and place them on the chair.

"You're sure? Aren't you worried that we're repeating their—" Hardin begins.

"No, we are not. We're nothing like them." I stop him. I don't want anyone else getting into his head, not tonight.

Hardin doesn't look convinced, but I force myself not to focus on that right now.

"What do you want me to do about your dad? Kick him out?" he asks. He moves to sit on the bed with his back against the headboard while I grab his dirty jeans and socks from the floor. Hardin's arms lift to rest behind his head, fully displaying his toned, inked body.

"No, don't kick him out. Please." I crawl into bed, and he pulls me onto his lap.

"I won't," he assures me. "Not tonight, at least." I look up for a smile, but there isn't one.

"I'm so confused," I groan into his chest.

"I can help with that." He lifts his pelvis, and I'm forced forward, using my palms to steady myself against his exposed chest.

I roll my eyes. "Of course you can. Every problem looks like a nail when your first tool of choice is a hammer."

He smiles wickedly. "Are you saying you need to get nailed?"

Before I can bemoan his bad joke, he takes my chin between his long, busted fingers, and I find myself shifting my hips, rubbing against him. I'm vaguely aware of my period; I know Hardin certainly doesn't mind it.

"You need sleep, baby; it would be wrong to fuck you right now," he says softly.

I shamelessly pout. "No, it wouldn't," I say and slide my palms down his stomach.

"Oh no, you don't." He stops me.

I need a distraction, and Hardin is the perfect fix. "You started it," I whine. I sound desperate, because I am.

"I know, and I'm sorry for that. I'll take you in the car tomorrow." His fingers slip under the sweatshirt and begin to draw unknown shapes across my bare back. "And if you're a good girl, I'll even bend you over the desk at my father's house, just the way you like," he says into my ear.

My breathing hitches, and I playfully swat at him, and he laughs. His laugh is almost as distracting as sex would be. Almost.

"Besides, we don't want to make a mess in here tonight, do we? With your father out there? He'll probably see the blood on the sheets and assume I've killed you." He bites the inside of his cheek.

"Do *not* start that," I warn him. His cheesy menstrual jokes are not welcome right now.

"Ahh, baby, don't be like that." He pinches my behind, and I yelp, sliding further into his lap, "Go with the flow." He grins.

"You've used that one before." I smile back.

"Well, excuse me for not being original. I like to recycle my jokes about once a month."

I groan and try to roll off him, but he stops me and nuzzles my neck.

"You're disgusting," I say.

"Yeah, I'm just an old bloody rag, I suppose." He laughs and presses his lips to mine.

I roll my eyes. "Speaking of bloody rags, let me see your hand." I reach behind my back and gently grab him by the wrist. His middle finger is the worst, a thick gash spreads from knuckle to knuckle. "You should get this looked at, if it doesn't begin to heal tomorrow."

"I'm fine."

"This one, too." I run the pad of my index finger over the mangled skin on his ring finger.

"Stop fussing, woman, go to sleep," he grumbles.

I nod in agreement and drift off to the sound of him complaining about my father eating his Frosted Flakes again.

chapter one hundred and twenty-five

TESSA

I lay in bed for over two hours, waiting patiently for Hardin to wake up, before I gave up. By the time I've showered and am fully dressed, the kitchen is cleaned, and I've taken two ibuprofen to get rid of my cramps and massive headache. I make my way back to the bedroom to wake him up myself.

I gently shake his arm and whisper his name. It doesn't work.

"Hardin, wake up." I roughly grip his shoulder and recoil when the vision of my mother ripping my father's slumbering body off of the couch flashes into my mind. All morning I've been avoiding thoughts of my mother and the heartbreaking history lesson I was given last night. My father is still asleep; I imagine that her short visit has worn him out as well.

"No," he grumbles sleepily.

"If you won't get up, then I'll be going to your father's house alone," I say, slipping my feet into my flat shoes. I have many pairs of Toms, but I always find myself wearing the tan crocheted ones the most. Hardin calls them "hideous moccasins," but I love the comfortable shoes.

He groans and rolls over onto his stomach, pushing himself up onto his elbows. His eyes are still closed when he turns his head to me. "No, you won't."

I knew he wouldn't like that idea, which is precisely why I used it to get his behind out of the bed.

"Get up, then. I've already showered and everything," I whine. I'm anxious to get to Landon's house and see him, Ken, and Karen again. It feels like ages since I last saw that sweet woman in the strawberry-print apron that she hardly ever removes.

"Dammit." Hardin pouts, opening one eye. I stifle a giggle at the lazy expression covering his face. I'm tired, too, mentally and physically drained, but the idea of getting out of this apartment for the day has perked me up tremendously.

"Come here first." He opens the other eye and reaches out for me. The moment I'm beside him on the bed, he rolls his heavy body on top of mine, encasing me in his warmth. He purposely rubs his hardness against me, grinding his hips until he's perfectly nestled between my thighs, his morning erection pressing torturously into me.

"Morning." He's wide-awake now, and I can't help but laugh. He leisurely drags his hips in a circle again, and this time I try to wiggle free. He joins me in laughter but quickly silences me by covering my mouth with his. His tongue laps mine, gently caressing, hinting at an intention completely opposed to the sharp movements his hips are making.

"Are you plugged?" he whispers, still kissing me. His hands have moved to my chest, and my heart is thumping rapidly, making his sleepy voice barely audible.

"I am." I nod, only mildly cringing at the hideous term I have become used to. He pulls away, his eyes slowly raking over my face, and his tongue swiping along his bottom lip, wetting it.

The sound of kitchen cabinets opening and closing carries down the hallway, followed by a large belch, and then the crash of pans on the floor.

Hardin's eyes roll. "Fucking lovely." He stares down at me. "Well, I had planned on fucking you before we left, but now that Mr. Sunshine's awake . . ."

He climbs off of me and stands up, taking the blanket with him. "I'll be quick in the shower," he says with a scowl toward the door.

Hardin returns less than five minutes later just as I'm tucking in the corners of the bedsheet. The only article of clothing he's wearing is a white towel wrapped around his waist. I force my eyes away from his gorgeous inked body and up to his face while he walks over to the dresser and pulls out a signature black T-shirt. Pulling it down over his head, he steps into a pair of boxers.

"Last night was a fucking disaster." His eyes are focused on his busted hand as he buttons his jeans.

"Yeah." I sigh, trying to avoid any further conversation that revolves around my parents.

"Let's go." He grabs his keys and phone from the dresser and shoves them into his pockets. He pushes his wet hair back off his forehead and opens the bedroom door. "Well . . . ?" he impatiently remarks when I don't jump up right away. What happened to the playful Hardin from only minutes ago? If his bad mood continues this way, then I suspect that today will be just as bad as yesterday.

Without a word, I follow him through the door and down the hallway. The bathroom door is closed, and the water is on. I don't want to wait for my father to get out of the shower, but I also don't want to leave without telling him where we're going and making sure he doesn't need anything. *What does he do in this apartment while he's alone? Does he think about drugs all day? Does he have people over?*

I shake the second thought from my head. Hardin would find out if he brought bad friends around, and my father sure as heck wouldn't still be here if that were the case.

* * *

HARDIN STAYS QUIET during the drive to Ken and Karen's place. The only assurance I have that today isn't going to be a total wash is his hand resting on my thigh while he focuses on the road.

When we arrive, Hardin, as always, doesn't knock before walking inside. The sweet smell of maple syrup fills the house, and we follow the scent to the kitchen. Karen is standing next to the oven, a spatula is one hand while she waves the other through the air in conversation. An unfamiliar young woman is seated at one of the island stools. Her long brown hair is the only thing I see until she turns the stool around when Karen's attention is directed toward us.

"Tessa, Hardin!" Karen nearly shrieks with joy as she carefully places the spatula onto the counter and rushes over to wrap her arms around me. "It's been so long!" she exclaims, holding me at arm's length and then crushing me back to her body. Her warm welcome is exactly what I needed after last night.

"It's only been three weeks, Karen," Hardin rudely remarks.

Her smile dims a fraction, and she tucks her hair behind her ear.

I peer around her to take in all the baked goods around the kitchen. "What are you making?" I ask to distract her from her stepson's sour attitude.

"Maple cookies, maple cupcakes, maple squares, and maple muffins." Karen pulls me along gently while Hardin cowers in the corner, a deep frown set on his face.

Ignoring him, I look at the young woman again, unsure how to introduce myself.

"Oh!" Karen takes notice. "I'm sorry, I should have introduced you first thing." She gestures to the woman. "This is Sophia; her parents live just down the road."

Sophia smiles and reaches to shake my hand. "Nice to meet you," she says with a smile. She's beautiful, extremely beautiful.

Her eyes are bright and her smile warm; she's older than me, but she can't be much more than twenty-five.

"I'm Tessa, Landon's friend," I say.

Hardin coughs behind me, obviously displeased at my choice of words. I assume Sophia knows Landon, and since Hardin and I are . . . well, this morning it just seems easier to introduce myself this way.

"I haven't gotten to meet Landon yet," Sophia says. Her voice is soft and sweet, and I immediately like her.

"Oh?" I assumed she knew him, since her family lives down the road.

"Sophia has just graduated from the Culinary Institute of America in New York," Karen brags for her, and Sophia smiles. I don't blame her; if I'd just graduated from the best culinary school in the country, I'd let people brag for me, too. I mean, if I wasn't already doing it myself.

"I'm visiting my family, and I ran into Karen down the road . . . buying some syrup." She grins, eyeing the massive amount of maple-flavored goodies on display.

"Oh, and this is Hardin," I say to include my brooding man in the background.

She smiles at him. "Nice to meet you."

He doesn't even look at the poor woman and just says, "Yeah."

I in turn offer her a shrug and a sympathetic smile, then turn to Karen. "Where's Landon?"

Her eyes flicker to Hardin, then to me, before she answers, "He's upstairs . . . He hasn't been feeling well," she says. My stomach turns; there's something going on with my best friend, I know it.

"I'm going upstairs." Hardin turns to leave.

"Wait, I'll go," I offer. If something is going on with Landon, the last thing he needs is Hardin taunting him.

"No." Hardin shakes his head. *"I'll* go. Have some syrup cakes or whatever," he grumbles and takes two stairs at a time, giving me no chance to argue.

Karen and Sophia watch him go. "Hardin is Ken's son," Karen says. Despite his poor attitude today, she still smiles proudly at the mention of his name.

Sophia nods in understanding. "He's lovely," she lies, and the three of us burst into laughter.

chapter one hundred and twenty-six

HARDIN

Fortunately for both of us, Landon's not rubbing one out when I push his bedroom door open. Predictably, he's seated in the recliner against the wall with a textbook on his lap.

"What are you doing in here?" he asks, his voice hoarse.

"You knew we were coming." I take the liberty of sitting on the edge of his bed.

"I meant in my room," he clarifies.

I choose not to answer that; actually, I don't know why I'm in his room. I sure as hell didn't want to stay downstairs with three women obsessing over one another.

"You look like shit," I tell him.

"Thanks." He looks back down at the textbook.

"What's wrong with you? Why are you up here moping around?" I look around his normally tidy room to find it sort of messy—clean by my standards, but not by his and Tessa's.

"I'm not moping."

"If something's wrong, tell me. I'm really good at, like, caring," I say, hoping humor might help somehow.

He slams the book shut and stares at me. "Why would I tell you anything? So you can laugh at me?"

"No. I wouldn't," I say. I probably would. I had actually been planning on him telling me some stupid shit about getting a bad grade so I could take my frustrations out on him, but now that he's here, in front of me, looking all pitiful, making him miserable doesn't appeal to me as much as it did before.

"Just tell me, maybe I can help," I offer. I have no fucking idea why I just said that. We both know I'm shit at helping anyone. Look at what a fucking disaster last night turned out to be. Richard's words have been eating away at me all morning.

"Help me?" Landon gapes, obviously wary of my offer.

"Oh, come on, don't make me beat it out of you." I lie back on his bed and examine the blades of the ceiling fan, willing it to be summer already so I could enjoy the sensation of it cooling me down.

I hear his light chuckle and the sound of the book being placed on the desk beside him. "Dakota and I have ended things," he admits meekly.

I sit up quickly. *"What?"* That was the last thing I imagined would come from his mouth.

"Yeah, we've been trying to make it work . . ." He frowns, his eyes glossing over.

If he fucking cries, I'm out of here.

"Oh . . ." I say and look away.

"I think she's been wanting to end it for a while."

I glance at him again, not wanting to put too much focus on his sad features. He really is like a puppy, especially right now. I don't like puppies, though, except this one, maybe . . . My sudden animosity toward the curly-haired girl is strong.

"Why do you think that?" I ask.

He shrugs. "I don't know. She didn't come right out and say that she wanted to end it . . . It's just . . . she's been so busy lately, and she never returns my calls. It's like the closer it got to me coming to New York, the more distant she became."

"She's probably fucking someone else," I blurt out, and he flinches.

"No! She isn't like that," he says, defending her.

I probably shouldn't have said that. "Sorry." I shrug.

"She's not that type of girl at all," he tells me.

Neither was Tessa, but I had her shaking and moaning my name while she was still seeing Noah . . . though I keep that fact to myself for everyone's sake.

"Okay," I say agreeably.

"I've been dating her so long that I can't even remember what life was like before her." His voice is quiet and so full of sadness that it makes my chest tight. It's an odd feeling.

"I know what you mean," I say. Life before Tessa was nothing, only sloshed memories and darkness, and that's exactly what it would be like after her, too.

"Yeah, but at least you won't have to find out what it would be like *after.*"

"What makes you so sure?" I ask, noting that I'm taking away from his breakup announcement, but I must know the answer.

"I can't imagine anything would tear you two apart . . . nothing has so far." Landon says it like it's the most obvious answer in the world. Maybe it is to him; I wish it were that obvious to me.

"So what now? Are you still going to New York? You're supposed to be leaving in what . . . two weeks?"

"Yeah, and I don't know. I've worked so hard to get into NYU, and I've already enrolled in my summer classes and everything. It just seems like a waste not to go, but it seems pointless *to* go at the same time." His fingers rub circles over his temples. "I don't know what to do."

"You shouldn't go," I say. "It would be really awkward."

"It's a big city: we'll never run into each other. And besides, we'll still be friends."

"Sure, the whole 'friends' thing." I can't help but roll my eyes. "Why didn't you tell Tessa what was going on?" I ask him. She's going to be heartbroken for him.

"Tess has—" he begins.

"Tess-*a*," I correct him.

"—has enough on her plate. I don't want her worrying for me."

"You want me to keep this from her, don't you?" I point out. I can tell by his guilty expression that he does.

"Only for now, until she catches a break. She's too stressed lately, and I'm afraid one of these days something will tip her over the edge." His concern for my girl is strong, and slightly irritating, but I decide against my better judgment and keep my mouth closed.

I groan. "She'll kill me for this, you know that." But I don't want to tell her either. He's right: she has enough going on, and I'm to blame for ninety percent of it.

"There's more . . ." he begins.

Of course there is.

"It's my mom, she—" But a light knock at the door silences him.

"Landon? Hardin?" Tessa's voice sounds through the wood.

"Come in," Landon calls, all the while looking at me with pleading eyes to reaffirm my promise of keeping his breakup from Tessa.

"I know," I assure him as the door opens and Tessa steps inside carrying a plate and the thick smell of syrup with her.

"Karen wanted you two to try these." She rests the plate on the desk and looks at me, then quickly turns to Landon with a smile. "Try the maple squares first. Sophia taught us how to properly ice them . . . See the little flowers." Her small finger points to the clots of icing piled onto the brown crust. "She taught us how to make those; she's so lovely."

"Who?" Landon asks, his brow raised.

"Sophia; she just left to go back to her parents' house down the road. Your mother really went crazy getting tons of baking secrets from her." Tessa smiles and brings a square to her mouth.

I knew she'd like that girl. I could tell instantly that the three of them would squeal over one another in the kitchen—it's why I had to bolt.

"Oh." Landon shrugs and reaches for a square. Tessa apprehensively holds the plate out to me and I shake my head, declining. Her shoulders slump but she doesn't say anything.

"I'll have a square," I mumble, wanting her frown to go away. I've been an asshole all morning. She perks up and hands me one. The so-called flowers on the top look like globs of yellow snot. "You must have iced this one," I tease her, pulling her by the wrist to sit on my lap.

"That was a practice one!" She defends herself with her defiant lift of the chin. I can tell she's confused by my sudden shift in mood. Actually, so am I.

"Sure, baby." I grin and she flicks a piece of the yellow icing onto my shirt.

She pouts. "I'm no chef, okay?"

I look at Landon, who has his mouth full of cupcake while he stares at the ground. I dip my finger onto my shirt to remove the icing, and before Tessa can stop me, I wipe my finger across her nose, smearing the hideous yellow across it.

"Hardin!" She tries to wipe it off, but I gather her hands in mine, the pastries falling to the floor.

"Oh, come on, guys!" Landon shakes his head at us. "My room's already a mess!"

Ignoring him, I resume licking the icing from Tessa's scrunched-up nose.

"I'll help you clean up!" She laughs as my tongue runs along her cheek.

"You know, I miss the days when you wouldn't even hold her hand in front of me," Landon complains. He bends down to collect the broken squares and smashed cupcakes from his floor.

I sure as hell don't miss those days, and I hope Tessa doesn't either.

"DID YOU LIKE the maple squares, Hardin?" Karen asks while pulling a ham from the oven and sliding it onto a cutting board.

"They were okay." I shrug my shoulders and take a seat at the table. When Tessa shoots me a glare from the seat next to me, and I backtrack. "They were good," I say, earning a smile from my girl. I've finally begun to realize that the tiniest things make her smile. It's weird as hell, but it works, so I'm going with it.

My father turns to me. "How is your graduation packet coming along?" He lifts his glass of water and takes a sip, looking much better than he did when I saw him in his office last week.

"Good, it's completed. I'm not going to walk, remember?" I know he remembers; he's just hoping that I've changed my mind.

"What do you mean, you're not going to walk?" Tessa interrupts, which causes Karen to look up and stop carving the ham.

Fucking hell. "I'm not walking in that graduation, I'm having my diploma mailed," I reply sternly. This isn't going to turn into a trample-Hardin-and-change-his-mind thing.

"Why not?" Tessa asks, which makes my father look pleased. That asshole planned this, I know he did.

"I don't want to." I look at Landon for backup, but he's avoiding my gaze. So much for our bonding shit earlier; it's clear that he's back on Team Tessa. "Don't push it right now, I'm not walking, and I won't be changing my mind," I say to her, loud enough that everyone will hear me so there won't be any mistaking the finality of my decision.

"We'll talk about it later," she threatens with flushed cheeks.

Sure, Tess, sure.

Karen comes over with the ham on a serving platter, looking pretty proud of her creation. I suppose she should; admittedly it smells pretty good. I wonder if she found a way to use maple syrup on it, too.

"Your mum said you've decided to go to England," my father says. He doesn't seem uncomfortable speaking on the topic in front of Karen. I suppose they've been together long enough that him talking about my mum isn't awkward.

"Yes." I give him a one-word answer and take a bite of ham to signal that I'm done with the table chat.

"You're going, too, right, Tessa?" he asks her.

"Yes, I have to finalize my passport, but I'm going."

The smile on her face knocks my irritation down a notch.

"It will be an amazing experience for you; I know you told me how much you love England. I hate to ruin it for you, though, but modern London isn't quite like the London in your novels." He grins at her, and she laughs.

"Thank you for the warning, I'm aware that Dickens's London fog was actually smog."

Tessa fits in so well with my father and his new family, much better than I do. If it wasn't for her, I wouldn't be speaking to any of them.

"Have Hardin take you down to Chawton, it's less than two hours from Hampstead, where Trish lives," my father suggests.

I had planned on taking her there anyway, thanks.

"That would be lovely." Tessa turns to me; her hand moves under the table, and she squeezes my thigh. I know she wants me to be a good sport throughout this dinner, but my father is making it difficult. "I've heard a lot about Hampstead," she adds.

"It's changed a lot over the years. It's not the small, quiet village it was when I lived there. Real estate prices have skyrocketed," he tells her. Like she gives a fuck about the real estate in my hometown.

"There are plenty of places to see—how long will you be staying?" he asks.

"Three days." Tessa answers for both of us. I don't plan on taking her anywhere except Chawton. I thoroughly plan to keep her locked away so her weekend won't be ruined by any of my ghosts.

"I was thinking . . ." My father presses a cloth napkin to his mouth. "I called around to a few places this morning and I found a really nice facility for your father."

Tessa's fork drops from her hand and clatters onto her plate. Landon, Karen, and my father are all staring at her, waiting for her to speak.

"What?" I break the silence so she doesn't have to.

"I found a really nice treatment facility; they offer a three-month program for recovering . . ."

Tessa whimpers next to me. It's such a low sound that no one else hears it, but it resonates throughout my entire body. *How dare he bring this shit up to her in front of an audience at the dinner table!*

". . . the best in Washington, though we could look elsewhere, too, if you'd like." His voice is soft, and I don't hear a hint of judgment in it, but her cheeks are flushed in embarrassment, and I want to rip my father's fucking head clear off.

"This isn't the time to bring this shit up to her," I warn him.

Tessa jerks slightly at my harsh tone. "It's okay, Hardin." Her eyes plead with mine. "I'm just a little caught off guard," she politely says.

"No, Tessa, it's not okay." I turn to Ken. "How did you even know that her father is a junkie anyway?"

Tessa flinches again; I could break all the plates in this house for his bringing this up.

"Landon and I talked about it last night, and we both thought that discussing a rehabilitation plan with Tessa would be a good idea. It's very hard for addicts to get clean on their own," he says.

"You would know, wouldn't you?" The words are out before I can think them through.

My words didn't have the intended effect on my father, who just brushes the statement off with a smooth pause. When I look over to his wife, sadness is clear in her eyes. "Yes, as a recovering alcoholic, I *would* know," he replies.

"How much does it cost?" I ask him. I make enough money to fully support myself, and Tessa, but rehab? That shit's expensive.

"I would cover it," my father calmly answers.

"Hell, no." I try to stand from the table, but Tessa's grip on my arm is strong. I sit back down. "You aren't paying for it."

"Hardin, I'm more than willing to."

"Maybe the two of you should talk about this in the other room," Landon suggests.

What he's really saying is, *Don't talk about it in front of Tessa.* Her grip on my arm lets up, and my father gets to his feet at the same time that I do. Tessa doesn't look up from her plate as we go into the living room.

"I'm sorry," I hear Landon say just before I pin my father against the wall. I'm getting mad, enraged—I can feel the anger taking over.

My father pushes me off with more force than I'd expect.

"Why couldn't you bring this up to me before throwing it in her face at the fucking dinner table—in front of *everyone!"* I shout at him, squeezing my fists tight to my sides.

"I think Tessa should have some say in it, and I knew you'd refuse my offer to pay." His voice is calm, unlike mine. I'm pissed the hell off and my blood is boiling. I'm reminded of the many times I stormed out of family dinners at the Scott residence. It might as well be a damn tradition.

"You're damn right, I refuse. You don't need to be throwing your fucking money around to us—we don't need it."

"That's not my intention here. I just want to help you in any way that I can."

"How is sending her fuckup of a father to rehab going to help me?" I ask, even though I know the answer.

He sighs. "Because if he's well, then she's well. And she's the only way to help you. I know that, and so do you."

I let out a deep breath, not even arguing back, because he's right this time. I just need a few minutes to calm down, to bring myself back to reason.

chapter one hundred and twenty-seven

TESSA

I'm relieved when neither Hardin nor Ken come back into the dining room with a bloody nose or black eye.

As Ken sits back down and places his napkin on his lap, he says, "I apologize again for bringing that up at the table. I was completely out of line."

"It's okay, really. I really appreciate your offer." I force a smile. I do appreciate it, but it's too much to accept.

"We'll talk about it later," Hardin hums into my ear.

I nod and Karen stands up to clear the table. I've barely touched my food. The mention of my father's . . . problem . . . stole away my appetite.

Hardin pulls my chair closer to his. "Eat some dessert, at least."

But I'm cramping again; the ibuprofen has worn off, and my headache and cramps have returned with a vengeance. "I'll try," I agree.

Karen brings a tray stacked with mounds of her maple-flavored treats to the table, and I reach for a cupcake. Hardin grabs for a square, eyeing the perfectly iced flowers on top.

"I did that one," I lie.

He smiles at me, shaking his head.

"I wish we didn't have to leave," I say when he glances at the clock. I try not to think about the watch he gave away to pay my father's debt to the drug dealer. *Is rehab really the best thing for my father? Would he even accept the offer?*

"You're the one who packed up and moved to Seattle," he grumbles.

"I meant here, tonight," I clarify, hoping he'll catch on.

"Oh no . . . I'm not staying here."

"I want to," I say with a pout.

"Tessa, we're going home . . . to my apartment, where your dad is."

I frown; that's exactly why I don't want to go there. I need some time to think and breathe, and this house seems to be perfect for that, even with Ken's mention of rehab at the dinner table. It's always been a sort of sanctuary. I love this house, and being in that apartment has been torture since I arrived yesterday.

"Okay." I pick at the corner of my cupcake.

Finally Hardin sighs in defeat. "Fine, we'll stay."

I knew I'd get my way.

The remainder of our time at the table isn't as awkward as what came before. Landon is quiet, too quiet, and I fully intend to ask him what's wrong after I finish helping Karen clean up the kitchen.

"I've missed having you around here." Karen closes the dishwasher and turns to me, wiping her hands on a towel.

"I've missed being here so much." I lean back against the counter.

"I'm glad to hear it. You've become like a daughter to me; I want you to know that." Karen's bottom lip quivers, and her eyes shine under the bright lights of the kitchen.

"Are you all right?" I ask her, moving to stand next to the woman whom I've come to care for so much.

"Yes." She smiles. "I'm sorry, I've been so emotional lately." She shakes it off, and just like that, she's back to normal, presenting a reassuring smile.

"Are you ready for bed?" Hardin joins us in the kitchen, grabbing another maple square on his way over to me. I knew he liked them more than he let on.

"Go on, I'm just a mess." Karen hugs me and places a loving kiss on my cheek before Hardin wraps his arm around me, practically forcing me out of the kitchen.

I sigh as we make our way to the staircase. Something doesn't feel right. "I'm worried about her, and Landon," I say.

"They're fine, I'm sure," Hardin says as he leads me upstairs and to the door of his room. Landon's bedroom door is closed, and there's no light leaking out from beneath it. "He's sleeping."

Stepping into Hardin's bedroom, I immediately feel like it welcomes me, from the bay window to the new desk and chair, replacements for the ones Hardin destroyed the last time he was here. I've been at the house since then, but I didn't pay much attention. Now that I'm here again, I want to take in every detail.

"What?" Hardin's voice startles me from my own thoughts.

I look around the room, remembering the first time I stayed here with him. "I'm just reminiscing, that's all," I say, stepping out of my shoes.

He grins. "Reminiscing, huh?" In an instant, his black shirt is pulled up and over his head and tossed to me, dragging me deeper into my memories. "Care to share?" His jeans are next; he pushes them down his legs quickly, tossing them to the floor in a messy heap.

"Well . . ." I admire his inked torso in a leisurely fashion as he lifts his arms straight up, stretching his long body. "I was thinking about the first time I stayed here with you." It also happened to be the first time Hardin ever slept here.

"What about it?"

"Nothing specific." I shrug, undressing myself in front of his watchful gaze. I fold my jeans and shirt before tugging his black T-shirt over my head.

"Bra off." Hardin raises a brow at me; his tone is stern, and his eyes are a deep green.

I remove my bra and climb into the bed to lie next to him.

"Now, tell me what you were thinking about." He pulls me by the waist and rests his hand on my hip when I'm securely lying on my side, as close as possible to his body. His fingertips trace over the waistband of my lace panties, sending a chill down my spine that spreads through my entire body.

"I was just thinking about when Landon called me that night." I look up at him to gauge his expression. "You were making a giant mess of the place." I frown at the clear memory of broken china cabinets and porcelain dishes smashed into hundreds of pieces and scattered across the floor.

"Yeah, I was," he softly replies. The hand that isn't being used to trace circles onto my bare skin reaches up and gathers a lock of my hair. He twirls the strands slowly, never breaking eye contact with me.

"I was frightened," I admit. "Not of you, but of what you would say."

He frowns. "I confirmed your fear then, didn't I?"

"Yeah, I guess you did," I reply. "But you made up for your harsh words."

He chuckles, finally taking his eyes from mine. "Yeah, only to say more fucked-up shit the next day."

I know where he's going with this. I try to sit up, but his palm flattens on my hip and presses me down.

He speaks before I can. "I loved you even then."

"You did?"

He nods once, tightening his grip on my hip. "Yeah, I did."

"How did you know?" I quietly ask. Hardin has mentioned that this was the night he knew that he loved me, but he never elaborated. I'm hoping that he will now.

"I just did. And by the way, I know what you're doing." He smiles a bright smile.

"And what is that?" I place my palm on his stomach, covering the center of the moth that's drawn there.

"You're being nosy." He wraps the section of my hair he's been playing with around his fist and tugs playfully.

"I thought I was the hair-puller here." I giggle at my corny statement, and then he does, too.

"You are." He removes his hand from my hair, only for a moment, so he can gather the entire mass of messy blond waves. He tugs, pulling my head back so I'm forced to look at him.

"It's been too long." He dips his head down, gently leading me to sit up straight, and runs his nose along my exposed jaw and neckline. "I've been hard since your little tease this morning," he whispers, pressing the evidence between my thighs. The heat of his breath on my skin is almost unbearable—I'm wriggling under his dirty words and intense stare.

"You're going to take care of that, yeah?" he says more than asks.

He pulls his fistful of my hair down and back up again, gently forcing me to nod my head. I want to correct him and tell him that he, in fact, is the one who went about teasing me this morning, but I stay quiet. I like where this is going. Without a word, Hardin releases my hair and my hip and pulls himself up to his knees. His hands are cold as they push up the fabric of the T-shirt, exposing my bare stomach and chest. His fingers greedily reach for my breasts, and his tongue pushes into my mouth. I'm instantly ignited; all the stress from the last twenty-four hours is banished and Hardin fills all of my senses.

"Sit up, against the headboard," he instructs after removing the shirt completely. I do as he says, lowering my body until my shoulders rest halfway up the enormous slate-colored headboard.

Hardin's boxers are tugged down, and he lifts one knee at a time to remove them from his body.

"A little lower, baby." I reposition myself, and he nods in approval. Then he scoots across the bed, on his knees, and positions himself in front of me. My tongue slides out of my mouth, eager to be on his skin. My jaw relaxes, and Hardin wraps his fist around his erection, and I watch in awe as he brings it to my lips, pumping slowly. I open my mouth further, and Hardin's thumb glides over my bottom lip, dipping into my mouth only fractionally before his finger is . . . um, replaced. He pushes into my mouth slowly, savoring the sensation of every inch of him sliding over my tongue.

"Fuck," he groans from above me. I look up to see his eyes burning into me; one hand is grasping the top of the headboard to steady himself as he withdraws and pushes back in.

"More," he pants, and I wrap my hands around his rear, pulling him closer. My mouth coats him, and I take slow drags of him, enjoying this just as much as he does. He feels like silk across my tongue, and his rapid breathing and low calls of my name, telling me how good I am for him, how much he loves my mouth, make my entire body burn with need for him.

He keeps moving, in and out, in and out. "So fucking good. Look at me," he begs.

I blink up at his face again, taking in the way his brows have lowered, the way his bottom lip is pulled between his teeth, and the way his eyes are watching me. He hits the back of my throat repeatedly, and I notice the way the muscles along his stomach are expanding and tightening, signaling what is next.

As if he can read my mind, he groans. "Fuck, I'm going to come." His movements pick up and he's being more forceful now. I squeeze my thighs to relieve some of the pressure and suck harder. I'm surprised when he withdraws from my mouth and comes across my bare chest. With another moan of my name, he leans forward in exhaustion, his forehead pressed against the headboard. I wait patiently for him to catch his breath and lower his body to sit next to me.

His hand reaches over, and to my horror he slowly rubs his hand across the mess he made on my skin. He watches it, transfixed for a moment before meeting my eyes.

"All mine." He grins cheekily, pressing a soft kiss to my open mouth.

"I—" I stare down at my sticky chest.

"You like it." He smiles, and I don't deny it. "It looks good on you." I can tell by the way his eyes are focused on the shining skin that he really does think that.

"You're filthy" is all I can think to say.

"Yeah? And so are you." He nods to my chest and grabs me by the hips to yank me off of the bed.

I squeal, and he covers my mouth with one hand. "Shh, we don't want an audience while I'm fucking you over the desk, now, do we?"

chapter one hundred and twenty-eight

HARDIN

The smell of coffee fills my nostrils, and I reach for Tessa, knowing she's close by. When my search comes up empty, I open my eyes to find two cups of coffee resting on the dresser and Tessa packing her bag.

"What time is it?" I ask her, hoping she says it's still early.

"Nearly noon," she says instead.

Fuck, I've slept through half the damn day.

"I've already packed everything and had breakfast. Lunch will be ready soon," she tells me with a smile. She's already showered and gotten herself dressed. She's wearing those damn jeans again, the tight pair.

I force myself out of bed and try to keep myself from lashing out at her for not waking me earlier. "Cool," I respond and reach for my pants from the floor . . . only they aren't on the floor anymore.

"Here." Tessa hands me the jeans, folded, of course. "Are you okay?" She must sense my hostility.

"I'm fine."

"Hardin," she presses. I knew she fucking would.

"I'm okay; the weekend just went too fast, that's all."

Her smile is enough to melt the ice that had formed around my mood. "It really has," she agrees.

I hate this living-separate shit. I hate it so fucking much.

"We only have to get through until Thursday," she says, trying to make the distance seem less . . . distant.

"What did Karen make for lunch?" I change the subject. "Nothing involving maple syrup, I hope."

She laughs. "No, no syrup."

Landon is brooding at the table when we walk into the dining room at the same time as Karen, who's carrying a tray of sandwiches. Tessa sits down next to Landon, and I watch as she asks him if he's all right.

"I'm okay, just feeling a little off," he says.

I never thought I'd see the day he'd lie to *her*.

"Are you sure, because you've been acting so—"

"Tessa . . ." He reaches up, and I swear, if he puts his hand on hers . . . "I'm fine." He smiles, lowering his hand from the table. I quickly reach for her hand and them on my lap, covered with my own.

The boring table chat fades in and out. I don't participate, and all too soon it's time for me to drive Tessa back to Seattle. I'm once again reminded of what a fucking idiot I am for not moving there in the first place.

"I'll see you again before you leave, right?" Tessa's eyes water as Landon hugs her goodbye. I look away.

"Yeah, of course. Maybe I'll come up there to visit you once you're back from your visit to the queen?" he quips, making her smile. I appreciate his effort, especially since I'm going to be the one she loses her shit on when she finds out that him and Dakota broke up and I kept it from her.

Ten minutes later, I'm practically dragging Tessa's ass out of the house. Karen is much more upset than you would expect any reasonable person to be, and she tells Tessa that she loves her, which is pretty fucking weird.

"Does it make me a horrible person that I feel more comfortable around your family than my own?" Tessa asks me after fifteen minutes of driving in silence.

"Yes."

She glares at me, making me roll my eyes at her pretend anger. "Both of our families are fucked up," I say, and she nods, returning to her silence.

The closer my car gets to Seattle, the stronger the current of anxiety that's flowing through my chest. I don't want to spend the entire week away from her. Four days away from Tessa is a fucking lifetime.

The moment I get back, I'm heading straight to the gym.

chapter one hundred and twenty-nine

TESSA

On Monday morning I arrive for my appointment half an hour early and take a seat in one of the mass-produced, blue-checkered chairs in the waiting room, which, I can't help but notice, is nearly full, crying children and coughing women crowding the space. I try to keep myself occupied by flipping through a magazine, but the only one available is a parenting journal, full of diaper ads and "revolutionary" breast-feeding tips.

"Young? Theresa Young?" An elderly woman calls my name as she looks up from a clipboard. I stand quickly, sidestepping a toddler who's scooting around on the floor with a toy truck in his hand. The truck rolls over my shoe, and he giggles. I smile down at him, earning an adorable grin in return.

"How far along are you?" a woman, the boy's mother, I assume, asks. Her eyes dart to my stomach, and I instinctively place my hand on it.

An uncomfortable laugh escapes. "Oh! I'm not . . ."

"I'm sorry!" She flushes. "I just assumed, you don't look it . . . I just thought . . ." The fact that she's as uncomfortable as I am makes me feel lighter. Asking a woman how far along she is never ends well, especially when she isn't pregnant. The woman laughs. "Well, now you know for future reference when you're a mother yourself . . . the filter disappears!"

I don't allow my mind to go there; I don't have time to ponder the future and the fact that if I want a life with Hardin, I'll never be a mother. I'll never have an adorable toddler running a toy truck over my shoes or climbing onto my lap. I turn back to look at him one last time.

I smile politely and make my way to the nurse, who immediately hands me a small cup and instructs me to go to the restroom down the hall to complete the pregnancy test. Despite my period, I'm battling nerves at the idea. Hardin and I have been so careless lately, and the last thing we need is an unplanned pregnancy. It would push him over the edge. It could completely upend everything I want to do with my life, to have a baby now.

When I hand the full cup back to the nurse, she guides me into an empty room and wraps a blood-pressure cuff around my arm. "Uncross your legs, dear," she sweetly instructs, and I do as I'm told. After taking my temperature, the woman disappears, and a few minutes later I hear a knock on the door, and a distinguished-looking middle-aged man with mostly gray hair enters. He removes a pair of thick glasses and reaches a hand out to me.

"Dr. West. It's nice to meet you, Theresa," he introduces himself amiably. I was hoping for a female doctor, but he seems nice enough. I do wish he was less attractive, though; it would make things less awkward for me during this already uncomfortable experience.

Dr. West asks a lot of questions, most of which are absolutely horrifying. I have to tell him about Hardin and me having unprotected sex—on more than one occasion—during which I force myself to maintain eye contact with him. Halfway through the embarrassing ordeal, the nurse returns and places a piece of paper on top of the desk. Dr. West glances at it, and I hold my breath until he speaks.

He gives me a warm smile. "Well, you're not pregnant, so now we can begin."

And I let out the deep breath I didn't realize I was even holding.

He reels off many options, some of which I've never even heard of, before we settle on the shot.

"Before I give you the shot, I'll need to do a brief pelvic exam; is that okay?"

I nod and swallow my nervousness. I don't know why I'm so uncomfortable; he's only a doctor, and I'm an adult. I should have scheduled this appointment for after my period. I didn't think about the actual exam when I called for the appointment. I only wanted Hardin off my back.

"ALMOST FINISHED," Dr. West announces. The exam is proving to be quick and not nearly as awkward as I assumed it would be, which is a blessing.

He pops up, a deep line forming across his forehead. "Have you had a pelvic exam before?"

"No, I don't think so," I answer quietly. I know I haven't, but the last part of my response was a nervous add-on. My eyes turn to the screen in front of him, and he moves the probe around the bottom of my belly, across my pelvis.

"Hmm," he says to himself. My unease grows—was the test wrong, and there really *is* a baby in there after all? I begin to panic. I'm too young, and I haven't finished college, and Hardin and I are in such an in-between place and—

"I'm a little concerned about the size of your cervix," he finally says. "It's nothing to worry about at the moment, but I'd like to see you again to do further testing."

" 'Nothing to worry about'?" My mouth is dry, and my stomach is in knots. My palms start sweating. "What does that mean?"

"Nothing as of now . . . I can't be sure," he says—in a very unconvincing tone.

I pull myself up, pushing the gown back down. "What *could* it mean?"

"Well . . ." Dr. West pushes his thick glasses back up his nose. "Worst case would be infertility, but without further testing, there's no way to know just from this exam. I don't see any cysts, and that's a really good sign." He gestures to the screen.

My heart drops onto the cold tile floor. "What . . . what are the chances?" I can't hear my own voice or thoughts.

"I can't say. This isn't a diagnosis, Miss Young. What I mentioned is the worst-case scenario; please don't fret over it until we get some testing done. I want to go ahead with your shot today, get some blood drawn for some tests, and schedule a follow-up." After a moment he adds, "Okay?"

I nod, unable to speak. I just heard him say it wasn't a diagnosis, but it sure feels like one. I felt the dreadful, empty flutter of my nerves crawling up my spine at the first mention of a problem. Only the hammering of my heart can be heard in the quiet room. I'm sulking, and I know it, but I don't care.

"This happens all the time; don't trouble yourself over it. We'll clear it up; it's nothing, I'm sure," he says rather stiffly, and then exits the room, leaving me to deal with the cruel, sharp edges of the situation on my own. He isn't sure, nothing is certain; he seems fairly blasé about it—so why can't I shake the anxiety gnawing at me?

I'm given the birth-control shot by the nurse, who has suddenly turned into a mother hen, talking about her grandchildren and their love of her homemade cookies. I stay quiet mostly, only speaking enough to be polite. I feel nauseous.

She gives me a thorough briefing about my new contraceptive, going over the pros and cons that I've already heard from Dr. West. I'm thrilled to not have to deal with a period anymore, slightly concerned over the weight gain, but figure it's an even trade.

She tells me that since I'm on my period now, the shot will be effective immediately, but to wait three days to have unprotected sex, just to be safe. Then she reminds me that this won't protect me from STDs, only pregnancy.

After scheduling the dreaded follow-up appointment, I head straight downtown to take my passport photo and finalize the paperwork. Of course, it has already been paid for by Mr. Vance. I cringe at the amount of money everyone around me seems to have no problem spending on me.

Every single person I pass on the street seems to be pregnant or carrying a child in their arms. I shouldn't have pressed the doctor for information; now I'm going to be paranoid until my follow-up, which of course isn't for another three weeks. Three weeks to drive myself mad, three weeks to obsess over the chance that I might not be able to get pregnant. I don't know why the idea is so painful; I thought I had somewhat come to terms with the idea of not having children. I can't mention this to Hardin yet, not until I know for sure. Not that it will make a difference to his plans anyway.

I text Hardin when I get back to my car, telling him that my appointment went well, and head back to Christian and Kimberly's house. By the time I arrive, I've convinced myself that I'll spend the week avoiding the topic. There's no reason to worry myself when Dr. West assured me that nothing was definite at this point. The hollowness in my chest says otherwise, but I have to ignore it and move on for now. I'm going to England. For the first time in my life, I'm going to be traveling outside of the state of Washington, and I couldn't be more excited. Nervous, but excited.

chapter one hundred and thirty

HARDIN

Tessa looks like she could pass out any minute. She's shoved an ink pen between her teeth as she looks over her checklist again. Apparently traveling across the globe kicks her neurotic tendencies into high gear.

"Are you sure you have everything?" I sarcastically ask.

"What? Yes," she huffs, focused on the task of rechecking her carry-on bag for the tenth time since we arrived at the airport.

"If we don't go inside now, we're going to miss our flight," I warn her.

"I know." She looks up at me, her hand still digging around that damn bag. She's crazy—adorable as hell, but fucking nuts. "You're sure about leaving your car here?" she asks.

"Yes. That's what this *parking lot* is for: cars." I point up at the Long-Term Parking sign above our heads and say, "It's for cars with no commitment issues."

Tessa stares at me blankly, as if I've said nothing at all.

"Just give me the bag," I say, pulling the hideous thing from her shoulder. It's too heavy for her to be carrying around. The woman has packed half of her shit in this bag alone.

"I'll pull the case, then." She reaches for the handle of the wheelie suitcase.

"No, I've got it. Relax, would you? It'll be fine," I assure her.

I'll never forget how frantic she was this morning. Folding and refolding, packing and repacking our clothes until they fit perfectly in the case. I took it easy on her, because I know how beyond her element this trip is. Even though she's being as annoying as ever, I can't help but feel excited. Excited to be taking her on her first trip abroad, excited at the prospect of watching her blue-gray eyes widen at the clouds as we fly through them. I made sure she had a seat next to the window for that reason alone.

"Ready?" I ask her as the automatic doors open as if to greet us.

"No." She smiles nervously, and I lead her through the crowded airport.

"YOU'RE GOING TO PASS OUT on me, aren't you?" I lean over and whisper to Tessa. She's pale, and her small hands are shaking on her lap. I gather them in one of mine and offer her an assuring squeeze. She smiles at me, a nice change from the scowl that covered her face the entire time from the ticket kiosk until now.

That TSA agent was hitting on her; I recognized the stupid fucking grin on his face when she smiled at him. I have the same fucking grin. I had every right to tell him to fuck off, but of course she didn't agree, and she'd been scowling since she dragged me away, my middle finger high in the air at that asshole. "Thank God that guy's so nearsighted," she mumbled, and then kept looking back over her shoulder.

Her attitude only worsened when I pressed for her to do up her cardigan. The old man next to me is a fucking pervert, and Tessa's lucky she has the window seat and I can shield her from his eyes. Being stubborn, she refused to button the damn thing, leaving her tits on display for everyone to see. Granted, the shirt isn't that low cut, but when she bends down, you can see straight down it. She ignored my protests and claimed that I can't control her. I'm not trying to control her, I'm trying to prevent men from ogling over her not-so-subtle chest.

"No, I'm okay," she hesitantly answers. Her eyes give her away.

"We should be taking off anytime." I glance up at the flight attendant making her way through the cabin to check the overhead compartments for the third time. *They're all fucking closed, lady; let's get a move on it before I have to carry Tessa off of this plane.* Actually, halting the trip could work in my favor, really.

"Last chance to hop off of the plane. The tickets aren't refundable, but I'll go ahead and add them to your tab," I say, tucking her loose hair behind her ear, and she gives me the smallest smile I've ever seen. She's still mad, but her nerves are causing her to soften up toward me.

"Hardin," she quietly whines. She rests her head against the window and closes her eyes. I hate to see her so nervous; it makes me anxious, and this trip has me on fucking anxiety overload as it is. I lean across and pull the cover down over her window, hoping that will help.

"How much longer?" I impatiently bark at the flight attendant as she passes our row.

Her eyes move from Tessa to me, and she raises a snooty brow. "A few minutes." She forces a smile for the sake of her job. The man next to me shifts uncomfortably, and I wish I had purchased an extra ticket so I wouldn't have to worry about sitting this close to an obnoxious asshole. He smells like stale tobacco.

"It's been longer than a few—" I begin.

Tessa's hand reaches over to mine; her eyes are now open, pleading with me not to cause a scene. I take a deep breath, closing my eyes to heighten the drama of the act.

"Fine," I say, turning away from the attendant, who continues down the aisle.

"Thank you," Tessa mouths. Instead of resting her head against the window, she gently rests it against my arm. I tap her thigh and signal for her to lift up so I can put my arm around her. She nuzzles into me and sighs in contentment as I gently tighten my arm around her body. I love that sound.

The plane begins to move slowly down the runway, and Tessa's eyes screw shut.

By the time the plane is in the air, she has the window cover raised and her eyes are wide with wonder as she stares out at the rapidly shrinking landscape. "This is amazing." She grins. All the color has now seeped back into her face. She's glowing with excitement, and it's contagious as hell. I try to fight my grin, but it's impossible, as she babbles on about how everything "just looks so small."

"See, it wasn't so bad. We haven't crashed yet," I disdainfully remark.

In response, murmers and annoyed coughs start wafting through the nearly silent cabin, but I don't give a shit. Tessa understands my humor, for the most part at least, and she shoots me an eye roll and gives me a playful jab in the chest.

"Hush," she warns, and I chuckle.

After three hours, she's restless. I knew she would be; we've watched some of the shitty programming the airline sponsors and gone through the *SkyMall* magazine twice, both of us agreeing that a dog crate disguised as a television stand is certainly not worth two thousand dollars.

"It's going to be a long nine hours," I say to her.

"Only six now," she corrects me. Her fingers trace the infinity-heart tattoo above my wrist.

"Only six," I repeat. "Take a nap."

"I can't."

"Why not?"

She looks up at me. "What do you think my father is doing? I mean, I know Landon watched him last time you were away, but we'll be gone for three days this time."

Fuck. "He'll be fine." He's going to be annoyed, but he'll get over it and thank her later.

"I'm glad we declined your father's offer," she says.

Fucking hell. "Why?" I choke, searching her face.

"The rehab place is too expensive."

"And?"

"I don't feel comfortable with your father spending that amount of money on my father. It's not his responsibility, and we don't know for sure that my father is even—"

"He's a drug addict, Tessa." I know she still doesn't want to admit it, but she knows it's true. "And my father might as well pay for his treatment."

I need to call Landon as soon as we land to find out how the "intervention" went. As much as I hope her shitbag of a dad agreed to it, I feel guilty that Tessa wasn't in on the plan. I spent hours punching and kicking that bag at the gym, pondering this shit. At the end of it, the solution was simple. Either Richard takes his ass to rehab on my father's dime, or he's out of Tessa's life for good. I won't have his fucking addiction being a burden on her. I cause her enough fucking problems, and if anyone is going to cause her stress, it will be me. I sent Landon to do the intervention, to tell the man that he had to choose one or the other: rehab or no Tessa. I figured things wouldn't turn violent if Landon, as opposed to me, was in charge. As much as it eats at me that my father will be the one who's actually helping Tessa, since he's the one paying, I couldn't turn him down. I wanted to, but I couldn't.

"I don't know." She sighs, looking out the window. "I need to think about it."

"Well . . ." I begin, and she frowns at the tone of my voice.

"What did you do?" She narrows her eyes and pulls away from me. She can't go far; she's stuck sitting with me until we land.

"We'll talk about it later." I glance at the man next to me. These airlines should really make these seats wider. If the armrest between Tessa and me wasn't lifted, I'd be sitting on top of the guy.

Her eyes go wide. "You *sent* him, didn't you?" she whispers forcefully, careful not to cause a scene.

"I didn't send your father anywhere." It's true. I don't know whether he agreed to go or not.

"You tried, though, didn't you?"

"Perhaps," I admit.

She shakes her head in disbelief and leans back against the headrest, staring off into space.

"You're mad, huh?" I ask her.

She ignores me.

"Theresa . . ." My voice is too loud and has the effect on her that I intend it to have. Her eyes snap open, and she turns to me.

"I'm not mad," she whispers. "I'm just surprised, and I'm trying to figure out how I feel about it, okay?"

"Okay." Her reaction was much better than I had anticipated.

"I can't stand when you keep things from me. You do it, my mother does it . . . I'm not a child. I am capable of handling things that are thrown at me, wouldn't you say?"

I stop myself from uttering the first thought that comes to my mind. I'm getting better and better at this shit. "Yes," I calmly reply, "but that doesn't mean that I won't try and filter out the bullshit for you."

Her eyes soften, and she nods once. "I understand that, but I need you to stop keeping things from me. Anything that involves you, Landon, or my father, I need to know about. I always end up finding out anyway. Why prolong the inevitable?" she asks.

"Okay," I agree without elaborating. "From now on I won't keep shit from you." What I don't mention is that nothing from the past that I've kept from her counts; I'm only agreeing that from *this moment on* I will try not to keep her in the dark.

A flash of emotion moves over her face, but I can't read it. I almost think it is guilt. "Unless it's something that I'm better off not knowing," she softly adds.

Okay . . .

"What kind of things are we talking about here?" I ask her.

"Something that *you* would be better off not being told also counts. For example, the fact that my gynecologist is a male," she informs me.

"What?" Tessa's doctor being a male never crossed my mind. I didn't know that dude doctors did such things.

"See, you were better off not knowing that, weren't you?" She isn't even trying to hide her little smart-ass grin at my irritation and jealousy.

"You'll get a new doctor."

She slowly shakes her head at me, telling me she'll do no such thing. I lean over and whisper into her ear, "You're lucky the bathrooms on this thing are too small to fuck you in." Her breathing hitches, and she immediately squeezes her thighs together. I love her reaction to my filthy mouth; it's always instantaneous. Plus, I needed to distract her and change the subject for both of our sakes.

"I would press you against the door and fuck you against the wall." I move my hand farther up her closed thighs. "I would cover your mouth to muffle your screams."

She gulps.

"It would feel so fucking good, your legs wrapped around my waist, your fingers tugging at my hair."

Her eyes are wide, pupils blown, and fuck, I wish the bathrooms *weren't* so damn small. Literally, I can't even stretch out my arms in the tiny space. Here I paid over a thousand dollars per round-trip ticket—you'd think I could at least fuck my girl in the damn bathroom during the long flight.

"Squeezing your legs together won't make the ache disappear," I continue whispering into her ear. I lower her tray table so I can bring my hand to the juncture of her thighs. "Only I can." She looks like she's about to come from my words alone. "The rest of the flight is going to be pretty uncomfortable for you, what with soaking panties and all." I press a kiss beneath her ear, using my tongue to tease her further, and the man next to me coughs.

"Problem?" I ask him, not giving a fuck if he heard anything I said to her. He quickly shakes his head and returns his attention to the e-reader in his hand. I lean over, noting the first paragraph on the dimly lit page. I spot the name "Holden" and immediately chuckle. Only pretentious middle-aged men and bearded hipsters actually enjoy reading *The Catcher in the Rye.* What is so appealing about an overprivileged, teenage fucking stalker? Nothing.

"Shall I continue?" I lean back over to Tessa, who is now panting.

"No." She lifts her tray table, clicking it closed and ending my fun.

"Only five more hours now." I grin at her, ignoring how hard I am from the thought of how wet she must be right now.

"You're an asshole," she whispers. The smile that I love plays on her lips.

"And you love me," I counter, making that smile grow.

NAVIGATING THROUGH HEATHROW wasn't as bad as I remembered. We got our bags quickly. Tessa was quiet most of the time, and her hand in mine was the only assurance I needed that she wasn't too upset about the rehab shit. The rental car was ready for us, and

I watched in amusement as Tessa promptly walked to the wrong side of the vehicle.

By the time we make it to Hampstead, she's asleep. She tried to stay awake and stare out the window, taking it all in, but she couldn't keep her eyes open. The old town looks the same as it did the last time I was here—of course it does, why wouldn't it? It's only been a few months. For some reason I feel like the moment that I drove past the official Hampstead welcome sign with Tessa in the passenger seat, the village would have altered somehow.

As I pass the historic homes and tourist attractions, I finally arrive in the residential part of town. Contrary to popular belief, not everyone in Hampstead lives in a historic mansion and is rolling in wealth. All that is clear as I pull into my mum's gravel driveway. The old house looks like it could topple over any day now, and I'm glad to see the Sold sign on the lawn. Her future husband's house, just next door, is in much better shape than this shithole and about twice the size.

"Tessa." I call her out of her deep sleep. She's probably drooled all over the damn window.

My mum appears at the front door only seconds after the headlights hit her windows. She pushes open the screen door and rushes down the small steps like a madwoman. Tessa's eyes open, and she focuses on my mum, who now is pulling at the passenger-door handle to get to her. What is it with everyone liking her so much?

"Tessa! Hardin!" My mum's voice is high and overly excited as Tessa unbuckles her seat belt and climbs out of the car. Womanly hugs and greetings are exchanged while I grab the bags from the trunk.

"I'm so glad you two are here." My mum smiles, wiping a tear from her eyes. This is going to be a long weekend.

"Us, too." Tessa answers for me and allows my mum to pull her by the hand into the small house.

"I don't like tea, so there won't be any stereotypical English welcome here, but I made some coffee. I know you both love your coffee," my mum hums.

Tessa laughs, thanking her. My mum is keeping her distance from me, obviously trying not to set me off during the weekend of her wedding. The two women disappear into the kitchen, and I take the stairs to my old bedroom to get rid of these bags. I hear their laughter travel through the house, and I try to convince myself that nothing catastrophic will happen this weekend. Everything will be fine.

The room is empty except for my old twin bed and a dresser. The wallpaper has been stripped off, leaving a hideous trail of glue along the walls. My mum is obviously trying to get the place ready for the new owner, but seeing the place like this actually makes me feel a little strange.

chapter one hundred and thirty-one

TESSA

"I still can't believe you both came," Trish says to me. She hands me a cup of coffee—black, just the way I like it—and I smile at her thoughtfulness. She's a beautiful woman, with bright eyes and an equally bright smile—and she's dressed in a deep blue tracksuit.

"I'm so glad we could make it," I tell her. I take a glance at the clock on the oven; already 10 p.m. The long flight and time change have thrown me off.

"Me, too. If it wasn't for you, I know he wouldn't be here." She places her hand over mine. Unsure how to respond, I smile. She catches on to my discomfort and changes the subject.

"How was the flight? Did Hardin behave?" Her laugh is gentle, and I don't have the heart to tell her that her son was a complete tyrant throughout the security scan and half of the flight.

"He was fine." I take a sip of the steaming coffee just as Hardin joins us in the kitchen. The house is old and cramped, too many walls close off too much of the space. The only decorations are brown moving boxes piled in the corners, but I feel oddly comfortable and at ease in Hardin's childhood home. I can tell by the look on his face when he leans down to walk under the archway leading to the kitchen that he doesn't feel the same way about this house. These walls hold too many memories for him, and instantly my impression of the place begins to dim.

"What's with the wallpaper?" he asks.

"I was removing it all to paint before selling, but the new owners are planning to tear the house down anyway. They want to build an entirely new home on the lot," his mother explains. I like the idea of the house being demolished.

"Good, it's a shit house anyway," he grumbles and picks up my coffee cup to take a sip. "Are you tired?" He turns to me.

"I'm fine," I say, meaning it. I enjoy Trish's humor and warm company. I'm tired, but there'll be plenty of time to sleep. It's still fairly early.

"I've been staying at Mike's house, next door. I assumed you wouldn't want to stay there."

"Obviously not," Hardin replies. I take my coffee back from him, giving him a silent plea to be polite to his mother.

"Anyway"—Trish ignores his rude remark—"I have plans for her tomorrow, so I hope you can occupy yourself."

It takes me a moment to realize she's referring to me.

"What sort of plans?" Hardin doesn't seem pleased with the idea.

"Just prewedding things. I have an appointment for us at a spa in town, and then I'd love it if she'd go with me to the last fitting of my wedding dress."

"Of course," I say at the same time that Hardin asks, "How long will *that* take?"

"Just the afternoon, I'm sure," Trish assures her son. "That's only if you want to accompany me, Tessa. You don't have to, I just thought it would be nice for us to spend some time together while you're here."

"I'd love to." I smile at her. Hardin doesn't argue, which is good, because he would have lost.

"I'm glad." She smiles, too. "My friend Susan will be joining us for lunch. She's dying to meet you, she's been hearing about you for so long that she doesn't believe you exist, she—"

Hardin begins to choke on his coffee, interrupting his mother's excited rambling.

"Susan Kingsley?" He eyes Trish, his shoulders tight and his voice shaky.

"Yes . . . well, her name is no longer Kingsley, she's remarried." Trish stares back at him in a way that makes me feel like I've wandered into some sort of private conversation where I'm not wanted. Hardin stares back and forth between his mother and the wall before turning on his heel and leaving us alone in the kitchen.

"I'm going to head next door now for bed. If you need anything, let me know." The excitement in her voice has faded; she sounds drained. Trish leans over and gives me a quick kiss on the cheek before opening the back door and stepping outside.

I stand alone in the kitchen for a few minutes, finishing my coffee, which is pointless, because I need to go to sleep, but I finish it anyway and rinse the cup out in the sink before heading up the staircase to find Hardin. The upstairs hall is empty; torn wallpaper hangs on one side of the narrow passageway, and I can't help but compare Ken's magnificent house to this one; the differences are impossible to ignore.

"Hardin?" I call for him. All the doors are closed, and I don't feel comfortable opening them without knowing what's on the other side.

"Second door," he calls back. I follow his voice to the second door along the hallway and push it open. The handle sticks, and I have to use my foot to get the wood to budge.

Hardin is sitting on the edge of the bed, his head in his hands, when I enter. He looks up at me, and I walk over to him.

"What's wrong?" I ask, running my fingers through his messy hair.

"I shouldn't have brought you here," he says, taking me by surprise.

"Why?" I sit down on the bed next to him, keeping a few inches between our bodies.

"Because"—he sighs—". . . I just shouldn't have." He lies back against the mattress and throws his arm over his face, so I'm unable to read his expression.

"Hardin . . ."

"I'm tired, Tessa, go to sleep." His voice is muffled by his arm, but I know that this is his way of ending the conversation.

"Aren't you going to change?" I press, not wanting to go to bed without his shirt.

"No." He rolls over onto his stomach and reaches up to shut off the light.

chapter
one hundred and thirty-two

TESSA

When my alarm sounds at nine, I have to force myself to get out of bed. I barely slept; I was tossing and turning all night. The last time I checked the time it was three in the morning and I wasn't sure if I had gotten any sleep or if I had been awake the entire time.

Hardin is asleep, his arms crossed over his stomach. He didn't hold me last night, not once. The only contact we had consisted of his hands reaching for me in his sleep, just to make sure I was still there, before they went back to his stomach. His mood change doesn't completely surprise me. I know he didn't want to come here for the wedding, but the high level of his anxiety doesn't make much sense to me, especially since he refuses to talk to me about it. I'd like to ask him just how he expected to deal with me moving here with him if he doesn't even want me here for one weekend.

I brush my hand over his forehead, pushing the mass of hair away, and move down to touch the light stubble that darkens his jawline. His eyelids flutter and I quickly pull away and stand to my feet. I don't want to wake him, his sleep wasn't the least bit peaceful either. I wish I knew what was haunting him. I wish he hadn't closed down so abruptly. He revealed everything to me in the letter that he wrote me—and later destroyed—and while most of the things he referred to concerned terrible mistakes he'd made, I've dealt with them and moved on. Nothing he did in his past will cause any damage to our future. He needs to know this. He has to know this, or it will never work.

The bathroom isn't hard to find, and I wait patiently for the water to turn from brown to clear. The shower is loud and the water pressure is very strong, almost painful, but it does wonders for the tension I've accumulated in my back and shoulder muscles.

I'm fully dressed in a pair of jeans and a cream tank top, but I hesitate before pulling on a floral-print lace sweater. It doesn't have buttons, which means Hardin can't demand that I close it; he's lucky I'm not wearing the tank top alone. It's spring now, and here in Central London it feels like it.

Trish didn't give me a specific time for our little jaunt today, so I head downstairs to make a pot of coffee. An hour later, I return upstairs to grab my e-reader so I can read for a while. Hardin has turned over onto his back, and his face is set in a full frown. Without disturbing him, I quickly leave the room and find my way back to the kitchen table. A couple of hours pass, and I'm relieved when Trish comes walking through the back door. Her brown hair is pulled back, just like mine, in a low bun, and she's dressed in—what else—a tracksuit.

"I was hoping you'd be awake, I wanted to give you some time to sleep in after the long day you had yesterday." She smiles. "I'm ready whenever you are."

I glance toward the narrow staircase one last time, hoping that Hardin will stroll down it with a smile and a kiss goodbye, but that doesn't happen. I grab my purse and follow Trish out the back door.

chapter one hundred and thirty-three

HARDIN

When I reach for Tessa, she isn't in the bed. I don't know what time it is, but the sun is too damn bright, pouring through the uncovered windows like it's trying to force me awake. I slept like shit all night, and Tessa kept tossing and turning in her sleep. I was awake most of the night, keeping my distance from her restless body. I need to get a grip before I ruin this entire weekend for her, but I just can't seem to shake my paranoia. Not after my mum had the nerve to invite Susan Kingsley to have lunch with her and Tessa.

I don't bother changing my clothes, just brush my teeth and toss some water onto my hair. Tessa has taken a shower already; her toiletry bag is tucked away neatly in the otherwise empty cabinet.

When I get to the kitchen, the coffeepot is still hot and half full, and a rinsed coffee mug rests on the counter. Tessa and my mum must have already left; I should've spoken up and kept her from going. Why didn't I? This day can go one of two ways: Susan could be a complete bitch and make it hell for Tessa, or she could keep her goddamn mouth shut, and everything could be fine.

What the fuck am I supposed to do all day while my mum has Tessa prancing around town? I could go find them, it wouldn't be hard, but my mum would probably be upset, and after all, tomorrow is her wedding day. I promised Tess that I'd be on my best behavior this weekend, and even though I've already broken the promise, I don't need to make it any worse.

chapter
one hundred and thirty-four

TESSA

"Your hair looks so beautiful." Trish reaches a newly manicured hand across the table to touch my head.

"Thank you. I'm getting used to it." I smile, looking into the mirror directly behind our table. The woman at the spa was appalled that I had never dyed my hair before. After a few minutes of persuading, I agreed to darken it slightly, but only at the roots. The final color is a very light brown fading into my natural blond toward the ends. The difference is barely noticeable and looks much more natural than I expected. The color isn't permanent; it'll only last a month. I wasn't ready for a longer-term change, but the more I look at myself in the mirror, the more I like what I see.

The woman did wonders on my eyebrows, too, plucking them into a perfect arch, and my nails and toes are painted a deep red. I declined Trish's offer to get a Brazilian wax; as much as I've considered getting one, it would be awkward to do it with Hardin's mother, and I'm fine with shaving for now. During the walk to the car, Trish teases me about my flimsy shoes, the same way her son does, and I hold back from making a dig at her daily tracksuit-wearing.

I stare out the window the entire drive, taking in every single home, building, store, and person on the street.

"This is the place," Trish says minutes later as she pulls her car into a covered parking lot nestled between two small buildings. I follow her to the entrance of the smaller of the two.

I notice that there's moss covering the entirety of the brick building, and the sight of it calls forth my inner Landon, as references to *The Hobbit* pass through my mind. Landon would think the exact same thing if he were here, and we'd share a laugh while Hardin griped about how terrible the movies are and how they destroyed J.R.R. Tolkien's vision. Landon would argue back, as always, claiming that Hardin secretly loves the movies, and Hardin would flip him off. Selfishly, I imagine a place where Hardin, Landon, and I could live close to one another, a place where Landon and Dakota could live in Seattle, maybe in the same building as Hardin and me. A place where one of the few people who actually care about me won't be moving across the country in a few weeks.

"It's pretty warm today; do you want to eat outside?" Trish asks, gesturing to the metal tables lined along the terrace.

"That would be fine." I smile, following her to a table at the end of the row.

The waitress brings a pitcher of water to our table and places two glasses in front of us. Even the water looks better in England; the pitcher is filled with ice and perfectly shaped lemon circles.

Trish's eyes search the sidewalks. "We have one more joining us . . . she should be here any— There she is!"

I turn to see a tall brunette bustling across the street, her hands waving in the air. Her floor-length skirt and high heels are making it difficult for her to move as quickly as she appears to be trying to do.

"Susan!" Trish's face lights up at the woman's clumsy entrance.

"Trish, darling, how are you?" Susan leans down to kiss both of Trish's cheeks before turning to me and doing the same. I feel awkward as I smile uncomfortably, unsure whether or not I should return the unfamiliar greeting.

The woman's eyes are a deep blue, making for the most beautiful contrast with her pale skin and dark hair. She pulls away before I can decide what to do. "You must be Theresa; I've heard so many wonderful things about you." She smiles and surprises me by taking both of my hands into hers. She gently squeezes them and gives me a bright smile before pulling out the chair next to me and taking a seat.

"It's nice to meet you." I smile at her. I have no idea what to make of the woman. I know that I don't like the way that hearing her name affected Hardin last night, but she seems so lovely, it's confusing.

"Have you been waiting long?" she asks and turns around to hang her purse over the back of her chair.

"No, we just arrived. We had a full morning at the spa." Trish flips her glossy brown hair over her shoulder.

"I can see that; the two of you smell like a bundle of flowers." Susan laughs, filling her glass with water. Her accent is elegant and much thicker than Hardin's and Trish's.

Despite Hardin's mood change last night, I'm in love with England, especially this village. I did my research before we arrived, but the photographs on the internet don't do justice to the old-fashioned beauty of the area. I'm in awe as I gaze around, and wonder how something as simple as a cobblestone street lined with small cafés and shops could be so enchanting, so intriguing.

"Are you ready for your last fitting today?" Susan asks Trish. I continue to take in the surroundings, only vaguely listening to the women talk. My attention is drawn across the street to the quaint old buiding that houses the library. I can only imagine the collection of books it holds.

"Yes, I am, and if it doesn't fit this time, I think I'll have to sue the shop owner." Trish laughs. I turn my gaze to them and force myself to keep from gawking at the architecture until I can get Hardin to take me sightseeing properly.

"Well, seeing as how I *am* the owner, I may have a problem with that." Susan's laugh is low and very charming. I have to keep reminding myself to be cautious of her.

My imagination begins to wander as I stare at the beautiful woman. Has Hardin been with her intimately? He's mentioned having sexual encounters with older women—quite a few of them—but I've never allowed him to elaborate. Is Susan, with her wide blue eyes and long brown hair, one of them? I shudder at the thought. I sure hope not.

I ignore the pang of jealousy that comes with the thought and force myself to enjoy the mouthwatering sandwich that the waitress has just placed in front of me.

"So, Theresa, tell me about yourself." Susan stabs a piece of lettuce with her fork and brings it to her painted lips.

"You can call me Tessa," I nervously begin. "I'm finishing my freshman year at Washington Central, and I just moved to Seattle." I glance at Trish, who, for some reason, is frowning. Hardin must not have told her about my move, or maybe he did, and she's upset that he didn't move with me?

"I've heard that Seattle is a lovely city. I've never been to America"—Susan scrunches her nose—"but my husband has promised to take me this summer."

"You should definitely visit . . . it's nice," I remark stupidly. I'm sitting in a village right out of a storybook, and I'm saying that America is nice. Susan would probably hate the place. I'm nervous now, and my hands are slightly shaky as I pull my cell phone out of my bag to send a text message to Hardin. Just a simple I miss you.

The rest of lunch is filled with wedding talk, and I find that I can't help but like Susan. She just married her second husband last summer; she planned the wedding herself, and she has no children, only a niece and a nephew. She owns the bridal shop where Trish purchased her gown; it's one of five in North Central London. Her husband owns and operates three of the most popular pubs in the area, all within three miles of one another.

Susan's bridal shop is only a few blocks away from the restaurant, so we decide to walk. It's warm today, and the sun is bright; even the air seems more refreshing than it was in Washington. Hardin still hasn't responded to my text message, but somehow I knew he wouldn't.

"Champagne?" Susan offers the moment we step through the door of the small shop. The space is minimal, but it's decorated perfectly, old-fashioned and charming, black and white covering every inch.

"Oh no, thank you." I smile.

Trish takes her up on her offer and promises me that she'll only have one glass. I almost tell her to have as many as she wants, to enjoy herself, but I don't trust myself to drive in England; it feels odd enough in the passenger seat. As I watch Trish laugh and joke with Susan, I can't help but think about how different Trish and Hardin really are. She's so bubbly and lively, and Hardin is so . . . well, Hardin. I know they don't have much of a relationship, but I'd like to think that this visit could change that. Not completely—that's too much to ask—but hopefully Hardin will at least warm up to his mother on her wedding day.

"I'll be out in a minute; you can make yourself at home," Trish says to me before pulling the dressing room curtain closed. I take a seat on the plush white couch and laugh when I hear her cursing at Susan for pinching her with the zipper. Maybe she and Hardin are more alike than I thought.

"Excuse me." A female voice interrupts my thoughts, and I look up to meet the blue eyes of a very pregnant young woman.

"I'm sorry, have you seen Susan?" she asks, her eyes scanning the space.

"She's in there." I point to the curtain of the dressing room that Trish disappeared into with her wedding dress only minutes ago.

"Thank you." She smiles, sighing with what sounds like relief. "If she asks, I arrived right at two," the girl instructs me and smiles. She must work here. My eyes travel down to the name tag fastened to her white long-sleeve shirt.

NATALIE, it says.

I glance at the clock. It's five minutes past two. "Your secret is safe with me," I assure her.

The curtain pulls back, and Trish is revealed in her wedding gown. It's beautiful—*she's* absolutely beautiful in the simple, capped-sleeve gown.

"Wow," Natalie and I say at once.

Trish steps out, taking a look at herself in the full-length mirror, and wipes tears from her eyes.

"She does this at every fitting; this is the third," Natalie observes with a smile. I notice the tears welling up in her eyes and know that mine look the same. Her hand is pressed on her belly.

"She's beautiful. Mike is a lucky man." I smile toward Hardin's mum. Her focus is still on her reflection in the mirror, and I don't blame her.

"You know Trish?" the young woman politely asks.

"Yes." I turn to face her. "I'm . . ." Hardin and I are really going to have to discuss how introductions should go around here. "I'm with her son," I tell her, and her eyes widen.

"Natalie." Susan's voice resonates in the small shop. Trish has paled, her eyes moving back and forth between Natalie and me. I feel like I'm missing something. When I look back at Natalie, I take in the deep blue of her eyes, her brown hair, her pale skin.

Susan . . . I think. Is Susan this Natalie woman's mother? *Natalie* . . .

Holy shit. Natalie. *The* Natalie. The Natalie that haunted

Hardin's conscience, the small bit of one that he has. Natalie that Hardin chewed up and spit back out.

"You're Natalie," I say with realization.

She nods, keeping eye contact with me as Trish approaches us.

"Yes, I am." I can tell by her expression that she isn't sure how much I know about her, and she's even more unsure what to say about it. "You're her . . . you're . . . Tessa," she says. I can see her thoughts coming together.

"I'm . . ." I choke. I don't have the slightest idea what to say. Hardin told me that she was happy now, that she's forgiven him and made a new life for herself. The empathy that I feel for her is deep. "I'm sorry . . ." I end up saying.

"I'm going to get some more champagne. Trish, come along." Susan grabs Trish by the arm and gently leads her away. Trish turns her head, watching Natalie and me until she disappears through a door, gown and all.

"Sorry for what?" Natalie's eyes shine under the bright lights. I can't imagine this girl, the one in front of me, with my Hardin. She's so simple and beautiful, so unlike any of the girls from his past that I've encountered.

Nervous laughter falls from my lips. "I don't know . . ." What exactly *am* I apologizing for? I ask myself. "F-for what he did . . . to you."

"You *know*?" I hear the surprise in her voice as she continues to stare at me, trying to figure me out.

"I do," I say, suddenly embarrassed and feeling the need to explain. "And Hardin . . . he's different now. He deeply regrets what he did to you," I tell her. It won't make up for the past, but she has to know that the Hardin I know isn't the Hardin that she once knew.

"I ran into him recently," she reminds me. "He was . . . I don't know . . . *empty* when I saw him on the street. Is he doing better now?" I watch for judgment in her cloudy blue eyes, but there isn't a trace of it to be found.

"Yes, he really is," I say, trying not to look down at her stomach. She lifts her hand, and I see a gold band on her ring finger. I'm so happy that she's been able to turn her life around.

"He's done a lot of terrible things, and I know I'm way out of line here"—I swallow, trying not to lose my confidence—"but it was so important to him to know that you forgave him. It meant so much . . . thank you for finding the strength to do that."

To tell the truth, I don't think that Hardin regretted what he did to her as much as he should have, but her forgiveness did chip away at some of the bricks he's spent years building between himself and the rest of the world, and I know it gave him a little peace.

"You must really love him," she says softly after a long silence passes between us.

"I do, so very much." My eyes meet hers. We're connected, this woman whom Hardin hurt in such a terrible manner and I, in some strange way, and I feel the power of that connection. I can't begin to imagine how she felt, how deep the humiliation and pain he caused her actually was. She was abandoned not only by Hardin, but by her family. At the beginning, I was just like her, a game to him, until he fell in love with me. That's the difference between me and this sweet pregnant woman. He loves me, and he wasn't capable of loving her.

I can't help the disgusting thought that passes through my mind, the thought that if he *had* loved her, I wouldn't have him now, and I'm selfishly grateful that he didn't care for her the way he cares for me.

"Does he treat you well?" she surprises me by asking.

"Most of the time . . ." I can't help but smile at this terrible answer. "He's figuring it out." I finish on a note of certainty.

"Well, that's all I can hope for." She returns my smile.

"What do you mean?"

"I've prayed and prayed that Hardin would find his salvation, and I think it's finally happened." Her smile grows, and she touches her belly again. "Everyone deserves a second chance, even the worst sinners of all, don't you think?"

I am in awe of her. I can't say that if Hardin had done to me what he did to her, without so much as an apology, I'd be sending positive thoughts out for him the way that she is. I'd probably be wishing for his imminent demise, yet here she is, this compassionate woman, only wanting the best for him.

"I do." I agree with her despite my failure to understand how she could be so forgiving.

"I know you think I'm nuts"—Natalie lightly laughs—"but if it wasn't for Hardin, I wouldn't have met my Elijah, and I wouldn't be only days away from giving birth to our first son."

A shiver creeps up my spine at the thought that comes to my mind. Hardin was a stepping-stone in Natalie's life—actually, more like a massive bump in the road on her way to the life she deserves. I don't want Hardin to be a stepping-stone in my life, a painful memory, someone I'd be forced to forgive and come to terms with. I want Hardin to be my Elijah, my happy ending.

Sadness overtakes my fear as she brings my hand to her stomach, swollen in a way that mine most likely will never be, and I notice the gold band on her finger, something I most likely will never wear. I jump back at the movement against my hand, and Natalie laughs.

"The little guy's busy in there. I wish he'd come out already." She laughs again, and I can't help but put my hand back to feel the movement again. The baby in her belly kicks at my hand once more, and I join in her happiness. I can't help it—it's contagious.

"When are you due?" I ask, still mesmerized by the flutter against my palm.

"Two days ago. He's a stubborn one, this boy. I came back to work to stay on my feet in hopes that he'll decide to join us."

She speaks so tenderly of the unborn child. Will I ever have this? Will I have the glow in my cheeks and the tenderness in my voice? Will I ever feel the flutter of my baby kicking inside of my belly? I force myself to blink away my self-pity. Nothing is certain yet.

Nothing is certain as far as your diagnosis from Dr. West is concerned, but you can be sure that Hardin will never agree to father your children, a voice inside me mocks.

"Are you okay?" Natalie's voice pulls me from my thoughts.

"Yes, sorry. I was just daydreaming," I lie and pull my hand away from her belly.

"I'm really glad that I got to meet you while you're in town," she says just as Trish and Susan appear from the back room, a bouquet of flowers and a veil in Susan's hands. I glance at the clock; it's two thirty. I've been talking to Natalie long enough for Trish's cheeks to become slightly flushed and her glass empty.

"Give me five and I'll be ready; you may need to drive!" Trish laughs. I cringe at the thought, but when I consider the other option—calling Hardin—driving doesn't seem too bad.

"Take care, and congratulations again," I tell Natalie on my way out of the shop. Trish's dress is in my arms, and she's a few feet behind me.

"You, too, Tessa." Natalie smiles as the door closes.

"I can carry it, if it's too heavy," Trish says once we're on the sidewalk. "I can go get the car. I only had one glass, so I can drive just fine."

"It's okay, really," I say, even though I'm terrified to drive her car.

"No, really," she counters and takes her keys out of the front pocket of her jacket. "I can drive."

chapter one hundred and thirty-five

HARDIN

I've paced around the entire house over a hundred times, I've walked around this shitty neighborhood twice, I even called Landon. Now I'm stir-crazy, and Tessa isn't answering any of my calls. *Where the hell are they?*

I look at my phone; it's after three. How long could this spa shit take?

Adrenaline is coursing through me when I hear a car crunching over the gravel driveway. I go to a front window and see that it's my mum's. Tessa gets out first and walks to the back, pulling out a massive white bag. Something is different about her.

"I got it!" she calls to my mum as I open the screen door. I take the steps quickly and grab the stupid dress from her hands.

Her hair . . . what did she do to her hair?

"I'm going next door to get Mike!" my mum yells to us.

"What the hell did you do to your hair?" I repeat my thought out loud. Tessa frowns, and I watch the sparkle in her eyes dim drastically.

Shit.

"I'm just asking . . . it looks nice," I tell her and take another look. It does look nice. She always looks beautiful.

"I had it dyed . . . you don't like it?" She follows me into the house. I toss the bag onto the couch. "Be careful! That's your mother's wedding gown!" she shrieks, lifting the bottom of the bag from the floor. Her hair looks shinier than usual, too, and her eyebrows are different. Women do too much shit to impress men who can barely tell the difference.

"I don't have a problem with your hair, I was just surprised by it," I tell her, meaning it. It's not that different from the hair she left the house with—just a little darker toward the top, but it's basically the same.

"Good, because it's my hair and I'll wear it how I want it." She crosses her arms over her chest, and a laugh bursts through my lips.

"What?" She glowers. She's serious.

"Nothing. I'm just finding your whole almighty-powerful-woman-thing amusing, that's all." I continue to laugh.

"Well, I'm glad you find it amusing because that's how it is," she challenges.

"Okay." I grab the sleeve of her sweater and pull her to me, ignoring the cleavage on display beneath it. I get the feeling this wouldn't be a good time to call her on it.

"I'm serious, no more caveman shit," she says, a small smile breaking her scowl as she tugs at my chest.

"Okay, calm down. What the hell did my mum do to you?" I press my lips against her forehead, and relief floods through me because she hasn't mentioned Susan or Natalie. I'd much rather hear her cursing me out over her dyed hair than over my past.

"Nothing; you were rude about my hair and I figured it was a good time to warn you that things are changing around here." She bites her cheek to conceal a grin. She's teasing and testing, and it's fucking adorable.

"Sure, sure, no more caveman." I roll my eyes, and she pulls away. "I'm serious, I get it." I pull her back to me.

"I missed you today." She sighs into my chest, and I wrap my arms around her again.

"You did?" I ask, wanting her to confirm. She hasn't been reminded of my past after all. Everything is fine. This weekend will be fine.

"Yeah, especially while I was getting a massage. Eduardo's hands were even bigger than yours." Tessa giggles. Her giggles turn into shrieks as I lift her over my shoulder and head toward the stairs. I know for a fact she didn't get a damn massage by some man; if she had, she sure as hell wouldn't tell me about it and then start laughing.

See, I can lighten up on the caveman shit. Unless, of course, there's a real threat. Never mind that "unless"; this is Tessa we're talking about, and there's always someone trying to keep her from me.

The back door screeches open, and my mum's voice calls our names through the house just as I reach the halfway point of the staircase. I groan, and Tessa wiggles, begging me to put her down. I do as she wants, only because I've missed her all day and my mum will be extra obnoxious if I show Tessa too much affection in front of her and the neighbor.

"We're coming!" Tessa responds when I put her back on her feet.

"Actually, we aren't." I kiss the corner of her mouth, and she smiles.

"*You* aren't." She waggles her new eyebrows, and I smack her ass as she rushes down the stairs.

Most of the weight on my chest has been lifted. I behaved like a fucking idiot last night for no reason. My mum wouldn't have purposely taken Tessa around Natalie; why was I so worried?

"What do you two want to do for dinner? I was thinking we could go to Zara, the four of us." My mum turns to her soon-to-be husband as soon as we enter the living room. Tessa nods even though she has no idea what Zara is.

"I hate Zara. It's too crowded, and Tessa isn't going to like anything there," I grumble. Tessa would eat anything to keep the peace, but I know she wouldn't want to eat liver or pureed lamb for the first time in a situation where she'd feel obligated to smile and pretend that it's the best thing she's ever eaten.

"Blues Kitchen, then?" Mike suggests. Honestly, I don't want to go any fucking where.

"Too loud." I rest my elbows on the counter and pick at the edges where the Formica is chipping.

"Well, you decide and let us know," my mum says in exasperation. I know she's growing impatient with me, but I'm here, aren't I?

Glancing at the clock, I nod. It's only five; we won't need to leave for another hour. "I'm going upstairs," I tell them.

"We need to leave in ten minutes—you know how parking is around here," my mum says.

Great. I hurry out of the living room. I hear Tessa following behind me.

"Hey." She grabs the sleeve of my shirt as I reach the hallway.

I turn to face her.

"What?" I ask, trying to keep my tone as soft as possible despite my irritation.

"What's going on with you? If something's bothering you, just tell me and we can fix it," she offers with a nervous smile.

"How was your lunch today?" She hasn't brought it up, but I can't help but ask.

She catches on. "Oh . . ." Her eyes look down to the floor, and I press my thumb under her chin to make her look at me. "It was nice."

"What did you talk about?" I ask her. It obviously wasn't as bad as I thought it would be, but I can tell she's hesitant to discuss it.

"I met her . . . Natalie. I met her."

My blood runs cold. I slightly bend my knees to get a better look at her face. "And?"

"She's lovely," Tessa says. I wait for her to frown or for her eyes to give away her anger, but nothing comes.

"She's 'lovely'?" I repeat, completely and utterly confused by her response.

"Yes, she was so sweet . . . and very pregnant." Tessa smiles.

"And Susan?" I hesitantly ask.

"Susan was very fun and nice as well."

But . . . but Susan hated me for what I did to her niece. "It was okay, then?"

"Yes, Hardin. My day was fine. I missed you, but my day was fine." She reaches her hand out to grab my shirt and bring me closer to her. She looks so fucking beautiful in the dim lighting of the hallway. "Everything is fine, don't worry," she declares.

My head rests on top of hers, and she wraps her arms tightly around my waist.

She's comforting me? Tessa is comforting me, assuring me that everything will be okay, after coming face-to-face with the girl that I nearly destroyed. She says it will be okay . . . *Will it?*

"It never is, though," I whisper, almost hoping she won't hear the words. If she did hear them, she chooses not to respond.

"I don't want to go to dinner with them," I admit, breaking the silence between us. I really just want to take Tessa upstairs and lose myself in her, forget all the shit that's been torturing my mind all day, push all the ghosts and memories away and focus on her. I want hers to be the only damn voice in my head, and burying myself in her right now will ensure that it is.

"We have to—it's your mother's wedding weekend. We don't have to stay long." She stretches to kiss the top of my cheek, then her lips travel down to my jaw.

"I couldn't be more excited," I mutter sarcastically.

"Come on." Tessa leads me back into the living room, her

hand in mine, but the moment we join my mum and Mike, I drop her hand.

I sigh. "Well, let's go eat."

DINNER IS JUST AS TEDIOUS as I expected. My mum is keeping Tessa busy, chatting her ear off about weddings and the small guest list. She fills her in in on the family members that will be there, which isn't much from my mum's side; only one distant cousin will be attending since both of my mum's parents are dead and have been for years. Mike is quiet during the meal, like me, but he doesn't appear to be as bored as I am. He's watching my mum with an expression that makes me want to smack him in his head. It's sickening but somehow comforting. It's obvious that he loves her, so I guess he's not so bad.

"You're my only shot at grandchildren, Tessa," my mum teases as Mike pays the bill. Tessa chokes on her water, and I pat her on the back. She coughs a few times before apologizing, but when she recovers, her eyes are wide and she looks embarrassed. She's overreacting, but I'm sure she was caught off guard by my mum's crass and out-of-line statement.

Sensing my anger, my mum says, "I'm only teasing. I know you're still young," and childishly sticks her tongue out at me.

Young? It doesn't matter how fucking young we are, she doesn't need to be putting that shit in Tessa's head. We've already agreed: no children. My mum making Tessa feel guilty and obligated won't help anything—it'll only cause another fight. The majority of our fights have been over children and marriage. Neither of which I want, or will ever want. I want Tessa, every single day for the rest of forever, but I won't be marrying her. Richard's warning from the other night creeps its way into my head, but I push it away.

After dinner, my mum kisses Mike good night, and he heads to his house next door. She's following that stupid tradition of the groom not being able to see the bride before their wedding night. I think she's forgotten that this isn't her first rodeo; those stupid superstitions don't apply the second time around.

As much as I'm dying to take Tessa in my old bed, I can't do it with my mum in the house. This shitty place has no soundproofing, nothing. I can literally hear my mum each time she rolls over on her creaky mattress in the next room.

"I should have booked a hotel," I whine as Tessa undresses. I wish she'd sleep in a parka so I wouldn't be tormented all night by her half-naked body. She slips my T-shirt over her head, and I can't help but stare at the curve of her tits underneath the fabric, the slope of her full hips, the way her voluptuous thighs almost fill the bottom of my shirt so it hugs to her skin. I'm glad the shirt isn't too loose on her; it wouldn't look nearly as fucking good. It wouldn't make me this hard, and it sure as hell wouldn't make this night so damn long.

"Come here, baby." I hold my arms open to her, and she lays her head on my chest. I want to tell her how much it means to me that she handled the Natalie situation so well, but I can't find the right words. I think she knows; she has to know how terrified I was that something would come between us.

Within minutes she's asleep, clinging to me, and the words flow freely as I run my fingers over her hair.

"You're everything to me," I say.

I WAKE UP SWEATING. Tessa is still latched on to me, and I can barely breathe through the thick air. It's too hot in this house. My mum must have turned the damn heat on. It's spring now; there's no need. I unhook Tessa's limbs from around my body and wipe her sweat-soaked hair away from her forehead before walking downstairs to check the thermostat.

I'm half asleep when I turn the corner to the kitchen, but what I see next stops me in my tracks. I rub my eyes and even blink to clear the distorted image that has formed in front of me.

But it's still there . . . *they* are still there no matter how many times I blink.

My mum is sitting on top of the counter, her thighs parted. A man stands between them, his arms wrapped around her waist. Her hands are buried in his blond hair. His mouth is on hers, or hers on his—I don't fucking know—what I do know is that the man isn't Mike.

It's fucking Christian Vance.

chapter
one hundred and thirty-six

HARDIN

What? What is happening? For one of the few times in my life, I find myself speechless. My mum's hands move from Vance's hair down to his jaw, her mouth pushing harder against his.

I must have made a noise—probably a gasp, I don't fucking know—because my mum's eyes spring open and she immediately pushes at Vance's shoulders. His head quickly turns to me, his eyes go wide, and he steps away from the counter. How did they not hear me coming down the stairs? Why is he here, in this kitchen?

What the actual fuck is happening?

"Hardin!" my mum says, her voice high with panic as she jumps down from the kitchen counter.

"Hardin, I can—" Vance starts. I hold up my hand to silence them while my mouth and brain work together, trying to make sense of the fucked-up sight in front of me.

"How . . ." I begin, the jumbled words flying through my mind not really connecting. "How . . . ? " I repeat, my feet beginning to move backward. I want to get away from them as fast as I possibly can, but I need an explanation at the same time.

I look back and forth between the two of them, trying to reconcile the people before me with those that I thought I knew. But I fail to do so, and nothing makes sense.

My heels hit the back of the stairs, and my mum steps toward me. "It's not—" she begins.

I'm relieved to feel the familiar burn of anger beginning to chip away at my shock, sweeping over me and pushing away any vulnerability that may have been present seconds ago. Anger I can deal with—I revel in it; shock and stunned silence, not so much.

I'm walking toward them again before I realize what I'm doing, and my mum steps back, distancing herself from me, while Vance steps in front of her. What?

"What the fuck is wrong with you?" I interrupt her, ignoring the selfish tears shining in her eyes. "You're getting married tomorrow!"

"And you," I seethe at my old boss, "you're fucking engaged, and here you are about to fuck my mum on the goddamned kitchen counter!" I lower my hand and strike a harsh blow to the already damaged countertop. The cracking sound of the wood splintering excites me, makes me want more.

"Hardin!" my mum yells.

"Don't you fucking yell at me!" I nearly scream. I hear the rush of footsteps above me, a signal that our voices have woken Tessa up, and I know she's on her way to find me.

"Don't talk to your mother like that." Vance's voice isn't loud, but the threat in his tone is clear.

"You don't get to tell me what the fuck to do! You're no one—who the fuck are you?" My nails dig into my palms, and my anger grows, gathering into a large mass, ready to explode.

"I'm—" he begins, but my mum's hand wraps around his shoulder and pulls him back.

"Christian, don't," she begs him.

"Hardin?" Tessa's voice calls from the stairs, and she enters the kitchen only seconds later. She looks around the room, at the unexpected guest first, then her eyes settle on me as she comes to stand next to me. "Is everything okay?" she nearly whispers, wrapping her small hand around my arm.

"Everything is just fine! Perfect, really!" I pull my arm out of her grip and wave it in front of me. "Although you may want to warn your friend Kimberly that her beloved fiancé has been shagging my mum."

Tessa's eyes nearly fall out onto the floor at my words, but she remains silent. I wish she'd stayed upstairs, but I know if I were her, I wouldn't have either.

"Where is your lovely Kimberly? Staying at a nearby hotel with your son?" I ask Vance, sarcasm screaming through my words. I don't like Kimberly, she's fucking nosy and obnoxious, but she loves Vance, and I was under the strong impression that he was just as much in love with her. Clearly, I was wrong. He doesn't give a fuck about her or their upcoming wedding. If he did, this wouldn't be happening.

"Hardin, everyone just needs to calm down." My mum tries to defuse the situation. Her hand has dropped from Vance's shoulder.

"Calm down?" I scoff. She's unbelievable. "You're getting married tomorrow, and I find you here, in the middle of the night, laid out on the kitchen counter like a whore."

The moment the words hit the air, he's on me. Vance's body collides with mine, and my head smacks against the tile floor of the kitchen as he tackles me to the ground.

"Christian!" I hear my mum scream. He uses the weight of his body to hold me there, but I manage to get my hands out from under his grip. The moment that his fist connects with my nose, my adrenaline courses through me, taking me over, and all I see is red.

chapter one hundred and thirty-seven

TESSA

Am I dreaming? Please let this be a nightmare . . . what's happening surely can't be real.

Christian is on top of Hardin. When his fist connects with Hardin's nose, it makes the most awful sound. The sound burns my ears, and my heart plummets. Hardin's fist reaches up between them, delivering a blow of equal force to Christian's jaw, causing Christian's hold on him to slip.

Within seconds, Hardin rolls from under him and shoves his shoulders, pushing him back to the floor. I can't keep track of how many punches they exchange, and I can't tell who has the upper hand.

"Stop them!" I scream to Trish. Every part of me wants to step between them, knowing that if Hardin sees me he'll immediately stop, but the slight fear is there that he may be too angry, too out of control, and accidently do something that would later drive him mad with guilt.

"Hardin!" Trish grabs Hardin's bare shoulder in an attempt to pull him from the violence, but she goes unnoticed by the both of them.

Adding to the chaos, the back door is yanked open, revealing a panicked Mike. Oh God. "Trish? What is—" He blinks his eyes under his thick glasses as he registers what's happening.

Less than a second later, he joins the rumble, stepping behind Hardin and grabbing him by both of his arms. Large man that he is, Mike lifts him effortlessly and pushes him toward the wall. Christian scrambles to his feet, and Trish pushes him against the opposite wall. Hardin is shaking, fuming, breathing so heavily that I'm afraid he'll somehow damage his lungs. I rush to him, unsure what to do but needing to be close to him.

"What the hell is going on?" Mike's voice commands attention, demands it.

Everything is happening so quickly: the terror in Trish's brown eyes, the angry bruises covering Christian's face, the deep red trail of blood running from Hardin's nose to his mouth . . . it's all too much.

"Ask *them*!" Hardin shouts, tiny drops of red splattering onto his chest. He gestures to a frightened Trish and an angry Christian.

"Hardin," I gently say. "Let's go upstairs," I reach for his hand, trying to keep my own emotions at bay. I'm trembling and I feel the hot tears on my cheeks, but this isn't about me.

"No!" He jerks away from me. "Tell him! Tell him what you were fucking doing!" Hardin tries to lunge toward Christian again, but Mike quickly steps between them. I close my eyes for a moment, praying that Hardin won't assault him, too.

I'm in my old dorm room again, Hardin and Noah on either side of me, as Hardin forces me to confess my infidelity to the boy who I spent half of my life with. The look on Noah's face wasn't nearly as heartbreaking as the one I'm looking at right now. Mike's expression is a mixture of realization, confusion, and pain.

"Hardin, please don't do this," I beg.

"Hardin," I repeat, pleading with him not to embarrass this man. Trish needs to tell him in her own way, not in front of an audience. This isn't right.

"Fuck that! Fuck all of you!" Hardin screams, and his fist drives down against the cheap countertop, snapping it in two.

"I'm sure Mike won't mind if you two use the premises tomorrow." Hardin's voice lowers; each word is deliberately measured and cruel. "I'm sure he'd let you, seeing as he probably wasted a shitload of his money on this joke of a wedding." He half laughs.

A chill sets deep in my spine and I stare at the ground. There's no stopping him when he's like this; no one tries. Everyone is silent as Hardin continues.

"What a nice couple the two of you make. The engaged ex-wife of a drunk and his loyal best friend," he scoffs. "I'm sorry, Mike, but you're about five minutes late to the show. You missed the part where your bride had her tongue down his throat."

Christian tries to grab hold of Hardin again, but Trish leaps in front of him. Hardin and Christian eye each other like panthers.

I'm seeing an entirely new side to Christian. He's not playful or witty; anger is radiating from him in thick waves. The Christian that holds Kimberly by the waist and whispers how beautiful she is is nowhere to be found.

"You disrespectful little—" Christian says through his teeth.

"*I'm* disrespectful? You're the one going on and on to me about the glories of marriage, yet you've been having an affair with my mum!"

My mind can't wrap itself around this. Christian and Trish? Trish and Christian? It doesn't make sense. I know they've been friends for many years, and Hardin told me that Christian had taken Trish and him in, taken care of them, after Ken left. But an affair?

I never thought of Trish as the type who'd do such a thing, and Christian has always seemed so deeply in love with Kimberly. Kimberly . . . My heart aches for her; she loves him so much. She's in the middle of planning her dream wedding with her dream man, and now it's pretty clear that she doesn't know him at all. She'll be devastated. She has built a life with Christian and his son. No matter what I have to do, I will not let Hardin be the one to tell her. I will not let him humiliate and mock her the way he just did Mike.

"It's not like that!" Christian's temper is just as hot as Hardin's. His green eyes are glowing, burning with rage, and I know he wants nothing more than to wrap his hands around Hardin's neck.

Mike is silent, his eyes focused on his fiancée and her tearstained cheeks.

"I'm so sorry, this wasn't supposed to happen. I don't know—" Trish's voice breaks into a heartbreaking sob, and I look away.

Mike shakes his head, clearly rejecting her apology, and he stays silent as he strides across the small kitchen and walks out, slamming the back door behind him. Trish falls to her knees, her hands covering her face to muffle her cries.

Christian's shoulders slump, his anger momentarily replaced by concern as he kneels next to her, drawing her into his arms. Next to me, Hardin's breathing picks up again, his fists tighten at his sides, and I step in front of him, bringing my hands to his cheeks. My stomach turns at the sight of the blood, which has now reached his chin. His lips are stained crimson . . . so much blood.

"Don't," he warns me, pushing my hands away. He's staring behind me at his mother, wrapped in Christian's arms. The two of them seem to have forgotten that we're here—either that or they just don't care. I'm so confused.

"Hardin, please," I cry and raise my trembling hands to his face once more.

He finally looks at me, and I see the guilt rising behind his eyes.

"Please, let's go upstairs," I plead with him. His gaze stays on my face, and I force myself not to look away from his eyes as his anger slowly passes.

"Get me away from them," he stammers. "Get me out of here."

I drop my hands and wrap one around his arm, gently leading him from the kitchen. When we reach the staircase, Hardin halts.

"No . . . I want to leave this house," he says.

"Okay," I quickly agree. I want to leave the house, too. "I'll grab our bags; you go out to the car," I suggest.

"No, if I go out there . . ." He doesn't have to finish his sentence. I know exactly what will happen if he's left alone with his mother and Christian.

"Come upstairs—it won't take long," I promise him. I'm trying my best to keep calm, to be strong for him, and so far, it's working.

He lets me take the lead and follows me up the staircase and down the hall to the small bedroom. I hastily shove our things into our bags, not taking the time to pack them properly. I jump and stifle a scream when Hardin knocks over the dresser, and the heavy piece of furniture lands with a loud thud against the floor. Hardin kneels down and pulls out the first empty drawer. He tosses it to the side before grabbing the next. He's going to destroy everything in this room if I don't get him out of here.

Just as he flings the last drawer against the wall, I wrap my arms around his torso. "Come to the bathroom with me." I lead him down the hallway and close the door behind us. Grabbing a towel from the rack, I turn the faucet on and instruct him to sit on the toilet seat. His silence is chilling and I don't want to push him.

He doesn't speak or even flinch when I bring the hot towel to his cheek, dragging it across the blood pooled under his nose, across his lips, and down his chin.

"It's not broken," I quietly note after briefly examining his nose. His busted bottom lip is already swollen but no longer bleeding. My mind is still racing, flashing angry images of the two men assaulting each other.

He doesn't respond.

When most of the blood is removed, I rinse the stained towel and leave it in the sink. "I'm going to grab our bags. Stay here," I say, hoping he'll listen.

I hurry to the room to gather both of our bags and unzip the suitcase. Hardin is shirtless and barefoot, wearing only athletic shorts, and I'm dressed in just his T-shirt. I didn't have time to think about getting dressed, or even to be embarrassed about running downstairs half naked when I heard the shouting. I didn't know what I was expecting to find as I raced down the steps, but Christian and Trish having sex wasn't one of the scenarios that I ever could have anticipated.

Hardin remains quiet as I pull a clean T-shirt over his head and pull socks onto his bare feet. I dress myself in a sweatshirt and jeans, not giving a thought to my appearance. I rinse my hands again in the bathroom, trying to scrub the blood from under my fingernails.

Silence stretches between us as we reach the stairs, and Hardin takes both bags from me. He hisses in pain when he lifts the strap of my bag onto his shoulder, and I cringe as I picture the bruise beneath by his shirt.

I hear Trish's sobs and Christian's low voice comforting her as we exit the house. When we reach the rental car, Hardin turns around to face the house again, and I watch as a shudder passes through his shoulders.

"I can drive." I take the keys, but he quickly pulls them away from me.

"No, I'm driving," he finally says. I don't argue with him.

I want to ask where we're going, but I choose not to question him right now; he's barely coherent and I need to tread lightly. I place my hand on his, and I'm relieved that he doesn't jerk away from my touch.

Minutes feel like hours as we drive through the village in silence, each mile adding another layer of tension. I stare out the window and recognize the familiar street from this afternoon as we pass Susan's bridal shop. The memory of Trish wiping away tears, staring at herself in the mirror while dressed in her gown, brings tears to my own eyes. How could she do this? She's supposed to be getting married tomorrow; why would she do such a thing?

Hardin's voice snaps me back to the present. "This is so fucked up."

"I don't understand it," I say, gently squeezing his hand.

"Everything and everyone in my life is so fucked up," he says, his voice emotionless.

"I know," I agree with him; even though I couldn't disagree more, now is not the time to correct him.

Hardin slows the car as he pulls into the parking lot of a small motel. "We'll stay here tonight and leave in the morning," he says, staring out the windshield. "I don't know what to say about your job and where you'll live when we get back to the States," he continues, and climbs out of the car.

I was so busy worrying about Hardin and the violent scene in the kitchen that I momentarily forgot that the man rolling around on the floor with Hardin was not only my boss, but the man whose home I'm living in.

"Are you coming?" Hardin asks.

Instead of answering, I step out of the car and follow him into the motel in silence.

chapter one hundred and thirty-eight

TESSA

The man behind the desk gives Hardin the key to our room with a smile that Hardin does not return. I try my best to offer one to make up for it, but it comes off as forced and awkward, and the desk clerk looks away quickly.

In silence, we walk through the lobby to find the room. The hallway is long and narrow; religious paintings line the cream-colored walls, a handsome angel kneeling before a maiden in one, two lovers embracing in another. I shudder when my eyes drag across the last painting, meeting the black eyes of Lucifer himself right outside of our assigned room. I'm stuck staring into the empty eyes as I hurry behind Hardin into the room and flip the light switch, illuminating the dark space. He tosses my bag onto a wingback chair that sits in a corner and drops the suitcase by the door next to where I'm standing.

"I'm taking a shower," he says quietly. Without looking back, he walks into the bathroom and closes the door behind him.

I want to follow him, but I'm conflicted. I don't want to push him or upset him any more than he already is, but at the same time I want to make sure he's okay and I don't want him to wallow in this—not alone, at least.

I pull my shoes off, then my jeans and Hardin's shirt, and follow him into the small bathroom, completely naked. When I push the door open, he doesn't turn around. Steam has already begun to billow through the small space, filling it, covering Hardin's naked body with a cloud of vapor. His tattoos peek through, the black ink visible through the steam, drawing me toward him.

I step over the pile of his discarded clothes and stand behind him, keeping more than a foot of distance between us.

"I don't need you to—" Hardin begins, his voice flat.

"I know," I interrupt him. I know he's angry, hurt, and he's beginning to slip back behind the wall that I've fought so hard to demolish. He's been controlling his anger so well that I could kill Trish and Christian both for making him lose it that way.

Surprised by the dark direction my thoughts have taken, I shake them away.

Without another word, he draws back the shower curtain and steps into the cascading water. I take a breath, summoning every ounce of confidence I can muster, and step into the shower behind him. The water is scalding, barely tolerable, and I hide behind Hardin to avoid it. He must notice my discomfort, because he adjusts the water temperature.

I grab the small complimentary bottle of soap and squeeze it onto a cloth and carefully bring it to Hardin's back. He finches and tries to move forward, but I follow him, stepping closer.

"You don't have to talk to me, but I know you need me to be here right now." My voice is almost a whisper, lost between Hardin's deep breaths and the falling water.

Silent and still, he doesn't move as I brush the cloth across the letters etched into his skin. My tattoo.

Hardin turns to face me, allowing me to clean his chest now, his eyes studying every stroke of the cloth. I feel the anger radiating from of him, mixing with the clouds of hot vapor, and his eyes are burning into me. He looks as if he's going to explode. Before I can blink, both of his hands are pressed against my jaw, cupping my neck on either side. His mouth desperately collides against mine, and my lips part involuntarily under the rough contact. There is nothing gentle, nothing soft about his touch. My tongue meets his, and I pull his bottom lip between my teeth, gently tugging, avoiding his wound. He groans and presses me against the wet tile.

I hear myself whimper when he pulls his mouth from mine, but he quickly reestablishes contact and peppers rough kisses down the column of my neck and across my chest, then cups my breasts, rolling them beneath his busted and bruised hands while his mouth works back and forth, licking, sucking, biting. I roll my head back against the tile and bury my fingers in his hair, tugging the way I know he loves.

Without warning, he lowers his body even further, resting on his knees under the spraying water, and for a fleeting moment I'm reminded of something vague. But then he touches me again, and I just can't remember what it is.

chapter one hundred and thirty-nine

HARDIN

Tessa's fingers rake through my hair, bringing my mouth to her flushed, already swollen skin. Touching her, tasting her this way, pushes everything else from my tortured mind.

She cries out as my tongue laps around her, pulling tightly at the roots of my hair. Her hips lift from the tile, meeting my mouth, desperate for more.

Too soon, I stand back to my feet and lift one of her legs to wrap around my waist, following with the other. She groans as I lift her, entering her slowly.

"Fuuuuck . . ." I draw the word out, my voice almost a hiss as I'm overwhelmed by the warmth, the wetness, of feeling her without the barrier of a condom between us.

Her eyes roll back into her head as I push forward, withdrawing and filling her again. I fight every urge to slam into her, to fuck her so hard that I forget everything around us. Instead, I move slowly but allow my mouth and hands to be rough on her skin. Her arms tighten around my shoulders as my lips latch on to the skin just above the curve of her full breast. I can taste the blood rising to the surface underneath my tongue, and I pull away in time to see the faint pink mark left in my wake.

Her eyes dart down between us, examining it herself. She doesn't scold me or even frown at the bruise left by my lips; she only brings her lip between her teeth, staring almost adoringly at the mark. Tessa drags her fingernails down the slope of my back, and I press her harder against the tile wall. My fingers are pressed into her thighs, indenting her skin, and I thrust inside of her, repeating her name over and over.

Her legs tighten around my waist, and I push and pull, in and out, bringing both of us closer to our release.

"Hardin," she softly moans, her breathing erratic as she comes around me. The realization that I can come inside of her without worry brings me to the edge, pushing me over. I spill into her with a shout of her name.

"I love you." I press my lips against her temple before placing my forehead against hers to catch my breath.

"I love you," she gasps, her eyes closed. I stay inside of her, allowing myself to simply enjoy the feeling of skin on skin.

On my back, I can feel the heat leaving the water; we won't have more than ten minutes left of hot water. The idea of a cold shower in the middle of the night causes me to carefully help her back to her feet. As I withdraw from her, I watch shamelessly as the evidence of my orgasm seeps from between her legs. Fucking hell, that sight alone is worth waiting seven fucking months for.

I want to thank her, to tell her that I love her and that she brought me out of the darkness, not only tonight, but ever since the day she caught me off guard by kissing me in my old room at the frat house, but I can't find the words.

I turn the hot water up and stare at the wall. I sigh in relief when I feel the soft washcloth on my back, continuing what she started only minutes ago.

I turn around to face her, and as she brings the cloth to my neck, I stay silent. My anger is still around, lurking and simmering below the surface, but she's taken me beyond it in the way that only she can.

chapter one hundred and forty

TESSA

"My mum is so fucked up." Hardin finally speaks after long minutes of silence. My hand jerks at the sudden noise, but I quickly recover and return to bathing him as he continues. "I mean this is some shit right out of Tolstoy."

My mind scrambles through Tolstoy's works before landing on *The Kreutzer Sonata.* I shiver despite the heat of the shower.

"Kreutzer?" I ask, hoping I'm confused or that he and I have interpreted the dark story differently.

"Yes, of course." He's becoming emotionless again, crouching down behind that damn wall.

"I don't know if I would compare this . . . situation to something so dark," I softly argue. That story is filled with blood, jealousy, and rage, and I'd like to think this real-life one will have a better ending.

"Not completely, but yes," he answers as if he can read my mind.

I play the story line through my head, trying to see some connection to Hardin's mother's affair, but the only thing I can come up with has to do with Hardin himself and his beliefs about marriage. That causes me to shiver again.

"I didn't plan to ever marry, and I still don't, so no, it didn't change anything," he coldly responds.

I ignore the pain in my chest and focus on him. "Okay." I run the cloth down one arm, then the other, and when I look up, his eyes are closed.

"Whose story do you suppose we'll have?" he asks, taking the cloth from my hand.

"I don't know," I answer him honestly. I'd love nothing more than to know the answer to this question.

"Me neither." He pours more body wash onto the cloth and runs it across my chest.

"Couldn't we make our own story?" I look up into his troubled eyes.

"I don't think we can. You know this is going to end one of two ways," he says, shrugging his shoulders.

I know he's hurt and I know he's angry, but I don't want Trish's mistakes to affect our relationship and I can see Hardin making comparisons behind the green of his eyes.

I try to take the conversation in another direction. "What is it about all of this that bothers you the most? It's that the wedding is tomorrow . . . well, today," I correct myself. It's almost 4 a.m. now, and the wedding is, or was, supposed to start at two this afternoon. What happened after we left the house? Did Mike come back to talk to Trish, or did Christian and Trish finish what they started?

"I don't know." He sighs, dragging the cloth down my stomach and across my hips. "I don't really give a fuck about that wedding. I guess I just feel like they're both fucking liars."

"I'm sorry," I tell him.

"My mum is the one who'll be sorry. She's the one who sold her fucking house and cheated the night before her damn wedding." His touch becomes rough as his anger builds.

I stay quiet but remove the cloth from his hands and hang it on the rack behind me.

"And Vance, what kind of fucking asshole has an affair with the ex-wife of his best friend? My father and Christian Vance have known each other since they were kids." Hardin's tone is bitter—threatening, even. "I should call my father and see if he knows what a backstabbing whore—"

I reach my hand and cover his mouth before he can finish the harsh words. "She's still your mother," I softly remind him. I know he's angry, but he shouldn't call her names.

I remove my hand from his mouth so he can speak. "I don't give a fuck that she's my mother, and I don't give a fuck about Vance either. And the joke's going to be on him, because when I tell Kimberly about them and you quit your job, he'll be fucked," Hardin proudly declares, as if this would be the best form of revenge.

"You will *not* tell Kimberly." I look into his eyes, pleading. "If Christian doesn't tell her himself, then I will, but you will not embarrass her or harass her about it. I understand that you're angry at your mother and at Christian, but Kimberly is innocent here, and I don't want her to be hurt," I say firmly.

"Fine. You *will* quit, though," he says while turning his body around to rinse the foamy shampoo from his hair.

Sighing, I reach for the shampoo bottle in Hardin's hand but he pulls it away.

"I'm serious, you aren't working for him anymore."

I understand his anger, but this isn't the time to discuss my job. "We'll talk about it later," I tell him and finally manage to get the bottle into my hands. The water is growing colder by the minute, and I'd like to wash my hair.

"No!" He jerks it back. I'm trying to stay calm and be as gentle as possible with him, but he's making it difficult.

"I can't just quit my internship; it's not that simple. I'd have to inform the university, fill out a bunch of paperwork, and give a solid explanation of what happened. Then I would have to add classes to my schedule in the middle of the semester to make up for the credits I was receiving from Vance Publishing, and since the deadline for financial aid has already passed, I'd have to pay out of pocket. I can't simply just quit. I'll try to figure something out, but I need a little time, please." I give up on washing my hair.

"Tessa, I literally couldn't give less than a fuck about you having to file some paperwork; this is my family," he says, and I immediately feel guilty.

He's right, isn't he? I honestly don't know, but his busted lip and bruised nose make me feel that way. "I know, I'm sorry. I just need to find another internship first, that's all I'm asking." Why am I asking? "I mean saying . . . that's what I'm *saying* . . . that I need a little time. I'm already going to have to move into a hotel as it is . . ." The anxiety I feel at the prospect of being homeless, jobless, and once again friendless is taking me over.

"You won't be able to find another internship anyway, not a paying one," he harshly reminds me. I knew that already, but I was trying to force myself into believing that I had a slight chance.

"I don't know what I'm going to do, but I need some time. This is all such a mess." I step out of the shower and reach for a towel.

"Well, you don't have much time to figure it out. You should just move back to central Washington with me." His words stop me in my tracks.

"Move back *there*?" The very idea of it makes me nauseous. "I'm not moving back there, and after last weekend, I don't even want to visit the place again, let alone move back. That isn't an option." I wrap the towel around my wet body and leave the bathroom.

I reach for my phone and panic when I see five missed calls and two text messages. All from Christian. Both text messages are pleas to have Hardin call him right away.

"Hardin," I call to him.

"What?" he snaps. I roll my eyes and swallow my annoyance. "Christian has called, a lot."

He emerges from the bathroom with a towel wrapped around his waist. "And?"

"What if something happened to your mother? Don't you want to call and be sure she's okay?" I ask him. "Or I—"

"No, fuck both of them. Don't call them."

"Hardin, I really think—"

"No," he says, interrupting me.

"I already sent him a text, just to be sure your mother is okay," I admit.

He grimaces. "Of course you did."

"I know you're upset, but please stop taking it out on me. I'm really trying to be here for you, but you have to stop snapping at me. This isn't my fault."

"I'm sorry." His hands run over his wet hair. "Let's both just turn our cell phones off and get some sleep." His voice has calmed, and his eyes have softened tremendously. "My shirt is stained," he says, dragging the bloodied garment across the floor, "and I don't know where the other one is."

"I'll get it from the suitcase."

"Thank you." He sighs. The fact that he finds so much comfort in me wearing his clothing makes me happy, even in the middle of this disastrous night. I retrieve the shirt he wore earlier today and hand him clean boxers to sleep in before refolding the articles in the suitcase.

"I'm going to change our flight when I wake up. I can't concentrate right now." He sits on the edge of the bed for a moment before lying down.

"I can do it," I offer, pulling his laptop from the suitcase.

"Thanks," he grumbles, half asleep already.

Seconds later he mutters, "I wish I could take you away, far away." My hands are still on the keyboard and I wait for him to say something else, but he breaks into soft snores.

As I pull up the airline's website, my phone vibrates on the table. Christian's name comes up on the screen. I ignore the call, but when a second comes in, I grab the room key and quietly retreat to the hallway to answer.

I try to whisper. "Hello."

"Tessa? How is he?" he asks, panicked.

"He's . . . he's okay. His nose is bruised and swollen, his lip is busted, and he has a few bruises and cuts." I don't hide the hostility in my tone.

"Dammit," he breathes. "I'm so sorry that it came to this."

"Me, too," I snap at my boss and try to ignore the hideous painting in front of my eyes.

"I need to talk to him. I know he's confused and angry, but I need to explain some things to him."

"He doesn't want to talk to you, and honestly, why should he? He trusted you, and you know that his trust is not something he gives lightly." I lower my voice. "You're engaged to a lovely woman and Trish was supposed to be getting married tomorrow."

"She's still getting married," he says through the line.

"What?" I walk farther down the hall. I stop in front of the peaceful painting of the kneeling angel, but the more I look at it, the darker it becomes. Behind the angel is another; this second one's body almost translucent, and he's holding a double-edged dagger in his hand. The brown-haired maiden is watching him, a sinister smile on her face as she seems to wait for the assault on the kneeling angel. The second angel's expression is contorted, his naked body all planes and angles as he prepares to stab the first angel. I look away and focus on the voice on the other end of the line.

"The wedding has not been canceled. Mike loves Trish, and

she loves him; they will still be married tomorrow despite my mistake." The words sound as if he's struggling to get them out.

I have so many questions to ask him, but I can't. He's my boss and his affair is with Hardin's mother; this is none of my business.

"I know what you must think of me, Tessa, but if I'm able to explain myself, maybe you both will understand."

"Hardin wants me to change our flight and leave in the morning," I inform him.

"He can't leave without saying goodbye to his mother. It will kill her."

"I don't think it's in the best interest of anyone to allow him to be in the same room as her," I warn and walk back to the room, stopping just outside the door.

"I understand your need to protect him, and it pleases me greatly to see how fiercely loyal you are to him. But Trish has had a hard enough life as it is, and it's time for her to have some happiness. I don't expect him to show for the wedding, but please do what you can to have him at least say goodbye to her. God knows how long it will be before he comes back to England." Christian sighs.

"I don't know." I run my fingers along the bronze frame of the Lucifer painting. "I'll see what I can do, but I can't promise anything. I won't push him."

"I understand. Thank you." The relief in his voice is clear.

"Christian?" I say just before hanging up.

"Yes, Tessa?"

"Will you tell Kimberly?" I hold my breath and wait for his answer to my highly inappropriate question.

"Of course I'll tell her," he softly responds, his accent thick and smooth. "I love her more than—"

"Okay." I'm trying to understand, but the only image that's coming to mind is Kimberly smiling in their kitchen, her head tipped back in laughter and Christian's eyes sparkling as he watches her in amazement, as if she's the only woman in his world. Does he look at Trish that way?

"Thank you. Let me know if you need anything. Again, I'm sorry for what you saw earlier, and I hope that your opinion of me hasn't been completely destroyed," he says and hangs up the phone.

I take one last glance at the hideous monster on the wall and walk back into the hotel room.

chapter one hundred and forty-one

HARDIN

Where are you?" His angry voice booms down the hall, creeping into the kitchen. The front door slams, and I jump down from the kitchen chair, grabbing my book. My shoulder knocks into the bottle on the table, sending it crashing to the ground into too many pieces. The brown liquid covers the floor, and I hurry to hide it before he finds me and sees what I did.

"Trish! I know you're here!" He yells again. His voice is closer now. My small hands pull the towel from the stove and throw it onto the floor to cover the mess I made.

"Where's your mum?"

I jerk back at the sound of his voice. "She's . . . she's not here," I tell him, standing to my feet.

"What the fuck did you do?" he shouts, pushing past me and seeing the big mess I made. I didn't mean to make the mess. I knew he would be angry.

"That bottle of scotch was older than you," he says. I look up to his red face and he stumbles. "You broke my fucking bottle." My dad's voice is slow. It always sounds like this when he comes home lately.

I back away, taking small steps. If I can just get to the stairs, I can get away. He's too drunk to follow me. He fell down them last time.

"What's that?" His angry eyes focus on my book.

I hug it tighter to my chest. No. Not this one, too.

"Come here, boy." He circles around me.

"Please don't," I beg the man as he rips my favorite book from my hands. Miss Johnson says that I'm a good reader, better than anyone else in fifth year.

"You broke my bottle, so I get to break something of yours." He smiles. I back away as he tears the book in two and rips out the pages. I cover my ears and watch as Gatsby and Daisy float around the room in a white storm. He grabs some of the pages in the air and rips them into small pieces.

I can't be a baby, I can't cry. It's just a book. It's just a book. My eyes are burning, but I'm not a baby, so I can't cry.

"You're just like him, you know? With your stupid fucking books," he slurs.

Just like who? Jay Gatsby? He doesn't read as much as me.

"She thinks I'm stupid, but I'm not." He grabs the back of the chair to keep from falling. "I know what she did." Suddenly his face goes still, and I think my dad is going to cry.

"Clean up this shit," he groans and leaves me alone in the kitchen, kicking the binding of my book as he leaves.

"HARDIN! HARDIN, WAKE UP!" A voice calls me from my mum's kitchen. "Hardin, it's only a dream. Please wake up."

When my eyes fly open, I'm met with worried eyes and an unfamiliar-looking ceiling above my head. It takes me a moment to realize that I'm not in my mum's kitchen after all. There's no spilled scotch or ripped-up novel.

"I'm so sorry for leaving you in here alone. I just went to get some breakfast. I didn't think—" Her voice breaks off into a sob, and she wraps her arms around my sweat-covered back.

"Shh . . ." I smooth her hair. "I'm fine." I blink a few times.

"Do you want to talk about it?" she quietly asks.

"No, I can't even remember it, really," I tell her. The dream has turned blurry, fading out more with each stroke of her hand across the bare skin between my shoulder blades.

I let her hold me for a few minutes before breaking away. "I got breakfast for you," she says, wiping her nose with the sleeve of my sweatshirt she's wearing. "Sorry." She smiles shyly, holding the snot-covered sleeve up in front of me.

I can't help but laugh, my nightmare forgotten. "There have been worse things on that sweatshirt," I cheekily remind her, trying to make her laugh. My thoughts travel back to when she jacked me off in the apartment while I was wearing said sweatshirt, and quite the mess was made.

Her cheeks flush, and I reach for the tray of food next to her. She has piled it high with different types of bread, fruit, cheese, and even a small box of Frosted Flakes.

"I had to fight an old woman for that." She grins, nodding toward the cereal.

"You did no such thing," I tease her as she brings a grape to her lips.

"I would have," she insists.

The mood has shifted drastically since our arrival in the middle of the night. "Did you change the flight?" I ask her and tear into the Frosted Flakes, not bothering to pour them into the small bowl she put on the tray.

"I wanted to talk about that with you." Her voice lowers. She didn't change the flight. I sigh and wait for her to finish. "I talked to Christian last night . . . well, this morning."

"*What? Why?* I told you—" I stand up, knocking the cereal box onto the tray.

"I know you did, but just hear me out," she begs.

"Fine." I sit back on the bed and wait for her explanation.

"He said he's really sorry and that he needs to explain all of this to you. I understand if you don't want to hear it. If you don't want to talk to either of them, Christian or your mother, I'll get online and change the flight now. I just wanted to give you the option first. I know you care for him . . ." Her eyes begin to water again.

"I don't," I assure her.

"Do you want me to change the tickets?" she asks.

"Yes," I tell her. She frowns and leans over to lift my laptop from the nightstand next to the bed. "What else did he say?" I ask hesitantly. It doesn't matter, but I'm curious.

"The wedding is still on," she informs me.

What the fuck?

"And he says he's going to tell Kimberly everything and that he loves her more than his own life." Tessa's bottom lip begins to tremble at the mention of her betrayed friend.

"Mike is fucking stupid, then—maybe he does belong with my mum after all."

"I don't know what made him forgive her so quickly, but he did." Tessa pauses and looks at me like she's trying to gauge my mood. "Christian asked me to have you at least say goodbye to your mother before we leave. He knows you won't go to the wedding, but he wants you to tell her goodbye." She rushes the words.

"Hell, no. No fucking way. I'm getting dressed and we're getting the fuck out of this shithole." I wave my hand around the overly expensive motel room.

"Okay," she agrees.

That was easy. Too easy. "What do you mean, *okay*?" I ask her.

"Nothing. I just meant okay. I understand if you don't want to say goodbye to your mom." She shrugs her shoulders and tucks her messy hair behind both ears.

"You do?"

"Yes." She smiles a weak smile. "I know I'm hard on you sometimes, but I'm going to support you on this. You're completely justified here."

"Okay," I say, more than a little relieved. I thought she'd fight me and even try to force me to go to the wedding. "I can't wait to go back." I rub my fingers over my temples.

"Yeah, me, too," Tessa weakly replies.

Where the fuck is she going to live? After what happened here she can't just go back to Vance's house, but she won't come to my place either. I don't know what she's going to do, but I do know that I want to rip Vance's fucking head from his body for making her return to the States complicated.

I wish I could get her a job with me at Bolthouse, but it's impossible. She's not even a sophomore, and paying internships at publishing houses don't come along every day, even to graduates. There's no way she'll find another, especially in Seattle, not until she's further along in her degree, or even finished with it.

I take the laptop from her hands to finish the task of changing our flight. I shouldn't have agreed to come to the UK in the first place. Vance talked me into bringing Tessa, only to ruin the entire damn trip himself.

"I just need to get the stuff from the bathroom and we can head to the airport," Tessa says, tucking my dirty clothes into the top pocket of the suitcase. A defeated-looking frown covers her face, and her brows are drawn together. I want to smooth away the deep worry line between them. I hate the way her shoulders are slumped, and I know without a doubt that they're bearing the burden of my troubles. I love Tessa and I love her compassion; I just wish she wouldn't carry my problems along with her own. I can carry my problems myself.

"Are you all right?" I ask her. She looks up and plasters the most unconvincing smile onto her face that I've ever seen.

"Yeah, are you?" she asks back, her worry line deepening.

"Not if you aren't. Tessa. Don't worry about me."

"I'm not," she lies.

"Tess . . ." I cross the room and stand in front of her, pulling the shirt from her hands that I've just watched her fold at least ten times within the last two minutes. "I'm fine, okay? I'm still pissed off and shit, but I know you're worried that I'm going to snap. I won't." I look down at my busted hands. "Well, not again, anyway." I correct myself with a small laugh.

"I know. It's just that you've been controlling your anger so well, and I don't want anything to jeopardize your progress."

"I know." I run my hand over my hair and try to think clearly without getting angry.

"I'm really proud of you already, for how you handled that situation. Christian was the one who attacked you," she says.

"Come here." I hold my arms out, and she graciously steps into them, nuzzling her face into my chest. "Even if he hadn't come at me, the fight still would have happened. I know I'd have made the first move if he hadn't," I tell her. My hands move under the hem of her shirt, and she flinches at the coldness of my touch against the warm skin of her back.

"I know," she agrees.

"Since you're off until Wednesday, we'll stay at my father's house until you—" The vibrating of her cell phone interrupts me.

Both of our eyes dart to the table. "I won't answer it," she announces.

I let go of Tessa and grab her phone. Looking at the screen, I take a breath before answering. "Stop fucking harassing Tessa; if you want to talk to me, then you can call me. Don't bring her into this shit," I say before he can even say hello.

"I did call you. You shut your phone off," Christian says.

"And why do you think that is?" I huff. "If I wanted to talk to you, I would have, but since I don't, stop fucking bothering me."

"Hardin, I know you're mad, but we need to talk about this."

"There isn't anything to talk about!" I shout. Tessa watches with worried eyes as I try to control my temper.

"Yes, there is. There's a lot to talk about. All I'm asking for is fifteen minutes." His voice is pleading.

"Why should I talk with you?"

"Because I know you feel betrayed and I want to explain myself. You're important to me, and to your mom," he says.

"So now you two are forming some kind of united front against me? Fuck off." My hands are shaking.

"You can act like you don't give a fuck about either of us, but your anger shows that you do."

I pull the phone away from my ear and have to stop myself from smashing it into pieces against the wall.

"Fifteen minutes," I hear him repeat. "The wedding isn't scheduled to begin for a few hours. All the men are meeting for lunch at Gabriel's bar. You should meet me there."

I bring the phone to my ear again. "You want me to meet you at a bar? Are you fucking stupid?" A drink sounds good right about now . . . the burn of hot whiskey on my tongue . . .

"Not to drink, only to talk. A public place would be the best spot for us to meet, for obvious reasons." He sighs. "We can meet somewhere else if you want."

"No, Gabriel's is fine," I agree. Tessa's eyes go wide, and she tilts her head slightly, obviously confused by my change of heart. It's not affection that makes me want to hear him out; it's purely curiosity. He claims that there's an explanation for all of this, and I want to hear it. Otherwise, my barely existent relationship with my mum won't exist at all.

"Okay . . ." I can tell he didn't expect me to agree. "It's noon now. I'll meet you there at one."

"Sure," I snap. I don't know how this little meeting could possibly not end in blows.

"You should bring Tessa by Heath—that's where Kim and Smith will be. It's only a few miles from Gabriel's, and Kimberly could really use a friend right now." I want to laugh at the note of shame in his voice. Fucking asshole.

"Tessa will be coming with me," I tell him.

"Do you really want to bring her into a potentially violent situation . . . again?" he asks.

Yes. Yes, I do. No, I don't. I don't want to be out of her sight, but she's seen enough violence from me to last a lifetime.

"You're only saying that because you want her to comfort your fiancée after you fucking cheated on her," I growl.

"No." Vance pauses. "I just want to talk to you alone, and I don't think it would be especially wise of us to have either woman present."

"Fine. I'll fucking meet you in an hour." I hang up the phone and turn to Tessa. "He wants you to hang out with Kim while we talk."

"Does she know?" she quietly asks.

"Sounds like it."

"Are you sure you want to meet with him? I don't want you to feel like you have to."

"Do you think I should?" I ask her.

After a moment, she nods. "Yes. I do."

"Then I'll meet him." I pace across the room.

Tessa gets up from the bed and wraps her arms around my waist. "I love you, so much," she says against my bare chest.

"I love you." I'll never tire of hearing her say the words.

WHEN SHE STEPS out of the bathroom, I nearly choke on my breath. "Fuck." I cross the room in three steps.

"Does this look okay?" she asks, turning in a slow circle.

"Um, yeah." I nearly choke again. *Okay?* Is she fucking insane? The white dress that she wore to my father's wedding looks even better on her now than it did then.

"I could barely zip it." She smiles, embarrassed. She turns around and lifts her hair off of her back. "Can you zip the rest?"

I love that I've seen every inch of her hundreds of times, yet her cheeks still flush and she still holds on to some of her innocence. I haven't completely tainted her.

"Have you changed your mind? I don't want you to be uncomfortable." Tessa's voice is soft.

"Yes, I'm sure. All I'm doing is giving him fifteen minutes to listen to whatever bullshit he has to say." I sigh. I sure as hell don't want to go anywhere except to the damn airport, but after seeing the look on her face while she repacked that suitcase, I felt like I had to do this—not only for her, but for myself, too.

"I look like a fucking bum next to you," I tell her, and she smiles, her eyes running over my face and body.

"Please!" She laughs. I look down at my black shirt and ripped jeans. "You could have shaved," she comments with a smile. I can tell she's nervous and she's trying to lighten the mood. I couldn't be further from nervous . . . I just want to get this shit over with.

"You like this." I take her hand and rub it along the stubble on my jaw. "Especially between your legs." I bring her hand to my mouth and kiss her fingertips. She jerks her hand away as I wrap my lips around her index finger, and swats at my chest.

"You never stop," she playfully scolds me, and for a moment I forget about all of the bullshit.

"Nope, and I never will." I reach around to squeeze her ass with both hands, and she yelps.

The drive to Hampstead Heath, where Kimberly and Smith are staying, and to the park where we're meeting her, is nerve-racking. Tessa picks at her painted fingernails in the passenger seat and stares out the window.

"What if he didn't tell her? Should I?" she finally says as I pull through the gate. Despite her worry, I watch as her eyes take in the scenic view of the park. "Wow," she says, sounding many years younger than her age.

"I knew you'd like the Heath," I say.

"It's beautiful. How could someplace like this be in the middle of London?" She gapes at the surrounding landscape, one of the few places in the city that haven't been polluted by smog and office towers.

"There she is . . ." I drive slowly toward the blonde who's sitting on a bench. Smith is sitting on another bench about twenty feet away with a piece of a toy train on his lap. That little boy is so weird.

"If you need anything at all, please call me. I'll find my way to you," Tessa promises before getting out of the car.

"Same to you." I gently pull her across the console to kiss her. "I mean it. If anything goes wrong, call me immediately," I tell her.

"I'm more worried for you," she whispers against my lips.

"I'll be fine. Now go tell your friend how big of a shitbag her fiancé is." I kiss her again.

She frowns at me but stays quiet as she leaves the car and walks across the grass to meet Kimberly.

chapter one hundred and forty-two

TESSA

I try to gather my thoughts as I cross the grass to meet Kimberly. I don't know what to say to her, and I'm terrified that she may not be aware of what happened last night. I don't want to be the one to tell her—that's Christian's responsibility—but I don't think I have it in me to pretend like nothing happened if it turns out that she doesn't know.

My question is immediately answered when she turns around to face me. Her eyes, though covered mostly in shadows, are swollen and sad.

"I'm so sorry," I say. I sit down next to her on the bench, and she wraps her arms around me.

"I would cry, but I'm afraid I'm all dried up." She tries to force a smile that doesn't meet her eyes.

"I don't know what to say," I admit, glancing across the way at Smith, who, thankfully, is out of earshot.

"Well, you can start with helping me plan a double murder." Kimberly gathers her shoulder-length hair in one hand and pushes it to the side.

"I can do that." I half laugh. I wish I had even half of Kimberly's strength.

"Good." She smiles and squeezes my hand. "You look really hot today," she tells me.

"Thank you. You look beautiful," I tell her. Bright sunlight breaking through the overcast makes her pale blue beaded dress glitter.

"Are you going to the wedding?" she asks.

"No, I just wanted to look better than I'm feeling," I reply. "Are you going to the wedding?"

"Yeah, I am." She sighs. "I don't know what I'll do afterward, but I don't want to confuse Smith. He's a smart kid, and I don't want to alert him to anything that's going on." Her eyes focus on the little scientist and his train.

"Besides, Sasha's skanky ass is here with Max, and I'll be damned if I give her something to gossip about."

"Sasha came here with Max? What about Denise and Lillian?" Max's treachery knows no bounds.

"Exactly what I said! She has no shame, coming all the way to England to attend a wedding with a married man. I should beat the hell out of her to get some of this anger out." Kimberly is so tense you can practically see it emanating from her. I can't imagine the pain she must be feeling right now, and I admire the way she's holding herself together.

"Are you . . . I don't want to pry, but—"

"Tessa, all I do is pry. You're allowed to, too," she says with a warm smile.

"Are you going to stay with him? If you don't want to talk about it, we don't have to."

"I do want to talk about it. I have to talk about it, because if I don't, then I'm afraid I won't be able to stay as angry as I am." She grits her teeth. "I don't know if I'll stay with him. I love him, Tessa." She looks at Smith again. "And I love that little boy, even if he only talks to me once a week." She laughs weakly. "I wish I could say that I'm surprised by this, but honestly, I'm not."

"Why aren't you?" I ask without thinking.

"They have history, a long, deep history that I'm just not sure if I can compete with." Hurt fills her voice, and I blink back my tears.

"History?"

"Yes. I'm going to tell you something Christian told me not to tell you until he can tell Hardin, but I think you should know . . ."

chapter
one hundred and forty-three

HARDIN

Gabriel's is a pretentious bar set in the middle of the wealthiest section in Hampstead. Of course he'd choose this place to meet me. I park my rental car in the lot and walk toward the door. When I step inside the stuffy place, my eyes scan the room. Seated at a round table in the corner of the bar are Vance, Mike, Max, and that blonde. Why the fuck is she here? And more importantly, why is Mike sitting next to Vance as if he wasn't on the verge of fucking his fiancée less than twelve hours ago?

Everyone in the place is wearing a damn tie, except me. I hope I trailed dirt in behind me. A hostess tries to speak to me as I pass her, but I brush her off.

"Hardin, nice to see you." Max stands first and puts his hand out to shake. I ignore him.

"You wanted to talk—let's talk," I snap at Vance when I reach the table. He brings his glass, filled to the brim with liquor, to his mouth and gulps it down before standing.

Mike's eyes stay focused on the table and it takes all of my strength not to tell him how fucking stupid he is. He's always been a quiet man, the dependable neighbor that my mum would always pester for milk or eggs when she ran out.

"How's your trip going so far?" Sabrina's voice rings out.

I look at her, dumbfounded that she would even speak to me right now.

"Where's your wife?" I glare at Max. Next to him, the blonde's smile drops from her overly made-up face and she starts swirling her empty martini glass in small circles.

"Hardin . . ." Vance says, daring to try to shut me up.

"Fuck off," I bark at him. He stands to his feet. "I'm sure she and her daughter miss him while he's here parading around with a skan—"

"Enough," he says and he gently grabs me by the arm in an attempt to get me away from the table.

I jerk my arm from his grip. "Don't you fucking touch me."

Stephanie's shrill "Hey!" cuts through my growing anger. "That's no way to treat your father, now, is it?"

How fucking stupid is she? My father is back in Washington. "What?"

Her smile grows. "You heard me. You should really treat your old man with more respect."

"Sasha!" Max grabs her thin arm with brutal force, nearly dragging her to her feet.

"Oops, did I say something I wasn't supposed to?" Her laugh rings through the bar. She's a fucking idiot.

Confused, I look at Mike, who has no color left in his round face. He looks like he could pass out at any moment. My mind begins to shift, and I look over at Vance, who is equally pale and nervously shifting from one foot to the other.

Why are they being so dramatic over some dumb chick's random nonsense?

"You shut up, now." Max removes the woman from the table and practically drags her through the bar.

"She wasn't supposed to—" Vance runs his hand over his hair. "I was going to . . ." He balls his fists at his sides.

She wasn't supposed to *what*? Make some stupid comment about Vance being my father when clearly my father is . . .

I look at the panicked man in front of me, his green eyes on fire, his fingers frantically running over his hair . . .

It takes me a moment to realize that my hands are doing the exact same thing.

acknowledgments

I can't believe I'm writing acknowledgments for the third book already! Time has literally flown, wings and all, away from me, and I'm so grateful for this crazy ride. I have so many people in my life worth thanking, and I'm going to try and fit as many as I can here.

First, my readers and loyal Afternators. You guys never fail to amaze me with your support and love. You show up in numbers to every event I have, you tweet me about your day, you care about mine, and you are always my cyber-sidekicks everywhere I go. I feel as if we have this bond beyond the typical reader/writer relationship where we are more than that, more than friends, even. We are family, and I could never thank you enough for being there for me and for each other. We have one more book to go in this series, and I hope you feel the sense of pride and ownership as you always have. I love you all so freaking much, and you mean the world to me.

Adam Wilson, my superhero of an editor at Gallery. We have gotten through so much work together, and we've been a steam train at getting these books done at a super speed, with you making it "easy" for me. You teach me to be a better writer through your comments and jokes, and you get my sense of humor. I was afraid at first to have a "big, bad editor," but you've been everything I could have hoped for! Thank you!

Ashleigh Gardner, you have become a very close friend to me. I've said this before, but honestly, you're the type of woman I look up to. You're strong and fierce, but so sweet and silly at the same time. You always have excellent book recommendations, and you take me to strange food places and don't make me feel stupid for needing a fork to eat ceviche or when I don't understand something (un-food-related, too—haha). I really just admire you a lot, and I'm so happy for your new marriage, and I want to thank you for everything.

Candice Faktor, since we met, we had so much in common to the point where it was creepy. I knew instantly that you and Amy were my type of people, and I was so relieved when you turned out to be awesome. I love the way you speak about everything so passionately—we are alike in that way as well. You are always so genuine and so organic, and I'm just thankful to be working with you and consider you a friend.

Nazia Khan, thank you for helping me learn to speak in public and make it through an interview without becoming a total disaster. You always make things fun, and you only get a little mad at me when I give people my email address without telling you first (haha). You're a good friend to me now, too, and we are getting ready to go to AMA's (in actual life, not when you're reading this), and I'm so, so happy you are the one to come with me! Thanks for everything!

Caitlin, Zoe, Nick, Danielle, Kevin (both of you), Tarun, Rich, everyone at Wattpad—you guys are beyond a doubt the best team imaginable. I know none of you signed on to Wattpad thinking you would have to do so much for After and for me, and I want to thank you for welcoming me into the family and helping me with everything After-related and some things not. I can't wait to see what the future brings all of us! You guys are the most creative, most daring and fun group, and I care so much for all of you. Thank you for all the laughs, Nick's picture taking, the wine drinking, the rainy but super-awesome condo crawl, and the massive amounts of food that seem to be there every time I visit.

Allen and Ivan, without Wattpad I wouldn't have found myself, so thank you for creating one of the most important things in my life. I know others share this sentiment as well.

Kristin Dwyer, thank you for making me laugh and calling

me "dude" all the time. I'm so happy to work with you and appreciate all the hours of work you put into me. I really love you and your humor, your hard work, how you make me remember that the good always overcomes the bad, and everything else you do for me!

Everyone at Gallery who has welcomed me, the inexperienced, overly fangirlish, weirdo author who mostly has no idea what she's doing but loves doing it! I appreciate all of the work you all do for this project, from the sales team to the production team. Jen Bergstrom and Louise Burke, for letting Adam sign me up. Martin Karlow, I know you've worked so hard on this, and I'm grateful for that! Steve Breslin, as Adam says, "You keep this train somewhat on track!"

Christina and Lo, you two have been great mentors and friends to me, and I love you both!

To all the Tessas and Hardins in the world who love fiercely and make mistakes along the way.

All of my friends and family who have supported me since I let the cat out of the bag that I just happened to, you know, write four books without them knowing. I love you all.

Last but not least, my Jordan. You are everything to me, and I can't thank you enough for being my rock this last year and the many before. We are so lucky to have found each other so early in life, and it's been the best adventure growing up with you. You make me laugh and make me want to murder you (not actually, because I would sort of miss you, sometimes). I love you.